HADES AND PERSEPHONE

THE GOLDEN BLADE

Copyright © 2024 Heidi Hastings & Erica Hastings.

All rights reserved. No part of this publication may be reproduced, distributed, or transmitted in any form or by any means, including photocopying, recording, or other electronic or mechanical methods, without the prior written permission of the publisher, except in the case of brief quotations embodied in critical reviews and certain other noncommercial uses permitted by copyright law. For permission requests, write to the publisher, addressed "Attention: Permissions Coordinator," at the address below.

ISBN: 978-1-7344762-3-1

Library of Congress Control Number: 2024901688

Any references to historical events, real people, or real places are used fictitiously. Names, characters, and places are products of the author's imagination. Front cover image by Heidi Hastings.

Book design by Heidi Hastings.

First printing edition 2024.

Heidi Hastings

New York, NY.

10065

www.heidihastingsart.com

Based off the myth of Hades and Persephone

Written by Heidi Hastings and Erica Hastings

Illustrations: Heidi Hastings

Chapter dividers: DG-Market

@hadesandpersephonebook

SPECIAL THANKS

A very special thanks to Hope, Mom, Heather, Emily, Megan,

Auntie-M, Poppy, Bebo and Baby E, Kosta, Nina, and our contest winner Micky Barnard @bookphenomena

Also, a big thanks to Pearl Hastings, for always believing.

HEIDI'S DEDICATION

To my Mother,

I love you always and forever.

& to Erica,

without you, this wouldn't have been possible.

ERICA'S DEDICATION

To Princess and Poppy, and my little Cerberus.

To my mother, for always being there.

& to Heidi,

for sharing this journey.

PROLOGUE

In the shadows, the king knelt alone in the dark, cold cavern. A single golden light gleamed dimly between his clenched, bloody fists, and drops trickled from his hands to the darkened floor in crimson rivulets. Two swords were crossed in the scabbard on his back, and the blue and golden glow of the blades illuminated the cavern in a combined greenish hue.

One of the Fates stepped forth, the light reflecting off her sunken face as a sickening, gleeful chuckle filled the silence. She gestured with her plump, swollen finger, her nose greedily sniffing the air, and a smile lifted her ruined mouth.

"We warned you, *king*," she cried in unison with her sisters. "She will bring about your destruction. You are *falling, falling*—the beginning of the end and the end of your beginning."

Hades exhaled as though awakening from a deep slumber and turned his face toward the voice. Sweat dripped from his brow, and his black hair, thick with blood and filth, was matted to his forehead. Embers in his gaze gleamed like fallen black stars, rising to meet the staring eye in the old crone's hand. The pupil of the eye dilated and constricted, greedily absorbing his focused stare.

The second Fate emerged from the shadows and inhaled the stale air. "Your immortal blood spills at your feet; I can taste death. But not yet. Your beloved will be the one to cut your thread. Are you prepared for the betrayal, oh king?"

Hades lowered his head, his eyes dropping to the golden thread he twisted between his hands. As his fingers met the end of the strand, he felt the thin, frayed edge. "What can I do?" he whispered.

The three Fates chanted in unison, "What is done cannot be undone." Their frenzied voices reached a deafening pitch, but the God remained still.

"But there is a way." The eye of the Fates twisted towards him. "The child. You must find his thread if you wish to save your kingdom."

His voice was low, the deep timber vibrating against the walls. "How much time do I have?"

The third Fate stepped forward, and finally, Hades lifted his head. Her empty, cavernous eye sockets were like a black abyss, and he flinched back, feeling that he could be pulled into the swirling darkness. Falling, falling. She pointed her finger toward the heavens.

"As the blood-red moon eclipses the sky, you were born this day to die."

CHAPTER 1
WAITING

Persephone had once again traveled down from the mountaintop into the mortal realm. It had been almost six months since she had seen her husband. The days stretched into months, with endless blue skies, green fields, and emptiness. In the serene solitude, she longed for even a glimpse of something that reminded her of him and the odd world she had grown to call home. Before, she had paid little attention to mortals' homage to the Underworld, but now she yearned for even a tiny taste of that dark kingdom. Covering her face with a thick wool scarf, she traveled during the early mornings to mortal libraries, pouring through books and studying every vase, manuscript, or fresco she could find. But months of searching had yet to yield results. Not a single statue of her husband was erected, and rarely was a work of art or story written of him in the mortal realm. Still, she would not be deterred.

The long brown robe hid her face as she poured through scrolls. Zeus, Aphrodite, and Hermes—even the lesser and demi-Gods—were repeatedly mentioned. A snort escaped her mouth as she came across yet another descriptive passage of Aphrodite's beauty. Persephone tried to force her rage down as she came across a series of stories devoted to Ares. She tossed the scroll on top of the other worthless manuscripts with shaking fingers, the pile tumbling loudly to the floor. Once again, no word of Hades. How could there not be more? It was like he did not exist, like he had been blotted from history, and it caused a strange panic to rise in her. She closed her eyes, remembering his mouth against hers.

"He is real," she whispered to herself. "You know he is real."

She lifted her head as she heard footsteps drawing near. A thin man with small tufts of brown hair approached her swiftly with a disapproving frown on his heavily wrinkled face. "May I be of some service? We request that our patrons not disturb other guests." He cast a disapproving eye at the scrolls on the floor. "Or mishandle our properties."

She pulled her scarf firmly around her face as she bent to pick up the discarded pile. "I apologize," she said in a low voice. She gathered the scrolls and stepped further into the darkness as the librarian continued to regard her disapprovingly. She had tried to avoid interacting with humans, but since she had already drawn his attention, she might as well ask him what he knew. "Please, tell me where I might find any literature or art depicting Hades?"

The old man gasped and raised an amulet around his neck to his lips. She briefly saw Zeus' face before it disappeared again into his clothing. "We do not speak that name aloud here, young woman," he hissed angrily.

"But why ever not?" she asked in surprise. "This is a place of learning. Is Hades not a God, too? At least you must have some documentation on his looks or what he is like. Or what kind of king he is?"

This time, the old man was thoroughly outraged, and he took a large sniff as he reached towards her and firmly removed the scrolls from her arms. "We certainly do not pollute our library with the dark words that may be dedicated to him. We know he is an elderly God that the living should never have to see. That is enough."

"Elderly?" she murmured, amused. "I always wondered if the King of the Underworld would not be a handsome God?"

The man raised his hands and let out a shriek. "Outrage! Blasphemy! Almighty Zeus, do you wish for death to find you? No one admires or prays to "the unseen." He does not care for prayers or praise. He

collects souls and sends his demon Gods to punish us as we live on this Earth." He gesticulated wildly to the door, shoving her forward. "Now pray leave and do not return here if you are looking for such depravity. You should pray to Almighty Zeus that "the unseen" does not seek you."

Before he could close the door, Persephone placed her hand lightly against it, halting the old man's movement. "Oh no, sir," she said with a wide smile, letting her eyes flash from the darkness of her hood. "We would not want him to find us now, would we? Think of all the wicked things he may do."

The man paused to stare at her and then closed the doors firmly in her face with a final, very loud sniff.

Persephone paused on the doorstep, troubled. That they should fear him did not surprise her, but that he be smitten from their history? If only they knew the evil they worshiped. She made her way to the forest slowly. Almost six months had passed since she had last seen her husband. Nearly six months since that night in the rose garden. He had left a rose behind; he had been there. So why had he never come to see her again? Since then, she had not heard anything—not even a single letter! It was like he vanished.

"What has happened to keep him from me?" Persephone whispered to herself.

Her thoughts raced with a thousand possibilities, each more horrifying than the previous. Why would Hades not contact her? She impatiently wiped a tear away with the back of her hand. Soon, he would come for her, and she would demand answers. In the meantime, her time above had been well-spent. She'd spent the long daylight hours at her mother's temple, pouring over texts, training, and honing her abilities, preparing for her return to the Underworld. She practiced alone in the forest, growing the most vigorous trees on Earth and pushing them swiftly through the ground to cover the woodland with a thick screen of leaves. Her efforts had resulted in one of the most magnificent forests the people of Earth had ever seen. When that wasn't enough, she'd ask her mother to train with her. They would travel far away from humankind so Demeter's supernatural calamities would not harm the mortals. Despite her reservations, Demeter never held back, and Persephone was thankful. She'd never let herself be weak again.

Closing her eyes, memories flooded back, and she marveled at the swift turns her life had taken. It all began with a curse—a golden love arrow—that had struck Hades' heart. But, no, that was not actually where their story began; it had started far earlier, with an anonymous letter—a sweet, tender letter—that had torn at her heartstrings. Hades and she had been communicating for months, writing to each other without ever having met. They fell in love and eventually planned a meeting where they would reveal their identities. But with a cruel twist of fate, Ares had shown up instead. Persephone closed her eyes tightly. She mistook the God of War for her lover, and Hades believed Persephone had scorned him. Hades had fled to the Underworld to drink from the Lethe, the River of Forgetfulness, washing away his memories of her, save a distant remembrance of love. Unbeknownst to Hades, the God of War had forced himself on Persephone, and she had borne a child from the encounter, a baby who had died.

And they may never have spoken again, but for Zeus, who tried to force Persephone to marry Ares. Demeter secretly worked with Aphrodite to remove her daughter from the clutches of the man who had violated her, but there was only one place in the world that Ares and Zeus could not go: the Underworld. Together, they shot an arrow of love at Hades, prompting the Lord of the Underworld to abduct Persephone to his realm. Their relationship had been rocky from the start, and she had misjudged him, blinded by fear. The spell became a curse because she could not reciprocate his love, but Hades tried to protect her.

One night, as the curse reached its zenith and madness consumed Hades, she was forced to flee the Underworld, unintentionally bringing the Underworld's seal to the surface. Ares, who had been watching and waiting, took advantage and attacked. But it was a mistake because Ares' rage taught her how much she loved Hades, not only by his sacrifice to accept the God of War's abuse in her place but hers, as she tried to force Ares to punish her instead. Finally, Persephone realized that Hades, not Ares, had written her love letters long ago. Hades took the pain from her soul, the scar on her heart, the heavy burden she carried from Ares' molestation, and the loss of her child. And then there was love for a while—a few beautiful moments together—until the God of War abducted her.

Hades came after her, first seeking Aphrodite, who provided him with a love arrow emblazoned with the letter A. The Goddess of Love told him to thrust it into Ares' heart to redirect his obsession with Persephone to Aphrodite.

And so, the God of War and the God of the Dead battled high on the mountain. As Ares pierced Hades with the golden blade, the God-killing sword, she was terrified Hades would die. Persephone ingested six pomegranate seeds, ensuring Hades and herself could never be separated, and then plunged the cursed golden arrow of love into the God of War's heart. And she thought it would be over, but she had been wrong. Zeus forced her to leave the Underworld for the other six months of the year. Now, she awaited her husband's return with bated breath.

She kept searching for the cataclysmic force she had felt after consuming the pomegranate, but it remained elusive. Sometimes, she imagined she could feel flutterings within her, but the more she sought it, the faster it seemed to slip from her grasp. It was like attempting to hold water; you could see it, touch it, and feel it, but you couldn't hold it. Though she tried to hide her doubts from her mother, she questioned if her Earthly abilities were sufficient. Was she anything more than a specialized greenskeeper? She pushed herself to the limit in her training to quiet her mind, but each night, when the moon was high in the sky, she lay awake, empty and suffering. Waiting.

She forced her mind back to the present. She had arrived at the forest that bordered the library, and as soon as the trees' canopy hid her, she started to sprint, her feet moving along the well-traveled trail. She jumped like a deer towards the river, where she used to wait for Hades' letters. The wind pushed against her until her feet rose, and she was swept over the treetops to the waters below. The violent eddy slowed, and her feet lightly touched the ground. So much had changed, and yet, she still sat by the river alone. She was no longer afraid of the location or the memories. Hades had removed the scar from her heart, removing her dread and anguish and sharing her sorrow. Every trip to this place felt like a victory; she'd regained this section of the forest, and it felt as good as the arrow she'd shot into Ares' heart—well, almost. She stared into the stream that flowed into the Styx to Hades but only saw a reflection of herself in its depths.

"Where are you?" she whispered to the river. "Do you forget me so easily?"

She waved her hands, and a scroll appeared. On the parchment, she wrote only one sentence. I love you. She had sent letters all spring.

She had sent letters all summer. And she waited for a letter that never came. No response was ever returned to her on the water. How could he leave her for so long with not even one word?

"Why is he so silent?" she asked the river. "Is something wrong?" In answer, the water splashed merrily against her hands, pushing her note towards the current. The water lapped at her with such pleasure that she could not help but laugh. "All right," she relented. "I will come in, but just for a moment."

She slid the woolen cape from her shoulders, then looked around cautiously, sensing no human or immortal presence. Her fingers unclasped the pin from her toga, and it fell to the ground. Sunlight glinted off her bronzed skin, and she breathed a sigh of relief as she stepped into the river, letting the cool water engulf her. Her pale nipples were just visible above the rippling water, and she let her long hair fall behind her as she inhaled the delicious woodland air. The current beneath her was powerful and throbbing with energy, and she let herself float to the river's bottom, where its life force beat.

She flattened her palms against the Earth as her feet made contact with the river's sandy bed. Closing her eyes, she let the stillness of the deep water wash over her, and through the emptiness, she heard a whisper, a voice calling to her. She reached her hand deep into the Earth, closing her eyes and praying, "Remember me." She rolled onto her back and stared at the water above her. The shadows danced over the surface, moving with the waves. A prickle of awareness traveled over her as she saw the shadows merge as someone above peered down at her, a vague, watery figure watching her. Pushing her feet against the river's bed, she shot quickly to the surface to glance hopefully at the shore.

There was movement from the periphery of her vision, and she turned her head, whispering his name. Her heart dropped in disappointment as she saw an enormous white swan emerge beneath a willow tree. It lifted its wide wingspan as it approached her, and Persephone held still, admiring the bird. When it was within an arm's reach of her, they gazed at one another, and Persephone felt herself blush as its eyes seemed to move over her pale breasts floating above the water.

"Not very wise, I agree," she said to the swan as she drew a garland of dark red roses over herself. She pulled some petals from the flowers and offered them carefully to the swan. "Are you hungry, my beautiful friend? You were not who I sought, but I do not mind sharing this

space with you."

The swan extended its elegant beak towards her hand and greedily gobbled the petals from her palm, tearing the delicate flesh on her skin. She yanked her hand back with a murmur of pain.

"You are starving, aren't you?"

There was a shallow cut on her palm, and she lifted it to her mouth, her tongue soothing the sting. The dark, curious eyes followed her movement.

"It's all right," she said softly to the bird, stroking the swan's silken neck.

The swan suddenly shot forward, its sharp beak yanking the garland from her breasts and ripped it to shreds. It grabbed the largest rose and then spread its wings, obscuring the sun as he abruptly flew from the forest. Persephone felt a chill run through her as she glanced at the red petals dancing on the water. Unbidden, her eyes shifted to where she had waited for Hades and instead met a monster.

"Perhaps it is unwise," she said to no one in particular, "to linger here after all."

CHAPTER 2
INVITATION

Persephone used the wind to allow her to swiftly reach her mother's temple, the forest the border between the mortal world and the Gods. Demeter was emerging from the entrance with a new bow in her hands as Persephone landed on the ground. She smiled at her mother's beautiful, exuberant face.

"Did you make that just today?" Persephone asked.

Demeter walked swiftly to her daughter, kissing her cheek. She held the bow to her for inspection, letting the sun glint off the fine craftsmanship. "Freshly carved, my love. What do you think? Shall we try it later?"

Persephone nodded her head. "Oh yes! But shall we eat first? I am famished."

Demeter laughed. "But of course. I had a premonition that you would return hungry."

"Where is Cerus?"

"He is waiting for you in the garden." Demeter smiled. "Terrifying the nymphs."

Persephone had discovered Cerus shortly after leaving the Underworld. She'd been achingly lonely, looking for something to occupy her time. An enormous white bull was said to be terrorizing adjacent villages, crushing crops, and trampling fields. The human men had been too afraid to approach the creature, and she had learned that they planned to shoot him to end his rampages. Persephone had moved quickly, seeking out the bull. She'd discovered him in a springtime meadow, pounding the ground beneath him with angry, powerful hooves. With a mighty snort, he had rushed at her, but the bull halted as she calmly observed him, white smoke pouring from his nostrils. She had lifted her hand, allowing him to smell her before petting his soft, wet nose.

"My name is Persephone," she had whispered kindly. "And your name is Cerus. The Earth told me of you. Cerus, would you like to come with me?" From that day onward, the bull spent all his time at their temple, exploring the fields and forests with her, safe from man's fury.

The bull rose to greet them as they entered the garden, and Persephone bent to kiss his head, brushing a hand on the soft fur between his dark eyes. As they settled into a spread of fruits and vegetables recently harvested from the forest, Cerus curled at her feet.

Demeter asked in a casual voice, "No word today, I take it."

Persephone paused as she lifted a fig to her mouth. "No," she answered slowly, forcing herself to take a bite. "I have not heard from him. But I know he is busy preparing for my return. I am sure it is hectic down in the Underworld. He has so much to do, and without me there, he does not have anyone to help him with the royal duties."

"Still," Demeter persisted, seemingly focused on arranging a plate of grapes, "how long does it take to tell you that he is well? It does not seem like the God I know to leave you without a word."

"It is unlike him," Persephone agreed in a small voice. "But I think that maybe he does not want to trouble me. He wanted to make sure that I could spend my time with you without worrying about him."

Demeter's gaze darkened. "But you do worry; I know you do. When was the last time you heard from him?"

A blush spread across Persephone's face. She would not share the details of their last passionate encounter. "That night, when I returned to your temple, he stopped by my room to tell me goodbye."

"I see. I wonder how Hades moved without Zeus knowing," Demeter asked thoughtfully, her gaze taking in her daughter's pink face and downcast eyes. "Well," she continued with a sigh, "men, both mortal and God, are strange. He was always the solitary type but kind and good. However, I do know one thing. He will be overjoyed when he sees you again. Of this, I am certain." Demeter picked up a nearby scroll. "I wanted to show you this as well, daughter, since you will leave soon. I have discovered a way to ensure the trees do not die this time. I will work to insulate the roots and allow the trees to sleep. They will lose their leaves, but they will be hibernating. If I can, I should be able to protect the forests. What do you think?"

Persephone took the scroll, scrutinizing it. "I think this is brilliant, mother." She glanced at Demeter. "I have a question," Persephone began tentatively.

"Yes, my dear," her mother asked, her dark curls bouncing as her head shot back up.

"How old were you when you decided to start a family?"

"Oh." Demeter sat back, considering the question. "Well, I was more or less your age. Young by Goddess standards, ancient by mortal ones," she chuckled. "Really, once I met Iasion, there was no question. I wanted everything with him. All the good things and even the bad. And how glad I am that I did," she finished with a smile, gently tugging Persephone's hair. "Why is it that you ask? Are you thinking of starting a family?"

Persephone took a long sip of the excellent honeyed tea her mother brewed so perfectly. She stirred the glass thoughtfully, watching as the honeysuckle leaves sank to the bottom. "I have just been wondering what our children may look like. I have imagined a little boy with his eyes," she mused wistfully. "I think he would be a good father. He would love his children fiercely, and I would love to have a baby."

"There were whispers," Demeter said carefully, her eyes downcast, "many years ago, on Olympus, that he was incapable of having children."

"What vicious rumors!" Persephone cried. "Why should he not be able to bear children?" Cerus looked up, glancing around for the cause of her distress. "You know how they lie, Mother! The Olympians believe that I am Zeus' child, which is certainly not true."

Demeter stood up, placing a calming hand on Persephone's shoulder. "I know; I know how they lie. I do not know the purpose of such a rumor, but lies do not always serve a purpose. Sometimes, they only exist to hurt."

Persephone grasped her mother's hand tightly. "I hate them. They torment the living; I will not allow them to torment us or the dead."

"Ah, my dear, sweet girl. How you have grown. I am so proud of the Goddess you have become. You are a fierce queen now."

"I will go to any length to defend the souls. They have a limited time with Zeus but an eternity with Hades and myself. It is my destiny to safeguard that." Demeter touched Persephone's cheek with her fingers. "You know what tomorrow is, Mother. Six months will have passed as the moon rises high in the sky."

Demeter's eyes flashed with pain, and as she opened her mouth to answer, they both looked up abruptly as a white dove descended towards them.

"That bird brings news from Olympus," Demeter murmured, her voice strained.

Demeter gently gripped the bird's leg and removed a white and gold scroll. As soon as its message was delivered, the bird snatched a nearby grape, shuffled its feathers, and flew skyward.

"It says you've been welcomed to Olympus. Zeus wishes to publicly recognize your position as Queen of the Underworld and celebrate your marriage to his brother."

Persephone's heart began to race wildly. "But if it's a celebration of our marriage, does that mean Hades will be there? He must be invited." She couldn't stop the enthusiasm in her voice.

"Persephone," Demeter interjected swiftly. "Hades hasn't been seen at Olympus since assuming his position in the Underworld." But Persephone was eagerly glancing at the invitation. "It has a personalized message for you," Demeter sighed as she handed it to her daughter.

Dearest daughter,

Tonight, Olympus will celebrate you for your illustrious marriage and your newly-found title as Queen of the Underworld. I require your presence at sunset. If your dear mother attempts to stop you, I will collect you myself. While your attendance is required, hers is not. Demeter, regretfully, shall not be attending.

Your loving father,

Zeus

"But you are not invited!"

"Of course not," Demeter replied, her voice tense. "He wants you alone; all the better to play his little games. He separates those of us who may be allies against him." Demeter fixed her gaze on her daughter. "The invitation is tonight. I do not think that is a coincidence."

"Tonight," Persephone said softly. "Then I have to—"

"Persephone, listen to me," Demeter said urgently, taking her daughter's hand. "Your head is in the clouds! There is a reason for the short notice. There's a reason why I wasn't invited. He left you no option; you must go, but go cautiously. Zeus never acts without a reason. He's about to make the next move in his game."

"What is the point of this game?"

"The same reason for murdering Iasion. Everything he does serves the same aim. Because he can, Persephone, simply because he can."

Persephone washed quickly. She knew her mother was right that there was another agenda to Zeus' invitation; his sudden role as the benevolent father was revolting. But tonight, she would see Hades. After six long months, they would be reunited. She would deal with whatever game Zeus was playing. She had gone through so much to be with Hades; this was another battle she must endure. And in truth, an encounter with Zeus was long overdue. She cleansed her skin with rose petals and eucalyptus oil. A nymph appeared to assist her in arranging her hair as she emerged from the bath, and Persephone kohl ringed her eyes in the same manner Jocasta had taught her. Tonight, she must look every inch the empress.

After thanking the wood nymph, she called to her mother, "May I borrow your pale pink—" Demeter entered the room before Persephone finished, holding out a garment with a troubled smile.

"I thought this one might do," Demeter said. She held a white toga with small golden leaves woven into the ivory cloth. "I wore this once when I was a young Goddess."

Persephone lightly caressed the delicate leaves. "It is beautiful."

Demeter helped her daughter dress, her lovely brow furrowed with worry. "Persephone, be wary if they try to lure you away from the crowd. Do not go alone with anyone. Trust none of them."

"I know, Mother, but you know I must go. I would eventually have to confront Zeus. And Hades will be there."

Demeter exhaled a frustrated breath. "I do not believe he will be there, Persephone. He has never been welcome on Olympus. And now, in the aftermath of Ares' loss, they are outraged and united in their opposition to him. It is naive to think differently."

"Then I will just appear and leave; they cannot keep me."

"Persephone!" Demeter chided, pacing nervously. "They are capable of anything, *anything*. After everything you've been through, your love still makes you weak and overly trusting." Demeter shook her head as Persephone opened her mouth to argue. "I understand why; love weakens me as well. To experience such love is both our greatest strength and our worst weakness." She drew her daughter to her, shielding her face as she embraced her, but Persephone could feel her mother trembling in her arms. "You are the reason I exist. The only way I can keep my fury under control. If you have a need, even a seed of doubt, send for me, and nothing will keep me from you."

Persephone and Demeter sat in the gardens, waiting. As the sun set below the horizon, a white stag galloped down the lush mountain, kneeling at the door to their shrine. Persephone stepped forward, but Demeter held a hand, preventing her from touching the animal.

"Persephone, I understand that you are the Queen of the Underworld now, but of the two of us, I understand more of Olympus. Never trust any animal that Zeus sends your way. She does not need your assistance," she said calmly to the stag.

Indignantly, the stag puffed. As the animal reared back fiercely, Cerus appeared, his head down as he went forward, thrusting his massive horns toward the stag. The deer bolted at the sight of the raging bull, bouncing back up the mountain with newfound vigor.

Demeter chuckled as Persephone soothed Cerus. "I had a hunch I liked that bull! He will transport you to Olympus."

"Do you want to visit Olympus, Cerus?" Persephone cooed. The bull agreed with a snort. Persephone raised her eyes to Demeter. "You know it will enrage Zeus that I rejected the steed he sent," she remarked.

"Yes," Demeter answered. "Yes, it will. And I do not care. " Demeter paused before raising her green eyes, tears glistening in their depths. "If Hades comes tonight, I might not see you again for another six months."

Persephone dashed into her mother's arms. "I know," she whispered. "It's why my heart is both sad and happy."

"I realize it's selfish," Demeter admitted, her voice wavering. "However, you are everything to me. But he's a good man and a good husband." The older Goddess stroked her daughter's hair. "Autumn is approaching, Persephone; I can feel it growing within me, an emptiness." Demeter abruptly pulled away and smiled at Persephone. "However, you must leave. Remember, no one, not even the animals, can be trusted."

Persephone kissed her mother goodbye, and they exchanged a fierce embrace before she mounted Cerus. Demeter kept her gaze fixed on her daughter; Persephone had no idea that as she soared toward Olympus, the Goddess of Spring became a beacon of pure light, and a tear traced down Demeter's cheek as the only thing she loved moved away from her until she vanished from sight.

CHAPTER 3
OLYMPUS

The blossoming trees' flowers floated down the mountainside, and the petals fell to form a rainbow bouquet in Persephone's hair. She gathered and braided them into a wreath for Cerus' neck. Her heart beat faster with each passing second. She hadn't been to Zeus' temple since she was a small child. How would the palace seem now? She'd see Zeus for the first time through the eyes of an adult. She'd been so well protected that she didn't know much about the Gods, but she knew enough. She recognized their fickleness, their cruelty, and none worse than their king.

As they soared higher, her trepidation also grew, and it felt as if a swarm of butterflies had taken flight in her stomach. Her decision to come here could have been a mistake, but then again, she didn't have much choice. When the King of Gods summoned you, you came.

She couldn't help but gasp when the palace finally came into view. She had forgotten how beautiful it was, appearing even more enormous than when she was a child. Pegasus sailed across the sky, the sun glinting gold across their ivory wings, and pink skies peeked out amid the white, gleaming temples buried high in the mountaintops. It was breathtaking. Cerus eventually reached the cliff's edge, where the golden gates stood, and Persephone dismounted, leaning to stroke the

enormous bull's neck. She thought he looked lovely with the flower garland around his snowy-white chest.

"Well done, sweet boy," Persephone crooned. She straightened as the palace doors opened slowly, her heart quickening.

A blonde nymph approached them, her ample hips sashaying with each step. "Queen Persephone," she mumbled as she adjusted the scarce feathers that covered her breasts. "You may leave your cow—" She shrieked as Cerus reared towards her, but Persephone stepped between them.

"Cerus does not belong to me." The bull huffed, and Persephone nodded. "And he takes offense at being called a cow. He will return to my mother's temple, where he resides as an honored guest."

The nymph uttered an incomprehensible noise before throwing one final glare at the bull and motioning for Persephone to follow her.

Persephone bent toward Cerus. "Thank you, my friend." The bull raised his soulful brown eyes to her, making a low, sorrowful bellow that wrenched Persephone's heart. It felt as though he were saying goodbye. "Do not worry, my dear friend; I will be back. Time is nothing between the best of friends."

She turned to follow the nymph, casting one last look at Cerus as he stood alone, a solitary pale figure. How misunderstood Cerus was; he had led such a lonely life before she had found him. Her heart twisted as the door closed, shutting Cerus away from her. Persephone swallowed the lump in her throat and realized the nymph was watching her.

"Are you going to cry?" she asked, aghast, insolent blue eyes sweeping over her.

"No," Persephone replied coolly.

The nymph gave her a nasty look and took her through several vast halls, each filled with large, exquisite marble carvings of the Gods and Goddesses. She finally brought Persephone to an expansive, vacant throne room. The nymph bowed low. "Your Highness," she mocked before slipping out the door, leaving Persephone alone.

Persephone gazed around the large chamber but saw no trace of Zeus or anyone else. She turned to inspect the arrangements for the purported party; white flowers crept up the marble columns, plush blue cushions lined silk-covered settees, and dripping wax candles were sprinkled about the room, casting soothing light throughout. She emitted a sound of happiness as she beheld the ivory petals that covered the ground and gigantic stone pots loaded with flowers of every shape and type. It was the ideal setting for an Olympian wedding. She reminded herself that it was only a pretty covering to disguise the ugly within, but she reasoned it wasn't the flowers' fault.

She turned quickly as she heard the heavy flutter of wings in the distance. The sound grew louder until a massive white swan emerged through the expansive palace windows. She watched in amusement as it landed on Zeus' throne; the bird was very daring. Persephone approached cautiously and gasped as she beheld the enormous red rose clenched in its beak. She thought in surprise that he must be the same bird from the river.

As a thunderclap filled the room, she stepped back, covering her face from the blinding lightning. Looking up again, she saw Zeus, King of Olympus, reclining on his throne. His hair was as white as the swan's whose form he had adopted, and white robes edged with gold thread clothed his large, muscular body. With a smirk on his lips, he inspected her while weaving the rose between his fingers. She hastily veiled her features in an inscrutable mask, yet she knew he could discern her astonishment beneath her practiced guise.

"Well, is this not a pleasant family reunion?" his voice boomed. "My dear, dear *daughter*. It has been so long since we met; you are quite a woman. How well you look." His thick lips curled in amusement as he brushed the rose against his teeth. "Though you looked even lovelier with nothing covering your pretty flesh."

He snapped his fingers, and a young boy with a golden vase entered the throne room. Zeus watched her as he let the flower fall into it, his finger tracing the stem slowly. He nodded for the child to depart, and his icy blue eyes swept over her before returning to meet her gaze. She stared back at him, observing the gold flaring along his iris' corners. "Come say hello to Papa."

Persephone felt her vision blur with anger, and she rooted herself firmly to the ground. "I am fine where I am. And you are not my father," she replied shortly. She pressed her palms into her skirts so he would not see her trembling hands. "If you wanted to be reunited with me, you had no need to watch me under the protection of a goose. You should have presented yourself to me as you are, not hide behind the form of another."

Zeus threw back his head and laughed, the substantial column of his throat moving as he swallowed. "Oh, child. You *are* delightful. I can see why he was so captivated. I will let you know that many women have been charmed by that *goose*. Besides, sweet Persephone, have you not yet learned the appeal of watching those you should not? It is so very decadent. How did a little flower like you come to beguile my brother? It must be a fascinating story."

Persephone stiffened. "I did not beguile anyone."

"Oh, come, child. We all know you have him wrapped around your tight, little..." He smiled, widening his eyes as she stiffened again. "Why, your little finger, of course."

"Perhaps you should ask your brother if you are so curious," Persephone replied coolly. She had been so sure she would not allow this King of Kings to subdue her, but her bravado was slipping away as she stood face-to-face with him. She felt like a country mouse before—well, a swan. Raising her eyes to his, they observed each other; she stood rigidly while Zeus sprawled, relaxed, and at ease, his large frame spread across his throne. As he inspected her, lightning bolts casually danced across his fingertips.

"Why exactly have you requested my presence here?" she asked in a tight voice. "Where is my husband?"

"Can't a father simply wish to see his daughter?" He stood, and she was taken aback as his tall form suddenly hovered over her, so close she could smell the scent of rain on his flesh. She refused to retreat, and for a moment, his face was pressed close to her own so that she could see her reflection in the inky darkness of his pupils. He grinned again as he stepped away, and she realized she had been holding her breath. "I asked you to come early so I could give you a tour of the palace. I have so many things to show you, my dear," he continued. "I love to share my treasures with my family."

"I would rather stay here."

"And I would rather you come with me." He gave her an ironic glance, knowing she could not refuse the King of Olympus. "Oh, kind lady, won't you accompany me?" Gesturing with his hand, she reluctantly

followed him from the throne room via a series of hallways. She remembered her mother's warning not to leave alone with a God, but Zeus was not leaving her a choice.

He came to a halt as a beautiful Goddess suddenly approached them. Long waves of ebony hair flowed past her slim waist, and her complexion glistened like moonlight. As she neared them, she raised dark brown eyes and sank into a deep bow, the edges of her purple gown pooling at her feet. Zeus moved his palm to her chin and lifted her face so that she stared up at him, but his eyes were on Persephone while he spoke.

"Persephone, this is Rhea. Savior of Olympians. My mother."

Persephone stifled a choking gasp. Her mind instantly rejected his statement. Hades had held Rhea as she died, and that death had destroyed him. She could feel Zeus' eyes on her as her mind tried to accept that this beautiful woman before her could not be real. And yet, she could see Hades in that perfect face, in the line of the nose, and in the tilt of the mouth. Persephone averted her gaze, unable to bear looking at her.

"It is a pleasure to meet you," Persephone murmured.

She could feel Rhea's gaze moving over her. "Welcome to Olympus. I will leave you with my son now."

"Isn't my mother beautiful?" Zeus inquired as he led her down another corridor.

Persephone made a murmur of assent, surveying the rooms they passed. The marble statues that lined the corner of this wing were far more provocative and disturbing: Apollo bowed between the legs of a mortal lady, and Aphrodite, who was enjoying the services of multiple Satyrs. Persephone clenched her fists as they passed a depiction of Poseidon's rape of Medusa. Even though his attack on the maiden had changed the trajectory of her life, both Gods and mortals blamed Medusa for her fate. As the passage grew darker, the statues seemed to take on a menacing appearance. The figures were wrenched into bizarre shapes, which created a horrible effect combined with the overly distorted expressions of pleasure engraved into their faces.

"Do you like my artwork?" Zeus questioned her with the same smile that always seemed to curl his mouth. "Perhaps we could add one of you in time."

"No, thank you," she replied coldly.

"Pity," he murmured, "but you may still change your mind. Here we are."

As they approached, two nymphs and a Satyr were manning the enormous golden doors. Persephone couldn't prevent the flush that grew across her cheeks as she noticed one of the nymphs had her face buried between the other's thighs while the Satyr stroked himself. When they spotted Zeus, they quickly rose and coiled their bodies around him. Zeus stroked his finger casually down one of the nymph's shoulders, halting when he reached the tip of her breast.

"See that my guest and I are not disturbed. We have important matters to discuss."

With a nod, Zeus untangled himself from the nymphs and seized Persephone's hand, dragging her forward. The door slammed shut behind them, and Persephone pulled her hand from his grasp. Where was Hades? Her dread was beginning to grow as she took in the surroundings. Once again, the room was stunning; there was an expansive marble balcony with breathtaking sunset views as crimson faded into pastel pink and pale columns with silvery blooms ran from floor to ceiling.

Her attention was pulled to a gigantic painting behind Zeus' desk, which filled the entire wall and depicted a naked goddess intertwined with a large, pale man, half-bull, half-God. The bull's enormous cock penetrated deep within the woman, and her lips were open in ecstasy as she yelled her delight. There was something familiar about the woman. As Persephone drew closer, she let out a gasp. The Goddess was Demeter.

Zeus sat, his feet propped up on his desk lazily. His gaze was guileless as he observed her closely. "Don't tell me you did not know, daughter?" he asked in sly surprise. "This one is one of my personal favorites. I keep it here so I can look upon it often and remember. Why, you may have been conceived that very day."

With a scornful scowl, she turned her back on the hideous depiction and faced the God. "Have you shown this to my mother? I think she might have something to say about its authenticity."

"Oh, it is authentic," he said softly. "Do you believe your mother is incapable of lying? A God is eternal. Do you genuinely think she has done nothing that she may want to conceal from you? Have you told your mother everything about *your* life?"

She did not allow him to see that his words had hurt her. "Where is Hades?" she asked. "I don't see why we should continue this pointless conversation."

"But don't *you* know where your husband is? It's still early days for him to neglect you. I'll have to speak with my brother." He laughed softly again at her expression. "Everything in due course. I'm curious as to what all the commotion is about. What is six months compared to the years I have waited to talk with you? But first," he added, swinging his long legs off the desk, "there's something I'd like to show you." He indicated an adjacent table holding a square black and white board. "Sit," he beckoned, motioning to a sumptuous velvet chaise.

The board was adorned with small figures, and she frowned as she leaned closer. She recognized Zeus, Hera, Apollo, Athena, and Aphrodite among the pale ivory carvings of the Olympians on his side. Hades, herself, Hypnos, Charon, and the Gods of the Underworld were engraved in black obsidian on the other side. There were other figures on the board that she could not place. All the figures, of course, were nude. She took up the figure of herself that had been set adjacent to an unclothed Hades. The pale breasts were thrust forward with small, erect nipples in a sensual posture, and the back was arched. The statue's small hand was nestled between her legs. Zeus held a naked Hera between his fingers but was gazing at Persephone.

"Why are they naked?" she asked, her brow arched with disapproval.

"I find it adds to the intrigue. This game is called chess. Have you heard of it?"

"My mother has explained the rules to me," she murmured.

Zeus nodded with a smile. "Ah yes, and I had shown her. What happy memories you're reviving! It has yet to be invented by mortals, but I guarantee you that it is highly fascinating. Have you ever played?

"Once or twice. We are too busy for games."

"Oh, daughter, you must always make time to play. I'm a sucker for a

good game. Your mother explained the rules, but now let a king show you because his fate is at stake. This is the queen," he continued with a smile, emphasizing the marble Hera in his palm. "She is positioned next to the king. The queen must keep her king safe at all costs. If the queen falls, the king will not be far behind."

He motioned to the figures at the front of the board on either side. "These are the pawns, the mortals." He stroked a long finger along the piece and lifted a female pawn near her face. "A pawn's objective is to lure out the queen. They are the first to fall in the game, readily sacrificed," he chuckled. "Pawns are gullible fools who are oblivious to the realities of their overlords."

He placed the pieces on the table and reached carefully across the board, his fingers lovingly grasping the minuscule Persephone. "The queen can move in any direction and take up as much room as she wishes. It is she who decides the king's fate." He frowned in mock distress. "But I wonder if I put you on the right side of my board. You are as much a part of Olympus as of the Underworld. Then again, perhaps you aren't a queen at all. Should I put you in front with the other pawns?"

"Why ask me?" Persephone asked as she watched his fingers move over the breasts of the statue. "It is *your* game."

"How very right you are. But I need to know where to place you before I can proceed. It has been quite worrisome for me. Which category do you belong in? Are you a pawn in this game? Or a queen? Are you dark or light?" He raised his eyes to hers. "Are you good or evil?"

She pulled the piece from his fingers, careful not to brush her skin against his, and placed it beside Hades. "I belong to the dark. I belong beside my king. And if you have forgotten that I am a queen, I have not. But I have no interest in playing this game with you." She felt a peculiar pull she hadn't felt since leaving the Underworld, and she could feel the fire flashing in her eyes. Zeus locked his attention on her for a brief moment before rising and moving away from the table.

"The truth is, Persephone, I have asked you here to find out how much Hades has told you. You knew that woman was not Rhea. I could see it in your eyes. I employed powerful magic to imitate her, and now you can expose me, but if you do, you will also expose him. Expose that he murdered his own mother. I haven't said anything about his crime, but how do you think the other Gods will respond if they learn the truth?" Zeus waved his fingers, and the minuscule figure of Hades fell from the board.

"And if you know of Rhea's death, you've heard of the God-killing sword. It has the potential to shake the foundations of Olympus. I know you dislike us, but what happens to the mortals and even your mother if our realm falls?" He stood over her as she bent to pick up the small Hades statue that had fallen at her feet. "What is the cost of honesty?

"Persephone, I know you don't believe me, but I only want what's best for both realms. He doesn't understand why I kept him away, but it was always for his protection. He's safe down there, and everyone else is safe because they don't know their immortality can be taken away with the swipe of a blade."

"I suppose," she replied, her voice quivering with the force of her emotion, "that your lies assuage your own guilt, but do not mistake me for a fool. You sentenced your brother to become an exile. So you can tell yourself a pretty falsehood, but it does not mean I am stupid enough to believe it."

Infuriated, Zeus pulled away from the table as lightning flared about his body like a furious whip. "He's a killer!" he spat. "He murdered my mother, and you act as if he is innocent." His wrath dissipated swiftly, vanishing like a summer downpour, and as he approached her once more, a charming ease graced his demeanor. "I adored him, my older brother, and continue to do so. But I can't pretend I'm not outraged by what he did and continues to do." He made a motion with his hand. "You know, this used to be his room."

She could not help her curiosity as she glanced around, imagining a young Hades standing on the balcony, gazing at the stars in the heavens. She wished she had known him then.

Zeus was speaking, almost as if to himself. "I recall the day I freed him from our father. He emerged a bloody, horrifying wreck, bruised and broken. When Cronus spat him up, he had a whip wrapped around him. Demons had tortured him endlessly." He leaned in closer, his blue eyes pleading. "It made him lose his mind. He takes pleasure in the pain of others. It is not his fault, but I feel compelled to warn you. Your mother should have warned you."

"That is a lie!" Persephone cried, pushing up against the table to stand. "He is a good man. His soul is better than anyone I have ever known. Certainly, better than yours."

"Good?" Zeus scoffed. "He plots, and he schemes, just like our father. I suppose it's all he's ever known. It is what he grew up believing to be normal. Our youth shapes us." He let out a long sigh. "He never belonged here. In Cronus, he learned cruelty. I don't blame him, Persephone, but to deny that something is unbalanced in him is to deny the truth." Persephone shivered when the light slipped behind a cloud, and Zeus' face was cast in shadow. Lightning suddenly flashed in his eyes, illuminating them like glowing orbs in the darkness.

"I've never met a more ruthless creature, God or mortal, than my brother. You should have seen him during the Titan Wars; he was as frigid as ice. He'd slaughter men with no qualms. I should have known he was dangerous then, but my love blinded me. I'm afraid for you, Persephone, because you married such a man. Can you tell me honestly that you never noticed anything troubling in his behavior in all your time down there?"

Persephone glanced straight ahead, an involuntary chill running down her spine as she recalled the night of the transit. He had been deranged. But it was not his fault; he had been cursed and had fought against it to protect her.

"You are cold; what a poor host I am," Zeus murmured. Persephone turned her head as he waved his fingers, watching as two cherubs appeared, lifting pudgy hands to pull the clouds from the sky. The daylight penetrated the corners of the room once more. "I'm taking a big risk by talking to you, Persephone," he said softly. "You love him, and I admire that, but please consider what I'm saying. I'm afraid he's taking advantage of you. He is determined to enlarge his kingdom by conceiving a child to inherit the throne. Tell me, Persephone," he urged as he halted squarely in front of her. "Are you pregnant?"

She jerked back as if struck. "That's none of your business," she spat. "Neither is my relationship with Hades."

"Tell me, tell the King of Olympus," he cajoled as he gripped her arms, and she felt herself slipping into his eyes, a compulsion spreading over her limbs until she was helpless against it.

"No!" she exclaimed. "No, I am not."

Tearing herself from his embrace, she turned to the balcony, tears brimming. Tremors ran through her, remnants of his overwhelming influence. She despised her own helplessness. Determination surged within her; she vowed to be stronger. Sensing his proximity, she steeled herself, but he did not touch her this time.

"And have you ever been pregnant?" he inquired quietly.

"No," she lied flatly. She would never share that sorrow with Zeus. He would have to tear those memories from the deepest recesses of her mind.

"Doesn't that strike you as odd? You are a fertility Goddess, but you are still barren. He has duped you, my child. He is powerless. Cronus harmed him so severely that he was unable to produce an heir. His sole hope is that a fertility Goddess will grant him his wish. To him, you are a means to an end, a broodmare, and a fertile body to grow his wicked seed. He's using you."

Persephone's mind flashed to the night in Elysium and how her husband had known she was a fertility Goddess. He had asked her if she wanted children. There was a quiet knock that interrupted her thoughts. Zeus moved back from Persephone, pulling open the door. "Apollo, bring her forth," he murmured.

The Sun God entered, clutching the arm of a tangerine-haired maiden. With dismay, Persephone observed the wild-eyed woman in his arms. She was mortal and in great distress. Apollo stood tall, with hair as golden as the first rays of the rising sun and a burnished gold complexion. As he passed his gaze over Persephone, his dark eyes gleamed in his lovely face, and he smiled. The juxtaposition of the emaciated figure in his arms and the virile Sun God was almost obscene. The woman's beautiful gray eyes darted around the room, the pulse at her neck beating wildly. She reminded Persephone of a rabbit who had detected the fox's scent and was prepared to die.

Apollo and Zeus each grasped one of the woman's arms and began to drag her. She fought wildly, but they pushed the woman to walk, her legs buckling furiously with each effort. The mortal's mouth opened as if to cry, but no sound emerged. Finally, they deposited her on the oversized chaise. Apollo gently leaned back and brought his lips to the mortal's brow. The woman instantly relaxed, her gray eyes fixed ahead. His dark gaze returned to the Goddess' face.

"Persephone," the Sun God murmured, "please allow me to present you to Cassandra."

Zeus grabbed Persephone's wrist and pulled her towards the chaise. When he let her go, she whirled and landed next to the now-tranquilized Cassandra. He studied them both with a wide smile.

"Cassandra has an exceptional gift; she can see the future."

The sound of her name seemed to awaken the woman, and Cassandra whipped her head from side to side.

"I am not mad," Cassandra howled. "I am not mad!" Her voice was harsh and raw. Persephone raised her hand to comfort the young woman, but Cassandra drew back, screaming, "No! Do not touch me!"

Cassandra's rapid breathing filled the room, and her eyes began to roll back in her head. Persephone swiftly reached out to catch her as she sank to the floor. Cassandra's eyes widened as their skin brushed against one another's, and her fingers clenched like claws around Persephone's flesh.

"I see a child," the woman cried out.

Persephone tried desperately to remove her hand from her arm, but her fingers were like iron bars.

Zeus suddenly stepped forward, his eyes gleaming. "A child? Where?" he demanded.

"Born in blood!" shrieked Cassandra. Her brows drew over her eyes, leaving a confused crease on her smooth brow. "He is…"

"He is what?" Zeus urged her.

Cassandra's unseeing eyes wandered wildly around the room. "I see the abyss." Persephone and Cassandra were now pulling at the pale hand of the mortal, clutching the Goddess' arm. Cassandra let out a sorrowful wail like a crazed animal. "And I'm being drawn into it. I do not understand; I'm frightened! Let go, let go!" she implored herself.

"Do not let go!" Zeus bellowed. "What more do you see?"

"I see nothingness! Oblivion," she wailed. "Gods, what is this?"

"Let go of me!" Persephone cried desperately.

Apollo moved forward, placing a hand on his father's shoulder. "Her mind is going to snap. We must stop this."

Zeus pushed Apollo away from him, irritated. "I do not care if her mind shatters," Zeus sneered. He moved forward again, peering at the mortal. "What more do you see?" he urged. "The blades—what is he going to do with them?"

"Betrayal," she moaned as her eyes rolled back into her head and her body rocked with convulsions.

"Father, he is the 'Unseen,' and she will never be able to see what you want; this mortal can grasp nothing. It's practically impossible to get a glimpse of that world. Not even I can. I am releasing her."

Apollo came forward quickly and bent to kiss Cassandra between the brows again, and she relaxed in the chair, dropping down as if asleep. Persephone let out a relieved gasp as the painful grip on her arm was released. She jumped from the chaise and looked down at the broken woman, suddenly silent, her titian hair cascading around her pale face.

Zeus approached them and shoved his face against Apollo's, his mouth drawn back in a snarl. "Interfere again, and you will regret it," he hissed.

Apollo said nothing but carefully took Cassandra's limp form into his arms. She awoke as she was being hoisted. "I'm not mad," she whispered. Her head turned, and her eyes darted wildly until they landed on Persephone. "Everything you believe to be true is a lie," she screamed suddenly. "Lies, lie! Wicked deceptions." Her throat ripped with frantic cries till her voice was hoarse and red spittle foamed from her mouth.

"I'm taking her now," Apollo muttered, his mouth grim. "She will not give you anything else." The Sun God exited the room, tenderly embracing the madwoman in his arms, and Persephone heard the echo of her tears until the door closed firmly behind them.

Persephone turned to face Zeus, the claw wounds on her forearms beginning to heal. "What was that?" she asked, her voice low with anger.

"I want you to see how deeply you are involved in his falsehoods. Cassandra can only say what is true. She is incapable of telling lies."

"You made that poor woman spew these words at me! You suppose I am so weak that I can be swayed by the words of a stranger."

"You are a fool," Zeus hissed. "Hades only cares about himself. I can see Demeter made a mistake by sheltering you and separating you from Olympus. You are just what he was looking for. A fertile goddess oblivious to our ways, ready to fall for the first person who said the right words to her. He took advantage of your naivety and your mother's contempt for me. You believe that because we are terrible, he must be good. You never considered that he could be just as wicked, if not worse."

"You don't know anything!" she cried.

"Stupid child. He can sway thoughts with his mind. How often has he hypnotized you without your knowledge? He is quite deadly. He has evolved into a creature of the Underworld."

"I know he almost gave his life for me! He was nearly killed in the battle with Ares."

Zeus slammed his hand against the desk so hard that the room rocked beneath her feet, and she gasped. Sizzles of lightning passed over him. "Don't make me laugh. What match is Ares over an upper God? He used deception to lure you into eating the seeds. He duped you into thinking you made the decision." He laughed, running his fingers through his silver hair. "You had no say in the matter; he made the decision for you. He now has you down there for six months a year to fuck till you bear him an heir. You'll see his brutality much more now that he has everything he desires. You and your mother were duped. Your mother foolishly sought the help of Venus, who persuaded Demeter to cast you into the Underworld—envious that her beloved Ares favored you."

Her body trembled with fury. "I would like to leave now."

"No, not yet. I have some questions for you, and you will answer them." Zeus went to his desk opening an ivory box covered with elaborate golden engravings. The interior was lined in pale blue silk, and there was an indentation where a sword had once been. He glared furiously at the empty box. "Can you explain where my golden blade from the Cyclops has gone?"

Persephone advanced and slammed the box shut. "Your vile rapist child has it."

Zeus laughed mirthlessly. "Every God on Olympus would be missing limbs if Ares possessed the sword. Furthermore, we have already scoured Ares' Mountain. We looked everywhere except where we couldn't go! Down below."

"And whose fault is that?" Persephone sneered. "Because of your rules, you exiled him and now blame him. He is a convenient victim because you would not allow him to defend himself here. I haven't visited my kingdom in six months. I don't believe he has your weapon. I don't think he wants your weapon. He doesn't want anything from you."

Zeus leaned on the desk, his gaze fixed on hers. "I want you to keep an eye on my brother. I'd like you to inform me or Hermes if he has the blade. He could control the lower world and the higher world with both blades. I don't think you comprehend the gravity of the situation, Persephone; the swords combined can do horrible things. Before his exile, he did something terrible on Olympus years ago."

Her eyes narrowed. "What did Hades supposedly do?"

"No, I will not tell you. I can see that you are not ready to hear the truth about your husband. The fact remains that my blade is missing. The two blades were given to us to balance the scales, and my brother misused them. Were he to possess both..." Zeus shuddered and shook his head.

Persephone drew in closer, and the aroma of a fresh rainstorm pricked her nostrils once more as she leaned toward the mighty God. "You tell lies. Just as you lie about being my father."

"Where is the deception? I am the father of all of my Olympians, whether by blood or by right. I can take care of you up here. You're at his mercy down there. He will turn on you, just like he has all of us. As he turned against his mother."

She tilted her chin, her eyes blazing. "You spew your lies so effectively that I almost think you believe them yourself. You assassinated my father. You're attempting to make me doubt my husband. He loves me."

Persephone fell back as Zeus moved closer, standing almost nose-to-nose with her. "He only loves himself. He needed you to love him so he wouldn't go insane. Wasn't it all so convenient how it all turned out? All of this was orchestrated by him. He, like Cronus, possesses the power of foresight. He knew, Persephone, that Ares would rape you, Aphrodite would betray your mother, and you would never be free of the Underworld. Things will be drastically different for you now that you're imprisoned there for the next six months. But we waste time. There are more questions I need answered."

Zeus abruptly moved around the desk and wrapped his strong fingers around her forearm, pressing roughly over the fading wound that Cassandra had left. She struggled against him as he forced her to the balcony's edge. His hand extended into the air, and with a twist of his fingers, a mighty wind swelled around them. Before she could blink, they were whisked away from Olympus in a whirlwind, their bodies pushing against one another tightly as they flew quickly over the land below. Persephone let out a strangled shriek, attempting to extricate herself from the God as the storm whipped about them. The wind stopped, and she fell from the sky, landing hard on the rocky terrain below. They were encircled on all sides by barren mountains far from Olympus.

She jumped to her feet, tripping slightly as she spun around to face Zeus, who stood staring down at her. "Where have you taken me?" she demanded.

Zeus motioned behind her. "I have someone I would like you to meet."

Persephone turned to see a massive God dangling from the mountainside. His arms and legs were as enormous as tree trunks and spread wide by chains. As her gaze traveled over him, she exclaimed in horror: his abdomen had been split down the middle, and intestines poured from the gaping hole, blood, and fragments of torn organ trickling to the soil below. His graying, grizzled hair hung over his face, and he remained motionless as Zeus approached.

"Look at her," Zeus commanded. Zeus clenched his fists in the God's tangled hair, forcing him to raise his head. "I said, look at her, gaze into Demeter's daughter's face." Tired, dull eyes swept over Persephone, but his expression did not change. His gaze quickly fell again, and he resumed his bent posture. "So quiet now," Zeus spat on the ground, mixing his saliva with the pooling blood. He turned to Persephone. "Have you nothing to say to Prometheus?"

Persephone inhaled deeply; this helpless creature tied to a rock was a

Titan. She watched in anguish as a gigantic eagle swooped down from the sky, snatching entrails from Prometheus' stomach. The gray head remained still and bowed as the bird swallowed his intestines.

"Why are you doing this?" Persephone cried. As Zeus turned to face her, Prometheus offered a slight shake of his head, which only she saw. She paused, watching the bent head with uncertainty.

"Always sympathetic towards the traitor, aren't you, Persephone? Enough!" Zeus bellowed, causing rocks to tumble down the mountainside. "We squander our time with this fool and still have much to do tonight." He grasped Persephone's hand once more, and she felt a sizzle of electricity go through her, paralyzing her as he drew her to the edge of the mountain, and down, down, down they went, her stomach swooping until the wind surged up to meet them, drawing them back into the darkened sky towards Olympus.

As the wind began to slow, they once again appeared on Olympus' balcony, and Persephone stumbled as her feet suddenly connected to the ground. She turned as quickly as she could to face him; he was already storming towards her, pressing her towards the entrance of his study.

"Persephone, the time has come to choose a side. Either your husband or us." He tenderly wrapped his fingers around her slim throat. "In his world, you could be a significant asset. A pair of eyes to guide us. You unnecessarily isolate your mother and yourself. I can make the rules work for you. You are not obligated to stay down there. You have done nothing wrong."

Persephone maintained a rigid posture, her gaze fixed ahead. "You can bend them for me," she agreed, feeling his body jolt in surprise at her acquisition. "If you bend them for him as well," she finished.

He backed away from her, his blue eyes narrowing in anger. "So be it. I understand now that it was pointless to attempt to warn you. I have reached you far too late. Remember your decision. Keep in mind that you had choices. Everything that happens from now on is the result of your actions."

"My decisions!" Persephone cried. "What I witnessed in the palace tonight is revolting. You are repulsive. This kingdom's truth has been demonstrated to me."

"Strange thing—the truth," Zeus responded, smiling. "I have lived many years, and I can tell you, Gods nor mortals care for it. Just like you can't bear to hear the truth about your husband, the Gods can't accept that winter is something we will have to deal with for the rest of our lives. Ice floods across the country, crippling my dominion and destroying life as a result of the damage you and Demeter have caused the world. Who do you think they'll point the finger at? They will despise not only Hades but also his queen and her mother.

"When mortals die, his kingdom grows stronger, while mine weakens." His eyes narrowed. "*She*." His voice was strangled as if the word had stuck in his throat. "She did it to spite me, her terrible anguish of missing you and blaming me for the murder of that insipid mortal." He spat out the last syllable in disdain, then turned quickly to face the painting of Demeter.

Sensing his distraction, Persephone began to edge toward the balcony. She could escape this madness and let the wind carry her away if she could get close enough to the edge. Her mother had been right; she should never have come here.

"You looked exactly like her in the forest," Zeus remarked. As if sensing her retreat, his gaze was drawn back to her, and Persephone paused. "From a distance, it was like walking back in time. I felt like I was looking at Demeter." He came to an abrupt halt. "War is coming, Persephone; I will do all I can to safeguard the territories of my world. Safeguard my Olympians. I will protect you and your mother, even if she will punish me the moment you leave this realm. All these years, you walking this Earth was the only thing that kept her vengeance at bay."

"Demeter would never purposefully harm the innocent," Persephone retorted angrily. "Did you forget about the Olympians' role in this? Ares? Aphrodite? Demeter had no idea what was going on the last time. She now has a plan, and the mortals know winter is approaching. The animals are aware that they must prepare. The plants are also informed."

Zeus laughed heartily. "Oh, you're so naive. Olympus doesn't matter to her. She'll look forward to punishing me and my kingdom the moment you go. If you want to be an ally to the innocent, if you don't want mortals to perish, bring me my sword before your husband destroys Olympus."

"I told you," Persephone growled, her teeth clenched. "He does not have it."

His mouth curled in an unpleasant smile. "Remember, you can only blame yourself." As he examined her, he tilted his head.

"So, I am your enemy?"

"Oh, nothing so easy. Labels rather annoy me. You are both guilty and innocent. Daughter and adversary. You will see the truth one day, and I will be sorry for you. Regret is a great burden for the rest of one's life. When you are ready, I will welcome you back into my fold. Until then, certain ceremonies must be performed to ensure that my people do not perish and that the land is fertile when you return from the shadows." He moved to a table with a decanter of wine on it. He took it up and poured a small portion into two glasses. "The dust from the mountainside settles in the throat. You are caked in red dust."

She had been thinking about how dry her mouth felt. "No, thank you," she said as Zeus lifted a glass to her.

"How suspicious you are," he murmured. He drank from one and then handed it to Persephone. "Then take mine." He pressed it into her hand, and she took a tiny drink, just enough to wet her mouth, keeping her lips away from where he had touched the glass. He laughed and raised his own in salute before swallowing the entire contents.

"I will leave now," she said coolly. "There is no need for me to stay any longer. Your invitation was deceitful."

He turned again to look at the painting of Demeter, his face pensive. "I find it interesting," he continued as though she had not spoken, "that I have not seen you use your powers in all the hours you have spent with me. I wonder why that is."

She slowly set the glass down next to the decanter. "There is no need for me to grow anything here."

"Ah, yes," he said softly, "but those are not the only powers you have, are they, Dread Persephone?" His face swam before her suddenly, and she felt the room spinning.

"What did you call me?" she whispered, her voice seeming to come from a distance. She leaned against the wall to brace herself against a sudden wave of dizziness.

"Your name. Dread Persephone, the Bringer of Death," he said with a smile, coming nearer. "What is wrong?"

"The wine," she whispered as the room spun around her. "But you..."

He was standing very near her now. "Do you really think that you are my equal? I, who have lived for millennia? You really ought to learn to stop consuming fare from the Gods. What you drank has no effect on me but for a new, nubile Goddess? She will be feeling very disoriented after drinking even a small drop. You really are deliciously naive. Do not worry, daughter," he said softly as he pushed her to the floor, letting his fingers trail over her breast. She tumbled helplessly down, staring up at him mutely. "It is only to make you more docile for what is to come. It will wear off soon. I will not let anyone touch you… much."

She heard him clap his hands, and the door opened. She could see several nymphs standing over her, but she was paralyzed.

Zeus motioned to her prone form. "See that you wash and prepare my daughter for the celebration; she must leave a good first impression. And get rid of the rags she's wearing. She should be dressed as an empress, not in her mother's old clothes." She felt hands raise her and longed to scream, but her mouth stayed slack and silent. A rough hand caressed her face.

"See you soon, *daughter*."

CHAPTER 4
THE CELEBRATION

She was carried to a pale marble bedroom and placed on a plush, cushioned bed by the nymphs. They yanked her plain clothing from her body. Their hands trailed down her body, their gazes lingering over her breasts while she was soaked in cool, fragrant water. The chilly water was followed by strongly perfumed oils that they massaged into her skin, and she felt their hands sink between her knees before spreading the aroma down her thighs to her feet. She wanted to rip them off the bed and strike them, but she remained motionless like a helpless fool. Persephone's lips were smeared with dark berries by one of the nymphs, who then put honey over the crimson stain. Persephone's bottom lip dripped syrup, and a fair-haired nymph leaned forward and licked the excess off her mouth.

"You are magnificent," the nymph whispered against her ear. "Maybe later tonight, I may come to you if Zeus will allow it."

She stepped away from the silent Persephone and brushed the Goddess' hair, piling it high. Between the rich chestnut strands, the nymphs slid little diamonds. The maidens lifted Persephone from the bed and placed a thin toga over her head, shining like stars. Her head was crowned with a silver laurel wreath. The same fair nymph knelt between her legs, drawing her foot onto her lap, and began to put on silver sandals. Her fingers traveled up Persephone's calf before she set her foot down and held her other foot, performing the same movements on the other side. She made her way up Persephone's body, and the petite nymph rose on her toes once again to press her lips against the Goddess'.

"Iara," snapped one of the maidens behind Persephone. "Do not touch her. Zeus will be angry."

Iara glared. She stepped away, pouting. "He usually lets us play with them."

"Not this one; she is different. Help us move her now."

Iara followed her, and the nymphs carried her to a vast dining hall. The table was empty but piled high with strange delicacies—the horrible combination of meats was nauseating. The chamber was lit softly, and there was a raised dais towards the head of the table. Persephone was placed in a chair, and she wanted to scream as she felt her neck, back, and wrists being secured by light, translucent chains. Nobody would notice that she was imprisoned. She stared, terrified, as additional Gods began to flood the chamber. Each wore a basic white toga, and their features were partially hidden by golden masks, but she recognized a few of them.

Apollo's hands guided a flame-haired woman who moved slowly behind him—Cassandra, Persephone thought with a pang of dread and pity. Persephone watched as Hermes entered the room, holding his caduceus. His blue eyes flitted away from her as he caught her stare beneath his mask. More people arrived until the table was full, except for the seat next to her, which remained empty. Most upper Gods were present except for Athena, Artemis, and her mother; no potential allies were in attendance. When she looked around again, Persephone realized Ares wasn't there either. What should she do? Should she call her mother? But that would put Demeter in danger, and Persephone would never do that again. She tried to move her hands, urging her fingers to move, and imagined she saw a twitch. Suddenly, Persephone sensed movement in the periphery of her vision.

"How beautiful you look," a voice close to her ear said. Zeus. He shifted her chair slightly so that she could see him fully. Long, pale robes draped from his neck to his feet, and a hood was drawn over his white hair. The firm set of his jaw, with his eyes obscured, reminded her of her husband. "It could always be like this, Persephone," he said, motioning to the vast hall filled with the magnificent Gods. "You might be one of us. You discovered how to be content with my brother. You might be able to learn to be satisfied with me."

Zeus leaned in closer until the intense blue of his gaze was so close that she could see golden flecks in it. He placed his lips against her limp mouth and brushed his tongue over her lower lip. "You taste just like your mother," he whispered against her mouth.

Bile rose in her throat, and Persephone wanted to scream, to tear his tongue from his mouth, but she couldn't; she could not utter even a moan of protest. She shifted her gaze away from his—the only defiance she could muster—and he appeared to understand, anger making his blue eyes flinty.

"Then you'll find out the hard way."

Zeus abruptly threw back his hood, and the covered faces turned towards him, cheering. In the dimly lit chamber, a golden laurel wreath crowned his head. He was beautiful, this King of the Gods. When Zeus raised his hands, the crowd fell silent.

"My beloved Gods and Goddesses, I have invited you to join me on this special occasion to welcome my daughter, Persephone, Queen of the Underworld." The audience applauded, and Zeus returned his gaze to Persephone, a smile on his lips and venom in his eyes. "Unfortunately, my brother declined my invitation because he is not an Olympian. He cursed everyone and stated nothing at the gathering could convince him to return to this mountain." She could feel the crowd's gaze, her cheeks flushing at the insult, as she sat as docile as a doll.

"We would have been delighted to have had the beautiful Persephone as an Olympian, but because her husband is no longer one, we must sadly strip her of that status. Queen Persephone, on the other hand, has a new title." The corner of his mouth twisted up. "From today onward, Persephone will be known as the "Bearer of Death." Our world will wither and die when she leaves this realm. Some of our people will perish as winter sweeps across the land. We will suffer while she and her husband celebrate below." Cries of fury raced around the table. Zeus went on, this time allowing the mumbled whispers to continue. "Mortals will come to fear her name.

"Because the King of the Underworld is not here to tell the tale, my darling daughter and I have put together a play to entertain you about how the happy couple met." Zeus finally sat, and with a clap of his hands, the room went dark. He grasped the armrests of her chair and shifted her so she could view the high altar fully. She willed her voice out, but her throat spasmed in vain. "So you can see everything, my sweet," his words a soft caress against her lips. "This is a night you will never forget."

The nine Muses rushed into the room, and Persephone immediately recognized those dressed as her, Hades, and Demeter. The Muses began to dance as music filled the great hall. The act was a mockery of their relationship, depicting a completely different scenario far from the truth. Demeter was described as an overbearing mother and a crazed, jilted lover of Zeus. She kept his lovely and innocent child hidden on the border between Gods and mankind to punish him. As a result, Persephone grew to be odd and silly. Demeter shouted and bellowed with each marriage proposal, and Persephone wept as her mother rejected each God, ending her chance at escape from an obsessive mother.

But no matter how horribly they painted Demeter, it was nothing compared to the portrayal of her husband. He was depicted as a ruthless and despotic king who dragged the beautiful Persephone from Earth to the Underworld. On their wedding night, the actors portrayed him raping her. Her screams rang across the dark kingdom as blood saturated the bed. He denied her food and drink, training her to be less than an animal and gradually brainwashing her into adoring him. Persephone was a weak-minded child who fell for the first man she lay with. Meanwhile, Demeter devastated the Earth above, shrieking and howling like a frenzied madwoman, her hair wild about her face as she wailed her daughter's name.

And the crowd loved it. They booed when Hades raped his wife and wailed when the innocent Persephone became so hungry that she was forced to consume the pomegranate seeds, which her husband gladly shoved into her mouth. Hades had been right: Zeus would alter history, and everyone would believe him. The Gods were fixated on the scene before them, and they reveled in it—this twisted farce contrived by Zeus. Even if she miraculously rose from her chair and shouted the truth at them, they would never believe her. She, her mother, and Hades' characters had all been painted, and there was no erasing the ink. She could hear the Gods whispering among themselves: deluded,

naive child, her husband had "cast a spell on her."

However, two other Gods present were aware of the truth. Her gaze was drawn to Aphrodite, whose magnificent eyes were riveted on the stage, her perfect mouth curved in a smile. There would be no help there. Persephone's gaze traveled down the table and met Hermes'; she saw the truth in his stare and frown, but he remained mute. Nobody would speak on their behalf. From this point on, history will remember Hades as the villain who had to kidnap a reluctant bride and force her to adore him. He was a mad king in the eyes of this crowd. The Muses took their bows as the play finished, and the audience erupted in applause. They had enjoyed the drama, and the falsehood was always more appealing to the hungry mob than the truth. Wine flowed freely between the Gods, and they appeared high on the endorphins of the show, unaware or uncaring that it was a farce.

"Are you upset?" Zeus muttered, turning her face to rest against his shoulder. The chain around her neck tightened cruelly, and Zeus rubbed where it pressed against her furious pulse. "Nevertheless, I did it to shield you and your mother from culpability. Their rage should be directed towards him rather than at either of you. But we're not done yet." He slowly lifted her head, turning her face forward.

Two strong guards carried a large object with a silken blue cloth covering the stage.

"I had a new statue constructed to adorn the halls of Olympus. I am delighted for my brother that he has found such a docile and lovely wife." Zeus moved forward to tear the silken blanket from the enormous object, revealing a hideous statue of Hades carrying Persephone down into the Underworld. As he assaulted her, his face was flung back in laughter. Persephone's marbled face was stuck in a distorted scream, her arms grasping for salvation that would never arrive. "And now," he continued, "for the final performance, in honor of my beautiful daughter." He once more sat and drew Persephone's hand high onto his thigh. "I think you will enjoy this one," he whispered.

Dancing nymphs whirled about the chamber, making their way to the dais that the Muses had vacated. A young maiden dressed in long white robes was carried in and placed on the center of the marble altar. Her pale skin glistened in the candlelight, and her long chestnut hair cascaded to the floor. The hair was the identical color of her own, she realized with a cold shudder of foreboding. She urged her hands to move, yearning to be free. The young woman shifted restlessly on the altar, her eyes closed, chains on her ankles and wrists.

The Muses hurried forward to hold the maiden's arms and legs as Zeus stood, approaching the altar. The God took a large knife from his robes and sliced the fabric that covered the maiden, exposing her nude body as she writhed on the cold stone. A nymph brought him a golden chalice, and he bent down to pour it on the woman's lips. Zeus rose up and held the empty chalice towards the chamber after she had drunk heavily from it. Persephone shifted her gaze across the room, sensing the building excitement of the audience, their gazes fixated on Zeus. Nymphs were scattered about the chamber, handing out wine to each visitor. Persephone could smell the nutty fragrance that lingered in the air, and it pulled her back to a memory of when she had mixed the draft to put her husband to sleep. The wine was heavily laced with poppies.

Zeus let out a boisterous laugh. "We smuggled these flowers from the Underworld for this special occasion. Believe me, it was no easy feat; Lord Hades disapproves of trading between worlds." A nymph rushed forward to refill his cup, and he took an appreciative sip of the wine, the knife carelessly dangling from his other hand. "Ah, no one grows poppies like Hypnos, not even Demeter. It seems our little mortal enjoys this as well," Zeus said as his eyes moved to the restless form on the altar. "Would you like some more?"

Zeus took another sip from the chalice before kneeling to kiss the imprisoned mortal. She pushed forward as far as her chains would allow and licked Zeus' lips, tasting the drugged wine off his mouth. The Gods roared in delight, filling the room with foreboding laughter, and Zeus' gaze moved to Persephone as the mortal feasted on his lips. When every drop was gone, he rose up and moved to the edge of the stage. "As we lose the Queen of Spring to the Underworld, our world will wither and die. This sacrifice will be made to Queen Persephone, who, henceforth, shall be known as the 'Queen of Shades, Queen of Death, who rules the Kingdom of the Damned.'"

He lifted the knife into the air, his gaze fixed on Persephone. Her mind screamed in agony, her immobile body twitching helplessly with the desire to move as she understood what he meant to do. He shook his head, a smirk on his lips, knowing she couldn't lift a finger. The room trembled as lightning arced across the sky.

"I call this day 'The Secular Games,'" he continued, "and one day, men will sacrifice innocent lives to the great Hades and Persephone. May the blood of this young virgin replenish the Earth for my daughter's return."

The Olympians slammed their fists on the table and shouted, "For the Dreaded Queen," over and over. Zeus' white teeth glinted as his gaze returned to Persephone's face, and he turned and raised the knife high before plunging it into the intoxicated woman's heart. Persephone's mind was filled with mute, terrible screams as the woman's body wrenched in pain, too drugged to even groan.

Zeus raised his glass in his blood-splattered hand. "To Queen Persephone, Bringer of Destruction."

The Gods lifted their cups and drank greedily. The woman on the altar was choking on blood, but Zeus had left the knife embedded in her chest, causing her to bleed slowly. Zeus stripped off his garments, revealing his tanned, muscular skin beneath; his massive cock protruded, erect, and engorged as he kneeled down to the dying maiden. "She doesn't have to die a virgin," he laughed as he mounted her. The Gods began to rise, pressing closer to the stage, as Zeus violated the dying woman.

The other Gods began to remove their garments as music erupted. While nymphs surrounded Dionysus, Hermes eagerly slid between Aphrodite's legs. Apollo and Cassandra went to a secluded area. As Apollo bent to her breast, her low whispering could still be heard: "I'm not mad, I'm not mad."

Persephone's gaze swept across the scene, the horrible sound of thrusting filling the room, flesh against flesh. This young mortal deserved so much more; her precious life was discarded as easily as if it were less than refuse. The young maiden was dying, her soul between worlds, as much a citizen of her kingdom now as Zeus'. Persephone closed her eyes and willed the sounds and images of their heinous celebration away until she found a faint, fluttering heartbeat that lured her closer. Death. It called to her and whispered to her to come nearer. Somehow, before Persephone could understand how her soul was linked to the dying woman, she saw the mortal's golden thread unravel strand by strand as she died. The maiden gasped as her lungs filled with fluid and blood, her intoxicated, panicked mind oblivious to her impending death.

Breathe with me, Persephone said softly into her mind. Persephone willed her own light to mingle with the woman's until they breathed. Persephone saw flashes of the woman's life and pushed the most joyful memories to the surface until there was no Zeus, no room, and no Gods, only sweet memories of childhood and happiness; she felt the maiden smile. And it was then, as her soul wrapped protectively around the dying, that it awakened; that tiny seed of power within her soul burst to life, and her mouth finally moved.

"Tu autem condemnabitur."

The candlelight went out, and she felt the chains snap, releasing her. A burning, white glow pulsed from her skin, illuminating the room. The air was filled with confused screams as she lifted her hands and floated towards the dais. The maiden's gaze was drawn to her, her beautiful, tranquil smile still resting on her lips. Persephone's eyes became a green flame as their gazes met, and the mortal's eyes dilated. Persephone raised her hand, and the knife was lifted from her chest as the woman collapsed, exhaling her last breath.

Zeus was crouching down, watching her, his eyes fixed on her levitating form. Her gaze landed on the statue of Hades and herself, and she lifted her hand, causing the statue to shatter into a million fragments that flew across the room like daggers. The Gods were fleeing, but the drugged wine made them clumsy, making them ideal targets, and Persephone lifted her hand, a shard impaling Hermes' back as he ran. Aphrodite raced forward, her lovely face contorted with horror as she dragged him out of the room. The dining room began to fracture as Persephone raised her arms again, the chairs and tables crumbling like children's toys. Zeus stood motionless as debris whizzed past him. Finally, he moved, stepping casually over the dead mortal at his feet.

"I met the queen at last," he greeted, bowing as he levitated into the air. "You are formidable, but you appeared too late, I fear. They will remember that you sat there, never saying a word. You never stopped me from sacrificing that maiden. I never got to finish with her. Perhaps I should finish with you," he mocked. He flexed his fingers, and lethal lightning arced across his hands, his motions erratic and his eyes clouded by the effects of the poppy. "What do you say, queen? Shall I sample my brother's leftovers?"

Something within her seemed to split at his mocking, disgusting words, the weak control she had on the dark magic ebbing away as something surged free from deep within her. The shadowy awareness that emerged was both her and not her, and its intensity was terrifying. She attempted to push it back inside her, but the magic was too powerful.

"I say this," the dark Persephone hissed as she brought down the ceiling with a final lift of her hands, and Zeus emitted a garbled yell before falling back.

"You crazy bitch!" he yelled as marble splattered across the hall. "You indoctrinated whore, bring me my sword before I start a war with you!"

The room began to disintegrate around her, the floors splintering, and she tried to flee, but she realized she couldn't stop the flood of angry magic spilling from her fingertips. Panic overtook her, yet the more frantic she became, the more control slid from her grasp. In the face of her rage, the entire palace could crumble. Gods, how did she stop this? She could feel Zeus' wrathful stare as she battled to regain control. As the room began to shatter, Persephone tumbled to the floor, her dazzling light fading as vast chunks of the room fell dangerously close to her. On the opposite side of the chamber, she could just make out the enraged God in the shadows; his blue eyes narrowed on her. His arm was extended in an attempt to reach her, but he was unsteady due to his drunkenness. She stood, fleeing the hall, as his voice echoed behind her.

"From the flame to the fire! You run towards your doom!"

Persephone sprinted through a labyrinth of dimly lit corridors, gasping for air as she pressed against a cold pillar. Opposite her loomed Zeus' throne room; the urgent need to move conflicted with her labored breathing. She berated herself for not heeding the warnings of Demeter and Hades; their admonitions had been painfully correct. Legs trembling, she collapsed to the floor, desperate to catch her breath. Panic set in as she noticed blood on her arms, futile attempts to wipe it away, only staining her robes further. The perversion she witnessed surpassed her wildest imagination, and the Gods had reveled in the debauchery.

A chilling realization gripped her when she heard the night fill with shouts, realizing the disgusting revelry persisted behind the closed doors of the throne room. The air in the temple hung thick with the scent of incense, opiates, and lingering passion. Anguish and frustration drove her to slam her fists against the ground, but it was too late. The opportunity to make a difference had slipped through her fingers, and the consequences of the Gods' immoral revelry were inescapable. *She* was too late!

As she watched the maiden die, she suddenly felt a dark power fill her. And she had held that power in her control for a brief period, but it had rapidly slipped from her hands. She was aware of the dangers of a God who was unable to maintain control of their powers, and she had told herself that this would never be her, that she would never be that selfish God. However, she had nearly been. And now she was in a much more perilous scenario than before, her vulnerability obvious. The drug Zeus had given her was still coursing through her blood, and her muscles jerked from exhaustion. She had been practicing for six months and could hardly move.

Persephone ducked swiftly as she noticed movement at the far end of the dimly lit hall. A man sagged in the doorway, his shadowy figure unsteadily moving. The moonlight revealed his body, but it was too dark to see his face. His sweaty chest glistened, and he was bare from the waist up. The man paused as he passed the throne room, sighing at the noises. With a grunt, he tossed a heavy sack over his shoulder, and something tumbled from it, rolling down the corridor until it came to a stop at her feet, and she let out a horrified gasp. It was a decapitated head! The severed head shifted direction as she scrambled to stand, and she stared at it in horror. The visage staring back at her was the distorted, lifeless face of Theo, the man she had reunited with his wife. She had saved him from death. How was this possible? Her gaze lifted, and she moved down the long corridor until she locked eyes with the shadowed man, and her breath caught in her throat. His head was cocked like a fox stalking its prey as he stood motionless.

"No," she whispered, terror filling her. For it was the God of War who stared back at her.

She fled from the hall, forcing her legs to pump when they wanted to collapse. She abruptly stopped when she recognized the doors of Zeus' office. Her best chance was on the balcony. She tried to turn the handle, but the door was locked. Vines pushed out of her palms and into the lock, but her hands were made clumsy by exhaustion and fear. A snarl echoed down the corridor. Ares had tracked her down. He locked his gaze on her before charging down the corridor, his boots pounding on the marble floor. She cried out, raised her hands, and shot a forest of briars at him.

"You think those will stop me?" he growled. He pulled his sword from its sheath and began hacking a path. Persephone returned to the lock and again inserted the vine, twisting and turning desperately.

"Come on, come on," she cried.

The lock gave way with a final twist of her hand, and she yanked the doors open, closing them in Ares's face as he reached where she had been standing seconds before. The violent beating of his fists trembled the door; she lifted her hands to sprout gigantic thorny trees, thrusting spiky needles through the keyhole so that they covered the outside of the door. Her entire body trembled with fury, exhaustion, and fear. As she moved past the chess board, she flung out her arm, hurling the Olympian pieces across the room.

"Bastard!" she yelled, her ire focused on the tiny statue of Zeus. "You sick bastard!" She pressed her hands against her face. "You coward," she chastised herself in disgust. "You ran again." With a soft sob, she stepped towards the chess table, raising the obsidian Hades and clutching it tightly against her chest. "I am not a fool," she whispered in the stillness. "You have not deceived me."

She ran to the balcony, clutching the chess piece, and stared into the quiet summer night, the lush green leaves lighted by the moon, the sky still and peaceful, and she wanted to scream. She attempted to conjure enough wind to lower herself to the ground far below but was too weak. She screamed in frustration as the moon hung high in the sky, her voice echoing loudly in the valley. "Where have you gone?" she cried. "You promised that you would be here. I need you." She impatiently wiped the tears off her cheeks. "I need you," she repeated again. "You said you would return in six months!" But there was no answering voice in the silent night—only damning silence. "Fine," she said in a low voice. "I will make you come."

She extended her hands upward to blast chilly air through the clouds and bring snow to the land. Dew fell from the sky, and instead of a blizzard, hundreds of snowdrop flowers blossomed up and around the balcony.

"My powers are useless," she said in a hollow voice, staring down at her hands in disgust.

What sort of Goddess was she? She had fled Ares after everything; after months of training, it had all meant nothing. She ought to have remained and challenged him! Though the pounding on the door had ceased, she knew Ares would never give up that easily. If she could not fly down, she would have to climb. She got to her feet and glanced over the balcony.

Lightning flashed across the horizon, illuminating the palace as she stepped over the balcony. Low thunderclaps rumbled so strongly that she could feel the trembling in her chest. Dark clouds were moving quickly over the moon, and a fierce wind blew through the valley, uprooting trees. She reached out to catch one of their leaves as it whirled past her; it was a lovely shade of gold. Her heart stuttered. Autumn had arrived. The once warm summer night rapidly changed to a frigid one. Persephone gasped as a brilliant light suddenly shone from the sky. There, in the stars, was the constellation of a bull, and she recognized the figure.

"Cerus," she cried. "I will come back for you," she whispered to the stars, a tear slipping down her face. How had her precious friend been sent to the heavens?

Another clap of thunder shook the balcony. Persephone straightened, standing as sleet began to fall from the sky, soaking through her clothes. He was coming. As Persephone turned her head toward Demeter's temple in the east, her heart twisted.

A voice was carried by the wind. "Farewell, my daughter. Let winter take you to the safety of the Underworld."

"Mother," Persephone whispered back. "I will miss you."

CHAPTER 5
THE SHADOW

The sound of thunder resounded in the wind as one last hooded figure emerged from the shadows. It slipped silently through the temple, moving down the dimly lit hallways, a thin crescent moon dully illuminating its path. The shadowy form effortlessly climbed onto the balcony and entered the royal chamber. Its head was lowered, taking in the drowsy, jumbled bodies on the floor. The once gentle summer breeze now brought bitter cold, and the bare bodies shivered, oblivious to the storm that raged outside. The masked phantom crept stealthily through the intertwined figures, bending to inspect each woman's face. Sprawled between Hermes and Apollo was Aphrodite; between two mortal men, Hera was lying, and Pan was lying on top of Enyo, his flute thrust in between her legs. The figure paused, surveying the room, and Dionysus stretched out and grasped the hooded figure's muscular, lean calf. He pointed drunkenly to the five nymphs lying across his abdomen.

"Ah, a man," he slurred. "Come and join our bouquet of lovers. I could use a man's strong mouth around my balls." As Dionysus peeked up at the shrouded figure, red eyes glared at the inebriated God from beneath the hood. The merry God fell back with a peep of fear.

A deep voice emerged from beneath the cloak. "If you are so in need of a man's touch, then I will gladly rip off your balls and shove them into your mouth. You can suck on them before shitting them out, Dionysus." The God of Wine hid his ruddy face in a nymph's large, pale breast. "Another time then," the hooded figure said politely as he continued to weave through the orgy.

He emitted a strangled cry as his gaze shifted from the gyrating bodies on the floor to the enormous throne. Hera's marble chair was strewn with an abandoned figure, her beautiful chestnut hair the only thing covering her bare, broken body. She held a single red rose, and a large silver crown sat carelessly atop her head. He hurried forward, inhaling heavily, his hands trembling as he separated the matted hair to reveal a young, mortal woman's face, still with the quietness of death. He gently lowered her back to the chair.

A low laugh rumbled from the shadows. "Do you like my new queen, brother?" The words were hissed, and Hades turned to see a tall, cloaked figure near the door.

"Zeus," Hades greeted softly. The white figure threw back his hood, and Hades' dark eyes met his sibling's sterling, cold blue.

"I am afraid a mock queen was the best I could do for now. As you see, my wife is otherwise occupied," he said with a smile as he began to circle the room. "The great Hades. Have you come to join in the fun? Or are you still fucking corpses?" He gestured to the dead body on his throne. "Maybe I will let you take her when I send you slinking back into the pit you call home. I doubt you would know the difference between that and your wife."

Hades' gaze moved to the young girl on the throne. "And where is my wife?" he asked softly.

Zeus shook his finger at him mockingly. "Ah, but if you lose it and I find it, I get to keep it. As it happens, my *daughter* is hiding. Unfortunately, it turns out she is as much a prude as her mother and my corpse-fucking brother. But I can fix that; she shall be taken under her father's wings."

"It is fortunate then that there is no part of you in her blood." Hades stepped closer to the throne and placed his hands over the mortal's eyes, closing them. He lifted the girl's hair and saw the jagged knife wound over her heart. When he turned to face his brother, his eyes glowed purple. "I see that time has taught you nothing. Why did you kill this woman?"

"Ah, brother," he began, his full lips lifting in a smile. "Because I wanted to." He raised his hand to his head thoughtfully. "No, better yet, because I could. And your wife watched as I did it, and would you believe it, she did not say a word in protest."

"You are right. I do not believe it," Hades replied. "You have not changed, Aene'ius."

Zeus' lips curled back. "Do not call me that. That name died the same way as yours. When you became Underworld filth, I became the God of the Gods."

Hades turned, and his eyes moved over the room. "Months turn to years, and eternity stretches before us, but you remain the same. You have no respect for those you consider weaker than you, but your entire existence hinges on worshipping those you so easily discard. You will never change." He gestured to the drunken Gods. "*This* will never change."

Thunder rumbled through the temple, and an icy wind swept over the inebriated deities. Snowflakes began to fall on the marbled floor, and the Gods marveled as they touched the delicate ice, Aphrodite licking the white flakes from a nymph's mouth.

Zeus cocked his head to the side, his blue eyes darkening as they moved over his brother's face. "You have something that belongs to me."

Hades gazed leisurely over each God until he finally touched upon Zeus again. "As do you."

Zeus laughed. "Everything the sun touches belongs to me, brother." Zeus stepped closer to him so their faces almost touched, and he leaned forward to whisper in his ear. "And when this is finished, *nothing* will be yours. I will own the dark and the light, hold it all in my fist, and crush you."

Hades smiled, letting his teeth show. "Take care, Aene'ius. Be sure that it does not reach back for you as you reach into the darkness."

Zeus drew back, a smoldering hatred in his blue eyes. As he circled Hades, lightning illuminated the temple. "You are bold to step foot on Olympus, tell me. What has given you the courage to leave your

crypt?"

Hades' purple gaze pierced his brothers' icy one. "It turns out there is one thing that can tempt me back onto this shithole of a mountain. It is six months to the day, and that is why you brought her here, right? Where is she?"

"Do you really think I would make it that easy? Just deliver her to you. I will watch you lose everything, starting with your wife."

The freezing air began to rouse the Gods from their slumber, and several started to push unsteadily from the floor.

"It is unfortunate you will not tell me," Hades murmured, turning to outstretch his hand. As he did so, a golden beam of light streamed from the center of his forehead, flowing to each Olympian's third eye. They moaned in unison, collapsing to the floor in pain as he probed each of their minds at the same time, searching for Persephone. Cassandra's hysterical screams merged with the Gods, and the mortals in the room tried to crawl away.

"Underworld filth! You will not touch the Olympians," Zeus bellowed.

Zeus raised his hands and hurled a powerful bolt of silver lightning at Hades. The King of the Underworld kept his light focused on the Olympians but lifted one of his hands, grasping the bolt of light as it arced towards him before dropping it to the ground. As it shattered, the Olympians were thrown against the wall, and their cries echoed as the lightning wrapped around them, sizzling their immortal flesh. Hades closed his eyes and allowed his soul to search for its other half.

Persephone. The dark whisper moved through the temple, and the walls trembled as it passed.

"You are not taking her! She belongs to me!" Zeus shouted. White lightning flashed from his hands towards Hades, whose eyes opened just in time to counter with his own purple energy. Hades stepped closer to the king, laughing, as silver light pressed against violet, and the energy hissed and cracked through the air.

"You are drugged; you drink too much and have gotten lazy." Hades laughed softly. He pressed the purple light forward until the silver light burned out, and the King of the Underworld stood face-to-face with the King of Olympus. Hades took Zeus' hand, bending the wrist until it almost snapped. "You cannot possess what is free." Zeus looked down at their hands and lifted his head with a smile. Hades' nose began to bleed, and Zeus' laugh was low.

"There is nothing I cannot have. I will enjoy watching your life flow from your body."

Hades gripped his arm tighter. "You have your children fight your battles for you as you rape and pillage the Earth." He twisted his opposite hand to probe Zeus' mind, forcing memories to the surface. He watched as his brother kissed Persephone with blood-stained lips. "Just like her mother?" Hades hissed.

Zeus' face twisted angrily, his breathing heavy. His eyes were still heavily lidded from the opiates. "Yes. Just like her."

Hades raised his hand to strike again when he felt something move against his spirit—something pure, light, and beautiful.

"Hades!" a voice cried from across the room. He turned slowly, and she stood at the throne room's entrance. Everything he had hoped for in the previous six months stood right before him. Her beautiful face was beaming with joy, and she looked like spring, sunshine, and everything he had ever desired. Looking at her, he lowered his hand and softened his expression.

"Persephone," he said quietly. He extended his arm, beckoning her to come to him.

Zeus' eyes narrowed as he watched Persephone walk towards Hades, her gaze fixed on her husband, seeing only him.

"I will not allow this!" Zeus bellowed.

Arcs of lightning flashed across his eyes, obscuring his pupils with silver. His white hair stood on end as he raised his arms. Deadly lightning bolts shot from his eyes, and with another rage-filled scream, a bolt of electricity blasted the King of the Dead in the shoulder. Hades moved quickly, raising his hands to form a dark forcefield around Persephone and himself, preventing Zeus from reaching them. The lightning pulsed furiously against the shield, desperate to enter. Zeus levitated high above the ground as the wind blew wildly across the room. The King of Gods' power was returning as the effects of Hypnos' poppies wore off.

"Persephone," Hades called, with an urgency to his voice. "Come to me now."

Zeus' terrible eyes moved to her, and he lifted his hand towards her, blasting powerful wind towards them, but Hades' shield held. "Persephone, I warn you for a final time," Zeus bellowed. "Go with him, and you will watch your kingdom burn."

Hades shook his head, yelling through the storm, "Persephone, do not listen to him. Come with me."

"Do not go with him!" Zeus demanded. "He is dangerous! He will destroy you."

"By law, she must come with me, by your law! The same rule holds me there."

"I can rewrite the law," Zeus spat. "I hold the very power of the galaxy at my fingertips."

"Not this time," Hades snarled.

The Gods of the Dead and Olympus fell silent as Persephone moved until she had closed the final distance between herself and her choice. Zeus' malevolent gaze followed her as she circled her arms around Hades' neck. She raised her face and let her green eyes travel over the raging God above them.

"I told you, the "Dreaded Queen" stands with her king. She will *always* stand with her king." When she looked at Hades, his eyes were filled entirely with black, and the depths were so dark and deep that she was afraid she would be sucked into the blackness. A tendril of fear curled around her. He looked like a demon. She could feel his powerful body tremble with a violent rage beneath her fingers. "Hades," she whispered. "Take us away from here."

Black smoke began to drift from the room's shadows. Despite everything that had happened, Persephone had never seen him lose control so completely in all their time together. Veins glowed black beneath his skin, and he shifted his gaze, the black eyes locking onto her, and she couldn't take her gaze away from him. The Olympians covered their ears as Hades began to chant in an ancient language, the words strange and terrible, and their frightened screams echoed in the wind. She felt herself falling, falling into the darkness of his eyes and then screamed as she was drawn into the shadow.

Zeus was thrown back past the throne as a massive blast of blue fire and smoke filled the temple. As he landed, the marble cracked, and he quickly righted himself, his eyes darting around the room, but the King and Queen of Death had vanished. His rage echoed through the snow-covered mountains.

As Hades carried his queen through the sky, the wind howled, the mighty tempest swirling around them. Their bodies were intertwined, and Persephone pressed her face against his neck, her lengthy hair blowing behind her. She took a deep breath, inhaling his enticing scent. She tilted her head to look up at him as she felt his fingers on her face. She felt shy after all this time as her beautiful, powerful husband stared down at her, finding it difficult to meet his gaze. Snow eddies formed, and as lightning arced across the frozen night sky, Hades gently touched Persephone's face. His dark eyes were fixed on her, and the corners of his mouth were lifted. She traced the dimple on one edge of his lips with her fingers.

"Persephone," he whispered, pulling her tightly against him. "Did you think I would not come for you?"

Her tears had frozen into ice on her cheeks. "I thought you had forgotten me."

"Never," he said quietly. "I could never forget you. I told you, remember, I'll come for you when the first snow falls on the mountains." Storm clouds shattered the moonlight, casting strange shadows across his face, half-light, half-dark. Her angel and her devil. Diamonds fell from the strands as he brushed his hands through her hair, tumbling to the Earth far below. "You are etched so deeply in my soul, Persephone, that the very fibers of it are weaved from you. I will always come for you. I will always wait. Whatever you need, I will be for you." His lips traced her ear, and Persephone shivered.

"Hades," she breathed.

He raised his head and gently brushed his lips against hers. She jerked her head nervously, then laughed sheepishly. "I'm sorry," she said, blushing. "It's been so long, and I've forgotten how to do it right."

As he looked down at her, he smiled tenderly. "Dear little wife, I will remind you."

Then, as his mouth moved over hers, she was consumed by his taste and heat. They rose higher and higher into the frigid night sky, but all she could feel was him pressing against her body and the growing need that drew at her. His teeth pressed against her lower lip, and she groaned. As his tongue pushed into her mouth, she felt as if he was possessing her, consuming her, until the air she breathed was filled with his essence.

"Open your eyes, Persephone."

Her eyes opened dazedly, and when she looked down, she saw the rich, green grass of Elysium, the beautiful island suspended above the turquoise sea.

"But how?"

The sun was setting over the pink horizon as their feet reached the lush grass. "I thought you might prefer this to the last time you came into this world. As King of the Underworld, I have the right to enter any part of my domain, as do you, Queen Persephone." His hand brushed against her shoulder and tugged at her gown's sleeve. "A gift from Olympus?"

Persephone's green eyes met his. "An unwelcome gift."

Hades' eyes became darker. "He should never have touched you." His fingers slowly pulled the gown from her shoulders, and a wicked smile curved his mouth. "It is a sin for anything to cover you."

Hades traced his lips across her skin as the gown slipped from her, and she shivered in the warm air. Hades straightened, his face still and taut, as she stood naked, the setting sun behind her. His high cheekbones were flushed, and his chest moved quickly. "You are so beautiful." He held her silver dress loosely in his hand and pushed a silver flame from his palm, the fabric quickly burning in the bright light. His lips curled as the dress in his hands turned to ash, and the flaming light danced in his dark eyes. With a laugh, he let the ash fall from his fingers, drawing his cape from behind him to wrap around her. "Happy Anniversary, my lovely wife," he said softly, kissing the tip of her nose. He took her

hand in his, his fingers lovingly trailing over her wrist pulse. "Come with me; I have a surprise for you."

They laughed as they ran through the fields. He suddenly vanished, only to reappear behind her, pulling her tightly against him. He pressed his lips against hers over and over until she was dizzy from the taste of him. When he finally let go of her, they were racing through the forests of Elysium once more. Persephone's heart leaped as she saw a small temple appear on the horizon. They were near Hades' small hut on the cliff. He drew her into his arms and twirled her so her back was against him, his lips nuzzling her throat.

"Tell me you love me," he breathed against her.

"I do love you," she said solemnly, her heart twisting painfully as she remembered how he had asked this of her once before.

"Tell me you'll never forget, no matter how dark the nights are or how much space and time pass between us."

"Never!" she cried. She tried to turn to face Hades, but he held her firmly in her arms.

"No, not yet," he murmured, his tongue pressing against the rapidly beating pulse in her delicate neck. He bit down gently, and she shivered against him. "Your anniversary present is coming. Look."

As she turned her face up, Persephone exhaled. Millions of stars twinkled in the endless night. In the center of them, stood a flawless constellation of pulsing starlight, an embracing couple with their arms tightly entwined, together for eternity.

"So that you would never forget. 'That he would love me just as I am, and I would take him just as he is.' Under the stars," his voice a cajoling whisper against her ear. "I have waited for you before I even knew your name."

She shivered as she recalled that evil voice from Olympus, telling her how her husband had spent years searching for the ideal victim for his game. No, she would not give in. She refused to water the seed of uncertainty that Zeus had planted. She would not allow him to manipulate her. The thought vanished from her mind as she cocked her head back to look up at him.

"And now I am yours," she said softly.

"Yes," he smiled at her. "What shall I do with you?" He took her hand and tugged her so that she went with him, and they closed the distance to the hut's entrance. With a wave of his hand, the door opened. The soft breeze of the night pulled tendrils of hair across her face. "Will you want your old room?" he asked with mock seriousness. "Or will you share mine?"

"Hmm," she said, pretending to contemplate the question. "I think... yours." And she wrapped her arms fiercely around his neck, pressing her lips against his.

He made a low sound in his throat as he pulled her against him. They tumbled through the door of his room, and she giggled as it hit the wall with a loud thud. The stunning black roses scattered around the floor caused Persephone to exhale in pleasure, but she was soon sidetracked when his hands settled on her again. His lips pushed against hers, and he moved her backward until she felt the large bed behind her. She uttered a small cry as she unexpectedly slid, sprawling amidst the blankets and roses. His throat convulsed as his black eyes swept over her. His gaze moved slowly over her body before settling on her flushed face. She lifted a self-conscious hand to her hair, which seemed to break his reverie, a self-derisive smile pulling his mouth. He lowered one knee to the mattress, which slumped slightly under his weight. She stared in fascination as he crept closer to her before stopping between her legs.

"What shall I do now?" he asked softly, one of his hands tracing the smooth flesh of one of her calves. Slowly, he drew his cape from her shoulders so she lay naked beneath him.

His hand was mesmerizing on her skin, and it took several attempts before she could find her voice. "I-I..." Her voice cut off as she felt his hand move higher on her thigh.

A smile curled his mouth as he watched her. "Yes?" he inquired, his voice politely inquisitive as his fingers moved to the hollow behind her knee. She bit her lip, wondering how such an area could feel so erotic when he touched it. "No answer? Well, don't worry, I have some ideas."

He bent between her legs, pulling her thighs apart. "You are so pretty," he mused. His fingers traced her almost reverently as he found that small bud where all her sensations centered. He brushed it softly at first and then more firmly, and she could not help the deep groan that escaped her lips. "You know what mortals call this?" he whispered, his breath tantalizing her sensitive flesh. She stared down at him, eyes wide and dilated, her lips swollen from his mouth.

"Wha–what?"

"You're not paying attention," he scolded. "Do you know what this," he asked again, tracing carefully around the anatomy in question, "is called?"

She shook her head frantically. "I don't know."

"They call it kleitoris, the little hill. It seems like a rather poor description of such a delectable area. Tell me, Persephone. Did you touch yourself here as you waited for me? Did you bring yourself pleasure?" His fingers moved the aching peak, but every time he came close, he drew away again until, finally, she gave a frustrated cry.

"Please," she whimpered.

"Tell me, little wife. Did you touch yourself?" A furious blush covered her face. "How lovely you are when you are embarrassed. But I require an answer." He rested his head against her thigh, his dark eyes focused on her face as he stroked her swollen flesh lightly. "Tell me."

"Yes," she whimpered.

"Good girl."

She gave a cry as his mouth covered her "little hill," his tongue flicking over and over against the small, pulsing bud. Stars burst behind her eyes, and she cried out as a powerful orgasm moved over, ripples of pleasure dancing over her body as he continued to lick and suck at her. Before she could come down from the high, his tongue pushed inside her, drinking the liquid from her body. She fell back helplessly as his tongue thrust inside her, sweat beading her face. He replaced his mouth with his fingers, first sliding one into her and stretching her. She gasped as he added a second, and he smiled up at her from between her legs, his black hair covering his eyes. As he thrust into her, he watched her face hungrily, absorbing her pleasure.

"Come again," he demanded. Persephone grasped his wrist, afraid of the overwhelming sensations, but he clasped her hand, pulling it to her side. "Let me pleasure you," he whispered. When she once again felt the pleasure culminating, he replaced his fingers with his mouth, drinking her response as she cried out in pleasure.

She fell back, gasping as she struggled to catch her breath, and only then did he remove his mouth. He moved up her body, pressing his mouth against her hip and her stomach, until finally he reached her breasts.

"Now, what shall we do with these?" his wicked voice whispered.

He traced the outline of a nipple, then drew it into his mouth, flicking the pink bud with his tongue. She pressed her fingers into his hair, pulling him closer. He smiled as he moved to her other breast, lavishing it with the same intent attention. Once he was satisfied, he entirely covered her body until he hovered over her face-to-face. He bent over her, biting her lower lip before covering her mouth. His tongue pressed into her mouth, and she tasted herself on him; and the scent was strangely erotic. His mouth moved over hers for endless moments until, finally, he drew back again.

"Any ideas what I should do now?"

She brought her hand to his shoulder, and he groaned as she touched him. She traced her hand down his body and felt him tremble at her touch. "Off," she demanded, yanking at his clothes. He laughed again, quickly pulling his robes from himself to throw them across the room. His beautiful body was exposed, and she resumed her perusal, running her fingers over his arms and chest. Shyly, she touched the large, pulsing anatomy between his thighs.

"And what do the mortals call this?" she whispered.

He smiled down at her. "They call it *phallus*, but you, my wife, can call it whatever you want."

Her fingers traced the veins running along the thick shaft. "I think I shall call it mine."

"Yes," he groaned, his eyes closed as though in ecstasy or torment. "I am yours."

"Show me," she urged, sitting up. "Show me what pleases you."

"The most sensitive part is here." He took her fingers, tracing the smooth flesh just beneath the head of his cock. "Stroke it like this." He tightened her hand over his shaft, his large hand showing her how to touch him and how to bring him pleasure. When she bent, letting her tongue trail over the large head, he groaned so loudly that she stopped abruptly, afraid she had hurt him.

"Did I do something wrong?" she asked, biting her lip.

His laugh was self-deprecating. "Gods no. You bring me pleasure I could never have imagined. But I think," he said, sitting up to fall back on his haunches, "that I can stand not a moment more of not being inside you." Gently, he drew her over him so that she straddled his lap. He lifted her, capturing her mouth as he brought her hips back down again. The tip of his cock entered her, and he paused, sweat beading his face. As he filled her and stretched her, he swallowed her cries. Their eyes locked, and Hades drew back, staring down at her.

"I love you," he whispered, brushing the hair from her damp forehead.

"I love you," she answered softly, smiling at him.

His lips were gentle on hers as he began to lower her slowly, giving her time to adjust to the thickness of him. Just when she thought she could not take any more, when she thought that surely it must be all of him, he kept going, pushing into her molten heat, until finally he was fully sheathed by her.

"Fuck," he groaned. "Are you all right?"

Her answer was to wrap her legs around his back, pulling him deeper into her. He gasped, angling his hands over her hips. He lifted her over and over again, filling her thoroughly each time. Their mouths caught each other's desperately, a sense of urgency driving them both.

"Take me to the heavens," he whispered, and she felt his fingers more on her. What had he called it? But suddenly, all thought fled her mind. She felt that wild pleasure again, expanding until it overcame her, and she shook with her release, a gold light flashing behind her eyes. She heard his rough cry, and he climaxed beneath her, spilling into her.

She collapsed against him, and he fell back onto the bed, holding her tightly against his chest. Persephone traced her fingers over his chest.

"I think you may turn me into a hedonist," she said severely, at which Hades laughed. Her fingers reached the thin diagonal scar that still lay across his heart. She bent forward, pressing her lips against it, her long hair trailing over him. "I hate seeing this," she murmured.

He stroked her face, brushing her hair back so he could see her expression. "I don't. It is a reminder for me of our love. Of all that we have been through, I am glad to wear this mark so that all who see it may know of my love for you." He took her hand and brought it to his mouth, letting his lips brush her fingertips. "Remember our wedding night?" He laughed at the expression on her face. "You hated me so much."

Persephone laughed, too, bringing her face close to him. "Well, you," she replied, jabbing a finger against his chest for emphasis, "did little to improve the situation. You stormed about like a great wraith! You wanted me to think you were some monster."

The dimple appeared at the corner of his mouth again. "I *am* a monster, but I am your monster."

"You aren't a monster," Persephone cried indignantly.

Hades brushed his lips against her. "Still seeing the man and not the beast," he murmured.

He turned her over gently and kissed her on the nose before getting up from the bed to move towards the side table, which held a decanter of wine. He poured two glasses of the rubied liquid and returned to bed. Persephone couldn't avoid focusing on the still-prominent, protruding erection between his legs.

"Later, my insatiable wife," he grinned down at her, following her gaze. She took the glass from him as haughtily as she could, with flaming cheeks, as he settled next to her again. "Tell me," he continued, the laughter fading from his eyes, "what occurred during the celebration on Olympus."

"Oh," Persephone replied in a low voice. "Hades, I could never have imagined how truly evil they could be."

His dark eyes moved over her face. "I know of the horrors that lie in the beautiful mountains of the Gods. Tell me," he urged, taking her hand.

Persephone told him of the sudden invitation from Zeus, how the King of Gods had taken her to that lonely mountain where Prometheus was chained. She could not tell him of the false Rhea that walked Olympus;

she could not bear to force him to relive that burden he always carried with him. It would be like throwing salt over a festering wound.

"He took you to see the Titan," Hades mused, his fingers tracing her palm. "That is curious. What did Prometheus say to you?"

"He could not say very much," Persephone said sadly. "He was chained to the mountain, and birds were eating him. It was terrible!" she cried. "And Zeus seemed to think that he should know me. But I have only ever heard Prometheus' name in stories."

His fingers stroked her palm thoughtfully. "What happened next?"

"When Prometheus refused to speak, Zeus hurled us back to Olympus. It was then." She paused and lifted her gaze to his face. "I was very foolish again," she said, her voice small and harsh. "I accepted the wine he offered and he had added something to it so I could not move or speak. They chained me to a chair, and I had to watch him lie with a smile on his face while I sat there like a fool, never saying a word against him! He had the Muses perform for the Gods and portrayed my mother as a jealous harpy, you like a depraved lunatic, and myself like a blundering fool. But, worst of all," she paused, taking a deep breath. "Worst of all, he butchered an innocent child, and I just sat and watched like a coward." Persephone jerked away from his comforting touch and sat up, pulling her legs against her chest. "I did nothing to help her."

Hades pulled her against him, his heart beating steadily against her back. "Persephone, do you think you are the first good person who had to watch helplessly as Zeus destroyed an innocent? He has played this game numerous times, making you feel the guilt he should have felt for his depravity. But, remember, sweet Goddess, he held the knife, not you."

"I feel as guilty as if it had been me," Persephone said sadly, wiping her tears on her arm impatiently. "But at least I have the satisfaction of tearing down the dining room," she finished with a shaky laugh.

Hades let out a whoop of laughter. "Ah, I wish I had seen that."

"I felt a dark power overcome me as my soul touched hers as she was dying."

He played with her fingers contemplatively. "How did you call upon that power?"

Her brow furrowed. "It is hard to describe, but I felt it calling to me, and..." Hades' entire body jerked suddenly, and Persephone sat up, staring down at him. "What's wrong!"

A look of panic crossed his face, but it vanished so quickly that she wondered if she imagined it. "Nothing," he answered with a laugh. "My body is recovering from your lasciviousness."

Persephone laughed, too, but it quickly faded from her eyes. "Hades... when I left the dining room, I saw Ares. He had been carrying a bag that he dropped, and," she turned to him, pressing her face against him, "it had Theo's head in it. Do you remember the man I sent back up to join his wife? How could that be possible? Why would someone have done that to him? He was a good man. I saw that, and I *felt* that."

Hades lifted his hand to stroke her hair. "I am sorry, Persephone, I was not there to protect you."

She lifted her tear-stained face to his and shook her head. "No," she said fiercely, "you should not be sorry. You have always been there when I needed you. Perhaps I needed to see what was on the mountains of Olympus." They were silent momentarily, and then she asked again, "Why do you think they intervened with Theo? It cannot be a coincidence."

Hades shook his head. "There is no such thing, not truly. They sought him out because of his association with us. They were afraid of his happiness."

"But why?" she whispered.

"Because the King and Queen of the Underworld had dared to give a mortal hope and life. The Olympians feared that he might spread the word of the good deeds of Queen Persephone and the dark kingdom in which she ruled. Hope is a dangerous thing, Persephone."

Her face paled. "So I sent Theo back, only to die again."

"He would always die again, my love. You sent him back because you are compassionate and kind; Theo knew that."

Persephone stared ahead at the blue flames flickering in the hearth. "My actions seem to have unwanted consequences. I feel like I throw a pebble into the water, and the ripples move out like tidal waves, consuming everything in their path. It makes me afraid to act."

Hades turned her to face him, and his fingers were tight on her shoulders, his expression fierce. "No. That is how he wants you to feel—alone and fearful. But you are not alone. You are a queen, a Goddess, and you rule with me at your side."

Persephone brushed her lips against his. "Thank you," she said softly. "There was something else," Persephone began reluctantly. "I saw a mural of my mother and Zeus. He depicted them as lovers, but I know that is a lie.

Hades' hand stroked her hair, but he paused briefly before resuming the gentle caress. "Your mother was once a young Goddess, Persephone. Zeus is a master storyteller, and by the time he is finished, the lies are so carefully interwoven with the truth that they cannot be separated. My brother did not end up with the queen he wanted. He did not love his first or second wife, and I do not believe he loves Hera. It is a mutual arrangement of distrust between them. He hates that our souls are connected and envies people with soul mates like you and me. He hated Iasion and Demeter the same way.

"But why?" Persephone asked. "Why does he hate so much?"

"Because he will never be able to have it, he cannot. You cannot love another when you are absorbed in your self-love. He is more in love with himself than he could ever be with another. " Hades' fingers moved against her chest so that her heart beat against his fingertips. "We are connected, you and I. A thread runs from my heart to yours, a shining thread of destiny that binds us together. "

Persephone tilted her head back to look up into his dark eyes. "Why did you not write to me, Hades? I waited all summer for even a word from you."

Lights danced in the black embers of his gaze. "First, I wanted you to spend time with your mother without my interference. How can you enjoy your days in the sunshine when the God of Hell is reminding you of darkness? Second, as you know, there were consequences to the winter. We had to restore the Underworld, and I did not want to trouble you with problems while you were above. I have been consumed by work these past several months, preparing for your return."

A frown formed between her brows. "But couldn't you have written about your work, even if it was just a note?"

"I am sorry, my love," Hades interjected and pressed his lips against hers, his ebony hair brushing over her face as he bent over her. "I did not know the best course of action; I have never had a wife," he whispered with a smile. "I have brought so many shadows into your life that I thought perhaps it was best to let you have a period without them."

"I never want to be without you," she said against his lips. "There is no light without you. How can you not know that?"

"I will make it up to you," he whispered into her mouth. "I will wrap my shadows around you so you will never be free from me." For a moment, they were lost in the movement of their lips against one another, and then he drew back so that he hovered above her. "Did anything else happen on the mountain?"

Her mind rushed back to Zeus' madness as he questioned her about the swords and his demand to know whether she was pregnant, but something held her back from sharing this with Hades. She knew Hades did not possess Zeus' sword and that he had no need of it. Demeter's revelation that Hades couldn't have children reverberated in her head. She would never pressure him or make him feel guilty. Perhaps Zeus had explicitly asked her the question for her to ask her husband and hurt him. Repeating Zeus' words might only harm her husband; they would either become parents or not. She refused to play along with Zeus' attempts to trick her or to sour their relationship.

Persephone shook her head. "Just more false words. I am where I am meant to be. With you." They held still, content to simply be together. Persephone felt dampness on her face and lifted her fingers to wipe away the wetness. "What?" she murmured, puzzled, but jumped up when she saw the blood smeared on her hands. "Hades!" she cried, turning around. Blood was dropping steadily from his nose. "You are bleeding!"

He lifted a hand, wiping carelessly at the blood. "It is nothing. It has happened occasionally since I was struck on the mountaintop."

Persephone lifted her gown to wipe away the blood smeared on his face. "It does not seem like nothing," she replied, worry creasing her brow. "Why is your wound still troubling you?" She lifted the blanket from him to look at his abdomen, where he had been struck and saw a small, white scar similar to the one on his chest. "But--"

He took her hand and lifted it to his lips. "You worry needlessly. Some wounds take longer to heal, even if you can no longer see them." He moved her fingers to the scar over his heart. "And some scars are worth having." She frowned at him still. "If you are worried, wife, I *need* your healing touch." His large hand pulled hers from his chest and moved it lower. "Can you guess where?"

"You are wicked to try and distract me," she scowled.

When he wrapped her fingers around that significant part of him, she couldn't help the gasp that escaped her lips. "Oh, yes, wife. Let me show you how wicked I can be."

CHAPTER 6
THE BALL

*P*erephone.

A low voice in her ear startled her, and she sat up, looking around the room, but she was alone. She felt Hades' side of the bed, but the blankets were cool. Hades must have left after he woke, letting her sleep. It must have been a dream. With a contented sigh, she fell back into bed. The first rays of light penetrated the hut, warming her skin. She felt delightfully rested for the first time in a very long time, her body sore in the most delicious places. She was tempted to go back to sleep but looked toward the door wistfully, wondering where Hades was. Suddenly, she caught sight of a stunning black toga lying over the dresser. Standing up, she inspected the dress and noticed that the fabric was woven with tiny golden threads in the form of pomegranates. Elegant, skeleton fingers secured the dress' shoulders, and the clasp was a skull whose ruby eyes twinkled rather rakishly at her.

"Beautiful," she murmured, touching the glittering eyes.

She giggled, suddenly giddy with happiness, and pulled the garment over her head, feeling incredibly alive. The clothing was secured by locking each of the tiny bony fingers together, and she tried to close the clasp, but the miniature appendages kept slipping from her grasp.

She jumped in surprise as she felt cool hands touch hers. Her husband's dark shadow was behind her in the enormous hematite mirror, his face hidden by his messy black hair. He could be a stranger, except she would recognize him by his touch and smell. Slowly, he placed his fingers around the gown's clasps while she watched transfixed. When he raised his head, his dark eyes watched her in the mirror, and she shivered.

His hands slid down slowly, first touching the exposed swell of one breast, then the other, following along her belly until he reached the point where her thighs met. Her breath caught in her throat as he tugged the gown's hem higher and higher until the vee between her legs was exposed in the mirror. His focused gaze was fixed on her image in the mirror, and she blushed at the sight. Her hands moved to cover herself, but he shook his head, and she let them fall. While one of his hands held her dress high, the other moved lower, cupping her. The mirrored Persephone gasped and lowered her eyes in embarrassment.

"No, Persephone. Watch."

His voice was a bewitching whisper in her ear, or did he say it into her mind? Her eyes flew open as those long fingers curled into her, and she cried out. Her flesh was still swollen and aching from the night before as he entered her slowly. As the welcoming wetness spread across his hand, his pace increased. Her head fell to his shoulder, and her cheeks flushed with embarrassment and arousal as she watched the erotic couple in the mirror as she shamelessly rode his hand. He teased her mercilessly, and just as she almost reached a peak of pleasure, he pulled her back again, slowing the thrust of his fingers. She let out a whimper of frustration, and he gave a husky laugh.

"Patience," he whispered. He lifted his fingers, bringing them to her mouth. "Taste," he demanded. He rubbed his fingers against her bottom lip, and her tongue followed his path, tasting her essence. He groaned and bent his head, capturing her lower lip. "Now we start again."

Down his hand went, his fingers thrusting into her, spreading the wetness. Finally, just as she thought she would go mad, he turned her suddenly, lifting her up to wrap her legs tightly around him as he thrust all the way into her. She gave a cry of pleasure in shock at the large intrusion, helplessly suspended as he drove into her. She felt his mouth on her neck, and she arched back, relishing in the feel of him filling her, completing her, and consuming her. The world fell apart around her as she shattered in endless pleasure.

They walked hand in hand from the temple. As Hades smiled down at her, sunlight streamed from the endless sky. He was so handsome that her breath caught in her throat, and she averted her gaze so he wouldn't see the tears in her eyes. She never expected to experience such joy.

"I wish we could stay here longer," Hades said softly. "But we have a ball to attend tonight."

Persephone groaned. "Oh, Hades, I would rather not. I don't enjoy them."

"You will enjoy this one," he replied, laughing.

"I hate parties," she grumbled.

Hades laughed, and he pulled her along beside him. "Don't be grumpy," he admonished.

Her husband looked so carefree walking beside her, but as Persephone stared at the perfect azure sky, a cloud temporarily obscured the light, and Zeus' warning played in her mind. Had the promise of war simply been an idle threat? Or did the King of Gods know something she didn't?

"Hades, what if the Olympians did attack us? Would we be ready?"

"I have not been idle in your absence, my love," Hades replied enigmatically.

"Zeus said something about his sword missing, and if it could be returned, then perhaps we could avoid a war."

Hades abruptly came to a halt and turned his wife to face him. "Let me guess what my brother said. He said that if the thing he seeks is returned, he will again be a benevolent God. It's a story I've heard many times, Persephone. Fear is how he gets what he wants so easily. Even if you comply with everything he requests, he is just as likely to slit your throat with a smile. War with Zeus is never avoidable, but if I had his weapon, I would gladly return it." He cupped both of his hands around her face. "You look beautiful."

Persephone bit her lip. "But Hades," Persephone persisted. "Zeus said he would watch our kingdom burn. He seems obsessed."

"Zeus says many things, none of which interest me today."

He suddenly took her in his arms and twirled her until she was breathless and laughing. "You aren't being serious!" she cried. "I am worried."

"I am always serious," he replied, pulling her back toward the water. "I seriously do not wish to discuss my brother. I seriously love my wife."

"But Hades," she said, pulling back on his arm so he could look back at her. "I have a feeling something is wrong."

He put his finger on her parted lips. "I despise the mere mention of his name on your lips. Sweet wife, I am well acquainted with the King of the Gods. I don't believe we need to be concerned about him for now." He stroked the side of her mouth. "Agreed?" She fixed her gaze solemnly on him for a few seconds before nodding her agreement. "All right," he murmured. "It's time for the first of many reunions."

He motioned towards the water, and Persephone cried out in delight as she saw Orphnaeus and Aethon waiting for them at the shore. She approached the mare slowly in case the horse had forgotten about her, but as soon as Aethon locked her dark eyes on Persephone, she neighed and raced forward, rubbing her long nose against Persephone's neck. The Goddess laughed out loud, delighted that the mare remembered her.

"I missed you as well," Persephone said softly, stroking her soft ears and bristly mane. "And you too, Orphnaeus," she grinned, feeling his nose press against her back.

"Are you ready to go?" Hades asked behind her. For an answer, she turned over her shoulder and gave him a joyful smile. Hades lifted her onto Aethon's back before mounting Orphnaeus, who tapped his hooves impatiently. "Let us go see your kingdom, Queen Persephone." Hades whistled softly, and Orphnaeus began to gallop, the mare racing close behind him.

Even though she was prepared, Persephone couldn't help but gasp as they raced across the endless blue sea. The King and Queen of the Dead rode side by side, and she didn't close her eyes when the world turned upside down as the steeds dove deep into the azure waters. Gleaming lights flashed by, souls dancing on the waves, and Persephone was mesmerized by the beauty of it all. Finally, the world righted itself, and they sped past the water wall into the Kingdom of the Damned. How different this trip was from the last; they relaxed and set their own pace, and the demons who had previously pursued them finally laid to rest.

She leaned in close and whispered into Aethon's ear, "I think we can beat them, don't you?"

Persephone laughed as Aethon neighed her answer and pulled forward, her long legs moving ahead of the stallion as Orphaneous snorted. She looked behind her, her hair and dress pulling in the wind, and Hades gave her an enigmatic smile, his gaze sliding over her possessively.

Queens should come before kings, his voice whispered in her mind. *And besides, I enjoy the view.*

She dashed forward as light as the wind. The steed's hooves thundered over the choppy waters, and as the castle came into view, she abruptly pulled back, tightening her thighs to bring Aethon to a halt. She could see newly built gates carved from black diamonds stretching as far as the eye could see around the castle's entrance. The size of the fortress astounded Persephone. This was no longer just a palace; it was a stronghold. Hades, like Zeus, appeared to be preparing for a battle.

Hades positioned Orphnaeus next to her and smiled. "I told you I've been very busy."

War. The word made her tremble in fear. Zeus had warned her it was coming. When Hades lifted his hand, the gates unlocked, and the wall of water collapsed behind them, concealing the path they had just taken.

"Come, my Queen."

She gazed over the palace as they galloped towards the massive black gates. The dark, ornate castle built into the obsidian mountains of the Underworld rose before her. Mist floated off the river, and water flowed through the palace's various towers, eventually falling into the swirling rivers of the Styx and Acheron below. The temples carved into the black mountainside shone with golden lights. The Olympians would describe this ebony palace as strange and bizarre, but it was home to her; it was where she had loved and been loved, and her heart leaped joyfully as they approached the entrance. They sped through the tall entryways, and she smiled at Hades, extending her hand to him. An angry, mournful cry echoed overhead, and Persephone glanced up, her hand soothing the mare, who shuffled uneasily.

"What was that?" Persephone cried.

"Those are the Furies," Hades shouted over the horses' hooves. "They are guarding the river before making their rounds in Tartarus. Look."

Persephone looked up into the sky and saw them. Three winged women flew high above, their skin red and burnt like leather, and their wings stretched out like giant bats from their bodies. They were too high above to see their faces, but Persephone shivered as one of the creatures' gleaming red eyes stared down at her before looping back to join her sisters. Their wails followed them as they approached the palace's entrance. Persephone stroked Aethon, but the mare had become uncharacteristically nervous, her powerful body trembling beneath the Goddess'.

"What are they guarding?"

"Our home."

They began to slow as the palace's steps came into view.

"I am happy to be home," she said softly.

"Home," Hades repeated with an answering grin.

"I cannot wait to see Olive and Cerberus!"

Finally, they reached the palace steps, and a familiar figure stood at the door.

"Charon," Hades greeted as he leaped down. He helped Persephone dismount, and they moved towards the steps.

The ferryman was predictably quiet as they approached, but Persephone's eyes moved behind Charon as another dark figure stepped from the shadows. The cloaked figure was taller and broader than the River Guide but stood as silently as Charon did, with knives wrapped

around his belt and chest strap and a dark hood draped over a helmet that completely covered his face.

Hades noticed her eyes on the figure and drew her towards him. "This is your personal guard."

"My guard?" she repeated in amazement. "I have no need of a guard." Her eyebrows drew down over her eyes as she stared at the quiet man. "Forgive me," she continued, addressing the silent wraith, "but I do not need additional protection."

"But I disagree," Hades said. "You are my most precious commodity, and I want to protect you well. Our guards are called *Maketes,* and you may call them that. They do not speak, for they should listen. You may think of him as your shadow."

She arched an eyebrow at her husband, shooting him a look that promised they would speak more about this later. "Where can I find Olive?"

"He is in our room, Persephone, wait," Hades called. "There is something I need to tell you."

She hurried forward and blew him a kiss. "I am sorry, Hades, but I must see him! Come and find me when you are finished." Hades stepped forward, but the silent guard moved before him, stalking the hall behind her light form. Hades noticed the guard took care not to step on the trail of flowers that followed behind her.

Persephone rushed through the corridors, eager to reach Hades' chambers. As she walked, she noticed tiny blue crystals streaked with white threads embedded along the corridor floor. She did not recognize the stone; she would have to ask Hades later. But right now, she wanted to rest in Hades' chambers. No, she reminded herself with a smile; it was no longer just his room.

"Ours," she whispered happily, her face bright.

She moved lightly as if soaring through the corridors, and the phrase tasted good in her mouth. She slowed her stride as the fine hairs on her neck pricked, tilting her head to see a shadow following her. Her heart skipped a beat, and then she remembered her guard.

"I forgot you were going to be following me," she murmured. If she didn't know better, she'd think the tall, motionless figure was just another statue in the long hall. "What is your actual name?" she inquired, her voice echoing in the marbled atrium. But he did not answer her. "Very well," she said, returning to walk again, "someday you'll tell me your name." When she arrived at the room's doors, she pushed them open with a broad smile.

"Olive," she cried, but the room was empty except for a voluptuous woman bent over Hades' bed, long red hair cascading down her back. The form straightened at the sound of the door, and Persephone realized she was staring at a lovely nymph. Fiery red hair hung to her knees, and she clutched a pair of robes in her pale hands. A peach gown hugged her petite frame and ample breasts, which threatened to spill over the low-cut top. Persephone had never seen a nymph as a servant in the castle, and seeing the lovely maiden leaning over Hades' bed made her feel—what was that feeling in her chest? Jealousy? Surprise? Her handmaidens were souls, but Hades had always gotten by alone. The nymph's blue eyes passed over her, then she turned dismissively and resumed folding the robes she held.

Singing and laughter grew louder in the hall until three very excited, very dear faces pushed into the room.

"Jocasta!" Persephone cried. The older woman attempted to bow, but Persephone drew her up and fiercely embraced her. "I am overjoyed to see you!" She then drew the two younger maidens into her arms, and when she let them go, they were flushed and beaming with pride and embarrassment at her informality.

Jocasta sighed and wiped her eyes. "We've been waiting for six months! We've missed you so much. And we've brought someone you might want to see." Olive dashed into the room, his long legs slipping on the marble floor. When he saw Persephone, he grunted softly and ran towards her, crashing over a table that held several clay vases. Persephone rushed towards him.

"My precious Olive," she cooed as she snatched him into her arms. She kissed the soft, downy fur between his eyes as the deer rubbed his face against her chest. "I missed you terribly." She fingered the lovely flower garland that hung around his neck.

"Those just bloomed last night," Jocasta said softly. "It was like they knew you would be returning soon. I thought you might enjoy seeing them around the little one's neck."

"They are beautiful," Persephone murmured. "Thank you for taking care of him while I was gone."

Persephone looked up as the nymph let out a loud, frustrated sigh from across the room. "That fawn is a menace," she muttered, shooting Olive an intense look of dislike. "I'll talk to Hades about getting him out of the castle again."

A wave of indignation pushed against Persephone's chest.

"Hold your tongue," Jocasta snarled before Persephone could say anything. "That fawn is the favorite pet of the queen."

Insolently, the nymph let her gaze wander over Jocasta. "Well, it's not like she's ever here."

Jocasta reached her full height. "Don't you recognize an empress when you see one? You should bow before your queen."

Her blue eyes widened as she looked at Persephone, and she fell to her knees quickly. "Oh, Your Highness," she said, lowering her beautiful face. "I had no idea it was you. I assumed you were a servant. I was expecting you to look different."

Jocasta and Persephone exchanged a glance. The elderly handmaiden shook her head, her eyes narrowing. Persephone moved forward, one hand lightly resting on Jocasta's, Olive clasped against her chest.

"What is your name?"

"Minthe, Your Majesty."

"Minthe, you may leave my room. My ladies and I wish to be alone."

Minthe shook her head and lifted her face, a subservient smile on her lips that contrasted with the malicious gleam in her eyes. "I only answer to Hades, my Queen; I am his servant. And this is also his room. He's asked me to stay here until he gets back. I couldn't defy the king. After being alone for so long, he relies on me to serve *all* his needs."

Persephone flushed. Did she imagine the implied meaning in her words? "All right," Persephone answered softly. "Then we will leave you to the important task of folding his robes." Persephone turned on her heel, hearing her handmaidens close behind her.

Jocasta was fuming beside her. "That nymph's nerve," she muttered furiously. "She believes she is superior to the rest of us. You'd think she was the queen of this palace." She looked at Persephone and pursed her lips, clearly resisting the urge to say more. "Please accept my apologies, Your Highness. I spoke out of turn."

Persephone pressed her face against Olive's head. "You do not need to apologize to me. How long has she been here?"

Jocasta huffed. "He found that nymph by the Cocytus and brought her here. He rode her back on his horse!" She smacked her lips emphatically as though she were tasting something unpleasant. "His personal dresser. He'd never needed anyone to dress him before. "

"He carried her back on his horse?" Persephone felt her cheeks flush. She, too, had been carried to the Underworld on Orphnaeus' back. "What is she like?"

"As sweet as a honey cake around the king, but as mean as a snake to the rest of us. She's nosy as well. We've caught her going through your room several times."

"What possible reason could she have to enter my room?"

"Jealousy. Minthe wants what you have. I believe she has taken some of your belongings, though I could never prove it; I've noticed things missing." Jocasta pushed open the door to Persephone's old bedroom. Flowers of various sizes and colors were draped around the room, and the floor was covered in a soft, rainbow-colored blanket of blooms.

"So lovely," Persephone murmured. She kneeled down and placed Olive on the canopied floor.

Jocasta made a clapping motion with her hands. "Phoebe! Cleo! Prepare yourselves. We have a lot of work to do to get the queen ready for the ball."

The younger servants got to work, pulling soaps and perfumes from the shelves.

Persephone lifted a perfumed bottle. "How much time does my husband spend with her?" she asked softly.

Jocasta frowned. "I've said too much. Now I have worried you, and I did not want to do that so early in your return."

"Please," Persephone begged. "I'd like to know."

"As his personal servant, she looks after him all day. They are always locked away together." Jocasta spoke quietly so the other two women wouldn't hear her.

Persephone swallowed and forced herself to say the words that had become stuck in her throat. "And at night?"

The older servant paused. "I've been avoiding that hall section for quite some time. It was made clear that my presence there was not welcome."

"By who?"

"By Minthe."

"And the king?"

"And by the king," she admitted sadly.

Jocasta's words brought a heavy weight to Persephone's chest. Footsteps sounded in the hall, and Persephone crept to the darkened foyer, instantly recognizing her husband's shadow. She watched as Hades entered his chambers. A soft, feminine laugh echoed down the hall as the doors closed behind him. *Maybe there was another reason he hadn't written to you in six months*—a voice whispered in her mind—*perhaps you are not enough for him.*

An abrupt scream interrupted Persephone's thoughts; the handmaidens were staring at a dark corner of the room. Persephone was startled when she noticed her protector's tall shadow. She realized she hadn't seen him entering the rooms at all.

"I apologize," she said quickly. "It appears that I, too, have a new companion. This is my unnamed guardian. Hades has told him to follow me—for the time being."

"Well," Jocasta said after a moment, "he should give us privacy while we prepare you for the ball."

Four pairs of eyes peered at the darkened corner, but he remained motionless and silent as if he were nothing more than a shadow.

"Please leave," said Persephone. The guard simply leaned against the wall more comfortably. She sighed, exhausted. She really didn't have the energy to battle her new guard. "It seems there is another member of the palace who only listens to my husband," she murmured. "Very well then; you're welcome to join us." She returned her attention to the handmaidens with a bright smile. "Ladies! What finery have you prepared for this evening?"

"Oh, Your Majesty, we have been sewing for six long months, preparing patiently for your return." Phoebe's face lit up with a charming smile. "You have so many gowns to choose from, each more beautiful than the last." They began pulling dresses from the trunk, pressed against the edge of her bed, all different colors, and twirling them around for her to admire their work. "But tonight, we wanted to dress you in green." Phoebe took out a stunning emerald gown. "Like the forest."

Persephone stroked the soft fabric, the cool green soothing and peaceful; the image of Hades and Minthe, on the other hand, made her feel anything but tranquil. "You have worked so hard, and each gown is truly a masterpiece, but tonight, I think I would like to wear red like the pomegranate. Do you have anything similar to that shade?"

"Oh, yes, we have the exact one! You will look stunning," Cleo said with a dreamy sigh. The handmaiden pulled out a deep ruby-red toga with one shoulder clasped with a golden serpent. Yards of silken fabric were used to make the train of the gown. Cleo held it out for Persephone to examine, and she let her hand trail down the skirt.

"I have an idea," Persephone said mischievously. Her gaze was drawn to the man in the shadows. "May I?" she inquired, gesturing towards the weapon in his belt. He gave an almost imperceptible nod of his head. He removed the blade so quickly from his belt that it was nearly a blur before passing it to her with a gloved hand. She unsheathed it with a soft swish and smiled as she returned her attention to the handmaidens. "I believe a minor change will be appropriate for the situation. What do you think about a slit all the way up to here?" Cleo took the knife from her hands as Persephone pointed to the very top of her thigh, and Phoebe squealed with delight.

"You'll be the most beautiful Goddess at the ball," Cleo said, beaming.

Phoebe took the dress to finish the alterations, and Jocasta got to work after another disapproving look at the shadow in the corner. Jocasta expertly gathered Persephone's hair, twisting the long length so it rested high on her head, and brushed it until it gleamed.

Jocasta manipulated small tendrils to rest against Persephone's face and neck. "The sun kissed your hair," Jocasta noted. "It has gold threads in it."

Persephone examined her hair in the large mirror, noticing the pale blond streaks. She smiled at Jocasta, and the servant couldn't help but notice it didn't reach her eyes. "I spent every day in the sun."

"Well, it's quite lovely. It suits you."

Cleo appeared behind her and began spritzing her vigorously with a glass bottle. The scent of fig blossoms filled the air, and Persephone could almost imagine herself back at Demeter's temple if she closed her eyes. But there was no time for reflection as Phoebe approached her with a tray full of pots. Persephone's eyes were kohl-rimmed, and she had coral powder applied to her cheeks and lips.

"I think it's time to get dressed," Jocasta said. Several sets of arms whirled Persephone, and she glanced uncertainly at the warrior, who was still facing them. How would they get rid of the blasted man? But the handmaidens were always resourceful. Cleo and Phoebe quickly drew a changing cloth around them. As the guard drew closer, his tall outline was visible on the other side of the fabric, with the firelight highlighting his shadow.

"I don't think the king's intention was ever to have you watch everything his wife does," Jocasta said loudly and rudely. "You may defend her behind that curtain."

To Persephone's surprise, the shadow remained still, and Jocasta gave a small sigh of relief. "I don't know what this palace is coming to," she muttered. "Now, raise your arms." Jocasta lightly tapped Persephone's fingers as she attempted to unfasten her own gown. "No, Your Majesty, allow us to assist you." Jocasta's deft fingers quickly removed the dress, and the red toga was draped over Persephone's head. The maid-servant kneeled and tugged at the gown's edges, ensuring everything was in order. The changing sheet was discarded after Jocasta gave an approving nod.

"You look so beautiful, Queen Persephone. Truly, there has never been a more beautiful Goddess."

Persephone laughed. "You are too kind, Jocasta. But I am nothing special. I am only beautiful with the help of talented women."

"You are stunning. Look." Jocasta returned her to the mirror. A Goddess returned her gaze with large, mysterious green eyes, coral lips, and golden hair. Persephone almost didn't recognize the woman in the mirror, and a tingle of emotion moved over her. She'd changed so much but could only hope it was for the better. She still wondered if she was enough inside, where it mattered.

"We will inform the king that you are prepared, Your Majesty." The handmaidens rushed from the room with a snap of Jocasta's fingers, trailing behind her like happy ducklings, leaving Persephone alone. But she was not entirely alone, she mused, remembering her shadow.

She took the knife from the vanity and approached the warrior. "I appreciate you letting me borrow this." He lifted his gloved hand, palm up, and she dropped the weapon into it. He tucked the knife into his belt before resuming his statue-like position. She walked around her room, her fingers running over the flowers cascading down the wall. "Better than when I left you," she murmured. "Did someone care for you in my absence?" She leaned closer to a nearby violet, whispering against the soft petals. In response, a small green vine wrapped loosely around her wrist. She closed her eyes and saw her husband, his dark head bowed, tending to the garden. "Oh," she said, smiling.

A tall form pressed itself intimately behind her, strong fingers pressing against her shoulders. "My flower is talking to the flowers." In her ear, Hades' voice was a mesmerizing whisper. His fingers moved, and she felt him pull at the diamond clip Jocasta had used to secure her hair. Her long, sun-kissed hair tumbled down her back like a waterfall. "You smell so good."

"You shouldn't have done that," she scolded. "Jocasta will be annoyed."

He laughed, and as she turned, his arms encircled her, pressing her against the wall. Her eyes moved over him, and she noticed that, despite his impeccable attire, more pale skin was visible than usual. The black toga dipped low in the front, slipping past his lower obliques and exposing his broad chest. Gold leafing on the scars on his chest and stomach highlighted his wounds.

Her fingers traced the golden scar on his chest. "This is a new look," she said slowly. "Who did these paintings?"

Hades let one of his hands fall, his fingers touching the deep gash on his stomach. "Minthe took a creative license. Do you like them?"

Maketes had moved closer to the entrance to Hades, close enough to hear their conversation. She didn't want to fight before a stranger, so she dropped her hand and remained motionless. "I don't believe you need ornamental designs to look like a king."

His laugh was deep. "I am glad that you think so."

"I like you exactly how you are," she said softly.

His brow furrowed in response to her words, his stance tense as he looked down at his torso, his fingers trembling as he traced the golden scar across his chest. His body jerked as he looked at her, and his black eyes widened.

"What's the matter?" she asked in concern, taking a step closer.

His long black hair covered his face as he shook his head. She lifted her hands to touch the golden dust that floated around him. The color of the paint. He was still smiling when she looked up.

"I, too, am tired from last night. I had a very ravenous lover."

"But–"

He took a step closer to her. "What is bothering you, wife?" His fingers lifted her chin, and she looked into his deep, dark eyes. How she loved him, she thought, and her heart twisted at the strength of the emotion within it. And how both weak and strong that love made her.

She lowered her eyes. "Perhaps I am nervous about the ball and who will be there."

"It will be a more intimate but grander affair. I have had some time to plan."

She drew his hand to hers and interlaced her slender fingers with his. "Do you remember last year?"

"Ah, yes," he said, laughing. "You thought I was taking you to the abyss."

"And now I would gladly accompany you into the abyss." Her voice was solemn. "Would you go with me?"

A pained expression crossed his face. "I would go into the abyss with you, Persephone," he said quietly, his hands trembling against hers. "I'd die for you."

She opened her mouth, wanting to voice her anxieties, when a cough from behind them caused Hades to step back, wiping a trail of blood from his face as he turned away. Minthe's red hair came into view.

"I apologize for interrupting, Your Majesty," the nymph said, her pale blue eyes fixed on Hades, "but I just wanted to double-check your attire." She was holding a paintbrush and a seashell filled with gold paint. "May I finish with you?"

Persephone gasped as Hades parted his robes to allow her better access, and the nymph's lush body moved towards him. Minthe was so close to him that their skin had to be touching as she brushed the paintbrush against his flesh. Persephone pressed her nails into her palms as jealousy simmered. She'd never felt that twisted emotion before and despised the wretched, consuming sensation. She reminded herself that Hades had every right to have a servant. Minthe pursed her lips as she blew on the gold paint. As the nymph drew away, her gaze moved to Persephone's face, and as she ran her fingers over Hades' smooth chest, she smiled, her long fingernails like daggers against his skin. Minthe's smile had vanished when she looked up at Hades, replaced by an innocent, guileless expression, and Persephone knew her face was flushed with anger.

"I believe you are finished, Your Majesty," Minthe said breathlessly.

"Thank you, Minthe," he said as he re-tied his robes. Hades smiled down at the nymph as she bowed low. Minthe sashayed out of the room without looking back, the door softly closing behind her as her apricot gown vanished from view. Hades turned around, a smile still on his lips. It faded as he observed Persephone's expression.

"Do you have something you wish to say?"

"Is there anything you need to tell me?" she asked, trying to keep her voice pleasant.

He looked perplexed momentarily before shifting his gaze to the recently vacated door. "In your absence, Persephone, Minthe has been assisting me. She is simply a servant, albeit a very loyal servant."

"I'm just curious why you need a dresser when you've never needed one before."

"Since I now have a lovely wife, I thought it was time I made some changes so that you could live as a queen should, in a normal palace with a normal husband."

He drew her close and pressed her head against his chest, scent tickling her nose. She inhaled deeply, the alluring, familiar scent of bergamot soothing and enticing her. There was a more subtle, elusive scent that she couldn't place—something new. His fingers traced down her back, distracting her.

"Is it possible, my love, that you're just a little jealous?"

"I'm not jealous," she snorted.

Persephone lifted her head and gave him a ferocious look as Hades laughed. "Pardon me, Persephone, but I can't help but laugh. If I could only show you how much you consume me, you'd realize there's no need for jealousy. On the other hand," he murmured, letting his fingers trace the sleeves of her dress. "I am jealous of the fabric you wear, the air that you breathe, anything that gets to touch you. My hands should be covering you. When you left," he continued, "I realized that changes were required. I have increased the number of positions in the castle. Minthe is one of them, as is your guard. As we proceed through the palace, you will notice more changes." He ran his hand through her hair and brushed his lips against hers. "Do not put anyone between us who does not belong."

"I don't want anyone between us," she said softly against his lips.

He drew back just enough to be able to look down at her. "There will never be. Have I ever given you reason to doubt me?" She shook her head. "I know a lot has changed, but what is between you and me will never change. Persephone, all I ask is that you trust me. All of this will make sense in time. We'll talk later tonight so I can explain everything. I was going to warn you about Minthe earlier, but you ran down the hall." He took her hand in his and brought it up to his mouth. "Will you accompany me to greet our guests?"

Persephone looked up at him, his dark eyes familiar, but she couldn't recapture her earlier joy. "Yes," Persephone agreed quietly. "However, I have more questions for you before the night is done."

He gave a mock bow, his eyes twinkling. "As always, wife, I am available to you."

She hoped that this moment would begin a new era for her, that she would enter the ballroom with the grace of a queen. But as Hades led her through the corridors, her shadowed guard trailing behind them, old insecurities resurfaced, whispering the same relentless doubt: that she'd never be quite enough.

Hades led her to an unfamiliar large sapphire door, and she realized how much of the castle she had overlooked in her brief visit to the Underworld. Two cloaked guards stood at the entrance in identical garb to her guard. Hades raised his fisted hand, and when he opened his palm, the door's locks unfastened and slowly opened. Persephone hesitated, nervous, but with a gentle squeeze on her arm, they started moving forward.

They entered the large ballroom, tiled in elaborate marble of various colors; massive, jeweled columns encircled the room; it was extravagant and grand. The crowd quickly drew Persephone's attention, which greeted them with thunderous applause, both Gods and spirits cheering. She attempted to withdraw subtly, but the king led her to the center of the floor and bowed over her hand. She felt like she was looking into the hungry eyes of a wolf when his eyes rose to hers. Music filled the hall as a trio of spirits expertly played the kithara, lyre, and aulos, and then Persephone and Hades were whirling across the floor, the crowd applauding.

"I despise sharing you," he whispered into her ear.

Persephone willed her body to relax. He moved effortlessly, unhindered by pain or uncertainty, as it had been the last time they danced. In comparison, she felt stiff and awkward, anxiety filling her as the crowd pressed in closer. He nodded, and some guests joined them on the dance floor. Distracted, she took the wrong step, turning left when she should have turned right, and she felt herself fall until his strong arms caught her and quickly redirected her. He twirled her, taking advantage of her momentum to make the movement appear effortless.

"I did not know you danced so well," she murmured.

"Ah," he replied, bending closer, "but there are many things you have to learn about me. Tonight, I will show you."

A chill moved down Persephone's spine at the predatory gleam in his eyes.

When the music stopped, Hades bowed low, and the crowd surged forward, dividing them. It was now time to pay homage to the other Gods, and her palms began to sweat as faces pressed in on her. She despised the frivolity of false pleasantry but turned to greet the first visitor with a bright smile. A familiar, dark figure approached her, and she gasped in surprise. Hypnos, the God of Sleep, advanced, his long, dark robes trailing behind him. As he passed, several Gods couldn't help but yawn, and one spirit even toppled over, with other guests rushing forward to help him up. It appeared that Hypnos' soporific effect extended beyond his cave.

The God bowed low, gracefully rising to watch her from beneath his dark hood. "It is good to see you again, queen. I see you bear no ill effects from the poppies Hades and I supplied to Olympus."

"I thought Zeus smuggled them," Persephone said in surprise.

"Zeus believed he was receiving a good deal. He had no idea he was assisting us in a setup. Turning a king into a fool is second to turning a fool into a king. I'm sorry to say that I don't have to work very hard to achieve either."

Persephone felt her eyes become heavier as he tapped one finger against his forearm; the movement was mesmerizing. She blinked quickly, returning her gaze to him, and she couldn't help but wonder what the face was like behind the shadows.

"Those poppies were extra potent," Hypnos was saying. "After all, you remember the ones." Persephone shook her head emphatically, nervously looking around, and Hypnos laughed silkily from beneath the shroud. "Regardless, Hades came up with a brilliant plan. The Olympians cannot resist the lure of the poppy, especially the king. It ensured that you could be removed safely from their clutches. Perhaps

Hades should thank you; weren't you the one who reminded him of the use of the poppy and the importance of the nightly ritual of slumber?" Hypnos ran his finger along the lapel of his robes. "I have reason to recall how much your husband despises sleeping."

A beautiful, raven-haired goddess stepped forward, her skin gleaming in the candlelight. When she lifted her gaze to Persephone's, it was like looking into infinite starlight. To Persephone's surprise, Hypnos joined arms with the lovely Goddess. "This is Nyx, our mother."

Persephone looked around, surprised. "*Our* mother?"

"Oh, you didn't know?" Charon moved forward, taking Nyx's other arm. "Charon is my brother." Though she couldn't see Hypnos' face, she could tell he was pleased with her surprise. "Do you not see the familial resemblance? Our other brother would have loved to come, but he makes people uncomfortable. Perhaps it's a family trait."

"Do not tease her, Hypnos," Nyx admonished. "It is nice to have two of my children together."

Persephone felt a thrill as Nyx reached for her hand, the same tingly feeling she had when she stood at the edge of a mountain or let the wind carry her through the sky: freedom, infinity, and not a little danger. Her eyes were unlike any others she had ever seen, with hints of purple, blue, and pink blending with the darker edges of her pupils. They were like peering into the night sky or a galaxy. Persephone felt conspicuous next to this stunning, ancient Goddess, like a child playing make-believe in her mother's clothing.

"My sons are very fond of you," Nyx continued, smiling tenderly at Charon. "Charon has told me a lot about his lovely queen."

"Oh." Persephone looked at Charon. The River Guide remained silent as usual, and Persephone was taken aback by the unexpected compliment. "Well, Hades implicitly trusts Charon. He is devoted to his king."

Nyx smiled at Persephone as she leaned forward. "He is a God of few words," Nyx whispered, "but once his loyalty is given, it does not waver. That devotion extends to you. I hope you remember this."

Persephone blinked. Was she talking about Charon or Hades? The ancient Goddess beamed at her, her hooded sons on either side, like

matching bookends. The River God, the God of Sleep, and the Goddess of the Night formed an enigmatic trio. Nyx leaned forward.

"Did you enjoy your gifts?"

"Gifts?" inquired Persephone.

"Hades created the constellation, of course. He'd been working on it for a long time. He showed it to you?"

Persephone nodded. "Yes, it was so beautiful."

"But did you know he also requested that I send you your friend, Cerus? I saw how close you got to the bull. Even in the heavens, he was mischievous, so I wasn't surprised to see him misbehaving on Earth. I wasn't sure he'd take to anyone, but Hades was confident he'd take to you. And he was correct. So, when I knew you were leaving the Upper Realms, I returned him to the stars to await your return. He would not have survived without you. Humans would never have let him live without your protection. But he will return to you when spring returns to the Earth."

"Oh, thank you," Persephone said, her eyes welling up with tears. "Cerus has provided me with great comfort."

Hypnos cocked his head, his gaze shifting behind her. She turned to see her guard's dark shadow hovering near the wall. "You've returned after a long absence. Is it everything you expected it to be?"

"There have been some changes, which I suppose is to be expected."

"It is a fact of life that change must occur," Nyx replied kindly. "We either allow change to reshape us or allow it to break us."

"Sometimes I just want things to be the same," Persephone admitted quietly.

"What matters remains unchanged," Hades suddenly said behind her.

The Gods and Goddesses bowed low to the Lord of the Underworld.

"Hades," Nyx greeted, moving her luminous eyes over him.

Hades made a low bow. "Nyx," he said quietly. He took Persephone's hand, drawing her to stand before him. "What do you think of my wife?"

Nyx's gaze was drawn to Persephone. "*Anima tua*," she softly said.

Hades' grip on her hand tightened. "Perhaps you should ask your mother to dance with you, Hypnos," Hades continued, his gaze fixed on their entwined hands. "If I recall correctly, she is exceptionally quick on her feet."

There was a brief pause at the evident and rude dismissal. Persephone flushed, her gaze drawn to Nyx, but the Goddess remained calm, her curious gaze sweeping over Hades. Taking the not-so-subtle hint, Hypnos nodded and began to back away, holding Nyx's arm tight against him. "Pleasant dreams, Your Highness," he said, turning his hooded face slightly, his voice lighter than a whisper.

Souls and Gods of the Underworld whirled madly across the candlelit floor as the trio was lost in the ballroom. The rhythmic steps of the dancers captivated Persephone. She had always enjoyed watching others dance, admiring their graceful movements and connection with their partner, if only for the duration of the dance. The dancers' dresses and togas swirled in brilliant colors, creating a kaleidoscope of brightness.

"I want to show you something if you're tired of watching the dancers," Hades murmured into her ear.

"But the guests-"

"They will keep. As you can see, they are swamped." Hades raised his hand, and the music picked up speed with several jubilant cries from the audience. "Come on, queen. Our rudeness will go unnoticed."

"Speaking of rudeness, that reminds me. Why did you dismiss Nyx and her sons?" she asked. "It was rude."

"I *am* rude," he laughed. "That is one of the few benefits of being the king. Besides, I wanted to be alone with you."

He drew her behind him, greeting subjects as he walked until he reached a quiet corner of the room. His hand brushed against the paneled wall, causing a portion to swing open. Hades motioned for Persephone to follow. She looked around the ballroom before exiting through the hidden doorway. Hades trailed her closely. She turned to look around the room as the door closed behind him. The walls were carved of striking dark blue and black azurite, the crystals' sharp peaks reaching high up into the ceiling. As she touched the beautiful, hard stone, she felt a calm wave over her.

"What is this room?" she inquired softly.

"I had this room built specifically for you. A place where you can go when you miss the world above." He motioned to the stone. "Azurite soothes the mind. Besides, I sense you've had some reservations since returning."

She ran her fingers over the dark crystal's sharpened tips, the razor-sharp edge pressing against her skin. "Things are a little different than I expected."

"Different isn't always a bad thing."

She turned to face him, her gaze fixed on him. "No, it is not always negative. And not always for the better. It just is sometimes." She glanced at the concealed doorway. " It appears you succeeded in keeping my shadow from following me."

"You don't need your guard when I'm with you."

"I don't believe I need a guard at all."

He'd gotten closer to her. "I protect my palace, I protect my people, and you think I will do nothing to protect the one I place above all others? Don't you know me better than that?"

Persephone lowered her gaze so he couldn't see the pain in her green eyes. "I guess there's still a lot I don't know about you."

He spun her around, pressing her against him, his fingers pressing into her back. "You know me," he snarled. "You know the parts of me that are important." He let her go and took a step back, surveying her. "Pull up your skirts."

She hesitated, biting her lip. "But your guests, there are people just outside."

"I know," he answered, his voice a dark whisper. "And they will never know. Now lift your skirts."

Persephone closed her eyes and began to raise her dress. As she felt the cool air on her thighs, he was there suddenly, pleasuring her and coaxing her until everything fell away but them, and while her mind cautioned discretion, her body rejoiced, caring for nothing else as the God of the Dead worshiped her.

They lay on the floor, exhausted and satisfied.

"We must be returning; we must have been missed by now."

Hades sighed and rose to his feet. "As you command." She stood up and began to wipe her legs discreetly when his hands stopped her. He leaned close, his lips against her ear, whispering, "No, leave it. I want to know that while everyone else is dancing and having polite conversation, you're walking around with the evidence of my love between your thighs."

"But…" His fingers traced the delicate outline of her ears, down her neck, between her breasts, and finally to her abdomen, cutting off her protest abruptly.

"My seed will take root here soon." He laughed as she stiffened against him. "But I'm not in a hurry, my love. It's enough to know you're mine. Let us return now to our guests as my oh-so-proper wife has decreed."

He pressed against the wall paneling again, and they reentered the ballroom's darkened corner. Persephone glanced at Hades, who appeared at ease after their interlude. He could not know how his words brought a chill of foreboding, dampening the pleasure he had just provided her. She was not ready for another child. She had told him that. But did he plan to pressure her now?

As decadent drinks flowed through the opulent ballroom, tendrils of smoke rose from the brims of goblets. Persephone overheard a hushed conversation among a group of river nymphs.

"I heard a drop of the Lethe or Acheron were used in some of these," one giggled.

"A little pleasure with pain," another tittered as they unabashedly gulped down the steaming libations.

Persephone frowned at the trivial use of the sacred river waters but was distracted as Hades grasped her hand

He led her through the crowd to a dimly lit emerald-carved room. The long table was piled high with silver platters of the most delectable fare. The table was a veritable feast for the eyes, with steaming, sizzling meats, cakes shaped in various sizes, sparkling with adornments, and many brightly colored vegetables and fruits from Elysium. Gods and souls began to pour in behind them, taking their seats at the large table as deep red wine overflowed in ruby cups.

Hades sat at the head, Persephone on his right, and Nyx suddenly slid into the seat on Hades' left, cutting off Minthe, who had been heading towards the chair with vigorous determination. The nymph's eyes narrowed, but then she saw who had thwarted her, and she paled before letting out a rude huff, moving further down the table. Hades poured a glass of red wine for Persephone, seemingly oblivious as he pressed the goblet into her hand. How bold the nymph was to assume that she would have a seat beside the king, Persephone thought, taking a sip of the wine.

"You haven't had an opportunity to meet everyone yet," Hades said softly. He nodded subtly toward a fair, silver-headed Goddess. "That is Lethe. Her river flows through the Underworld. The Furies are the women seated next to her in leather gowns. When we first arrived, you saw them flying outside. Styx is the Goddess with bluish hair who rules over her river here, the water that flows from above to below. Her waters are what brought me your letters. She also punishes those who break oaths." He smiled at her as she sipped her wine. "Keep your marriage vows while Styx is around."

Persephone did not return his smile; instead, she looked further down the table. Minthe now sat at the opposite end of the table, staring intently at Hades. The nymph, sensing Persephone's gaze, shot her a look of dislike, and Persephone let her gaze pass over her. The Gods of the Underworld were darker in appearance than the Olympians, and they sparkled like frost on a winter's night.

The discussion, events she was unaware of, and names she didn't recognize moved across the table. She felt completely out of place as bits of conversation drifted to her. She knew nothing about these Gods, and as they whispered and laughed together, a feeling of loneliness swept over her. How foolish she had been to think she belonged here. She was no more a part of this world than she was of Olympus. Zeus was correct in one respect: her upbringing had shielded her from the ways of the Gods, both above and below. Why had Hades waited so long to marry? These Goddesses were far more interesting and worldly than she was. She crossed her legs in shame, fearful that the Gods would sense what had just happened between her and her husband, and she felt overwhelmed by her ignorance and inexperience. When she raised her eyes, she found Nyx's luminous eyes fixed upon her thoughtfully.

Hades' large hand covered hers.

Persephone, why don't you speak with our guests?

It is difficult for me to contribute to this conversation. I know very little of what is being discussed.

His fingers traced over the soft flesh of her palm. *But you can learn, as I did. I was once new to this world as well; they will welcome you if they feel you want to be part of it.*

She shifted her gaze to him. He was a true king of his domain, confident and beautiful, sitting at the head of the table. And how miserable and insignificant she was. A peahen amongst peacocks. *I will try*, she conceded.

"I think the king must be very happy for the return of his queen," Nyx said suddenly, drawing their attention to her. "I have never seen him throw such a large party in his palace. In fact, I have never seen Hades at a gathering of the Gods." The table, humming with conversation, fell silent as the Goddess spoke, everyone leaning in eagerly to hear her sweet voice.

Persephone blushed and sipped her wine, desperately trying to think of something clever. Why was she so bad at this? The beautiful Goddess' attention made her feel too large and clumsy, and she despised the entire party staring at her. She looked at Hades, who nodded encouragingly.

"Have you known Hades for a long time?" she asked finally. Good Gods, they would likely think Hades had married a fool.

Nyx smiled enigmatically. "On a relative scale. I've known him since the day he was born. He has never been much of a social being. His dislike of trivialities earned him my respect many years ago."

Hades chuckled. "Come now, Nyx, do not tell her what a bore I am. I intended to keep it hidden for the first few hundred years."

Nyx focused on him, crossing her fingers to rest her chin on her hands. "Hades, you are not a bore; I find you very interesting right now."

Hades began to serve Persephone portions of the vibrantly colored vegetables. "Truly? I am humbled."

"I always find discovering new facets in one's character intriguing. After a while, you believe you know everything about someone, then pft!" She moved her fingers, causing small streams of black smoke to unfurl from her fingertips. "Yes, I remember watching you as a young God on Olympus; you were far more boring then. If I recall correctly, you detested drawing attention to yourself."

Persephone, transfixed by Nyx's words, chuckled. "I've always suspected you were shy. Tell me about him when he lived on Olympus."

Nyx smiled at her eagerness and raised her gaze to the heavens, deep in thought. "He was alone and brooding at the time, very studious, always outlining how the day should be structured or drawing a map. He was not the King of the Dead then but the God of Wealth. He had little time for the palace's inanity and depravity and even less time for lies. It's a good thing Hades was able to get away from Olympus. It did not suit him."

"That is correct," Persephone said with a smile. "He will not put up with nonsense."

"I am organized," mumbled Hades. "A kingdom should be well-run."

"But life is not always straightforward, Pluto."

"Do not call me that," Hades snapped, his voice low and cold as he stared at his plate. Persephone was taken aback as he again showed disrespect to the ancient Goddess.

Nyx's expression remained calm. "But isn't that who you are?"

"I do not like it."

"You do not like who you are?"

"I do not like that name," he growled in a low voice. "My feet are firmly planted on the ground, not floating through the cosmos. Besides, I was banished from the heavens long ago."

Nyx gave him a small smile. "Banishment does not change who you are. You are a part of the Universe, child. You always wanted to follow the rules, but when will you realize that we came from Chaos and that the Universe is Chaos? Nothing in our lives runs smoothly or according to plan. We can't control the discord more than the wind can control fire."

"Order exists in Chaos," Hades snapped. "You sprang from him, and you follow the same obvious pattern every sunset since the beginning of your birth. You are the epitome of structure and order."

"But is there truly a pattern? No two sunsets are alike, and no matter how hard you try, you can never duplicate one. So it is with life. Every action causes tiny modifications to the Universe's fabric, which you may only notice once they weave a larger shift. The seas' tides are never the same, and neither is the moon's pull. A pattern, too, cannot be truly repeated. In my efforts to restore order, I have actually unleashed Chaos. Sometimes, there are minor disruptions; other times, there are major disasters. He's always there, waiting, order nothing more than a template for him to write his history on."

Hades kept his gaze lowered. "Do you seek to warn me, Goddess?"

The midnight eyes never wavered from Hades' bent head. "Right now, I'm just chatting with an old friend." Nyx laughed softly, and the tension dissipated as she turned to face Persephone. "As his old friend, I have no hesitation in telling you a few stories. I recall Hades politely declining invitations to his brother's events. I would watch him avoid Zeus' parties night after night, preferring to be alone. He'd sulk out of the dining room and disappear to gaze at the night sky. Many a beautiful God or Goddess tried to persuade him otherwise, but he would not be swayed. However, even a mountain can be worn down over time if the water is persistent. He avoided their attempts at corruption for a long time," she concluded thoughtfully.

"Avoided the orgies," he corrected. He had relaxed once more and poured another glass of the fine wine. "You never frequented them either, Nyx."

"You recall correctly. But I observed the Olympians' depravity from the night sky. I learned much about those Gods during those early days on Olympus simply by watching."

"And did you learn everything you needed to know?" Hades inquired, thoughtfully twirling his glass.

"Oh, one can never learn everything. But I learned to avoid those particular parties."

"I, too, dislike large gatherings," Persephone admitted shyly. "However, this one appears much more pleasant than the Olympus parties."

"I can see that you're a good match for each other. Your lightness entices Pluto's darkness," Nyx said softly. "Your husband was never one of the Olympians. He did not enjoy the orgies either, did you, Pluto?"

Nyx was looking at Hades, but Hades was staring at Persephone, his fingers trailing over her arm. "No, I did not. What happens between lovers is personal. I've never felt compelled to share."

Nyx gave Persephone a smile. "Did you hear what your husband said? He is not a fan of sex at parties."

Persephone's cheeks flushed, and she couldn't stop herself from crossing her legs, tightening them in embarrassment. Between her thighs, she could still feel the sticky residue of their encounter. "Oh," she said, her voice high-pitched.

Even as Nyx addressed Hades, her large, luminous eyes stayed Persephone. "You are extremely fortunate to have discovered such an extraordinary Goddess. Faithfulness is uncommon among men and even less so among Gods. It's nice to see it after all these years." Nyx's gaze moved down the table, and Persephone paled, knowing the Goddess was looking at Minthe. "Or am I assuming too much?"

"Do you remember what you asked me about the blood moon, Hades?" Nyx went on, unfazed by their lack of response. She'd leaned in closer, her voice soft enough not to be overheard.

Hades was finally forced to look at the ancient Goddess; his dark eyes were guarded. "That was a long time ago."

"Surely not long enough for you to forget. It seemed vital to you at the time. The blood moon is getting closer, Pluto, but you no longer ask me for answers." Her black hair partially covered her face as she tilted her head, intently observing him.

"Do you have an answer for me then?" His voice was clipped.

"I don't think you would like what I say."

One of the Furies was leaning close in an apparent attempt to eavesdrop. When it proved futile, she abruptly stood up, her large wings folded behind her as she bowed low. "Hades!" she shouted. "Tell us about the Olympians; how did it feel to be back on the mountaintop after so many years?"

Hades shook his head, but the other Gods had joined in, thumping their glasses, demanding a story. Persephone looked across the table impatiently at Nyx, who smiled benignly at her. What exactly did she mean by the blood moon? She had a gut feeling that everything Nyx said was deliberate. She trusted the ancient Goddess, though she could not say precisely why. Something about her told Persephone that Nyx did not play games.

The king suddenly leaned forward. When he raised his hand, the audience fell silent. "It was exactly the same as when I left years ago. And yet...his cruelty is worse than ever, more brazen than ever, more callous to his subjects and the Gods. He is dangerous because he wields so much power."

"You should have been High King," a voice exclaimed.

The silver-haired river Goddess rose and bowed low. "Regardless, thank the Gods, you are our king. We follow you, and only you. You are our monarch, our heavenly father."

Styx rose to her feet. "We will follow you wherever you lead us. And if war breaks out, we will be by your side. The rivers may run red with your enemies' blood."

Persephone was taken aback by the fervent gleam in the expressions of the Underworld Gods as she looked down at the table. This felt like fanaticism to her, and she looked at her husband, sure that he would stop such obsequious praise, but he was smiling and his dark eyes swept the table in approval. Hades' face was gleaming, tiny beads of sweat dotting his brow. Persephone noticed him glancing at Minthe, who was smiling at him, her pupils large and dilated. The heat of their shared glance ignited a silent turmoil within Persephone.

The crowd fell silent as Nyx stood. "Such adoration," she began, her stare passing over each person at the table. Her gaze was drawn to Minthe, and the nymph's gaze darted away nervously. "Its intensity

seems familiar, though I've not seen it in this hall before." As her ancient eyes moved over them, the bowed Goddesses took their seats clumsily. "Because this is a joyous occasion, I will give the following salute, for we are gathered to celebrate the return of the Goddess, are we not?" Everyone raised their glasses in response except Hades, who stared at Nyx with dark, expressionless eyes.

"To the Underworld's king and queen," Nyx went on. "May the ancients guard them. May they never forget the corruption of power and that true strength lies in the sacrifice of love and those whose hearts remain true." The audience fell silent as Nyx spoke, and she raised her glass once more. "To the queen and her king."

"The king and his queen," the crowd chanted.

Nyx eyed Hades as she took a deep drink. "They did not get it quite right, did they, Pluto? Queens before kings." Persephone had to strain to hear her voice because it was so soft.

The Gods drank silently from their goblets, and Persephone sipped from her cup uneasily. Was Nyx trying to warn them? Why was she so troubled? It was a party, and Hades was just trying to be a good host, yet she was unsettled. The silence was broken by an argument, and raised voices could be heard behind closed doors.

A voice screamed loudly, "Where is she? Where is my daughter? Persephone!"

Persephone leaped from her seat. That voice was familiar to her. The guests' curious gazes turned to Persephone.

"Father," she whispered. She hurried away from the table, but Hades was ahead, striding abruptly to the dining room doors. He tried to shut them in her face, but she blew them open and stepped through. Behind her, the doors slammed shut.

"Do not dare try to lock me in!" she shouted angrily. She peered around Hades' tall form and saw her handsome father imprisoned by large, hooded guards on either side.

"Release him," she demanded, her voice as sharp as a whip. They let go of his arms as she dashed to her father, wrapping her arms around his neck. For long stretches of silence, they embraced each other tightly. When she stepped back, she saw her father's face contorted with rage as he stared at Hades.

"Will you or I tell her?" Iasion inquired, his voice shaking with fury.

Persephone turned to face her husband, then to her father; Hades' face was calm and contemptuous, while her father's was enraged and passionate. What had happened to enrage her normally serene father? She cried out in frustration when neither of them spoke. "Can someone please explain what this is about?"

Iasion was so angry that he became breathless as he began to pace the hall. "You have a right to know. I'd heard about your return and knew he'd keep me from you. I'd be doing your mother and yourself a disservice if I didn't tell you what I've seen. He has been unfaithful to you. When his wife is away, he brings a whore to his temple. I despise a woman who cheats on her husband, but there are no words for a husband who breaks his vows. None of them will be said in front of my daughter."

Persephone felt the blood leave her face. *No*, her mind cried, *no, it cannot be.*

Hades grabbed Iasion's arm and dragged him across the room, away from the guards and Persephone. Hades spoke in a low, enraged tone. "You have no idea what you are talking about."

Iasion tried to yank Hades' arm off, but Hades only tightened his grip. "Am I supposed to deny my own eyes?"

"That 'whore' decorated and prepared the temple for the return of my wife. She has been a loyal servant, whereas you have been a disobedient one. You are doing your daughter a great disservice by coming here. You have caused irreversible damage." He hauled Iasion onto a nearby balcony.

"Leave him alone!" Persephone screamed and reached for her father. As the door slammed shut behind them, Hades held up his free hand, his dark eyes flashing. Persephone dashed to the door, raising her hands and blasting a powerful wind at it, but it didn't move.

"How dare you!" she yelled. "If you don't let me in, I'll never forgive you." She pounded on the door until she was pulled against a firm chest by solid arms. She looked into her guard's hooded face. "Leave me alone, you great oaf!" she snarled. She pushed and raged at him, but his firm grip never wavered. He didn't budge even when she dug her sharp teeth into his arm. She finally lay motionless and exhausted, breathless with helpless rage. A sliver of glass on the door allowed her to see Hades and Iasion.

She watched as Iasion raged at Hades while her husband stood like a vast, silent wraith. Hades' face was in shadow, so she couldn't tell if he was speaking, but Iasion's face suddenly turned pale, and he fell to his knees, bowing his head to Hades' feet. "No," she whispered. Hades put a hand on her father's bowed head. Her husband stepped back, allowing Iasion to rise, and motioned for the man to follow behind him. When they returned through the doors, the guard let her go. As he entered the hall, Iasion bowed his head.

Hades stood between her and her father. "Iasion has something to say to you. He was wrong - weren't you wrong, Iasion?"

Iasion lifted his green eyes, but instead of looking at Persephone, he only watched Hades. "Yes, your Highness."

"Minthe is not my whore?"

"No, King Hades."

Persephone moved towards her father, but Hades stepped firmly between them. "And because Iasion was so foolish as to shout in a room full of Gods where I had carefully hidden him, Iasion must now hide somewhere else. Is that also correct- Iasion?"

Her father lifted his head, and his eyes were filled with tears. "That is also correct."

Hades moved in closer so that only Persephone and Iasion could hear. "And because there is a weapon in existence that has the potential to shatter his immortal soul into oblivion, and he has a powerful enemy out there, Iasion will hide where I tell him and cease contact with his daughter until this situation is resolved?"

"What?" Persephone exclaimed. "No! You can't do it!"

Iasion bowed as if she hadn't said anything. "Yes."

Hades drew his arms across his chest. "Say your farewells."

Persephone's mouth dropped open in shock. "You're not serious," she finally said. When neither responded, she moved to her father, shaking his hand. Even as his head remained bowed, she felt his cold fingers tighten around hers. "You are insane if you believe I will allow you to exile my father. I'll stay with him. If he needs to hide, I'll go with him. I will not abandon him."

"I'm doing it for your father," Hades said quietly. "You cannot accompany him to his destination. If he stays here, he will surely die. And not a mortal's death this time, but a final, permanent one. I've been protecting your father all this time, but his folly has rendered it all in vain. He must depart, and you will not accompany him. He's already in serious danger. He should never have come to the palace."

Persephone stepped in front of her father, blocking him from Hades. "I'll say it again," she said, trembling. "You're deluded if you think I'll abandon him."

"You are a loyal daughter, but I refuse your offer," Hades said coldly. "He must travel alone."

"I will not allow it," snarled Persephone. "What happened out there? I deserve to know!"

"Daughter," Iasion interjected, his voice soft and sad. "I must make the journey alone. I assure you everything will be fine, but it is best for everyone if I follow the king's orders. I made a mistake."

Persephone looked at her father, tears welling up in her eyes. "No, Father," she cried. "I can keep you safe. I cannot let you go!" She threw herself into his arms and felt his fingers gently stroke her hair. He kissed her on the cheek, and she heard an urgent whisper in her ear. "Do not trust them, Persephone." Persephone drew back, fear coursing down her spine as she locked her eyes on Iasion's emerald gaze.

As Hades approached, Iasion drew back. The king waved his hand, and a goblet appeared. He traced the cup's delicate rim without looking up. "Iasion, you know what to do."

Iasion's green eyes shifted to his daughter. "Persephone, I love you."

"Father," she cried, but his form had already begun to waver, and when she reached where he had stood, she embraced only empty air. She stood motionless in the corridor. "Where is he?" she inquired quietly. When he didn't respond, she charged at Hades, shoving him hard.

"Where has he gone?" she yelled.

Hades grasped her wrists with one hand and held the rubied goblet filled with swirling blue water in the other. "I'm afraid I can't tell you what I don't know." Hades raised the cup to his lips, and she realized too late that it contained Lethe water, the River of Forgetfulness; she reached for his arm, attempting to shake the goblet from his grasp, but he had already swallowed the pale, glowing water.

She sobbed and fell to her knees. "How could you do this? How could you be so cruel to us?"

His fingers caressed her hair, but she jerked away. "Lose him now or lose him forever, Persephone," he said gently above her. "In time, you will understand."

She jumped up, her face ravaged by grief as she turned to face him. "I will never understand. I'm conscious of two things. My father accused you of being unfaithful, and you then exiled him. That's what I know!"

Hades' mouth thinned. "This isn't the time."

"When is the right time! When will I get an honest answer from you!"

Charon stepped through the dining hall doors. She could see the guests crammed into the doorway, staring in astonishment at the scene. Before the doors closed again, she caught a brief glimpse of Nyx standing behind the crowd, her glowing eyes fixed on Hades.

"Charon, please inform our guests that we have retired for the night," Hades said.

"I'm not going to retire with you," Persephone snarled.

"You're causing a scene," Hades muttered.

"Oh, and we wouldn't want that, would we?"

"You will come with me, and I will answer your questions. Charon, go now."

Charon bowed his head and slipped back through the doors, and Persephone bolted down the halls to her old room. She was faster now and slammed the doors of her bedroom shut behind her before anyone could stop her. Her heart was pounding, and Persephone slid down the wall as her legs gave way beneath her. The sweat on her brow mingled with her tears, and she wiped her face impatiently.

"How could you?" she whispered. Her father's accusations caused physical pain in her heart. She had not even been allowed to speak to him privately. *Do not trust them*, he had whispered. Who did he mean? Hades? Her father had voiced the fear she'd felt since first seeing Minthe. Her cheeks burned with anger and humiliation, and her eyes stung tears at a betrayal she did not want to believe.

A pounding came on the door, and Persephone lifted her head.

Persephone. His voice pressed in her mind. *Persephone,* his voice was cajoling. *Let me explain to you. You do not have to answer, but I wish to be able to explain why I had to hide your father. I've been protecting him all along; don't I deserve a chance to explain why I had to send him away?*

She leaned back on the wall, wiping the tears from her face. Hades' hand had shielded Iasion for all these years, but her father's words were like poison in her chest.

Persephone, please trust me enough to let me explain. Do not acquit me without trial.

And Gods helped her; she wanted to believe in him. Foolish, foolish heart, her mind whispered. It's not like she could avoid him indefinitely. She was the Queen of the Underworld, *his* queen, and she was here for six months. She would not judge another person without hearing their defense; therefore, she should grant her husband this right. She stood, paused, and then pulled open the door. Her husband was leaning against the door frame, his dark eyes fixed on her, his face weary. She moved, allowing him to enter, then sat on the ground, letting the soft grass beneath her cradle her body. Hades was wise enough to keep his distance, standing against the wall, and casually lifted his hand to light a blazing fire in the hearth.

"I knew I'd have to make sure Zeus didn't find out about your father's rescue when I brought him to the Underworld," he began in a low voice. "I have carefully hidden your father all this time, and now the guards, the Gods, and souls in that room know of his existence. It's why he should never have left the fields of Elysium and why I warned him never to enter this palace. I haven't told you everything yet. You are correct; war is on its way. I believe the Underworld has a spy. If your father's whereabouts were known, he could be harmed or used to manipulate you in ways that neither he, you, nor I would want.

"Zeus still hates Iasion. In fact, time has only allowed his hatred to fester. He will be enraged to learn that he lives well within the Underworld, which he will learn soon. He'll come after him. If he finds him, he will use the sword to extinguish his soul. There is no turning back now." Hades' eyes moved over Persephone. "I hate seeing you cry. If there was another way, I would have found it. But the moment your father stepped foot in the palace, he had to leave. I had no choice. How much worse would it be for you to lose him forever?"

"A spy?" she murmured, considering his words carefully. "And who do you think is the infiltrator?"

"It could be someone in that room tonight. Or it could be a servant, even a soul. Trust no one, for Zeus, has eyes and ears everywhere. That is partially why I wished to hold the ball, to see if I could discover any inconsistencies."

She drew her knees up to her chest and rested her head against them, her face turned away from him. "And did you?"

"Your father arrived before I could continue with my investigation." His voice came to a halt. "Why don't you ask me what you want to know?"

She swallowed hard and closed her eyes. "Are you unfaithful to me?

"Never!" His voice was raw with emotion. "Persephone, I could never betray you."

"And yet, when my father confronted you, he was suddenly banished, and your special servant remains. I see the way she looks at you; I am not foolish. I know that others suspect it as well."

"I could never betray you. After all we have been through, don't you believe that?" When she said nothing, he gave a weary sigh."There is more regarding Minthe. I have not told you, but it is not what you think. As you are aware, I have been busy since your departure."

"Yes, I am aware of that. What does this have to do with Minthe?"

"I've been guarding our borders, having meetings with the Gods of the Underworld. Our palace is on the other side of the Coyctus, a river that could give the Olympians an advantage in battle. Only the wall separates the upper and lower worlds without the river. I've attended numerous meetings to guarantee that this river is effectively protected."

"But I thought the wall was secure?"

"There is nothing that is impenetrable."

It was impossible to fathom the impassable barrier encircling the Underworld crumbling, but she was a young Goddess and had never seen Gods at war; Hades had. He had fought in one of the bloodiest wars the Earth had ever known. "How did you keep the border secure? Additional security?"

He shifted his eyes to hers, his face expressionless. "Extra guards were one way. And, of course, expanding the wall's perimeter, but I obtained a very significant pact."

"With whom?"

"Minthe. Or, more specifically, her father. He is the Coyctus King, with whom I require an alliance. Minthe is their princess."

"I see," Persephone responded after a little pause. "So a king's daughter is satisfied to work as a servant in your household?"

"He is satisfied for her to be a servant in *my* household. Cronus' son, Zeus' brother, Poseidon's brother, and King of the Underworld. He does not want to lose his important position, and I will work with him to keep it within his family. He wanted Minthe to learn about the Underworld, for me to mentor him for a time."

She was silent as she considered what he had revealed. "When will I see my father again?" she asked finally.

His eyes closed. "You will see him again before stepping on the upper world."

Persephone raised her eyes to the carvings of Eros and Psyche. She had promised herself that she would not allow the words of others to persuade her against her will, but how could she so easily dismiss her father's words? And how was she to know who was manipulating her? She looks at her husband, her very handsome, very enigmatic husband. She knew very little about the world. That was confirmed tonight.

"I'm tired," she admitted, "and I'd like to go to bed."

"Without me?"

She averted her gaze but then felt his hand on her shoulder.

"Persephone, please do not banish me. I've waited so long to be able to hold you again. Allow me to hold you tonight. Allow me to be with you. I wish that things had not happened as they did. I wish your father had not crossed the threshold into my palace, but he did. I wish I did not have to change things here, but I must. I only ask that you trust in me and give me time to prove that I am the husband you thought I was."

She wanted to say no. Hurtful words hovered hot on her tongue, but she held them back. Hades had sacrificed so much for her, and they had wasted so much time before with misunderstandings and mistrust. She could see the wisdom in his words that her father was in peril. But what about Minthe? How she wanted to believe him.

"You can stay," she whispered.

As they lay in bed, Persephone replayed her husband's assurances in her mind. Yet, the seeds of doubt, planted by her father's unsettling revelations and amplified by the cautious whispers of Jocasta, had taken root in the fertile soil of her mind. She lay beside Hades in the vast expanse of their bed, but an invisible chasm widened between them. Her love for Hades warred with the fear that she was a naive fool, willingly closing her eyes to the shadows in their life. As sleep finally claimed her, Persephone began wondering just how well she knew her husband.

CHAPTER 7
HIDDEN FOREST

That night, she had a dream about her husband. As they floated high in the starry sky, he embraced her in his arms. A storm roared around them, and he leaned in closer, protecting her with his body and engulfing her in his warmth. Her attention was drawn to the gentle flutter of wings, and she turned to see a single black moth flying out of the darkness, moving closer and closer. It circled around her, the hum of its wings filling her ears till the fluttering drowned out the storm's noise.

"I'm coming for him," it whispered. "I'm coming."

The moth suddenly expanded to the size of a massive black-winged beast, ripping Hades from her arms. She screamed and tried to cling to him, but the thing was too powerful. Then she found herself alone in the dark, sobbing.

Persephone, a voice called.

Her eyes fluttered open, and suddenly, the pomegranate tree stood before her, its fruit throbbing, weeping blood. A shadowy figure materialized, lurking behind the tree, beckoning her. Its lips moved in a terrible parody of a smile as it whispered, "*Summum malum.*" And the shadow was racing towards her, and Persephone fell back, recoiling in terror.

And then she was falling, descending into light and shadow, and when the world came back into focus, she was standing in a valley, her gaze locked on the mountain high above.

Tendrils of smoke snaked down the mountainside, reaching for her. Cries burst from all directions at once, agonizing fearful voices, and she covered her ears, unable to bear the sound. She began to cough and gasp as the smoke filled her lungs. When she looked up, a flash of green light filled the valley, and she saw her husband floating in the iridescent hue, his eyes closed.

Help me, Hades, she cried into his mind.

His eyes flashed open, and fear crossed his face.

"I don't want you here," he growled. "Persephone, run! Run!"

A massive blast descended from the summit towards the Earth, amplifying her cries of pain and panic as the ground crumbled beneath her feet. Far below, a winged form awaited her, and she was falling, plummeting into nothingness.

Abruptly, she awoke to the disorienting feeling of falling through the air. A surprised gasp of pain escaped her as she crashed onto cold, unyielding ground.

"Wha-what?" she mumbled, dazed. When she touched her head, warm liquid smeared her fingertips. Blood. Her ears rang as she lifted herself slowly, leaning against the wall for support. She stared around the unfamiliar, darkly lit passageway. Dear Gods, she had been sleepwalking.

Long shadows flickered across the walls as if they were reaching out to her. She needed to get back to her room. Shivering, she rushed through the dimly lit halls, arms crossed across her breast. The corridor was dark and cold, and she was dressed only in a flimsy night rail. Every now and then, she glanced behind her. She could almost imagine something close behind her in the dark, reaching for her. She exhaled gratefully when she noticed a light in a nearby corridor. This area was familiar; she was close to the throne room. She paused, glancing into the darkness.

"Who is there?" she called out, her voice trembling. There was no response, but she could feel something out of sight, watching. Shuddering, she turned. She crept in softly when she reached their room, not wanting to wake Hades. But as she peered into the bed, it was empty.

"Hades?" she whispered.

The heavy draperies at the windows fluttered in the chilly night air. She moved towards them, gazing through the window below, but the palace's outside remained still and calm. She noticed a tiny, dark figure on the floor. Olive was huddled beneath the draperies, his little body curled up against the cold night air.

"What are you doing down here, sweetling?" she murmured.

She caressed his soft fur, finding comfort in the warmth of his small body. Persephone crawled into bed with Olive in her arms, trembling with fear. Pulling the blankets up to her chin, she sat upright, determined to keep her eyes from closing. As the hours passed, she repeatedly fought the urge to let her eyelids droop, forcing them open each time. Her gaze fixated on the empty space beside her, the fear of what might happen in the night keeping her wide awake.

"Hades," she whispered, "where are you?"

As the first rays of light reached the chamber, Persephone had finally fallen asleep, Olive's tiny body nestled protectively against hers. Her dreams had been turbulent and disturbing.

Her eyes opened as a featherlight touch brushed against her. Olive's brown eyes stared into hers. She stiffened as she became aware of a presence next to her. Hades was deeply asleep beside her. He lay atop the sheets, apparently too exhausted to crawl beneath. His wrists were bruised, and there were black shadows beneath his eyes.

"You're awake," he murmured abruptly without opening his eyes.

She straightened, embarrassed at being caught staring. "Yes." She took a deep breath and then asked the question on her mind. "Where were you last night?"

"Last night?" he repeated, his brows furrowing. "Last night..." He was silent for so long that she wondered if he would respond. "I couldn't sleep," he finally answered. "I didn't want to bother you. I frequently have sleepless nights."

She scrutinized his face. Was he lying to her? Would she even notice if he was? Her fingertips trailed over the bruising on his wrists. "And where did these come from?"

His eyes opened at her touch, and he lifted his wrist to examine the marks as if they had also surprised him. When his gaze met hers, he suddenly jumped up, pulling her towards him.

"What happened?" he questioned, his voice gruff, his fingers soothing as he stroked her bloodied brow. "What did you do?"

"It's nothing," she answered hurriedly, pulling away, wishing she'd washed her hair last night. "I— tripped."

As he peered down at her, his grip on her was firm. "And fell on your head? When you went to bed last night, you were fine. Did you take a midnight stroll?"

"I suppose I also couldn't sleep."

Their eyes locked, each feeling what was left unsaid. Though the cut had already healed, Hades raised his hand to alleviate any leftover pain. His fingers sifted through her hair, massaging her head tenderly. "Persephone, it is unsafe to stroll around the palace at night."

"But you do," she murmured, her body melting under his touch despite her reservations. "Doesn't the queen have to follow the king?"

"No," he replied. "The queen must be guarded because she has the key to the kingdom in her heart. Why aren't you sleeping?"

"I had bad dreams. Why are *you* not sleeping?"

His eyes were shrouded in shadows. "Bad dreams," he echoed. He hesitated as though considering his words carefully. "I think tonight, perhaps, it would be best if you sleep in your own room."

Her heart sank at his words. "Why?"

"You need sleep, and I'm concerned my restlessness may bother you."

"But I don't want to sleep without you," Persephone admitted, her hurt evident in her voice. "We have been apart for so long. All I want is to be with you."

His eyes flickered away from her, his fists clenched tightly in the sheets. "As I do you, but I worry I will disrupt your sleep."

"It does not bother me. I only worry about you."

"And I do not want you worrying."

"And yet," she persisted, "I will still worry. I can't just turn it off, you know." Don't shut me out, she wanted to scream. But there was a distance between them, and she could not bridge that space, so she locked the words tightly in her chest.

"Only until you rest." He traced the dark circles under her eyes. "You are more important than anything. You must stay well and rest."

"Don't you need rest, too?" she argued.

"For the wicked, sleep is rarely easy to come by. Besides, I am a beast of the shadows; we do not need as much sleep," he teased with a small smile.

She bit back her protests; she would not beg him more than she already had. "Very well, if it's what you want, I will sleep in my room."

Silence stretched between them, heavy and painful. It felt like they had taken a giant step backward in their relationship.

He took her hand in his. "Persephone–" But she never knew what he meant to say as his eyes were drawn to the door. "A visitor has arrived," he said suddenly.

Questions lingered on her tongue, but they died with his words. She suppressed a groan. "Who?" She was not in the mood for company, her mind still foggy from the night's interrupted sleep.

"It is a distinguished visitor. He is upset that he was not permitted to attend the ball."

"Truly?" Persephone inquired, leaping towards the bed. She grabbed a dressing gown and quickly wrapped it around herself. "Who is it, Hades? I should first get dressed."

He grimaced and shook his head. "I can't make him wait. In fact, I've kept him waiting long enough. I believe he is upset with me."

With trepidation, Persephone chewed her bottom lip. "Oh dear," she muttered, pulling her hair into a loose braid. "Very well, you may allow him in." As he pulled the door open, the sound of heavy breathing filled the room, and Persephone looked up curiously at the empty entryway. She was thrown aback as a little, warm body shoved against her.

"Cerberus!" she exclaimed. Three tiny pink tongues licked her face vigorously, and she laughed, kissing the tiny black snouts that crowded against her. He was as little as a puppy as he cuddled against her neck.

"You see," Hades remarked solemnly. "He is enraged."

"Oh, poor Cerberus. Where has he been keeping you?" she asked the dog, soothingly stroking his trembling little body.

"Cerberus has been stationed at Tartarus' gates. But he's been distracted since catching your fragrance, which I completely understand. He grew to his current size because he knew you were coming, rendering him completely useless to defend the gates."

"You are quite clever," she said softly to the nearest head. Persephone stood up, cradling Cerberus in her arms, and Olive looked down at them, his tail wagging joyously. Looking at her husband, she noticed his intense focus on her. It should have been so natural for the four of them to be together, yet she felt strangely out of place.

Hades bent to stroke one of Cerberus' necks before straightening. "I have a few things to attend to with Charon. I thought you might like spending the morning reconnecting with old friends."

With his dark hair and black eyes, he looked every inch the wicked prince, and the sight made her treacherous heart melt. He stepped closer, drawing her against his chest; his touch was a balm for her soul. He had the scent of the forest after a summer shower. Was that where he'd been the night before? Dear Gods, she wished to bridge this strange gap between them. They could overcome it if he had been unfaithful and would only be honest with her. *If* he still loved her.

Do you know how I love you, his mind whispered to hers. His muscular body trembled against Persephone's as she touched her lips to his. He took a step back, putting some distance between them. His face was flushed, and beads of sweat dripped from his brow.

"Hades? What is wrong?" she asked in concern.

"I have to — I have to go," he mumbled, his eyes dazed. "I —" His gaze shifted to hers, and gold flashed in his irises.

"But," she mumbled, offering her hand to him. "I can tell you're not feeling well. I'm sure there's something I can do to help. I could come to the royal room and help you sort the souls."

"No!" he exclaimed, his voice firm. He swallowed, his throat convulsing, and then smiled, but his lips twisted in anguish rather than pleasure. "No," he repeated again more gently. "I simply want you to re-familiarize yourself with this world. I'm sure I don't have to tell you not to go too far from the castle." He approached her, kissing the top of Persephone's head and then Cerberus' nearest head, and then swept from the room.

She stared after him, wondering what had just happened. The door was suddenly shoved open as the handmaidens burst in. A mug of steaming hot wine was thrust into Persephone's hands. Phoebe reached for Cerberus but was startled by the violent roar the small heads let out. Persephone repressed a laugh at the maid's terrified face. Right now, the little mouths could only nip, but Cerberus was very particular about who he allowed to touch him.

"Best to leave Cerberus to me, even when he is small," Persephone advised the maid kindly. Cleo and Jocasta exited and returned with trays of food, silk gowns, and aromatic scent bottles.

Jocasta fixed her gaze on Persephone. "How did you sleep?"

Persephone grimaced as she caught sight of herself in the mirror. "I'm afraid no amount of your sorcery will make me presentable."

Jocasta tsked and drew the curtains from the windows. Persephone glanced at her bed and smiled. Cerberus and Olive were curled tightly around one another. Their friendship had been surprising, the ferocious guard of the Underworld and the little fawn, but a reminder that one may sometimes find friends in unexpected places. After undressing, a dark blue gown was pulled over her head; blue beading ran over her breasts and down the front of the gown. A gold necklace filled with sapphires was placed around her neck, and Persephone lifted her hair so Jocasta could fasten it. The gentle flow of conversation hummed around her, and the familiarity of it was soothing after her restless night and the tension with her husband.

"So," Persephone began, "what else has been happening in my absence these six months?"

"Well," Cleo began as she tried different styles in Persephone's hair, "the king has been building up the castle. In fact, no one has ever seen such expansions, they say. Even the oldest souls!"

"The outside of the palace?"

"Yes, Your Majesty, but the inside as well," Phoebe said emphatically. " For certain events—-" Phoebe halted and stared at Jocasta, who was organizing the food.

Persephone looked at Jocasta in the mirror. "For what events?"

"Well," Jocasta explained as she approached the queen with a plate of honeyed pears and a pitcher of mulled wine. "He looks to be expanding this wing, which houses the royal family."

"The family!" Persephone exclaimed, perplexed, as the platter was placed before her. "But there's only him and me, and Olive and Cerberus don't take up much room." Cerberus made a low sound. "Well, Cerberus doesn't normally take up that much space," she clarified.

"Perhaps he was considering a more Godly addition to his family."

"Godly," Persephone repeated softly.

Phoebe was so giddy with happiness that she almost screamed. "He's added a bedroom in this hall," she exclaimed. "It's for a baby!"

"A baby," Persephone said quietly. "But—has he stated it was designed for a baby?"

Phoebe cast a thoughtful glance up towards the ceiling. "Well...noooo, not quite. But I'm guessing it's a nursery. He's worked on it for a long time."

"Have you looked at the room?" Persephone inquired.

"Nooo…" Phoebe stated once again. "But it's only off these halls, so it must be for a family member."

"Can you tell me where it is?"

"Down the corridor, up the stairs."

Persephone laughed with relief. "Up the stairs? For a nursery? Oh, Phoebe, you must be mistaken."

Jocasta was looking in the mirror at Persephone. "We could be mistaken. We were just excited and thought, Perhaps..." Jocasta bent her head in response to Persephone's stillness. "We have been presumptuous."

The room was quiet, then Cleo spoke out again, this time in a happy but quiet tone. "Well, I can't wait to dress a little baby! It would enliven the atmosphere."

After finishing her hair and being satisfied that she required nothing else from them, the three women exited the room, their lively chat fading as the doors closed behind them.

Persephone's smile vanished as soon as they left. She couldn't shake the image of that quiet, little face in the forest. Her precious baby had been so silent and still in her arms. She blinked back her tears. No, she was not prepared for another child, not yet. There was no urgency for them; they had eternity ahead of them. Only Hades knew she'd lost a child, and he, more than anyone else, should understand why she needed time. She recalled a flower that mortals used to avoid pregnancy: silphium.

The queen checked behind her to make sure she was alone. Her guard had yet to appear, which surprised her, but she was grateful for the privacy. She frowned. And he hadn't been there last night either when she had been sleepwalking. Not a very good guard, she mused, but still, she would not complain. She needed time alone. She produced a tiny silphium seed with a wave of her hand, holding it between her fingers for a long time as she pondered it.

After that night in the garden, she had prayed for another child, but something was holding her back now. She knew what had changed if she was honest with herself. Cassandra's warning had, regrettably, made her nervous. Persephone felt a chill from the memories of the mortal, the darkness and death that had been in her gaze. She couldn't bear the thought of losing another baby. Her mother had told her that her husband was sterile, and Zeus had echoed her mother's words. But, on the other hand, she was supposedly extraordinarily prolific, maybe fertile enough to compensate for her husband's infertility.

It's why he chose you, a small voice in her head said. She jerked back, her gaze fixed on her mirror. Those were Zeus' words. Who do you trust more? She chastised herself. The answer seemed obvious. She placed the small seed in a silver box on her bedside, hidden beneath her jewelry.

Her thoughts returned to the ostensible nursery. "I'll look into it myself," she mumbled, pushing herself up from the vanity. She carefully tucked the blankets around the sleeping Olive and Cerberus before silently pushing open the room doors.

There was no guard, and even better, no Minthe lurking near the doorway. Then again, Minthe was not likely to linger when Hades was absent. Persephone treaded softly through the dim hallway until she reached the stairway Phoebe had pointed out. The shadowed and musty corridor caused Persephone's spine to tingle as she ventured away from the well-lit rooms. "Stop being silly," she scolded herself, yet she persisted in maintaining a hushed pace. She noticed the delicate blue and white crystals along the dim passageways, a new addition to the otherwise dark surroundings.

She climbed till she came to two massive ebony marble doors with beautiful gold embossment. She was taken with the beauty of the doorway. The entryway was engraved with an ancient tongue with mysterious symbols whispering a long-forgotten language. The wood, carved with celestial constellations, seemed to pulsate beneath her touch. She ran her fingers over the writing, a shiver trailing down her spine. This doorway felt... alive. What mysteries lay concealed beyond this threshold? Would Hades share this with her, or was it another unanswered question? A frown creased her forehead as she drew back, the air thick with an unsettling energy.

She paused before turning the doorknob, and to her surprise, the door opened. Her amazement turned to shock, and she scrambled backward with a gasp. The door led to a little ledge that gave way sharply to a precipitous drop into the Acheron River. This was not a room but rather a trap for the unwary. Over the river, a large stone edifice hung in the air. The hanging structure resembled a miniature fortress; the rocks of the construction were dark and dense, and molten magma flashed be-

tween the cracks of the stone. She noticed bars across the windows. It was not a room but a prison. The chilly wind whipped the fabric of her gown, causing her to shudder as she looked down at the frigid depths of the Acheron. Falling into those waters would be excruciating.

Persephone walked carefully to the edge of the marble floor and looked down. The turbulent water below rushed rapidly, and one wrong step would plunge you deep into the River of Pain. The only way to cross the river was by lowering a drawbridge from the stronghold over the river. She tried to summon the drawbridge with her powers, but it did not budge. How did one reach the other side? She mentally calculated the distance between the door's steps and the structure. Perhaps she could leap to the opposite side and peer through the windows. Or maybe, she considered in grim amusement, she would fall into the river and be ripped apart by excruciating pain. Before she could decide, a hard hand abruptly drew her back, and she turned to see the tall, hooded guard behind her.

He quickly yanked her back from the threshold, and she stumbled. He drew a long key from his dark robes, locking the dark stone doors. Then he swept past her without a word.

She stomped after him. "What is that room?" she demanded. He didn't acknowledge her, continuing to walk down the stairs. She snatched his arm and spun him around to face her. "I asked you a question."

He shook his head and pointed to his lips, which were, of course, covered. He motioned for her to follow him. She swept after him, cursing beneath her breath. His movements indicated stealth, so they crept down the corridor and across the courtyard until they arrived at the royal gates. Aethon waited for them just beyond the dark wall.

She looked at the mare in confusion. "I don't understand," Persephone began. "I want to know—what are you doing!" she sputtered angrily as the soldier effortlessly lifted her onto the back of the horse. Before she could protest further, he gently tapped the mare's hindquarters, and then she was speeding through the Underworld. She clenched her fists, enraged by the guard's arrogance. She tried to stop Aethon, but the horse continued galloping. Finally, the mare began to slow, and Persephone saw Orphneaus standing at a nearby river inlet that led to a reedy marshland.

Persephone dismounted and approached the stallion. The mare exchanged greetings with her partner, bumping noses with him.

"What are you doing here? Where is Hades?" Persephone asked, gently stroking Orphneaus' mane. If Hades had abandoned his horse, then he must be nearby. Persephone glanced around but saw no sign of her husband.

"Hades," she called tentatively.

"Hermes, I want you to bear witness...everything goes to her and her alone." It was Hades' voice, but it sounded distant, almost like a faint echo, and a shiver moved over her.

"Hades," she shouted, more urgently this time. "Where are you?" She stepped into the rocky marsh, where the wind swept through the reeds, carrying soft whispers on the breeze. She followed the faint murmurs until she arrived at a lone tree in the swampland. The tree's center was split by a large, hollowed opening, and the whispers intensified, appearing to originate from within this hollow. Persephone crouched down, her gaze fixed on the mysterious darkness within the tree, and a faint glow shimmered from within the opening.

"Hades?" she called tentatively into the aperture.

She returned her gaze to the horses grazing safely alongside the river before deciding. She knelt, easing herself into the tree's hollowed fissure, and gasped when she emerged on the other side.

It was as though she had stepped into another Universe within the hollowed tree. A diamond forest unfolded endlessly, with miles and miles of crystallized trees. Their radiance reflected on the crystal ground below, creating a surreal landscape. Persephone couldn't resist curling her fingers around a cool branch vibrating at her touch. The hum grew louder, and she heard it again—a deeper voice than before, merging with hundreds of other voices echoing from within the crystal limbs and resonating across the enchanting forest.

"I am a part of the Underworld. I am the Queen of Shades, and I rule..."

The voice vanished and was replaced by a single voice that wrapped around her and engulfed her. *"You are stronger than you realize."*

She gasped. "Hades?" she cried.

A repetitive, gentle thumping drew her attention, and she realized the low, rhythmic hum was coming from a massive tree in the center. Unlike the other trees in the jeweled forest, this gigantic, gnarled tree's twisted, naked limbs were devoid of ornamentation. She realized the sound she heard was the tree's heartbeat, and she could feel the flow of life through the massive root system that ran deep. This tree was alive, not just a gem in a kingdom of riches; its roots were linked to all the other trees in the forest, millions of silver cords extending from the enormous tree's base to the others. A single source of life with no beginning or end.

She felt the tree's awareness move against her as a silver corded root pushed from the ground, wrapping around her ankle, leg, and torso until it reached her heart. Her eyes widened as a massive cluster of crystals appeared in her hands, and as some of the crystals tumbled from her hand, a small sapling sprouted beneath the mother tree.

"I do not understand," she breathed into the wilderness. But her words only added to the symphony of whispers as they echoed off the gleaming trees. "I don't understand," she whispered again.

She closed her eyes, letting her fingers close over the crystals still in her hand, and when she opened her hand, a small crystal branch lay in her palm. A smile spread across her face. She bowed low to the mother tree and raced back through the forest, returning to the hollow, the doorway she had entered from.

Aethon and Orphneaus still waited on the river's bank as she exited the tree. Persephone turned back to the wetlands, pressing her hand into the tree's hollow once more, but the doorway had closed, her hand touching rough bark. It was only a tree once more. Persephone approached the horses thoughtfully, stroking the crystal branch she still held. She looked for Hades one last time before leaping onto Aethon's back, Orphneaus trotting happily behind them. If Hades had been there, he would simply have to return on foot.

As Persephone entered the gates, she saw the courtyard bustling with activity, but no one questioned her as she made her way to the palace stairs. Like her husband, her bodyguard had vanished, which was good for him, as she was still simmering with anger at his highhandedness. She crept up the stairway and silently went to Hades' study. She paused, glancing around, but it was exactly as she remembered, full of ornate items and well-worn books. At least some things had stayed the same, she mused. She crept in until she found what she was looking for, carefully tucking a map, scrolls, and books in her arms. She crept out and ran to her private room.

Olive and Cerberus appeared in the corridor and trotted behind her as she crept past Hades' chamber. Persephone opened her bedroom door, ushering them inside. After locking the door behind her, she sat on the grassy floor of her old room, absentmindedly plucking a peach from a nearby tree. Spreading the scrolls and books on the floor, she bit into the fruit and carefully placed the crystalized branch next to the scrolls. Cerberus approached it, sniffing it eagerly. Persephone laughed and moved it away from him.

"Not this branch, Ceb," she muttered, brushing his bristly back.

He sighed with disapproval. Cerberus chose to retreat to the luxurious bed, spinning three times before sliding beneath the sumptuous blankets while Olive curled tightly against her side.

Engrossed in the teachings, she began to browse through the scrolls. She had no idea each crystal had a secret meaning, like flowers. Amethyst was thought to improve intuition, while black tourmaline was used for protection. She looked up at the jade on the ceiling before flipping through the manuscript: jade protects you from harm and allows you to open your heart to love. She took the book and made her way to the pink quartz fireplace. Stroking her fingertips over the gorgeous engravings of Eros and Psyche, she paged to the section on rose quartz. This stone symbolizes unconditional love and the attraction of soul mates. She hurriedly flipped through the book until she came across the pure quartz crystals strung from the tree in her room; this crystal amplified other stones and minerals, making them stronger. Paging through the book, she located the tiny blue crystal that grew in the palace halls: blue kyanite. It was a truth-awakening crystal.

She returned to the grassy patch beside Olive and carefully examined the clear quartz branch before returning to her book - clear quartz was the master healer's jewel. She looked up at her emerald bed. He'd told her a year earlier that emeralds promoted romantic love, and he'd been right. She paged through the book until she reached the chapter on emeralds and closed the book slowly with a sinking heart. Emerald was also supposed to help couples with trouble conceiving a child.

What a well-planned room she had. Every inch had been painstakingly adorned with a secret meeting. Was it a coincidence? This room was designed with a single objective: to promote romance and the beginning of a family. Cassandra's enraged face flashed before her, and she recalled the warnings from Olympus. *Everything you believe is a lie.* She picked up the text to take her mind off the memories, reading that some rare stones take years to form. However, she had grown one in the crystal forest in mere seconds. How was that possible, she mused, and could she do it again.

She placed both hands on the ground, recalling the great tree's strength as it touched her, the roots that ran deep within the Earth. She felt a tiny seed of power blossom within her, and it grew until the energy flowed through her hands. She opened her eyes to find a little green stone before her. She held it up to her face, overjoyed, admiring the various shades of green reflected off its smooth surface. Excitedly, she flipped the book open, scanning the pages until she located the green gemstone. Malachite. It signified manifestation, transformation, and personal empowerment. She jumped to her feet, startling Olive. She could do more than simply grow flowers! Anxious to share her news with her husband, she rushed to the door pulling it open.

She paused as voices echoed down the corridor. Hades was coming down the stairs with Minthe by his side. The nymph was securing the belt of her emerald toga with delicate fingers. Minthe giggled as she approached him and suddenly reached for his hand.

"Last night, I forgot my emerald clip. I'd better go get it."

She entered Hades' chamber and reappeared carrying an emerald pin. Minthe kissed his cheek while standing on her tiptoes and muttered something into his ear before they moved down another hallway, vanishing from view. Persephone quietly shut the door.

With a loud sob, she collapsed to the floor. The pair had looked like lovers as they walked down the hall. How naive she had been to believe he would have been content to wait for her. Everything Zeus said came rushing back to her. Had Persephone even been his first choice? Or was she simply the means to an heir? Cerberus jumped from the bed and approached her, and she drew the small dog into her arms. Persephone jumped up as the latch to her room opened, Cerberus clutched in her arms.

The hooded guard stood in the doorway. He stepped forward and paused, staring at the books and parchment strewn across the floor.

"Nice of you to appear again," she snapped, too incensed to be polite. "I would like some answers—"

Her voice came to a sudden stop as the guard suddenly leaped toward the door. He pressed his ear against it like an overly inquisitive houseguest.

Despite the heaviness in her heart, an incredulous laugh escaped her lips. "Have you taken leave of your senses?"

He abandoned his post by the doorway, darting towards her study material. Outraged, she shrieked as he seized the crystal branch, shattered it with a practiced motion, and callously tossed the shards into the fireplace. The scrolls and books almost received a similar fate, but he moved away from the fire at her snarl and discreetly hid them beneath her mattress.

Turning toward her, the guard urgently gestured at her tear-streaked face, leaning in to roughly wipe away the evidence of her sorrow.

"What do you think you're— ompf!"

He grasped her arm, yanking her towards the bed, as he pulled down the sheets. "Get off me!" she fumed. She gasped in surprise as he pushed her roughly to the bed. "What are you doing?" Persephone hissed. "You're insane."

From the doorway, she could hear the echo of footsteps drawing nearer, and Persephone could guess who it was. As the guard moved into the shadows, he raised his finger to his lips. Persephone frowned as she realized he didn't want her to tell her husband about the crystals. She furrowed her brows at him, questioning, but he shook his head.

The door opened abruptly, and Hades stood in the doorway. As her eyes moved over him, she noticed the beginnings of a bruise on his neck, the shape disturbingly similar to that of an open mouth, and her heart plummeted.

His gaze traversed the room, coming to a halt in the corner to examine the silent guard before returning to Persephone. "I've been looking for you. Why are you in your old rooms?"

Her brows drew down in confusion. "I thought this was going to be my room. You said so this morning." She paused, studying him. "Don't you remember?"

Hades smiled softly. "Ah, I did say that, didn't I? However, I have changed my mind. I want you to sleep next to me."

"But–"

He bent, taking her hand, brushing it across his face. "I wanted to see what you did today. How was your first day back?"

From the corner of her eye, she noticed Maketes stiffen, and her eyes drifted to the bruising on her husband's neck. "I found myself quite tired," she said quietly. "So I spent the day in my room."

"You were exhausted from the previous night. Well, I am glad to hear you are rested, for I've been working on a surprise for you. We're going to a festival this evening."

"A festival?"

"Yes, there will be a celebration at the Cocytus. You should dress warmly. The river on the Cocytus side is freezing."

Her face fell at his words, but she stood quickly, turning to hide her expression from his overly perceptive eyes. "We are going to Minthe's home?"

"I decided it was about time for an introduction. I'd like to ensure my allies are acquainted with our queen."

"And I presume your allies are also mine?"

"Of course," Hades responded, laughing. He came up behind her, but she turned away and walked closer to the fire. "I am lucky to have you with me to keep me warm. The Cocytus can be deadly cold."

"But perhaps you don't need me to keep you warm any longer," she quipped.

Hades erupted with laughter. "Not this again. Minthe, as previously established, is the daughter of a river God. I employ his daughter because the Cocytus is an important waterway for securing our borders."

"Isn't the Cocytus near Elysium?"

"It is near Elysium." He moved in closer, his hands running down her back. She shivered as she stared into the fire's flames. "I did not know," his low voice continued behind her, "that I also had gained an inquisitor and a wife. Please ask me directly what you want to know."

She turned to face him, shifting her weight. "My father saw you with her in Elysium."

Hades gave her a disgruntled expression. "Yes, we discussed this. As I told you, she was there to prepare the temple for your homecoming."

"Yes, and I've been wondering why Jocasta didn't prepare the temple for me. She knows me better than your... apprentice."

"Thinking can be a dangerous thing," he teased. "I find it easier to instruct Minthe. I brought her there to make you feel at ease."

Her emerald eyes were solemnly fixated on his face. "How thoughtful of you. Is your personal servant for my benefit as well?"

He laughed once more. "I shudder to think of the fantastical story you've concocted. You should write plays. Ask me directly what you want to know."

"But you've already answered my questions," Persephone said softly.

Hades kept a wary eye on her. "I certainly hope so, wife. Those who seek trouble frequently find it."

Cerberus suddenly jumped from the bed, a deep growl vibrating in his throat. He was no longer a puppy but had grown to the size of a full-grown wolf, complete with gleaming golden eyes, his three heads riveted on Hades.

"Cerberus," Persephone exclaimed, surprised. "What's the matter?"

"I probably smell like Tartarus filth. I was near the gates earlier." Cerberus went closer to Hades, tentatively sniffing him with one snout. The dog withdrew and sat on his haunches by Persephone, apparently satisfied.

"You have a devoted companion," Hades said, smiling.

"And a good thing," Persephone said, petting Cerberus. "Loyalty is so hard to come by."

"So it is," Hades murmured, his black gaze fixed on the dog. "I've got something for you." He reached into his robes, pulling out a golden necklace with a beautiful pale stone dangling from the center. The large stone had a moonlight white shimmer, encircled by three smaller aqua stones.

"It's beautiful," she mused. "What is the stone?"

"Moonstone," said Hades. She made a mental note to look up the stone's meaning in her book later. He took her hand in his and curled her fingers around the necklace. "I'll leave you to prepare." His foot brushed against something on the floor as he approached the door. He bent, holding the little malachite stone between his fingers as he straightened.

"Where did you get this?" he said, flipping it over to examine it.

She shook her head. "I'm not sure." While the lie flowed easily from her lips, their dishonesty broke her heart.

"How interesting." He ran his fingertips over the stone again before placing it on the dresser. Before he reached the door, he turned. "One more thing, Persephone; I think it's important to mention, given what happened the last time I gave you a necklace. Make no effort to ingest the moonstone; it would be quite terrible to consume *that* stone." He swept from the room with a wink.

Persephone moved to pick up the small green stone. It still held the warmth of his hands, and she fisted the stone, pressing it against her heart.

CHAPTER 8
THE COCYTUS

The night was warm as they journeyed through the Underworld in a golden chariot. Several carriages followed them, and Persephone was certain Minthe would be among them. She yanked at her gown's long sleeves, the evergreen toga with its pools of cloth far too warm for the current environment. An evergreen cape was wrapped around her shoulders, secured by a large golden clasp, and sweat dripped down her back. Wisps of tendrils broke free from the elaborate coil of hair piled high on her head as the wind swirled around them. Her golden laurel wreath glistened in the moonlight, and the maidens had even ground evergreen jewels into a fine powder that sparkled on her lids. Once Jocasta had learned where Persephone was going, she let out an unholy war cry, and the maidens were as ferocious in their preparations as if they were preparing for battle. Her final glance in the mirror had assured her that she appeared mysterious and majestic, but she felt hollow inside.

Persephone had cornered Maketes as soon as Hades had left her room. She demanded an explanation for the secret prison, crystal forest, and her husband's erratic behavior. Maketes knew something clearly, and he did not seem to trust her husband. But despite her demands, pleas, and not-so-veiled threats, her guard remained unmoved. He merely stood there as she thrust parchment and quills at him, refusing to speak, write, or do anything! He defied her every effort until finally, the handmaidens arrived as Maketes' unwitting rescuers, and she could not question him further. Persephone's eyes blazed at him as Jocasta began to brush her hair, assuring him that the interrogation was far from finished.

She glanced at her husband, who appeared serene as he directed the chariot. He was dressed in long dark robes with a high collar trimmed in scarlet and a long red cape draped over his shoulders. His four horses drew the carriage, with Orphaneous and Aethon in front, and one of his hands covered Persephone's while the other held the reins. They traveled fast through the Underworld, and it was quiet, for the animals and spirits had already nestled in for the night. As they saw the tall, golden Elysium gates in the distance, Persephone strained her ears. Quiet sobbing resonated in the night air.

"What is that noise?" Persephone asked in concern, glancing around them.

"That is the people of Cocytus; it is their nature to be filled with sorrow."

As they drew nearer, the temperature suddenly plummeted, and Persephone shivered, pulling her cape closer around her. Hades lowered his gaze and encircled her with his arm. "I did warn you it would be cold. Cocytus is on the very edge of the Underworld."

She frowned, remembering Minthe's bitter expression. "It doesn't sound like a pleasant environment."

"That is just their nature. Minthe didn't belong there. I am glad she left."

Persephone clutched the small green stone she had placed in the pockets of her dress earlier, allowing the coolness of the crystal to comfort her. "Why is it such a desolate place?"

"They are spirits trapped between two worlds. They could not pay for passage into the Underworld and were forced to wander for one hundred years to repay their debt. His subjects see the world in dull shades of gray and cry for the loss of feeling anything deeply, good or bad. It is a sad way to live, is it not? Theirs is the River of Lamentation. They are required by law to keep the river frozen, or else their tears will fill the river and flood the Underworld. The frigid Cocytus progressively warms where the river runs into the Styx, allowing the people's tears to flow forever."

Persephone's brow furrowed. "So, they were unable to have the ritual coins placed over them," she said softly, remembering Olive. "That seems so very wrong. Is there nothing we can do for them?"

"In truth, Persephone, the debt is not real. They are taught that they must pay passage in the upper world. So real is their belief that it becomes a rule of a kind. Regrettably, I have little control over what they were taught above, and myths can sometimes become truth."

"That is so sad," Persephone murmured.

"Eventually, they will pass into our realm."

"But only once they have paid their debt?" Hades nodded. "And when they finally come to the Underworld, do you find their time in Cocytus has altered them?"

"Oh yes," Hades responded quietly. "They are forever altered." His voice instantly cheered. "I have made a deal with their commander, and the people of Cocytus will side with us in a war. As you can see, they are near the entrance to our kingdom. It would provide an additional layer of security."

The chariot slowed, and Hades raised his fist, allowing the gates to open.

"Perhaps war could be avoided if you and Zeus could speak about it," Persephone continued as they passed through the gates.

"Nothing can be discussed with Zeus. Nothing can stop him if he has determined that war is necessary."

"But isn't it worth the try? War could be avoided if you could aid in locating his weapon. Even if he refuses to compromise, if we could just find the sword, we could deliver it to him—"

Hades raised an eyebrow at her. "Should I find his weapon? The one with which I was almost killed?" His dark hair covered his eyes as he shook his head. "My brother's compassion on Olympus left an impression on you."

Persephone tensed. "I'm not worried about your brother; I'm worried about a war that may destroy everything. I'm worried about you."

"I will not try to bargain with Zeus, Persephone. I know my brother. If that means war, so be it."

"Even if many people will die?"

His features contorted as a dark smile swept across his face. "But my people are already dead," he said quietly.

She stared at him in appalled shock. "What a horrible thing to say! The living do not deserve to die in this war."

"Oh, of course, I forgot. My sweet little wife is always so concerned about the mortals. But in war, someone has to lose. Where does your loyalty lie?"

She looked up at him, horrified by the venom in his remarks. "My loyalty lies with the innocent, regardless of whether they are in our kingdom or above."

"So speaks a Goddess who has never actually faced war."

Hurt flooded her at his words, at the anger in his voice, and she moved away from him, trying to yank her hand from his.

"Persephone." She shook her head, and he turned her to look at him, even as he guided the horses with his other hand. "I am sorry, Persephone, forgive me," he said softly. "I spoke out of turn. I've been in battle before, and it's brutal and unfair. But you don't deserve to have my frustrations directed at you." She said nothing, her body tense. "Please, I don't want to fight. You know I love you."

"Do you?" she asked, her voice trembling. "I begin to wonder."

"I do." He brought her fingers up to his lips and kissed them. "Remember it."

She stayed silent, letting her eyes travel over the horizon, hoping the sting of his words would fade away. She understood he was anxious, but so was she. He had never disrespected her before, always seeming to have valued her opinion, even welcomed it. She averted her head, brushing away useless tears with the back of her fingers as they froze to ice on her cheeks.

As they traveled into Cocytus, the landscape began to change; the black mountains were replaced by jagged stones gleaming with frost. Some rocks had fractured from the freezing temperatures, and turquoise ice glistened inside the broken surface. The wind carried a somber cry as it whistled over the iced water of the Cocytus. Their steeds slowed, and Persephone glanced around for a glimpse of the palace, obscured by ice and snow. When Hades lifted his hand, the mist began to lift, and a kingdom appeared in the receding fog. The palace was smaller than theirs but was impressively austere, covered with ice crystals.

A carriage pulled up alongside them, and a servant dashed back to open the door. Minthe appeared in a pale mesh toga, her pink nipples stiffened by the cold and elevated beneath the thin cloth. As she neared their chariot, she lifted her hand, her gaze fixed on the king. "I can't wait to welcome you inside," she exclaimed. As she spoke, a crowd gathered at the palace entryway, descending the flight of steps.

Hades climbed out of the chariot and extended his hand to Persephone. They stood alongside Minthe, watching Cocytus' King descend. The King of the Cocytus was as austere as his palace, with silver hair and icy blue eyes, his expression mournful and remote. He and his entourage sank to their knees as he approached Hades and Persephone.

"King Hades," he greeted monotonously, "we are delighted to welcome you back to Cocytus." He raised his gaze, his chilly blue eyes dismissive as they moved over Persephone.

When Hades urged him to stand, they gripped each other's forearms. "It gives me great pleasure to return to your kingdom. I want you to meet the Queen of the Underworld, Queen Persephone."

"Welcome to Cocytus," said the King of Cocytus, bending his head and shielding his expression from her.

Persephone stepped back as the procession moved ahead, watching the king and his daughter swarm around Hades like ants invading a beehive. She turned away in disgust, returning to the chariot to ensure the horses were adequately protected from the cold. She untied her cape and slung it over Aethon's back before bending forward to speak in the mare's ear.

"I wish I could stay with you, but I will return soon." Orphnaeus neighed in protest, and Persephone chuckled at what she assumed was indignant displeasure on his face. "All right, let me see." She paused, then spun her fingers, soft, green moss blankets covering Orphnae-

us, Nyctaeus, and Alastor. Their sweet brays of contentment made her grin.

The sound of a voice beside her startled her. "Are you coming?" She whirled around to see Hades. Minthe stood back with a sour expression while Cocytus stood motionless.

"Yes," Persephone said quietly.

Hades removed his cloak and draped it over Persephone's shoulders before offering her his arm. Persephone felt Minthe's gaze on her back as they ascended the palace stairs.

Once in the hall, they were introduced to members of the palace. Each had precisely the same expression: icy, detached, and cold. Their hair and skin were a frosty silver, and frozen tears adorned the inner corners of their pale eyes like sorrowful diamond accessories. Persephone's heart ached for these souls who had lost their ability to feel joy. A lead servant started a tour through the palace. She had foolishly hoped that the inside of the castle would be warmer, but ice crystals hung from the ceilings, and frost covered all the surfaces.

She drew closer to the aloof King of Cocytus. She smiled at him, but his face grew infinitesimally more sour. She broadened her smile to nearly obscene proportions and noticed Hades' lips twitching in amusement. "Your palace is magnificent," Persephone exclaimed, beaming. "Did Minthe grow up here?"

Cocytus did not glance at Persephone as she spoke, his incredible blue eyes fixed on the path ahead. "Minthe was born here, but her mother was a nymph from above, my lover. My queen brought me much sadness. I thought a nymph would make me... happy, and she did for a while until I found she also made many of my male subjects happy. However, the people of this river love Minthe for her smile, which brings them immense happiness. One day, I hope to see her sit on the throne and be called queen, with a suitable king by her side."

"I am confident she shares your desires," Persephone muttered. Cocytus must be upset that Hades already has a queen on his throne. And yet, a parent with such lofty goals had sent his daughter to work as a servant in Hades' palace. Unless— did he suppose there was a chance Hades would select another wife?

The Cocytus King was strange; he seemed to feel neither satisfaction nor displeasure as he showed them about the palace. While he stated phrases that should have communicated pride, his flat, monotone voice revealed none of those emotions. They were eventually escorted to a vast dining hall, with a large table carved from ice dominating the space. A window was opened, emitting a chilly breeze and revealing a vista of the frozen river below. Hades sat to the king's right, Persephone next to her husband, and Minthe sat directly across from them. Her husband murmured to a servant, who returned with a large fur blanket, and Hades tucked it carefully around his wife.

A swarm of servants entered, carrying trays piled high with chilled wine, iced fruits, cold soups, and iced creams. The lively Minthe monopolized the conversation at the table, which was stilted and uninteresting. Persephone gazed at the food in disappointment, hoping for something to warm her. The meal was so cold that iced smoke rolled off the plates. She gingerly took some of the offered fruit and suppressed a scream when her tooth cracked as she bit into a frozen blueberry. She grimaced and discretely pushed the plate of treacherous fruit away. A bowl of chilled soup was placed in front of her, and she took a cautious drink, shivering as she did so.

Hades' voice entered her mind, and there was laughter in his words. *The food here is dangerous; I should have warned you.*

Persephone took a sip of the chilled wine. *The food served here cannot help with anyone's mood. It is too frozen to taste anything. The more I eat, the colder I get.*

They cannot consume warm foods, or their tears will overflow and flood the Underworld.

Persephone shivered, and Hades leaned closer to her. *Poor, little wife. Let me warm you.* His large thigh pressed against hers. The heat from his skin seeped into her, and she leaned into his warmth. His long fingers moved over her leg beneath the table, and she held her breath as he stroked her leg. His touch moved higher and higher until he touched the apex between her thighs. *Are you cold here, too?*

Hades, no! she thought firmly.

His hand cupped her, and she smothered a gasp. She noticed Minthe watching them from across the table, her eyes narrowed, and Persephone could not help the flush that spread over her face as his hand continued to move against her. He rubbed her through the thin fabric of her toga, and the sensation of the soft material pressing against her sensitive parts was overwhelming. Shame that she was allowing her husband to pleasure her at the dinner table caused her to wrap her fingers around his wrist, and for a moment, he stopped, but she realized he was inching her gown upward.

Their hands began a battle beneath the table until one caught her wrists, imprisoning her. His other hand was beneath the fabric now, his fingers moving over her, tracing her. She knew she was wet, and she bit her lips to keep from lifting her hips, sweat beginning to pool on her forehead. One fingertip occasionally tapped at the little bundle of nerves where so much sensation centered, but then he would move away again, continuing his lazy perusal.

Once or twice, she thought maybe someone asked her a question. They likely thought her mad, and she heard Hades' soft laugh in her mind. Just as she thought she may scream in frustration, she felt his hands at her entrance, one long finger pushing inside her, and to her everlasting shame, a small moan of pleasure escaped her lips. The nymph leaned forward suddenly, holding a platter in her hands.

"King Hades, won't you try this?" Her eyes flickered between Hades and his wife.

Hades paused, his fingers still resting beneath her gown as he looked at the nymph with the first hint of irritation Persephone had seen. Reluctantly, he withdrew his fingers and accepted the platter from Minthe. "How considerate," Hades murmured. "My wife adores fruit." Hades took a frozen strawberry from the dish and traced Persephone's lips with the thawing fruit, staining her mouth with the juice. When she bit down, he watched the scarlet liquid that dripped from her lips with his dark eyes.

Tell me, he whispered in her mind, *are you still cold?*

Persephone shook her head and saw Minthe's furious gaze fixed on them.

Desserts and refreshing drinks were served. Persephone hastily sipped an iced beverage, refusing to look at Hades, who was smiling beside her. She waited for her blush to fade, astonished at her own behavior. Finally, the King of Cocytus rose to his feet, disinterestedly regarding his visitors. "We have arranged a celebration for Your Highnesses."

The king and queen were led to a vast arena open to the freezing night sky, frost sparkling like stars far above. Persephone shuddered as she looked up at the endless blackness above them. They were led to a large seating area, which, given the opulence, was almost certainly designed for the royal family. Cocytus sat to Hades' left, and Persephone sat on Hades' right on ice-rimmed benches. Minthe, curiously, was absent. Persephone almost cried in relief as a servant again appeared with a fur blanket, spreading it over her lap. The arena started to fill up with souls, and it seemed as if the entire kingdom of Cocytus had gathered for whatever Cocytus had planned.

A loud gong rang, and nymphs stepped onto the floor, their pale blue skin gleaming in the faint light, thin gauzy fabric covering them. An unusual instrument began to play, and the ice nymphs started dancing, whirling across the room like snowflakes. Their lithe limbs bowed in odd contortions as they glided fluidly across the room, silvery-white hair streaming behind them in perfect synchronicity. The dancers spun in smaller and smaller circles, spinning around each other until they created the shape of a pulsing flower.

A vibrant flame pushed through the center, and Minthe emerged, her red hair gleaming. She was naked save for the brilliant crystals that decorated her voluptuous figure. The audience politely applauded, likely equivalent to a standing ovation in Cocytus. Minthe joined the other nymphs in their dance, the music accelerating as they whirled faster and faster, their rhythmic movements enthralling.

Persephone turned towards her husband and Cocytus, who were staring intently at the dancers. While Persephone was startled by the smile of delight on Cocytus' typically expressionless face, her husband's face astonished her; lights flashed in his eyes, and his pupils dilated so that only an amber rim could be seen. He stared ahead, his attention solely on the movement of the dancers.

The dancers were now moving erratically, the contortions overtly sexual, and the nymphs began crawling across the floor. Persephone knew before she even moved which direction Minthe would head in. The fiery-haired princess was soon standing immediately in front of the royal box. Her hands caressed her sumptuous shape, squeezing her own breasts, and her gaze was fixated on Hades as she gyrated to the music. She bowed and contorted in front of them over and over, oblivious to the fact that her father was watching as she exposed herself. The crystals on her breasts began to melt as she gyrated, displaying her pink nipples, which she thrust forward repeatedly towards Hades. The music had reached a fever pitch, and Minthe fell into a split posture as the last music note faded. The audience stood and applauded.

Minthe bowed deeply. Hades rose then, extending a hand towards Minthe to help her rise. As she stood, she pressed a kiss against his cheek, brushing her naked breasts against him. The eyes of the crowd were turned towards the royal box; the naked princess standing close to the king, the jilted queen looking on—it must be quite amusing for the audience. The entertainment of the dance was nothing compared to the farce that had been made of her. Persephone knew her cheeks were pink with anger, but she stared ahead, letting no expression touch her face. Minthe let her gaze wander over Persephone, and a contented smirk graced her lips as she turned to join the other nymphs.

"Is my daughter not a skilled dancer?" Cocytus asked as Hades sat, but his cold blue eyes were fixed on Persephone.

"She is exceptionally talented," Hades murmured.

"We have missed your visits," Cocytus said in hushed tones to Hades. "You know they need not stop."

"I have been busy these last few months. And now it is more difficult…"

At these words, Cocytus and her husband turned towards Persephone. Cocytus' countenance was unreadable, but Hades' eyes gleamed amber, and his mouth was framed by a cruel smirk. Who was this man sitting next to her? Persephone thought she knew him, but he revealed a new, unpleasant facet of his character every day. How long had he known Minthe? Cocytus' remarks suggested a long and intimate connection. Persephone flushed and turned her head, not wanting her husband or Cocytus to notice the sheen of tears in her eyes. The phrase repeated in her mind - *How well do you know your husband?*

The crowd had become a sea of bland faces once more, and the stadium began to fill with faint whispers of desultory discussion. Minthe had returned, a shimmering blue toga now covering her form. She stood with her back to them, a green comb shining in her hair. Minthe moved to the center floor as the nymphs departed the arena, and the audience fell silent once more. A gleaming silver horse trotted through the open doors that the nymphs had just left, coming to stand behind Minthe.

The princess lifted the glittering reins in one hand. "Who amongst you will challenge me to a race?" Her imperious voice rang out loudly around the arena.

Hades locked eyes with the nymph, and Persephone watched as a smile formed across his face. Minthe grinned back, and Persephone's jealousy and rage exploded, and she leaped from her seat before she could think.

"I will challenge you." Persephone's voice was soft, yet every soul in the stadium could hear it.

Hades grasped her hand and drew her closer as murmurs echoed across the crowd. "What are you doing?" he snarled angrily. "A queen cannot challenge the princess."

She gave him a cool look. "I'm only continuing the spectacle you created. Shouldn't we keep up the show? Let us place a wager."

"What wager?" he asked suspiciously.

"If I win, she will no longer be your servant."

He made a noise of disgust. "What if you lose?"

"Then I will not say another word against her."

He pulled her down roughly to her seat. "I am trying to establish an alliance," he hissed. "By your folly, you jeopardize everything."

"Oh, I see quite plainly what you've been establishing while I have been absent. While you strengthen your relations with your borders, you lose the one you had with your wife."

"Your jealousy will lead to trouble."

"Your infidelity has already accomplished that. Take the wager; think how delighted you will be if I lose. Your mistress will be welcome to share a castle with your wife."

Hades shook his head, abruptly releasing her hand. "Very well. *If* you win," he answered coldly.

Persephone untied Hades' cloak from her neck and placed it on his chair. She then shifted her focus to Cocytus, who had clearly been eavesdropping on their heated whispers. "Thank you for your hospitality, King Cocytus. If our enemies have neighbors like you, I doubt anyone would bother crossing to the Underworld."

Persephone stormed from the box, walking through the crowd of sad-eyed observers. She closed her eyes and whispered, "Aethon." The crowd gasped as the black horse emerged from the shadows, her golden hooves stomping the freezing ground, steam blowing from her nostrils. Persephone moved to greet the mare, petting her muzzle tenderly. "Thank you for coming," she greeted quietly. She jumped up quickly, mounting the mare bareback, and then bent forward. "Aethon, swifter than an arrow – today, my friend, you live up to your name."

Minthe stood in the center of the stadium and addressed the audience loudly. "The Queen of the Underworld will be a formidable opponent, but it will make my victory over her all the sweeter. " Minthe nodded, and a servant brought her an elegant, white saddle, placing it on the silver steed. A stepping stool was brought forward, and Minthe mounted her steed.

A silver-clad guard stepped forward. "The rules of the race are straightforward," he announced in a desultory voice. "Whoever crosses the finish line at the arena's perimeter will be declared the winner."

Minthe studied her fingernails while they waited for the track to be positioned. "You do not belong down here," she said sweetly.

Persephone brushed her fingers through Aethon's mane, keeping her eyes fixed on the mare. "I don't belong where? This prison? I do not believe anyone actually belongs here. I have never seen a kingdom that existed only by ransom before."

"How dare you?" Minthe spat, her exquisite face twisted with anger. "You pathetic—"

Persephone raised her gaze and allowed her wrath to show in her eyes. The nymph drew back, afraid at what she saw in the queen's eyes. "Be careful, Minthe," Persephone cautioned quietly. "You have not even begun to see how far I dare."

The guard raised his hand. "Are you both ready?" he inquired politely.

Both women nodded their heads. Persephone bowed low on Aethon as Minthe's fingers gripped her reins loosely.

Persephone felt a tingling run down her spine and turned back to look at Hades in the royal box. His dark visage was disapproving, his black eyes fixed on her; she turned around quickly. She did not need that distraction. They took off as soon as the guard lowered his first. Persephone and Aethon moved in unison. Her horse was clearly more skilled, and Persephone knew she was a superb rider. Minthe could be seen lagging behind her, a bitter, frenzied expression on her face as she thrashed her horse viciously with a pale blue whip. Persephone frowned and leaned forward. Anyone who had to lash a horse was not fit to ride.

Suddenly, large black, jagged diamonds pushed through the ice directly before Aethon. At the last moment, she had to make a sharp turn to avoid striking them, and Aethon skidded over the ice, slamming them both into the wall. Persephone quickly repositioned them and stroked Aethon soothingly.

"Be careful, girl," she whispered.

She jockeyed back in place, but more rocks jutted up from the ground, diverting their path. She slowed as they swerved around one impediment after another. The moment they dodged one treacherous hazard, another broke through the frost. Where were they coming from, she wondered desperately.

Persephone glanced towards Minthe, whose path remained unobstructed. With foreboding, she looked behind her. Her husband was lazily weaving his fingers through the air, and when Persephone turned, another rock pushed up, blocking her path. Persephone swallowed her despairing cry. Minthe had finally caught up with her, and she had her husband to thank. The nymph's malicious laughter rang back, and she clearly knew who was aiding her.

"Es kòrakas," Persephone whispered.

But his treachery spurred her forward, and she expertly led Aethon down the perilous path. They well avoided the traps, Aethon gaining up speed despite the greater complexity. The throng cried out in sorrow as the gap between the Goddess and the nymph shrunk.

"Green is the perfect color for you, Queen Persephone," Minthe called

to her as Persephone dodged yet another rock. "You are filled with envy."

"I have a proposition," Persephone called to her. "If you cross the finish line before me, you can have my bedroom. If I cross before you, I will take your horse."

As another boulder pushed up before Aethon, Minthe smiled vindictively. "I accept with pleasure."

Persephone and Aethon vaulted over the stones in their path, her horse leaping forward, Persephone's spruce toga whipping behind them like green wings. Persephone heard Minthe's outraged scream as the Goddess of Spring crossed the finish line, and the crowd wailed in unison, causing sheets of ice to pelt down on the arena like frozen tears.

Persephone raised her gaze to the royal box, where her husband stood in the darkness, peering down at them. His eyes flared amber in the shadows, and she could see his chest rise and fall in furious gasps. And Persephone felt afraid for the first time in a very long time.

CHAPTER 9
ALONE

Minthe was left at the Cocytus, and Persephone elected to ride back on Aethon, anxious to avoid her irate husband. Minthe's silver horse trailed behind them. Hades had already abandoned the chariot when she arrived at the palace, his dark form marching through the doors. Persephone sighed, dismounting.

Persephone talked as she led Aethon and the new mare, Boreas, to the stables. "Fresh oats and apples will be served. A soft bed of hay to sleep in. Doesn't that sound lovely," she said soothingly. Persephone exhaled with relief as they arrived at the stables. She washed the sweat from both mares and requested that extra carrots be brought for them after supper. Her victory today would not have been possible without Aethon, and she wanted to ensure that the mare felt her triumph, even if Persephone herself did not.

Persephone approached the palace doors and hesitated, her heart racing with anxiety. She wished she could also spend the night in the stables with them. She felt uneasy in her own home. Why had he stayed with her after the curse was broken if he loved someone else? The curse had forced them together, but she would have understood if it wasn't what he wanted. Unless... she was just a means to an end. She shook her head. She was too tired to try to unravel the mystery tonight.

But she dreaded going inside, dreading sleeping, dreading seeing her husband. Her feet moved up the stairs hesitantly. But one thing was certain. She could no longer deny that something was terribly wrong with her husband.

Persephone lay motionless on her bed, Olive's soft, rhythmic snores filling the room.

A low voice broke the silence. "What were you thinking?"

She looked up, startled, to see her husband standing over her. He had changed out of his formal dress and was wearing basic black robes, but she could still see the animosity in his eyes. A scowl crossed her face.

"I wish to be alone," she answered coolly.

"And I wish you hadn't behaved so foolishly. Have you lost your senses? I am trying to protect our kingdom, our people, and you muddle it up with jealousy over nothing!"

Persephone attempted and failed to keep her calm. "I'd appreciate it if you gave me more credit than that. You can try all you want to deny it, but I'm not a fool. You purposefully pulled those rocks up from the ground to aid her victory. You attempted to game the system." She laughed bitterly. "But once a cheater, always a cheater, I suppose."

His hands shook, and he was so enraged that his nose began to bleed. He wiped away the blood impatiently. "It was an uneven playing field, and you know it! You are a Goddess. What impression does it make on Cocytus to see the Queen of the Underworld acting like a spoiled child."

"A child! In case you have forgotten, you are married! To me," she said, her voice trembling with emotion. "In your attempt to secure your borders, it seems *my* husband has forgotten that he has a wife."

His dark eyes flashed. "I have not forgotten," he replied in a low voice.

"That must be very inconvenient for you when you sleep with your mistress."

"*Your* husband is not sleeping with Minthe."

She shook her head and stared ahead. "So much has changed since my return. I thought I would be so happy here this time, but now—"

"But now?" he prompted.

"But now I wonder where your loyalties actually lie."

He looked at her incredulously, raking his hands through his hair, his eyes widening. "I'm at a loss for words. No matter how much I reassure you, you do not believe me."

The silence was heavy between them as they stared at each other, black eyes blazing into green, and she felt her heart breaking. All the trauma they had endured together, all the sacrifices had led to this. The void between them felt wider than ever. He may as well be a stranger standing before her.

"I don't believe you, Hades. You have been lying to me since my return. Maybe even before then."

"And yet, despite believing the worst of me, you still want me," he whispered, pulling the toga from his body. "What does that say about you, little wife?"

She turned her head, refusing to look at him. "I don't!" she denied. "I don't want to see you tonight."

He descended quickly on her, seizing her mouth in his with a vicious kiss, and to her horror, she responded with equal rage and ferocity. He ripped the toga from her as she tore his robes from him like an animal. She let out a surprised cry as he yanked her from the bed, pushing her down onto the rug. The embers of the fire reflected in his eyes.

"I like it when you are angry; it reminds me of that night on the mountaintop and the fire in your eyes. The power inside you." He pressed himself hard against her. "I must make you angry more often."

She was feverish, high on arousal, rage, and sorrow. And while Hades tormented her with his mouth, she felt herself being swept away by the magic that was his touch.

"Do not pretend you do not want me, my wicked, jealous queen. Show me your anger." He flipped until she lay on top of him. "Show how much you hate me."

She pushed harder down on him, and he grabbed her tighter, smiling with a devilish grin, and she wanted to weep at this twisted farce of love. Suddenly, she felt a presence wrap gently around her.

I love you, Persephone.

She drew back, confused. "I don't understand," she whispered. But then he was pushing inside her. As his body moved beneath her, she felt her husband's aura kiss the back of her neck as she writhed on top of his body. She shivered at its touch. She could feel the hands of her husband pulling at her and the soul of her husband grasping for her, and it was overwhelming.

"What are you doing to me?" she breathed.

The phantom touch then slid between her legs, and her body arched back in bliss or anguish—she couldn't tell which. As she fell into the darkness, she felt the heat from his seed pour down her legs.

He walked along the corridor, his footfall the only sound in the otherwise silent passage. He could feel the other pressing him, but he was weakening. He'd have everything soon, very soon. He would hold the world in his palm and crush it to dust. As he passed a mirror, he looked at his reflection and smiled at the amber-colored eyes that returned his gaze. For a split second, a purple flare appeared before quickly vanishing. Satisfied, he continued to move along the corridor, a gleeful chuckle rising from his throat until he was fully shrouded by the shadows, disappearing into the darkness.

CHAPTER 10
GREEN LIGHT

That night, Persephone stood again at the summit of the mountain. Turbulent wind blasted between the mountain peaks, and burning sparks erupted as green bolts of energy exploded all around her. And there, on the highest cliff, Hades fought against a shadow. The blue and golden swords clashed repeatedly as ruby blood ran down the slope in rivulets, leaving sticky pools at her feet. Behind the king, a black-winged creature crept like a dreadful shade, but Hades' focus was on the swords, and he did not see the malignant entity that moved behind him. Persephone shouted a warning, and the king's attention was pulled to his wife.

But it was too late for him. The dark form now stood behind Hades like a second shadow, spreading its massive wings wider and wider until the wings seemed to emerge from Hades' own body. Hades looked down at her as the wings folded tightly about him, engulfing him.

"Wake up, Persephone," he called, extending his hand to her. And she could see him shouting, mouthing the words, but his voice was barely a whisper in her ear, like a fluttering moth.

Pomegranates began to fall from the sky, bursting as they fell, weeping their blood. The fruits started to cover Persephone, smothering her,

and she was choking, suffocating beneath their weight.

Wake up.

She jerked from sleep, her body drenched with sweat. She lay motionless for a few moments, allowing her rapid breathing to settle. She groaned and then paused, stunned. She was lying on the ground outside. She had been sleepwalking again! She scrambled into a sitting position quickly before leaping to her feet.

A gentle breeze pulled her attention to a shaded tree in the darkness, and a chill passed over her. The tree bent low over a rippling lake, and she recognized its heavy, spherical fruit. It was the pomegranate tree, and she could just make out a gravestone beneath its branches. Dear Gods, she had walked to Rhea's grave.

A whisper echoed in the wind, but the voices were so faint she couldn't make out the words.

Persephone stared into the shadows, peering into the darkness beyond the tree. "Who is there?" she demanded, but her voice trembled.

But no one answered her. She turned on her heel, running away from that tree of death, away from her dreams, fear mounting in her heart.

Her feet were dragging behind her when she reached the central hall of the palace, her eyes bleary from tiredness. She paused suddenly as she passed Hades' study. Behind the closed doors, she could just make out hushed voices. Cautiously, she drew closer. She pressed her ear against the door, not making a sound.

The deep, smoky tone of her husband spoke in a cold voice. "You owe me."

"She is going to be suspicious," another voice replied, low and harsh. Had she heard that voice before?

"She is already suspicious. I did not ask you down here for your opinion. I have set forth a task, and you will follow it. Word for word. Do you understand? Leave Persephone to me."

Her hands trembled. More proof that her husband was hiding things from her, lying to her.

Their voices became more distant, and she heard the adjacent door open and close. She paused, listening for a few moments, but only heard quiet. Hades and his nocturnal visitor had left the study. She was exhausted, but she knew she had to investigate. Cautiously, she opened the door, terrified of seeing her husband's gloomy visage, but the room was empty. She rushed to the desk, combing through the heaps of papers and ancient parchments. Despite her haste, she was careful to leave everything exactly as it was. Her husband had an unmatched attention to detail and would notice anything unusual.

An enormous map of the Underworld and Tartarus lay open beneath the stack of scrolls, with certain sections of Tartarus crossed off. Three names were written on the map in the sprawling handwriting of her husband: Arges, Brontes, and Steropes. She recognized those names; she had studied them when reading about the Titanomachy, the ten-year battle the Titans had fought in Thessaly. They were the three blacksmiths who had forged the weapons for the Gods. She looked again at the map but could make no sense of it. With a frustrated sigh, she put it down; she knew nothing of Tartarus.

"Who are you looking for?" she murmured.

Another strange object was sitting on the desk, a globe sliced into layers that floated to form a round sphere. On top was Chaos, followed by Aether, Olympus, the Underworld, and the final, deepest layer: Tartarus. The Earth rotated, and little stars of the Aether sparkled around it… it seemed as if he were mapping out the cosmos. Miniature planets circled along with the Earth, each etched with golden symbols. She found the small planet with his symbol on the solar system's outskirts. It was far away from the rest, an outcast even amongst the cosmos. She stroked the little planet thoughtfully with her finger, its smooth surface quivering violently against her fingertip.

As she turned away from his desk, a stream of light caught her eye.

In the corner of the room, a giant crystal cluster radiated an emerald hue identical to what she had seen in her dream. She paused, hesitant to approach that frightening green light that reminded her of her nightmares. But she moved closer, slowly raising her hand to the crystal. A whoosh filled her body as her fingers brushed over it, and she was abruptly plunging forward, space and time whirling around her. The spinning stopped abruptly, and she was staring at the reflection of a Satyr in a crystal mirror. She raised her hand only to see him raise his hand and realized she was seeing things through his eyes. In her head, a deep melancholy voice echoed:

I weep for the future of man. Though they do not realize it, what was meant to be a new beginning is merely the beginning of the end. Has the rise of the Olympians created a better world? The Golden Age for mortals is over, and the prosperity of man is to be no more. Shortly after the Olympians' victory, I saw it - the most evil of acts. A green and dreadful light, so evil that I could hardly look at it as it moved through the valley. It descended from the mountaintop, destroying the mortals like a disease, and yet, it was worse than a plague, for it did not kill them, and there was no cure. It was to be a fatal wound that could never be healed. They will never be whole again.

His memories mingled in her thoughts, and the crystal around them began to crack, wind rushing through the fissures, tugging them closer until they were plunging into it, and she was suddenly alone, hovering above the Earth. Humans walked the world below but weren't like any she'd seen before. They had four limbs and four legs, and their joy was evident as their laughter reverberated high into the heavens. They ran freely through the land, just like the other creatures of the forest. The Satyr's voice returned, weaker than before.

Humans were once pure, not troubled by jealousy, envy, or greed. They were guardians of the Earth, the champion of other creatures; they sought only to be free and answered to no God. But some grew afraid of the mortals' power and autonomy. The Olympians feared what they might become. So, he split them, cutting them into two so they would never be complete. Even for a God, dividing a soul is an unfathomable evil, but this metamorphosis would eliminate any threat mortals could pose to the Gods. Forever, humanity will search the Earth for its divided half, soul mates forever yearning to be reunited. Desperate, the mortals soon turned to the Gods, praying for what was lost but would never be found. For every split soul, the Gods now had two souls that could worship them, thus multiplying their power.

War swept across the Earth, followed by famine, disease, and treachery of an unforgiving Creator. The divided human souls gave the Olympians a more extensive, far-reaching kingdom and devoted worshipers, never knowing that those they prayed to had brought about their misery. The humans look bizarre after the dark magic: two arms and two legs. They wail like swine for love. Their greedy hands are raised to an unforgiving God, begging for riches, love, and anything to fill the void of emptiness within them. Oh, I weep for the people of Earth. I looked there upon the mountaintop and saw him in the emerald glow when he removed his helm, that wretched God, Hades…

She looked up and saw him then - younger, colder, a vengeful God hovering high over the mountain. His long, black hair swept around him, his beautiful face contorted with fury as he stared down at the humans. *No! Not him. Anyone but him*, her mind cried out. The God lifted his hands, a blue sword held in one and a golden blade held in the other, and as he raised them high overhead, a green blast moved over the Earth, causing it to tremble. As the smoke settled, the God watched the humans squirm on the ground below like worms. His face showed no remorse as he placed the blue sword on the scabbard on his back, the golden blade still clenched tightly in his fist.

"Hades," she whispered; this heartless deity who had committed this unfathomable violation bore no resemblance to her husband. The God bowed his head, then abruptly turned, his searing stare fixed on Persephone. His gaze burned into hers, and she could not look away. But how could this be? This was Satyr's memory; she was only an observer. And yet, she knew he saw *her* and not the Satyr. His flaming black eyes showed no contrition, and she feared this wicked God. She was gripped in terror when he abruptly lifted his arms, dissolving into dazzling green flames, wondering whether he would shatter her with the golden God slayer.

By splitting the souls of the humans with terrible weapons, one blue, one golden, he ensured they could never more be joined, the Satyr whispered.

The mournful wails of mortals echoed loudly, and Persephone felt tears streaming down her face until she could bear it no more.

Please, she whispered, *take me back.*

She jerked her hands free from the crystal and tumbled backward into the present, once more, standing alone in Hades' study. The crystal's green brilliance faded, and she saw it was nothing more than a Lemurian seed crystal with a red core with drops of blood imprisoned within. Bile rose in her throat, and she pressed her hand against her churning stomach.

She covered her mouth to keep from screaming at what she had just witnessed. Oh, how could he have done such a monstrous thing? Zeus had warned her, and he had been correct: her husband had done something horrific on Olympus. She could never have imagined him guilty of such a crime, but she had witnessed it with her own eyes. Hades had cautioned her before that he deserved punishment and more for his crimes; he had surrendered himself to Eurynomos out of guilt. *I am the villain in this story*, he had said.

"Looking for something?" a dark voice asked.

She froze, a chill moving down her spine as she turned. Hades leaned against the entrance of his study, blocking the exit with his towering, muscular figure. She couldn't get the image of him in the skies, blasting the humanity below, out of her head. Her stomach clenched tightly.

"I… am looking for Olive." Her voice trembled, and she knew he would recognize the sound of fear and smell it on her. "I thought maybe he may have come in here," she finished lamely. She watched him with wary eyes, but he remained against the door, engulfed by shadows.

"Olive never ventures in here.

Gods, she was a terrible liar, she thought frantically, and her husband was a bloodhound for deception.

"Well," she hedged as she stepped away from the crystal. "I was looking for Olive. But then, since I couldn't sleep, I searched your library for a book to read." She lifted one hand to smooth her hair but quickly yanked it back down when she noticed it was trembling. Gesturing to his desk, she pulled a book from the edge. "Gemology," she said, holding it up. "It was most instructive."

"What a studious little wife I have," he mused. "I had no idea you were interested in gemstones. What did you learn?"

"Um, well," she looked around frantically. "Take your desk, for example; it is likely made of rubies to help you focus?" He nodded his head. "Rubies are also utilized to boost attention, according to what I've read."

He stepped from the door, the light from the room touching his dark beauty. His black eyes flickered with amusement, and he circled her, cutting off any potential escape.

"Or perhaps," he murmured as he approached her, "I used ruby because it signifies passion."

He was so near to her now that his heat combined with hers and repulsion mixed with love, the paradox of emotions bringing tears to her eyes. He leaned closer, pressing his body against the desk, and she could feel his erection between her legs. And Gods help her, her body trembled in response. When his lips moved against her neck, she made a yelp of desperation, slipping beneath his arm. She snatched the book from the desk, clutching it against her chest.

"How interesting," she replied, "because I am very passionate about reading... this book. It must be due to your rubies." She forced a nervous smile, her fingers tightening around the pilfered book. "It will be just the thing," she continued. "Goodnight!" She had just reached the handle, opening the door, when she felt him behind her. His fingertips closed the door with a subtle but definite thump, barring her escape.

"Where are you going?" he murmured against her neck.

"To read—"

"You really are a terrible liar, Persephone." His tone was like ice, and he moved closer, a predator closing in on its prey. She felt his fingers close over hers as he took the book from her slack hands and tossed it to the floor.

"I suppose I do not have as much practice as you," she replied stiffly.

He laughed, and his hand lifted, reaching to fasten the lock on the door. "Nothing that time cannot remedy." He turned her abruptly, his fingers tight on her upper arms, and when he looked down at her, his dark eyes glowed amber at the edges. He chuckled, a hollow sound that sent shivers down her spine. "Would you like to tell me what you are really searching for?"

Her eyes met his with a glare. "You tell me your secrets; maybe I'll tell mine."

"Oh, sweet lady," he whispered, "are you truly prepared to witness the depths of my secrets? Once the curtains are drawn, the shadows revealed, there's no retreat. Delving into the recesses of my soul may lead you down a path from which there's no return. But it seems fate has left us no other choice. Come," he said.

He pulled her hand into his and led her to the center of the room. A beautiful blue stone levitated before them as he raised his other hand, rolling gently in the air. "Blue sapphire," he explained. "This stone represents loyalty, truth, and honesty. These are all qualities desirable in a wife, don't you think? This stone, I think you will find, is particularly special."

Roughly, he pulled her hand towards the stone, placing her palm over the spiky edges. She struggled against his grasp, but he forced her hand back to it. "I only want you to place your hand upon the stone. Don't you trust me?"

"I only want to be allowed to leave this room," she spat, fighting his hold on her furiously.

"All in due time," he murmured. He bent forward, biting the lobe of her ear, and she trembled in fury, fury at him, but even more so at herself, that she still desired him. As he moved her palm higher on the crystal, his voice was as honeyed as a serpent in her ear. "How can you not trust me when you can still feel the heat of me between your legs? Even now, my seed may be taking root in your womb." His tongue caressed the delicate shell of her ear. "Trust me."

She said nothing, waiting, knowing that he was playing with her, knowing she could not escape him.

"No answer," he murmured. "Trust is so very precarious. But I have a greater problem than your lack of trust in me. I find myself wondering where *your* loyalties lie. I do not like when people lie to *me*." His voice was casual, but when she looked up at him, his eyes were cruel. "I especially dislike it when my wife lies to me."

The gemstone suddenly began to sparkle. The stone seemed to come to life, drawing her hand closer and squeezing her palm against the sharp clusters until the edges of the crystal punctured her skin. She was stunned into silence as she realized he was intending to torture her. She bit her lower lip to keep from sobbing as her blood dripped onto the floor.

"This stone, as I said, encourages honesty. Let us make the first question easy: do you still trust me?"

She bit her bottom lip hard until the metallic taste of her blood rushed over her tongue, but she could feel the stone's compulsion working on her as it tore and ripped through muscle and bone. She tried to strengthen her mental fortress, but her response seemed to rise from her lips like a bird soaring to freedom.

"No," she gasped.

"And were you, my recalcitrant bride, searching for Olive?"

"No," she admitted quickly.

Hades released her hand and moved towards the rows of books. He let his fingers trail over the spines before moving to his desk to study the items on it. "And were you here studying gems in my library?"

He asked the question nonchalantly, and she couldn't help but cry out in anguish as she strained against the urge to answer. The word was once again ripped from her throat. "No!"

He moved closer, his full mouth curving. He almost looked tender as he peered down at Persephone, and she wanted so badly to wipe that treacherous smile from his face. She spit the blood from her mouth at his feet. "Almost done," he murmured, stroking back her damp hair. "And what, wife, did you come here to find?"

"The truth."

"The truth is not in this room. What were you looking for?"

"Answers. Zeus' sword."

The corner of his mouth turned up. "Sadly, his sword is not here either. You will have difficulty finding it since it is not in my possession. What did Zeus ask you on the mountain?"

She tried again to remove her hand, but he forced it tighter into the stone, and fresh blood gushed from her palm. The edges of the rock began to penetrate the back of her hand, shredding muscle and tendon. He traced the edges of the blue stone. "You hurt yourself needlessly," he soothed. "What did Zeus ask of you on the mountaintop?" he asked again.

Her knees buckled, and he lifted her against him. "To spy on you."

Hades hissed. "What have you seen? What do you know?"

Her mind raced to conceal the truth, and she realized she might respond in veiled truths, prolonging the inquisition until he was tired of it. Or until she surrendered to the pain. As she lifted her head, her emerald eyes blazed into his. "Something I did not expect."

"Tell me. I demand you tell me what you have seen."

"I have seen the frailty of the Gods."

Hades laughed. "You know I can make this last, don't you? How long would it take you to bleed from your palm so you would be unconscious? A very long time, I think. And then we could just start again until I learn everything I want to know."

She forced herself to smile at him, her lips stained garishly with blood. "Then do it," she hissed. "You keep asking, and I will keep evading until six months have passed. My mother may collect whatever remains of me."

His dark eyes blazed as he lifted his hand to the sapphire, pulling it from her palm with a soft laugh. She stood still, not making a sound as her ruined hand was released. He set the bloodied gem on the table, his back to her.

"I think that is sufficient for the time being. I must say, you impress me with your fortitude. But if you would think for a moment, you would realize why your deception is unwarranted." He turned around, amber fire blazing in his eyes. "I saw you." The words hissed from his lips like a serpent. "All those years ago, I saw you from the mountaintop. Dressed just as you are now."

She fell back, stunned. "But that was a Satyr's vision. It was only a memory."

He moved closer to her, and his smile was malevolent. "But nevertheless, as I gazed down on the village amid the smoke and destruction, I saw you. I scoured the land for the crystal generated from that Satyr's lifeforce when he died, simply for a chance to see you again. And now, millennia later, you're here. Mine."

Fear and shock subdued her into an eerie silence, gradually enveloping her until she quivered under the weight of these overpowering emotions. "You've known me all this time," she whispered. "You let me believe we met by happenstance by the river."

"Yes, the river led me to you. Some would call it fate."

"Fate," Persephone said, her voice tight. "Carefully arranged at your hand."

"Yes, I always meant to have you." He circled her, letting his fingers trail over her shoulders possessively. "Did your mother not warn you how dangerous it is to tread into the beast's lair? Your past, future, and present now belong to me."

"And what of the humans? What about what you did to them? You show no remorse for what you did. I saw you with my own eyes. You destroyed them! You ripped apart their souls. Why did you do such a thing?"

He stood before her, unashamed. "You speak like a child. Innocence is a luxury a king cannot afford. I did what was necessary."

"How could that have been necessary! The humans were peaceful; they hurt no one! There can never be forgiveness for such a crime."

"Ah, but I do not ask for forgiveness; I do not need your forgiveness."

She stared at him, stunned. "You... you do not regret it?"

"I do not," he answered, facing her shocked expression and lifting the bloodied sapphire in his fingers. "It's clear you don't believe me." He clenched his fist around the sapphire, allowing the spiky edges to penetrate his skin, and blood dripped down his fist. "I do not regret it," he said again, smiling at her.

"Then you are worse," she whispered, "than anyone I have ever known."

His eyes held a glint of malevolence that sent shivers down Persephone's spine. "My dear, you've always been blinded by your own naivety."

"So I was right the first time, then," she said. "I am, and always have been, your prisoner."

"Thanks to you, my sweet, you are my prisoner. A very favored prisoner." He laughed. "I could not believe it when you ate the pomegranate seeds of your own accord." He lifted the slender wrist of her damaged hand, pressing the wound against his lips, kissing it.

She ripped her hand from his grasp. "Was everything you ever told me a lie, a game to trap me down here with you?"

He smiled. "No— and yes."

"That makes no sense! Stop talking in riddles!" she yelled.

"But you love puzzles, do you not? You were so eager, after all, to find the clues hidden in my office."

"I will not be a part of this! I will find a way to break free from this hell you've created."

Hades' expression turned dark, and he snarled, pulling her against him. "You think to leave me? I will never let you go."

The memories of the Satyr swirled in her mind, mixing with her other memories: Hades in Elysium, sitting by the fire with her father, the night she had bared her soul to him. How could it all have been a lie? She could not reconcile this God with the one she had loved. But he had admitted his crimes. She had been such a fool, over and over again. And she was still a fool.

"I can see how foolish I have been. What a wicked game you've played with me," Persephone said quietly. "I believed you loved me."

He looked down at her, no warmth in his eyes. "But I do love you. Let me show you how much."

Hurt, yearning, betrayal—her scorn for him and herself whirled violently within her. She felt an overwhelming rage swelling within her. Persephone lifted her ruined hand, blasting him with a mighty, dark wind. She made a fist, holding him tightly against the wall, and had only a fleeting glimpse of his enraged face before sprinting to the door. As her trembling fingers removed the bolt, she glanced backward at Hades. His eyes glowed with unearthly fire, and as their gazes locked, her lips trembled. Then she fled the empty hall, racing through the corridors until she reached the front doors. She threw them open and fled from the palace, rushing across the Underworld, away from the man she loved and despised.

CHAPTER 11
THE MOURNING FIELDS

Persephone ran blindly away, seeing nothing, overcome by grief. It felt like death–the loss of her love. As her tears fell, they crystallized and shattered against the Earth. The night was still dark, and the terrain became mountainous, with mist wrapping around her like icy fingers. Snow pelted her skin, but she kept running across gorges and between mountains, her feet carrying her far away. It was not until a large cavern appeared before her, blocking her path, that she finally collapsed to the ground, exhausted and sobbing, the cold rain drenching her.

"I loved you," she cried to the darkness. "I trusted you. Dumb, stupid girl," she whispered.

Flashes of the Satyr vision played before her, the humans wailing in pain and fear, and she was overcome with melancholy and regret. A reprehensible crime for which he felt no remorse. A drop of her blood dripped to the barren Earth from her still injured hand, and a single purple flower blossomed from it, yellow streaks at its heart. It was an iris, the symbol of hope. She burst into tears.

"I will make it right," she promised the flower. She sat up slowly on her knees, bowing in front of the cavern's entrance. It was dark and desolate, and she could sense no life within the cave. "I will right the wrong and heal those spirits who have yet to find their other half." She lifted her face, letting the cold rain mingle with her tears. Her fingertips pushed into the Earth, and she remembered the ancient tree of life in the crystal forest, the cords of life that snaked below them, reaching deep into the planet's center, each root linked to a powerful single source. She could sense the same strength deep inside herself, though it burned quietly now, the flame of hope almost extinguished. "Help me," she pleaded quietly to the Earth. "Let me find my way back. Give me the strength to find my faith in humanity once more."

The tiny light flared suddenly, fierce magic bursting free within her, traveling through her fingertips as green meadows filled the stone cavern. Massive willow trees bowed their heads in grief across the long-stretched fields while bushes of pink bleeding hearts exploded through the grass. Tears streamed down her face as magic flowed effortlessly through her limbs, watering the Earth. Millions of cords flashed through her mind, each entwined with the next, and within them was the cord that ran between him and herself, the unbreakable connection they shared. She despised it, and yet it was part of her, so tightly wound around her own soul that she could not separate their threads. They were not two but one, their cords entwined endlessly throughout eternity. As she sobbed, the storm intensified, forming ponds and lakes.

As love and hatred whirled through her, a strange, ancient force moved against her, enveloping her, wrapping around her soul over and over until a light-filled her, poured from her, and she glistened like sunlight, floating high into the cavern, lighting the sky and illuminating the new world she had created. Flashes of memories, some her own, mingled with strange visions, moments of people and places she did not recognize, flashed across her consciousness.

The cords began vibrating, twisting faster until they formed a golden key. As Persephone reached for it, a drop of blood from her hand fell on its surface, creating a rose quartz handle. She gripped the handle, and the light suddenly extinguished from her body, and she plummeted from the sky, landing hard on the ground below. Her breath hissed out, the fall knocking the air from her lungs. She rolled onto her back and stared at the ceiling, gasping as she looked around the cavern. The cave had been transformed.

"The Mourning Fields," she breathed, christening the new land. "This shall be a place for souls to wait, a resting stop, in hopes that they can find their shattered halves." She sat up and sketched a heart in the dirt with her finger. "Two halves of the same whole, for those who have squandered a lifetime on love unreturned." She bowed again to the Earth. "Thank you," she whispered.

The steady pounding of the rain abated, and she realized the storm had finally ended. She stood on unsteady legs. Enormous rose quartz doors had materialized at the entrance, and she pushed them shut with the last of her strength, slipping the key into the lock.

Hades would send someone to look for her; she did not want them to find this refuge. She glanced in the direction of the palace. No, she was not ready to return. She turned sharply and moved in the opposite direction. She reached the edge of a mountain and peered up at the high precipice. It seemed a good enough place to hide. With a weary sigh, she began to pull herself up the rocks. She eventually made it to level ground, breathless and exhausted. She gasped when she saw a towering shadow standing several feet away, but the figure remained motionless. She gave a sigh of relief as she peered closer. It was a statue.

She walked towards the structure, studying the massive sculpture. There were two enormous faces, one side depicting a handsome young man, while the other showed an elderly man with a cunning, bearded expression. Why, these were the same faces on the goblets in Elysium. She admired the carving's artistry before succumbing to exhaustion and slumping on the ground. She let her head rest against the statue's cool marble and inhaled deeply, filling her lungs with the chilly night air.

"I do not want him to be a monster," she whispered. "I know there was good in him, that there must be."

Only the wind spoke as it passed over the mountain. Persephone needed to make plans to decide how she would live out these next six months, but she was exhausted. But she was wise enough to realize that Zeus was correct about one thing: the golden sword must be located. She had witnessed firsthand the danger of having a single owner of both the God-killing blades. Zeus was still threatening war until his sword was restored. They must be kept apart or, better yet, eradicated. But how?

Hades denied having Zeus' weapon, but she could no longer trust him.

He had control of the blue blade; had he stolen the golden blade? And for what purpose? Her thoughts raced around in circles as the night grew darker, but she was no closer to finding an answer. Her eyelids began to droop, and as her head lowered, she leaned on the statue's lips.

"Persephooneeeee…" She sprang up, her heart pounding, turning to stare at the statue.

"Bring him back," a voice cried deep within the figure as another voice danced in the wind. "I will always find you."

She placed her hand on the stone and felt an ancient magic within. "What is this?" she whispered. "Who speaks to me?"

The voices had vanished, leaving only the wailing wind to interrupt the silence. Persephone shuddered, the mountain no longer feeling like a sanctuary. Standing, she rushed down the rocky path. She saw a familiar hooded figure in the distance as she reached the craggy terrain below. She recognized Maketes right away; his tall, rangy form was conspicuous. So, he had sent her personal watch guard after her rather than coming himself.

She hid behind a huge boulder and watched him stare up the mountain. She muttered a curse. He must be an exceptional tracker. He was now charging up the cliff towards her. She sighed and sat down behind the stone. She didn't want to fight Maketes; she only wanted to be alone. She was suddenly grabbed by rough hands. She twisted from his grasp, trying to escape back towards the cliff, but he pounced quickly, grabbing her calf. They rolled down the mountainside, the rough surface of the rocks tearing their skin. They finally landed with a painful thud, and she rose with a groan. The guard was already up, kneeling in front of her.

"Go away," she said rudely. Maketes chuckled, and her eyes narrowed in suspicion. "I thought you weren't allowed to speak?"

"It is not that I cannot speak; I *choose* not to. I find few people are worth talking to. Most of the time, it allows me to do my job more easily." His voice was rough, as if rusty from disuse.

She yearned to stand up and run away from him, but her muscles refused to cooperate. "And what exactly is your job? Serving my husband's whims?" Persephone quipped.

"That is part of my job. You look wretched," the guard said bluntly as he examined her.

"How charming of you to say," she snapped. Maketes reached for her, and she kicked at him.

"Only a fool picks a fight when running on fumes." A nonchalant shrug followed. "But, if you're in the mood for a scuffle, I'm game. Either way, I'm taking you back to the palace. Whether you know it or not, it's for your own damn good."

She shot him a withering look. "Ah, the classic 'it's for your own good' routine. How original. I think I liked you better before you could talk."

He laughed. "Luckily, I don't give a fuck what you think. I have a job, and you're coming with me."

"Ah yes, your job. You aren't a very good guard. Where do you go for hours on end?" she demanded.

"Sometimes I am needed elsewhere," he replied cryptically.

Her gaze narrowed. "What's behind that door my husband erected? And why do you possess a key?"

"I have a key because he granted me one. As for what lies within, I'm as in the dark as you are."

"How did you know about the crystal forest in the swamplands?"

"What forest?"

An exasperated noise escaped her. "Why did you not want me to tell my husband?"

He paused, choosing his words with deliberate care. "It serves everyone's interest for him not to be privy to every discovery you might've stumbled upon that day."

His enigmatic words left her with a headache, her expression souring. She had no inclination for a battle of wits but needed to stall until her strength returned. "And now that you've found your voice, your real name, perhaps?"

"My name is not worth repeating," he replied in a low whisper.

"How did my husband find you?"

"He didn't. I found him."

"And why did you *find* him?"

"I believed that I could do good in his service."

"And here you are," she said icily, "hunting me. Does that seem like a good use of your time?"

Though she couldn't see his face, she knew Maketes' eyes moved over her, taking in her bloodied hand, her unkempt look. "It looks like you've been doing a shit job of taking care of yourself. We waste time. Are you coming back willingly or not?"

"Not!"

He sighed, muttering foul words under his breath. "There is no need to treat me like an enemy. You have enough of those."

She drew in a breath at his words. What did he know? "And who is my enemy?"

"You tell me."

"You know," she said thoughtfully, "you may be the most unhelpful person I have ever met."

He stood up and moved closer to her. "Stay away!" she hissed. "How did you find me, anyway? I am miles from the palace."

"You are not so hard to track. I followed the scent of a garden." He sighed wearily when she kicked at him again. "Even if I do not collect you, he will send others. I am not the only new addition to the palace, and I think you would find them less caring of your feelings than I am."

She scoffed rudely. "I would find that hard to believe."

He moved closer, his massive, powerful frame towering over her, and something about it made her heartbeat quicken. He offered a gloved hand to her.

"At least let me help you stand. Then, if you would like, you can attempt to pummel me."

She eyed him. "Fine," she muttered.

She reluctantly placed her smaller hand into his large one, and he drew her upwards. She gave an "ompf" of surprise as she fell against him, and as he righted her, she felt his fingers press hard between her neck and shoulder. Fury filled her, and she tried to fight back, but blackness pressed against her vision, and then she saw nothing.

When she woke, hard, impersonal hands carried her through the castle halls. She glanced up to see Maketes' shrouded face.

"Put me down," she hissed. Maketes shook his head and continued his long strides through the darkened corridors. "You great oaf, release me!" She struggled violently in his arms, but he continued walking, unbothered by her protests.

"You are too tired to walk, Your *Majesty*," he replied, his obsequious emphasis on the word carrying his habitual undertone of rudeness.

A sudden thought occurred to her, and she pulled at Maketes' shirt, trying to draw his attention. He slowed his stride and looked down at her.

"Do not," she began, then cleared her throat. "Please, do not take me to my husband. I would like to go to my private rooms."

His head tilted as he looked down at her. "Why? What happened?"

She rolled her eyes. "Don't you find it a little ironic that *you* expect me to answer your questions?" He didn't move, and she gave a frustrated sigh. "Suffice it to say, it would be better for us both if I did not see him and he did not see me."

He started walking again, and she was taken aback when he approached a wall and pressed several spots in the stone. A door swung open, and he quickly spirited up a secret stairwell as though she weighed nothing. How did he know so much about the palace? He pressed against the wall again at the top of the steps, and a door sprang open from the stone again. She realized they were in her bedroom as they stepped through the doorway.

"How many secret entrances are there to my room?" she muttered, disturbed.

Maketes deposited her unceremoniously onto the mattress, and a muffled "oomph" escaped her lips as she bounced across the bed. Olive, who had been sleeping comfortably, stretched enthusiastically before settling comfortably onto her lap. She brushed back her hair impatiently, glaring at the guard.

"You can go now," she said coolly. "You've returned me to my prison, so consider your job well done."

But he didn't move, staring down at her. "Are you all right?" Maketes asked in his low voice.

Perhaps it was the sudden compassion in his gruff voice, but suddenly, the fear, the sorrow, and the loneliness of her life culminated in her chest, and a loud sob was torn from her throat. She turned her head away as her body trembled.

"I am sorry," she whispered. "I have just had an awful day."

"Have you had a good day since you've been here?" he asked sarcastically.

She surprised herself by laughing. "No, actually," she admitted.

He was silent for several moments. "Has someone... done something to you. Your husband—?"

"Does it matter? Does what happened to me really matter? You will continue serving Hades as he bids, regardless of my wants." She lifted her face then, staring at the tall man above her. "I do not think it is my destiny to be happy. I thought maybe– once." She broke off again as another sob welled. "I am sorry!"

The guard was silent, and finally, Persephone pushed her tears back down, temporarily sealing her anguish behind a barrier. Gods, how embarrassing to cry before her surly guard. But there was something almost comforting in his bluntness, an honesty that she appreciated. "Don't tell my husband that I was crying."

Maketes' hand convulsed at his side, and he fisted it tightly. "As I said, sharing everything with your husband is unnecessary." He turned as if to leave but halted, returning his gaze to her. "Your hand? Did he do that?"

As she curled her now-healed hand against her body, she looked up at the guard, knowing he saw the answer in her eyes.

"I will guard your door tonight. No one will enter."

The door closed quietly behind him. Persephone sat still in the darkness, afraid to allow herself to sleep, fearful of what her dreams would bring. What tormented her at night—that thing that waited for her in the shadows? The unwelcome thought entered her mind that perhaps there was nothing in the blackness, that it was just an empty abyss animated only by her subconscious fears. Was her mind breaking as the world shattered around her? She reflected on what it may feel like to go insane. Was one aware of the microscopic cracks in their sanity?

Despite her uneasy thoughts, sleep drew her in. Her eyes closed repeatedly, but each time, she jerked awake, unwilling to succumb to the unsettling blackness. But the allure of Hypnos' realm soon proved too much for her, and she succumbed to the unknown darkness of sleep.

CHAPTER 12
THE DEVIL WITHIN

The hematite room was dark and frigid, the air heavy with the scent of incense. The dark, reflective stone covered the room from floor to ceiling, and the king sat in front of a crystal mirror, his complexion flushed with anger. A large hood was pulled over his head, obscuring his eyes, and the reflected light from the crystals created shadows on his angular features. Dark shapes seemed to move in the shadows around him, reaching towards him, and the edges of his robes swayed as though pulled by greedy fingers.

A low voice echoed from deep within the darkness. "Let me gaze upon it."

Hades closed his weary eyes, and the blue-flamed sword appeared in his grasp.

"Come closer," growled the voice.

The king approached the hematite mirror, holding the sword up. Hades glanced into the mirror at his reflection, who was empty-handed and avaricious, his amber eyes fixated on the sword.

"Magnificent," the reflection whispered. "Now show me the other." Again, Hades knew what he wanted, so he summoned the golden blade. He lifted it in his other hand, and it glinted in the darkness, a beacon of light that the shadows clung to. The figure in the mirror reached for it but could not hold it. A rage-filled scream filled the room. "Let me hold them," it hissed.

The King of Death stood still and lifted both hands, slamming the swords into the stone floor. "No." His voice was harsh, and sweat beaded his pale skin.

"No?" the voice jeered dangerously. "How long do you think you can defy me?"

As if bent by an invisible hand, Hades fell to his knees, and the reflection grew taller, looming over his prone figure.

"Bring. Them. To. Me."

Blood poured from Hades' nose and mouth as he lifted his head. "I will not."

"Your nobility grows tiresome, king."

"As does your treachery," Hades said, his voice impassive, even as blood pooled beneath him.

The reflection began to pace agitatedly. "I can guess what stays your hand. It's her, is it not? Your *love*," the voice mocked. "And what a special thing it has been for you. Love has brought a once-mighty king to his knees. And now you bow to me," the reflection laughed, filling the room with the dreadful sound.

"That is what you do not understand, what you can never understand," Hades replied softly. "We gladly suffer for those we love."

"Oh, and you will suffer," the voice promised.

"Then why do you not kill me and let us be done with it."

The reflection smiled. "Very well. Take out your dagger and slice your palm." The king's movements were jerky as he lifted a dagger from beneath his robes, slicing his palm until blood poured down his arm.

The reflection licked his lips; his gaze was fixed on the gushing blood. "Very good. Now, lift your dagger and slice your face." Hades drew the dagger down his left cheek, his black eyes expressionless as blood poured from the cut. "Shall I make you cut your other cheek now?

Maybe that scar on your chest? I could make you carve out your heart if I wanted to, make you eat it." Hades was silent, making no effort to wipe away the blood that splattered around him. The reflection sighed. "Always so quiet. But I think that is enough for now. Remember, I can kill you how and when I want. But first, I will make you suffer."

Hades stood then, bursting through the invisible hold. He slammed his fist against the glass. Purple eyes blazed into amber ones. "Free me from this," Hades hissed. Golden dust flew from the king's skin, settling around him like gold-colored snow.

The reflection had moved backward, his eyes on the flecks of gold. "Temper, temper, king." The mirrored Hades wagged his finger. "Your little displays of defiance cost you. How much more can your soul withstand? Even now, the threads unravel."

All you have to do is give me the blades. The voice whispered into his mind, cajoling, enthralling.

Hades raised his head, his eyes blazing. "You shall never have them."

The reflection's face contorted in fury. "I shall have them and her. And when the last breath of life finally flows from you, you will know that I have taken what you love and destroyed it. I shall shatter the light inside of her, and the best part will be that she will believe it was you, her love, who broke her."

A wind began to flow through the room, whipping around Hades. "*Occultis aperta,*" he whispered, lifting his hands, and the swords vanished. Golden dust mingled with coagulated blood on his flesh.

"So be it," the reflection said with hard eyes. "The end will be the same, but you will destroy yourself in the process."

Hades' body burned as if a poison moved through his veins, and he fell to the floor in anguish, writhing in pain.

"You cannot win. You lost the battle that day on the mountain."

"He who holds the weapons holds the power," Hades whispered.

"And he who controls the man who carries them wields it," the voice mocked.

Whispers came from the darkness, soft at first but growing louder and louder until hundreds of voices hissed at him. Hades shuddered as memories wrapped around him, replaying the darkest moments of his life: Rhea falling as his sword pierced her; the evil he had committed on the mountainside; his dark deeds repeated in his mind until he screamed his agony. He was falling into blackness, and suddenly, the visions vanished, and Persephone was there. He reached for her, but a shadow stood behind her. A blade suddenly pushed through her, and she cried in anguish before falling to the ground and collapsing next to Rhea, with rubied pomegranate trees growing around them. He saw his hooded face standing over them, holding the golden blade high.

"No!" Hades cried.

The reflection laughed. *Your disobedience will not go unpunished. Beg me for mercy, and I might be kinder in my punishment.*

Hades could feel his consciousness fading, and he looked at the mirror, staring into those translucent eyes. "Fuck you," he whispered.

Wrong answer.

The reflection became a dark shadow as it approached the mirror's edge. One leg stepped through, then another, until the entire body emerged. The figure transformed into a black mist, hanging over the king's prostrate figure. As the fog began to push into him, flowing down his throat, his body convulsed as it filled him, possessing him.

"Go to her," the shadow whispered. "Go to your queen."

Hades' eyes opened, amber lights dancing in them, and he stood slowly, walking unseeing through the halls.

Orphnaeus was waiting at the palace's entrance, and the king mounted his steed, galloping through the Underworld, leaping across the rivers of lava, and dodging endless caverns. His horse whinnied and jumped over a frightened spirit blocking his way - not even pausing in its stride. He did not stop until he reached the ancient castle made of ice, standing tall and shining white against the darkness. She was waiting for him, standing on top of the icy steps - draped in a long ivory fur cape, her naked body on full display beneath. There was an icy gleam in her eye and a cruel smile across her rubied lips. She opened her arms to greet him and he leaped from his horse - straight into her clutches, her lips cold against feverish ones.

His mouth tasted like a kingdom, like power. Minthe ran her milk-white fingers through his ebony hair, studying his face intensely. His eyes were like the night sky, his skin was burning, and he smelled like the mist of the Styx. Minthe pulled him close to her breasts; she tugged at his hands, guiding them from the small of her back to cup both breasts in their fullness - closing her eyes as she kissed him deeply.

A tear washed down his cheek, and she licked it away, laughing. "You make me feel like a Goddess." She moaned. "I love you."

Hades ran his hands through her hair, yanking her head back, anger shining in his eyes. She could feel the desperation inside him, like he was a man fighting for his life. The heat of his body burned into her skin painfully, as if she were being branded by fire.

His voice smoldered angrily, "I hate you." And then he was kissing her cruelly as she rubbed her body hard against his.

He pulled away, and golden dust washed off him, dancing in the wind, "Stop resisting." She smiled. "Give into the pleasure I have to offer." He relaxed, and she led his lips to one of her large breasts, moaning as he suckled.

Licking his ear, she whispered, "I ache for you between my thighs. Come, king, tonight you shall worship me."

She led him up the palace stairs, guiding him into the castle, and her footsteps reverberated over the ice as she led him to her final destination: her bed-chamber.

CHAPTER 13
THE THRONE ROOM

The world was shrouded in golden mist, and Persephone knew there was something she must find, but she couldn't remember what it was. When she turned around, she saw a hooded figure rushing through the swirling mist.

"Wait," shouted Persephone. "Who are you!"

She ran after them, her feet gliding softly across the Earth as a shadowed forest spread around her. Pomegranates swirled on the black leaves, golden mist tracing veins across the fruit. The cloaked figure dashed between the trees, cradling something in its arms, and Persephone tried to reach them, but they were too fast.

"Wait," she cried, panting.

But then the stranger vanished into shadows, leaving her alone once more.

The Earth tilted suddenly, and she slid back into that endless darkness, down, down, down. She stood once more at the mountain's base, and there he was, the King of the Dead. As the humans writhed around him, Hades was fighting a shadow. She stared in dread as she realized he was losing. The shadow grew more powerful as blood streamed from Hades' scarred body. The wraith raised a golden blade before she could cry a warning and stabbed Hades' abdomen. The shadow exploded into a million black moths, covering her husband and obliterating all light.

"No," she cried. She flew through the void, her voice echoing in the darkness. "Tell me what happened! Where are you?"

She felt his palm caress her cheek, but then he was pushing her away as he died, and she plummeted into nothing, into blackness.

"Open your eyes," he whispered.

Persephone woke up gasping, her body drenched in sweat. The dream still clung to her head like spider webs, and she tried to piece it together, but the details were already fading from her memory. She struggled, raising her head to look around, then let it drop to the ground with a groan.

"Of course," she whispered.

Resolutely, she pushed herself up and stood silently in the darkness, observing the pomegranate tree. With only a slight hesitation, she moved forward, brushing her hand over the fruit.

"What is happening to me?" she whispered softly, but there was no answer.

Slowly, she made her way back to the palace. It felt like she was living a nightmare. Paranoia slithered into her thoughts, a relentless whisper that cast doubt on the loyalty of those she once considered allies. If Hades, whom she had trusted implicitly, could betray her, it seemed no sanctuary was left. Her father was gone, and her mother was stuck in the upper realms. Jocasta, she trusted, yet confiding in her would mean exposing the soul to danger. Maketes remained an enigma, his motives unclear. There was no one to turn to.

Persephone's mouth gaped open as she approached her bedroom and saw the figure in the doorway. Minthe had returned to the palace and stood holding a serving tray at the room's threshold. Hades had reneged on their bargain. The nymph's smile was cunning as she turned to the queen.

Minthe cooed, "Your Highness." Her arrogant gaze swept over Persephone's nightgown. "Why are you rambling about the palace in that ancient gown? You could catch your death." The nymph positively beamed at the prospect of Persephone's imagined demise.

"What are you doing here?" Persephone demanded.

"Why, I am to be your personal dresser. Did Hades—" She narrowed her blue eyes in malicious pleasure. "I mean, the king, not tell you?"

Persephone pushed past her, entering her room. Her heart pounded angrily, but she bent down to pet the still-slumbering Olive. So Hades had not dismissed her as he had promised her. She did not know why she was surprised, why the predictable betrayal still could shatter her heart, but it did. It was evident that his affection or love for her, if any, was gone.

Minthe tsked as she placed the tray on a table. "I thought a husband and wife were supposed to share everything. When I marry, I know I will."

"You can leave," Persephone said coolly, her head and heart pounding. "I have no need of you."

"I am to help you dress. King Hades bade you join him in the throne room this morning; he told me so as we woke."

So that was why he had not looked for her last night; he had been with his lover. Persephone's heart clenched tightly in her chest. Minthe's face was lit with a malicious smile, and it was clear that she hoped Persephone would shatter at her words. And she would, but later, not in front of this silly, shallow creature. She had to hold herself together for now; she needed to find her father, locate the golden blade, and ensure that the war that Zeus had promised would not come to fruition.

A thought occurred to her: she was being so predictable, the angry, jilted wife. She devised her first strategy. With a smile on her face, Persephone turned to Minthe. "How considerate you have been, Minthe, to warm my husband's bed. Why don't you bring me a gown for the day?"

Minthe gave her an odd look before turning to the wardrobe and taking out a long, black toga. The train of the gown was constructed of yards of black silk that poured behind the garment like a river. "He said you were supposed to wear this." Minthe curled her lips, clearly envious that Hades was still interested in her wardrobe. As the nymph approached, she stepped right over a patch of flowers, stomping them ruthlessly beneath her tiny, delicate feet. Minthe looked up at Persephone innocently. "Oh dear," she exclaimed, "did you grow these weeds on purpose?"

Persephone bit her tongue as she sensed the flowers' anguish. "I will restore them after you leave," she said calmly. "Where are my previous handmaidens?" Minthe looked blank. "Jocasta?"

"Oh, that old bat," Minthe muttered. "She has been dismissed. Her presence and those insipid nieces are no longer required at the palace." Persephone had shifted to the dressing chair, and her hands trembled as she heard the news. She hid them beneath her dressing gown, away from the nymph's probing gaze. Minthe stared at Persephone in the mirror. "Does that bother you?"

Persephone waved her hand. "Oh, no," Persephone lied with a sweet smile. "It matters little to me who dresses me." Persephone stood, then casually began to move closer to the door. A pleasant wind flowed across the room as Persephone swirled her fingers behind her back. The wind began to whirl as the movement of her fingers intensified, and Minthe glanced about, startled, as it began to pull her hair.

"What is happening!" the nymph exclaimed, her eyes darting about the chamber for the source of the wind.

"These winds happen sometimes," Persephone replied, all polite concern. "I am afraid they can be rather brisk. It is probably due to the terrain I have created."

Minthe screamed as the little whirlwind surrounded her, dragging her across the room as she was engulfed in the gale. "Make it stop!" she shrieked.

"I am afraid I cannot. We do not know exactly how the winds will blow. It is best to give into it."

"Why is it not pulling at you?" Minthe raged.

"It's highly unpredictable. Jocasta was used to it. I would have thought she had warned you before she left. Well, nothing to do now, I'm afraid, except let it play out," Persephone sighed as Minthe began to twirl within the whirlwind. Persephone knocked on the door, which was opened by Maketes. "Best to give her a wide berth, Maketes!

She's coming through!"

Maketes jumped back, and Minthe swept past him, all red hair and wild eyes. "I will dress myself today, do not worry!" Persephone called down the hall to the spinning nymph. The whirlwind carried her away, her screams and curses moving down the hall until there was blissful silence.

Maketes stared through the doorway, and Persephone gave him her best innocent expression.

"Is there something you wish to say?" Persephone asked with wide eyes.

Maketes shook his head. "Just that I have never noticed whirlwinds in the palace before."

"Hmm," Persephone replied in a sweet voice. "Well, now you know. You ought to be careful lest you get swept up in one."

"I shall watch my step," he murmured politely as he resumed his position against the wall.

With a cheerful smile, she closed the door. It fell instantly from her face, and she moved to pick up the toga Minthe had laid out. So, he wanted her to wear this gown. She looked at it, frowning. She could thwart him and choose another dress. But then again, all the gowns here were ones Hades had designed for her. So what did it matter what she was wearing?

She moved across the room to sit at her desk and retrieved a blank scroll from the drawer. Dipping a reed into ink, she began to jot notes,

Golden blade

Minthe

My father

Dreams

Sleepwalking

Splitting of the souls

The crystal forest

She examined the list with care. On the edge of the page, she scribbled Hades' name and drew lines to Minthe, her father, and the soul splitting. Next to her father's name, she wrote: "Find him." She paused, and then, next to the golden blade, she wrote Zeus' name. Her gaze narrowed as she nibbled on the end of the reed. None of it made any sense. She sighed in frustration and shoved away from the desk. She must not linger too long, or he would look for her. She tucked the list beneath the mattress with the books and scrolls that Maketes had hidden and returned her attention to the toga Hades had left for her.

Gold was engraved into the skirt, forming words, but she didn't recognize the language; perhaps the writing was an ancient dialect. She had little trouble slipping the robe over her head, but the fastenings were challenging. She fumbled with a large golden chain hooked to the skirt but couldn't reach it. By the time she had turned in a third circle trying to secure it, she huffed a frustrated sigh. Resolutely, she moved to the door and poked her face through.

"Maketes?" His dark form moved into the doorway.

"Yes?"

She frowned up at him, wondering how she could ask him. She was unaccustomed to men touching her other than her husband. But that was nonsense. He was her guard, and she would choose Maketes between him and Minthe any day. Besides, he had already carried her unconscious body back to the palace.

Even so, her face reddened terribly as she asked, "I was wondering if you would help me with something?"

She took a step back as his large frame moved through the doorway. He seemed to peer around the room.

"What are you looking for?" she asked curiously.

"Just wondering if another whirlwind will appear."

Persephone bit her lip to keep from giggling. "I have hypothesized that they form in proportion to my level of annoyance."

"Then I will try not to annoy you. What do you need help with?"

"Well," she began, blushing again. "I am having trouble reaching the back of my gown to fasten, and there is no one else to ask—"

He stepped close to her. "Turn around," he said in his rough voice. She heard the clink of metal as his hands moved up the back of her dress, and it felt strange to have another man so close to her. "All done," he murmured.

She stepped away from him. "Thank you."

"What else do you need help with?" He moved forward, lifting sparkling hair pins from the small table. "Shall I?"

She raised her eyebrows. "Really?"

He laughed softly. "You would be surprised how many times I helped my mother. Sit." His hands moved deftly over the pins, placing them into her long, sun-streaked hair.

"Do you know where Jocasta is?" she asked quietly.

He shook his head. "No."

"And my father, do you know where he was sent?"

"No," he rasped.

Maketes worked silently, his fingers surprisingly gentle in her hair.

"How long has Hades been having an affair with Minthe?" The question spilled from her lips before she knew she meant to ask it. His hands paused, and when she looked up, she saw his covered face staring into the mirror. She hated the bitter laugh that escaped her lips. "Come now, Maketes," she said softly. "I am not an idiot, at least not completely. I would like to know when it started. Was it before he met me?"

"Will the truth not hurt you more?" he whispered roughly.

"Not any more than a lie."

He stood behind her, frozen like a dark statue, but finally, he shook his head. "I wish I could tell you, but I cannot."

"Because you do not know?" she queried.

"I cannot," he repeated again.

He finished placing the last pin in her hair, and she stood, letting the black gown trail behind her.

"Thank you," she said again. She let the cold mask settle over her face once more. "Shall we go to face my husband?"

Turning on her heel, she preceded him out of the room. She felt his dark presence behind her as they moved through the halls, and she made her way to the throne room. The doors were closed, and she hurried forward, but at the last moment, Maketes appeared in front of her, his hands covering the handles.

"Have you been there since your return?"

"No," she frowned at him.

"It is a bit different now."

"In what way?"

"I will let you see for yourself, but I felt it best to warn you." Maketes pushed the handles, and the palace doors swung forward.

The guard stepped back, bowing as Persephone entered, and she could not help the gasp that escaped her lips. The two thrones had been shattered into a massive mound of obsidian rocks piled in the center of the room. Hades lounged at the top of the giant, cracked throne with a laurel crown on his head, reading a scroll. In his other hand, he carelessly held a glass of wine. The River Goddesses, Lethe, and Styx, bowed at his feet, speaking softly. Persephone noticed that they were dressed in armor. To the side of the throne room were unfamiliar faces, and scantily dressed servants held up plates of food and drinks.

His gaze lifted to hers, sending a surge of complex emotions through her—pain, the bitter taste of hatred, and the haunting echoes of love and longing. He waved his hands, clearly dismissing the River Goddesses. They bowed to Persephone as they passed her.

Once she reached the bottom of the jagged throne, she lifted her eyes to her indolent husband. "Do I dare ask what happened to the thrones?"

He lifted a shoulder carelessly, revealing his powerful chest beneath his toga. "I had them crushed to create a more practical chair. Those old thrones were so tedious, were they not? And besides, with you being down here only six months, there was no reason for it to sit empty." He nodded, and a servant rushed to place a golden laurel crown on her head. "It will be more comfortable for you, a queen sitting at the feet of her king." He eyed her, his eyes slumberous, but she was not fooled into believing he was anything other than alert. "Sit," he demanded softly.

"I will not."

His eyes flared. "Must you defy me in everything?"

"No, not everything," she said sweetly, "only when I think your ideas are absurd, though that seems to be the majority of your thoughts these days."

His face flushed, the air crackled, and she knew what would happen. An incredible force lifted her from the ground, forcing her compliance with a careless sweep of his fingertips. She landed in an inelegant heap on the stone pile, causing some attendees to titter.

"There now. Was that really so difficult?"

With a nod of Hades' head, a servant rushed forward, pressing a glass of wine in her hand. Without looking at her husband, she poured it into the center of the fractured throne. She heard his low laugh behind her.

"I have to thank you," she said, still facing forward, "for my new servant. How generous it is of you to share your lover with me."

"You think I broke our deal, but I did not. You said that Minthe would no longer be my servant, and she is not. She is yours. A gift for my darling wife. You should be more careful the next time you attempt to bargain with me."

She looked back at him, fluttering her eyelashes like the idiot he clearly believed her to be. "How thoughtful. Who could ask for more? And the best present is that she may warm your bed at night instead of me."

His eyes darkened. "But no one could warm me like my Dread Queen, who has fire in her eyes and anger in her heart. The destroyer, my destroyer."

"Do not call me that," she snapped.

Hades leaned forward, and she shivered as his heat touched her. "But you are my dark queen. You have destroyed me for anyone else," he whispered. His hands moved to her pale neck. "You consume my mind until nothing else matters but the thought of fucking you." His fingers tightened around her slender throat, making it difficult to breathe.

He sat back, reclining against the throne, and she took a shaky breath. "Shall we sort the souls? Guards open the gates," he called abruptly, his gaze fixed on her, a smirk on his lips.

The Judges were the first to arrive. They bowed politely before the throne, greeting Persephone coldly. She wasn't one of their favorites, but she nodded to them as they sat on their bench. A vast swarm of souls were then led inside the room. Guards stood around the crowd, shoving them roughly, and there were souls of all ages, from infants to an ancient soul, who had to be close to a century old. The children were sobbing, and even the elderly seemed terrified.

"Have these souls not been sorted?" she exclaimed. "Will we not greet the children first?"

Hades waved his hand carelessly. "Oh, we do not do that anymore. I have a new method. It is much quicker to greet them all at once. Saves us all time."

"Clumping them all together is not a method," Persephone retorted. "How will they get to know you? How can you ensure you do not need to help the children find someone to watch them?"

"They can sort that out themselves. My job is simply to deliver them, like livestock. I merely provide the transportation."

"Like... livestock," Persephone repeated slowly. "Regardless of what is between us, you must understand this is not right."

He leaned forward, brushing his fingers against her shoulder, a seemingly loving movement until they tightened painfully on her flesh. "With war on the horizon, certainly you are not dictating what is right and proper to me? Tell me, wife, exactly how many wars have you fought? You offer the meaningless opinion of a woman, full of complaints but no remedy."

She jerked her shoulder away from him. With a flick of his fingers, Hades summoned a servant to bring him a new glass of wine. Persephone looked around the throng, noticing their dread and distrust. She landed on a face that she recognized and gasped. "Theo!" she exclaimed. She motioned towards the man, but he backed away, sliding deeper into the crowd. "Theo, come forward," she cried again.

The crowd parted until he stood in the center of the room, a pretty blonde soul clutching tightly at his side. She could only guess that this was his wife. So she died too, Persephone thought sadly.

"Theo, do you not remember me?" she asked, standing. "It seems so long ago that we last met." A shadow passed over her eyes. "You did not keep your promise."

"What promise was that?" He spoke cautiously, and Persephone noted the trepidation in his wife's eyes as she drew nearer.

"To live a long life. Tell me, what ended not only your life but your wife's as well?"

Theo glanced at his wife, but the soul shook her head firmly. "My wife's name is Selene. We were murdered." As he spoke, something strange happened. His voice slowed, and between the couples' clasped hands, Persephone saw golden threads, weaved together and glittering between them. The threads were connected to both, entwined as her own was helplessly entwined with Hades.

"Soulmates," she whispered, her eyes alight with gold. Suddenly, time reverted to normal, and she looked into Theo's blue eyes again. "Tell me," she asked again, her voice soft, "who hurt you."

Theo and Selene exchanged a meaningful glance. "I– I do not remember," he finally answered.

Persephone moved closer, speaking softly. "Do not be afraid. I saw Ares holding your... holding your bodies. Tell me what happened." But Selene only grew paler.

"We do not know who it was," Theo said again, his eyes lowered.

"Very well. You have suffered much during your lifetime but will find peace within the Underworld. You shall live in Asphodel," Persephone declared. "You will fear no more, my friend."

A sob of relief spilled from Theo's lips, and he turned to embrace his wife, both collapsing to the ground.

The King of the Dead slowly rose from his ebony throne, and uneasy silence fell over the crowd. Each step he took seemed to reverberate on the throne room floor, shadows trailing behind him. His eyes gleamed with a malicious light as he surveyed the couple.

"How very touching. But I am afraid my wife has spoken too soon. Theo, you have broken a promise to Queen Persephone. I shall, as she decreed, place your wife in Asphodel, but you will be sent to the River of Fire for one year until your debt is paid. You must pay for breaking an oath to the Queen of the Underworld."

The couple cried out as Persephone's eyes blazed at her husband. "What an oath!" she exclaimed. "That was no oath, just me wishing him well! He was murdered." She moved closer, adding in a quiet voice, "And you know who was responsible. He would have no way to defend himself against the God of War."

"But it was you who declared it a promise," Hades retorted, his voice booming like a tempest. "And in being so foolish as to be murdered, he broke his promise to you." His obsidian eyes locked onto hers. "There are rules that must be followed, and you, my queen, must learn to speak more carefully when you impart sentences to souls. Every word you utter has meaning."

Persephone stepped closer to Hades. "Please don't do this."

Selene was sobbing now, and Theo looked desperately from his wife to the queen. A look of resolve crossed his face as he stepped forward, but as he opened his lips, a thin black string weaved from the corner of his mouth through his upper and lower lips, stitching his mouth shut. As Theo furiously tugged at his mouth, Selene shrieked in fear, and Persephone's face paled. She turned to face her husband, who was smirking. The souls in the room were pressing themselves against the wall in terror.

"Let him speak," her voice trembled.

"I do not wish him to speak."

"He wants to tell us the truth! What is wrong with you!" she cried. "We do not treat our subjects like this."

Hades began to circle them again. "Not only did Theo break a promise to the Queen of the Underworld, but he drew the attention of the God of War. I must lock Theo away for one year to protect the people of Asphodel from Ares."

"You have built up the walls of our kingdom higher than ever. How could Ares find his way down here?"

"Did you forget that he did it before?" Hades' voice grew louder, gesturing to the frightened crowd around them. "Do you not care for the people? Do you not want *them* to be safe? You would send this man to live amongst them and make them ripe for slaughter. Have they not suffered enough?"

Cries of fear and outrage poured from the souls, and several began pointing to the couple in the center of the room.

"We should conclude our talk in private," Persephone said quickly, aware of the crowd's growing uneasiness.

"Why? Do the people not deserve to hear?" His voice was a loud boom across the throne room. "At Theo's sentencing, you thwarted the rules of the Underworld, and this is what transpires when rules are disregarded. It threatens the safety of all souls."

"This is wrong," Persephone spoke in a low voice. "*You* are wrong."

The room was taut with tension. The Judges were standing in shock, their heads synchronized as they looked back and forth between Hades and Persephone.

"Wrong?" Hades repeated. "No mortal can cheat death. Theo should never have been allowed to leave our world to spread rumors among the living. *You* should have never allowed it. His wife would have eventually joined him if he had waited here. You did this." The king turned toward Theo then. "And you... did you not tell mortals about your experience with the queen, Theo?" Hades raised his hand, and the stitch was pulled with a snap from Theo's lips, and the man gave a cry of pain.

"King Hades–" Theo began, trembling.

"Bow when you speak to me," Hades snarled.

Theo fell to his knees. "I–I did speak of the queen's goodness. I only wished to spread your good word and the kindness of the beautiful queen. I let them know that death is not something to fear and that when we go, we may go peacefully into the next life."

"And in doing so, you made the mortals not fear death."

"Only to comfort them, Your Majesty," Theo cried. "Why must they live in so much fear?"

Dark veins began to wrap around Hades' throat, traveling upward until they reached his eyes, filling them with blackness. "Because death is something to fear," he said, his voice a deadly rasp and the souls scattered, pressing against the wall. "I am someone to fear."

As Hades snapped his fingers, the room was plunged into darkness. The sound resonated, and something in the shadows began to repeat the snap, mimicking the pattern. Suddenly, a single crimson orb peered from the darkness. Shuffling footsteps echoed through the throne room, a macabre sound in the oppressive silence. The shadows clung to the evil form, obscuring it from view, and the air filled with the unmistakable odor of death and decay. With dawning horror, she realized who Hades had summoned.

"No," she gasped.

She lifted her hands, and several candles flared. All eyes were drawn towards the sound, and she peered into the darkness as the footsteps drew nearer. A bloody claw landed first, smearing entrails along the floor. He was close enough now that she could hear the incessant smacking of his tongue, the dragging of his broken wing as it lay worthless on the floor. A second claw appeared, and he stepped from the shadows, towering above the crowd. Eurynomos. The movement drew Persephone's eyes, and she noticed shadowy beings crawling across the ceiling, hanging like bats as they stared down. Their eyes flashed red as they watched the souls below, their heads twisted backward, hideous, distorted effigies of men who had followed their master from the most bottomless pits of the Underworld.

The souls screamed in terror, and Persephone looked towards Hades in shock. He smiled back at her, his eyes demonic.

"Eurynomos was kind enough to bring back your heads from Olympus."

The demon's one eye was riveted on Hades while a damaged, sightless white globe hung from the monster's other side. Persephone had stabbed it out herself just last year. A stained, burlap bag was clutched in one claw, but at Hades' words, Eurynomos let the bag fall from his grip. The mortal craniums of Theo and his wife rolled out, coming to rest in the center of the room. Theo and his wife both gasped, shocked to see their lifeless blue faces. Maggots crawled from the long-dead corpses, and Theo's wife fainted in his arms, overcome with shock.

"Since you have enlisted my wife to help you break the rules, I will ensure that you never step foot on Earth again," Hades sneered at Theo, his canines sharp. The demons around the room hissed with pleasure. "No man can cheat death; no man can cheat his king."

Before Persephone could understand what he intended, Hades snapped his fingers, and Eurynomos moaned in delight as he bent to feast. He gobbled Theo's head first, bones crunching as he ate. Screams filled the hall. By desecrating their mortal flesh in such a way, Hades had ensured that they could never again cross the barrier to the mortal land.

"Excellent work, Eurynomos," Hades said soothingly to the demon.

Persephone opened her eyes, staring ahead. She could feel the ancient magic shimmering inside her, rising, and she welcomed it. If she let it grow, she could smite this foul beast. She had been wrong to let Eurynomos live and so terribly mistaken to have felt compassion for this wretched creature. Of its own accord, the magic began to swell within her, and she could feel the shadowed power of it bubbling in her veins. Hades' hand suddenly snaked around her wrist.

"No," he whispered. Gold dust settled on her wrist where he touched her, and when she turned around, Eurynomos had finished his meal. Hades released her, snapping his fingers a third time, and the demon and its minions vanished, engulfed by foul, black smoke.

As the fumes cleared, two guards pushed through the doorway. They hauled Theo from the ground, where he was trying to rouse his wife. Selene struggled to stand, swaying as Theo was pulled from her grasp.

"Theo!" she cried. "No!"

For a moment, their hands clasped one another's, but as they were pulled apart, Persephone heard the wrenching tear of their threads, a soul being ripped from its mate, and her spirit wept for theirs. As the doors thudded behind the guards and Theo, Selene collapsed.

The crowd was still pressed against the wall, huddled like wounded animals, their eyes hollow from the atrocities they had just witnessed. The room was filled with the sounds of children's muffled wailing. Persephone knelt before Selene and took her hand in hers. As she murmured in Selene's ear, she bent low so no one could see her face. "I will find him."

The woman did not move, and Persephone stood again. She felt Hades' hands on her back, and she stiffened as he leaned in close to her and whispered, "What will my clever little wife do now?"

She jerked away from him, climbing the throne as she faced the crowd. "I have created a new realm," she shouted. The crowd grew quiet as she spoke. She could feel her husband's eyes on her, but she did not look at him. "It is not Elysium, but a stopping place to wait until your soul's mate returns. We will also welcome those whose love is unrequited and whose mate was never found. This place will provide you with tranquility and allow you to rest until—"

Her gaze shifted to her husband, who stared at her with an incomprehensible look. She returned his gaze boldly. "Until your love, the other half of your soul, returns. Every soul has a companion, a single being who completes it. Until you are reunited, you may stay there. It is called Mourning Fields."

A few people in the crowd smiled cautiously, drawing closer as she spoke.

"What an astonishing coincidence, my dear wife," Hades murmured, his smile chilling. "I have already compiled a list of names that would be perfect for such a place."

Despite his pleasant demeanor, she was wary of his newfound good humor. "As you say, that is an amazing coincidence," she replied cautiously. "Where is your list?" She held out her hand to him, but he shook his head.

"But you already have it," he smiled. He stepped towards the throne, lifting the long black train of Persephone's gown. "It is here; embroidered into the skirts of your gown are the names of souls desperate for love. Read them aloud, and we shall see if they find their soul's mate."

With her fingers trembling, Persephone raised her skirt, and the gold threads now glistened in familiar names. "Rastus," she read aloud quietly. Selene jerked and raised her swollen, tear-stained face. It was the name of the man who had raped Selene, the man Theo had killed. "King Tantalus." She stopped. "What is this list?" she demanded, throwing her skirts down in disgust. "You wish for the criminals of Tartarus to be liberated so they can find their soulmate? You wish for Rastus the rapist to find love?"

Hades turned to the crowd, and his voice resonated through the hall. "But do they not deserve love? Is not everyone worthy of affection? Would you, my loving wife, refuse them this?"

"You are twisting my words," Persephone growled. "You placed Tantalus in Tartarus yourself, and now you want to release him? They will not be permitted in the Mourning Fields. They committed heinous crimes!"

"In that case," he continued ruthlessly, "according to your logic, some members of this group should be sent to Tartarus."

The assembly erupted in outcry. "No!" she interjected quickly. "I think that individuals should be forgiven, but some actions are inexcusable."

"And what about your crimes, wife?" he asked softly. "You returned Theo, and in doing so, you broke a sacred rule of the Underworld."

"That is not true—"

"You violated the Underworld's laws. Your hasty actions put the laws of our land in jeopardy."

Her anger grew, and she sensed a dangerous power flare simmer within her. "Stop it," she said in a hushed tone.

"You as good as killed Theo yourself."

Before she could stop it, her fury erupted in a blast of power. She rapidly turned, shifting her power away from the crowd, shattering fractures in the wall behind the thrones. At the same time, Hades moved his fingers, and a massive chunk of the marble wall began to crumble above the spirits. As the wall fell, Persephone spun, flinging the spirits out of harm's way. But as she stepped closer, intending to offer comfort, the spirits backed away, fear and suspicion in their gazes.

"Oh dear, look what you've done," he softly said behind her.

As she swung around to face him, her eyes glittered with fury. His lips were twisted in a contented smile, but when he turned to face the crowd, his face was filled with solicitous concern for the souls. "I believe we should postpone the sorting until tomorrow. The queen is unwell." He looked at the Judges. "Please direct the souls back to the river, and we will greet them another day."

The Judges exchanged glances, followed by a hushed discussion. Minos advanced, bowing. "But, Your Highness," he began, his voice tentative. "These spirits have already waited for weeks and, in some cases, months. The river is becoming overcrowded."

"Then another day won't matter," Hades interrupted impatiently. He grasped Persephone's arm and she tried to jerk it from his grasp, but his fingers tightened painfully. "Go now; the queen needs rest." Minos looked uncertain, and Hades stepped closer, his eyes dangerous. "Do you really wish to quarrel with me, Minos?"

With a bow, the Judge hastily returned to his brothers and began to usher the souls from the room. As the spirits passed, she was conscious of their condemning stares. She could hear dissenting voices in the crowd and shuddered as she deciphered their words. *The mad queen*, they whispered. The door closed when the last soul left, and she was left alone with her husband.

"You put on quite a performance," she said, trembling with suppressed fury.

His gaze swept over her, and he smiled when it came to rest on her face. "You make it so easy, wife. Your feelings are clearly visible on your oh-so-expressive face. When you're angry, when you're joyful, when I make you come." He grasped her chin with his fingers. "It's all written on your beautiful face.'

She flushed. "What do you want from me? Do you want me to leave? I can live elsewhere in the Underworld until the six months have passed."

His eyes darkened. "I warned you, you will not leave me. And I do not hate you, I am in love with you."

"I do not think you know the meaning of the word. Release me." She yanked her arm, and his fingers shackled her wrist.

"Where do you think you are going?"

"Don't worry," she sneered. "I won't interfere with whatever plans you have today. In fact, I only wish to be as far from you as possible."

"But I want you near me," he replied.

"But I *do not* want you near me."

He chuckled softly, releasing her. "I sense you have more questions for me."

"You are deliberately sabotaging the Mourning Fields. Why?" she demanded.

"I meant what I said. Do all souls not deserve love? People can change."

" I have felt Ratus' soul. There was no good in it, not even a drop. He felt no remorse for the violence he had committed."

"How pessimistic you have become."

"And how optimistic you have become. Which reminds me," Persephone continued, her voice trembling. "I was so very surprised to see Eurynomos here. What interesting friendships you have made in my absence! The last I remembered, we both agreed that he was foul."

"I find that even one such as Eurynomos has a purpose. Did you not stay my hand when I meant to slay him? Was it not you who pleaded for mercy?"

"So that he may live," she hissed. "Not so he could be brought into the palace and devour the heads of your subjects."

"Eurynomos has proven useful. For instance, he tells me of my wife's strange wanderings. Which reminds me: do not go near the statue of Janus again. If you had stepped inside, you could be trapped for eternity."

"I do not know what you are talking about."

"The two-faced statue next to the Mourning Fields. Eurynomos saw you near it. It is best to avoid Janus."

She turned and locked her gaze on him. "You sent Eurynomos to spy on me!" Her voice was incredulous. "Do you not remember what he did last time? And you not only let him loose in the Underworld, but you sent him to me!"

"As I said, he has his uses," Hades murmured, smiling faintly. "He is now a kind of pet; you were never in danger. How beautiful you look in your gown." His fingertips stroked the softness of her flesh as he fondled the strap over her shoulder.

She pulled away from him.

"If you like it so much, you wear it," she spat. She turned then, grasping the train of the dress between her hands, where the wicked names glittered in gold, pulling hard. The fabric split, and she threw it towards Hades. He caught it in one hand, his eyes glowing. "Your friends' names, so you don't forget them."

He flipped the material over slowly, his gaze scanning the scrawled names. When he lifted his eyes to hers, he had a horrified expression.

"Persephone, leave this place," he urged quietly. "Leave immediately and do not return."

Her cheeks flushed. "Are you insane? You just told me that I cannot leave."

"Find a place away from here where I cannot find you." He dropped the clothing on the ground and grasped her arm, bringing it to his face. Though the scar was no longer visible, he traced the path where the sapphire stone had pierced her palm. His eyes were filled with wrath as he raised them to hers. "Next time," he growled, "finish me."

Her lips trembled, and then she pulled away from him. "Why do you play games with me?" she cried. "You hurt me and then pretend to regret it." She looked at him sadly. "Why did we suffer through everything just to end like this? What was it all for? You tricked me into loving you, only to turn around and mock me. Zeus was right about you."

"Do not mention my brother's name here!" he snarled. His tall frame trembled, and he remained motionless as shivers ran through him. He took a deep breath. "You are here because of your love for me." He had his head cocked to the side as if he was listening to something. He said in hushed tones, "She does not have a choice but to release me. Help me. I am too weak to let her go."

A chill ran up her spine. "Who are you talking to?" she whispered.

He did not respond but stood motionless, like a magnificent princely statue. Persephone's brow furrowed. "Hades?" He did not move. She walked over to him and gently caressed his forearm, but he stared straight ahead, unresponsive. She regarded him warily, leaning closer. His pupils were dilated and fixed on a distant spot. She wondered if he was hypnotized. "Hades?" *Hades,* her mind whispered to him.

He stumbled suddenly, crying out in pain as he fell back.

"What is wrong?" she cried. "What is happening to you?"

He shifted as if in discomfort, his breathing becoming laborious.

Slowly, the trembling subsided, and when he turned back to face her, his eyes were burning with fire.

"Don't say I didn't warn you," he whispered, his lips parted in a smile.

Persephone reached the room of the door, and Maketes was there. He took one look at her disheveled figure, her torn clothes, her swollen, bruised lips, and his body tensed.

"What happened?" his gravelly voice demanded.

"I'm not in the mood for a fight," she answered in a small voice. "I just want to be alone."

She could sense that he wanted to argue, but finally, he inclined his head, opening the door. When it closed behind her, her knees crumbled beneath her, and she crawled into bed, her body shivering. She felt broken, shattered. She lifted the blankets high over her body, curling on her side. Dear Gods, he had been like an animal, and she had been no better. It was sick. She still felt his possession on her skin, between her legs… in her heart. He had mounted her like a stallion, thrusting inside her, and as he began to orgasm inside her, he had whispered into her ear: "Give me an heir," and those words had turned her frenzied passion to ice. She had run from the throne room, his seed dripping down her legs, and he had been content to watch her go with a lazy smile, his goal accomplished. As she understood everything Zeus had told her was true, a tear streamed down her cheek. She was no more than a fertile womb for his future prince. And yet, despite everything, their twisted love still bonded them together like an unbreakable curse. She loved and hated him, but most of all, she hated herself for the weakness inside her.

Finally, she sank into a weary sleep, only to be thrust into the clutches of the darker nightmares that awaited in the shadows.

CHAPTER 14
RIVER OF FIRE

She knew death. The blackness washed over her, and she existed in the nothingness until she, too, became nothing. It was an eternity, yet somehow only moments, when a gleaming light pulsed from the blackness, engulfing her.

"I love you," he whispered.

As the king's voice echoed, she gasped, life filling her lungs, and she cried out as she fell into being once more, her body ripped from the blanket of blackness. She was standing in a darkened meadow. A thunderous heartbeat moved through the landscape, and the ground shook with its rhythm. Her pulse joined with the Earth's life force in a single heartbeat.

As green energy rushed through the sky, it illuminated the mountains that encircled her. She knew where she was, and, with dread, she looked towards the cliffs.

Hades stood on the mountain, battling the shadow once more. He held the glowing blue sword in one hand and a gleaming silver bident in the other. His death would repeat, again and again, an endless battle, always culminating in the same ending. Helplessly, she reached toward him, trying to open her mouth, but she was held, unable to move. She looked down at her body in dawning horror. The roots of the pomegranate tree had encircled her, consumed her, and the tree itself was growing from her. She could only scream silently as the shadow thrust and the golden blade ripped through the flesh of his arm.

Blue fought with gold, and green lightning sparked from the blades with each strike, flooding the sky with tumultuous energy. Hades' mouth was moving, and strange, ancient words were whispered across the land. Gold shimmered like a halo around him, the dust collecting to form golden threads that grew around him. The Earth trembled, cracking and fragmenting, and Hades' shadowy opponent moved forward, striking a blow as he slashed Hades across the abdomen. The king roared a scream, and Persephone cried out with him, his pain echoing inside her, and she writhed in agony, fruits tumbling from her branches. As she looked up from the valley, the shadow's hand snaked out and grasped the king's chest, thrusting its hand inside to clutch Hades' heart. But the shadow could not hold it; it recoiled in pain, shrieking a deafening cry.

The king seized the shadow's wrist, clenching his fist so that the shadow held his heart. *Where there is light, darkness cannot enter.* His voice pressed into her mind as the wraith pushed back from the king, retreating and fleeing into the dark night that had created it. Hades stood alone, the wind blowing his dark hair across his face, his cape and robes billowing in the storm. He lifted the blue-flame sword, placing it in a scabbard on his back, the bident still clutched in his hand. He stepped to the mountain's edge and looked down at her, his purple eyes blazing with unease.

"Persephone," his voice thundered around her, "Open your eyes." His voice echoed through the cursed valley. "Open them," he demanded.

Persephone woke with a pounding heart. Already, the dream was slipping from her consciousness, but she trembled at the aftermath. She kept dreaming of the mountain, of her death, and of his. Why did her subconscious punish her? She brushed her hair from her face, the feverish feeling from the night before still remaining. How long had it been since she had actually slept through the night? She tried to sit up, but her left wrist was yanked back down.

"What?" she murmured.

She twisted her head back, noting with surprise that she wasn't sleepwalking but was still lying in her bed, and then realized why: her wrist were tied to the bedpost.

"How long have you been sleepwalking?" Hades' deep voice asked.

She jerked in surprise, his voice both a soothing balm and torment. When she lifted her eyes, he stood over her, dark and glorious, but his gaze made her catch her breath. For a brief moment, she imagined him looking at her with the eyes she remembered, filled with love, concern, and something more profound, the tie that only he and she shared. Her heart ached from the unrelenting pull she felt towards him, the unquenchable flame. Oh, how she wished it could be simple, that they could love each other, and that would be enough. But they'd never have that easy love; theirs had been tainted and twisted from the start, a love that was born to die.

"I found you in the hall last night," he continued, his black eyes fixed on her, sparking with an intensity she could not decipher. "You were walking towards the palace doors. I led you back here, but you kept trying to get up. Hence, the rope. It's why you have been waking up with injuries, isn't it? Sleepwalking is dangerous in the best of circumstances."

"And I think we can all agree that these aren't the best circumstances," she said softly. She yanked on the rope. "Will you untie me?"

"I must confess," he muttered softly, "that seeing you so much at my mercy is intriguing." He lifted his hand to her face, and she forced herself to remain still. His fingers were gentle as they touched her skin, a stark contrast to his painful, twisted touch the night before. Deftly, he unknotted the tie that held her wrist. He stepped back, and his face was once again shrouded in shadows. "So, why are you sleepwalking?"

His false concern enraged her, mostly because she wanted it so badly to be real. So she forced her heart to harden instead of melting. "You needn't play the concerned husband when we are alone," she snapped. "Save your theatrics for when you have an audience."

"But just think, the sooner you tell me," he murmured, "the sooner I will leave."

She thoughtfully stroked her wrist, attempting to recall her dream. Although the parts were jumbled, the terror lingered. She trembled as she remembered that he had been dying. He was still studying her as she lifted her eyes. "I had a bad dream," she admitted.

"And what did you dream about?"

"In fact, I dreamed of you." Her brow furrowed. "You were yelling at me. You did not want me there, you seemed..."

"I seemed what?" he enquired; his voice was impassive and calming.

"You were—" She paused; she could not force her mouth to say the word. "Sick."

He laughed. "Well, I think we can both agree that I am sick. Why was I yelling at you?"

She rose from the bed, swiftly moving away from him. "I have hazy memories of my dreams, parts of images, and emotions. You were trying to warn me." She examined herself in the mirror, absently noting the dark hollows beneath her eyes and the troubled expression on her face. Her husband was a shadow in the background, and she spun around abruptly, her luminous eyes locking on him. "You were afraid."

"Of what?"

Her thoughts raced back to the shadowy apparition that had battled her husband. "Of a shadow."

"Where there is light, darkness cannot enter." His voice was a whisper.

"What?" Persephone asked breathlessly. "What did you say?"

"Nothing," Hades replied. She looked into his dark eyes, which were fathomless pools and could discern nothing from his gaze. "And are you being a good queen and listening to what I say?"

She shook her head, managing to give him a scornful look. "What do you think?"

He moved back to stand deeper in the shadows, but she knew he was watching her. "Perhaps you should heed my warning, Persephone."

Open your eyes.

Her body jerked. Had Hades spoken aloud, or was it a memory from a dream? Gods, her head ached. She pushed her hand hard against her pulsing head. "You think I am so weak that I will run from a fight?"

No, his voice pressed into her mind, *I think you are a formidable queen.*

"Hades," she whispered, stepping towards him. He was wiping at his face as he emerged from the darkened corner, blood pouring down his chin. She stopped, apprehensive at the expression in his eyes and the smile she had come to hate playing around his lips. "Why do you still bleed?"

He shrugged. "I told you, old wounds. I am fine. Never better, in fact."

She moved closer, suspicion growing in her mind. "Lift your robes."

"Oh, wife," he laughed. "You are insatiable." He yanked his robes apart, revealing his flat stomach and broad chest; only two thin scars marred his chest and abdomen. "See," he smirked. "As I said, never better."

What had she been expecting? That her dreams were true? That there was some explanation for his behavior. Her dreams were nothing more than nightmares, the summation of her worries. Her brow was speckled with cold sweat, and she wiped it away with a trembling hand. Her entire body ached, even her bones. She grabbed a robe from her closet, cinching it tightly around her narrow waist. At this rate, if she lost any more weight, she would need a whole new wardrobe.

She strode from the room, walking onto the balcony. Though she wanted nothing more than to lay back in bed and sleep, she had to get started on her plans. First, she would try to find Jocasta, make sure she was all right, and find out what she knew. And she needed to get rid of Hades to do so.

She sensed his presence behind her but stared ahead, her gaze fixed on the rivers below. "What are your plans for today?"

"I am already late for a meeting with the Judges."

"Will you sort the souls?"

"Most likely."

She could be sure he would not look for her if she offered to accompany him. She knew he would not want her anywhere near the throne room. "Shall I come? I have some ideas—"

"I think not. I know how very *distressing* you found it yesterday."

She gazed into the swirling water of the Styx. The water bubbled strangely, the current erratic, and she wondered distantly if a storm was coming. Her husband was still speaking, something about how she needed to rest. She let her face slump in mock defeat and completed her performance with a disappointed sigh.

His hand caressed her shoulder. "I am sure you will find something to occupy yourself. Do not wander too far. I will send someone to check on you."

She turned to watch him fasten his cape with a pin shaped like a golden arrow. Once the door closed behind him, she waited patiently for a few moments. She pressed her ear to the door and heard only silence. When she opened the door slowly, Maketes stood in the hall with a breakfast tray.

She gave him an exuberant smile. "Come in!"

He placed the tray on the table, and Persephone opened the lid to reveal a delicious, rich, steaming soup and a thick loaf of bread.

"Would you like some?" she asked.

Maketes shook his head and walked over to the balcony, where Persephone began to eat hurriedly, dipping enormous slices of bread into the warm dish. The hot soup revived her, and she could feel some of the fog lifting from her mind. She cast a pensive glance toward the guard occasionally during her breakfast. Finally, she pushed the tray away and beamed as she approached Maketes.

"What are you so happy about?" he asked sourly.

"Maketes, can I trust you?" Persephone inquired with a genuine tone.

"You shouldn't trust anyone," Maketes replied gruffly.

Persephone chuckled, a glint of mischief in her eyes. "Ever the optimist," she mused. "But I am afraid I must trust you because no one else is left."

"How flattering," he muttered, sarcasm dripping from his words.

Undeterred, she waved her hand dismissively. "Nonetheless, despite your warnings, rudeness, and lack of finesse, I do trust you." He crossed his arms over his chest, and she continued hurriedly. "But you should know before you agree that if you aid me, my husband will likely retaliate. Though I will do my best to shield you from him, I cannot guarantee it."

"You are making this sound so appealing; how could I possibly resist," he retorted. "And what is so important that I am risking my neck for?"

"First, we will go look for Jocasta. I want to ensure she is well and have questions for her."

Maketes leaned against the wall, crossing one long leg over the other. "And the second task?"

"Our ability to complete the second task will be contingent on the first."

"That is to say, the second task is much more idiotic." He took a step forward, his large frame towering above her. "He'll send someone to follow your activities. You know that."

"Yes," Persephone murmured. "I know he will. Someone, but not himself. So, I reason that I only need to confuse Minthe, most likely, or possibly a one-eyed demon. Neither of them will pay too close attention. Let me see if this will work." She felt the flowers push from her fingertips, so she drew on the colors she needed and sculpted them. A replica of Persephone lay on the bed, entirely made completely of exquisite little flowers. It wouldn't deceive anyone up close but would be reasonably convincing from the doorway.

Maketes gave a low whistle. "Quite a talent. But I think you underestimate your husband's attention to detail."

Persephone tucked the blankets over the blooming Persephone and then drew the drapes. "My husband will not come himself," she reminded him.

He scoffed. "I think you underestimate your husband."

"Still, she will give us a little extra time." She lifted the tray to him. "While I dress, you can return my tray and perhaps mention that I am feeling unwell and shall be lying down."

He took the tray from her arms. "I bow to your superior knowledge of deception. I will return as soon as possible." With a nod, he departed.

She dressed quickly. Belatedly, she wondered if she was a fool to trust her guard. He had been gone longer than expected—far longer than it took to return to the kitchens—and she was almost ready to leave without him when a knock sounded on the door. She opened it, ushering Maketes inside.

"I thought perhaps you had changed your mind," she confessed nervously.

"Now, why would I do something like that?"

"It takes courage to disobey my husband."

"Courage," Maketes murmured, "or insanity."

"Well, which is it?"

"I am afraid that for me, it is both."

She couldn't help but laugh. Maketes presented her with a simple woolen cloak.

"Where did you get this?"

"I borrowed it. You may find it more useful to remain anonymous in the plain clothes of a mortal."

Persephone drew the woolen cloak over her shoulders, fastening the hood. He pressed on the wall, and the secret passageway opened. Maketes and Persephone moved stealthily, the guard leading her through other hidden passages. It took longer than expected; the passageways twisted and dark, but finally, he opened a door in the wall, and they stood outside the palace. Maketes took her to a paddock, where two saddled horses awaited them.

She stroked the silvery mane of Boreas, and the mare gave a gentle neigh.

"Excellent work, Maketes," she murmured. "Where is Aethon?"

"If your horse were to leave the palace, it would arouse suspicions. If we are to deceive, we should deceive well."

"What a devious mind you have, Maketes," she said cheerfully. "That will be useful. First, we shall go to Asphodel."

They mounted their horses and took off quickly, only slowing once they reached the outskirts of Asphodel. Persephone stiffened as she observed a group of rugged men dispersed across the entryway, heavy weapons slung over their shoulders. They gave Maketes a nod, clearly recognizing him as a guard from the palace. The fields were nearly empty except for a few spirits who gazed at the newcomers suspiciously.

"Who are those guards?" Persephone asked.

Maketes hesitated. "They are men who committed crimes for which the Judges recommended they be sent to Tartarus. The king authorized them to spend part of their sentence as guardians of the Underworld."

"Authorized," Persephone repeated.

"I should say that he demanded it," Maketes said plainly.

Persephone rode in silence, lost in tumultuous thoughts. They eventually came upon a small group of citizens. The spirits huddled close together, talking in hushed tones, but as outsiders from the palace approached, they dispersed quickly. Hurriedly, Persephone dismounted and approached a nearby woman who had been glancing at her furtively.

"Can you tell me where Jocasta and her nieces are? They were once handmaidens at the palace."

The woman looked fearfully towards the guards. She gestured for Persephone and Maketes to move closer and then turned so they faced away from the men. She jerked her head towards a cottage high on a hill in the distance. "They live there now." The woman hurried away quickly.

They walked their horses, passing only a few people. The Meadows appeared nearly devoid of life; even the animals seemed to hide. She gasped as they passed through a grove of trees on their way to Asphodel's core. A gilded figure of Hades was erected high in the field, surrounded by offerings of fruits and gifts. Several spirits bowed before the statue, praying at its feet. A young man with an unpleasant expression turned to face them as they approached. His gaze shifted to Maketes.

"You come from the palace?"

Maketes spread his hands, indicating his uniform. "Oh no," Maketes said sarcastically, "doesn't my attire scream 'countryside' to you?"

"You come on the king's business," the man deduced, his voice dripping with venom.

"A true visionary, aren't you? Perhaps you should join the oracles at Delphi."

"Maketes," Persephone chastised. She turned to the young man. "Why are you concerned if we come from the palace?"

"Because we haven't seen the king or the queen in months! You could tell him to come himself next time instead of sending more guards, but I suppose it's easier to turn his back on his people if he does not have to see them!"

An older woman came up behind the young man, her face fearful.

"Hush, Argus," she admonished in a harsh tone.

His face softened as he turned to the woman. "I only say what others are thinking, Mother. The king has abandoned his people. He sits in his palace with his riches while we suffer! Our loved ones are denied access to the Meadows; they are held in the palace dungeons awaiting their release."

"Please," the woman said softly, her eyes pleadingly directed at them. "He means no harm."

Maketes shook his head. "Then he best keep his mouth shut before his tongue ties a noose around his neck."

The woman paled, but Argus spat on the ground. "I will not stay silent! The king has his interests fixed skyward. And the queen is deranged. The people are neglected while he seeks to please his wife. She is not content to only rule the Underworld." He gesticulated wildly. "She is the Goddess of Spring." He laughed, "Look at this place! Asphodel was never bleak until she came. She cares nothing for us."

Persephone gasped and stepped forward, but Maketes moved forward deftly before her. "Where did you hear the queen was mad?"

The man burst out laughing, his hands outstretched in front of him. "The whole village knows. She plays with the souls, convincing them that she will assist them just to murder them again. While the cities turn to ice, she smiles. We're being held in a jail here!"

Maketes took a threatening step forward. "You are a fool," he rasped. "And if you do not temper your language, you will be in an altogether different prison. We will be on our way. When you talk of treason, remember that you are endangering more than yourself." Maketes let his gaze rest on the woman beside Argus, and the young man's face paled.

As Persephone moved past them, she saw Argus' mother dragging him away, speaking to him in hushed, harsh tones.

"Come on," Maketes said. "We shouldn't stay here too long."

Side by side, they made their way towards Jocasta's dwelling.

"Someone has been spreading rumors," Persephone said, trembling.

"Spreading them very effectively," Maketes replied in his harsh tones. "You're in a perilous situation. One false step and your kingdom will crumble. Be careful of your next move."

Her mind flashed back to the chess board in Zeus' private quarters. Gods, she hated games. "I cannot believe—" Her voice broke, and she took a calming breath. "It's hard to realize how much has changed, that my husband has permitted this." She glanced at Maketes. She had confided this much in him; she may as well trust him. "I've been thinking," she said quietly, "trying to make sense of everything. A few months ago, I was still at my mother's temple when I heard a voice. It cautioned me of a potential danger. I'm unsure who it was, but it warned me of impending peril."

Maketes stopped, and she almost barreled into him as he turned to face her. "What did it say?" he demanded, his voice rough.

"It said that the game was just beginning, that he was coming for him."

"Coming for your husband?" She nodded. "But who spoke to you?"

"I do not know. I wondered… but now I believe--" Persephone moved closer to the guard, whispering. "Maketes, I believe it was my husband's voice I heard that summer's night. He is coming for someone. And I've dreamed of him since I've been down here, and I'm afraid." Her hand tightened convulsively around the bridle.

"Do you fear your husband, or do you fear for him?"

She resumed her progress up the lonely hillside. "Both," she whispered.

As they neared the front of the modest home, Persephone handed the horse's bridle to Maketes. "I would like to make this visit alone."

"I await your return with bated breath."

She gave him a look, then pulled back her hood. She hesitated slightly before knocking on the door, waiting as she heard soft footsteps approach.

"Who is it?" a voice called out.

"It is Persephone," she replied softly.

The door was yanked open quickly, and several pairs of arms pulled her inside.

"Oh, Your Majesty," Cleo said breathlessly. "We never dreamed, never thought—"

Phoebe frantically straightened the room, picking up discarded garments from the floor. "We are in a state of disarray at the moment, my lady," she interjected in a frantic voice.

Footsteps sounded around the corner. "What is this racket!" Jocasta chided, and then her eyes landed on Persephone. "Oh, Your Highness." Suddenly, Jocasta was crying, raising her dress to her face to cover her dripping eyes.

Persephone rushed forward, taking the older woman into her arms. "What is wrong!" she cried.

Jocasta shook her head, too overcome to speak, so Cleo stepped forward. "They informed us that you, Your Majesty, were dissatisfied with us. You no longer need our services, and we were to vacate the premises immediately. Our family has a long history of service to the palace. It was quite difficult for Auntie."

Persephone's face darkened. "Who told you such lies?"

"Lord Hades," Cleo tattled without hesitation.

"Then he did so without my permission," Persephone said fiercely. "I have never been displeased by anything you have done. I would never throw out my friends."

Jocasta began howling at those words, and Persephone and Cleo escorted the older woman to a nearby chaise to lie down.

Persephone sat next to her and took Jocasta's hand into hers. "Please listen to me. I *never* said that. I would never speak to you in such a way."

Jocasta wiped her eyes. "Oh, I knew he was lying, yet it still hurt to be easily dismissed. However, the hardest part was that we did not get to say our final goodbyes to you. There were certain things we needed to tell you." Jocasta raised her eyes to Cleo. "We must inform her immediately."

Cleo sat on the other side of Jocasta. "Who serves you now?" she inquired quietly.

The youthful soul's eyes were filled with knowledge and pity. "Minthe," Persephone answered. Cleo and Jocasta exchanged a significant glance.

"That nymph is incapable of dressing herself, let alone an empress," Jocasta growled. "Tell her, Cleo."

Cleo shook her head in dismay. "She is far more heinous than you can fathom, my lady. She is wicked." Cleo leaned forward and whispered, "In her chamber, she dances naked and commits atrocities. She casts spells of shadowed magic. Oh, the wicked things she does!"

"What kind of wicked things?"

Cleo closed her eyes. "It would be too shameful to say, but I seen it in her room. When she is alone."

"Saw," Phoebe corrected, pausing as she fluffed a cushion. "You saw."

"Hush, Phoebe!" Jocasta cried, and Cleo glared at her sister.

"Where?" Persephone asked, drawing Cleo's attention back.

"At the very end of the hall, I seen it... er, I saw it in Lord Hades' room. There is an opening from his room to hers."

"How long has Hades known Minthe?" Persephone asked Jocasta.

"Minthe claims they have known one another for years, but I have never seen the king with a woman. Not until you came."

"But he could have visited her at the Cocytus."

Jocasta and Persephone exchanged looks. "He could have," the older woman admitted.

"And what about in Elysium? They could have met there."

"I do not know; we rarely accompanied him there."

"What else have you seen?" They hesitated, but Persephone would not be deterred. "You may as well tell me everything. I have a strong suspicion."

"We have never *seen* nothing," Jocasta replied, "but we have heard them together... in his room."

"What did you hear?"

The woman lowered her eyes, and Persephone understood. Her silly heart twisted in agony, but her expression remained calm. The good souls were already distressed enough.

"I seen something!" Cleo cried again. "In her room, Queen Persephone. You must go to her room. In Lord Hades' room, peer through an opening behind the bed. Please don't ask me to repeat what I seen."

"Saw," Persephone overheard Phoebe mutter once more.

"What else?"

Jocasta frowned. "He seemed concerned for your safety. All summer, he prepared for your return. He had the souls ready for the kingdom, making it a stronghold. He told us his only concern was your safety."

"My safety? But that seems strange when he—"

"Yes," Jocasta agreed sadly. "And yet, he seems to think you are in danger."

"Danger!" Persephone repeated thoughtfully. "From whom?"

"I do not know. We heard the king say the name Ares. This is all we know. I wish we could tell you more or help you somehow."

"You have helped me more than you could possibly know with your kindness and loyalty." Persephone stood, and the women leaped to their feet. She gave each of them a fierce hug. When she embraced Jocasta, she stood back, taking her hands. "I want you to know how much I appreciate your friendship. I will send for you when the time is right, but it is too risky for now. The palace is not safe for you. Inform no one that I talked to you."

"Take care, Queen Persephone," Jocasta said solemnly.

Persephone pulled the hood over her face once more and left the small cottage. Maketes stood with the horses exactly where she had left him. She averted her face, wiping the tears from her cheeks discreetly.

"Did you find what you expected?" he asked.

"More or less," she answered in a muffled voice.

"Where do we go now?"

She sniffed, but her voice was calm as she replied, "Now, we find Hypnos."

Maketes made a noise. "Hypnos is unpredictable. Why do you wish to see him?"

"I have questions about my dreams," she answered. She didn't want to tell the guard that she was starting to doubt her ability to tell the difference between reality and the monsters that stalked her in her nightmares.

"What about them?"

She gave him a sidelong glance. "Why? Are you a specialist in dreams?"

Maketes snorted. "Hardly. However, I have had enough nightmares to make me fear their master. If you search for Hypnos, you may discover more questions than answers."

"Then I will be no worse off than I am now. Come, I know the way." He hesitated, and she gave him a sardonic look. "If you are scared, I can promise you that I will not let Hypnos hurt you."

His muffled displeasure rang in her ears as she reared her horse and headed towards Hypnos' lair. She followed the River Lethe till they arrived at the cave, surrounded by crimson flowers. Persephone dismounted, overwhelmed by flashbacks to her last visit. The chasm between Hades and herself had never been greater. Yet this time, there was no curse to explain his strange behavior, no answer that would grant forgiveness. She glanced at Maketes, and she realized he really did seem nervous. And why not? Hypnos knew the darkest nightmares that haunted all souls. Maketes may not be ready to face that dark God.

"Stay here, Maketes," she said briskly. "I will be back soon."

"I will come with you—" But his grip on his bridle was tight, and Persephone shook her head.

"I think it would be better to speak to Hypnos alone."

Maketes' fingers twitched, but reluctantly, he conceded. "Very well, but I will come after you if you stay too long. You can tell Hypnos that his poisonous little flowers won't slow me down."

She laughed, but her heartbeat quickened as she stood at Hypnos' dark cave entrance. Reluctantly, she crossed the threshold, and the air was warm and damp, the delicate, nutty aroma of the poppies caressing her senses. Her head spun in response to the overwhelming perfume of the blooms, and she blinked repeatedly, resisting the urge to close her eyes.

"Hypnos?" she whispered. There was no answer, so she moved deeper into the cave. The cavern looked deserted. "Hypnos?" she called more loudly this time.

Something was unsettling about speaking aloud in this quiet fortress, warning her to keep silent in this dark, slumberous world. The feeble light from the entryway dimmed as she moved farther inside. A fluttering noise disturbed the deep solitude, reverberating off the cavern's walls like a thousand wings suddenly taking flight. She stared into the bleak abyss, startled at the emergence of a shadowy figure ahead of her. A sigh of relief escaped her lips when she realized it was only an ebony bed. Fighting a yawn, Persephone contemplated how enjoyable it would be to lie down.

"Hypnos?" she called again.

"He's not here." Persephone whirled to face the speaker, her heart in her throat.

Even in the dim light, she could recognize that the God facing her was exquisite, a living embodiment of manly perfection. His stature was imposing and muscular, with an armor-draped torso and a cloak cascading down his back. Long, dark hair curled tenderly over the angular structure of his jaw, which was softened by perfectly formed lips. His nose was a sharp blade, masculine, and, in fact, all that a nose should be. His face was so perfectly sculpted that she could imagine he was made of marble. But it was not the beauty of his form that she was focused on, but rather his blazing red eyes. They looked like the eyes of a nightmare, and she was frightened by this magnificent creature. She wanted to run away from him, but her sleep-deprived brain didn't seem able to send the message to her feet.

"Oh," she stammered. "Who– who are you?"

"You don't know?" he asked, his voice echoing strangely in the profound stillness of the cavern.

Persephone shook her head, mesmerized by the God's blazing eyes.

"I know all creatures," he murmured, "from their birth until their last breath. I am the end and the beginning, the final equalizer."

She shivered at his enigmatic words. "What is your name?"

"But you know who I am, queen. You have seen me in the fields, the forests, and the sky. Where there is life, there I will be. "

Persephone trembled. "What is your name?" she demanded again.

"I... am... Death." Something dark spread behind him, and she realized beneath his cape were massive black wings, like those of a great moth.

She gasped. "You are–"

"Thanatos." He uttered his name like a curse, a promise, and his crimson eyes flamed at her.

"I have seen you," she whispered. "You have been in my dreams. You—you have been following my husband." His wings fluttered, but he said nothing. "I want to know why you are following Hades. What do you want of him? Is he in danger?"

"Since death was invented, neither God nor man is safe. He is a king and has made the dreadful mistake of being a king who cares for his people," he whispered.

"Is there nothing I can do to help him?" she asked, her voice trembling.

"Your husband walks a path stained with the blood of choices he has made. There is no turning back."

"I don't believe that! We have the power to change fate if we want to!"

He scoffed cruelly. "Then you know little if you believe that. Fate is a river that flows, and you are merely a leaf adrift upon its currents. You cannot change destiny. I have heard the threads snapping and unraveling. Your husband's fate is far beyond your grasp." His eyes blazed at her. "You should be concerned for your own future."

Persephone's gaze hardened. "I want to know what you're doing in my dreams."

He moved closer to her, circling Persephone, his movements like a predatory waltz. "Awake or asleep, I need no invitation." A sinister smile played on his lips as he regarded her. "You are treading into darkness. The path you walk leads to the edge of oblivion, and every step you take will bind you further to the shadows. It was a mistake for you to come here."

His words brought a chill of foreboding over her. "But I am seeking answers from Hypnos. About my dreams."

"My brother is not here." She was taken aback as she realized she was looking at one of Nyx's other offspring.

He turned those red eyes on her. "However, now that I've seen you, I've discovered that you've piqued my curiosity. My brother kept me from you last time, but no longer."

"What do you mean?" she asked, panic causing her slumberous eyes to widen.

He lifted his head as though smelling the air. "There is an odor to it; that's how I find them. Before they even know, it beckons me. By the time they understand, they never accept it gracefully. They always beg for more time, for mercy, but once the path is set, it cannot be reversed. Once I am summoned, there is only one way forward."

"Wh—what?"

"The sweet scent of decay. It clings to you. Death is catching," he whispered. She stepped back in fear, and his wings fanned before her, barring her passage, his eyes demonic in his lovely face. Her gown blew behind her from the powerful force of his enormous wings. "You shall not leave! You have been marked!"

His hand was reaching for her when suddenly, a red mist filled the cave, and Persephone became instantly disoriented. The poppies were filling the cavern with their perfume. Panicked, she began to fall, and she saw Thanatos was also falling, so they landed clumsily next to each other. His red eyes were the last thing she saw before her eyes closed, and his beautiful lips whispered a promise: "I am coming for you."

She found herself lying on a lovely, fragrant bed when her eyes opened. As her heavy eyelids rose reluctantly, she noticed with a dazed surprise that the robed form of Hypnos was hovering over her. He extended a hand, and she paused before allowing him to hoist her to her feet. She looked down and realized she had been lying on a makeshift bed of poppies.

"Queen Persephone," Hypnos greeted softly in his sweet voice.

She yawned in response, then looked apprehensive around the cave as her memories returned.

"Looking for Thanatos?" Hypnos guessed, reading her mind. "I have lulled him to sleep; indeed, if I had not appeared at the time, I did—" His voice faltered, and she shivered at his unspoken insinuation. "Regardless, he is resting. It is best to avoid Thanatos. He will find you if he needs to; he always does."

She trembled as she gazed toward the ebony bed and saw the dark body slumbering on it. "Do you often drug your brother?" she asked.

Hypnos glided closer to her. "Whenever possible, I aid him in resting.

When he is awake, his mind wanders, and Thanatos, with a wandering mind, can be a frightening thing to behold. We are not just brothers; you see, we are twins. I can sense when he is becoming agitated. He has taken an interest in you. That is… troubling," Hypnos said serenely.

Persephone made a noise somewhat near a snort. "He seems to want to add me to his collection of bones, but I must admit, I am not quite ready." She stared at the still form on the bed. "He is not a particularly endearing subject."

"No, Thanatos is generally unwelcome wherever he goes. But should the wolf be penalized for its moon-seeking behavior? Like all of us, Thanatos will constantly pursue what inspires his soul. Not everyone is motivated by goodness. Some find peace helping a loved one, while others may turn to the poppy or drink. And love itself may be impure. A man may yearn for a lost love, withering to nothing but bone over a long-forgotten memory. A mother may watch her baby begot of love and go hungry for a drop of poppy on her lips.

"For my brother, peace is found in the ultimate voyage, in the final breath of life. *Memento mori.* It is only natural that he sometimes looks for it in places he shouldn't." Hypnos tilted his head toward Persephone. "But you did not come here to speak of Thanatos. Tell me, queen, why do you seek me. Do you wish for another elixir for your husband? I am afraid that I am unwilling to supply it after last time. Unless *you* have developed a taste? That would be highly unexpected."

"No," she said sluggishly, trying to organize her thoughts. "My dreams," she said, "I want to know what they mean."

"Your dreams?" he repeated, confusion in his voice. "But you have not been dreaming."

"What?" she asked, her voice a thin thread.

"You have not been dreaming," he repeated. "I have not seen your dreams since your return to the Underworld. Under normal circumstances, I would investigate, but your husband clarified that I was not welcome at the palace."

She gaped at him. "But— this is impossible. Everyone dreams. My dreams have been so vivid that I have been sleepwalking!"

"What have you been seeing?" Did she imagine the reluctance in his voice?

"I—I see my husband. He is in pain, and your brother is pursuing him! Hades is always engaged in combat with a shadowy entity, and there is a green light—"

Hypnos lifted his hand. "No," he said emphatically. "No more. As I already stated, you are not dreaming."

"Then what do I see at night?"

Hypnos' hooded face was turned toward her, and silence stretched between them as he studied her.

"Some places are so dark that even dreams cannot flourish there." He appeared to be battling an internal conflict before speaking again; his voice was so low that she needed to lean in close to hear him. "I warned you once, queen, to be careful, and I will repeat this warning now. Take care not to venture too far into the darkness, for men have gotten lost and never found their way back. How much more valuable would a queen be to the monsters that lurk in the shadows. I must tend to my brother now, for he will awaken soon. You would be wise not to be here when he wakes. Farewell, queen."

He pressed a poppy to her lips, and she collapsed into darkness.

Persephone awoke with a start. A face hovered above her, its features swimming in and out of view.

"Wh–what?"

Suddenly, Maketes came into focus.

"Nice of you to join us," his gravelly voice greeted.

She was lying outside Hypnos' cave on a bed of his cursed, infernal poppies and sat up fuming.

"Hypnos put me to sleep!" she hissed. She stood, and poppies tumbled off of her. Enraged, she pulled the wretched little flowers from her hair and gown. Her hands and legs trembled as she fought against the effects of the poppy.

"I warned you not to trust him."

"How do you know so much about the Underworld Gods?" Persephone snapped.

"I eavesdrop," Maketes admitted unabashedly.

"Of course you do," she muttered.

"And how was the God of Sleep? Did he tell you everything you needed to know?"

Persephone brushed her hand against Boreas before mounting her swiftly. She stifled a yawn. "More or less."

"Well, which is it, more or less?"

She glared at him, and he reared his steed with a laugh so that he was facing the same direction as Persephone. "Fine," he muttered. "Don't tell me."

"Stop distracting me. I need to find someone—a soul named Theo. He was sentenced to the River of Fire. Has your eavesdropping told you anything about that place?" she asked sarcastically.

Maketes let out a low whistle. "In fact, it has. Are you sure you want to go there? It is a wicked place."

"I made a promise," she replied resolutely. "And it is my fault Theo is there. I will understand if you do not wish to accompany me; if you do not wish Hades to know, you should return soon."

"But I hear the Underworld's dungeons are lovely this time of year. Follow me," he called excitement edging his voice. Before she could protest, he was already steering his horse away. "I know a shortcut!"

As they left the meadows, the ground became more dangerous, and the horses had to move slowly across the rough terrain. Steam erupted from red rocks protruding from the Earth. Maketes suddenly slowed, pulling beside her. He extended a hand toward her horse, bringing them to a halt, his head raised alertly.

"Do you hear that?"

"No." She glanced around, worried. "What is it?"

"We are being hunted." He motioned for her to move their horses behind a large boulder, and they stood silently, waiting. As her ears adjusted to the quiet, she could hear the slapping of a wet tongue and the sound of a wing dragging across the stone.

"Eurynomos," she whispered. "Hades must have sent him."

"Ah, it seems the makeshift Persephone has been discovered," he murmured. Maketes sniffed the air. "He smells like shit, shouldn't be too hard to avoid." He swung his horse around. "Follow me. We will take a different path. The wind is blowing our scent to him."

Maketes led them along a winding route, dodging expertly around large boulders. As they neared their destination, the temperature began to climb. They rode till they came to a river, at which point Maketes slowed. "I think we have lost him."

Persephone glanced around. Sharp, jagged rocks punctured the Earth, and the river ran with viscous molten lava that churned slowly. Periodically, enormous flames erupted from the surface, splattering on the ground. It seemed they had reached the River of Fire.

"Do not let the flames touch you," Maketes cautioned, "unless you want the flesh seared from your bone."

On the opposite side of the river was a colossal stronghold, and as they approached, a stone bridge was dropped. With a raised hand, an armed guard stepped out.

"Halt!" he called. "You may go no further."

"We seek one of your occupants. Theo," Persephone said in a low voice.

The guard shook his head. "We do not allow our prisoners to leave. You must turn around."

She brought her horse closer. "You have imprisoned an innocent man."

The guard shook his head once more. "I take my orders from the king. You are trespassing. If you do not leave, I will have no choice but to treat you as a threat."

Persephone touched her hood, preparing to lower it, when a low voice spoke behind her. "Jason, bring her Theo." Persephone turned in amazement to see Maketes raise his hand, one of his fingers gleaming with a golden ring.

The guard had fallen to his knees, his face pale. "My lord, I did not know–"

"Off your knees. Bring forth, Theo. Oh, and Jason?" The guard jumped to his feet, eager to obey, but when he heard his name, he turned to face Maketes."Hold your tongue."

The guard paled and bowed again, then rushed back over the bridge.

Persephone turned to her guard in astonishment. "My lord?" she queried.

Maketes shrugged. The golden ring had vanished from his gloved hands. "I trained him years ago when he was alive."

"You are a nobleman?"

Maketes laughed roughly. "A prince."

A booming horn erupted in the lofty fortress, startling Persephone. She was drawn to the swirling river as something moved inside the depths. A molten monstrosity composed entirely of black rock rose from the boiling liquid, its eyes aglow with gleaming orange stones. It dipped its hand into the lava, and an agonizing cry pierced the air as a shattered, burned body was retrieved and hurled carelessly over the bridge. Persephone's breath caught. Theo.

His body was severely scorched, with blisters covering his flesh, and he lay motionless, his wrists and legs shackled with iron chains. Persephone shouted, leaping from her saddle and sprinting ahead. She kneeled beside Theo, Maketes close behind her. The molten beast turned to face them, bowing low, and she had the strangest feeling that he was bowing to Maketes before it leaped back into the blazing river.

She shifted her focus to Theo. "Let me heal you," she whispered.

Theo could barely move his lips. "No, my Queen, I beg you. My fresh skin sizzling was the most agonizing experience I have ever felt. I do not want to repeat it once they put me back." He tried to smile at her, but his face was a twisted grimace of pain. "It is easier this way."

"I am not putting you back in there," she vowed fiercely. "I know you are innocent. Forgive me, Theo."

"You tried to help me. To do right."

"I know who murdered you. I saw Ares with your head in the upper world." She felt Maketes stiffen beside her at the mention of the volatile War God.

Theo's burnt, melted lids looked up at her, his blue eyes hazy. "You think Ares murdered me?"

"Yes."

"No," Theo whispered, "it was not him." He hesitated, his pained eyes brimming with compassion. "My lady, it was your husband."

Persephone's soul cried out in response to his words. "Tell me," she demanded.

"It was as he said. I praised your good deed, preaching of the kindness and goodness of the Underworld. One night, I sensed a presence watching me, a malevolent shadow, as my wife slept. He was there when I turned around as though he had stepped from the shadows themselves. I still remember his eyes," he moaned, his throat convulsing. "They burned with an amber fire, and he informed me that I had outlived my usefulness. He said I was informing too many mortals about my visit to the Underworld and that I had evaded death. He pulled his bident and immediately attacked my wife. I attempted to stop him but was impotent in the face of such a powerful God. Then he turned to me, and I have no more memories."

Persephone felt lightheaded at Theo's words. *Murderer*, her mind whispered. Hades had murdered not only this man but his wife, too, in cold blood.

"Thank you for telling me, Theo," she said gently. She pressed her hand to his shoulder, attempting to push healing warmth into him, but it was as though the flow of energy was blocked. "We must go."

She all but lifted Theo. She felt a hand on her shoulder. It was the river guard.

"You cannot take him!" he cried.

She lifted her hands, the shackles on Theo's wrists and ankles crumbling to dust. The guard gave a cry of surprise and fell back. She helped Theo mount Boreas, then turned around to face the guard.

"He must stay here," the guard said again.

"Let us leave, for your sake. I do not wish to hurt you." She let sparks flare in her eyes, and they glowed beneath her hood. The guard fell back, his terrified gaze on her face. She raised her hand, her fingertips sparking, when Maketes rushed from behind her, delivering a well-placed punch to the guard's face. Jason collapsed instantly to the ground, entirely unconscious.

She gave him a surprised glance, and he offered a rusty laugh. "At times, a punch is just as effective as your fiery magic. What shall we do with him? " he asked, jerking his head towards Theo.

"We will go to Asphodel," she stated matter-of-factly. "And then we must hide them so Hades will never find them."

Maketes mounted his horse and then glanced back at her. Persephone had jumped behind Theo, holding the injured man on the horse.

"He will know it was you," Maketes said softly.

"I do not care," Persephone said, her voice steely. "Let us go." Persephone closed her eyes, and she could feel the direction of Theo's wife, the location of her soul within the Meadows.

They rode back to Asphodel, the mantle of night enveloping them. Maketes occasionally hesitated and altered routes, but they eventually arrived at Theo's wife's hut. Selene had left her hut to stand warily at the door at the noise of the horses, but she let out a cry at the sight of her husband. Persephone helped lower Theo to the ground. The couple embraced, sobbing, but they had no time to waste.

"You can rest soon, Theo. Maketes," she said as she dismounted, "will you stay here? When I am finished, I will come for you."

Maketes hesitated. "Don't do anything stupid."

"Now, why would I do that?" Maketes made a dubious noise. Her face softened as she looked at the couple. "Come," she urged. "We must move swiftly. People will already be looking for Theo."

Persephone led them through the darkened meadows until they reached a cave, the soothing sound of a creek bubbling nearby. It was a beautiful and peaceful spot. "Theo," Persephone said quietly, "I will enchant this land so that none will see it. You and your wife may live peacefully but cannot leave this area. Do you understand? If you leave here, my husband will find you and never let you go."

Theo limped forward, his eyes still beautiful in his burned face. "Are you sure, my queen? You take a great risk by helping me again. All I wish is for Selene to be safe. That was all I ever wanted."

Persephone nodded her head, placing her hand on his arm. "I am sure. Live well, Theo," she whispered one final time and stepped back. Her last view was of them moving toward the water, their golden threads entwined and shining in the black night.

She summoned her inner light and allowed the magic to expand, but this time, she could connect it to the couple's soul link, strengthening the spell. Two soulmates reunited. She stretched her hand to the Earth, imploring it to supply her with what she needed, and she sprinkled the salt that materialized in her palm over the entryway. Words poured from her lips so rapidly that she couldn't identify their origins, but she understood their meaning. Gold illuminated her hands, their threads clutched between her fingers as she bound and braided the strands. Theo and Selene faded from view as the final thread was fastened.

Her legs shook beneath her, but she pushed herself to move. If she was discovered, Theo and Selene would be in jeopardy. Even though the trek back to the hut was relatively flat, it was strenuous in her weakened state, and she had to stop repeatedly to rest. Maketes was waiting for her when Persephone arrived. She stumbled, and he reached out to aid her.

"You little idiot," he breathed as he looked at her. "What have you done to weaken yourself so much?" His voice was blazing with anger.

"I did what needed to be done."

He shook his head. "You're the queen," he chastised, "not some reckless child. You put your entire kingdom at risk by jeopardizing your safety."

Her cheeks flushed at his rebuke. "I did what was right."

"You're not just risking your neck; you're exhausting yourself and dragging the kingdom down. Ultimately, you may be the only thing between your people and war."

She closed her eyes, weary. "Say no more of it, Maketes. I did what I needed to do, for an innocent man and for the sake of my soul." Her eyes abruptly opened, her emerald gaze glowing like stars in the gathering darkness. Something was calling to her, whispers in the wind. "Do you hear them?" Persephone asked urgently.

Maketes turned around, listening intently. "I hear nothing."

Her eyes dilated, and she cocked her head. Maketes took a step closer and shook her shoulder. "What is it?" he inquired huskily.

"Something in the Mourning Fields. Evil is coming."

Maketes blocked her path. "No," he said simply.

Her eyes remained glazed as she attempted to walk past him. "I must go. Something is wrong. I can feel it."

"And you believe you are fit to fight?" he sneered. "You are so frail that you are scarcely able to stand." Unexpectedly, he reached out, lightly pushing her shoulder, and she tripped, just righting herself before collapsing.

Her angry gaze shifted to his; his point was well made. "I do not have to listen to you, *Prince* of the Upper World."

"You say it like it's a bad thing. You need to have a greater regard for princes, given that your father was one."

She moved back to look up at him. "How did you know that?"

"I am familiar with you, queen. I am aware that you are not prepared for combat."

Her eyes closed tightly. "But the souls are suffering."

"Use your head. Have you considered the possibility of someone attempting to lure you there when you are already weak?"

"You are right," she conceded. "I am not ready ... yet." Her eyes were weary as she returned her gaze to the guard. "You should return without me; there is no reason for them to know you helped me."

Maketes shook his head. "I'm no coward. I knew the risk when I agreed to come with you."

They mounted their horses, and Persephone looked towards the area where Theo and his wife were safely hidden. She regretted nothing; she would do it again; she would do it a million times over. The horses took off and moved as silent shadows over the dark land.

CHAPTER 15
POUND OF FLESH

They made no attempt to hide their entrance at the front steps, and Persephone could feel hostile eyes on them as attendants led their horses to the stables. As they reached the palace doors, Maketes halted abruptly.

"I have matters to attend to," he grumbled.

"Oh," Persephone murmured, caught off guard. "Another mysterious task, I presume?"

Maketes offered a noncommittal grunt. Despite his rough exterior, Persephone had found an odd comfort in his surly presence.

"Very well," she conceded, attempting to inject a note of bravery into her voice. "I suppose it's best if I face the king alone. Perhaps you should find a place to hide for a while."

Maketes snorted. "I will leave the hide and seek to the king's guards. Be careful; he will be out for blood."

Persephone looked up at the towering palace, a shiver running down her spine. She turned back to Maketes, but to her astonishment, the surly guardian had already vanished into the shadows, leaving her to face the looming palace alone.

"Of course," she muttered to herself. "Why am I surprised?"

Taking a deep breath, she walked through the doors. Cleo's comments echoed in her mind as she moved quickly, pausing before her husband's bed-chamber. She placed her hand on the door and slowly drew the door open; the room was empty. Her husband's tempting scent tickled her nose, and again, she noticed something new about it, some enigmatic fragrance that caused her to frown. She shook her head. She needed to hurry. Cleo had said that the latch was behind the bed. She almost prayed she wouldn't find it, but as she slipped her hand along the wall, her fingers found it easily.

She retracted the clasp with a sinking heart, revealing a peephole in the wall. Thick black carpets and crimson velvet drapes covered the hidden space, and the room was illuminated by candles. Persephone stood on her tiptoes as she heard heavy breathing. It took only moments to locate Minthe, who thrashed naked on the floor before the feet of an obsidian statue of Hades.

The nude statue matched every portion of Hades' anatomy, including the large, jutting part between its legs. Minthe lay within a circle that was drawn in red, and the nymph was thrusting a smooth, sparkling moonstone into herself, twisting in delight as she moaned. Persephone saw a small, broken figure near the circle on an altar, and she suppressed her cry of rage. An animal had been drained of blood. Dark words poured from Minthe's mouth, and Persephone's skin crawled as she discerned the meaning. *Let the darkness grow in my womb.*

The sweaty nymph grasped one of the candles, pouring the hot, red wax down her body. She gasped with pleasure-pain, then climbed up the statue of Hades, mounting it, groaning as she penetrated herself with its stone cock between her thighs. Her breasts bounced with each thrust, and she wailed in delight. "Fill my womb with a child," she cried. She licked the face of the statue and flung her head back in ecstasy, her red hair tossing and her eyes rolling back in her head.

Persephone recoiled in disgust. With trembling hands, she re-latched the peephole and exited the room. She approached her own room and opened the door cautiously. Her bed had been destroyed, and the delicately placed flowers strewn throughout the room. Persephone rushed in, heaving a sigh of relief when she discovered Cerberus cuddled around Olive in the corner of the room. She kneeled to both of them and touched one of Cerberus' heads before doing the same to Olive's.

"Thank you, Cebbie, for protecting him," she whispered. The dog winked and gazed up at her with three identical golden eyes.

She bent before her bed, removing the books from beneath her mattress. She tabbed to the section on moonstone and read the inscription: "Promotes fertility, conception, and pregnancy." She walked over to her dressing table and removed the necklace Hades had given her. Moonstone. Another necklace with a double meaning: the first had duped her into becoming a prisoner, whereas this one was to trick her into pregnancy.

"Bastard," she hissed.

Her life was spiraling out of control, and she could not stop it—a pawn in another's hands. Her head pounded fiercely. She was imprisoned in a nightmare that she had unwittingly assisted in orchestrating. It was as if she knew two men: one was her lover, the one in whom she would place her ultimate trust, and the other was a deranged psychopath capable of terrible evil. Minthe's delighted yells echoed in her ears, and she lifted her hands to her temples, squeezing them tightly. Where was the truth? Zeus' warning echoed like the whisper of a serpent in her ear. Minthe and her husband were lovers, and clearly, Minthe was attempting to become pregnant. But Hades could not have children. And that's where she came in. The fertile womb. Her heart clenched painfully.

A hard fist banged against her door, and Persephone jumped. She wiped the sweat from her forehead, hid the books beneath her bed again, and cautiously opened the door. Minthe stood at the entrance, now fully clothed. Her contemptuous blue eyes moved over Persephone's disheveled appearance. She held out a gown, and when Persephone made no effort to take it, Minthe threw it at her. "This is for tonight."

"Tonight?"

"For dinner," she snapped with annoyance. "With Hades. I will help you dress."

Minthe attempted to move forward, but Persephone held up her hand. At the corner of the nymph's neck was a trace of blood. "I have no need of you," Persephone said. "In fact, I have no further need of you at all. You are dismissed."

The nymph's face twisted angrily. "You do not have authority. Hades is my master. He will not allow me to be dismissed."

"You misunderstand. Hades can do whatever he wants with you. But I do not want you around me. Is that simple enough for you to understand, or do I need to speak in fewer syllables?"

Olive poked his head through the doorway. Minthe's face lit up with a malicious smile as she stepped forward, kicking the fawn as hard as possible. Persephone swung towards Minthe, her eyes flaming with rage, as Olive cried out in pain. Cerberus suddenly loomed in the doorway, enormous with hackles raised, and Minthe's gleeful smile vanished instantly. The three heads were fixed on the nymph, their throats heaving with a deep growl. Green vines snaked up Minthe's legs, enveloping her, as Persephone raised her hands. The Goddess moved closer, gripping her fists so tightly that the vines were agonizingly tight.

"They burn!" Minthe screamed. "They are burning me!"

"Their leaves are poisonous," Persephone replied with a smile, her teeth sharp. "Return to my door again, and I will stuff them down your throat. Harm an innocent creature again, and I will watch you burn." With a flick of her fingers, she dislodged the vines from the nymph. "Ask your lord if he has an antidote for that poison," she advised softly. The nymph's body was already covered with searing welts from the vines, her lovely face swollen and red. Minthe blubbered as she staggered away from Persephone, her lips retracted in horror.

Persephone scooped up the garment and escorted the now diminutive Cerberus back inside her room, shutting the door. She bent toward Olive, cradling the young fawn in her arms. The tiny deer was shaking but was quickly regaining his composure; Persephone scrutinized him, pushing healing warmth into him, before lovingly tucking him into her bed. She swept the room clean, discarding the flowers. When the room was in order, she examined the gown her husband had chosen for her. The dress was gleaming silver, fitted at the waist, and adorned with yards of star-studded skirts. Two crescent moons clasped her breasts, forcing them upward. There was no fabric covering her breasts, leaving her entirely exposed.

"Ugh," she muttered in disgust. "I am not going to wear this."

She dashed to the closet, only to discover that everything except an exquisite beaded silver shawl had been removed. With an annoyed sigh, she began to dress. She carefully slid the shawl over her shoulders and down the front of the dress, fastening it firmly. She pinned her hair high on her head with a crescent moon pin from her dressing table and fastened diamond earrings that hung like chandeliers, framing her face. She went to the mirror and rubbed the dark circles beneath her eyes, but they remained firmly in place. Persephone walked to the back of the room, dipped a cloth in the pond, and pressed it against her aching brow. She wished she could lay down, but there was no time. She rushed to the mirror at the last moment and slipped the moonstone necklace inside her skirt.

Cerberus snarled deep in his throat as a knock sounded on the door. The sickening sweetness of decaying flesh warned her first, and as the door pushed open, she recoiled, gazing up at the colossal figure. Eurynomos.

The demon's voice was beautiful, and his orb-like eye glowed in the dim hall light. "Follow us."

Persephone glanced at the bed, and Cerberus and her exchanged looks. She knew the dog would guard Olive if Minthe came back. But, it was unlikely the nymph would return anytime soon; the poison from those vines would keep her busy. She followed the beast down the corridor, the stench of blood and rotting flesh nauseating. The tiny blue stones she had noticed on the palace floors were growing, spreading across the floor and the hall, and she saw her reflection in the stones. As the demon's damaged wing smeared across the floor, a path of slime spread across the beautiful crystals.

Whether it was the putrid stench, her lack of sleep, the disintegration of her marriage, or some combination of the three, she felt strangely lightheaded. Black dots danced around her vision, and she leaned against the wall for support.

"Does it feel unwell?"

"It feels fine," Persephone snapped, forcing herself to stand rigid. "Are you escorting me to dinner, or am I to be your dinner?"

Eurynomos licked his lips but continued on his way. "Oh no, we eat when the king says we eat." The long tongue shot out, licking at a maggot crawling on its face.

Persephone made no response as she was escorted inside the upper tower. It was one of her favorite areas in the palace, with the windows providing a breathtaking view of the Underworld's three rivers. It seemed so long since she had sat with Hades here. The table and fireplace mantle were adorned with lush red flowers, and candles flickered around the room. A feast had been laid out: oysters, honeyed figs, wild fowl, and a rainbow-colored assortment of fruits and vegetables.

Eurynomos slid back into her field of vision. "We never thanked you," he hissed, his voice a serpent's whisper, "for sparing our life. How delightful it is to realize that every wretched choice we make is a consequence of your pitiful mercy. You may believe yourself virtuous, but every ounce of suffering I cause now rests squarely on your shoulders—your burden, your curse."

Persephone jerked at the memory of Eurynomos devouring Theo's head in the throne room, and Eurynomos' mouth pulled back in a macabre smile. She gazed ahead, her ears ringing with the pull of the demon's wing until all was silent. The demon's words stung her deeply, and she cursed his power over her. How much evil would Eurynomos unleash because she had asked Hades to spare his life? With trembling hands, she poured herself a glass of rich, red wine from the table, gulping it quickly.

After pouring a second glass, she looked down at the churning rivers. Hades had bared his soul to her in this room, confessing the tragedy of his mother's death. It had seemed so genuine, but plainly, he was an expert at deception, and she was a fool; a match made in heaven, she thought bitterly. She gasped at the touch of cool hands on her shoulders. They traced her bare arms, fondling the shawl clasped tightly over her breasts.

"Good evening," he murmured, whirling her around to face him. She caught her breath at the sight of him and bit her lower lip hard to stop it from trembling. "How beautiful you look. I thought tonight," he continued, "that you and I could dine alone—no servants, no interruptions." He eyed the shawl over her shoulders. "Do you not like your dress? I had it specially made for my queen."

"Then I wonder why Minthe isn't wearing it," she answered sweetly.

Hades laughed lightly. "Ah, but you know that you are my queen." His dark eyes pierced her. He lifted his hand again to her shoulder, but she jerked back.

"I prefer for you not to touch me."

He laughed. "And do you believe I give a damn what you prefer?"

"You once did," she murmured in a hushed tone.

As she attempted to withdraw from him, his hand snaked out, wrapping around her arm with a possessive grip. The tips of his fingers traced the fragile skin of her wrist, coaxing her hand toward his mouth. He pressed his lips to her palm, his gaze on her hungrily. A shiver coursed through her, and she jerked her hand away, moving to sit at the far end of the table.

Hades sat at the head of the table. His dark eyes were fixed on his wife, an enigmatic smirk playing on his lips. He began piling food onto his plate and poured himself a glass of wine. Persephone picked up a fig and rolled it carelessly between her hands. Despite her assurances to herself that she would not be frightened, she was. She had taken a stand against the Lord of Darkness and must be prepared to pay her pound of flesh. And she knew that he would make her pay; the only question was what form it would come in. Her husband was very clever in exacting revenge. Therefore, if her heart was beating slightly faster than usual, that was understandable.

He observed her over the rim of his glass. "Are you dissatisfied with the food?" he inquired solicitously. "Shall I call Eurynomos back and see if he can procure something more you like?"

Persephone gave him a disgusted look and then dished herself a spoonful of mashed fruit. Hades raised his glass in salute. "To my lovely wife. May she receive precisely what she is due." Hades drank deeply, and Persephone took a sip from her glass as she processed his enigmatic words. He picked up a long, glittering knife and sliced off a piece of meat. "Minthe mentioned that you had shown her a new plant. She was most agitated about the effects of it."

Persephone smiled sweetly. "Oh?" she asked. "Be sure to tell her that there are many more plants that I intend to study. It's a shame I haven't yet discovered a treatment for their effects. Only the tincture of time, I'm afraid." His amused expression informed her she would never make it as an actress. "Perhaps you should be careful, too; some toxins can remain on the skin for quite some time. It would be such a

shame for a certain portion of your anatomy to get burned. After all, you spend so much time together; there's no telling what parts of you may rub against one another," she finished with a snap of her teeth.

He chuckled. "What a lucky man I am to have a wife so concerned about the health of, what did you call it? My anatomy?"

She smiled at him as she bit down hard into a fig.

"Tell me, wife, what else did you do today besides torment the servants?"

She maintained a focused look on the abused fig, knowing well that he was toying with her. "Nothing noteworthy. I'm sure your day was far more interesting. How are you spending your time now? Between the illicit affair and all the changes in the palace, you must find yourself quite busy."

He raised an eyebrow but did not bother to deny the accusations. "Oh, I did nothing noteworthy," he echoed. He reclined in his chair, his long fingers caressing the stem of his wine glass. "However, were we not speaking of you? Did you spend the entire day in your room? Or did you perhaps get some exercise? A stroll by the rivers of the Underworld is such a pleasant way to cool one's head, do you not think?"

He knew what she had done. She couldn't help the chill of foreboding that went down her spine. She took a long drink from her wine, her face impassive. "Well, that would depend on why my head needed cooling and whether it would be served to Eurynomos afterward." She frowned. "Or should I call him your pet? It is so hard to keep up with your current whims. Oh, I just had the most wonderful thought. Imagine Eurynomos, dressed in matching outfits with you and Minthe—what a charming little trio you would make!" He had been taking a sip of wine but choked, looking up at her. She let her eyes moisten as if overwhelmed by the endearing image. "Would you mind passing the wine?" she asked cheerfully.

"Are you sure you have not had enough?" he asked dryly as he passed her the decanter.

"But, dear husband, I find that when I am in your company, it makes the evening pass so much more pleasantly."

He looked down at the table, a smile curving his lips. "So, you spent a quiet day at home."

"Isn't that what an obedient queen is obliged to do?"

He made a noncommittal noise. "Yes," he murmured, "if only I possessed one of those obedient wives." His black eyes blazed up at her, and she couldn't ignore their hypnotic intensity. "Would you like to know what I overheard?" he asked in his silken voice. "I heard you did not spend the day in your room but rather were assisting in the release of criminals, defying the express orders of your king. However, these are almost certainly just malicious rumors."

She licked her lips anxiously, even as she attempted a tranquil smile at him. "As they say, only fools believe rumors."

"And am I a fool, Persephone?"

"No," she answered softly, "you are not a fool."

"I believe the time has come for me to become more involved in your affairs. Tell me, my wife, are you not yet with child? Our joyful little family would be complete with a son. It would keep you out of trouble, and a king, after all, requires an heir."

"I am not with child," Persephone replied through gritted teeth.

His eyes gleamed as he observed her. "But it is strange, is it not, that a fertility Goddess should be so... infertile?"

She gave him a cold look but remained silent. His gaze lowered to her breasts, a deliberate, contemplative perusal, and she struggled to keep her arms at her side. "While you appear like a fertility Goddess, you seem somewhat frigid compared to the other deities who share that special distinction. But all your parts seem to be in working order." His head tilted, and a smirk appeared on his lips. She had come to understand that this was when he was at his most lethal when he smiled at her while coldly calculating his vengeance; he was a beautiful, smiling serpent. "Do you have an explanation for your inability to conceive?"

"I do not," she said stiffly.

"Oh, you must have some notion," he said softly, "after all, conceiving would be difficult while ingesting these, wouldn't it?" He raised his hand and flung the contents of his palm onto the table's center. The silphium seed rolled towards her, and a cold chill moved over her.

Persephone launched herself from her chair. "You have been spying on me!"

"And you have been lying to me," Hades growled as he rose from his seat.

She yanked the necklace from her pocket and tossed it across the table so it landed next to the seed. "You have deceived me a million times over! I trust nothing you say. Any gift you have ever given me was done for a reason."

Hades took fast strides towards her, looming over her. With a hard hand, he yanked the shawl from her shoulders, exposing her breasts. "I am a king," he shouted vehemently. He circled her wrists, forcing her breasts forward, and his gaze was possessive as he traced the soft flesh. "You answer to *me*. Everything you are belongs to me."

"I belong to no one," she hissed. She twisted suddenly, wrenching herself free from his grasp. She pulled the cape from his shoulders as she spun and wrapped it quickly over her body. "You should ask Minthe to bear the fruits of your loins. She is the perfect match for you."

He smashed his fist into the table, causing a sudden crash as food dishes tumbled to the floor. He turned abruptly, picking up the wine decanter and bringing it to his lips. He carelessly flung the bottle on the ground after emptying it, the glass shattering. His composure had been regained as he confronted her again.

"With Minthe, I am not interested in having children," he said. "None of this makes a difference; you and I each have little secrets. A tiny seed cannot prevent a fertility goddess from being impregnated. Your little outbursts will have no effect on my control." He opened his hand, and he held the tiny seed once more. He examined it, held it to the light, and then crushed the seed between his fingertip and thumb. He lifted his eyes to hers. "You, my darling, are a rule breaker. I will assist you in breaking that nasty habit, even if it means destroying and reshaping you."

Persephone tipped her head forward, her eyes glittering. "And you think you have such power over me."

His dark gaze pierced her. "I think you remain very susceptible to me, Persephone. And I always get what I want. You shall submit to my will, sooner or later." He raised his voice. "Bring her in."

Persephone gasped as Boreas was brought in by a servant: the horse was frozen, encased in ice!

"What have you done to her!" Persephone cried.

"You have proven remarkably resistant against torture. Let us see how you fare when I destroy your accomplices in your crime. Your criminal guard has vanished for the time being, so that leaves Boreas. Poor, innocent Boreas. Did you give her a choice as you brought her on your illicit little journey? Tell me where Theo is," he demanded.

She stared at Boreas. "Don't do this," she pleaded to Hades. She grasped his arm. "Please!"

He wrapped his fingers around her, pulling her against him. "Tell. Me. Where. He. Is."

"No!"

"Then watch," he whispered, holding her head forward. "Watch what happens to those who defy me. You will bend to me, or you will break."

With a snap of his fingers, the ice around Boreas began to melt, and the horse's black eyes blinked in horror. With every drip of ice, the horse, too, began to melt, and the horse cried out in fear and pain as it disintegrated into nothingness until the mare was nothing more than a puddle of water on the floor.

"See what you made me do?" he whispered gently into her ear. "I will take everything from you, piece by piece."

"I hate you!" she cried, tears streaming down her face.

He released her suddenly, and she stumbled back. Hades smiled at her and began prowling towards her when the room suddenly went black. She froze as something brushed across her, a touch caressing her arm.

Run, his voice said.

"Come here," he snarled.

Her mind raced, and she stumbled out of the room, blindly fleeing through the dark corridors. The entire castle was pitch black. Persephone knew he must be pursuing her, but she couldn't hear anything. She skittered to a halt as she saw the door of his study. After slipping inside, Persephone frantically felt along the walls until her fingers moved over the invisibility helmet, quickly jamming it over her head before fleeing down the passage. Once she reached the outer doors, she began sprinting. If she could get to the surface of the Underworld, Persephone could find the one person she could always trust. Demeter.

Persephone raced deep into the Underworld, and it seemed to take forever before she reached the giant, black diamond gates at the very edge of Hell. She ran her hands along it, desperately seeking the door's clasp, but she could not find it. She glanced behind her, and the night was still silent, but her instinct told her to keep moving. Furtively, she followed along the edges of the gates. The fortress traveled for miles, and she finally paused when she reached a lagoon. Exhausted, she removed the helmet, flustered and out of breath. She surveyed the tranquil water before scampering over the rocks, gentle ripples disrupting the smoothness as she immersed herself.

The water was warm, and it poured through sections of the gate, forming minute turquoise waterfalls. She reached her hand through the openings, but the water repelled her like a magical force field. It was impossible to get past the fortress. She was inescapably trapped in this place. There would be no help from the outside world for her, no ally to assist her. She waded through the lagoon and had just reached the edge of the slippery rock when something enormous slithered past her. Fear caused her heart to skip a beat, and she remained perfectly still, terrified to draw the attention of whatever monstrous beast lurked in the depths.

"Do not move," a deep voice commanded.

She looked up and saw her husband standing at the rocky entrance to the lagoon, but instead of anger, he looked frightened. Something had sliced through his robes, tearing at his flesh, and his face was pale, his black eyes as fathomless as the deep water that surrounded her. Even though he had repeatedly deceived her, the sight of blood flowing down his body caused her physical pain. He looked down and saw the helmet in her hand, and his voice entered her mind.

Put the helmet on. Now.

As she did so, she felt a powerful force propel her away from the lagoon just as a massive monster, part snake, half female, broke through the surface. Hades whirled, dragging his bident out of the darkness and driving it deep into the Earth, sending a powerful blast slamming into the beast as it roared in wrath.

"You dare to enter my territory," the creature bellowed. "Give me Typhon!"

The top half of her form was that of a beautiful maiden, complete with vibrant green eyes and lush, red lips. Her long green hair framed her head like a crown, trailing down her narrow waist and blending with the green serpent's tail that made up her lower half. The scales on her tail glistened in the dim light of the night sky.

Hades twisted his bident, holding it between him and the beast. "Echidna," he sighed, "we discuss this yearly. He is imprisoned in Tartarus for crimes against the Olympians."

"And what of their crimes!" she shrieked.

The monster aimed her tail toward the king, and he jumped high into the air as thick, dark venom splattered onto Hades' arm, searing his flesh. Hades' face tensed as he gripped his arm, healing the burns rapidly. Persephone had given a cry of distress, and the creature turned her ferocious gaze toward the noise. Again, she raised her hands but aimed her poison at Persephone this time. Hades leaped into the water, yanking the tail of the snake hard. With a flick, the tail wrapped around him, and he vanished into the darkness below, his body scraping hard against the rocks. Blood poured into the lake, painting it red.

In an instant, the trees around the lagoon bowed, their branches reaching down into the murky water below, and the king was dragged out of the lagoon's depths and deposited on the shoreline. Persephone lowered her hands, releasing the trees, and moved close to the water, the helmet held at her side.

"Who are you?" Persephone demanded, standing directly before Hades to shield him from the creature's view.

The beautiful face twisted in derision as she eyed the Goddess. "Well, well," she hissed. "The king has a little protector."

Hades tried to stand, but he stumbled to the ground, and Persephone's head whipped towards him, shocked at his weakness.

"Come here," he called desperately. "Get away from the water!"

She eyed him worriedly but turned back to the creature.

"The Dark King loves you," Echidna said suddenly, her lips curving with malicious pleasure. Large jets of poison erupted from her hands, and Persephone formed a massive crystal wall around the shoreline, shielding Hades and herself from the poison.

"You shall not touch him!" Persephone cried. "I am the queen of this realm, and I demand that you stop!"

"You hold no dominion over me!" Echidna shrieked. More poison spattered from the snake's fingertips, and Persephone held the crystal shield high. "I admire your tenacity to protect your mate," Echidna hissed. "But I would be doing him a favor. He reeks of death. He is dying."

Persephone's heart stuttered as she turned to look at Hades, even as she held the shield high. He made no response to Echidna's claims, but he still lay on the ground, a pool of blood expanding beneath him. She returned her attention to the snake, though she was cognizant of Hades' attempts to stand behind her, his legs unsteady, but slowly he began to make his way towards her.

"But you are in our kingdom," Persephone replied, her voice menacing, "and you will not threaten the king."

The trees bent to grip the snake, entwining her in their massive branches. Persephone lifted her hands, wrapping sarpagandha around the snake's body. Echidna recoiled, screeching in fury. Persephone let lemongrass pour from her fingers, the tall, fragrant plant sprouting for miles until they were covered by it. Hades stood unsteadily behind her, blasting a blinding light where the creature had stood. He grabbed her hand, and they ran through the grass until they reached the safety of the castle. Hades breathed heavily when they reached the front gates, and she had to support him into the palace. The hour was late, and they did not meet anyone as she helped carry him through the halls. He gestured towards a door, and she opened it, leading them into a small room dominated by red and green columns. There seemed to be no end to the rooms she still had to discover in the palace.

Helping him to sit on a chaise, she poured them both a glass of wine, thrusting the goblet into his hands. She stared down at him, noting the sweat on his forehead and the unhealed wounds across his chest and arms.

"What," she began in a shaky voice, "is happening to you?"

His eyes were enigmatic as he stared up at her. He took a long sip of the wine, saying nothing.

In frustration, she grasped his arm, the warm flesh enticing beneath her hand, and she let go quickly. "Tell me! Stop these games. What did she mean that you were dying? Who is she?"

"Echidna," he responded. "Mate to Typhon. Cerberus' mother, as a matter of fact."

Persephone frowned at that. "Truly?"

Hades nodded. "I'm afraid so."

She shook her head. "You are trying to distract me. Why did she think that you were dying?"

Hades raised his hands, pressing against the wounds over his body, healing them carelessly. "No one knows why Echidna says what she says. She battles for Typhon's freedom at least once a year, which generally ends with her spitting poison at me. I appear to irritate her."

Persephone eyed him. "I know the feeling," she muttered. She was tempted to leave him, to get as far away from him as she could, but something in his gaze, some hint of vulnerability, held her. "Tell me," she said quietly, "why you are so different. All I want is the truth."

"The truth," he murmured, staring at her. "That is the one thing I cannot give you. Persephone." He reached for her suddenly, and his arms were trembling. "I love you." He said her name like a prayer, like a curse, and then his lips moved over hers. His lips were frantic, restless, and his eyes wild. She pulled back to look into the face of the man she loved, and it was a stranger looking back at her.

"I won't stop," he breathed. "I will never stop. He cannot stop me; you cannot stop me." Golden ash fell from his body until the light left his eyes, and he promptly passed out.

CHAPTER 16
TRAINING

A hand shook her awake. "Persephone, wake up." His voice was urgent in her ear, and she saw her husband looming over her. "Come with me, quickly."

Without question, she put her hand in his. But then she remembered that she no longer trusted him. He pulled her into his arms, and her doubts vanished, and she realized how foolish she had been. Of course, she trusted him; she loved him. He was her other half, the completion of her soul. He held her against his chest, and she felt that indescribable pull, that sense of completeness, as their bodies met. Raising a finger to his lips, he took her hand, leading her down a spiral staircase. Threads of gold dangled from the ceiling, swinging as they passed by.

"I want you to find my thread," he whispered. Persephone moved farther into the tunnel, examining the seemingly infinite golden strands, before returning to him, shaking her head.

"It is impossible!" she cried. "There are too many."

"Do not search with your eyes." He raised her hand, pulling her fingers into a fist. "Concentrate. Call it to you." She frowned, willing herself to locate his thread of fate, but it refused to appear in her grasp.

"I cannot," she whispered, shutting her eyes tightly. "It is because–"

Hades leaned forward, pulling her against his chest so that his heartbeat thumped against her back. "Because you do not love me?" he finished for her, his voice gentle.

"You hurt me. I feel it here." She lifted her hand to her heart. "It is broken. I am afraid to love you."

His arms tightened around her. "What did you used to love about me?"

"Your selflessness."

"And…"

"Your kindness."

"What else?"

Her brow furrowed as she remembered. "It was as if you held the key to my heart in the notes you wrote me by the river. Our love echoed in our first kiss, the tender caress of our first touch. I felt it when you selflessly rescued my father and when you saved my life on the unforgiving mountain. It was every ordinary moment that became extraordinary in your presence. It was you – every shadow and every light." A tear rolled down her cheek. "It was in our goodbye, the belief that you would wait for me and I would wait for you. Time, distance, and space were supposed to mean nothing between us because our love was meant to fill that void."

She opened her eyes and gasped. A golden glow filled her grasp. Hades loosened his grip, and she unfolded her fingers to reveal his thread of fate. It was tarnished and spoiled, and the ends of the thread were thin, unraveling. She turned around to face him, fear trembling through her.

"What has happened to it?" she cried.

He closed her fingers around the thread. "I give this to you under one condition. You must never pull it again in my presence. Do you understand?"

"But what–"

"Promise me, Persephone!"

"I promise," she whispered.

His fingertips stroked her neck, and she realized she was wearing the necklace he had given her so long ago. It had once gleamed with six pomegranate seeds, but she had consumed them on Ares' mountainside, sealing her fate in the Underworld—to Hades. A locket now hung in place of the crimson fruit, intricate constellations engraved on the surface. Persephone delicately touched the gleaming gold, and Hades' fingers gently intertwined with hers as he opened the locket, enclosing his thread within.

"It is yours now, Persephone," he said softly. He drew her closer to him, his lips soft and compelling against her. He abruptly stepped back, releasing her with a gasp as he slipped further into the shadows.

"When you want to pull my thread, think only of the man you once loved. Understand?"

She nodded.

"We must go." He pulled her hand into his, and they found the spiral stairs, ascending swiftly. A green light illuminated the area, making the atmosphere thick and suffocating. Hades paused, staring at her, his face illuminated by the eerie light. "There is a secret," Hades whispered. "Something I have not told you—"

"Tell me," she urged. He gave a cry of pain, leaning against the stone wall, hunching in agony.

"Persephone I…"

"Tell me!" she cried, rushing to him.

The king pulled the blue-flamed sword from the scabbard on his back. He ripped open his robes, and blood covered his abdomen, the scar from the mountain festering and raw.

"Help me," he whispered.

He lifted the blade high, and she cried out, rushing forward to stop him, but she was too late as he plunged the sword into his abdomen, dragging the blade up to his sternum through bone and muscle. He let out a heavy gasp and pulled the blade up further, tearing open his skin; his ribs were golden, and inside his chest were two hearts, contracting in different rhythms.

He lifted his purple eyes to her and said, "Open your eyes, Persephone."

She moved closer, tears streaming down her face. On one heart was a deep scar—the scar he had taken from her. She lifted her hand to touch it, and as her fingers traced the thick, white tissue, she was filled with a memory so painful and dark that they both screamed as she disappeared into blackness.

Her eyes shot open. She was lying in bed. It had only been another nightmare, she reassured herself, her breathing coming in quick, painful gasps. It was only a dream. But Hypnos' words came unbeckoned to her, that she had not been dreaming since her return to the Underworld. She gasped as a tall shadow moved towards her.

Hades stood over her, wrapping a long leather scabbard around his chest. "You are awake," he said briskly. "I thought we would begin training today." He gestured to a beautiful white velvet toga across her dressing table with golden armbands. "Put this on."

"What training?" she demanded. "Shouldn't you be resting?"

"Why?"

"You passed out yesterday." Her eyes narrowed at him. "Don't you remember?"

"I am fine," he said, indicating the subject was closed. So they weren't going to discuss what had happened by the lagoon. They weren't going to discuss his erratic, bizarre behavior or Echidna's claim that he was dying. She was just supposed to pretend none of it had happened.

"You didn't seem fine yesterday," she persisted. "Why–"

"Get dressed," he interrupted, tossing the toga to her. "We don't have time to discuss this." Her mouth thinned as she glared at his stony face. Stubborn ass, she thought, seething.

"I don't want to train with you," she said rudely.

"Then the next several hours will be very unpleasant for you."

Her eyes narrowed. "I dreamt of you again."

Was it possible that she imagined the uneasiness in his gaze? "And what was I doing this time?"

"You are always warning me."

"Against what?"

"I do not know," she answered, frustrated. "But it feels like there is something wrong, that there is something wrong with *you*."

"But do I not look like the picture of health?" Hades asked lightly. "Perhaps I am in danger from being with you, the 'bringer of destruction.' My little harbinger of death." He smiled. "All who see you should fear for their immortal souls."

"Do not call me that," she snapped.

"All of us, my darling, are capable of destruction." With hooded eyes, he observed her. "Even you. Now get dressed."

"I'm not going with you," she fumed, crossing her arms over her chest.

He reached down suddenly and drew her up against him, his fingers tracing the contours of her curves. "Shall I dress you?"

She pulled away from him, but he maintained his grip, running his hands over her lightly before ripping off her robe, the delicate fabric tearing easily in his grasp. As he traced over her breasts, her breathing became ragged. He reached out abruptly, grasping the toga and then quickly shoving it over her head before securing the fastenings with careful hands. Finally, he released her, and she spun away from him, fuming. Her anger died as she noticed the dark circles beneath his eyes and the shadows in his gaze.

Before she could say anything, he twisted his fingers, and the chamber spun, whirling wildly, until they found themselves in a vast cavern, the walls adorned with weaponry. A fireplace cast a golden glow on the stone, and Hades drew two swords from the wall, nonchalantly handing one to her. She examined the swords closely, but they were just well-made weapons, not the blue and golden ones.

He smiled, reading her easily. "I told you I do not have Zeus' sword."

She made no reply as he pressed one of the weapons into her hand.

A bident materialized in his other hand, and her eyes widened as she recognized it was the same weapon he had held in her dream; he scabbarded it on his back. He suddenly advanced towards her, his large

form intimidating, and she knew this was what he had looked like during the Titan Wars—a furious, beautiful soldier. She stepped back, but his fingers effortlessly gripped her wrist, manipulating her sword hand to force her grip to loosen.

"Relax these two fingers to guide your weapon. Your sword should function as an extension of your arm. Hold it too loosely, and you are easily unarmed."

To illustrate, he raised his sword against hers, and she came dangerously close to dropping her weapon as their blades collided. He grinned at her irritated expression.

"Hold it too tightly, and your movements will be constricted." She raised her gaze to his, and their eyes connected, black to green, and she felt the connection thrill her soul. "Focus." He whispered. He lifted his hands to her face and traced the gentle contours of her jaw. "Keep your eyes open." Her gaze shot back to his as he echoed the words from her dream. "Look away for a moment, and your enemy may strike while you are distracted. Rest assured, Persephone, they will do everything possible to divert your attention."

Hades returned to a corner of the cave, holding a living fawn in his arms. She could hear the quiet flutter of its heart and the blood flowing through its body. From the same corner emerged a large doe, her soulful eyes on Hades as her baby was taken from her. He placed the small deer on the floor, and it began to roam the room. It moved closer to her and settled at Persephone's feet as the doe paced anxiously.

"Where are we?" Persephone demanded. "Why did you bring these deer from above?" She bent to soothe the fawn, stroking its fur.

Hades stepped in front of her, raising her sword arm. "I brought you to this place to train you. That is what matters. Whenever you pull your blade in a war, do not fight unless you intend to slay what is on the other end of your weapon." Hades gestured to the doe. "Kill it."

She moved her gaze to his, thinking she had misheard him. "What?"

"You heard what I said."

She looked at the deer's soft, soulful brown eyes fringed with dark lashes. "I will not," she cried.

"We will heal her afterward, but I cannot teach you to properly heal unless you kill the deer first." She dropped her arm. He observed her mulish expression and sighed. "Would you not like to heal Theo of his burns?"

Her eyes widened. "How did you know—"

"You think I do not know what happens to those in the River of Fire? And I know how you want to help him; why not let me show you how?"

"You know," she said in a conversational tone, "I believe you may be insane. Last night, you lost your mind thinking that I helped him, and now you wish to show me how to aid him further."

"I am of a changeable mind, perhaps."

"You never were before," Persephone said in disgust.

"Your anger toward me has consumed you," Hades said softly. "It makes you weak. Let go of the anger, Persephone, or you will burn in the flames." He pointed his sword towards the animal, his eyes blazing. "Persephone, stab the deer. If you do not, I will."

"You will not!" she cried. "Why can't you show me how to heal Theo without causing an innocent animal pain?" She shook her head defiantly. "No, I will not kill this creature, especially in the presence of her baby. The mother of this fawn has done nothing wrong."

She threw down her weapon in disgust. "I do not want to fight anyone. I disagree with war. I am the Goddess of the Spring, not a War God!"

"You are the Queen of the Underworld! You are death and darkness and fear! It's time you learn that." She crossed her arms, her eyes blazing at him. "You will not harm the deer, even knowing I will heal her?" he asked in a dark voice.

Persephone made a disdainful noise. "I am not so stupid to believe what you tell me."

"You are wise then," he hissed, "but you will do as I say." He lunged towards her, eyes flashing with rage. "Persephone, I swear to the Gods, pick up that fucking sword right now."

When she remained motionless, he waved his hand, and the blade shot back into her hand, pushing firmly against her palm. He repositioned her before him and curled his palm over hers, strengthening her grasp on the blade. He dragged her across the room, and the fawn leaped from the ground, sensing sudden danger. She stood behind her mother, her brown eyes watching helplessly as doom approached. Persephone bucked wildly, trying to free herself from him, but his grip was implacable. He ushered her forward until they were immediately in front of the doe.

"You resist, and yet you will still be the one to kill her. The day will come when something good must die at your hands. " He lifted her arm high, and tears blurred her vision as she stared down at the doe. She felt his fingers caress her wrist, and then the sword descended, piercing the animal's heart in a swift blow. The animal cried, and the fawn curled her body around her mother. He released her arm, and Persephone fell to the ground, pressing her hands against the deer's wound as blood gushed around them.

"You are a monster," she cried as the doe's eyes dimmed. "There was no reason to kill this animal!"

"Concentrate," he admonished coldly. "You waste time arguing with me. Pour every ounce of magic into healing the beast."

She focused, thinking of her love for little Olive. He had been left in the forest after a hunter had taken his mother, and his loneliness had called to her. Placing her hands on the deer, she attempted to keep her mind on the doe, but when she lifted her hands, blood still poured from the gaping wound. She eyed the fawn, sensing its fear and despair as it nuzzled its mother. Persephone made a slight noise of distress. Hades took her hands and gently placed them back on the doe.

"You are focusing on the wrong deer," he whispered. "She has died. Look up." Persephone glanced above them to see the floating soul of the deer above their heads, her sad eyes staring down at her baby.

"Grab her soul."

"What! How?"

"With your own. Trust yourself, Persephone," he urged. "I know you have felt that call inside you; the souls reach for you."

She felt the truth of his words resonate within her soul. She had first felt that power when she connected with the mortal's soul on Olympus. She raised her hand, and her fingertips glistened, gold pulsating from her as she stretched her arm, gently directing the throbbing light toward the doe. With the utmost care, she grasped the soul, feeling its sweet, gentle life force, and Persephone gasped at the feeling of the bounding life force against her own. It was like holding a butterfly in her fingers. Slowly, she weaved the soul back into the deer, placing it within her body.

His voice was less than a whisper. "Now, watch its life and feel that life force pulse through you."

The doe gleamed with a golden aura, and Persephone closed her eyes, seeing all the doe had seen—the forests she had run through as a fawn, the tribe of deer she was a part of, the birth of her baby. She could sense a golden warmth permeating the room. Persephone's eyes shot open to see millions of clusters of threads surrounding them; it was the deer's life force. Death had severed the threads into tiny, innumerable pieces. She sensed innately what she needed to do and waved her hands repeatedly, weaving the strands together, somehow knowing just how they should fit.

As she gathered the threads together, the wound on the deer began to close, shrinking in size as her fingers stroked softly over the sparkling strands. Finally, as she weaved the last thread, the gap on the doe's chest was sealed. The doe's eyelids slowly opened, and her trusting brown eyes raised to meet hers. Persephone gasped, her hand trembling in wonder as she touched the animal's face.

Hades kneeled beside her, gently stroking the deer's chest. "How did you do that?" His voice was incredulous.

She looked at him, bewildered. "I only did as you instructed."

He shook his head in amazement. "I assumed you would repair her skin and reconnect her spirit to her body. But the deer has been rewoven; you altered its threads - like a Fate."

"I only healed her," she replied, confused. "I did what you do."

He shook his head and was close enough to her that she could see the purple border on his iris. "You altered the deer's strands of fate. I do not cure in this manner; I only restore the flesh, but you healed her soul."

Persephone frowned. "It's the same when I create a flower or a tree. It is nothing."

He eyed her speculatively. "What you did, only a primordial can do. Have you ever grown anything besides vegetation?"

"I recently grew a crystal," she admitted reluctantly.

His eyes lowered. "Show me how you grow the crystals."

She lifted her hands obediently and noticed the tips of her fingers gleaming. Several green crystals materialized in front of them. Hades kneeled to pick one up and gently held it in his hand.

Hades regarded her with awe. "You hold the power of creation in your hands."

She shook her head and gazed down at the deer once again. "You are a far more accomplished healer than I am."

"I can heal, Persephone, but I am incapable of weaving existence. I cannot create a flower, a tree, or anything else with... life. I should have suspected." He took both her hands, bringing them up to his lips. He flipped her palms over and traced the crisscrossing lines that ran through the middle. "My mother was a fertility goddess. I've always marveled at the power of creation. If I had that gift, I would have a hundred children." His eyes darkened as he looked at her, and she tried to draw her hands away. His grip tightened, but eventually, he released her, stepping back. "Injure it again," he demanded suddenly, pointing to the doe.

She let out an exasperated sound. "I will not hurt this poor animal just so you can train me. I thought you would teach me how to fight, not kill."

"We are getting there, but unless you are prepared to kill, what is the use of fighting?" He considered her, his black eyes taking in her stubborn face. "Very well," he sighed. "We will try a different approach. Hold out your sword."

"And you will leave the mother alone?"

"Yes."

Her eyes narrowed in sudden suspicion. "And the baby as well?"

"Yes, I will not hurt her baby." He snapped his fingers, and the deer vanished. "Now raise your sword." He drew closer as she lifted her arm. "Lunge forward with your rear leg extended." She did it with impeccable form but resembled a dancer carrying a prop rather than a warrior wielding a sword. He continued striding towards her until the blade's tip came to rest against his chest. Her eyes widened, and she attempted to withdraw but was frozen.

"What are you doing?" she cried. "Stop this!" To her horror, he continued to step forward, and she felt the weapon tighten in her hand as it began to rip through skin and muscle. "Stop!" she cried.

"You must learn that sometimes you must hurt before you can heal. Everything you are can crumble, and you will rise from the flame renewed," he murmured. Her face was lifted to meet his, and as he gazed down at her, his long black hair tickled her face. His mouth held a gentle smile despite the immense pain he must be in. "Push it all the way through, Persephone. Deliver the killing blow."

When she remained still, he advanced again, coming closer to her until she began to back away, desperately attempting to withdraw the sword. He moved forward until the sword's hilt was embedded in his chest.

"How could you?" she whispered, shutting her eyes tightly.

"Now release me, Persephone, free me from the pain. Open your eyes, Persephone." She jolted as he repeated the words from her dream and lifted her eyes to his. "Don't let me suffer," he urged softly. She raised her hands to the hilt, but they slipped on the blood.

He grunted in discomfort, and she let her hands fall.

"Certainly, you will not leave me with a blade in my chest. Pull harder." He placed his hand over hers and pressed them against the hilt. "Together," he whispered. With his hand over hers, they pulled the blade from his chest. It brought back vivid recollections of when the arrow was embedded in his heart, and bittersweet memories clashed in her head, choking her. He sank to the ground as the blade slipped from his flesh, his hand covering the massive hole that was spewing blood. She collapsed alongside him, anxiously pressing her fingers to his wound. He encircled her hand with his own.

"There's no need to be scared, Persephone," he said with a smile.

"Mortal weapons cannot kill me. Concentrate."

She closed her eyes and focused, and memories flooded her mind. She could see him being born so tiny and with a full head of black hair. She watched Rhea clutching him to her breast, and then suddenly—darkness. Her eyes flew open, and his eyes were fixed on her face.

His fingers clenched convulsively around hers, and his face blanched. "You do not need to watch my life," he murmured breathlessly. "It is not relevant. Focus."

She drew in her breath. Fresh blood covered their hands, and she could feel the course of his life's force in his veins, the ebb and flow of his heart. It was more difficult to unite with the soul of a powerful God than the deer, but she felt herself falling deeper, following the source of the golden light inside him. She gasped as it began to touch her. She felt unconditional love running through his body; warmth filled her hands at the pureness of it, but something was wrong. There was a darkness there, a sickness. She moved closer, trying to inspect the shadow, when she felt his hands on her face.

"Look at me," he whispered, "only at me."

He brushed his lips against hers. She paused, then pressed her lips to his, and she was lost in his taste and his mouth's sweetness. As she pulled back, a light-flooded around him, engulfing him. His hair floated around his face, and even his clothes were lifted as though he were flying, the golden glow illuminating him. He wrapped her in his arms and pulled her close to him.

"Your soul soothes mine," he whispered. She looked down at his chest and saw that the sword wound had healed with no trace of a scar.

She was still so close to him that she could see the flecks of gold in his eyes. "What happened to us?" she whispered. "Did you ever love me?"

His face became shadowed. "I have never stopped loving you."

"Then why--"

He suddenly paled and clutched his abdomen.

"What is wrong?" she implored. "Tell me!"

He stood suddenly and turned away from her. "I have taught you enough for today. I think it is time you learned the sword now."

"But you said we were done training..."

"And we are. I am not the one who is going to teach you." He cocked his head to the side, looking towards the entrance of the cave. "He is."

He motioned his hand towards the cavern's opening, and Maketes sauntered through. She stood to greet the guard but paused as he lifted his hands to his helmet. She watched as though in slow motion as his face was revealed for the first time.

Tawny blond hair tumbled from the helmet, followed by a strong jaw, sensual lips, a bold nose, and striking blue eyes. She recoiled as if struck. It was impossible, and yet, here he was. For underneath Maketes' helmet was none other than her greatest enemy, the man who had tried his best to destroy her, the God of War.

"What is this?" she gasped. She looked at her husband, expecting shock or rage, but his face was dark and implacable.

Hades walked to the entrance of the cave to stand next to Ares. "He is your trainer."

"You... you knew?"

"I brought him down here. How much time do we have, Ares?"

"The diversion will soon be over," the War God responded enigmatically, his voice gravelly.

"What are you talking about?" she yelled. "You are sick! Both of you." An incredulous laugh bubbled from her lips. "To think that after everything, I still felt you possessed a semblance of goodness. I could never fathom such treachery. That it should be you--" Her voice broke. "How much more do you think I will endure from you? I am leaving."

Hades stepped in front of her, pulling her back inside. "Fight him!" he growled.

"No! He's disgusting, and you're disgusting. I hate him!" Her legs were trembling so badly she was afraid that she would fall. "I hate you!"

"You think you have seen the worst of humanity?" he seethed. "You have not begun to see the evil of the Gods. Take your sword."

"You know what he did to me!"

"I am teaching you a lesson."

Ares shook his head, stepping back. "I told you, I do not think this is a good idea."

Hades flew to his side, striking him with a hard blow. The War God's head swung back. "I did not bring you down here to think." Ares absorbed the blow, making no attempt to defend himself. She was shocked at Ares' subservience to her husband. The War God looked like a young man beside the virile, ancient God. Zeus' words returned to her, warning that Ares could never have defeated such a mighty God as Hades.

"He did your bidding, didn't he? He has acted on your orders this whole time. When he—"

Both Gods turned towards her, and she noticed Hades' wrathful face, but Ares was the one who caught her attention. She was nearly convinced she saw agonizing guilt in his face and contrition in his blue eyes. This was the ultimate blow, the final betrayal that would drive her insane. And she could not bear it, would not take it. She lifted her hands in desperation, enclosing herself in a crystal prison. She curled into a tight ball, pressing her knees to her chest as she rocked back and forth, her mind racing with horrible visions, and she gasped for air. Ares on the banks of the river. Ares by the river. Kissing him. Trusting him. His savageness as he had held her down and forced himself upon her. And Ares was Hades' servant.

"I cannot breathe," Persephone whispered.

She sensed Hades on the other side, tearing furiously at the crystal barrier she had constructed around herself. The rocks were broken by a blow, and he reached for her, but she would not allow him to touch her. She was vaguely aware of him yelling as he stretched his arm, her name on his lips, but she was withdrawing farther inside herself, out of his reach. As Persephone faded away, she sensed the appearance of the other. Darkness began to rise within her, flowing through her and enveloping her.

As his fingertips brushed across her, a massive wall of black fire erupted from her, scorching and lethal. She stayed hunched on the ground as darkness flowed from her, hurling Ares across the cavern and slamming his body into the wall. Hades maintained his position, his hands forming a forcefield around him as he watched the cavern erupt in flames. Amethyst and granite smashed into a thousand bits around him as the Earth jolted beneath his feet.

Persephone's awareness had faded, and she was content to hand over control to the other. She felt comfortable in this solitude, far from where anything could harm her. Suddenly, she sensed a voice echoing within her, much like the moon's call to the sea—a compulsion she could not resist.

Persephone. Come back to me.

Her heart hammered in her chest, and she was aware that the wretched organ was syncing with his, her consciousness returning. She was being summoned back against her will. Around her, the magic began to fade, and she felt utterly powerless without the dark energy to support her. Her body slumped to the floor as the final drop of magic drained from her.

"Persephone," he whispered, cradling her in his arms. "Do you understand now?" She raised her swollen eyes and caught a glimpse of the visage of the War God looming above them.

"Yes," Ares rasped. "She has the power of the King of the Underworld."

"No, she has so much more than that," Hades said.

She focused her gaze on Hades, seeing starlight reflected in his eyes.

"You lied to me from the beginning," she whispered.

"Yes," Hades admitted.

She closed her eyes, and tears slipped from them. "Why?"

"Because I was weak," he said softly. "I loved you before the cosmos spoke your name. Forgive me." She felt dampness on her face; as her eyes connected to him, he cried out in pain, hunching over.

"Hades," Ares intervened, his voice urgent. "You must go. There is no time."

"I don't understand," Persephone cried as he moved away from her.

"Persephone," Hades said as he stood. "You must learn that you are stronger than your fear. You are the dark queen and will do what you must." He raced out of the room before she could respond, his cape trailing after him like the ghostly wings of a moth as he vanished from view.

She remained still on the ground while Ares stood over her.

"Pick up your sword," he growled.

Her eyes lifted to his, and her stare was filled with loathing. "I do not answer to you."

Ares let out a low whistle and clenched his fist. Two soldiers materialized alongside him, bent in battle formation.

"Hades predicted you would be difficult. I have sent many men to their graves, and thanks to your husband, I can call them back again and again. Stand up!" he hissed.

When she remained still, Ares waved his hand, and one of the soldiers leaped forward, his arm raised as he slammed a sword at her. Persephone spun quickly, evading the warrior's attack. As she moved, she clutched her blade and sank into a squat.

"You fight with the timidity of a coward," he scoffed. "You retaliate but lack the confidence to hit your adversary."

"You call me a coward," she said in a low, furious voice. "Maybe I am. But better that than a rapist."

His eyes glowed, but he only raised his palms, encouraging the warriors forward once again. They continuously swung at her, attempting to deliver devastating blows, but she evaded their attempts. Minutes passed, hours passed, and they chased her fiercely, but she never raised her blade except to deflect their attacks. She cried out in pain when she was too slow, and one of the soldiers hit his mark, the sword piercing deeply into her arm.

Ares paced the floor, his gaze narrowing. "You are weak! Do you believe the Gods will be merciful to you? Raise your sword! Defend your kingdom!"

Even as he spoke, his soldiers pursued her. "What do you know of honor, oh Prince?" she spat as she dodged another strike.

"I did not lie. I am a Prince of Olympus,"

"Prince Rapist and King Defiler. Like father, like son."

"Shut the fuck up," he bellowed. His hands were clenched at his sides, and in his rage, his men slowed and became awkward, allowing her to race away from them.

"Oh, I must have struck a nerve," she laughed. "I am glad."

Ares' face smoothed, and she could see him struggle to reign in his rage and calm that famous temper. "When you struck me on the mountainside," he sneered, "I saw a queen. Now I see a little girl who still runs from her nightmares." He raised his hand, and the warriors faded away. "You have let your uncertainty weaken you." She kept a wary eye on him as he circled her. "Think of what I have done. Do you not want to see me suffer?"

He bent to pick up the sword Hades had left behind, gently running his finger along the blade. "I have watched for eternity as men fought for things they could never own and died for Gods that never knew their names. And you, who have so much to lose, will not even lift your sword. Tell me, Persephone, what will it take to motivate you? You think it is a crime to kill, but how many will suffer because of your inaction? You allowed Eurynomos to go free. Your mother remains above ground, surrounded by enemies. And Hades..." His eyes simmered. "Are you not willing to battle for your soulmate?"

"Do not speak to me of him!" she said in a dangerous voice.

"You think he has betrayed you," Ares snarled, "and still you do not raise your hand. How much more will you take? Weak. Useless. Fight! Let your anger out!"

Ares raised his palm, and fire burst from its center. He rubbed the flame along the sword, igniting it in a hellish blaze.

"Very well," he mocked. "If you will not fight like a Goddess, you will lose like a coward!"

He rushed forward, and she just had time to step back before his blade destroyed the ground on which she stood. "Put your left foot ahead of your right. Defend yourself!" He advanced again, and she dove too slowly, causing his blade to sear her flesh. The touch of the flame was agonizing, and her eyes filled with tears. "Is there nothing that will motivate you? Are you not going to defend your people? Perhaps you lack the proper motivation?"

He lifted his hand, and Olive appeared before them. Ares' eyes blazed while Olive looked up at the War God trustingly. "What do you love more? Which is it—your honor or your friend? Will you allow me to harm him yet again?" As his sword approached the fawn, Persephone lifted her blade, blocking his, and her arms trembled with the impact.

"Do not touch him," she screamed. She lifted her hand, and Olive vanished.

"Then fight me, or I will rip him apart again and again until you learn your lesson."

She raised her palm, revealing a pink oleander in her hand. She twisted the blossom towards her blade, drenching it with the petal's juices. Ares laughed, pleased.

"Excellent," he said. "Teach me a lesson now."

She approached him and swung her blade in his direction; he smiled, effortlessly deflecting her sword. "You lack ability. You strike too soon, which exposes your weaknesses. When you remove the blade's protection from your body, you never know when your adversary may strike." He pounced on her, viciously hitting her till her flesh sizzled and she collapsed to the ground. He hauled her up by the gown, repositioning her on her feet. "You are far too slow! Watch for my weaknesses, find my mistakes, and strike me!" He advanced towards her, and again and again, he burned her. "You are wretched at this," he snarled.

However, she was observing him and eventually realized her advantage. She lacked ability, but he was becoming complacent. She lifted her blade to a point where she could see his gaze locked on her exposed stomach. As he raised his blade towards her, she rapidly dropped hers to intercept it, utilizing the momentum to slam her foot on his groin, throwing him off balance. She made sure to deliver a vicious kick to his testicles before slicing him severely in the abdomen as he fell to the ground, scarlet blood flying like raindrops. He laughed as he felt the wound.

"Very good." He jumped to his feet, pushing his entrails carelessly back into his body as his skin slowly closed. "Again."

She had no idea how long she had been in the cavern with Ares roaring at her and them both doing their best to dismember the other, but by the time they were through, she was severely burned, and his body was trembling from the effects of the oleander.

"Enough," he eventually said. He snapped his fingers, and a soldier materialized. "Hector, return her to the palace."

"I don't require an escort."

"Your husband disagrees," Ares spat. "Either Hector can take you, or I can." She was limping from the burns on her calves but moved forward, anxious to be away from the War God. He raised a hand as she passed him, and she jerked away. "Remember what I said. You have no friends left in the palace."

She paused. "Why did you pretend to be kind? Why did you help me?"

He shook his head. "You saw what you wanted to see."

She took a step closer to him. "When the time is right," she stated quietly, "I will find you and watch you burn." She turned on her heel and stepped from the cave, leaving the War God alone in the shadows.

The phantom guard trailed behind her. She raised her face to the black, starless sky. She stood for long moments, allowing the night's calm to fill her, praying it would offer her peace, but there was none. She eventually turned and made her way to the palace. At this late hour, the courtyard was deserted, but she could see one of the Furies perched on one of the tall towers.

As she entered the palace's threshold, the ghostly warrior faded away. She closed the door, leaving a trace of blood behind. Her hands were raw from the many hours spent clutching a blade. Allowing her senses to wander, she sought Hades and quickly felt his presence. Again, she detected something different in the rhythm of his heart, but she could not discern what it was.

She followed the trail of his life force until she stood just outside the throne room doors, listening to the cadence of his blood. She closed her eyes tightly, then raised her hands against the door, pushing hard. Hades was floating directly in front of his throne. Long black hair dangled across his face, obscuring his features. Olive stood before him, his little face lifted, while Cerberus paced the room, occasionally howling as he looked back toward Hades'.

The king looked worse than she did, with deep, bloody wounds gashed across him. His hair was soaked with sweat, and dirt was smeared across his clothes and embedded in his skin. She moved closer and parted his hair. His eyes stared sightlessly ahead, but amber flickered like fire in the black depths. She put her hand over the deep gashes on his arms and gasped. There was conflict in his soul; he was hunting, searching for something, but it was just out of reach; there was darkness; there was death. She pulled back, clutching her hand to her chest.

"Hades?"

He did not move. Tremors moved through his muscles, but his eyes remained unfocused. She shook him firmly.

"Hades," she repeated again, more urgently. She closed her eyes, concentrating on his breathing and pulse rhythm. It was there, but … her brows furrowed. Something was wrong. Panicked, she called out his name again. "Hades!" She slapped him hard, but he remained locked away. "Come back and face me!"

The only noise was Cerberus' erratic pants. Suddenly, Hades' eyes flickered, and a deep gasp filled the room as he awoke. Cerberus and Olive gathered beneath him, concern evident on the four faces.

"Where did you go?" Persephone asked quietly. Fine tremors ran over him though the room was warm. She stepped closer to him and could smell the sweat on his skin. "What were you looking for?"

A flash of desolation filled his eyes before they closed tightly. "I seek answers to questions I should have asked long ago." His voice was soft and weary.

"And did you find them?"

"I only ever find more questions," he whispered.

Worry consumed her, but the pain from the cave, both physical and, far more importantly, psychological, forced angry words to spill from her lips.

"I have a question for you," she said, her voice shaking with emotion.

"I would like to know why you brought a rapist and a murderer here? I asked you this once before, and like a fool, I believed you when you denied it. Did you arrange for him to meet me by the river that day?"

He turned suddenly, righting himself, and she could fully see his face; it, too, was covered in bruises and blood. His lip was split, and blood slowly trickled down his chin. "No! Do you believe I am capable of such a thing?"

"Maybe you just wanted to play games with me, destroy me, and force me to come here! Or maybe you did not have a reason! I do not know! I do not know you anymore. All I know is that you knew that he, above all others—" Her voice cut off abruptly, and she closed her eyes tightly, unwilling to let tears fall. When her eyes reopened, their emerald depths were filled with hatred. "That you've let him re-enter my life. It is unforgivable."

His eyes closed, and his throat convulsed as if the movement were painful. "He will teach you what I have been unable to teach you. There is nothing I would not do to protect you, even if it meant facing your hatred. In time, you will understand—"

"I will never understand!" she cried, her voice quivering. "I will never forgive you."

Hades gazed at the retreating figure of the woman he loved, her feet soundless on the marble floor. As the door slammed behind her, he closed his eyes tightly, wishing desperately to unleash the truth that was imprisoned within him.

CHAPTER 17
TARTARUS

In the blue-hued night, Hades pulled a blood-red cape over his shoulders, fastening it to a leather belt firmly tightened across his chest. There was someone that he must find, but they had proven surprisingly elusive. Tonight, he would end his pursuit. He positioned his shoulder shield in place, his fingers remembering the movements that had once been part of his daily life. It was part of his old armor from the war, back when he was bronzed by the sun instead of the heat of Hell.

This armor had once felt like a second skin, the metal molding lovingly to his flesh. If he closed his eyes, he could still imagine the stench of blood, the endless fields of rotting corpses, and the relentless scorching of the sun. He shook his head, forcing those particular memories from his mind.

He crept down the halls, making one last stop. He entered her room, then let his eyes move over his wife. Her sleep was restless; long dark hair spread behind her as she tossed on the pillow. His hand trailed from her shoulder to her wrist before moving to her hand to trace the lifeline on her palm. Eternity was a long time, yet he could feel time slipping through his fingers; he was unraveling. He bent low to her ear.

"I am sorry, Persephone," he whispered softly.

Her brows drew together in a frown, and he stroked her face until she slept soundly again. As he turned to leave, he felt a pull on his cape. Her hand had reached out in her sleep, grasping his cape tightly. Gently, he released her hand, tucking her arm beneath the covers. He stared down at her and finally forced himself to retreat, slipping silently out of the room.

Like a shadow, he made his way to the rubied room, quickly locating the secret panel in the wall. He pulled out the blue and golden blades, one clasped in each fist, and then placed the weapons into the scabbard on his back. He moved to the wall and drew the golden whip Ares had left in the Underworld, tying it to the side of his belt before grabbing his golden bident. Tonight, he would find the answers he sought. Heading to the stables, he led Orphnaeus from his stall. He stroked the stallion's mane and bent forward as the horse greeted him with a soft snort.

"Tonight, we ride back into Hell, old friend."

Hades chuckled as Orphnaeus pounded his hoof excitedly as he leaped on his back. They rode through the Underworld like two ghosts, making no noise to disturb the dark night. Soldiers were now patrolling portions of the Underworld, but the king was wise enough to dodge their traps. Orphneaus remembered the path and began the gradual descent until they came to the colossal iron gates of Tartarus.

The gates were surrounded by craggy, dark mountains, and Cerberus sat by the massive doors, patiently waiting for his master. As Hades came into sight, Cerberus' tail began to wag wildly. He lifted up on his hind legs, inviting Hades to stroke his soft necks as Hades bent down. He picked up the tiny pup and slung his plump body over his shoulder.

"Good boy," he murmured soothingly. Hades surveyed the landscape, and he suddenly smiled. "Gyges!"

Suddenly, the entire side of one of the mountains shifted as an enormous giant with hundreds of hands and heads stepped from the shadows. Gyges was a Hecatonchires known as the Hundred-Handed Ones. They were rare creatures, tall and robust as mountains and twice as wide. Their unusual appearance made them shy away from others; the world was not kind to those who were different.

Gyges extended his hands, and thousands of enormous, callused fingers swayed like blades of grass dancing in the breeze. The creature grimaced, the heavy weight of the limbs and heads making him appear in constant pain. In truth, a mortal might say he was rather wretched-looking, deformed, and ugly, but to Hades, he was stunning, a creature that seemed to have stepped forth from a dream.

"Gyges," Hades greeted warmly.

"Back again?"

His many cadenced voices boomed across the barren land, causing gigantic cascades of rocks to tumble down the mountainside. Gyges was the protector of the gates of Tartarus, but Hades had first met the Hecatonchires during the God War when he had been set free by the Olympians to help the Gods win the war. He later returned to guard the gates so his brother Cronus could never escape. Much to Gyges disgust, Cerberus often joined Gyges to patrol the gates.

"My favorite uncle," Hades said with a smile. "I feel we will have success tonight." Gyges gently lowered one of his fingers to Hades, who lifted his much smaller hand to touch the giant's large pointer finger.

"I've scoured Tartarus to the point where my skin is blistering. My search has been fruitless all summer, but there is one last region to look at. The Shadowed Mountains. Think, nephew." Gyges carefully tapped the top of Hades' head, leaving his black hair in disarray. "It would be easier for him to hide in the darkness. It draws in the wicked."

Hades nodded and ran his hand over his thick mane before lifting his face to his uncle. The many rough-skinned faces of the giant smiled down at him, save one perpetually grumpy face that only frowned unhappily, reminding Hades of the suffering Gyges had once endured. In addition to their blood, Gyges and Hades shared another bond; both had been cruelly imprisoned against their will by Cronus.

"He changed us," Hades murmured his thoughts aloud. "For better or for worse, I do not know."

Gyges regarded him for a long time, knowing he spoke of Cronus. "But you are an honorable God."

"Am I?"

Gyges' eyes were sorrowful as he regarded the dark God. "I should not have assisted you all those years ago. You would not be imprisoned here if I had not opened these gates. You would not be….."

Hades stroked Cerberus' ear, who gave a wide yawn, untroubled by Gyges' mournful cries. "It is not your fault for my bad decisions," Hades replied. "Besides, you and I know I did not belong in the heavens."

"You should have been High King," Gyges cried, pointing his hands high. "Different Immortals rule the heavens, but nothing has changed. And a new God sits on the throne, but it is the same prison. Why did so many die only to change the head of the snake?"

Hades studied the gates of Tartarus contemplatively. "I am where I belong. With whom I belong. They underestimated this dark world. It was…" Hades' voice firmed. "It *is* a refuge for mortals."

"There are whispers that your wife is mending what was broken."

Hades' head shot up. "I want her to stay out of it."

"Stay out of it, nephew? She can never stay out of it. She will write the fate of the world, whether you like it or not. Do not push her away."

The king lowered his eyes. "Let us not discuss it."

The Hecatonchires shrugged, and his many shoulders caused a powerful wind to push through the land. "You try to protect her but do not help her by concealing the truth. Eventually, she will know. You should be the one to tell her."

"Tell her what?" Hades asked with a bitter laugh. "That I am a coward? That I destroyed my people's lives? That I am fucking Minthe?"

Gyges shook his head slowly. "Not in that order."

Hades shifted on his horse and placed the slumbering Cerberus in a satchel attached to the saddle.

"I know, uncle."

Gyges leaned close to Hades. "I wish I could help you more."

"You have. You have guarded these gates for many years, Gyges. And you know my secrets and have not turned from me."

His uncle's eyes scanned the horizon. "Aren't you worried you will be followed?"

Hades looked up at the mountains, and his eyes flashed with anger. "I will not be followed here. Cowards do not enter Tartarus."

"No," Gyges agreed, "but sometimes fools will tread where cowards will not. Be careful, nephew."

"Don't forget, uncle," Hades replied with a smile. "I have Cerberus."

One of Cerberus' snouts poked out at the mention of his name, and Hades petted it absently.

"That dog," Gyges scoffed.

"And the Furies will circle around and make sure I am safe. They make their rounds as we speak."

"I do not think it is safe for an Olympian to stay too long in Tartarus."

Hades mounted Orphnaeus, his bident clasped firmly in his hand. "But I am no Olympian."

"Then good luck, nephew."

Gyges stepped forward, lifting his massive arms, and his hundreds of hands pulled at the heavy iron doors. It sounded like the Earth was being torn apart, and the ground shifted beneath Orphnaeus' feet. The Hecatonchires grunted as the gates burned and throbbed in his hands. The red-hot iron scorched so intensely it would melt a mortal's hands, but the Hecatonchires' skin could withstand the heat of even the core of Tartarus and still stay intact. Hot red steam billowed outward, hitting Hades in the face.

The fierce air was so scorching that he could taste it. It had a disturbing smell, like the taste of moldered iron that spewed up through the Earth's core. The scent always unnerved him and seemed to stay with him for days after, and no amount of scrubbing could wash him clean. It reminded him of war and memories he would prefer to leave forgotten.

He urged Orphnaeus forward with a cry, and they galloped swiftly towards the fumes. Hades glanced towards his uncle, and he saw that one glaring face again until the gates slammed with a loud crash behind him, and they crossed the threshold into Tartarus.

Hades scanned the scorching expanse before him—here was the actual desolation of the Underworld. It was a barren, rocky landscape blazed with molten iron and heat, stretching endlessly. Massive plateaus rose from the Earth, erupting with lethal steam from fissures and lava waterfalls across the landscape. This kingdom did not require the sun or moon to illuminate its atrocities. This was the absence of hope.

Wicked souls wailed in agony, and their screams were like music to his ears. Demons swarmed towards the gates that had unexpectedly opened. The king lifted his hand; brilliant light pushed the creatures back, and their cries were deafening. Other beasts inside the lair seemed to sense that their warden had arrived, and they flew towards Hades. He cut them down one by one with his bident. Tilting his head, he saw the Furies circling high in the sky above.

He pointed his bident to the north and shouted, "Fly ahead and clear a path." The Furies swooped down, annihilating all demons in their path.

Hades charged over the scorched Earth, and Orphnaeus' golden hooves pounded furiously against the smoldering rock. Tonight, Hades was determined to locate the one who had forged the swords. The three brothers, Arges, Steropes, and Brontes, were prominent Cyclopes who were immortalized in myth, but there was one not written into legend.

The Master Crafter had been left out of myth and history by Zeus, for he was too dangerous for mortals and Gods alike to know of his existence. And it was easy to keep him hidden, for the Unnamed One preferred the confines of his cage and had chosen to stay in the shadows when Zeus released the other one-eyed beasts from the gates. The Unnamed One knew he was safe in Tartarus, for as foolhardy as Zeus was, he did not dare enter this prison. A God may be confined here much too easily, and if Hades had adversaries in Tartarus, so had his brother. However, captivity did not bother Hades; he had spent his whole existence imprisoned, and this time, when he thundered through Tartarus, it was not for vengeance but to protect those he loved.

Hades looked towards the twin peaks of the Shadowed Mountains. The three brothers had lived on an opposite volcano millennia ago, forging weapons from anger and desperation in the hope of escape.

The fourth was a mystery to him but could give him the answers he sought.

"She is not safe as long as the weapons exist," he whispered aloud. "He will destroy her. He will destroy all of us."

As they soared over the smoky terrain, the heat intensified. The air was oppressive and vile, and Hades' lungs burned as heat singed his flesh and bronzed his skin. Out of the corner of his eye, he saw movement and glanced backward to see slimy snake-like creatures trailing behind them. Hades reared the horse to a stop as dark tentacles pushed through the ground.

"Damn," he mumbled.

These were the fingers of Typhon, the monster that had been Cerberus' father. Some of the beast's slithering, serpent-like appendages had been severed from his body years ago during his forced passage through the Gates of Tartarus, and these foul serpents still did their master's bidding. Hades spurred Orphnaeus forward, but the tentacles wrapped securely around the stallion's legs. Knocked off balance, Orphnaeus tumbled, and Hades sprang off his back, swinging his bident to slaughter the snakes as he fell through the air. He landed behind Orphnaeus and crouched, yanking the tentacles from the horse's flank, grimacing as they sank their poisonous fangs into his flesh.

He struck the serpents continuously, but twenty more rose from the Earth to cling to the horse for every ten he removed. The snakes had lamprey-like jaws and bit deeply into Orphnaeus, ripping enormous chunks of flesh off his side. The horse screamed in agony as more of the creatures fell mercilessly on him, eventually driving him to the ground. Hades pushed his hands forward to create a forcefield between the creatures and his horse.

"Hold on, my friend," he whispered. Hades grabbed the satchel to locate Cerberus, but the pup must have been tossed in the fall. He searched frantically for the dog but could not find him. "Fuck," he muttered under his breath. "Cerberus!" he bellowed. "Cerberus come!"

The monsters thudded deafeningly against the forcefield, their bloody mouths hitting the magical walls and staining them crimson with blood. Some serpents began burrowing into the ground, and the Earth trembled beneath his feet.

Gyges, Hades said telepathically, *Open the gates. I am sending someone through.* Hades stomped at the tentacles bursting through the ground, then placed his hands on Orphneaus. "I am sorry, Orphneaus, I should not have brought you here."

The stallion looked at Hades lovingly, giving a soft neigh. He stroked one hand over the horse's chest, and Hades closed his eyes, concentrating. He felt the stallion begin to fade away, and when his eyes opened, Orphneaus was gone, safely out of Tartarus. Standing, he surveyed the land beyond the forcefield while the snakes pounded at the shield incessantly. His eyes moved quickly over the rough rocks, but he could not see Cerberus. Where was the dog?

"Cerberus," he called again.

There was no response. Had the snakes covered the Hellhound, devouring Cerberus? The thought was unbearable, and Hades turned to face the creatures. With a nod, the forcefield lowered as he grabbed the whip from his belt, slashing it through the air to slice the beasts in half.

"Typhon!" Hades yelled, his voice resonant. "I will bury what is left of you in the fires of Etna." He crashed the whip hard against the ground. "I am the son of Cronus, King of Darkness, and I do not fear you."

The snakes rushed towards him, springing upon him by the hundreds and encircling him with their tentacles. Their flat lips cut into the body of the king, greedily draining his ancient blood like giant leeches. Hades' flesh was shredded as he pulled them off, hurling the monsters into the air. But as soon as one serpent was gone, another took its place.

"Fucking Typhon," Hades growled.

The king felt his veins beat with darkness as golden ash swirled around him. He lifted his bident high, slamming it hard on the Earth with a resounding blow as a massive purple blast hurled the serpents far, ripping them apart. However, hundreds more slithered from the Earth, rushing out like a black wave. The serpents attacked in unison, ripping into his flesh and grabbing onto muscles and tendons. His vision began to blur, and he swayed, dizzy from pain and poison. He grabbed the golden blade from his back and aimed it towards the snakes, the weapon glowing and hissing in his palm.

"I warn you, I will extinguish your life force. If you descend upon me,

you will never live to feast off of flesh again."

As though his words were a cry of battle, the tentacles swarmed over him, and he stumbled against the assault. He felt himself sinking, drowning in that black sea of serpents when a rage-filled howl roared through the haze.

A massive Cerberus erupted beneath the rocks, his eyes ablaze with gold fire. He began to tear through the serpents, snapping the creatures in his enormous jaws. They tried to latch onto the Hellhound, but his thick coat and skin shielded him from their poisonous fangs. His tail had been transformed into a serpent, and it snappped and hissed at its paternal counterparts. Cerberus stomped them with his massive paws, moving relentlessly through the swarm towards the king, his teeth tearing and gnashing. His saliva held a poison of its own, and the snakes squealed in agony as he devoured them. One of Cerberus' heads opened its jaws, spewing scorching black smoke and jets of fire that burned the serpents to ash.

At the same time, all three heads were flung back as Cerberus let forth an unholy howl that rocked the grounds of Tartarus. His call drew the Furies, who swooped down to scoop up the remaining, scattering beasts, carrying them away to obliterate them in the giant volcano in the west. When he reached his master, the nearest head gently nudged him with his large, wet nose, whimpering until, at last, the king groaned. Cerberus sat back on his haunches, staring adoringly at Hades as he sat up. Cerberus chomped at the air, attempting to collect gold particles that floated around the king. Hades laughed and then grimaced in pain.

"Thank you, Cerberus." He lifted a hand, and the nearest head licked it, the pink tongue engulfing his entire arm. Hades glanced at Cerberus' paws and noticed the purple bloom of the wolf's bane spread across the rocks. A new patch of flowers grew as another drop of saliva dripped from Cerberus' jaw. "Your poison has begun to bloom," Hades observed with a grin. "Your mistress, Cerberus, has taught you well."

Cerberus panted contentedly. Hades rapidly repaired his wounds as best he could after confirming the hound was uninjured. "Soon, it will be too dangerous to venture into these lands, my friend. Perhaps it does not matter because soon nothing will be left of me." Cerberus whimpered. "Come. Let us go onward." The Hellhound lifted a paw, and Hades leaped up, sitting astride his gigantic back. They soared

over the terrain towards the twin mountains until the foothills grew tall and the dim light of Tartarus grew darker.

"Strange that a forger would live away from the volcano," Hades mused.

Cerberus' pace slowed, and Hades leaped from his back, landing softly on the ground in a crouch. He ran his hand across the jagged rock of the mountainside. Unusual markings were carved into the stone: planets, astrological maps, and symbols in a language so ancient that most Gods couldn't read it, but Hades could. He had been taught long ago by a dark Goddess who, like him, did not fit in with the world above. She had taught him the old magic the Olympians feared, and many had forgotten existed. He had whispered this magic over Persephone in Elysium when he had taken her pain away. That day seems so distant now as if it had been a dream. He closed his eyes and recalled holding her in the sea as she confided her secrets. Powerful secrets. That day, he had taken her pain and placed the wound on his heart. The weight of the scar was heavy on his chest. Now, he carried the burden, and he was glad of it.

He refocused on the carvings and the task before him; thin sheets of metal had been pounded into the designs and ignited in a green hue as he touched them, revealing carvings of four Cyclops forging weapons and helmets and gifting them to the Gods. Each panel he touched began to glow, revealing further etchings: a giant eye shining down on two men holding swords pointed towards the heavens, one in blue and the other in gold; a single man holding a green blade, pointing it down towards the Earth. Suddenly, the etchings stopped.

"Forger!" the king bellowed, his voice echoing across Tartarus. There was no answer. Hades leaped up, grasping the edges of the jagged mountainside, and began climbing the steep cliff until he reached the highest of the twin peaks. The amber flame of Tartarus lit the high mountain. "Unnamed One, show yourself!"

The ground began to shake, and a massive blue eye appeared at the edge of a mountain. Hades tightly grasped his bident and stared into the colossal orb. The eye was beautiful; the iris reflected infinity with whirling stars and planets, but in the center was an inky black pupil that left him with a feeling of despair, like a black hole in the core of a galaxy, a reminder that death was at the center of life.

"I seek answers from you," Hades said, lowering his weapon.

The eye blinked once, and then a giant hand appeared, gesturing for the king to follow him. Hades moved to the edge of the mountain. The Cyclops was moving down the mountainside, astonishingly nimble for such a giant creature. Hades quickly jumped across the rocks to the ground, following the beast down the enormous stone stairs that led beneath the mountain. Cerberus paced behind him.

Once in his lair, the Cyclops turned to face Hades. The blacksmith's hair hung in long, dark strands, and his body was filthy, his fingernails encrusted with dirt and grime. The smell emanating from him was revolting, and only a thin scrap of ancient fabric covered his groin, which was barely visible beneath his enormous, overhanging belly.

"What is your name?" Hades asked finally.

"I have no name," the Cyclops smiled, showing a mouthful of enormous, malformed teeth. His voice was raspy from disuse, and his breath was like the air of Tartarus—foul and putrid. Cerberus walked hesitantly to the cavern's entrance, his sensitive noses overwhelmed by the stench, but he would not abandon Hades.

"You forged the swords," Hades stated.

"That was long ago, *king*. Oh, yes," the Cyclops laughed at Hades' surprise. "I know who you are."

Hades pulled the silver sword from its scabbard, and the smile fell from the blacksmith's face. It ignited in a blue flame as he pointed it toward the Cyclops, who stepped closer, mesmerized by the light.

"It has been so long since I have seen it. One of my greatest creations," he cooed lovingly to the sword, the glow of the blade reflecting in his enormous eye. His giant tongue licked his lips, spittle frothing on his chin. "Let me hold it."

Hades drew his hand back, removing the sword from the creature's reach, and the Cyclops frowned. "Tell me how they were made? What gives them such power?"

The Cyclops walked to a table and raised a big stone mug filled with boiling lava, drinking from it with a pleasurable sigh. "Not everyone sided with Zeus, and not everyone sided with Cronus. I sided with my father, Uranus. I warned my brothers that Zeus would kill them once their usefulness expired, but they disregarded my warning. My foolish brothers focused on weapons of protection while I focused on weapons of destruction. Destruction cloaked in the *illusion* of protection." The Cyclops drank another mouthful of lava, wiping his lips clean of the flames.

"How were they made?" Hades demanded again, shaking the sword.

"Forged from Chaos, weaved from the entrails of Ophiotaurus…and," he continued slyly, "dipped in the blood of Uranus."

A shiver of dread coursed down the king's spine, and the Cyclops watched him with a malevolent eye. "How can that be?" Hades asked slowly.

The Cyclops smiled his ghastly grin again. "Foolish Gods, always so eager to receive what is freely given. But everything has a price."

Hades extended his hand and entered the mind of the forger. He watched the Cyclops clumsily make his way to the center of Tartarus and plunge his long arm into the black pit of Chaos, yanking from it a dark, terrible emptiness that swirled in disorder. He spilled Uranus' blood upon the dark matter and uttered a horrible curse in the ancient language as he forged the blackness into a large sheet of iron. As he wielded the swords, his own blood flowed on them.

Hades fell back, disconnecting from the memory, and stared at the Cyclops, who watched him with a smile.

"Those who go where they are not welcome seldom like what they find," the Cyclops sneered.

"Why would you create such weapons!"

Suddenly, the creature's eye narrowed and was filled with malice. "The Gods are vile. You should be wiped from the Earth," he spat. "Vain and selfish beings who care only for their own glory. You bring destruction wherever you go. Zeus murdered my brothers to prevent them from forging thunderbolts for anyone else. They taught Hephaestus their secrets, and the King of Olympus exterminated and slaughtered them just like I knew he would. You cannot put your faith in the Gods."

"You sentenced not only the Gods but all other creatures to damnation by such a creation!" Hades raged.

The Cyclops' deep voice shook the mountain. "To destroy the snake, you must kill what nourishes it."

"My mother is dead because of this sword!"

"Foolish little God," he smirked, "you killed her yourself. I watched you all those years ago in the distance. Watched as you rammed her through. I merely created the weapon, but you ruined her with it. It is in your blood to kill your own. You used them as I knew you would, helpless against such power."

"Tell me how to destroy the blades," Hades demanded. "So, I can end this." He took his other hand and unsheathed the golden blade from the scabbard, and the sword gleamed with golden fire. He crossed both swords into an X, and the flames' colors cast a green hue in the cavern.

The Cyclops began to laugh. "You should not be able to grasp both weapons, *king*."

Hades shook his head. "Tell me how to wipe them from existence!"

The blacksmith sneered at the king. "There is one way, but a selfish immortal would never do it."

"Tell me!" Hades shouted.

"Would you give up your kingdom?"

"Yes."

"Would you give up your power?"

"Yes."

"Would you give up your life?"

Hades paused, glaring up at the giant, and the Cyclops laughed. "A selfish immortal could never do the impossible. You can destroy the blades only by giving up your life." The forger chuckled again, stirring his cup with a femur bone. He lifted the bone to his mouth, taking a satisfying bite before washing it down with another large swallow of the molten grog. "From the looks of it, you do not have much longer to live. But you will still cling to immortality because the longer you live, the greater your desire to survive." He cackled meerily.

"But how can I destroy the blades once I am dead!"

The giant ignored him, still roaring in boisterous laughter and shaking the cave as his belly jiggled. "I knew you would destroy one another," he smirked, wiping a tear of mirth from his eye.

The king's hands shook. "I swore to destroy these weapons."

"Abolish them, and I will build more."

Hades stepped forward, his eyes glowing purple. "I know." His voice was silky as he moved closer, and Cerberus had bent low, watching from the entrance of the cave with golden eyes. The Cyclops moved back warily as the Pluto symbol illuminated the king's forehead. "I saw it in your soul," Hades hissed. "I see it now—the same hatred pouring out of you as it did when you forged the weapon in my hand. Through these weapons, you have given death life."

The king jumped high into the air and, with both blades, sliced the Cyclop's eye, blinding him. The creature let out a cry of rage, flailing his enormous hands. His cup of molten lava splashed across the room as he stumbled and stomped the floor, trying to smash the King of the Underworld like an ant.

Hades quickly slashed with the sword, and the Cyclops' hands tumbled to the ground with a sickening thud as thick black blood arced across the room. He scored again, delivering a mortal blow to the Cyclops' chest. The blacksmith howled his impotent fury.

"If you have no hands, you cannot wield. You are the destroyer of worlds."

"You destroyed yourself," the Cyclops screamed in pain. "Your souls are the Chaos from which you sprang."

"You are from the same Creator!"

"You are of a cursed lineage! Cursed by Uranus as he was overthrown. Cursed to repeat the same fate that was cast upon him. To be betrayed by your children, to betray your children, and to be dethroned repeatedly. I have done my part in helping to destroy you, and I am glad."

The edges of Hades' pupils began to spread until the entire eye was replaced by black. "I would give my child the world; I would give my child my life. I am not cursed to hate my kin."

The Cyclops yelled, "But you cannot have children, and you are dying."

Hades lifted his arms high, and black veins pulsed from the center of his heart to the tips of his fingertips. The ancient words began to flow from his mouth, and the Earth around them shook as he touched the blades to each other. The swords glowed brighter, casting green lights across his face, and energy pulsed from the blades, ripping through the mountain. Cerberus leaped into the room, grasping Hades' cloak with his teeth to yank him from the cavern as it crashed down around them. Hades' last vision of the Cyclops was him thrashing wildly as rocks began to crush his body. Cerberus pulled again, and then they were running up the stairs and away from the mountain as it crumbled to dust around them.

Dirt covered them as they looked at the mountain's peaks. Only one mountain stood; the lair of the Cyclops had been wholly destroyed. Hades sheathed the swords and then climbed atop Cerberus. "Take me to the center of Tartarus."

They traveled deep within the kingdom until the landscape began to change. The atmosphere became increasingly suffocating and putrid. Blood dripped from the sky, gathering in red pools on the ground below. Though Hades had traveled to Tartarus countless times, he was still unfamiliar with much of this vast realm. It made him uneasy to go deeper into this world, but he had no choice; he needed answers and would do whatever was necessary to get them. Down, down, down they went, deeper into Hell. The air grew stiller, the silence thicker, for not even the demons ventured this far. Yet, he could detect something hovering in the quiet, hiding in the dense heaviness.

"We are here," he said abruptly.

He jumped off of Cerberus, surveying the area. The ground beneath his boots was mushy and pulpy. It was covered in thick crimson and purple vein-like structures that pulsated with life, the rhythmic sloshing, creating a cadence that grew louder as Hades moved towards the center. The veins and vessels converged, forming a massive, bulging black hole. Hades stood over the emptiness, gazing into the abyss. He knelt and reached his hand into the pit, drawing it back up. It was nothing but air.

He paused for a time, staring contemplatively at his hands.

"Stay here," he cautioned Cerberus before bending again and pressing his body through the darkness.

He could hear the Hellhound's whines as he pushed through the narrow passage. The tunnel was too narrow for him to stand, forcing him to crawl on his hands and knees. He caught his breath as the slick pounding of the arteries encompassed him, the oppressive darkness pressing in from all sides. It was suffocating and claustrophobic, but he forced his mind to be still as his body pushed forward on his elbows and knees. A terrible squelching noise filled the dense passageway each time he inched forward. It seemed that he went on like that for hours, seeing only darkness, until he abruptly came to a halt, suddenly cautious. The blackness ahead was different, darker than it had been, and he imagined he could feel movement. He began to edge backward, sensing a presence.

Suddenly, the darkness moved toward him, gripping him, pulling him into the emptiness, and down, down, down he fell.

An infinity of nothingness spread before him, and Hades drifted alone. He knew where he was—between Heaven and Hell, betwixt realms—and he waited patiently, poised in oblivion. Moments passed, an eternity in the blackness until a gleaming white dot appeared on the pitch-black horizon. His body was curiously feather-light in the nothingness. The King of the Dead was filled with tranquility and joy as the light shimmered in the distance. It seemed familiar, like a flashback to a long-forgotten memory, and his heart flooded with happiness.

"Who are you?" he called to the light.

His voice was hollow, the words resonating oddly through the darkness. He pushed his way through the nothingness, desperate to reach the small dot, but the further he traveled, the more distant the light became. As the white light faded, a sense of bereftness overcame him; losing that tiny glow was nearly too great to bear.

"Come back!" he pleaded. "Do not leave me!"

Suddenly, something raced forward, a potent and intangible presence vibrating in the ether. The emptiness reverberated in waves that pulsated towards him, flinging him back.

"You dare to venture here," a low voice thundered. "You are owed nothing. You will find nothing. You are nothing."

Nothing—the word swirled around Hades, pulling at his skin and devouring him. He tried to push through the darkness, reaching his hands towards that gentle light in the distance, but it was barely visible now.

"I seek to destroy the blades forged by the Unnamed One," he called out, but the only answer was silence. Hades swam deeper into the darkness. "Tell me about the child, Persephone's son. Is he here?"

"I answer to no God," the ancient voice laughed, the bitter sound filling the space around him. "I am Protogenoi, the Master of Fate. I am the beginning, and I will be your end. I am the nothingness you sprang from, and I will be the oblivion yet to come."

Hades sensed a change in the darkness, a schism in the emptiness, and mayhem erupted from the void all at once. Disorder swirled about him, attempting to infiltrate his consciousness. He felt as if he were drowning in feelings as he was dragged into memories and dreams. Visions of Persephone swirled—different variations of her, every color of hair and eye color, every possible version. She loved him, and she hated him; she was both his rebirth and his death.

She merged suddenly with Demeter, and they were two halves of one whole, spinning until their features blurred. They faded abruptly, and he found himself gazing into a mirror. No, it was not a mirror but another version of himself. He was the ruler of the Upper World, perched on the pale marble throne but still imprisoned within Cronus, clawing to be free. Behind the throne stood another version of himself, nude and white-haired, who smiled knowingly as he approached Hades. Hades tried to wrench himself from the visions, but the emptiness encircled him, and he plummeted deeper into Chaos' abyss.

His red cape began to attack him like an animal, like a wave of blood pushing against him, and Hades began to fight, but when he looked down at his body, he was a child again, his tiny hands helpless and soft. Suddenly, the cloak fell away like a curtain, and he looked up to see his mother bending toward him. Just as she was about to reach him, she was ripped apart, and he was screaming when a cool hand stroked his arm, pulling him from the madness.

"Come with me, little one," the voice whispered.

And then he was falling, and the darkness enveloped him once more.

Hades sat up abruptly, gasping for breath. He was conscious of the pulsing, damp marshland between him as he tried to piece together what had happened. He had come to Tartarus in search of Chaos. Someone had saved him. He had been brought back from the void. Just as he remembered the voice in the darkness, a shadow passed over him, and he glanced up to see his rescuer.

"Hello, Pluto," the figure greeted.

The blurred image above him finally righted itself. "Nyx," he gasped breathlessly.

Stars twinkled in her eyes as she gazed at him. "While it is always pleasant to see you, I must ask, what were you doing inside Chaos? You are too inexperienced to navigate through it. Lucky for you, it was morning, and I was returning home. Cerberus was concerned; that is how I knew to look for you." The puppy-sized Cerberus sighed as she rubbed one of his ears. "He is a very loyal companion."

Hades attempted to stand, but she gently pushed him back down. He tumbled as helplessly as a child under her firm hand.

"Rest," she demanded. "Now, what were you doing?"

He regarded her wearily. He knew Nyx well enough that she would not allow him to leave without an explanation. "I was seeking answers," he answered lamely.

One perfect brow arched. "And you thought to find them within Chaos? You will find no answers there, only more questions."

Hades pressed a trembling hand against his head. "But I felt a presence there. Something was trying to reach me. A white light, do you know what it meant, who it could be? It felt… familiar."

Nyx's face was troubled. "No one has ever traveled to the very center of Chaos or has any idea what is within. You should not return there, Pluto. Even the elder Gods do not dare to seek his heart."

When Hades opened his mouth to speak, he began to vomit. While he dry-heaved, she knelt behind him, gently brushing his hair back.

"That will teach you not to attempt such a feat again," she scolded kindly. When he had finally finished retching, she gently placed the King of the Dead in her lap, wiping the sweat from his brow. His eyes closed wearily, letting her cool fingers soothe him, the touch reminiscent of his mother. "Tell me why you sought him," she urged. "It is not like you to be so reckless."

"I am trying to right a wrong." He laughed mirthlessly. "Well, many wrongs. I have done such bad things, Nyx, such unforgivable things." He pushed his hands through his hair, dust, and dirt falling from the thick locks.

"We all have done bad, Pluto; it is difficult to avoid when you live an eternity. Evil conceals itself in such lovely packages that it is much too late by the time you have removed the covering to see what is beneath." She paused and then asked, "I have known you for the better part of your life. I do not believe you are wicked. Are you sorry for what you did?"

"Yes," he replied in a low, trembling voice. "However, regret alone is insufficient to atone. I do not seek redemption, for I know that that is impossible. But if only I could reverse some of the harm that I unleashed on the world."

"Hades." He opened his eyes to meet hers. "I do not think you have felt well for some time, my child," she said softly. His eyes lowered, and she drew his face toward her. "Why don't you tell me the whole story? You will find that I am quite incapable of being shocked."

He shook his head and struggled to sit up. "Not until I tell Persephone." Nyx rose to her feet and extended a hand to him. The Goddess hauled him to his feet, and as he staggered, her brows drew down over her unfathomable eyes.

"Tell me," she urged again. When Hades said nothing, her gaze swept over him with careful perusal, lingering on his eyes. "Oh, poor sweet child," she murmured. As though her sympathy was his undoing, he fell towards her, sobbing into her arms. "I know," she murmured, gently cradling him as if he were a child. "I noticed you were not quite yourself at the ball. A bit too sociable and glancing down the far end of the table at your lover. How long has this been happening?"

"Too long. I want this to end, to be free of this," he choked out, "but..."

She tightened her grip on him. "Gaia will guide you. If you pray to her."

"Until Persephone came..."

"She will be fine. She is strong."

"She will despise me."

Nyx drew back, holding him up. "There is one who could help you."

"Tell me. I will do anything."

She turned so they both faced east. She raised her hand, gesturing to a fiery castle far in the distance, and Hades shook his head, falling back from her as a shadow crossed his face.

"No," he growled. "Not him. Anyone but him. I detest him."

"But does your hatred override your love for Persephone?"

"He is a monster; he would never help me."

"He *became* a monster, but there was a time when he was not. He once was a great ruler until the curse of Uranus took hold."

"A curse is no excuse," he uttered harshly.

Her fingers traced exactly where the pale scar traced across his chest, though it was hidden by his clothing. "You, above all others, understand the power of a curse."

"I fought it."

"Yes," she answered softly. "You battled valiantly. Do you still fight against what haunts you now?"

His dark eyes narrowed. "That is not fair."

"The Cosmos are not fair, little Pluto. You must try to forgive your father. Hatred is a fertile soil in which darkness might flourish. There is hope for Cronus. Your father was not born evil. Uranus cursed him, the first curse uttered into this Universe."

Hades began pacing, agitated at the prospect of having to turn to the one person he despised the most. "What happened when I was inside him is unforgivable. What those demons did to me..." He shook his head as if trying to shake the memory from his mind. "I can never forget. Cronus had to have heard my screams for help. Why did he not help me? If he had, our fates would all be different."

Nyx's eyes sparkled, sorrow spinning deep within her heavenly gaze. "I am so very sorry for what happened to you as a boy. But don't you see that his fate would be different, too? You view Cronus through the eyes of a hurt child, but you must look at him through the wisdom of man," she insisted. "He has suffered as you have; he can understand you in a way that no one else ever will." She gestured again to the distant castle. "He knows the deep magic, Pluto. He could help. He may be the only one who can."

Hades stayed silent as his thoughts became a tangle of emotions and memories he longed to forget. The pictures of Chaos pulsated in his thoughts, and he collapsed abruptly, gripped with nausea as he retched once more. Nyx grabbed his arm as he slumped against her.

"He thought it was the mother," he mumbled, "but it was the daughter. She mustn't know. She is in danger."

Nyx lifted him to his feet, taking his clammy hand in hers while she traced the lifeline on his palm with her index finger and frowned. "Chaos leaves the mind scattered," she said soothingly, "but your thoughts will clear soon. Wait a day before deciding, for you might regret it later. Come, you should leave this place; it has already taken too much of you."

She led him to Cerberus, who, with a nod from Nyx, grew rapidly again. She assisted Hades in mounting and then leaped up to sit behind him, steadying him. When they arrived at the gates, Nyx jumped down, pounding on the door. Hades struggled off Cerberus as Gyges wrenched open the doors.

Nyx moved forward and grasped his hands. "Tell her, my child. No matter how difficult it is." Her eyes moved over him. "Tell her before you are unable to. Now go, " she said gently, "and do not seek Chaos again."

She gave Cerberus one last rub before the gates closed behind them. Hades heard a soft whisper and turned. Nyx was just visible behind the wall, her eyes glowing like stars in the darkness of Tartarus.

"Let me know when you are ready to see your father, and I will guide you to the castle myself. The Blood Moon draws near. Adjust your eyes, Pluto, to see what is so clearly in front of you." With a wave of her hand, the gates slammed shut, and the Goddess of the Night vanished from sight.

Gyges stood over Hades, his gaze riveted on the golden dust swirling behind his nephew like fireflies. Orphnaeus moved around the giant and nuzzled Hades softly.

"Nephew—" Gyges began.

Hades lifted a hand, halting Gyges' words. "I know, uncle. I know."

"I wish I could help," Gyges said in his thick voice, lifting enormous hands to wipe the tears from his faces.

"You do help, uncle. You have always helped," Hades replied emphatically. "I must go now. Dawn is approaching, and I cannot be discovered here."

The king raised his hand again, and Gyges bent his nearest fingers toward him, the contact expressing the love their words could not. Hades mounted Orphnaeus, pulling the cape's hood over his head and saluting Gyges before spurring the steed forward, with Cerberus following close behind. As dawn broke over the horizon, the Giant of Tartarus wept, for he saw death in the glittering ash that swirled behind the king.

Hades leaned heavily upon Orphnaeus as the stallion thundered across the landscape. Suddenly, he detected a second pattern of hoofbeats behind them, and he swiveled the horse rapidly, surveying the horizon.

"Who is there?" he shouted. There was no answer. Hades lifted his bident, which erupted into blue flames, illuminating the pathway. It was empty. "Show yourself," he demanded, but only the wind answered, blowing eerily through the desolate hollow.

Cerberus was perfectly calm, sensing no threat, so Hades turned again, urging Orphnaeus forward. At the point where the path led to the palace, Hades ordered Cerberus to return to the castle, and the hound took a different route as he and Orphnaeus continued northward. From the Gates of the Underworld, they ascended the steep mountain and sped across the frigid plains of Earth. Tiny snowflakes fell from the sky, and Hades shivered in the frigid air. The black steed's golden hooves plowed through the ice until they reached the summit of a mountain: Mount Othrys. Orphnaeus started ascending until they arrived at a large, abandoned temple. Slowing the stallion, Hades dismounted, guiding him to the entrance, where he would be protected from the elements.

As if in a dream, he began to wander the empty corridors of the abandoned palace. It had been long forgotten, and snow and ice poured through the shattered windows, mixing with the decaying vegetation on the marbled flooring. Blood dripped from his wounds, coloring the morning's pristine snow scarlet. He went through the crumbling corridors until he came to what had once been a bedroom. His fingertips brushed the walls; he could sense the life that had once been here, its triumphs and tragedies. It was dead to the world now, the lives of all those who had lived there long forgotten, their sorrows and successes obliterated from memory. He approached a window to observe the first faint rays over the icy horizon. He heard a quiet footstep and turned, simultaneously pulling the blue-flamed sword from the scabbard on his back. His hand trembled when he realized he was aiming the weapon at his wife. She stood in the doorway, holding his helmet of invisibility in her hand.

"Persephone," he admonished harshly, sheathing the blade swiftly. "What are you doing here?"

Without a word, she moved forward, pushing the cloak from his shoulders to study him. Deep gashes on his torso were still bleeding profusely. He was covered in grime and muck, and the heat of Tartarus had bronzed the skin beneath. Her eyes followed a rivulet of blood that traveled from his chest to the snow below. He let out a startled gasp as she wrapped her arms around him, pressing her head against his heart. Instantly, he encircled her with his arms, burrowing his face in her hair.

"Persephone." He repeated her name as if it were a talisman that would keep the demons at bay, and for a time, maybe it would.

"Why won't you let me in?" she asked sadly. "Where do you go night after night to suffer such injuries?"

He tightened his embrace. "I seek to right my wrongs."

She raised her face, and he committed the hue of her gaze to his memory until the lush green was seared into his consciousness. Her gaze softened as she looked at him. "Let me help you, Hades."

He pulled her closer so that she could not look into his eyes, terrified that she would slip into the depths of the darkness that lay within him. "Persephone, I cannot. Come," he said, taking her hand. "Watch the sunrise with me. Let that be enough for now."

He escorted her to the expansive balcony, where she could see the sun beginning to rise over the snow-capped mountain peaks. How many more dawns did he have left? He trembled as the frigid air flowed over him, a stark, welcome contrast to the stinking heat of Tartarus. After the turmoil of Chaos, the stillness of the new day felt sacrosanct, and he allowed the cold to cleanse him, willing it to remove the jumbled images from his mind.

"Where do you go?" Persephone asked again.

"Someplace... unpleasant."

"Where?"

"Please, Persephone." He stood behind her, and he leaned against the balcony for support. "For the moment, let us enjoy the stillness of the dawn, just you and I." It broke his shattered heart, after all that he had done to her, that she still cared for him. It would be far better if she did not. And yet, selfishly, his poor, withered heart could not help but rejoice at her nearness. Lifting her hand, he kissed the palm, and just the touch of her flesh against his mouth was enough. It was enough that she stood beside him. It was enough that she had loved him, loved him enough still to try to help him. "It's enough," he whispered.

"What?" she asked. She had turned to look up at him, and he bent, kissing her forehead.

Although the feeble rays of sunlight fought to penetrate the bitter winter air, Hades closed his eyes and allowed the chilly rays to brush his face. He would remember standing at the dawn of a new day with the one he loved best in his arms.

"Hades, I can feel your torment," Persephone said. "Tell me, please! What is the answer to all of this?"

"The answer is there for you to see. Can you see the truth, Persephone?" He took her hand and brought it to the scar over his heart. "Can you not feel my answer?"

Her eyes filled with tears. "I do not understand. Sometimes, I feel you are two men! " His body tightened; she was so close, and he wanted to scream out his answer, but his mouth remained frozen, the truth locked away.

"I wish I could make you understand," he breathed. "But I am afraid I do not always understand myself. It is quite disturbing to look in the mirror and not recognize who is looking back." He tilted her face upward. "I feel the conflicting emotions inside of you; doubt and fear have festered. It makes it so hard to see reality."

She paused to reflect on his comments. "Then start at the beginning," she insisted.

"The beginning?" he asked quietly.

"Yes."

"In the beginning, I was born here." He gestured to the room with his hand. "In this castle, I was like many other babes, born with love from my mother's womb. I was not called Hades then, but our true names died long ago. Only shadows walk these halls now."

She looked around the ruins, the snow whirling throughout the temple. His gaze wandered to the far end of the room. "Here I was born." His eyes trailed up to the opposite end of the room. "And there I died." He shook his head at her confusion. "No, not death in absolutes, but it was in this room that my innocence died. Maybe that's how it's supposed to be, death nibbling away at you until all that's left is a hollow shell, and you yearn for nothingness to fill the void. Until you yearn to be nothing." He paused, then lifted his hand to hers. "Would you like to see more?"

She nodded and slipped her small hand into his larger one. His fingers encircled hers, and he guided her along the desolate passageways. They arrived in a colossal room. A tall, decaying ivory throne stood in the center, surrounded by windows that offered breathtaking views of the valley below.

The king brushed his hand over the throne, the fragile stone crumbling to dust beneath his fingers. "Do you believe in forgiveness? Can an evil man be redeemed?"

She hesitated, remembering the evil she had seen him do, remembering the soul that she herself had condemned to Tartarus. "If the man regrets his actions, then goodness is still inside him. If there is still goodness, there can be forgiveness."

He turned to her and held her hand against his face. His skin felt cool beneath her hand, as cold as the winter air that blew around them. "I want to believe that."

Her fingers stroked his cheek. "Is it you who needs forgiveness?" she asked softly. "Or your father?"

Hades closed his eyes tightly, and when he opened them, they were burning as though with fever. "Both. My father... and myself. I hate him, but I am no better. I have done unspeakable things. You know what I have done." He dropped her hand and tried to turn away from her. "I should have never let you near me; I should never have touched you. I knew it was wrong, but I was weak."

"Hades--"

He smiled down at her wistfully. "You are still so sweet after everything I have done to you; instead of cursing me, you will tell me there is still good inside me. But there is not."

"No, do not say that! I know there is good inside of you! I have seen it repeatedly and watched you sacrifice yourself for others. Something has happened. Start from the beginning," she implored again. "What of your father?"

"My father was cursed after dethroning Uranus. I sometimes wonder if Uranus had not damned him if... if he could have loved me."

She looked up at him, shocked. "But he was wicked. He tormented you."

"Did he?" His voice was strained, the effects of Chaos still pounding in his mind. "Or was it another hand that forced Cronus to act against his will? Is it only the outcome that we remember, or does the story of how the villain was shaped matter?" He turned to look out at the frozen horizon. "I have hated him for so long," he laughed bitterly, raking his hand through his hair. "No, not hated. That is too tame a word. Loathed. Despised. I wanted to rip the fibers of his being to shreds so that he would cease to exist. But maybe he was doing the world a favor by imprisoning us. Perhaps he saw the evil I would do. And he was a righteous king, good to his people. Under him, mortals lived long, happy lives. His reign was known as "The Golden Age of Man." The people loved him, and he protected them." He lowered his eyes, and she saw his hands clench the balcony so tightly it crumbled beneath his fingers. "He loved them more than he loved me."

"Is that why you did it?" she asked softly. "To punish him?"

He turned to her as though shocked at her question, his eyes wide. "No," he answered fervently. "No."

"Then why?" She moved forward and shook his arm. "Why did you do it?"

He leaned wearily against a timeworn column. "I was weak and foolish. It was long ago. I think, Persephone that I know the answer to my question. There is no forgiveness for me; some crimes cannot be forgiven. Perhaps this is my penance," he said, looking at her. The light from the rising sun reflected on her face- the light in the darkness.

"What is?" she asked, confused.

"You are so beautiful. What a selfish deed I have done in marrying you."

He turned his back to her, and she saw it then, the cool winter sun glinting against its brilliance: the Golden Blade. For a brief moment, she was rendered speechless by shock, and then she charged forward angrily, roughly twisting him to face her.

"You lied to me about Zeus' sword!" she hissed, almost blinded by her wrath.

His black eyes were fathomless as he watched her. "Yes," he admitted quietly.

"You promised me, time and time again, that you did not have his weapon! You swore to me!" She put her hands to her head, staring at him wildly. "Don't you see what you have done? You have unleashed war upon your people, and for what! Tell me! Tell me what was so important that you have risked everything!" When he said nothing, she lunged towards the sword, attempting to pull it from his back. "Give me the blade!" she demanded.

"No."

"People are going to get hurt, including you! There is no need for him to know it was you. I will tell Zeus I found it; I can return it anonymously; I can slip it into his bed at night, and he can think he just misplaced it! I do not care how it is returned, but we cannot keep it!" She reached for the weapon again, and Hades effortlessly prevented her from getting it. With an unholy cry, she launched herself towards him, determined to pull it from him. In an insultingly short amount of time, he had both her wrists captured in one hand, effectively subduing her. She was exhaling short, furious gasps, and hearing his calm, steady breaths enraged her more.

"Persephone, stop," he ordered calmly.

"What happened to the love of your people?" she spat, beginning her struggles anew. "You have abandoned them. You have abandoned me."

"It is for love that I took it. For them and you."

An unpleasant laugh escaped her lips. "It is selfishness. It is for power. Zeus told me you would seek the swords to control all the kingdoms." She pulled back enough to see him, his dark, beautiful face hovering above hers. "I didn't believe him then."

His grip on her wrists tightened, anger flashing in his dark eyes. "Do you believe it now?"

"Give me a reason not to," she spat.

"You do not trust me?"

"You know I don't."

"Good," he murmured softly under his breath. He drew her closer, pressing her head against his chest, and she was so astonished that she let him. "I pray that is enough to keep you safe. I want to take you away from all this, but there is no place we can run, no place that is safe for us."

"What are you talking about!"

She stepped back, and he let her go.

"The evil is within me. I carry it wherever I go; no matter where we run, you will not be free of it. Don't you see it, Persephone? Can you not see it?" *See me*, he whispered into her mind.

"What evil?" she asked.

"It's right in front of you." He held his arms out. "Can't you see?"

She let out a noise of disgust. "You speak in riddles, just like your Olympian friends."

"You look with your eyes, but they deceive you. You only see me; if you look closer, you will see—"

He suddenly cried out in pain and collapsed to his knees. She raced forward, but he raised his hand, halting her as he stood clumsily. When he faced her, his nose was bleeding, and his eyes mirrored the golden dawn, lights flickering like fireflies in the endless depths. He approached her, his gait unsteady. "It will not matter soon," he said softly. "My father once ruled all the kingdoms, and now he sits alone in Tartarus. The sins of the father were always mine to bear."

"You said you did not believe that," she said, her voice barely audible.

"All love turns to ash and is reborn in death." He pulled her to him abruptly, and she struggled against him this time, but he tightened his grip. "You loved me once, did you not?"

"I did love you," she whispered.

"And your love has died."

She said nothing, tears silently streaming down her face. Love, fear, and hate—how could she feel so many emotions at once? She wept for him and for herself. She felt his fingers tracing her cheeks, wiping away the tears.

"Be brave, Persephone," he said into her ear. "Do not doubt yourself; you are stronger than you know. You will survive this, and that is all that matters." Footsteps crunched in the snow behind them, and Hades spoke to the newcomer without lifting his head. "I instructed you to watch her," he said, his voice cold.

"I've been busy." Persephone tightened at the voice. Ares moved forward, a dark hood covering his face. "My schedule is rather full between Olympus, Aphrodite, and a war."

"What an unholy trio, " Persephone interjected, her voice angry. "And how perfect for you. Why don't you go back to your friends?"

"Do not let it happen again," Hades warned coolly, ignoring Persephone's outburst. He turned to his wife, and his voice softened. "Time for your training."

She backed away from him. "I will not go with him."

His fingertips traced the edge of her lips. "Oh, there, sweet wife, you are wrong."

He raised his arm, and the bident flew into his hand. He thumped the edge of it against the floor, and Persephone and Ares vanished into the Underworld. Her enraged face was the last thing he saw before she disappeared. He stood for endless moments, staring at where she had been, before abruptly turning and walking down a hall until he came to a stone rotunda. A marble statue of a beautiful Goddess stood in the center. Thick green ivy and wisteria grew around it; it had been centuries since it had been tended to, but the face was as beautiful and dear as it had ever been. Rhea. Hades collapsed to his knees, lifting his arms to embrace the cold stone.

"Mother. Protect her, for I do not have the strength."

As the sun rose high against the horizon, the King of the Dead hung his head and wept.

CHAPTER 18
THE GODDESS & THE SOLDIER

Persephone walked swiftly through the palace, trying to ignore the tall shadow at her back. Rage was trembling inside her like a living being, and she could feel the hum of anger singing in her veins.

"Do not follow me," she called out harshly.

There was no answering response, and though she could hear no footsteps behind her, she knew he must be trailing her. She rounded a corner, and Ares suddenly appeared in front of her, so close they almost collided. He threw back his cloak to reveal his pale hair and princely features. They had fooled her once, but they would not again.

"How did you get in front of me," she spat.

"I know many secrets of this palace," he replied with a smirk. "Are you ready to continue your lesson?"

"Are you ready to stop being a sadist?"

"Now where would be the fun in that? Besides," he said, leaning one muscular arm against the wall, "aren't you curious to see how Mourning Fields is doing?"

"Well, after my husband decided to fill it with the prisoners of Tartarus, I have less interest. Being around one rapist is quite enough for me."

He straightened, his hands in tight fists, and his cheekbones turned a deep shade of red. "*Den mas gamas*," he said angrily. "You think you know everything." He stopped abruptly, his mouth closing tightly, white brackets forming on either side of his lush lips. "I am tired of this. Take these." He pulled a sword from beneath his robe and forced it into her hand. She had been too distracted to notice, but she saw that he also had a bow slung over his shoulder. He roughly placed it into her arms and realized it was the pomegranate bow she had made on the mountainside. "Take care with that," Ares said coolly. "I prefer not to have another arrow shoved into my heart."

"Oh yes," she replied softly, "I wouldn't want to injure the poor little War God."

He turned and pointed his finger in her face. "What do you want from me? You want me to say sorry?"

She gave a bitter laugh. "Sorry? Words could never grant forgiveness for what you did. And I doubt you know the meaning of the word," she replied in a tight voice. "Why must *you* train me? If I must be trained, Athena could see to it."

Ares scoffed. "Athena. Do you forget what she did to Medusa? She would have cursed you the minute she learned you were no longer a virgin. Maybe she could carry your head on a shield."

Her hands tightened into fists. "And I have you to thank for that, don't I?"

"As I said, you seem so certain of everything."

"I am certain," she spat. "I was there; I witnessed it. I lived it."

"So did I!" he shouted. "You don't know—" Again, he cut off his words abruptly. He took a deep breath and then continued. "You disparage me every chance you get. Do not treat me as every God on Olympus does. I am not a fool. I remember, too," he said in a quiet voice.

"What an inconvenience it must be for you to remember, *defiler*."

He pulled her by the arm, and he was so fast she didn't have time to stop him. He yanked her against him. "Stop calling me that," he snarled in her face. The hand on her arm began to glow, burning with the deadly fire that lived inside the War God. "This is your last warning." She felt an answering call within herself, and her eyes sparked with an answering flame. Ares' eyes traveled over her face. "Gods, my father would love to use you as a weapon. Who would think that a forest Goddess could call fire to her?"

"Get your hands off me."

Ares' fingers tightened around her arms. "Make me, *queen*."

The glow in her gaze began to spread, obscuring her iris and pupil with golden flames.

Ares smiled. "You do not scare me. I am forged of fire." He leaned over and whispered in her ear. "I have seen terrors you can only imagine, and I grew up in the worst horror of all."

"And what is that?"

"Olympus." He let go of her abruptly. "There is a future, and if you do not train for it, Zeus will rip everything you love from you until you beg for death."

"I have already lost everything."

"You have shit for brains if you believe that," he sneered. "You wallow in the Gods' damn misery of the past, and as long as you are stuck there, you cannot prepare for the future."

"I don't wallow in the past!"

"Yes, you do, and it is exactly where he wants you. Alone and frightened like a lost little girl. We will go on foot," he said abruptly. She did not move, and so he pressed closer to her. "You may as well come. The sooner we go, the sooner I will leave you alone. I am nothing if not tenacious."

With a snarl, she turned on her foot, leading the way out of the palace. As they exited, he motioned for her to follow him, taking her through a path she had not seen before. Though she tried to drive his voice from her mind, she considered his words. The bastard was right; she had let the past consume her. She had fought so hard to let go of the anger in her heart, but she was filled with uncertainty and fear, and she found

herself relapsing back into old patterns. Scars she believed had healed had resurfaced and were festering. What happened to the Goddess who had begun over and was determined to influence her destiny? She hastily wiped away a tear.

"Tears don't help anything." he volunteered in his rough voice. She sniffed and glared at him.

"I don't think I need your advice," she snapped.

He shrugged, slowing as they stopped before the big rose quartz gates. "Persephone," he began tentatively, "there is something your husband has not told you, something you should know."

Her heart accelerated at his words. "What is it?" she demanded urgently. "Tell me."

Ares' hands trembled, and he looked in physical pain, his face pulled back in a grimace. "I—cannot." He suddenly sank into a crouch, studying the gates. "Wait," he whispered, yanking her down beside him. "These gates were supposed to be locked. Once the prisoners moved in, they were supposed to be closed to the outside world."

They regarded one another, and simultaneously, both drew their weapons. Ares beckoned with his hand, and they slipped through the gates into the shadowed valley within. Persephone gasped as the Mourning Fields came into sight. The fields had been burned, and smoke lingered thick in the air. The trees were still burning brightly, golden embers dancing within the branches. The fire had been recent.

"I am assuming it's not supposed to look like this?" he asked in a whisper, lifting a brow.

She shook her head. "It was to be a place of refuge. I poured every ounce of love into this land, and it's destroyed." She reached her hand to a nearby tree branch, and it cried out in pain to her. "Who did this?"

Ares' eyes gleamed, and he urged her forward. "Come, I hear something."

As they got closer, she could hear a woman's wailing voice in the distance. They quickened their pace, moving through the thick smoke until they came to a clearing. A man had pinned a woman to the ground, her dress torn to shreds as he slapped her viciously into compliance. Ares snarled, raising his sword when an arrow flew into the man's chest. The attacker was thrown back as two more ruby red arrows plummeted into him. Ares lowered his sword and glanced at Persephone, who held the bow expertly between her hands.

"As good a shot as ever, I see," Ares muttered.

Persephone ignored Ares, hurrying ahead. She knelt by the woman and swiftly pulled the garment together, covering her, before helping her up. The God followed more leisurely, stopping once he reached the man. The Tartarus prisoner sat up, looking at Ares before spitting at his feet. Ares tried to kick him in the face, but his foot passed right through him. The prisoner began to laugh, hurling insults at the God.

"Fuck," Ares growled in disgust. "How can we put them back into Tartarus if we can't touch them?"

Persephone approached him. "I think I might have an idea." Kneeling next to the prisoner, she pushed her hands into the soil; thick, black vines crawled out of the Earth, wrapping firmly around the man and chaining him to the ground. The prisoner fought and bucked against the shackles, his eyes bursting madly, but he could not escape.

"You like to hurt defenseless women?" she inquired softly.

The prisoner laughed again, baring his stained teeth and straining his hips grotesquely as he stared at her.

She made a noise of disgust, then lifted her arms, and a pale green light began to glow from her hands. As the light spilled from her palms, it reached the prisoner, and an enormous fluorite crystal developed around the man, trapping him inside. The man's face was eternally contorted in a terrified expression, his body forever imprisoned in green crystal.

Persephone turned to Ares with a satisfied smile. "He looks better that way, don't you think? Now, you'll be able to throw him into Tartarus."

Ares knocked his knuckles against the stone and laughed. "That is quite a trick."

"I suppose I have you to thank for it," she said reluctantly. "If Maketes had not put me on my horse, which led me to the crystal forest, I never would have known this gift was possible. How did you know it was there?"

Ares bent his head, his blond hair shielding his eyes. "You give me too much credit. Your husband instructed me to send you there, so I am sure whatever was in that forest was waiting for you."

"But...Hades acted as though he did not know I possessed this power. He was surprised when I told him."

Ares' eyes lifted, and the dark blue gaze stared into hers with startling intensity. "He probably was surprised. He drank Lethe water after giving the order. He's been doing that a lot lately."

She looked at him, stunned. "But...why would he do that?"

Ares shrugged his shoulders. "Why does anyone drink from the Lethe? There must be something he does not want to remember."

She huffed in frustration. "But why would Hades not want to remember? Tell me," she demanded. "What is going on?"

"Perhaps he has something to hide."

"Your answers are always so ambiguous," she scoffed. "You talk in riddles. If I did not know better, I would think *you* were trying to hide something."

"Of course I am," he snapped. "I am a God from Olympus; therefore, every word I say is a lie. We must refocus. I brought you here to train, and train you will. The prisoners here need to be disposed of. How would you like to help me round them up?"

"I would like nothing better than to help you dispose of them. We need to help her first, though."

Persephone moved, but Ares was already there. He bent to the ground and lifted his hand to the soul, helping her to stand. "Where are you from?" he asked in the softest voice Persephone had ever heard from him.

"Nearby," the soul whispered, her cheeks filled with tears. "My hut is very close to here. I was walking when I heard a voice calling me. I should never have come here; I was foolish, but it sounded like a child. I thought they needed help."

"You must not blame yourself. The wicked always know how to call on the innocent. What is your name?"

"Nadia," she whispered.

"Nadia. You have been very brave. Can you walk to your family if we take you to the entrance?"

She nodded vigorously. Quietly, they accompanied the woman to the door. Once they reached the threshold, Ares held up his hand. "Go directly home. Once there, lock your doors. This land is no longer safe. Tell all others not to venture here." The woman gave them both a grateful nod, her eyes brimming with tears.

"Who are you?" she whispered.

"We are no one," Ares replied. "Now go, and remember, do not come back here." With one final bow to them both, she took off, her form disappearing into the black night. When he turned, Persephone was watching him with wide eyes. "What?" he demanded, bristling.

"Nothing," Persephone replied, watching him warily.

"Let's go find these swine," Ares growled.

Together, they moved through the charred, blackened forest. "Why can our weapons touch them but not us?" Ares whispered to her. She looked at him in surprise. "You may think I am stupid, but I recognize what I am good at and what I am not. You're the authority on the dead, not me."

"My husband is the King of the Dead, not me."

"And you are the Queen of the Dead."

She hesitated and then furrowed her brow. "Well, I cannot know for certain, for I have never been to Tartarus, but I imagine you can touch them there. Souls can always touch other souls, but a safeguard must be built in case the prisoners ever escape the Underworld so they cannot harm living humans. Hades must have designed it so that Godly weapons could still harm them outside of it."

Ares nodded his head. "Always thinking ahead, that one."

"And yet he set them free," she replied, her voice harsh.

"Yes," he agreed. "And don't you think that is strange?"

The God of War led the way through the fields, seemingly following his nose, and she trusted him to find the trouble; after all, wasn't that what he did? He stopped abruptly and pulled them both down to the ashen ground. She fell with a quiet "oompf."

"Up ahead," he whispered, his voice edged with excitement at the prospect of battle. "Follow behind me." She moved to stand, and he pulled her back down. "The doe is only caught if she forgoes the safety of the forest. Do not reveal yourself before you're ready." He waited until she nodded her head, and then they began to crawl on their bellies until they reached the rest of the captives. A wall of villagers bowed on their knees before the large crowd. A leader appeared to have emerged from the Tartarus faction.

"You will do as we ask," yelled the leader. "Your families will be kept here to ensure your compliance."

"Who the fuck gave them those weapons?" Ares spoke quietly, his burning gaze fixed on the commander, who carried a long blade in one hand.

When one of the villagers muttered something, the leader grabbed his sword and rushed toward the villagers with murderous intent. The Goddess of Spring and the God of War exchanged glances before leaping from the ground and soaring toward the warriors with supernatural speed. While Ares cut and burned through the prisoners, Persephone switched between bow and blade. She bound the wicked souls down with vines and swiftly sprouted fluorite around them as they were knocked to the ground.

Several of the inmates surrounded Ares, who swore under his breath as he attempted to punch one and nearly fell through empty space. He swung one of the fluorite-encased souls like a club, sending another prisoner flying, and blasted their souls with fire. He laughed, well-pleased, then turned to watch with approbation as Persephone struck true with her blade repeatedly. Although these evil spirits were inadequate substitutes for Gods, it was nonetheless a worthwhile exercise. He called at her from across the terrain to improve her form. She snarled at him, and he kept incinerating the prisoners with a smirk, leaving the ash for Persephone to deal with. Persephone eventually encased the rest of the inmates in solid fluorite, and they turned to face the frightened villagers.

Ares let his sword drop to the ground and approached the souls with raised hands. "You are safe now. You all are from the Meadows?"

Persephone stood in the shadows as Ares dealt with the villagers, comforting them and leading them towards the gates. Persephone remained behind, staring at the ruined sanctuary. When Ares returned by himself, he gave her a quizzical look. "Ready to go?"

"I am to blame for this," she said quietly. "The Mourning fields were my idea."

"There you go again, thinking that you have power over what others do. You do not, this was not your fault."

"It is my fault," she replied in a quiet voice. "But I will right this wrong." She fell to the ground and dug her hands deep into the charred Earth. Her fingers pulsed with energy, and fresh grass sprang from the ground. Pink blossoms bloomed on the trees, and healing swept over the land. "When the time is right," she whispered, "this land will be ready to welcome those who need it. No one else shall trespass here." Persephone suddenly fell to the ground, the soft grass cushioning her body. Roughly, Ares pulled her to her feet.

"You have used too much power," he snarled, annoyed. "This place cannot be fixed overnight. Come, we must go."

With an arm supporting her, he led them from the Mourning Fields. Once outside the entrance, he laid her on the ground and withdrew the key from his cloak. Raising his arms, he closed the doors with a resounding thud, and after securing the lock, he turned towards Persephone. He fell back as an arrow flew into his chest. He looked down in surprise and pulled it out, fresh blood spurting from the injury. Another arrow whizzed through the air, striking him, followed by a third. Ares raised his eyes at the assailant.

Persephone stood tall and alert, her hands steady on the bow. She had tricked him; he admired her deceit, well, almost admired it, he amended, as another arrow flew into his chest.

"It's going to take a hell of a lot more than that to stop me, " he snarled, moving towards her. "I told you not to shoot me with that fucking bow again." He reached her and yanked the bow from her hand, but not before several more arrows had pierced his chest. He threw the bow and towered over her. "Never turn on a soldier you just went into battle with."

Persephone latched onto his arm, her fingertips digging into his flesh. "I owe you no loyalty. You belong with the other rapists."

Ares smiled grimly at what he saw in her gaze: fire. It differed from his internal flame; he burned hot and out of control, but she was cold and deadly, fatally precise in her inferno. The War God staggered suddenly as large clusters of rubies pushed from the ground and began to form around him, imprisoning him. He tore them down, ripping the flesh from his hands, and crushed the ruby rocks beneath his fingers.

She walked towards him, her eyes blazing. "Tell me what is going on with my husband."

"I cannot!" he yelled angrily. He pulled his sword, crashing it upon the cluster, but the faster he tried to break the formations, the quicker they grew around him. "Stop this!" he demanded. "You are making a mistake!"

"Tell me!" She looked wicked, and he blasted her with fire, but it did not stop her even though her skin sizzled from it. "I will lock you in Tartarus with the other rapists unless you tell me."

"If you do, you will never know the truth."

"Did you work together to trap me here and hold me prisoner?"

He laughed mirthlessly. "Do not let hate consume you! You do not see what is plainly in front of you."

A ruby crystal burst through his chest, and he yelled out in pain.

"What does he want Zeus' sword for?"

"You are so blinded by hatred that you fall right into his hands. Fine!" he yelled, yanking the gem from his chest. "You want to know the truth?"

She had lifted her hands again, but at his words, she let her arms rest by her side. "Yes!"

He eyed the crystals, and with a motion of her hands, they crumbled to ash around him. He immediately turned on his heel, walking towards the rugged mountains on the horizon.

"Wait," Persephone called, "where are you going?"

Ares did not turn around. "To show you the truth."

CHAPTER 19
JANUS

His towering shape was silhouetted in the moonlight, and she followed behind him, a lonely, empty shadow. The terrain shifted, becoming rocky and as they began climbing, she realized she was familiar with the location. She had climbed this peak once before.

They climbed further and higher until they encountered a two-headed figure carved into the rock. She looked at the old and young faces, their mouths open as if they had asked a question in their dying moments that was now permanently etched in stone high on the cliff. Janus. She moved back, a shiver of fear moving over her, as soft murmuring danced across the desolate rocks.

"Why have you brought me here?" she asked in a low voice.

Ares stood before the statue, staring at both faces, his back to her. "Your mother did a very foolish thing by shielding you from the Gods," he said softly. The words so closely echoed Zeus' that she trembled. He abruptly turned to face her, and she was startled by the similarity of his features to Hades and was reminded that the same blood ran through them. "You asked for the truth," the God continued. "You want your greatest lesson? Step inside." He gestured toward the cavernous mouth of the statue.

"I am not going in there," she said flatly, crossing her arms.

He moved, his eyes gleaming in the darkness. "You said you wanted answers. Afraid to look the truth in the face?"

Her eyes narrowed. "Hades warned me not to go in there."

"I thought you did not trust Hades," he laughed, giving her a disdainful look.

"I don't trust you either," she hissed.

Suddenly, he leapt forward, shoving her roughly into Janus' open mouth. Her cry was muffled as he fell beside her, and the mouth slammed shut behind them, leaving them in complete darkness.

"You idiot!" she cried. "We are trapped inside!" She groped desperately for the edge of the statue's wall, but all she gripped was the dark air surrounding them. She felt a wave of mindless terror wash over her, the blackness closing in on her.

"Such little faith," he mocked. "Still afraid of the dark, Persephone?"

His voice was near her, and she spun around, cursing the pointless tears in her eyes. She despised the darkness, despised that she longed for Hades to come and save her, and despised the knowledge that he would never come. She brushed away her tears and moved forward, preparing to shatter the statue's mouth if necessary, when she felt firm fingers lock around her wrist.

"Stay still, Persephone. Love him enough to stay." Ares's voice was so gentle that she wasn't sure it was real in the darkness. She jumped in surprise as his voice abruptly reverberated loudly. "Janus, show us the life of Hades."

The darkness dissolved, spinning into light and color until the landscape took shape. They were standing at the entrance to a massive temple. Persephone looked around with wide eyes; stars shone above them, illuminating the landscape far down with their calm, benevolent light. She knew this place. They were atop Mount Othrys, the Titans' residence, the very area where she had stood with Hades earlier this morning. The temple, however, was not as Persephone remembered; instead of the dilapidated, abandoned structure, it was flourishing with life, a cherished dwelling. The silence was broken by sobbing. She glanced at Ares, who stood motionless in the darkness.

"What is this?" she asked, fear pounding in her chest. "Is this real?"

"It was real." The crying became louder and Ares' eyes gleamed in the darkness."I wonder who is crying?" he asked softly.

She stared at his shadow before turning on her heel, following the sound. The soft sobbing guided her to a doorway. She hesitated, then pushed it open to enter a blue room, identifying the source of the noise. A beautiful woman lay on a bed, her long black hair tousled around a tear-stained face. Persephone stared at her, for she looked achingly familiar.

The woman ignored Persephone's unexpected appearance and bent over a sleeping newborn at her breast, lovingly caressing his forehead with her ruby lips. The infant's sweet lips pulled at his mother's breast, unaffected by the tears that dropped on his precious face as he suckled. The sky outside the window was turbulent; a storm was coming. As though Persephone had awakened the sky with her thought, thunder and lightning suddenly fractured the soft night air.

Persephone gasped as a creature unexpectedly entered the chamber. She couldn't call him God because he was much too powerful, far too … everything. As his massive presence filled the room, the air itself seemed to constrict to make way for him. His long, silvery hair cascaded down his back, and his face would have been stunning if not for the expression on it. His gleaming silver eyes bulged with madness, and black, pulsating veins traced the contours of his skin and pupils.

He stalked towards the beautiful mother. At the last moment, the mother turned to face this wrathful beast, her eyes melancholy and knowing. Persephone exclaimed, finally recognizing the face. Rhea. And the child at her breast— Hades! And the mad-eyed creature— Cronus. Persephone moved in closer, just inches away from the Titans and the Mother of Gods, and wept for the baby who would soon suffer so much.

Cronus was muttering beneath his breath, his eyes wild. "B for baby. B for blood. B for betrayer," he whispered. His visage suddenly contorted with an unnerving mix of anguish and rage and his eyes moved to the child. "He will overthrow me. He will steal my throne! The father's misdeeds must be paid forward!" the Titan King roared. "I have seen it!" Spit bubbled from his lips and he suddenly leapt forward, attempting to snatch the baby. Rhea screamed, burying her fingers into him.

"He is just a baby!" Rhea cried.

"He is a traitor! Give me him!" Cronus bellowed.

"No!" Rhea screamed.

"Uranus has cursed me! Do you want me to end up like him? Do you not love me?"

"I do love you!" She lowered her gaze to the child in her arms. "I love what we have made. He is innocent! He should not pay for crimes he knows nothing about. Do not do this!" she cried. "I beg you, do not do this!"

Cronus snarled and reached for the child, but Rhea whirled away. "Aidoneus is your son! You owe him your protection, at whatever cost. At the cost of your life! Of my life!"

"He is a betrayer! He must pay for his future crimes!"

Rhea ran to the balcony, but visions of the past and future whirled around her as Cronus' frenzy hurled time fragments around the chamber. She swayed in panic as she plummeted through space, and he grasped her securely in his arms, crushing the sleeping infant between them.

"He is cursed because of your greed to rule the Heavens," she wept.

He slapped her hard, the sound reverberating loudly across the room, and Rhea and the child collapsed to the ground. Rhea twisted at the last moment, so her back hit the ground, cushioning the baby's fall.

"You chose him over me!"

"As you should. You have lost your mind," she gasped as she climbed to her knees, her face bloodied and reddened. Cronus leaned down, his hands tight on her hair, and she struggled in his grip. He dragged her across the room, his fingers cruelly pressing into her scalp. She screamed, one hand around his, the other tightly clutching her infant. "Help me, mother," she begged. "Please help me."

Cronus yanked her up suddenly, pressing her tightly against him. His silvery eyes closed tightly as he dug his fingers into her back. "I will lose you. I see that I will lose you completely! You will be less than dust, less than nothing." His pupils dilated, filled with horror and frenzy—chaotic lunacy.

Her blood was smeared over his flesh as she stroked his arm. She shifted her gaze from the sleeping infant between them to the enraged Titan, who stood staring at them with wild eyes. "You might not," she breathed in panic, attempting to infuse her voice with a calming tone. "Your visions do not always come true. It may be that you're not seeing things clearly."

It was the wrong thing to say. He yanked the baby from her arms and Rhea fell to her knees, her lips ripping apart in a keening wail. Persephone reached out a hand to console the babe, his small face twisted in protest after being torn from his mother, but she was merely a ghost in this moment, her fingers touching nothing but air. Rhea lifted her hands towards her baby.

"Give him to me, please. Let me say goodbye," she pleaded. "If you love me, please let me say goodbye to him."

Cronus stared down at her and finally, slowly, allowed Rhea to take the infant from his arms.

"Stay in my sight," he muttered.

Rhea clutched the infant firmly and staggered to the room's nearest window. Cronus waited in the shadows, golden embers dancing in his eyes. The mother sat by the window, cradling the infant in her arms and murmuring in his ear so softly that Persephone couldn't make out the words. As the first rays of sunrise pierced the horizon, Rhea raised the infant so that the sunlight kissed his little face. Rhea glowed in the early dawn, and the infant was half cast in shadows and half in light. Cronus roared and yanked the infant away from the welcoming light of morning, and Rhea cried out, her voice like that of a dying animal. She attempted to wrest the infant away from him once more, but Cronus held him tightly.

"Do not use the sickle," she cried.

Cronus hissed and stormed out of the room like a cursed wind, crushing the infant in his merciless grasp. Rhea rushed towards them as the door slammed shut. She screamed and yanked on the sealed door, ripping the flesh from her fingers, but it wouldn't budge. The sound of Rhea's screams followed Persephone as she glided through the entrance like a ghost.

Cronus sat on the throne, his gaze fixed on the newborn in his arms. The baby wrapped his little hand around one of Cronus' massive fingers. The Titan stroked one finger over the pale face of the dark-haired child thoughtfully. Persephone saw the amber lights in Cronus' eyes fade to a beautiful silver light for a brief moment, as the baby looked at him with solemn black eyes. Persephone knelt at Cronus' feet and put her arms around the infant, whispering soft, reassuring words to him that he couldn't understand.

"You are not alone, little one," she whispered, tears welling up in her eyes. "I will stay with you, I will not leave you."

The baby cooed softly, and Cronus' eyes hardened.

"I cannot let you live!" he muttered. "You are blood betrayer, you are my death. You hold the power of my life within you, and as blood pumps through you, my own life force slows. I formed you into being, and now I will erase you!"

Persephone cried out as he lifted the baby up to his mouth and ripped the child apart with his teeth as Aidoneus let out a small, terrible scream. The baby's blood dripped from Cronus' lips onto the floor, where Persephone screamed incessantly. Cronus' eyes grew dim as he stared down at his bloodied hands, and he cried out in horror. "No! Please, Gaia, no. My son, not my son." His despairing cries blended with those of Persephone, and she leapt in shock when she felt a touch on her back.

"Time to leave this memory," Ares said. Time spun around them again, and when the colors righted, they were in a dark cavern.

A dark-haired boy stood deep in the shadows. As Persephone stepped closer, she saw his hands had been bound above his head; he was chained to the wall. Dark shapes moved around him, circling him, moving closer and closer, until one of the shadows stepped from the darkness. She recognized his wretched form: Eurynomos. Other shapeless forms continued to move, oily and foul in the darkness. The boy's face was covered in sludge and bruises, his features swollen beyond recognition. He did not lift his eyes as the demon drew closer.

"What am I?" he whispered.

"You are nothing," the voices replied, as beautiful as they were wicked.

Days became years, and years became millennia. The boy did not know what he looked like or what he was, but he grew despite the demons who feasted on him. Each day he became more handsome and strong, and the demons could see how striking he was behind the sludge and dirt and hated him more. They chained him tight by the neck to the wall and beat him with a golden whip until he could bear no others such as himself. The boy's screams were terrible, but his pain was music to the creatures' ears. They molested him and feasted on his flesh, but still, the boy grew more beautiful.

Persephone cried out in anguish and moved towards the child. She reached her hand towards him, but instead of passing through him, her hand touched the cool skin of his face. His brows furrowed. She lowered her hand to his, entwining their fingers tightly.

He looked in shock at their entangled hands and then lifted his black gaze to hers. She stared back in mutual disbelief. He could *see* her.

"Bear this," she whispered, "know that there are those who love you, and know that I love you. You will step from this darkness to the light. I swear this to you. Do not let them break you! This is just a moment, a flicker in time. Endure this. That's all you have to do. Survive." Their eyes locked, and then Eurynomos stepped through her, and she felt their connection sever.

Even as Eurynomos tore a chunk of flesh from the boy's arm, the boy smiled. For the first time in his life, he felt a reason to live. The hope of seeing her face again filled his heart, and the horror that surrounded him became tolerable with the faith that he would someday see her again. The green-eyed woman had promised him that one day he would step into the light. In his innocence, he asked the demons what the vision of her was, and they told him she was only a dream.

"She is nothing, she does not exist. There is no world beyond this."

Their voices were no longer beautiful but disjointed, painful to his sensitive ears. The demons were afraid because if the boy believed in her, he would hope, and hope was dangerous. Hope allowed you to endure all things and never be broken. So, though the demons told him not to believe, it was too late; that delicate emotion had taken root in him and would not die. So, as they tore at his flesh and violated his body, his mind was not touched, for he was filled with golden dreams, and the tiny flame lit his soul in the darkness, a place they could never destroy. Sometimes in the black cavern he could see her watching him, keeping vigil over him, and he would keep his eyes fixed on her so that he felt nothing except peace.

One day, another was swallowed and shared the cell next to him, and now Aidoneus was no longer alone. He would put his hand through the cell and grasp the infant's tiny fingers. The demons feasted on the baby, and the boy begged for them to take whatever they wanted from his flesh, so long as they left the tiny creature alone. Now the boy took twice the punishment and twice the beating and grew full of hatred, but as they whipped him, he still dreamed of the woman with the green eyes, and she filled his thoughts. And so the time passed.

Suddenly, the darkness began to swirl, and Ares and Persephone watched as both Gods were spat up by their father. Cronus' silvery hair whirled from sight as he abandoned his sons and his palace while a young, white haired God knelt beside his brothers and bathed the grime and saliva from their flesh, carefully unwrapping the golden whip from Aidoenus' flesh. For the first time, they learned they were Gods, imprisoned within Cronus. Aidoneus and Asphaleius, the future Gods of the Dead and the Sea.

"My name is Aene'ius," the young Zeus whispered. "Will you fight beside me my brothers? He must be stopped. They must all be stopped."

Time swirled again, and Persephone watched her husband fight in the war. It was a trial by fire for Aidoeneus, but he learned the sword and his powers swiftly as he fought against the Titans. He was impervious to pain or injury, for he had known nothing but agony since his first memory. He slaughtered with the most heinous blows, and his rage erupted like smoke billowing from a forest fire. At night, he would watch the young Olympian Gods make love in the forest and dance naked in the moonlight. Aidoneus sat alone in the darkness, and though he was approached again and again to join in their revelry, he merely turned away, allowing no one to touch him. He watched as Aene'ius secured alliances in dubious ways with the Titanesses, luring them in with his charm and his body.

Persephone followed Aene'ius and noticed that he had a dangerous ability, which he kept carefully hidden from his brother. If an unyielding Titaness resisted his advances, he would abduct her, violating the Goddesses' will. Before the attack was over, the unwavering Goddess was left captivated by him, bouncing up and down on his cock in jubilee, laughing, and pledging loyalty to him in the night. It was as if he had hypnotized them, and the non-consensual turned into a seemingly consensual union. Soon, many Titaness were on the side of the Olympians, and eventually Aene'ius married Metis, who was extremely cunning and wise. He watched as the two plotted and schemed, their fair heads bent over maps and scrolls Aidoneus attended the wedding, but he knew it was only a marriage of convenience, and there was no love between his brother and the Titaness.

By day, he battled, lost in blood and death, but at night he would go to the forest, far from the other immortals, and wander through the woodland to dream of the woman with the eyes of the forest, hoping that one day he would find her. Persephone followed him, letting her hands trail where his own had touched, willing him to know she was near. He paused suddenly, slowly turning, until their eyes collided. She stepped back, shocked and as he reached for her, fire grew around them. Time whirled again.

She watched as the three brothers crept into the Underworld, meeting in secret with three Cyclops: Arges, Brontes, and Steropes. The Cyclops gave them weapons of magic to defeat the Titans in exchange for their release from the imprisonment the Titans had enforced on them: thunderbolts to Aene'ius, a trident to Asphaleius, and a helmet of invisibility to Aidoneus.

With the weapons, Aene'ius struck Cronus down with a mighty blow, and as Aene'ius smote his father, Cronus echoed a terrible curse that danced through the heavens and shattered the lightning that pulsed from Aene'ius' fingertips.

"The sins of the father shall be repaid. Your child will overthrow you and take your kingdom. All you have done shall turn to ash. "

Persephone had seen the look on the young God's face as Cronus had spoken—the fury and fear on Zeus' face. As Aene'ius descended from the sky and was swarmed by Gods hoisting him aloft, hailing his courage and cunning, a rage shimmered inside him that he carefully concealed from the other Gods.

When the Olympians won the war, the Cyclops, who were now freed from their prison, returned to Aene'ius and Aidoneus with a secret gift. Brontes bowed in pride.

"A gift from our brother who stays hidden in the shadows of Tartarus." The weapons were pulled from an intricately carved box that only a true craftsman could have carved: a golden sword for Aene'ius and a silver blade for Aidoneus. "Keep them secret," Brontes warned. "They are the only weapons capable of slaying a God. To Aidoneus, the blue-flamed sword. To Aene'ius, the golden blade. Only you can lift your individual blades, unless you grant another permission. We offer them to you so that you can prevent another being from acquiring such power, and so that the future is one of equality."

Persephone watched as Arges pulled Aene'ius aside, whispering into his ear as he handed him the golden blade.

A divine council was formed on Olympus, and the three brothers sat on ivory thrones. The Titans, who had sided with Cronus, were tried and sent to Tartarus for eternity.

In the first few months after the war, Aene'ius threw lavish parties, which always culminated in orgies, the Gods and Titans consumed by sex, drunk off their pleasure and victory. "The cult of Aene'ius," Aidoneus' brother called them. To Aidoneus' chagrin, Asphaleius had followed his younger brother to leisure. Aene'ius tried many times to entice his raven-haired brother into the arms of a Goddess or a large-breasted Titaness, but Aidoneus was adamant in his celibacy. His time within Cronus had made him unwilling to be touched by others, but as the years passed, his loneliness grew as he wondered how he would ever meet the green-eyed woman.

One night, Aene'ius brought a dark-haired, amber-eyed goddess to Aidoneus. A golden crown held back her long black hair, and at the center of the headpiece was a crescent moon. Something glittered in her amber eyes that made him shiver, but she was beautiful, and he had been lonely for so long. A large black dog sat beside her with gleaming, golden eyes much like his mistress'.

"You and Hecate will get along splendidly." Aene'ius winked.

Silently, Hecate extended her hand, and after hesitating, Aidoneus took it, wrapping his longer fingers around her delicate ones. She smiled and led him down the halls until she reached the threshold of his room.

Without pause, she opened the door and drew him and her dog inside. Her full lips brushed against his own, and he drew back in surprise as she touched her tongue against the seam of his mouth. He shivered, and she laughed softly.

"How untried you are," she murmured. "Are you sure you are Aene'ius' brother?"

Aidoneus did not respond but pressed his lips more urgently against hers, and she laughed again, teaching him what she liked and how to please her. Suddenly, she pushed him down on the bed.

"Watch," she whispered. Slowly, she stripped off her gown, revealing creamy breasts with dark nipples and a narrow waist that tapered to full, lush hips. She moved to the bed and then crawled atop him, smiling. "I will be your first." With a twist of her wrist, a silver dagger appeared in her hand, and he felt a moment of fear before she began to slash the toga from his body, the blade coming perilously close to his aroused flesh. She tossed the shreds over the edge of the bed carelessly, letting the cold tip of the dagger trail down his skin. "Your body is broken," she murmured thoughtfully.

He shifted, embarrassed by the scars.

"I healed," he replied in a rough voice.

"Some parts did," she murmured, "and other scars you will bear for eternity." She sat back and spread her legs, letting him see the feminine parts of her as she ran her fingers down his abdomen before tracing the long length of his shaft. "You are so big," she purred. "Too bad you cannot bear children."

He sat up quickly, grasping her wrist to halt her movement. "What?"

Her eyes lifted reluctantly from his groin. "When they beat you. You are unable to bear children from the wounds."

Aidoneus frowned. "That cannot be true. I am a God, I will heal eventually."

She smiled enigmatically and a little sadly. "Not all wounds heal."

"But I see no wounds," he replied, trying to push back the dread her matter-of-fact tone brought him.

"Invisible wounds are the worst; they fester where no one can see," she replied, not unkindly. "I know what they did to you," she whispered.

She let her knife trace just above his jutting manhood, and he jerked from the bed, striding to the balcony. The cool night air touched his face, and he breathed deeply, closing his eyes. It was so easy to remember those dark days he had spent within Cronus. How much it had hurt, the endless torment— no, he could not relive those moments.

"Do not be mad," her voice cajoled behind him. She pressed her lithe body against his back, and he turned to her. "Do not hate the truth-bearer." Her pale skin shone like stars in the moonlight. "Only fools hate the truth. Let me teach you that this," her hand reached down between them, stroking his cock again, "can be worth so much more than just bearing children. Come back here."

Her amber eyes blazed into his own, and almost against his will, Aidoneus' feet carried him back towards the bed. She ran her fingers up his arm, and he shivered. "I have been looking for such a unique God. You spent such time in the darkness that it reshaped you." She pushed him back on the bed and crawled between his legs. "I sense a power in you. You are different from the others. There is rage within you, a swirling darkness that you try to suppress. Let me help you draw it out. I will help you feed it and nurture it."

"Stop!" Aidoneus pleaded. "I do not want to think about those times."

"But you think of them every day," she whispered. "You lie to yourself." As she licked the head of his cock, his retort died on his lips, and she gazed up at him with her dark mane and golden gaze, he was reminded of a hungry wolf. "You have remarkable powers you have not properly tapped into. I will teach you the shadow magic, I will teach you how to wield your pain into power." She bent her head once more, licking his long shaft. "Fill me with your shadow," she whispered, and Aidoneus almost laughed, wondering if she was talking to him or his cock, but her tongue on him silenced all thought. "Let me take you to where Chaos reigns."

He groaned with delight, but then something pushed against his awareness, a darkness, a shadow filled with such emptiness that it terrified him. Part of him welcomed it, wished for the all-encompassing emptiness, and that scared him more than anything else, the longing for the abyss, for nothingness. He pushed himself out of bed and crashed hard on the floor.

Hecate stood over him then, and she seemed taller, her pupils narrow slits like the cunning glare of a serpent. "Oh, Aidoneus. Aren't you tired of being afraid? Aren't you ready to take control of what is inside you?"

"No," he denied, his voice a growl. "I do not wish it. I wish to forget."

"Forget." Her laugh was low. "When the marks are so deep inside you, they are etched on your soul? Do you truly believe you can forget? You cannot be that naive."

"Yes! I do not want to remember!"

"But are you sure that there was nothing worth remembering?"

He gasped as her eyes blazed green, for it was the green-eyed woman of his dreams who stood before him. She bent down, and he felt feverish with desire as he lifted his face to hers, pressing his lips desperately against her mouth. She kneeled beside him, and he bent his head, so heated with longing that he could not stop himself. He pressed hard kisses against her soft breasts, drawing one tip into his mouth, and the green-eyed woman moaned her pleasure. He drank in her voice, but something was wrong; the voice was different—huskier, deadlier. He fell back and looked into the amber eyes of Hecate. The witch smiled at him, and he scrambled back from her, breathing hard, his body trembling with unspent desire.

"Did you just hypnotize me?" he asked angrily. The need he felt was so acute that he felt shattered as reality closed around him.

"Yes," she admitted with a smile. "Would you like me to teach you how?"

"No," he answered in a low voice, his black eyes blazing. "You play games with me, and I have had enough of that. I do not dwell in darkness anymore. Get out."

She stared at him with a smile, then walked slowly to his door, making no effort to cover her lush, nude body. With a flick of her fingers, the black dog materialized by her side. She bent to pick up her dagger and turned to look at him over her shoulder. When she faced him, she was transformed into an ancient crone, her beautiful face and body sagging and wrinkled. He blinked, and suddenly she stood young and strong before him, a knowing smile on her lips.

"We will meet again, Aidoneus, when you reach the crossroads of your darkest moment." Her golden eyes flickered. "You should not fear the darkness. There is freedom in the shadows. Never forget the one who bore you those scars," she said as she waved her blade at him. "He dwelled in the sunshine and devoured you as the first rays of light filled the sky. You will never be free until you embrace both sides of your soul: the light and the darkness. The harder you try to outrun from the darkness, the faster it will consume you. Till we meet again, Aidoneus."

The door closed quietly behind her, and Aidoneus slumped to the ground, trembling, ashamed of the fear that coursed through him at the dark memories that she had awakened.

"I will forget," he promised himself. "I do not want to remember."

The night swirled away, and suddenly it was dawn. Aidoneus left his room and found Aene'ius sleeping in the throne room, his robes in disarray. He lifted his head as Aidoneus approached and grinned.

"Brother," Aene'ius greeted. "Tell me, did you finally reach that blissful little peak, that culmination of all desires?" He studied Aidoneus' face and laughed. "It seems not. You look far too tense."

Aidoneus scowled. "Why did you send her to me?"

Aene'ius laughed again. "Oh, come now, brother, you cannot tell me she did not appeal to you. I saw how you looked at her." He sighed. "In any case, it matters not, for she has returned to the Underworld now."

"Have you laid with her before?" he asked suspiciously.

Aene'ius laughed with a visible shudder. "Gods, no, that witch terrifies me. I am afraid she would cut off my cock and use it as a wand to conjure the dead."

"And yet, you thought I would be interested?"

"Well, the bouncing titties of a nubile, young Goddess don't appeal to you, so I thought perhaps that you would like that moody little witch."

"What I would like is for you to stop interfering in my private life."

Aidoneus glanced around the throne room, ensuring they were alone. "She said I was impotent," he admitted suddenly in a low voice.

There was silence while Aene'ius kept his head bent. "Ah," he said finally. "Hecate is rarely wrong. Her gift of foresight is quite strong. I'm afraid if she says it, it is true, brother."

Aidoneus sat next to his brother on the floor, utterly dejected by his brother's words. The demons had taken everything from him, even his future. Aene'ius slung his arm around Aidoneus' shoulders . "Being barren is a blessing! At least your children can never overthrow you. You can fuck all day and never have to worry about leaving a trail of brats! I am envious."

"But I want a family."

"You have one on Olympus."

"It's not the same," he sighed. "I want a wife and children. A family to fill my home."

"Well, I envy you. Metis is pregnant," Aene'ius bemoaned. Aidoneus' head jerked up, but the congratulatory words died on his lips at his brother's expression. "I do not want the child," he admitted. "I should never have married Metis. I don't know what I was thinking. It was the war. I was sick with stress, and she was so devious in tricking me into marriage and just as cunning in getting pregnant. I would admire her trickery," he frowned, "had I not been on the receiving end of it."

"That is not how I remember it. You seemed more than willing to partner with Metis."

Aene'ius narrowed his eyes, playfully mocking. "Whose side are you on? In any case, it is best to avoid procreating. Metis will probably get fat and I will be saddled with an unattractive wife," he pouted, shuddering. "Imagine going to bed with someone that large."

Aidoneus gave him an incredulous look. "How can you feel that way? Don't you regret not being raised together, by our mother and father? We were robbed of our childhood. I would love to have to start a family and give a child everything I did not have."

Aene'ius leaned forward, plucking an apple from a nearby platter that had been laid to energize the guests of last night's orgy. He bit into the juicy fruit, his white teeth a stark contrast against the vivid green.

"Brother, I was raised by a beautiful nymph on Crete who nursed me from her tit until I was a man. My childhood was remarkable. And I don't wish to be robbed of my newly acquired throne. Rodents in the forest have offspring. You are a God. Fuck the rest."

"What good are powers if they cannot give me the one thing I desire?" Aidoneus argued. Aene'ius gave him a disgusted look. "What good is being the God of Wealth when the only riches I seek are those I am unable to grasp? I am envious of those rodents."

Aene'ius finished off the apple, licking the juice from his fingers and hurling the core to the center of the throne room. He laughed at his brother's outraged expression. "If I do not give the servants things to do, then they would have no reason to be here, would they?" He waved his hand. "Listen, brother mine, if you want a wife and family, you have to fuck, and you are doing a piss poor job at that. Why don't you try fucking for a few hundred years and see how you like it first? Then say if you are envious of a rodent.

"I say that you are blessed beyond measure to have a family," Aidoneus insisted stubbornly.

"Oh brother," Aene'ius sighed, "as my family grows so do my problems. Be glad you were not gifted with beauty. Look where it has gotten me, entangled with a fat wife."

"I am indeed fortunate to have been born so malformed," Aidoneus murmured drily. "Nonetheless, it seems I am destined to be alone."

Aene'ius looked at Aidoneus with mock despair. "Is there no one who takes your fancy?"

Aidoneus hesitated and his brother's blue eyes widened. "There is!" Aene'ius flipped onto his stomach, and rested his jaw on his fist, batting his eyelashes. "Do tell."

He could not help but to laugh at the ridiculous expression on Aene'ius' face, but as he thought of the green-eyed woman, his laughter died. "I saw her first when I was a child. I thought she was a vision, but at various points in my life I have seen her. She has followed me my entire existence and I feel she is… waiting for me?" He shook his head. "I do not know exactly how to describe it."

"How do you know she was not a dream?"

"She was as real as you are now."

"She must be a Goddess then," Aene'ius mused, "for her to follow you for so long and not age." Aidoneus grunted his agreement, for he had thought the same thing. "She has green eyes? Demeter has lovely green eyes," he continued contemplatively. "I would love to practice making babies with her."

"You said babies were for forest rodents."

"Well for the right incentive, I would not mind being a rodent," Aene'ius laughed.

Aidoneus' eyes narrowed. "Leave Demeter alone; she is an Earth child and far too virtuous for you. Content yourself with your own kind."

"My own kind? Brother, don't you know that all of creation belongs to me?" he asked lightly. "Besides, I do not believe another God has taken Demeter's fancy. Just imagine being the first to explore her fertile lands."

"I would rather not," Aidoneus uttered. "Besides, you are married and Metis is pregnant. Leave Demeter alone."

Aene'ius smiled and the colors whirled again.

Aidoneus strode past the orgies on the floor—he was content now to wander the forest and spend his days in a little temple he had constructed on the edge of Olympus. In the quiet refuge, he would write out plans for the kingdom, organizing new laws and topics the court should discuss in the coming months. Some days, Demeter would join him, and they would sit by the lake and laugh about the virtuous Gods on the mountain. In some ways, the exquisite forest Goddess resembled the green-eyed woman. They shared the same purity in their eyes, but Aidoenus was never enticed by Demeter. He considered her a close friend and treasured their time together.

The picture whirled again, and Persephone watched as the Gods on the mountain began to discover that Aidoneus was the responsible brother, while Aene'ius was most content between a lover's legs. Metis noticed it too, and in time, she alerted Aene'ius to the danger of his older brother being more respected when he was the king's firstborn son. Aene'ius listened to this news with displeasure, and Persephone saw the same gleam in his eye that he had worn as Cronus had shouted his curse. There was danger in the truth that Aidoneus uttered, raising fears and plans that may alter the entire structure of Olympus and redistribute power among the Gods. If Aidoneus' intentions were put into action, Aene'ius' autonomy would be taken away. His older brother had consistently shown that he would not succumb to corruption. Metis cautioned against trusting those who could not be influenced.

The husband and wife devised a strategy: Metis would first disseminate rumors that Aidoneus had spent too much time within Cronus and still secretly supported his father. It would be simple for some in the palace to suspect him after sowing the first seed of suspicion. His hesitation to accept a lover would come back to haunt him. He did not lie with God or Goddess and he did not dance naked under the moon with them. He talked too little and observed too much. Why did he refuse to reside within the castle walls? What did he do in the forest? He was not one of them and he would never be one of them.

Meanwhile, Aene'ius would begin to gradually break his brother down; disobedience must not be tolerated, Metis warned her husband, but do it gently, slowly, so that Aidoneus would not realize what was happening.

"I rescued you," Aene'ius would say when Aidoneus disagreed with him. "Without me, you would still live inside Cronus," Aene'ius would interject when Aidoneus argued that his plans for the kingdom were unjust and he was wielding too much power. "I sacrificed my life to save you from our father." Aidoneus hesitated, and their plot began to take root. The Gods began to chatter with skepticism; while some claimed that Aene'ius, with his scandals and orgies, should not be trusted, many more feared Aidoneus and his upbringing, and still more were afraid to speak out against the fair-haired God who was growing in power.

Rhea now lived on Olympus, and she assured the Gods that both her sons were trustworthy, but the whispers grew, and mistrust spread. Aidoneus' mother would visit him in his temple, encouraging him to spend more time at the palace and lay to rest the rumors against him.

"Aidoneus," she whispered one day in hushed tones. "You are the rightful heir to the throne. You are the eldest son of Cronus. You are wise and kind, let people see what I see. I love all my children, but you." Her beautiful eyes raised to his. "You have goodness in your soul. You put others above yourself. That is a rare gift, what any person would desire in a king." She grasped her hand in his. "Come back to Olympus, let them see you, and they will love you as I love you."

But Aidoneus refused. Though he loved his mother, he knew that he was too different from them and that no matter how he tried, they would never accept him.

When Metis devised a plan to tell Aene'ius that a display of strength would be needed to unify the kingdom, he told Metis that if they could grow the empire and double their power, he would be the true King of Olympia. Another threat would bring the Gods together, and he would be far more powerful than Cronus had ever been. They just needed to find a villain. And who better to play that part than mortals?

Cronus had cherished the humans under his rule, his reign depicted as the 'golden age' of man. The Olympians feared Cronus, so why not fear what he had loved as well? Aene'ius convened a special council and warned the Gods about the perils of humanity. Their strength in numbers and their lust for power made them as dangerous as the Titans. Aene'ius feared that Cronus had imparted a portion of his powers to them, and soon, the Gods would be at war again.

Fear gripped the council, and as their cries of outrage filled the room, Aene'ius raised his hand. He told them he had devised a plan: he would split the creatures in half, and in turn, they would be weaker in strength and the Gods would have twice as many worshipers to boost their influence. The Gods marveled at the idea and almost unanimously voted in agreement with the plan. Only Aidoneus and another Titan, Prometheus, vehemently disapproved. Aidoneus argued fiercely, and when the council refused to listen, he stormed out of the meeting, refusing to grant agreement. Aene'ius hid his smile.

After the council departed, Aene'ius found Prometheus and told the Titan that he could reshape the humans into a better version of themselves after they were split. It was only necessary to remove the power that Cronus had imparted to them, and they would otherwise remain unharmed. After considerable deliberation, Prometheus was convinced that he could better the lives of people and therefore consented to the proposal. Aene'ius grinned and said that Prometheus' next mission would be to persuade his beloved brother of the plan. So the Titan went on to meet the king's dark-haired brother in order to convince him.

Prometheus found Aidoneus in the forest.

"I thought you agreed that this was wrong," Aidoneus replied in a low voice after Prometheus explained Aene'ius' scheme. "You disappoint me."

"They will do it anyway," Prometheus answered. "At the very least, if we help, we can make sure that the humans survive."

"So we must go along with what we know to be wrong? I will not stand with the council, I disagree with this course of action, I disagree with my brother. What was said in that room was nothing more than fear mongering. Just because Cronus loved them does not make them wicked. They are peaceful beings, they hold no power from Cronus. They will allow fear to drive their actions. And you would allow them to be harmed?"

"You are wrong, Aidoneus! I do not wish to harm the humans, I wish to ensure that their lives continue. All of Olympus is against us. We cannot hold out against the rest of the Gods."

"There are others," he murmured.

Prometheus shook his head. "They do not sit on the council. It will do no good if we try to oppose them, but if we agree, we can ensure the humans are protected."

"What exactly did my brother propose?"

The Titan answered in a hushed voice, looking over his shoulder as though he were afraid of being overhead. "If you use the helmet of invisibility, Aene'ius said he would lend you the golden blade the Cyclops had given them, and the souls can be divided for eternity. Aene'ius would hurl a powerful bolt of lightning to the ground, fooling the Gods into believing he had divided the mortals while never having to reveal the power of the weapons. No one would know it was you," Prometheus insisted.

"I would know," Aidoneus growled. "I will not do it. I do not agree with Aene'ius."

A dark voice sounded behind Aidoneus and Prometheus. "All that I have done for you, saving you from that prison where they beat you, and you preach disloyalty." Aene'ius stepped from the shadows and tears shimmered in the blue depths of his eyes. "I washed the mud off you and raised you to the status of king, and you repay me with treachery. You claim you want a family, yet you don't even trust your own brother. You do not know what Cronus was like, you were safely hidden in the depths of him, but I remember." As Aene'ius continued, Aidoneus' heart pierced with guilt. Coward, the demons whispered in his mind. "I would rather eradicate man all together, but I am sparing them for Prometheus and you. Any creature that Cronus protects is evil. How can you not believe that brother? I merely wish to protect this world, but I need your help. I cannot do this alone."

Time began to whirl once again. Metis made certain that rumors spread throughout the castle: Aidoneus allied with Cronus by supporting mortals and was ungrateful for his brother's protection. The Gods began to scowl at the raven-haired sibling, and a cloud of mistrust gathered about him. He was viewed as an outsider and, despite Rhea's encouragement, spent an increasing amount of time in the forest, away from the other Olympians.

Aene'ius found him out in the wilderness one day and implored his brother once again.

"The mortals must be divided. The Gods are skeptical of you. They claim you adore Cronus in your chamber and yet desire to follow in his footsteps. Should I believe what I'm hearing? We recently finished a ten-year conflict, and you're okay with another war?" His blue eyes were filled with tears. "How can you repay me with betrayal? Consider what we've given up to be together, brother."

"I don't want another war," Aidoneus said. "It's just that I don't think mortals pose a threat."

Aene'ius looked at him with scorn. "Do you really think Cronus would leave without imparting a portion of his power to his favored creatures? Humans are a crime against nature. When the next war comes upon us, they will turn against us and fight for their true king."

"I don't believe that."

"You were in Cronus before the last war began. How could you possibly understand the beginnings of conflict?"

"We just ended ten years of conflict."

"But you didn't watch it happen. I witnessed what a cruel God can do, and the mortals loved their king." Aene'ius came behind his brother and swung his arm over his shoulder, as he had done so often since they had been reunited. "The mortals will not die. We are not going to kill them; we are going to *alter* them—make them less of a threat." He whispered in Aidoneus' ear, "Do it for her. For your green-eyed spirit. To keep her safe. Do it for our mother. Mortals are dangerous. Cronus imparted them with power that they should never have had, I saw what they were like before. They were not meant to be united in such a way; it is against the laws of nature itself. We are merely righting the wrong that our father did. Do we not owe the world that much? The sins of the father, Aidoneus, must be repaid. Think how much we have all sacrificed; the mortals must sacrifice a little too. Trust me, did I not save you from Cronus?"

And so, out of guilt, out of a moment of treacherous weakness, and out of the need for his brother's love, he agreed to the act. When he held the swords high and felt the splitting of their souls, he could feel his spirit shatter from the weight of his immoral crime. This had not been justified, but instead, an unforgivable act, a transgression that could never be righted. Screams of pain echoed through the valley, and the smell of burnt flesh covered the land. The creatures' souls were broken, and their lifespans were drastically shortened.

He looked in speechless horror at the destruction he had wrought, and then he saw *her*—her beautiful green eyes shone with tears, horror in their emerald depths. He turned his head, unable to bear the revulsion in her gaze. He was worse than the demons who had destroyed him; he was the very personification of evil. With a wave of his hand, he vanished, and time whirled again. They were in the palace, and Aidoneus was striding towards the throne room, which was full of immortals cheering and carousing at Aene'ius' success.

"Get out!" Aidoneus bellowed.

Aene'ius sat on the throne with a laurel wreath atop his beautiful silvery hair. He eyed Aidoneus with an enigmatic smile.

"It seems my brother wishes to speak with me." He gave a lofty wave of his hand, dismissing his adoring admirers. "Go now, so that I may speak with him."

Aidoneus could hear the mutterings of mistrust as the crowd scattered, and he scowled at them, causing a couple of the Gods to yelp in terror. Finally, the door slammed shut as the final figure fled, leaving the siblings alone in the royal chamber.

"Whatever is wrong, brother?" Aene'ius asked finally. "You deserve a hero's welcome!"

"You lied to me," Aidoneus replied, his low voice vibrating in rage.

"About what, exactly?"

Aidoneus wiped impatiently at the tears on his face. "The humans were never meant to split! Cronus never imparted them with any powers. I severed their very beings!" He ran his hands through his hair in agitation, closing his eyes tightly. "I could feel the wrongness of it." His eyes flashed open. "I am no more than your unpaid assassin." He threw the golden blade to the ground, and it vanished from sight as Aene'ius stood.

"Calm yourself, brother. You did as your king commanded, that is all that matters."

Aidoneus stepped back, as though struck. "All that matters?" he repeated. "Blind allegiance. You speak, but I only hear Cronus' words coming from your lips."

Aene'ius hissed, and lightning struck the chamber. "You speak of treachery, then, brother." He looked at Aidoneus and, with much difficulty, smiled again. "Come now, in time you will see I am correct. We have no reason to disagree. When one attacks their opponent, they must utterly demolish them. For the benefit of the Gods. For the benefit of our family."

"Could you not hear their agony? They were free creatures of this land and now they are prisoners to it. They will never be free on this Earth again, they will be bound by base emotions, by hatred, by greed and loss." Aidoenus looked at his brother's face and fell back, as if struck. "You were well aware that they were never a threat. This was never about fear; you couldn't abide the fact that they didn't seek the Gods' approval, that they didn't need us. It was all about control."

"We did what needed to be done. You cannot judge me; you also played a role in this. Do not act like you are better than me."

"Yes," Aidoneus acknowledged, "I altered them; I will forever bear this dark deed and will despise myself for what I did. I deserve no absolution for my crimes." Aidoneus put his hands to his head, a searing agony piercing his brow. His wrath grew, and black smoke billowed from his eyes, curling up around his face. "But a king who believes this was just and who feels no remorse," Aidoneus asked quietly, "does that king deserve a throne?" His eyes were entirely black now, and Aene'ius backed away from him, staggering slightly.

"You treacherous viper!" snarled Aene'ius . "If you were not my brother, I would smite you. I am the King of the Universe. For these foolish creatures, you would ruin everything. Your precious mortals are not dead!"

"They're dead inside!" Aidoneus shouted as he appeared in front of Aene'ius like a dark wind. He pushed him up against the wall, one hand on the King of Kings' throat. "How could you do something like this to your people?" His grip on the king's neck tightened. "You are unfit to rule."

Metis flung open the door, and the Gods rushed in, terrified to see the dark Aidoneus holding his pale-haired sibling against the wall. When Aidoneus turned his head to face the crowd, they noted his dark visage and the new emblem that had appeared on his brow, the luminous symbol of Pluto. He resembled a raven-haired Cronus, and they recoiled in horror. Aidoneus let his hand fall as Rhea stepped forward, her beautiful eyes begging. As the king fell, the brothers exchanged glances, and Aene'ius grinned up at him so that only Aidoneus could see, until he was encircled by his loving subjects, letting out a soft groan of pain. Aidoneus let his sight rest on Rhea's saddened eyes before storming out of the chamber, past the Gods.

That night on Olympus was a party. The revelries persisted for weeks, and the palace, which had previously functioned as a location for building civilization, had been reduced to little more than a haven for pleasure. Wine flowed like blood from the ivory fountains, and Olympus was only concerned with gratification. They sang songs and chanted Aene'ius' name. The King of Olympus spent his nights with a new mistress, a pale-haired Titaness named Mnemosyne, whom he had duped into joining him in the form of a shepherd. She burst out laughing when he removed his disguise, and she reveled in his cock, foretelling the future.

"I see the curse of Cronus," she wailed.

Aene'ius placed his fingers on her clit. "How do I avoid his curse? I do not want to be overthrown."

"Metis, carries twins. The son could dethrone you."

"How can I prevent this?"

She laughed, riding him harder - pounding her tight channel down onto his throbbing member and smiling as she felt it slide deep inside of her, making the vision become clearer. "You must imprison Metis as Cronus did his children. If you swallow her, you will gain her wisdom. If your son dies - your throne is safe. The girl shall be a great warrior and fight for you."

Aene'ius bit her lip roughly in gratitude and pushed himself deeper into her, angling his hips so his cock filled her, and she arched her back, feeling another wave of pleasure come over her body, mindlessly fucking. If she had looked closer she would have seen that Aene'ius was unmoved by passion, his eyes coldly focused as he watched her. "What else do you see?"

"A Goddess," she said breathlessly, her golden hair sticking to her sweaty flesh.

"A Goddess?" Zeus asked, rubbing his hands up her waist over her smooth skin, squeezing her soft breasts so that pain merged with pleasure.

"The child of the green-eyed Goddess. I see two fathers. Prometheus has seen the vision. He knows the other who could dethrone you. There will be a war."

"Tell me more about this war," he whispered, as he shifted their position. She cried out in ecstasy as he entered her from behind, deeper this time, thrusting inside her relentlessly. It was sex unlike any she had experienced before and the prophecies poured from her lips freely.

"A war between brothers," she gasped. "I see you and the dark-haired brother. He fights against you."

"How do I defeat him?"

"A Goddess of the Earth. Do not let them join together. Their union will bear fruit that could sit on your throne."

"But he is infertile."

"Not with her. She is as fertile as the richest soil." His hands gripped tightly onto her hips, pulling them up higher so that she took all of him in and she choked out, "The High God."

He tugged her face to look into his eyes, his fingers rough on her chin. "The High God?" he demanded ruthlessly.

"Gaia, the Highest Goddess favors the White-Haired God."

Zeus sighed in relief. Mnemosyne could feel his cock swelling inside her, and then he pulled himself out with precision before slamming back hard into her again. She screamed so loudly that all of Olympus could hear her shaking in euphoria until her eyes rolled back in her head and the prophecy slipped from her mind.

Time slipped again. Rhea sat beside Aidoneus in his hut, stroking his hair as he told her what had happened on the mountainside.

"The swords are evil," Rhea breathed. "They should never have been forged. That Aene'ius should hold one—" Rhea shook her head. "He should never have been allowed to become king. He is dangerous, bloated on power. He must be stopped."

Aidoneus raised his head, his eyes puffy and red, his face exhausted. "I don't know what to do."

Rhea stroked his face gently. "You must forgive yourself, Aidoneus. You were manipulated. He is…" Her eyes closed tightly, her face filled with pain. "He is evil." She embraced Aidoneus. "Promise me, do not let this destroy you!"

"I am destroyed, mother," he whispered, a tear falling from his cheek. "I became death on the mountainside that day and as the mortal souls cracked, so did my own. I am broken."

Aidoneus lay in his mother's arms until, finally, he fell into an exhausted slumber and Rhea held him tightly, weeping for her dark-haired son, for all he had suffered, and all the suffering that was yet to come.

Time bent and Aidoneus stood at the foot of the mountain, peering up at the palace. He turned around and walked through the forest to his modest temple. Animals gathered around the entryway, and he smiled at them, grateful for their companionship. He moved to an easel, picking up a paintbrush, as he examined a large fresco he had been working on. Carefully, he began to grind azurite and malachite crystals to make the greenish-blue pigment he needed for the sky, the process soothing, as he blended the colors into a fine powder. He seldom used his powers now, content to live like a mortal, grateful for the simple pleasures of life.

One night, he heard laughter and was taken in by the pleasant sound. He proceeded softly through the thick foliage till he came across Demeter and a young man. A mortal, he realized with surprise. She caressed his dark hair, muttering something to him, and they exchanged glances before he bent and kissed the tip of her nose. Her joy made her shine, and Hades grinned, pleased to see his friend happy. He quickly withdrew, evidently having intruded on a private moment between lovers. He returned to his shrine to resume his painting silently. Sometime later, Demeter appeared in the doorway, looking jubilant as she tried to sneak up on Aidoneus.

"Hello, Demeter," Aidoneus greeted, his back still to her.

She giggled and sat on the ground, carefully picking up a brown rabbit who was curled against Aidoneus' feet. "I should have known you would know I was there! Does nothing ever surprise you?"

Aidoneus turned and smiled at the pretty, young Goddess. "I am surprised every day. When a king tells the truth, when a man is loyal to his lover."

She shook her head at his pessimism. "Are you surprised by me?" Demeter asked. "I sensed you for a moment in the forest."

The God shook his head. "No." Aidoneus smiled. "I am sorry I intruded. But I was glad to see you happy."

"You did not intrude," Demeter laughed. "I wish you had stayed; I would like for you to meet him." She buried her face in the rabbit's soft fur. "I have never met anyone like him."

Aidoneus laughed softly. "That is because he's human, and *you* are used to wicked Gods."

She looked up at that. "Not all Gods are wicked."

"Really? Name one."

"You are not wicked."

His smile wavered. "No, Demeter. I am the most wicked of them all."

"The *most* wicked?" She gestured to the fresco. "Painting an orange tree alone in a temple? My eyes wither from such dark deeds!" she exclaimed dramatically.

But he did not smile back at her. Her dark hair partially covered her face as she watched him. Again, she reminded him of the green-eyed Goddess. Pain flashed through him as he remembered the revulsion in her eyes as she had watched him on the mountainside.

"Come," Demeter said softly, interrupting his thoughts. She patted the space beside her. "Come and sit beside me. For if you are wicked, then it cannot be such a bad thing."

He hesitated, but finally set his paintbrush down and sat beside her, stretching out his long legs. She placed the rabbit in his lap.

"Julias will make you feel better," Demeter said firmly. "He always helps me."

They stroked his velvety fur in companionable silence for a few moments.

"What happened?" Demeter asked finally. "Something has changed in you. You are so sad now, won't you share the burden with me?"

Aidoneus shook his head. "Because I was weak, I caused... others to suffer. Sharing my burden would lessen it. And I do not deserve that."

She grasped his hand and they sat there together, thunder rumbling quietly through the trees, and though he knew he did not deserve it, he found comfort in her closeness.

"I wish you would tell me. There is sorrow in life, but there are some good things too," Demeter insisted. "We triumphed in the war. Aene'ius is now on the throne, and Cronus is safely imprisoned. The lands are once again in order. If you haven't forgiven yourself yet, maybe you will eventually."

Even though he laughed, the sound was harsh. His grip on her hand tightened. "I am glad that you see good in the world, that hope lives in your heart. I would wish it no other way, but I caution you, Demeter, not to put your faith in the Gods. Make your own way in this world, keep to yourself, out of their sight. Now, tell me of your young man."

Demeter beamed at him. "Oh, Aidoneus, he is so wonderful. He's a prince; he was galloping around on a piece of his kingdom that I happened to be tending. I was ready to whisk him away in a powerful wind because he was interfering with the sowing of wheat seeds, but I am awfully glad that I didn't, for he could not have known that I was assisting the seeds in their germination. When I saw his eyes," she sighed blissfully, " I knew, I just knew he was the other half of my soul. I actually lost count of how many seeds I planted that day. I'm afraid that the region will be overwhelmed by an overabundance of harvest."

"The people will grow positively plump from your benevolence," Aidoneus murmured.

She laughed. "Do you want to know a secret?"

"But of course."

"Come closer then." He leaned in and she pressed her lips against his ear. "I am going to marry him," she whispered. At her words, a large arc of lightning flashed across the sky, and she scowled at the window. "This wretched storm," she mused. "It will tear up all the flowers that are just beginning to bloom."

Aidoneus smiled down at her. "Little mischievous Demeter is going to marry a mortal. I suppose that will make you a princess."

"Yes," she laughed. "It is hard to imagine, is it not?"

"It is, and yet it is not. Will you be a good little wife?" he teased.

She spit her tongue out at him. "If he will be a good little husband." He actually chuckled, and Demeter grinned, pleased that the darkness had left his eyes for a moment. "One day you will marry and be as happy as I am now."

Aidoneus stood abruptly and faced the fresco before turning back to her. "No," he replied softly. "I will not marry."

She frowned at him. "Whyever not!"

"There is no one I wish to marry who would wish to marry me."

"But maybe someday, surely."

"No." His voice was harsher than he intended, so he smiled to soften the word.

She opened her mouth when another rumble of thunder shook the small temple, distracting her. She sat up on her knees suddenly, lifting the rabbit with her, and they both watched him with soft, pleading eyes.

"Please, oh great Aidoneus, grant me the use of your forest temple!"

He looked down at her, suppressing a smile. "For what purpose?"

"To make merry! To rest! To have a tryst!"

"You want to kick me out of my refuge?" he asked with mock ferocity.

"Only for tonight," she argued, unimpressed by his frown. "It is raining after all, and he *is* mortal. He could catch a chill, and I want him around for a long time."

Aidoneus extended his arm, helping her to stand. The sweet Goddess looked up at him with such innocence that it made his heart twist in fear for her. Olympus was not kind to the innocent, but he would do his best to guard her. "I will abandon my temple," he said finally, not allowing any of these thoughts to show on his face, "but under one condition."

She let out a victorious yelp, turning in a jovial circle as she shouted, "Anything! Name it! No price is too high!"

When she turned around to face him, he scowled at her. "Do not paint a wedding scene over my fresco."

She wrapped her arms around him, kissing his cheek. "I knew I could depend on you. I will not touch your fresco; you have my word."

"Very well then, I will leave you, but first..." Aidoneus waved his hand, and a black rose appeared, the edges trimmed in gold. He placed it carefully in her palm and curled her fingers over it.

"That is beautiful!" Demeter beamed as she examined the rose petals. "Perhaps you are, after all, a God of the Forest!"

"I merely adorned the beauty you created, Goddess of the Forest," he replied, bowing with a smile. "Congratulations, beautiful Demeter. I wish you much joy."

As Aidoneus wrapped his arms around her, lightning struck the temple, and he peered out into the forest to see a dark figure standing far in the distance, observing them. Aene'ius.

Aidoneus left her in the temple to wait for her lover, and as he passed the dense trees at the entrance, he imagined he could see the green-eyed woman watching him, but when he turned, he only saw the dark outline of the forest. He roamed through the night until the storm Demeter had forecast erupted, but he made no move to seek shelter. He let the water rain on him, hoping it would cleanse him but knowing it wouldn't. Lightning flashed in front of him, illuminating a figure. Aene'ius' blue eyes flashed in the brief flash of light, filled with hate.

"You are secretly meeting with Demeter?" Aene'ius hissed.

Aidoneus looked at him coldly. "Since you've taken to eavesdropping, I assume the thunder must have reduced your hearing. My friendship with Demeter is no secret." He made to move past when Aene'ius roughly grabbed Aidoneus' shoulder. He shook him off impatiently, but Aene'ius blocked his path.

"I do not want you with Demeter," he commanded.

Aidoneus laughed incredulously. "Months of wanting me to fuck everything that moves on Olympus, but you are upset I embrace Demeter? Why?"

"She is not right for you. Any Goddess but her."

"As much as I find this conversation fascinating, I have nothing further to add." He shouldered past Aene'ius.

"I command you not to see her again."

Aidoneus stopped at that and turned to face his brother. He stepped closer, his black eyes blazing. "You command me? I will speak with who I want, embrace who I want, and fuck who I want—when I want, how I want. Do you understand? You are not my master."

Aene'ius snarled, and his fingers twitched with rage as white lightning curled around his fingertips. "I warn you, Aidoneus, I am not to be defied."

"You *warn* me? You think I am one of your Gods on the mountain who fears you. I do not fear you, *brother*. The day you held any sway over me died that day I held the golden blade." He pushed the silver-haired God aside. "Get out of my way. You are not my king."

As Aidoneus turned his back, a powerful urge of intuition caused him to fly high, and as he lifted from the ground, lightning blasted the very spot he had been standing, shattering a nearby Cypress tree to ash.

Aidoneus turned to him in horror as he landed on the ground. "You were going to blast me as if I were Cronus? When my back was turned?"

His brother's blue eyes bulged with madness. "I saved you from him. You forfeited your life to me the moment I rescued you from his jaws! I own you!"

"Cronus thought my life belonged to him as well," Aidoneus said in a low voice. "Any debt I owe you, I have repaid many times over."

Aene'ius hunched over in a coughing fit, and Aidoneus paused as he studied Aene'ius' face; blood and flesh were trickling from his mouth.

"What have you done, brother?" he whispered.

The king wiped at his lips. "I did what I had to do to secure my throne."

"Where is your wife?" Aidoneus demanded, his voice rasping.

Aene'ius rubbed his stomach, laughing. "I am with child." His face twitched, and suddenly Aene'ius was howling with mirth until his boisterous laughter filled the forest.

Aidoneus fell back in horror as he realized Aene'ius had swallowed Metis and the children within her. "You are just like Cronus."

Aene'ius' grin suddenly vanished, and his face twisted, deforming his perfect features so that he looked almost demonic. "He cursed me! I did not fight a war to have a son sit on what I won. The throne is mine."

"What have you won? Do you think this is some sort of game? We fought the war not to rule but to dethrone a mad king."

"I am not giving my throne to a son," Aene'ius snarled.

"Not *a* son. *Your* son, your very blood! Your kingdoms should be passed to your offspring, to a new generation. Be happy that you can have a family. I would give anything to–"

"To what?" Aene'ius interrupted, raising his eyes in anger. "Is that what you hope for? Does Demeter lick your wounds, hoping to make them fertile?"

"Enough!" Aidoneus yelled.

But Aene'ius was past reasoning. "Does she ride your broken body in hopes she will grow a child from a fruitless wasteland?"

Aidoneus' eyes grew black, and with a snarl, he lunged towards his brother, moving so fast that Aene'ius did not have time to draw back. The Dark God landed on top of his brother and delivered a series of swift, powerful punches that echoed as loudly as the thunder that rumbled across the sky. Aene'ius gasped but lifted his hand as lightning arced above them. Electricity surged through him, and the golden blade materialized in his grasp. His blue eyes stood out starkly in his bloodied face, and Aidoneus drew back, his eyes wide in shock.

"You dare to draw that sword here," Aidoneus growled. Aidoneus raised his hand, attempting to pull the hilt of the sword from his brother, but it remained firmly in the king's grasp.

"Ah ah ah," Aene'ius smiled to reveal crimson-stained teeth, "you cannot yield my weapon without my permission. Remember?" His smile suddenly vanished. "Pull out your blade."

"I will not," Aidoneus stated flatly. "I will not fight you." He stood abruptly and began to walk away when Aene'ius spoke again.

"You are not fighting me. I need you to help me dispose of the Cyclops."

Aidoneus stopped but did not turn around. "Why?"

"I've been thinking that the Cyclops know too much about these weapons. It puts us in danger. Besides, I have a new forger. Hephaestus will make my thunderbolts now."

Aidoneus gave him an incredulous look. "I see. And so you sought out your executioner to do your bidding?"

"Don't be ridiculous. It is for both our safety and the safety of all the

Gods. The Cyclops themselves made us promise to keep the blades a secret. Well, it will only be a secret if they no longer know."

"And what will happen when you no longer wish for *me* to know the secret?"

Aene'ius waved his hand as though this were inconsequential. "But you are blood. You can trust blood."

"And yet you killed your own blood. Aren't the Titans and Olympians going to wonder where the Cyclops *and* Metis went?"

"That blood was tainted," Aene'ius replied, his voice annoyed. "I am married to Mnemosyne now. No one will remember a thing. No one questions me."

Aidoneus made a noise of disgust. "I will remember. The Cyclops showed loyalty at great peril to themselves. I will not help you. Find another servant to do your bidding."

"What makes you so morally superior?" Aene'ius scoffed, his eyes narrowing in something close to loathing, the golden blade's gleam reflected in his burning blue eyes.

"Superior? No, I do not call it superior. I would not kill my wife so that my throne could be secured. I would not kill a child so that others could call me master. I would die for them. I would suffer for them. It is the way any creature would behave towards the ones they loved."

"Love!" Aene'ius hissed. "You speak of it as though you have felt it. Your own father could not bear the sight of you."

"True," Aidoneus replied softly. "But I have felt a love that calms my soul, guiding it to be a better man. I have felt the kindle of hope that love can light the darkest of places. That flame burns in me still; it will always burn within me."

The rain poured around the brothers, and as lightning arced across the sky, their faces were illuminated in the forest, dark and light. The pale God's face almost looked fearful as he watched his shadowed brother.

With an unsteady laugh, the king shook his head. "No woman has such power. Love is nothing but a false emotion, a weakness."

"You are wrong," Aidoneus whispered. "There is no greater power than to hold another's needs above your own."

"And the needs of your king?"

Aidoenus' face hardened. "I told you, I have no king."

"Blasphemous words," Aene'ius breathed. "You will not seek out the Cyclops?"

"I will not."

"So, we are to part enemies."

"You are not my enemy," the dark one replied, "but you are no longer my friend." With those words, the dark God slipped from the forest like a shadow, leaving the King of Gods alone with the ghosts that now lived inside him.

Aene'ius knew now that the vision of the green-eyed woman kept his brother from doing the dark deeds he instructed him to do. If he could eliminate the memory or taint it in some way, he would have control over Aidoneus.

As Aidoneus slept in the forest, Mnemosyne sat astride Aene'ius, wailing with prophecies in the darkness.

"Tell me how to control Aidoneus." She closed her eyes and let out a deep moan as she felt the head of his shaft penetrate her. As he ruthlessly pushed deeper, she opened her mouth and gasped with feverish pleasure.

"Banish the fertile goddess from his mind. She leads him towards righteousness."

"Will you help me?"

"I will help you," she moaned, "and in return, you will aid our children."

His fingers tightened painfully on her arms. "You are pregnant?"

She stared down at him and began to twist her hips sinuously. "I am, but you need not fear. My Muses will spread your name so that humans will revere you and your powers will grow. The mortals will erect statues, build temples, and write poetry, all devoted to you. You shall go down in history as the savior of the Gods. You will have more worshipers than any and be the most powerful God."

Aene'ius smiled and rewarded Mnemosyne by thrusting his own hips to meet hers. "Daughters. I do not fear daughters."

"You need not fear all your children, for children can help you attain power," she whispered, leaning back on him with another groan as her eyes rolled back in her head. "Use your offspring to attain more power."

"How do I keep my brother from bearing a child?"

"Your brother is most vulnerable alone. Leave him abandoned in the darkness. Isolation is how you can control him."

"Tonight, you must help me," he urged her. "For us and the sake of our children."

"It will not be easy. Aidoneus guards his mind well. I will not be able to enter it from afar."

"Then we will go to him. You will show me who guards his heart from me."

So late in the night, when the dark moon was high in the sky, they snuck through the forest into the temple deep within the trees. As Aidoneus slept, Mnemosyne ran her fingers through his dark locks.

"Show me the green-eyed woman," Aene'ius demanded.

Mnemosyne extended her hand, and Aene'ius eagerly gripped her fingers. She smiled, for she unwisely believed he was delighted at her touch. Aidoneus' face twisted as she began to probe his mind, and Mnemosyne shook her head, her own brow furrowed.

"I do not know if I can do it," she breathed. "He will not allow me to enter, even in his deep slumber."

Aene'ius' hand twisted, and his face was ugly as he looked at his wife. "You will find a way," he snarled. "Do not disappoint me."

"But it hurts," she whispered.

"I do not care," Aene'ius replied, his voice cold. "Find a way."

Mnemosyne shrank away from him, but Aene'ius' forced her hand tightly against Aidoneus' head. Reluctantly, her mind began to probe once more, and she was filled with agony as she pushed into his presence, sweat beading her smooth forehead. Aene'ius watched impatiently, his blue eyes narrowed into slits. It took hours for her to force her way through his defenses, looking for a point of weakness, but finally she found it—a memory so dark and so painful that she was able to push through to him. She gave a small whimper of pain as her mind touched the dark prince's. Aene'ius swelled with power as, for the first time, he was able to violate his brother's mind.

She took him to the dark memory—that moment that was close to the surface of Aidoneus' mind—the day he split the humans. Watching from the mountaintop, through the fire and devastation, Aene'ius' eyes moved greedily through the memory, smiling at the suffering below him and giddy at the power of the golden blade. His gaze scanned the horizon and then saw her, and in his ignorance and haste, he mistook the green-eyed woman for Demeter. He could see the despair in her eyes as she watched the mortal souls rip in half, and he was jubilant that she had witnessed his brother's downfall. As Aidoneus' eyes moved to the Goddess below, a powerful sensation filled Aene'ius, and he realized in shock that this was the connection between the dark God's and the green-eyed Goddess' souls; it was so overwhelming and powerful that he grasped his own heart painfully as emotion overcame him. It was like nothing he had ever experienced.

Aene'ius floated endlessly in this oblivion, with a feeling of wholeness and selflessness so divine that it was complete fulfillment. As Aidoenus looked away in shame, the feeling vanished, and Aene'ius snarled as the pure sensation disappeared too, leaving him empty and desolate once again. Aene'ius now knew what lived inside his brother, and he was filled with envy. Why should his brother be allowed to feel what he himself has never experienced? He did not deserve this connection. It should not have belonged to a mere prince but to the king himself. He turned his covetous gaze to the green-eyed woman. He would not allow his brother to have something that should belong to him.

"Banish the woman from his mind," he hissed to Mnemosyne.

"But you told me you only wanted to see her. It could break his mind to remove this memory!"

This time Aene'ius let electricity burn Mnemosyne's soft flesh and she cried out, almost severing her connection to the dark God.

"And I have changed my mind. Take all the memories of her."

So she pulled the memories from Aidoenus' forehead, and tears streamed down his face as the visions of the green-eyed woman were taken in the quiet night, every memory of her wiped from existence. When Mnemosyne looked upon Aene'ius, she knew she had made a mistake in letting him see the girl. His eyes were callously cold, and there was no love in their depths for her. For a brief moment, he felt a soulmate connection, and he yearned for more. Nothing less would satisfy him. Aene'ius looked at the white, swirling magic she held in her palm and reached for it, but she drew back from him. In anger and fear, she whispered dark words so that Aidoneus' memories vanished, forever erased, for she knew Aene'ius would become addicted to what he had just experienced.

He grabbed her wrist tightly, bending the fragile bones. "I wanted his visions," he snarled.

"It is too late, they are gone. They were not yours to have," she replied in a low voice, her lower lip trembling.

"Everything is mine! All that I want in this world belongs to me and me alone. You betrayed me tonight, you do not get a second chance." He grabbed her arm tightly and she made a strangled sound as he pushed her to her knees. "I want you to insert a new memory into his mind."

She could read Aene'ius' thoughts and pushed away from him in horror, feeling as though she had just awakened from a deep slumber, seeing him clearly for the first time—the beauty of his face and the ugliness of his soul.

"And what will happen if I do not?"

He stepped closer to her, bending over her. "The real question is, what will happen if you do? If you do this, our children will not suffer the way I intend them to if you do not." He reached down, squeezing her abdomen painfully, and she quickly laid her hands back on Aidoneus. "Smart girl," he praised, releasing her. "First, he must go to the Cyclops. Next, embed into his mind a plot of revenge to kill Cronus."

She closed her eyes, but did as she was told. The dark-haired God twisted against the bed, his face contorting in pain as thoughts were pressed into his mind.

Aene'ius ran his finger down her cheek, and she could see his erection as he stood in front of her. "Mnemosyne, you are so beautiful."

The betrayers left the temple, and when Aidoneus woke, he felt a void inside of him. Sweet memories danced just out of reach, but like all dreams, the more he reached for them, the quicker they moved from his grasp. Sunlight filled his temples, but he shivered in the soft light. Something had changed within him; he felt as though a curtain had been pulled over his soul so that light could never touch him. The loneliness of eternity stretched before him, and he wanted to cry out in despair.

He glanced up sharply as he felt a presence; Aene'ius was moving toward him, his white-blond hair gleaming in the sunlight, his beautiful lips pulled back in a jubilant smile.

"Good morning, brother," he greeted. He paused as he looked down at Aidoneus. "You look wretched. Rough night?"

Aidoneus hung his head, his dark hair obscuring his eyes. "Just a headache," he murmured.

Aene'ius made a sympathetic noise as he sat down on his bed. "I too ache, brother, for I do not love my wife."

"Why does that not surprise me?" Aidoneus muttered. "Why do you insist on marrying when you do not love them to begin with?"

"Because I want to *believe* in love, don't you?" There was an inquisitive gleam in Aene'ius' eyes that Aidoneus did not notice.

He shook his dark head. "Why believe in what does not exist?" Again, he did not notice the satisfied smile on Aene'ius' face.

"Oh brother," Aene'ius moaned sympathetically, "you are wiser than I. I yearn for love. Her lips were around my cock last night when I realized that she just does not fill my soul. There's no..." He snapped his fingers, and a hint of white lightning sizzled. "Spark," he finished with a smile.

Aidoneus grimaced. "Fill your soul? When did you suddenly care for true love?"

"I would love to be deep inside a Goddess who loved me." Aene'ius twisted his face in disgust as he thought of his wife. "Not these ancient Titaness who are hungry for power."

"I do not know how you make the women you violate fall in love with you. Your cock is more persuasive than your crown."

"I've been dreaming of Demeter. Me between her legs and ambrosia flowing from her like honey, thick and sweet."

Aidoneus frowned, for he did not like him speaking of Demeter in such a way. "Why are you in my room? You do not come around unless you have a need for something."

Aene'ius smirked, extending his hand so that the golden blade appeared in his grasp. "I need you to *visit* the Cyclops. Remember? I cannot have four forgers."

Aidoneus stood, agitated. "For a man who has more lovers than fingers, I do not see why having four blacksmiths should upset you."

"They know our secret." Aene'ius whispered, his cold eyes narrowing. "They are dangerous. You agreed last night; did you forget?"

Aidoneus hesitated, for Aene'ius' words sparked a memory, but it felt wrong, distant, and blurred in his mind. He made a non-committal noise. "Why does it have to be me?"

"It is what I wish. You are the only one I trust. You will find them in the Caucasus Mountains. You promised me," Aene'ius continued, looking at him expectantly.

Aidoneus did not know why he had agreed to it; he did not want to go into the mountains to find the Cyclops; he did not want to hurt them. And yet, there was a rage inside him that he could not deny—a hunger to punish others for the emptiness that he felt. Was he so base as to seek retribution from those with whom he had no quarrel?

"I will speak with them," he replied, reaching for the golden blade in Aene'ius' hand.

Aene'ius pulled his hand back. "Speak with them. And then destroy them. For my good as well as your own. Five cannot keep a secret."

Aidoneus lifted a brow. "And how do you feel about two keeping a secret?"

"Do not be foolish, brother. I could never hurt someone I care about."

"Like your wife and your unborn children?"

"Nonsense. How could I care about a child I never met?" Aene'ius stepped back, inspecting his brother with approval. "That black toga suits you; it's perfect to wear to an execution. Let me know when you return."

Aene'ius extended the sword, but Aidoneus shook his head.

"I have no need for your weapon." His own blue-flamed sword appeared, and as Aidoneus left his temple, he pulled a black hood over his head, letting no light touch his face.

Aidoneus walked into the temple on the mountaintop, surveying the marbled halls with distaste. The other Gods backed away from the ferocious dark God who had been absent from their halls for so long. He looked like a harbinger of doom, with a sword at his side and a hood over his head; he was not one of them, and he did not wish to be one of them. As their fearful eyes moved over him, he felt hatred swell inside. Their whispers were loud as he passed—how strange and sullen Aene'ius' brother was, how unlike his brothers. He was almost on the balcony when a hand grabbed him. He looked down to see Demeter.

Her smile fell as she looked up at him. "What has happened?" she asked, her face creased in concern.

"Nothing," he growled.

"It is not nothing," she persisted, "you look—"

"Stay away from this place," he interrupted harshly. "You should know better than to be here. I thought better of you than that. I thought you were different."

Her face fell, hurt shining in her beautiful eyes, and for some reason the sight made him physically ill. He opened his mouth to apologize, but she was already turning away from him, and as more Gods filled the room, she vanished into the crowd. Like a great bat, he pushed away in disgust and jumped from the balcony to soar towards the mountains of the Caucasus, away from his brother's palace, where he should have found solace but found only condemnation. Despite his brother's demands, Aidoneus had devised a plan to hide the brothers. They did not deserve the fate that Aene'ius was so callously ready to serve them. He flew up the rugged cliffs, levitating above the ground, before landing softly. The terrain was abandoned, and a chill of foreboding went down his spine as he moved through the rocks.

"Brontes? Arges? " Aidoneus called.

When there was no answer, he continued to weave his way to the brothers' home. He felt death first, the stillness of it, and as he walked closer, recognized the sweet, sickening stench of it. He spotted the slain bodies of two of the brothers lying across the entrance of the cave where they lived.

Aidoneus cursed, and threw down the sword, moving towards the Cycloops. As Aidoneus got closer, one of the brothers moved, and the God bent over him, grasping his enormous hand tightly in his own. Brontes. Mortal wounds penetrated deep into the Cyclops' chest, and Steropes lay still beside him, forever silent.

"Aidoneus," the Cyclops gasped. "Your brother— betrayed us. It is not— safe with him. We should never have trusted— him. My belt," his giant eye rolled to indicate the leather belt across his waist. "Take– the weapon."

The God lifted the weapon. It was a bident, beautifully cast of gold and steel.

"For you," Brontes gasped. "A helmet is not enough."

"I do not deserve this," Aidoneus shook his head, gently laying the weapon next to Brontes. "Aene'ius sent me to kill you. And I have misused the sword already, I am not better than Aene'ius . "

Brontes shook his head, his gigantic eye focused on Aidoneus."If he believed you would have killed us, he would not have done it himself. You are – different. You have– kindness in your heart."

Aidoneus bent his head, touched at the words of the Cyclops. "Is it possible to save you?"

"He used the blade," Brontes breathed. "There is no helping my fate. I will join my brothers."

"Where is Arges?"

"Dead– inside." He lifted his great hand to engulf Steropes pale, cold hand in his own. "Do not–pity me little God – I would not wish to live in a world– without the ones I – love. Our fourth brother warned us. We should not have given Aene'ius such a weapon of destruction. We misplaced – our trust."

"What can I do?" Aidoneus asked. "He will continue to abuse these weapons. No being is safe so long as they exist."

"You must—merge the weapons."

"How?"

"Our brother will know." Brontes' body contorted in pain, his great eye closing.

"Tell me his name," Aidoneus said sharply. "Brontes, please, his name!"

His eye opened reluctantly, the pupil dilated. "He lives in– Tartarus. Seek him there. There is something else–something we have not told you. The golden blade–" Brontes whispered as his eye rolled back in his head, and then it opened no more. Brontes had joined his brothers in death.

Aidoneus circled the bodies, finding Arges in the cave. All had been murdered with the sword they had given Aene'ius. The other two brothers had been stabbed through the eyes, and all three bodies had been burned as though struck by lightning. Even the ground around them was charred. Aene'ius had attempted to cover up the murders by making it appear that lightning had struck by accident, but the brothers must have fought valiantly against the God. So Aene'ius had sent Aidoneus to clean up his slaughter.

He climbed up the giant's burnt face and grabbed the lid to pull it shut, accidentally stepping into the pale cornea, his feet sinking into the gelatin-like substance of the eye. He pulled the lid shut as best he could and said a prayer over the creatures. He did not want to bury them with magic; that would be too disrespectful. So, he spent the rest of the day digging three large graves to bury the brothers, then collecting their belongings, which were only a few maps and manuscripts that they had in their pockets. Aidoneus studied the maps. They contained information about Tartarus and the weapons they had forged. Aidoneus resized their belongings, folding them up and hiding them with magic. He began to drag the body of Brontes closer to the grave when, from the corner of his eye, he saw a shadow move amongst the rocks, and he bent to lift the bident near his feet.

"Who is there?" he asked harshly.

Prometheus' head peered out from behind a rock.

"Are you alone?" the Titan whispered.

Aidoneus leaned onto his bident, his eyebrows raised in surprise. "I am unless the dead have ears."

Prometheus kept his place behind the rock, his eyes full of shadows. "I carry a warning. Though it will not make sense to you now."

"A warning? And here I was hoping for good news," Aidoneus replied sarcastically.

Prometheus moved along the shadows of the mountain, approaching Aidoneus furtively. "You did not agree in splitting the mortal souls."

"I did not."

"I see it so much clearer now. He does not love his people. He fears them."

Aidoneus looked at the three graves. "He loves no one but himself," he said bitterly.

Prometheus cautiously stepped towards Aidoneus. "There is a way to stop him. In time, I pray you will remember my warning."

"Tell me your warning old God. Then let me bury these poor beasts."

"She shall bear a son stronger than the sire. The Gods will fear what her child can do."

"Who will bear this child?"

"I will not say her name – for fear her life will be put in danger. Do not ask me again for no God can pull her name from my lips."

"How can I help a woman I do not know?"

"You will come to know her, and you will carry her burden for her. In turn, she will protect your people."

"My people? I am no king."

Prometheus edged closer to peer intently at Aidoneus. "But you will be. You will be a great king. I have given men fire." At this, Aidoneus actually gaped at him, but Prometheus shook his head. "But most importantly I have buried the spark of fire in a man's soul, and he will pass it to his daughter. Through her, men will rise up and fight to protect the Land of Immortals."

"The Land of Immortals," Aidoneus repeated. "Olympus?" But Prometheus now stood as silent as the brothers at his feet and Aidoneus' brow furrowed. "Why do you tell me this?"

Prometheus pointed a finger towards Olympus. "Because you are not like them."

"I am nothing more than a grave digger," Aidoneus replied, looking down at the tombs of the brothers.

"Protect her life. At all costs," Prometheus whispered, his eyes bulging slightly.

Aidoenus shook his head, his long black hair tumbling over his face. "I could not even protect these poor creatures. You are mistaken in your choice of a defender."

The Titan's face contorted. "Promise me," Prometheus urged, grasping Aidoneus' arm. "You must promise me."

"I promise old God. I will protect your nameless woman, however I can." Aidoneus turned back to the Cyclops' body, pulling him into the deep grave and when he turned Prometheus was gone, leaving Aidoneus alone with the dead.

The night sky was dark when Aidoneus traveled back. He moved silently through the palace, intending to make his way to the forest, when a laugh echoed through the halls. He stiffened and changed his course, following the sound. He found them in a garden, lying under the stars, Aene'ius reclining on the ground while Demeter leaned primly against the fountain behind them. An elaborate feast was spread before them, and Aene'ius was idly fondling a ripe peach as he eyed the Goddess. His eyes narrowed at Aidoneus' approach, but then he was smiling, his face welcoming. Demeter looked up at Aidoneus with wide eyes.

"Brother, look at the bounty Demeter has created." He plucked a poppy from the ground, waving it wildly. "She even grew a few poppies that have made my wine quite divine." He took an appreciative sip of the liquid. "Ah, already she has enriched Olympus."

Aidoneus frowned down at her, and Demeter shot him a guilty look. Much to Aene'ius' chagrin, Aidoneus sat down on the soft blue cushion, joining them.

"I think Demeter can find much more appropriate uses for her powers than drugging your wine. Olympus has already found enough ways to be entirely useless without the potent addition of poppy." His eyes moved over Demeter, and she blushed furiously at his admonishment.

"I should go," she began.

Aene'ius popped a large, plump grape between his lips and raised a hand. Demeter sat back down, looking uncertainly between the brothers. "Do not be so dour, brother. I am going to induct Demeter as an Olympian; she would be an excellent Goddess of the Harvest, would she not? And of course, I must sample her powers first." Aene'ius leaned over to the statue of a man urinating wine. He filled Demeter's glass and handed it back to her with a smirk. "More piss, sweet Goddess?" He filled his own cup from a statue of a woman with wine flowing from both ample breasts.

"Thank you," she murmured. The young Goddess gave a tight smile and then lifted a large pear, passing it to Aidoneus with a hopeful look, her eyes imploring him to understand. "Aene'ius was kind enough to invite me. I thought perhaps you would be here as well."

Aidoneus took the pear, regarding Demeter with his black gaze before letting his eyes sweep over Aene'ius. "I was busy paying respects to old friends."

"My brother prefers a more lifeless crowd," Aene'ius interjected with a smile, his eyes hard as they moved between Demeter and Aidoneus.

He plopped another grape between his full lips, crushing it between strong white teeth. "Tell me, Demeter, why do we not see you at our parties? Are you shy? Do you not like Olympus? Are you a hermit like my brother?"

Demeter shifted uneasily on her pillow. "None of the above, I simply prefer more intimate conversation."

Aene'ius' eyes lingered over her breasts, and he said sincerely, "But I would prefer more *intimate* conversations with you."

The Goddess smiled tentatively, not understanding the double entendre, and Aidoneus had enough. Standing, he turned to Demeter. "It seems you have spent enough time in my brother's company, my friend. It is time for you to return to the forest. I believe that he has assessed your talents enough to come to a decision. " Before Aene'ius could speak, the elder brother helped Demeter to stand; the Goddess murmured her thanks, swiftly leaving the brothers. Aidoneus watched Demeter until she vanished from view, then turned to his brother, anger shimmering in his dark eyes.

"What games do you play with her?" he demanded in a low voice. "Leave her alone."

"But I do not wish to leave her alone."

"She is too good for you."

"Too good for me? A king?" Aene'ius scoffed. "She has been more than happy to spend the day with me."

"You pretend she had a choice. Besides, what about Mnemosyne?"

"She has outgrown her usefulness. She is pregnant with nine children, fat and boring. She does not fill my heart."

Aidoneus made a noise of disgust. "You have no heart to fill,"

Aene'ius turned to him with a smile. "But if I did, Demeter could fill it, no?"

"Your appetite can never be satiated. You devour anything that is novel or that can serve your purpose, and when it outlives its usefulness, you destroy it."

"But everything exists to serve my purpose," Aene'ius laughed, twirling his glass in his hand. He raised his beautiful blue eyes to his brother's face. "Did you do as I asked with our friends on the mountain?"

Aidoneus searched Aene'ius' face but found no remorse in his eyes. "I found the brothers already slaughtered by a mad God."

Aene'ius' nostrils flared. "But I have heard the only mad God here is you."

The dark brother bent to the light one, his voice soft. "We were born from madness, you and I. The same tainted blood runs in both of us. You believe you are better than others, but we are pits of emptiness, black holes that nothing will ever fill. We devour the stars and galaxies that lie in our path, but no light passes through us. I have seen your soul, the bleakness of it. I have seen you, brother, and someday, all will see what you are trying so hard to hide: that there is *nothing* inside of you."

Aidoneus swept from the garden, and Aene'ius' lips curled. The beautiful fair God leaned back, peering up at the night sky, as the light from the stars streamed down on him. He knew the stars shone only for him, that the sky existed only for him, and he tried to dismiss his brother's words; yet there was fear deep within his warped soul, for as he peered at the galaxy that belonged only to him, he felt what he always felt— nothing.

Persephone and Ares watched as the days flew by, memories dancing around them. At the birth of Athena, Aene'ius cleverly tricked Hera into marrying him, and the Muses spread Aene'ius' good name across the land. Hate began to consume Aidoneus, and he shunned all Gods and mortals alike. Rhea feared for her dark-haired son and she watched Aene'ius' carefully, hating what he had become.

Demeter was given a throne in Olympia and welcomed with a crown of flowers in her hair. Aidoneus worried for Demeter, but she would not heed his warning, and so he moved deeper into the forest until even she no longer visited. At night, Demeter would sneak from the palace to meet Iasion, and they would talk of the future. She missed the dark God who had been her friend, but she saw no evil in the Gods of Olympus, and their disagreement festered between them like an open wound.Aene'ius' infatuation with Demeter had not wavered, and he resented her the more she avoided him.

However, he was contented with a new hobby that occupied his time:

the indulgence of mortals. Since humans' souls had been ripped in half, he found they were desperate for love. The once joyful humans were now filled with discontent and spent their lives searching for the missing half of their soul, and Aene'ius ensured that soulmates would forever be kept apart. It would not do to allow the souls to join, for they were malleable and corruptible in their misery. Age and death would take care of what distance could not. Their sorrow sparked battles like the Earth had never seen before, and its soil turned scarlet with their blood. The greater their depravity, the more they sought the approbation of the Gods. They didn't comprehend their pain, but they prayed to the God who dwelt high in the sky to heal them, and Aene'ius grinned, for it was exactly as Metis had predicted. As a result, Aene'ius grew more powerful while mortals weakened, and plagues and starvation ravaged the regions.

When he snuck down to Earth and laid with a human for the first time, it was like ambrosia to him. They were so desperate for love that they would do anything he desired; no perversion was denied. He played games with them, watched them from the sky, manipulated them, and smiled. He sat on the throne, laughing with Asphaleius about how he had disguised himself as a swan and defiled a woman with his beak. He even abducted a young prince, making him serve as his cupbearer by day and in his bedroom at night. He took who he pleased and laughed at how they never knew the secret—that it was he who had broken them.

Mnemosyne's daughters, the Muses, inspired people to write poetry to the God, and moral history became saturated with Aene'ius. Aene'ius was no longer satisfied with his birth name, so he was renamed Zeus, Supreme Ruler of All Gods, and the Muses spread his fame far and wide. They would sing songs to him, dance, and put on performances, and he would sneak down to Earth in disguise, a beard covering his face, and make love to the prettiest people of his choice.

Mortals were his hobby, but the green-eyed Goddess, whom he had taken from his brother, was his obsession. He fantasized about being the first between her legs, and when the yearning became too strong, he secretly watched from the mountainside. He let out a rage-filled scream as she not only met with a mortal man, but lay with him; he had assumed she would be safe after Aidoneus was banished, but she had instead spread her legs for a pathetic human! A pitiful mortal had taken what was rightfully his, and he was blinded by jealousy. His eyes flashed with lightning as he heard her quiet moans of pleasure and saw the delight in her green eyes. He raised his hand to the heavens, and a dark storm swirled across the skies as he unleashed his fury.

From the clouds, a bolt of lightning crashed down and snatched Demeter's happiness, stealing the life of her lover. Aene'ius flew to the Earth below, determined to take what he was owed. Her cries of despair and agony echoed through the forest, and Aidoneus heard her. He flew towards the voice, his heart racing, but he was too late. She lay next to Iasion's scorched body, his charred hand clasped in hers, the flesh crumbling like dust in her fingers. Her skirts were ripped, and blood ran down her thighs. She was so still that Aidoneus' heart stopped, terrified that his brother had used the golden blade on her. He wrapped his fingers around her wrist and as he felt her fragile heartbeat, he let out a pent-up breath.

At his touch, her body began to tremble, and her eyes flashed open, dilated and unfocused.

She was murmuring, and her voice was so faint that Aidoneus had to bend to hear her. "Do not touch me, do not touch me, do not touch me."

"Demeter," he said gently, "Demeter, it is Aidoneus. Can you hear me."

Her eyes shot to him. "Aidoneus." Her face crumbled. "Help him," she pleaded. "Oh Gods, please help him."

She did not have to say who had violated her; Aidoneus' hands shook as he covered her with his cloak. He wanted to weep at the emptiness in her gaze, for he knew how it felt to be violated, to feel less than nothing. Aidoneus lifted his hand to the place where she was still holding her lover and gently attempted to loosen her grip.

"No!" she cried. "Do not take him from me."

"He is gone, Demeter, "Aidoneus said as softly as he could. "You must not remain here. Let me help you. I will return for him, but first I must see to you."

She shook her head, closing her eyes tightly. "I thought it would never end. I want to die," she whispered. "That he should have touched me. He has taken everything from me. I told him to stop and that I was pregnant. But he didn't," she sobbed, "he didn't stop."

Aidoneus gripped her hand tightly. "You are with a child?"

She nodded her head, tears leaking from the corners of her eyes.

"Let me help you, Demeter, it is what he would wish. For your child. Let me help you." With a sob, Demeter let go. She lifted herself to her knees and pressed her lips against her lover's burnt face.

"I love you," she whispered. "Forgive me."

Aidoneus picked her up, striding quickly from the cursed spot. Cool rain poured from the sky, and Aidoneus lifted his head as the small drops turned into white flakes, swiftly covering the ground, and he stared in wonder at the crystals. The temperature was dropping rapidly, colder than he had ever felt, and he hurried. As he reached his temple, he entered quickly, laying Demeter on the bed.

She turned her face away from him as he brought her a bowl of warm water. "Will you let me help you, Demeter?"

"You do not have to," she whispered. "I do not deserve your help. You tried to warn me, but I did not listen. Because of me, he is dead." She sobbed the last word, her sweet face crumbling. "Oh Gaia, I cannot bear it!"

"No," Aidoneus said fiercely. "You are not to blame. All you did was love him."

Gently, he began cleaning Demeter's legs, hands, and arms. He wanted to weep at the bruises on her skin, but he kept his face expressionless and his hands gentle as he removed the torn shards of clothing from her, quickly covering her with the soft blanket on his bed.

"When he was inside me, he turned into a minotaur," she whispered. "I thought my body would rip apart." She clutched her abdomen. "Is the baby unharmed?"

Aidoneus laid his hand over hers. "I feel her life pulsing inside you. Quiet your mind and listen. Iasion's love grows within you."

Demeter closed her eyes and concentrated. "I feel it," she whispered. Her eyes flew open suddenly. "Her?"

Aidoneus smiled. "A daughter."

Demeter placed her hands on her abdomen and sobbed. "I will shelter her away. I will not let her be part of their world." Thunder rumbled in the wind, and as she looked up at him, there was no hope in her gaze, only bitterness and fear. "You were right; the Gods are vile."

She shot from the bed suddenly before Aidoneus could stop her and rushed to the window, oblivious to the sheet falling from her naked body. She lifted her arms, and the storm raged wildly outside the windows, icy air blowing around them. "I will destroy his lands! He will be the King of Nothing!" Aidoneus moved behind her, watching in shock as the forest was covered in swirling, white crystals. "I shall cover the lands with my power! I shall name it snow, winter, and it will wipe out all life! I will watch his kingdom wither!" she screamed. Her eyes were blazing, and he saw no trace of the gentle-eyed Goddess he had first met.

"No, Demeter, you will not do that. You do not wish to harm innocents. Protect your daughter, shield her from Olympus and Olympians, but let her grow happy in the forest. It is what her father would want. Do not let your hatred for him outweigh your love for your daughter. Do not let it outweigh the goodness that lies within you. Nothing would please him more than to take that away from you."

Demeter suddenly crumbled at his words, the fire leaving her body as she fell to the ground. "I will hide her safe inside me for a hundred years. She is the only reason I will not destroy this world. My only reason for living."

He helped her to the bed and covered her again. "She is a good reason for existence. She was made in love, by love. I will bury Iasion."

Demeter gripped his hand tightly. "He said he wouldn't allow Iasion to be buried. That his soul will wander the Earth for eternity. Do you think this is true? "

Aidoneus hid his troubled gaze from Demeter and gave her a reassuring smile. "He will be given a true and proper burial." At his words, Demeter swung her legs over the bed. "What are you doing?" he asked with a frown.

"Give me a robe. "

"You must rest."

"I will, but first I am coming with you. I will bury my husband and the father of my child."

He studied the trembling line of her lips and then nodded his head. She gathered a few things from his temple and dressed in one of his black robes. Together, they moved through the dark night and the land was covered with heavy white—what had she called it—snow? Demeter had been unable to completely control her grief. Finally, they reached the spot where Iasion's broken body lay. Aidoneus picked up the charred remains, and the quiet night surrounded them, the frozen air hushed and still.

Aidoneus looked through the forest, seeing the dim light of his temple, and a strange premonition came to him, warning him that he would never again return to this sanctuary. How much more torment would his brother cause before everything was said and done? How much more suffering? Shaking off his reverie, he turned. Demeter held Iasion's hand as they brought the Earthly prince through the forest.

"Follow me," Demeter said softly. "There was a place he loved best in the world."

They carried Iasion's body up to a high cliff that overlooked the sea. In her arms, Demeter held a bundle of fabric that she spread over the ground. Aidoneus bent, placing Iasion's remains on the shroud. He opened his hand, and a large golden coin appeared in his palm. He passed it to Demeter, who kissed it before placing it against the mortal's lips. As he began to dig, Demeter anointed Iasion with oils and dressed him in the same black robes that Aidoneus and Demeter wore. When they were finished, they knelt once more by the prince, and Demeter sang softly, her sweet voice echoing in the cold morning air.

"Far down the valley and rivers below

There I shall meet you, young, strong, and whole.

Deep in the water, by the light of the moon

There I will find you; I'm coming soon."

And as the sun rose over the water, the Earth wept frozen tears, and Persephone's father was buried on the high, lonely cliff.

Time swayed again, and Aidoneus stood like a dark beacon at the entrance of Olympus. A white blur raced towards him, and Zeus materialized, shoving his brother hard so that his back shattered the mountainside behind him.

"I did not want him buried," Zeus snarled. "I forbade it!" He raced towards Aidoneus again, but the dark God had already leapt away, landing in a low crouch.

Aidoneus stared at his younger brother with revulsion in his black eyes. "You are a murderer and a rapist." He stood, gesturing to the kingdom surrounding them. "You have no right to this throne."

"And who would take it from me?" Zeus laughed, his blue eyes sizzling with silver light. "You?" He scoffed. "All of Olympus knows you are mad. Everyone knows you were ruined the moment Cronus swallowed you."

"I am ruined," Aidoneus agreed in a low voice. "But Demeter is not. She is pure and whole, and you took what she cherished most on the whim of a moment. Just because someone had something you thought belonged to you."

"You helped her keep her secret with that mortal. You undermined me. She is mine—mine to play with, mine to destroy. The world will remember that she wanted me; they will believe that I fathered the half-breed she carries in her womb." He spat on the ground. "They will remember what I wish for them too."

The elder brother drew closer, circling Zeus. "But I remember the truth, Aene'ius. I will always remember. Demeter will always remember."

"Do not call me that!" the king spat. "I am Zeus, the King of Kings!"

"You may change your clothes; you may change what you are called; but you cannot change your soul, and it is that dark, shattered part of you that makes you so unworthy."

Zeus flew towards Aidoneus again, but this time the brother was ready, and he lifted his arms wide. As the brothers collided, something strange happened—something that Aidoneus had never felt before. His own consciousness merged with Zeus', and he could see the wretched, broken fragments of Zeus' soul. There was no light there, no hope for redemption; it pulsed with every ugly emotion that had ever been felt, and deep within the center, hidden carefully, was a void.

As he saw Zeus' true form, Aidoneus fell into that black abyss as his brother's thoughts echoed around him.

Zeus relished in hopelessness and despair, for in those dark moments he could almost feel something. The more shattered the person, the easier it is for him to control them. Just as the demons kept Aidoneus broken within Cronus and used his baby brother against him, Zeus planned to manipulate Demeter for eternity through her daughter. Olympus was a prison, and the King of Olympus grew stronger each day, feasting on the captives who did not realize they were under his control, Gods and mortals alike.

To spread his ideologies, Zeus would defile, manipulate, marry, fuck, and bear more vain, narcissistic children. They would work together to shatter mankind's souls, and the people would sing and dance, erect statues, and say his name in prayer—Zeus, the most righteous of Gods. His only true talent was recruiting others to do his bidding, manipulating them for his own benefit. Aidoneus watched how he slept and married each Titaness to gain power. He watched him plot to destroy the humans with Metis. He could feel how each child was a tool to give him more power. Olympus was simply a much larger, better constructed belly of Cronus—all for the benefit of a mad king.

Aidoneus forced his hands away from his brother and fell back, gasping for breath. When he raised his face, he saw that Aene'ius was also breathing hard, shock in his storm-filled eyes.

"What did you do?" Aene'ius demanded.

"You never intended to be a just king," Aidoneus spat. "Your words against Cronus were not of concern; you only wanted to take his power and his throne."

Lightening arced across the room as Zeus took a threatening step closer. "I freed you, and I can put you back in your cell."

Aidoneus gestured to the gates of the palace. "All that you touch turns into a prison. Your palace. This world. But be careful, brother, for in time, your captives will rise against their jailer, and even immortality will not save you."

"I am the King of Kings, and I will have everything! I will have this world, and I will have Demeter!"

"Her heart belongs to the dead prince, and it always will. She has found her soulmate, and she will never love you. Even death will not stop her love." Aidoneous eyes glowed purple.

"Traitor," Zeus breathed. "I will take everything from you. Just as you took Demeter from me. When I am through with you, you will be left with nothing. You betrayed your king. You owe me your loyalty; you are bound by blood!"

At this, Aidoneus raised his head, and Zeus fell back. Again, the symbol of Pluto glowed on the dark God's forehead. "You are not my king. You are not my brother. I renounce you. I renounce all connection to you."

"When you find happiness," Zeus promised, his face contorted in loathing, "I will snatch it from you. Anything you build up, I will break down. I will never let you be happy."

Aidoneus turned. When he heard the unsheathing of a sword, he pulled out the blue-flamed sword, lifting it high to block the blow of the golden one. At first, Zeus' very being was lit with silver flames, but the king staggered back before the blades could touch. A powerful force emanated from the swords, pushing them apart. The swords were like the Sun and the Moon, rotating in the same orbit but never able to touch. Zeus' powerful chest heaved, and Aidoneus stepped back to look at his brother.

"So it is like that?" Aidoneus asked softly.

"Yes," Zeus breathed. "It is like that."

A powerful emotion swept through Aidoneus: sorrow, hatred, and remorse swirled within him until wicked Chaos consumed his soul. There was one deep within Tartarus who had unleashed this evil on the world—the bearer of the evil fruit. He turned on his heel, vanishing from Olympus. He would seek vengeance against the banished king. As he sped from the halls, he could not have known he would never enter them again as Aidoneus.

They watched him battle Cronus in Tartarus, and as Aidoneus lifted his killing blow, his mother, who had followed him from Olympus, flew between them, her chest pierced by the blue blade. He held her as she died in his arms, and the first pomegranate tree blossomed from her blood. His brothers gathered, harshly sentencing their sibling, and

Aidoneus was no more. He died that day, and the birth of Hades began alone in the darkness. The fall of Aidoneus begat the rise of Zeus. The dark prince was banished to the Land of the Dead, and fear of him spread among mortals and Gods alike.

Persephone watched him wander in the darkness, deeper into the shadows, until Eurynomous stepped from the blackness. Hades surrendered himself to the demon, rejoicing in the suffering he had earned and praying he would die, aware he would never have that absolution. Time swirled, and Hades emerged from his imprisonment, Cerberus in tow. Hecate appeared before him, a knowing smile on her face.

She led him from the darkness to a place engulfed in power and taught him shadow magic. Hades learned necromancy and divination there and eventually grew the Underworld from ashes into a strong and just kingdom. He punished evil souls severely, locking them away from innocents and healing the souls that were broken on Earth, placing them where they could live a simple but peaceful life for eternity. He would listen to their pain, touch their souls, and heal them, and as he did so, his thread would grow darker, knowing how he had assisted in their suffering. He promised himself that down here, they would never be broken again.

One day, when he thought he could bear no more, the Styx showed him a vision. In the water's reflection, he saw her, Demeter's daughter, and he was filled with hope. He felt at peace with the Universe for the first time in eternity. Persephone watched Hades look for her in the forest that wretched day she had been broken. She saw him seek amnestic refuge in the River Lethe after he read her letter and felt his heart breaking.

She saw the day he slipped the signet ring on her finger. "Someone must protect the dead. My riches, my power, my kingdom. Everything I have will be yours."

Time whorled, and they were on Ares' mountaintop, and a voice whispered in the blackness, "Did you think it would be that easy?"

Ares' hand suddenly covered her eyes, and he began pulling her. "Do not watch," he yelled. "The future can drive you to madness. Do not look at it, Persephone!"

She felt his hand grab hers and pull her, and they began to run as hundreds of voices rose around them. She could hear screaming and thunder splintering. The sound of war rose around them, cries of pain and death surrounded them, and a mighty wind pulled against them.

Hades' voice rose loudly above the others. "Claim your kingdom. He knows!"

The sound of a swift blade swished through the air, and they were running, knowing death hung just above them until suddenly they were outside the statue and stumbling into the black night of the Underworld. Persephone fell to the ground, trembling. When she raised her head, she saw that Ares' eyes were tightly closed and his hands trembled.

"Why did you show me that?" Her voice trembled.

Ares' eyes flashed open. "You do not know? Still?"

She stood, and her legs were unsteady; her face was furious. "You showed me Hades loved me once, but he cannot even remember it! If he ever felt love for me, he does not now! It is too late for that. You showed me the corruption of the Gods. I already hated them. I hate all of them!" she cried. "You showed me that all Gods should fall. Is that what you wanted? "

The War God stared at her incredulously. "You cannot see," he whispered through pale lips. "Do you not see it?"

"See what!"

"A man who had loved you before you existed! Do you really believe his feelings have changed? How can you possibly be so stupid?"

She closed her eyes tightly. "He has suffered so much. I do not fault the child. I do not fault the young God who was manipulated. He loved me once, but he—" Her voice broke, but she forced her lips to firm. "He does not love me like that anymore. He never will again. I wish I did not know!"

Ares shook his head. "Think, Persephone, of what you have seen."

Her eyes blazed. "Why must you speak in riddles? How do I know what I watched is even real? Tell me frankly what you mean."

He put his hands to his head, and his lips opened and then closed helplessly. "I cannot, for he will not let me!"

"Who? Who will not let you know! One of you is lying to me."

"You lie to yourself! You are so filled with self-righteous anger that you are blinded by stupidity."

Her head jerked back. "I want you gone by dawn. Do not come back here."

"He has done his job well," Ares spat. "Hatred has concealed who you fight against and your true enemy."

She stepped closer to him, and her eyes were filled with fire. "You are right. I am filled with hatred. For all Gods, for myself, and for you. I look within me, but I can find no forgiveness or absolution. I could not even protect my child." Tears filled her eyes, and she turned abruptly, unable to speak.

Persephone did not see how Ares stilled, his face pale and frightened. "There was a child?"

"Yes," she whispered. "My little boy, and he was perfect."

Ares' eyes widened. "Does Hades know? Does your husband know about the boy?"

"Do you think I could hide it from him?"

"Persephone, we must leave. You are not safe." Ares reached for her, but she pulled away from him.

"Do not touch me," she yelled. "Never touch me again."

"Where is he now? The child?"

"Feeling paternal?" she hissed. "I have seen how Cronus' line treats their children."

Ares flinched. "Don't you understand that your child could be the one Prometheus and Mnemosyne..."

"He's not," she cried. "I wish he was, but he is not."

"How do you know?"

"Because he died in my arms!" Her voice was a raw, broken cry. "Choking for life from the minute I bore him."

Ares lowered his head. "I am sorry, Persephone."

"I would almost believe you were if I didn't know the monster you are."

"No," he breathed. "For this, I am truly sorry."

Persephone moved to the mountain's edge, gazing towards the castle far on the horizon. Her eyes were dry, and a peculiar hollowness filled her as she stared toward the palace where she had once dreamed of happiness. "I am leaving now. For your sake, I hope our paths do not cross again."

CHAPTER 20
THE TRUTH

Persephone wandered back to the palace as if in a dream, oblivious to her surroundings. Janus' visions repeated repeatedly in her mind, but the memories were muddled. Her brain pounded incessantly as she attempted to understand what had been revealed, but Ares' had been correct. She was distraught, her head too disorganized to comprehend Janus' revelations. If only she could seek someone's counsel, but there was no one she could confide in or trust. Persephone was alone in this dark world.

As she entered the castle, it was silent and shadowed, and she made her way through the hallways until she came to Hades' quarters. The blue kyanite followed her footsteps and had grown up around Hades' doorway as though beckoning her inside. Her fingers reached the handle, but she paused as if a premonition had warned her not to enter. A faint muffled whimper could be heard through the door, and dread filled her. Persephone wished she could turn away from the broken sound, flee from that door, from this world, but she heard the cry again, and her heart sank as she recognized the call. It was the sound of death. Her fingers turned the doorknob almost of their own accord, and the door slowly opened, minutes stretching into eons as she examined the chamber, the horrors within searing in her consciousness.

Bodies were sprawled over the floor, their blood staining the walls. And there, in the center of the room, amidst the bodies with crimson, gaping throats, was Minthe atop her husband, her heavy breasts bouncing with every thrust. Long, red hair cascaded down her back as she rode him, and she gripped a ruby-stained dagger tightly in one hand. She threw her head back and screamed, not caring who heard as she bounced up and down on him like an animal. Blood was smeared across both of them, and she bent her head, licking the fluid from Hades' chest.

"I bind their blood to me," she screamed, throwing her head back. "I take their life force so that our power may grow." She rode his cock with abandon, relishing the feel of it deep inside her. "Don't stop. Fill me with your power!" Hades' eyes suddenly connected to Persephone, and there was no life within their depths; golden ash fell from his skin to mingle with clotted blood on the floor. Minthe moaned loudly—an animalistic sound that could be heard echoing down the castle hallways—and when she finally saw Persephone, a smile pulled at her lips, twisting her face. "He is mine," she whispered as she licked his face.

Persephone's gaze moved from Minthe, and she saw a tiny arm and foot in the pile of corpses, the small hand reaching for help that had never come. Horror pierced her chest, and he searched Hades' face for some trace of remorse, of regret, but instead, a smile curled his lips.

"You have lost everything, *queen*," Minthe sneered.

A gentle wind began to move through the room, and Hades sat up, watching Persephone intently.

"I have lost nothing, you fool," Persephone spoke, her voice so unlike her own, a harsh whip in the room that stank of death. "But you—you will be less than dust. I will wipe you from existence. First, I deal with the pawn. Then I come for the king. "Her eyes flashed red as she said this, and they stared into her husband, who lay prone on the floor, a slow smile spreading across his face.

Persephone smiled back, her teeth sharp points in her mouth, as she raised her arms high above her head, and the wind turned powerful and deadly as it began to pull Minthe from Hades, lifting her physically so that his giant, erect cock slid from her. The nymph reached her hands pathetically towards the king, her eyes wide and fearful.

"My love, help me!" But Hades did not move to help his lover; his eyes were only fixed on the glowing Goddess before them. The wind pulled Minthe towards the Queen of the Dead, and once she lay at her feet, Persephone smiled down at her, and Minthe knew true fear.

"Mercy!" Minthe cried. "Mercy, my queen!" As Persephone's eyes gleamed red, Minthe saw no retribution for her, and her face twisted in rage and terror. "He's going to marry me! And I will be queen of this realm; you cannot touch me; he will not allow you to touch me!"

But Persephone's gaze never wavered from the nymph. "You will be Queen of Nothing," she promised.

"He comes to me almost daily," Minthe's shrill voice shrieked as she struggled wildly against the wind. "You are as cold as ice to your husband, but he is warm between my thighs. I am as sweet as you are frigid!" In vain, she tried to lift her hand, clutching the dagger stained with the blood of innocents, but she was unable to move and was helplessly held. "My king! My king! Help me!"

"You have dealt death so freely," Persephone whispered. "Did you not know that for each deed we do and each grain we sow, there is a price to be paid? In the domain of the dead, you have defiled the living. Here is the price I demand."

The nymph's arm turned into a large root, twisting round and round. Minthe looked horrified at her hand, screaming as leaves began to sprout where her fingers should have been. She tried to turn her body to run, but pale roots burst from her mouth, eyes, and ears. Blood dripped off the vines, and the fragrant leaves burst forth. The plant screamed, twisting and tumbling over itself toward Hades. Persephone casually lifted her hand, and flames exploded as the plant tried to climb up the walls to escape the fire, but there was nowhere to crawl, nowhere to escape. The inferno burned brightly until all that was left were the ashes and seeds of the treacherous handmaiden.

The fire danced hot in Persephone's eyes as she finally turned her gaze to her husband, who sat still among the dead. His face was cast in light and shadow, and his eyes had a strange gleam.

"You cry no tears for your lover?" she hissed.

But he said nothing.

She leaped suddenly, grabbing his arm tightly and burning it with fire as she pulled him to his feet. "Answer me! You allow her to commit murder in your name; you break your vows with me and with your people, and you are unmoved still! I would respect you more had you fought for her! At least then, you would have stood for something."

His head was bent, his dark hair covering his face, and she was reminded of the young boy who had once been chained in Cronus. But this was no longer an innocent child. Roughly, she grabbed his chin, forcing his face up, and his amber eyes stared down into hers, an ugly smile pulling at his beautiful mouth. Her eyes narrowed as memories pulled at her, but he jerked away from her suddenly. He bent to pick up a seed, studying it carefully, uncaring that his bare feet stood in pools of blood.

He crushed it between his fingertips and turned to her with gleaming eyes. "Watching you destroy Minthe," he whispered softly, "I did not know you held such power. How has it been hidden from me? You are a true Goddess. Will you smite me, too? Teach me retribution? I would so much enjoy having you punish my sinful flesh." He let his hand travel down his naked body, and she saw his cock erect once more. His head tilted as he studied her, his eyes slumberous. "If I gave you the golden blade, do you think you could do it?"

She moved her eyes to his face, to those golden, unfamiliar eyes. "All things die; you told me that once."

"Oh, I never said that," he replied softly, his fingers carelessly moving over the head of his cock. "*I* will not die, but you, my Queen, I have not yet quite decided. But the more I see, the more captivated I become. I may let you rule by my side after all."

"But what if I have decided you are unfit to rule?" she asked, moving closer to the God of the Dead and her once beloved husband. "What if I have found you unworthy?"

He smiled then as though pleased. "And have you found me unworthy?"

"Yes," she whispered.

Around her, she could feel the spirits of the dead, their souls crying at their abrupt, untimely deaths. She heard them praying to her. She lifted her hands, and fire burst from her fingertips. White-hot flames moved over the bodies, and she felt the souls' pain ease; their connection to their bodies was severed so they could begin their next journey. Her eyes then moved to her husband, and she shifted so that the flames encircled him, hot and bright. She moved closer, her palms raised, studying his illuminated face.

"I am tired of this game. The truth," she hissed. "Tell me the truth."

"But where is the fun in that?" he replied. His eyes glinted. "Shall you attempt to imprison me?"

She allowed none of her sorrow to show in her eyes. "I will encase you in stone until I decide what is to be your fate."

Hades smiled. "But that sounds so very tedious." He lifted his hand and reached out to grasp the flames surrounding him. The fire turned into a blazing whip in his fingers, and he slashed it towards her. She jumped quickly from its path, but the tip of the searing lash scorched against her cheek. Her fingers touched the red-hot burn on her face.

"Want me to kiss it and make it better?" he mocked. Fury uncurled within her. Over and over, she pushed hot flames at him, but each time, he casually whipped them away. "Come, Persephone," he taunted. "I can feel your reluctance. Still, you hesitate to harm your beloved. You are weak after all this time."

She snarled and leaped so that she hovered above him. His head lifted up, and she aimed her palms toward him, but just as the deadly fire grew in her, their gazes met, and in his black eyes, there was endless sorrow.

Do it, she heard his voice urge her, but at his words, she felt the flames within her extinguish, and she fell to the ground, landing in a crouch.

Golden ash fell like snow in the room. "Magnificent," he breathed. "Give me that promise you made almost a year ago."

"Promise..." She repeated, her eyes wary. "What promise?" Her hands trembled as she stood, for a thought was growing within her—an answer so terrible she was afraid to give it life.

"You promised me 'anything, everything,'" he whispered from the shadows.

"I made no such promise."

"But you did, hoping I would leave him alone."

"Leave who alone?" she breathed.

"Your husband, as I was beating him."

Persephone gasped. "Who are you? You cannot be Ares."

The God laughed scornfully. "Do you think Ares could be this powerful? Do you think I would allow him to wield my blade?"

She looked carefully, staring into his eyes glowing gold with the fire of his whip. But it was not the flame of the fire that flickered in his eyes; the amber went all the way around his iris, familiar and yet unfamiliar.

"Who are you?" she demanded.

"Dread Persephone. I told you," he said softly, gesturing to the charred seeds of Minthe. "The pawn will draw out the queen."

"No," she whispered through pale lips.

"Checkmate," he smiled. "What a beautiful game you have played with me. You have helped me sacrifice your own king. It has been most enjoyable."

She locked her gaze on him, frightened. Her eyes moved over the crystal below, the blue kyanite, the stone of truth, and she saw him, the white-haired God, in the reflection. "Zeus," she gasped. As she spoke his name, the crystal shattered all around them, shards of blue glass spinning throughout the room, Zeus' face reflected in the spinning crystals.

Hades' hand rose, and the shards tumbled to the ground. "I told you I had eyes in your world. You were too naive to realize they were your husband's. He did warn you to trust no one." Hades' lips frowned. "In fact, he has been annoyingly persistent. Still," he continued, waving his hand carelessly, "it matters not. I will soon have everything I desire."

"Where is my husband?" Persephone demanded.

"Oh, he is still within this body. When I allow him to be," he finished with a smile.

She was overcome with shock, and she wanted to scream and howl.

How could she have been so blind? She wanted to rage at him, demand Hades' back, and collapse in despair, but she knew she must not show weakness. So she suppressed her feelings and glanced at him coolly while he studied her with amber eyes.

"What is it that you want?" she asked finally.

His eyes flickered in the darkness. "I want everything." He moved casually, lifting a decanter of wine from a nearby table. Persephone eyed the door, but he shook her husband's head, his back to her. "I would not do that if I were you. In fact, have a seat." He poured himself a glass of wine with one hand, and with the other, he twisted his fingers. She was pulled roughly and pushed hard against the bed, forced to lay back, unable to move.

He eyed her as he took a sip of wine. "That's better, isn't it? See how solicitous I am. I am sure that is rather a shock; don't blame yourself for failing to recognize that your husband was possessed. I'm sure he understands. Would you like a glass?" She lifted her eyes to him, and he laughed. "So full of fire," he murmured. "Now," he said, settling beside her on the bed. "Let me share my story with you so I can beguile you with my cleverness. I have so longed to confide in someone.

"Since you were a child, I knew I had to have you," he began, picking up a piece of her long hair to rub between his fingers. "I watched you grow on Olympus, but of course, Demeter noticed and hid you away, but it mattered not; I continued to observe you. As if anything can truly be hidden from me," he scoffed, letting his fingers trail down her paralyzed arm. "But between your mother and Hera, I knew I would need to act indirectly. If I married you to one of my sons, I could get you up to Olympus, and it would be so easy to make you my own."

His eyes narrowed. "But your meddlesome mother turned down every suitor and kept you locked safely away until one day I watched you sneak from her watchful eye, down by the river, where you read a love letter. Can you imagine my surprise when I saw that rose on top of the scroll? I knew it was *him*." He spit out the word with such contempt that his body trembled. "That despicable brother of mine. I watched and listened as you read his words aloud, smiling and so in love. Just like your bitch of a mother, you thought you could allow another to touch you. It almost drove me mad. He would have children with you, and his kingdom would grow larger with his offspring. He would have the happiness he did not deserve. It was not supposed to be like that.

Why should he have what I was never allowed? I was once thwarted with Demeter; I would not allow another to take you."

His face suddenly relaxed again, and he smiled at her. "So I knew I had to stop it, but how? My elder brother had the damnable gift of foresight like our cursed father; worse, he seemed to have some detestable connection to me. But he would never see it coming if I could act as another. So, I tried something I had never attempted before. The golden blade. When the Cyclops passed the sword to me, they whispered a secret. They had done something extra special for the King of Gods. Not only could it *kill* a God, but the golden blade could *possess* a God. But, they warned, it would leave my body vulnerable to attack, and I could only control one God at a time through it, which was terribly tedious. Now, imagine such a secret." He smiled, and it was chilling. "That is why I had to kill them; I could not allow them to tell anyone else, especially my most detested of brothers. So, I bided my time, waiting for the right opportunity. And finally, it came.

"I sought my accursed son, and it was so easy. Ares was never compliant with my requests; he was another blood traitor, always preaching and judging, but Hera would not allow me to get rid of him. He constantly questioned me, encouraging his harpy of a mother to demand my fidelity, but finally, I found a use for him, my *snake* of a son.

"I riled him to a fight, challenging him to a duel, and hot-head that he is, he accepted without thought. I then delivered the smallest of cuts to him, right here." His fingers traced Persephone's forearm. "Once the golden blade had been used on him, I could invade Ares' body. It was so easy! I couldn't believe I had waited so long to use it. So, I ventured down to Earth to watch you. You were so in love with that betrayer—you would give yourself to him that day. He couldn't be your first; I deserved that honor. Besides, what if you got pregnant? What if that traitor bore heirs? So, you see, it was with double pleasure that day that I found you by the river. To thwart my brother while I finally felt your sweet body around my cock and your blood spilling around me. Ah," he said, closing his eyes, "what a delightful afternoon it was."

Persephone's body shook at his words. "Ares--"

But her words were quickly cut off. "Oh yes," Zeus interrupted with a grin, his face alight with excitement. "How very cruel you have been to him. When he learned what I had used his body for, he was enraged and devastated. Seeing a son of mine act in such a way was revolting.

He should have been glad to serve his father. But instead, the fool was tormented and fought against each possession, but he could not stop me. All was working according to plan—you would marry Ares and move to Olympus, and I would have you whenever I wanted. But another meddlesome bitch intervened. Venus was furious. She had an understanding with Ares, and when she heard of the proposal between you and my son, she sought justice by coaxing Demeter into sending you into the hands of my enemy. But she later saw reason and became an ally when she convinced Hades to ram the arrow into my heart. He would believe he was shooting Ares, but really, it was me that the arrow would be driven into."

"But the arrow had Ares' name on it," she whispered.

"Oh no. You saw what was easy and were happily deceived. I knew I could not enter Hades as easily as I had with my son. I would need additional magic to secure his mind. And then it dawned on me. The curse of the golden arrow," Zeus sighed contentedly, flourishing his hand as though writing the letters in the air. "My greatest plan. The *A* never stood for Ares but for Aidoneus and Aene'ius." He smiled down at her. "I see that name means something to you. It was not a love arrow but an arrow cursed by my own magic, an arrow of death. When it was driven into my heart, it would open a connection between myself and the shooter. No one other than Aidoneus should have been able to shoot the arrow, so imagine my surprise when it was not my brother but *you* who was entwined by my magic."

He sat up suddenly and leaned over her, pressing his face against hers, his lips pulled back in a snarl. "If only *you* had not been the one to shoot that fucking arrow. My plan was two-fold: I would be able to enter Hades through the cut of the golden blade, and through the arrow, I would control his very heart. I was supposed to have instant control of his body, but it has taken longer than I would like. When you first plunged the arrow into him, I was taken ill as I have not been in my entire existence and forced to remain only a thread in a powerful God.

"I barely held onto my small grasp within him as he tried to push me out to regain control, but I held firm. It has been a slow and arduous process, and I am not patient. You have been immensely troublesome," he murmured, tracing Persephone's breast through the outline of her toga. "In time, I realized the possibility of possessing you held its own appeal. But I have been unable to breach you. For some reason, you remain beyond my touch." His fingers traced her face. "But you will not be for much longer. He is dying."

Her body jerked at his words despite his control over her. "Hades will find a way to push you out. He will draw you out like venom."

Zeus threw back her husband's dark head and guffawed. "But that is the best part. He cannot do a damn thing. I refuse to leave, and the only other option is to kill the host's body. Through him, you will bear my heirs, and I will have both the splendor of Olympus and the magic of the Underworld. My other brother has always deferred to his rightful king. All will be under my control." His fingers dropped to her neck and tightened slightly so her breath came in short gasps. "Even you." He let go abruptly, and she gasped, dragging air into her lungs.

"What will happen to him?" she demanded, her voice hoarse.

"His soul will fracture, and he will cease to exist. The golden blade has served its purpose— it is killing a God. And it is so much more pleasurable to draw it out. His body will become a shell I can pass through at leisure. I will be king of both realms." He traced his finger over her lips. "Do not be sad; you can still fuck your husband. After all, you have been fucking me all this time, and you did not know it, so what is the difference?"

Persephone felt shock as she realized his words were true; horrified shame filled her, and her body trembled, but she could not give in to those emotions yet. Soon, she could allow herself to shatter, but not before this greatest enemy who watched her so carefully. "I can come down here in the winter, and we can live in Elysium," he was saying. "When spring comes, we'll return to Olympus, and I'll fuck you in my rightful body." He laughed with amusement. "My little scheme has worked out better than I planned."

She stared up at her husband's beloved face, at the eyes that were not his, and hatred flared inside her so powerfully that even she was surprised as a golden bolt of energy burst from her. He fell back, giving a grunt of pain, and she was free, racing towards the door. Too soon, his fingers were on her arm, but she quickly let another burst of energy pulse from her, and he cursed. She was almost at the door when she heard his voice.

"Remember," he called in a sing-song voice, "if you attack me, you hurt him. It's his body you destroy, not mine. Perhaps I will just let the burns fester. You know he can still feel pain?"

Her fingers were on the door handle, and he made no move to stop her. She could leave now and try to get back to the Upper World, but she turned and saw her husband standing near the bed with burns across his arms and chest, and she hesitated. It was not him, not right now. There was no Hades in this God's eyes, but he was still somewhere inside that body, a prisoner once more. Just like when he was in Cronus. Oh, Gaia, how she wanted to fall on the floor and weep. She had seen glimpses of the real Hades pushing to the surface, she realized now. How could she leave him injured? Helplessly, she released the door and walked back to where Zeus stood. She placed her hands over the wounds, shivering at the feel of his cool skin beneath her hands. He felt very, very cold. Healing warmth covered the burns, and only unblemished skin remained when she lifted her palms.

He shackled her wrist with his fingers and studied her hands. "How easily you allow love to manipulate you. It is a weakness. The humans feel it, too, making them so pathetically frail, so far beneath the Gods. Perhaps the mortal's blood that runs in your veins makes you so prone to these inadequate emotions. Poor foolish girl, you do not know how to play this game. You will never understand our ways. Eurynomos," Zeus bellowed so suddenly that she jumped. "I have prepared rooms for you," Zeus continued more quietly, "but first, I have questions that need to be answered, and I am afraid that my sweet wife would not be honest with me without an incentive."

She heard the uneven gait of the demon, and Eurynomos entered, dragging the War God behind him, his enormous claws tearing into Ares' flesh. Persephone allowed her eyes to move over the demon, her heart beating rapidly as Hades' memories resurfaced in her. She promised herself that she would avenge Hades by destroying this creature. Never again would he touch an innocent. Eurynomos leaned his broken wing against the door, closing the foul beast inside with them.

Persephone's gaze moved to Ares, and she noticed that the War God shook his blond head, not meeting her eyes. His sullen stance was very much like Prometheus on the mountainside.

"Eurynomos," Zeus greeted. "How very punctual you always are. Please remind our lovely Goddess and my devoted son of what they spoke?"

Eurynomos's beak opened, and black ooze dripped from his broken beak. Persephone had the horrible notion the demon was attempting to smile. "There was a child," he hissed.

"Ah," Zeus responded with a pleasant smile. "And was there a child, Persephone? Did you lie to *Papa* on the mountain?" She said nothing, keeping her eyes stonily ahead, and Zeus gave an exaggerated sigh. "You know," he said, his voice still congenial, "the best part about possessing my brother, besides fucking you, is that I am able to use his powers. I find them quite useful." He twisted his hand, and she felt a ripping in her mind. She made a small whimper of pain and then cut off the noise abruptly. For endless moments, he probed mercilessly, but quickly, she forced him ruthlessly from her mind, securing the fortress of her memories. He released her and stood back, studying her. She noticed with satisfaction that he was breathing heavily.

"You are good at hiding your thoughts from your husband."

"But you are not my husband," she replied in a cold voice. "His powers in your hands are like a child playing with his father's tools, clumsy and inept."

Zeus' smile became tighter. "Hades has somehow managed to keep this secret from me, but that is no matter. There is always a weak link." He turned to his son. The War God's head was down, but as his father approached him, he raised his blond head, his blue eyes filled with loathing as he looked at his sire. A muscle ticked in his jaw, but he did not step back from the King of Gods. "My boy, my nuisance of a son, you have never been good at shielding your thoughts. It got me into much trouble with your detestable mother. I always considered you a waste of my Godly seed, but you have proven useful." Zeus lifted his hand, and Ares levitated off the ground. Through Hades' body, Zeus twisted his fingers and penetrated Ares' mind. Ares' limbs tensed in pain as he fought the invasion.

"Tell me about the child."

"Fuck you!" Ares spat, sweat beading on his face.

Zeus took a step forward and lifted his hand higher. Lightning ran through Ares, his body suspended as his limbs shook wildly. Persephone gasped and moved forward, but Ares shook his head again, even as he gasped for air.

"What do you know?" Zeus demanded.

"Come closer!" Ares gasped, and Zeus released him. Ares slumped to the ground, his lip bleeding where he had bitten it during the spasms.

Zeus moved nearer. "Tell me."

"Closer," Ares whispered. Zeus levitated, moving right beside his son. He bent his head urgently toward Ares' mouth.

"Fuck. You." Ares screamed, headbutting the God hard.

The king snarled, falling back, and another jolt of electricity moved through Ares, longer this time, his body spasming repeatedly.

Persephone raised her hands, but Hades' amber eyes shot at her. "Help him, and I will punish both Hades and him," Zeus growled, blood dripping down his face. Finally, he withdrew his hands and roughly penetrated his son's mind again. Persephone could see the moment he found what he sought. "Tell me."

Ares' voice was disjointed, and his eyes were unfocused. "When you possessed my body, a child was born by the green-eyed Goddess in the forest." Zeus released Ares, and he fell to the ground, gasping for breath. Zeus turned and dismissed the War God. Ares leaped up, lunging unsteadily toward his father in a blind rage, but Ares was weakened, and Zeus was fast and powerful. He pushed his son tightly against the wall. "If it were not for your wretched mother, I would have banished you from Olympus long ago."

He lifted his hands, hot white lightning flowed through Ares again, and his screams echoed through the room.

"Stop this," a quiet voice said. Zeus turned to see Persephone standing behind him. "He knows nothing else." Zeus released Ares, who dropped to the floor unconscious.

"I am your humble servant, Queen Persephone," he bowed sardonically. The king looked over to Eurynomos. "Remove him from my sight. I want to be alone with her."

The demon looked up at Zeus expectantly. "But Master, please repay me for my loyalty. I beg you for it now."

"Oh, very well," Zeus sighed. "But be quick about it." Zeus held up Hades' arm, and Eurynomos' tongue slithered out before opening his enormous jaws to bite Hades' flesh, groaning in delight as the blood dripped down his mouth. He licked his lips repeatedly, even bending to the floor to clean the drops of blood with his tongue, before carelessly grasping the unconscious Ares in one claw and pulling him from the room. The door closed behind them.

"So this is how you secured Eurynomos' compliance." Her voice quivered with rage even as she healed the gaping hole in Hades' arm.

Hades' eyes closed as though finding great pleasure in her touch. When they opened again, the amber still glowed at the edges. "Yes, he seems to have a strange addiction to Hades in particular. Such a small price to ask for loyalty. But we waste time; tell me about my son."

"Your son? Which one? You just had one of your offspring removed from the room after abusing him. Or perhaps you speak of the one you devoured? It is so hard to know which son you wish to know about."

Zeus waved a hand. "Those were all mistakes. My seed took root in foul ground. But *your son*, well, he would be something special. To have grown in your sacred womb, I might have use for such a son. Eurynomos tells me that you think he died?"

She looked past him, refusing to speak. Zeus rolled his eyes. He picked up the blade Minthe had used and held it against his face. "Give me an answer, or I will give him a wound. You don't want me to damage his oh-so-pretty face, do you?" Her eyes jumped to him. "Ah, I see I have your attention. Did you see the child die?" he asked again.

Her eyes lowered. "Yes."

"That is not possible. Gods do not die. Where did you bury him?" Persephone was silent, and he shook her roughly. "Where did you bury him?"

"He was taken," she snarled at him, her eyes flashing.

"By whom?"

"I do not know!"

"Describe them."

"I never saw the face. They wore a hood. I do not remember anything else."

"Where did they take him?"

"I do not know; they vanished before I could follow them. My child is dead, and someone stole his body. That is all I know."

Zeus released her and stared pensively at the wall. "Our son is alive. I will help you find him."

Persephone laughed mirthlessly, the sound low and harsh. "Like the way you helped yourself into my husband's body? The way you helped yourself to mine? I may be many things, but do not think I will ever be fool enough to trust you. I do not want you touching my child. Not even his corpse. Even that is too good for you."

Hades' eyes were cold. "I have been tolerant of you because it amuses me to be so, but tread carefully, Goddess. You seem to think you can dictate to me," Zeus taunted softly. "How do you think you will stop me when even my powerful brother was no match against me?"

"Truth," Persephone countered. "I will tell everyone the truth of what you have told me."

He walked toward her, laughing. "That is your counter? Oh, Persephone, what a weak, ineffectual move! I had so hoped to find a worthy opponent in you. If you tell people the truth, I am afraid they will think you are quite mad when your husband tells them otherwise." He put his hands on either side of her slender shoulders, and she looked into the mocking eyes of her husband. "The mad Queen Persephone is as insane as her mother, I am afraid. There are already whispers that you are not quite right. Don't you see Persephone? No one cares for the truth, Gods or mortals alike. It is why they are so very easy to play my games with." He was closer to her now. "Come, Persephone," he demanded, his eyes alight with flames, "tell me your next move."

She regarded him coolly. "If you need the body of an Underworld ruler, take mine. Leave him. He has suffered enough at your hands."

"Bargaining? How disappointing. I already have his body and will have yours soon enough. Besides, I have watched you train. I need the body of a warrior, and you are weak. You have always been weak. Even now, knowing your husband is all but dead, you are unable to deliver a blow to him. All that power is locked inside you, yet Ares will never make a fighter out of you. But have no fear; Papa will know how to help."

His words should not have had the power to affect her, but they did, like tiny cuts in old wounds. Weak. Ineffectual. Worthless. He let his eyes trail down her body.

"You were meant for one thing, and it seems like you are failing at that since you cannot procreate with this wretched body." He lifted one muscled shoulder. "It does not matter. When found, our son will sit on the throne of the Underworld during the summer. Once my soldiers invade, I will come down here, and you will sire more of my children. I assure you, my real body is not broken like this one."

"You will never break through our barriers," Persephone promised, green eyes blazing.

"But I already have. And once I have complete control over him, I will let myself fully in." He studied her. "I must admit I have been very annoyed by your persistence in distrusting me. If only you had been content, you could have lived in blissful ignorance. But I am relieved you know the truth now. Keeping up the good husband act was so very tiresome. And the best part is that you are held prisoner by your love for him; no shackles are necessary. Now we can have fun together. I have many skills to teach you."

Hades stood directly before her, and she stared into his beloved face, searching for something familiar in his eyes. Amber lights danced endlessly in the black depths.

"Hades?" she whispered, her voice trembling.

Blood dripped from his nose, and Zeus licked the blood from his lips. "He isn't here. Time for your first lesson."

CHAPTER 21
WOE OF THE WARRIOR

Persephone sat alone in a rotunda carved of larimar, the gemstone's vivid blue conveying a sense of peace. Her mind flashed back to the ferocious battle of wills she had waged against Zeus last night, a tumultuous clash that had left emotional scars far more profound than any physical ones. She forced her fists to unclench, determined to banish the haunting memories into the depths of her consciousness. The indelible touch of his possession, the lingering bruises on her skin— she knew they would fade with time. But the fight for her husband's life and the imminent war on the horizon demanded her unwavering focus. As her eyes traced the serene beauty of the surroundings, she found solace in the opulent chamber. Massive columns of chrysoprase rose to the ceiling, faux plants sculpted from malachite weaving between them. Above, a painted landscape depicted a soft, pink sunrise.

So while she sat in an oversized golden chair, her face serene, a perfect picture of a sedate, circumspect queen, her mind plotted war.

Calmly, she poured herself a hot goblet of wine. Taking a sip, she carefully cataloged each God and Goddess she had met, deciding who could be an ally and who would be a foe. How many of them had Zeus already corrupted? He would be expecting her to act, and he had played her so easily so far. Over and over, she considered each action she could take, wondering which one he would anticipate and how she could outwit this master of games. A knock sounded on the door, disturbing her reverie. Somehow, she already knew who stood on the other side of the solid wood.

"Let him in," she called lightly to the guard outside.

He was as tall and intimidating as ever but stood uncertainly at the room's entrance. They regarded one another, and then Persephone stood.

"Ares," she greeted softly, extending her hand.

The weight of her forgiveness, evident in her understanding gaze, lifted a burden he had carried for too long. Overwhelmed by emotion and remorse, he rushed forward, falling to his knees, trembling as he took her hand. "Forgive me," he whispered harshly.

She tightened her hand beneath his. "Ares," she said softly.

The War God stood, his heart pounding, and the words spilled forth from his lips as if a dam had burst. "You can't fathom the torment, the weight of the secret I've carried. I've yearned to confess, to expose the monstrous truth about that fucking monster, to apologize for the pain he inflicted on you." He closed his eyes, turning his head, and when his blue eyes opened, they burned with hatred. "I would *never* have subjected you to that—never."

Her hand reached out to touch his face, a gentle caress reminiscent of a mother's touch. Slowly, his eyes met hers, revealing what had always been concealed beneath the surface—a mixture of deep shame, remorse, and an unexpected kindness. The deep blue of his eyes shimmered with vulnerability, and he looked away, unable to meet her gaze.

"Ares," Persephone began, her voice filled with a poignant sincerity, "you are innocent of any wrongdoing toward me." She bowed her head. "You tried to warn and tell me the truth, but my hatred blinded me, and I refused to listen. It is I who should seek your forgiveness. Ares, will you be my friend? Will you stand by me, fight with me, and be my brother?" Her voice trembled with emotion.

Blue eyes locked onto green, and Ares genuinely smiled for the first time in their tumultuous history. His entire face radiated an inner light, and the tears on his cheeks only enhanced his beauty.

"I like you better than my sisters," his smoky voice replied, irreverent. "I will follow you into battle," he pledged, "and if necessary, I will die beside you. We will stop him, that fucking monster, and watch him burn!"

In the intensity of his gaze, the glint of retribution shone bright, and their hands clasped each other firmly, a promise. The unspoken words woven into that simple gesture conveyed a myriad of expressions, encapsulating a shared understanding known only to two souls bound by the same harrowing trauma.

"Come," Persephone said, leading him to the chair beside her. She felt him tense and followed the direction of his gaze. Olive was curled up at the foot of her chair, and she understood. Zeus had used Ares' body to kill her sweet friend. "It is alright, Ares; Olive is happy now."

Ares shook his head and kneeled before the fawn.

"Little one," he whispered, extending his hand. "I must ask for your forgiveness as well. Olive lifted his head and sniffed Ares with interest. Finally, his small pink tongue licked his fingers, seemingly granting absolution. Ares laughed shakily, standing to take the seat next to Persephone.

"You know," Persephone said thoughtfully, "I think Olive always knew it was not you who hurt him. I wish I had the wisdom of the creatures of the forest to see beyond what my eyes show me. Tell me, Ares," she continued in a quiet voice, "why can you speak to me now?"

"As Zeus entered Hades, his control over me was shattered, save one final spell, that I would be unable to speak the truth to anyone," Ares admitted, his voice a subdued but seething undercurrent of anger. "For all that time, I was nothing more than a puppet, manipulated in every move, my very words dictated by him just as much as my body." His hands tightened into fists. "And I could not even reveal the truth to anyone what had happened. The moment Zeus revealed the truth to you, it felt like the spell shattered, setting me free from the grip of his power." He removed the armor from his arm, revealing a long, diagonal wound. "This served as his entry point. Once he pierced me with the golden blade, he controlled me completely. It was the same with Hades. "

Her heart twisted like a vise in her chest. "You have spoken with my husband?" Persephone asked breathlessly.

"Yes," Ares replied. "He has never stopped loving you. Not even for a moment."

She gave a small cry, burrowing her head in her hands. "I have wronged him so!" she cried.

"No." Ares' voice was firm. "Zeus wants you to be tormented, doubt yourself, doubt Hades. If you are distracted, you are not a threat. Don't let him win. He must be stopped, and it is up to you to stop him."

"Me!"

Ares nodded his head. "Yes, it is why he fears you. Why he wants to make you feel small. You must stop him," Ares repeated again. "And I will help you."

Persephone lifted her head, wiping her eyes. "Yes," she whispered. "He must be stopped. At all costs."

"And you must forgive yourself," Ares urged.

Persephone shook her head. "Not yet," she said wistfully. "Not until I know Hades is safe again. Ares, I would like to hear your tale. If we can combine all we know, we may find a weakness, something we have not yet thought of."

Ares looked meaningfully towards the door. "He has eyes and ears everywhere."

"True," Persephone agreed. She lifted her hands, and red flowers grew along the door, pushing themselves through the keyhole. She lifted her hands, and a glittering blue gemstone pushed from the ground surrounding them. "Lapis lazuli," she explained. "And poppies to occupy my guard. They are not as potent as Hypnos' but will do the job fairly well."

"Very clever!" he laughed.

"Now, Ares, will you tell me your tale?"

Ares' smile faded as he studied his reflection in the blue stone and then quickly looked away as if he could not bear what he saw. "I sometimes wonder what I would be like if my parents hadn't raised me."

Persephone poured a steaming cup of hot wine and passed it to him. He took a sip gratefully. "The truth is, there is not much to my story. I was raised by selfish, negligent Gods, and, in turn, I became a selfish, negligent God. Even in my youth, I knew my father was self-centered and uncaring, and my mother was vindictive and manipulative." His eyes softened. "But I do love my mother, for she is capable of love, but she too is a product of her environment.

"For many years, I knew nothing but self-satisfaction and anger. My childhood was a battle; my father decreed that I would be the very Spirit of Battle, the God of War. I felt nothing for the men who died around me. Why should I? My father told me mortals lived to die and that their only purpose was serving the Gods. He told me that they were primitive beasts, incapable of feeling, and Gaia forgive me, for I followed him without question. But slowly, I began to see the truth of who he was."

He studied the ground. "I have children," he began softly. "I love them very much and have tried hard not to repeat my father's mistakes. You know that Aphrodite and I have an understanding. She has done great wrong by you but has also been abused by Zeus. He twisted and molded her until she did not know who she was. We secretly conceived a child who has grown into a God I love and respect.

"I am an adulterer, but she does not love her husband, and he only views her as a trophy. How ironic that the beautiful Goddess of Love, whom my father cruelly wed off to Hephaestus against her will, is trapped in a loveless marriage. My mother did not wish to marry Zeus; she was a strong Goddess and knew enough of Zeus' history to reject him. Again and again, he sought her hand, but each time she said no." Ares' face twisted in revulsion. "But of course, my father would not accept that.

"One night, my mother found a helpless bird with a broken wing caught in a storm. She took in the bird to nurse him, and then he transformed into the King of Gods. But this time, he did not ask. He forced himself on her, and out of shame, she agreed to marry him. But he could never make her forget what he had done to her. When she finally confided the truth of their relationship to me, I vowed to her that I would be a protector of mistreated women and that I would punish men who forced themselves on the innocent." His jaw tightened. "But I am always too late.

"I have a daughter, Alcippe, who is sweet and kind. She is a gentle spirit who is content with a simple life. One day, as she was walking by the sea, Poseidon's son, Halirrhotius, took her by force. He did what my father did to my mother—what he has done to so many women. I was going to rip the flesh from Halirrhotius' bones, but Poseidon protected his kin, and I could not reach him." Ares' fisted his hands. "In a tide of fury, I swept to Olympus to seek my father. I demanded Halirrhotius be brought to trial and punished for his crimes, but Zeus laughed. He said that I was pathetic and not a son of his.

"But I would no longer tolerate my father's insolence. I screamed my truth for all of Olympus to hear: that he was an unworthy king, a rapist, and a murderer. I told him that as long as he ruled Olympus, I would no longer be a part of it. He watched me with eyes filled with malice, and finally, he stood, challenging me to a battle. He drew the golden blade, and great pain overcame me as he sliced my flesh open. The pain was so unbearable I thought I would die.

"After that, my memories became blurry. Zeus used my form as he pleased, directing my thoughts and actions. I would wake up, and large chunks of time would be missing, but I began to piece together vague memories in my subconscious. I could feel his obsession with watching you. I knew he feared the girl with the green eyes, Demeter's daughter, who had been made in love. When he saw you writing to his brother, he was filled with madness and determined to break your soul connection. He thought he had stopped the prophecy and was safe, but he saw his destruction in you. He possessed me, but this time, he left me aware and punished me. He snuck down to the river, and it was there that you believed I was your lover.

"Zeus whispered in my mind that I was a snake. "You hate rapists," he whispered to me. "Then I shall make you one." Desperately, I tried to fight him, to break his hold on me, but he was too strong, and through my weakness, he committed a crime on your body for which I will never forgive myself. "He drug his fingers through his hair. "As he committed the deed, I screamed in rage, but my anger only fueled him. He turned me into what I despised most: himself.

"When I left you by the river, I could feel his pleasure, and it sickened me. He thought he had broken you and that you would never love again. Once more, he believed he was safe. But despite all odds, fate again led Hades to the soul that had called for him all those years ago. "He smiled ironically. "Who would believe fate would use Venus' hands to bring you back together? She changed the game by convincing your mother to hide you in the Underworld, hoping to keep Zeus from forcing you to marry me.

"Initially, my father's fury knew no bounds, but it transformed into amusement upon discovering the cursed arrow's existence. A love arrow, infused with Venus' potent magic, was destined to unravel Hades' sanity. Considering your trepidation towards men, the prospect of a cursed man, driven to madness and consumed by desire for you, seemed like a harbinger of ruin for both of you."

"But it didn't work out that way," Persephone said softly.

"No, it didn't go as planned. It was a risky gamble, but my father revels in the game of chance. His hope was that Hades would turn so monstrous and repulsive that you'd despise him. The intention was for you to flee the Underworld, never looking back, leaving Hades to spiral into madness under the influence of the love arrow. It would have provided the perfect excuse for my father to lock away his brother for good. However, the curse didn't drive Hades mad. Instead, his love for you became a soothing balm for his tormented soul. When Zeus realized that his scheme had backfired and that you two were falling in love, he wasn't just furious—his anger was beyond measure."

Ares closed his blue eyes momentarily as though in pain. "Once more, he used my body. I abducted you to lure Hades to the mountaintop, and if I died in the process, so much the better. Venus cursed an arrow that would allow Zeus to take control of Hades' body. This was his final attempt to stop the prophecy and prevent Hades from having a child with you. With the wound from the golden sword, he would enter Hades, and with the cursed arrow, he would control him. There was one mistake, though." Ares smiled at her. "Hades was supposed to plunge the arrow into my heart, and in that instant, Zeus would have gained complete and total access over your husband's body. He did not count on you shooting the arrow. You fucked Zeus' plans, and his control over Hades is moving much slower than Zeus intended.

"Through your soul connection to Hades, you could wield the arrow only intended for him. As you plunged the arrow into me, Zeus was overcome by weakness, and my body was released. As I was freed from prison, I reached for my uncle, desperate to explain. What a surprise it was when your husband's voice entered my mind! "I know," he whispered to me. Hades had realized the truth sometime during the battle, but he continued fighting for my soul. He saved me, and for that, I owe him everything. I was freed from his possession once Zeus struck Hades with the golden blade. The effort to hold the powerful king under his control consumes Zeus. Hades has become his only objective and obsession. I sought Hades in the Underworld to offer my allegiance to him.

"Together, we worked so that Zeus would have moments when he was forced to leave Hades' body. I discovered that when Zeus possesses a person, his body goes trance-like, leaving him vulnerable. So, I used this to our advantage. I would go to Olympus, tell my mother of Zeus' infidelity, and she would fly into rages, attacking his body with powerful magic, forcing him back on Olympus." Ares smiled at Persephone. "You should see my mother in one of her rages; it is truly a sight. It was during these moments that Hades was released from Zeus' hold. But his freedom was only ever temporary."

"So there were moments," Persephone said softly, "where my husband has been here?"

"Yes," Ares replied, his voice, for him, surprisingly gentle.

Persephone sat deep in thought.

"Is there a way to permanently force Zeus away from my husband?"

Ares shook his head. "We have only ever had brief respites from him. Zeus cannot be forced out. He will not leave until he chooses to do so."

"When he controlled you, were you ever able to fight against the possession?"

"I fought when I was aware but I was powerless against him. My wound is not as deep as Hades. When I, or rather Zeus, cut his flesh, I could feel it cut deep into his soul."

Persephone sat back, her face pale but her lips firm. "What can I do to save my husband?"

"Fight," he replied with a snarl. "Fight with everything inside you."

"Yes!" she cried. "With everything that is within me."

"But beware. I do not know how my father does it, but he makes his victims worship their attacker. He will try to make you love him so your loyalty will no longer lie with your husband."

Persephone shook her head. "Never," she said in a low voice.

"Many clever women have said the same thing, only to find themselves in his thrall. His manipulation will grow even worse now. Now that you know the truth, Zeus will change his strategy. The game begins anew."

"We will devise our own plan."

"Never forget he wants your kingdom." Ares placed his hand against the stone. "Persephone?"

"Yes?"

"Zeus wants a child, a son. He wants to set him on the throne of the Underworld, to taint him, to control him. It is what he has done to all his children. He will search for the first son, who died by the river."

"He will not touch him," Persephone hissed. "What do we do first?"

Ares smiled down at her with a trace of his usual swagger. "First, I think we let you see your husband."

CHAPTER 22
REUNION

Following his abrupt declaration, Ares swiftly ascended to Olympus, leaving Persephone alone in her room, anxiously twisting her fingers. Restless, she ventured into the kitchens, paying no mind to the inquisitive gazes of the servants. There, she assembled a tray laden with various sustenance—bread, cheese, and a steaming bowl of stew crafted from her garden's produce. Quietly, she carried it up the hidden staircase to her room. She felt nauseated but forced herself to eat, hoping it would quell her nerves. It hadn't. And that had been hours ago. She had been anxious when Ares had left, and that anxiety had since transformed into a frenetic, nerve-racking energy. Olive was curled up on her bed, long ago worn out by her endless pacing. She sat near the fire, then stood again, only to move once more to the door.

It was a shock when it finally opened, and she fell back, surveying the visitor with a mixture of trepidation and inexplicable longing. Hades stood in the doorway, his black robes covering him. She stared at him, afraid to move or even breathe. Who was standing before her now? Was this Zeus or her husband? He watched her with black eyes, and when she saw that purple edge on his pupil, she let out a sob, hiding her face in her hands.

Strong arms moved around her. "Hush," he whispered, his lips moving against her hands. "Let me see you, Persephone."

She shook her head, a desperate attempt to articulate words drowned by the choking sounds that escaped her. Gradually, she felt his arms around her as he lifted her, cradling her against the reassuring warmth of his chest. Her head found solace on the smooth fabric of his robe as great sobs wracked her body. Again, she tried to speak, but the words emerged in a tangled mess of incoherence. Hades tenderly caressed her hair, uttering soothing sounds that gradually quelled her cries as he laid her on the bed. As the storm of emotion subsided, she felt his hands cup her face. With a reluctant surrender, she allowed him to lift her chin. Tears stung her eyes as she turned her gaze to his, a silent exchange of understanding amid overwhelming emotions.

"How can you forgive me?" she whispered. "I knew something was wrong, but I did not see what was right in front of me. I have been such a fool, never seeing how you have been suffering." Her eyes closed tightly. "I am so ashamed."

His eyes burned with intensity, his voice carrying a raw edge. "Forgive?" he inquired, his lips briefly brushing against hers before he pressed his forehead to hers. "Forgive me for ever laying eyes on you, for leading you to this juncture." His eyes closed as he continued, "I should never have permitted myself to step out of the shadows. My existence was forged there, and I have unwittingly entangled you in the web of my madness."

"No," she said fiercely, her voice trembling. "Our love may have been forged in darkness, but it is made of the purest light." She bent forward, wrapping her arms around him tightly as though she could hold him to her. "Now that I know the truth, we can devise a plan."

"The truth," he murmured. "That I am both a man you love and abhor?"

"You're just one man," she exclaimed, kissing the palm of his hand. "The man I love. I love you." She encircled him with her arms, feeling the steady rhythm of his heart against her own. Closing her eyes, she immersed herself in the precious sensation. "Love brought us together, and love will be the force that unravels him. Throughout our existence, he's tried to tear us apart. Together, we'll conquer him."

Hades stroked her hair softly. "To sit with you, to finally be able to

speak freely with you, is better than any ambrosia. I was so afraid that you would never know."

She closed her eyes at his touch and then sat up, suddenly remembering the food. She gestured to the tray. "Would you like something to eat?"

He shook his head. "You are so sweet, my beautiful wife," he answered, tracing the outline of her lips. "But he will not let me eat." She had been lifting him a cup of hot wine, and he eyed the cup. "Or drink."

Her face fell. "You mean, all this time, you have been unable to eat?" He nodded his head. "But... can you not try? You need strength!"

"I cannot fight it; it weakens me. There is only one thing Zeus thirsts for, one thing that he craves." His eyes flashed with lust, gold shimmering in his gaze suddenly, and Persephone shrank back. The purple quickly edged back into his eyes. "No, Persephone. I must be careful. Even when he is gone, he is still there. I am never free. It draws him back like a moth to a flame if I fight."

She became acutely aware of Zeus' ever-present scrutiny, simmering just beneath the surface, a constant observer of their most intimate moments. This watchful gaze, spanning even before her birth, ignited a deep well of hatred within her. How much he had taken from them and how much he would still take.

"When I promised him anything and everything," she whispered, "he knew you were my weakness. If only I had known the darkness I was letting in."

"You share no blame," he growled, his fists tightly clenched in frustration. "This power struggle predates your existence—a game that unfolded ages before your birth."

"We will break this curse! Like last time."

Hades closed his eyes, and when they opened, they were bleak. "This is not a curse, Persephone. He is inside me. He is watching, listening, and controlling me to do his every command. Through the golden blade, he created a wound that he seeped into, and my soul is fracturing in the process. He will not stop until he takes everything I love and have built and burns it to the ground. There were times I crawled from the darkness, but when I was about to break through, I felt my immortal soul fracturing, and I thought I would die from the pain." He closed his eyes, his face creased in torment. "I was so afraid that I would die with you thinking I am a monster. "

"Hades," she breathed, fear wrapping tightly around her chest. "Are you dying?"

His eyes opened, and he tangled his fingers with hers. Persephone saw the answer in his eyes, and her strength crumbled. "Yes." His voice spoke that single word, and it was like poison to her soul.

She sprang from the bed, her lips forming a resolute "No" as she vehemently shook her head in denial.

He reached for her, and his hands were gentle on her arms. "I am dying, Persephone; my thread is unraveling."

"No. No," she reiterated, her fingers clenching tightly on his arms. "This can't be. You can't die. You must fight it! Just like you have before!"

"This time it is different, Persephone. He grows stronger every time I fight, and my life weakens. There is little time left. "At his words, she sobbed, jamming her fist into her mouth, and he brought her against him. "You must be brave. It is you he wants to destroy, and he is doing it through me."

She drew back, and her eyes were fierce. "I will not allow this."

"How ferocious you are," he whispered. "But even you cannot stop it. I have lived long enough. You are my concern now."

Rage unfurled within her like a tempest. "I don't care about myself!" she bellowed, wrestling against his hold. "Without you, what am I? Just a void in the shadows. Don't you see," she implored, her tear-blurred eyes pleading, "that the flame inside me only exists for you?"

"As mine burns for you," he answered softly. "Come," he urged. "Lay down with me; let me feel you next to me." She did not move, and he smiled. "We do not have much time before he returns. Don't you want to be with me? "

She nodded, yielding to his silent insistence as he guided her back to the bed. Nestled beside her, he enveloped her in his arms. She bit her tongue, knowing he wouldn't entertain any argument, prioritizing his safety over hers. Determination surged through her, vowing silently to find a solution or perish in the attempt. This so-called "game" was one she adamantly refused to lose.

"Tell me how it happened, how he possessed you," she demanded.

"On Ares' mountainside. He struck me with the Cyclops' blade."

"Ares said that you knew it was Zeus on the mountain."

"When the lightning twisted around his fingers, I suspected, but when he told me he would take everything from me, I knew it was Zeus. Ares had merely been an unwilling pawn."

"But why didn't you run?"

"And leave you alone? Allow Ares to perhaps die at his father's hands? He could have killed both of you. I knew he would keep his word to me when he said he would obliterate you. Besides, by the time I knew, it was too late. Ares never should have been able to lift my blade without my permission. Zeus was already inside me. He infected me the minute he slashed my stomach with the golden blade. But I realized that if he could lift my blade, I could lift his. If I had both weapons, I could figure out how to destroy them, and you would be safe. As I felt him merging with me within the Underworld, I called the golden blade to me." His fingers moved through her long hair. "And I have been hiding them ever since."

"Persephone, tell me what you remember of Prometheus. I know Ares took you to Janus."

"Prometheus," she whispered, furrowing her brow. "He said that he buried a spark in a mortal man that he would pass to his daughter and that she would bear a child stronger than Zeus."

He stared at her and then smiled. "That is you. You are the woman he prophesied."

"You think Prometheus meant me?" she asked incredulously. A frown tugged her face. "He said that you would carry a burden for her." Her voice trailed off as a horrible thought occurred to her, and she sat up, turning to him. "What burden did you carry for me in Elysium? What dark words did you whisper that night in the ocean? Tell me!" she demanded.

"That I may die so you may live," he stated simply.

She grasped his hands tightly. "Take it back!" she cried. "I will not allow you to die for me!"

"It is too late," he said softly, stroking her face. "What is done cannot be undone. I would do it a million times over; I would die a million times for you if necessary."

Dumbfounded, she gazed at him, her voice trembling when she finally spoke. "How could you presume to make such a decision for me? Offering your life for mine without my consent? You had no right! Sacrificing yourself for a cause that doesn't exist! I don't know how to thwart Zeus; there is no child! You're sacrificing yourself for a false promise!"

He brought his face next to hers. "But you *are* that woman. You may not know it now, but you will. I proudly did what I promised on the mountain an eternity ago. I would have died for the woman who would bear a true and noble king. But I would suffer eternity for you, dying again and again. There is nothing I would not give you. My life is a small sacrifice to have relinquished for the love that you have given me."

Tears blurred her eyes. "You have always believed me to be much more than I am. The most I am is a queen by marriage to you; I am nothing!"

Hades grasped her hand and traced the lifeline on her palm. "I see it in the lines of your thread, in the air that you breathe, in the very blood that courses through your veins. My brother fears you, Persephone, in a way he has never feared anyone else. Your nobility endures no matter what he has done or how he has come at you. He tried to break you in the forest; he wanted to break you with Minthe; he has treated you with unspeakable cruelty, and yet your soul remains untainted.

"In all the Gods, in all the mortals that he has met, only you have defied him, you, who are incorruptible. He is afraid and has done everything he can to diminish you. Zeus wants you to be that lost and frightened girl from the forest. He has spent these last months trying to bring you back to that frightened child. And yet the flame of hope still burns within you, as Prometheus said it would."

Persephone shivered at his words. He believed that she was something that she was not, and fear seized her, for if she was not powerful enough to stop Zeus, how would Hades be saved?

"What of my immortal life when you are gone?" she asked hollowly. "What would it be without you?"

"You will carve a new life."

"You think I will forget you? Like it would be that easy?" Her voice was a thread. "Your soul is the other half of mine. If you die, so will my spirit. Every day, I will remember and weep for the past. I will be in love with a ghost. "

"No," he murmured, pressing his lips against her palm. "You will live for your people." He smiled down at her. "But I am selfish enough to hope you will always hold a piece of your heart for me. Will you come with me? I need to show you something, and we haven't much time left. "She hesitated, and when he smiled down at her, her heart stuttered. "Persephone, please. I know I don't have the right to ask but trust me. For just a little bit longer. "

And she trusted him with her soul and heart, just not with his own life. Despite her anger and grief, she extended her hand to his. The simple interlocking of their fingers infused her with profound joy, causing tears to stream down her cheeks uncontrollably. They left the room silently, and he took her to yet another unknown part of the palace. He opened a door from a part of the wall, and it revealed a shadowed, spiral staircase. He led her down, and the door closed behind them, shutting them into the blackness. When they reached the bottom of the stairs, they stood in a black, empty cavern.

He turned to look at her, a smile on his lips. "I have left a bequest. I will give you the two most precious things closest to my heart. Your life and this kingdom."

A sudden realization gripped her. "The crystal forest…"

He nodded. "Yes. It was a way to show that you now possess all the powers of an Underworld ruler."

"So, the powerful, shadow magic I have felt—"

"I have bequeathed all my riches to you. Once the golden blade was used on me, the transition of power began."

"No! Take it back!"

"It is too late. Hermes himself was a witness to the contract. There will be no disputing it. Persephone," he said firmly, cutting off her furious protests, "you must listen. Do you know where we are?" He gestured around them. "This is the Cave of Fate."

She moved forward, peering into the blackness in dismay. "But the threads—where are they?"

"You asked what I was doing this summer, and I told you I was busy. The threads have been hidden in a new location. I erased my memory with the Lethe, so not even I know where the threads or the Fates are." He placed his hand against her heart. "But you know, whether you realize it or not, there is a great power in you—beyond mine, beyond any God. The heartbeat of this world lies within you, and when the time is right, you will find them."

Her thoughts returned to the dream when Hades had guided her to the Cave of Fates and entrusted her with his thread. She needed to find the locket, but how? Discreetly, she had searched both of their bedrooms for the locket, but it was nowhere to be found. Was it hidden by Hades? And how exactly did one unearth something from a dream? As they strolled through the vacant cavern, her mind raced with possibilities. Though she yearned to share her concerns with Hades, she knew she could not; doing so could endanger not only Hades' thread but the entirety of humanity. Zeus would return soon.

He took her hand, leading her further into the cavern.

"Zeus was always rash. He made a mistake giving me the Underworld." He laughed softly. "He thought it was a punishment. He did not realize the power this world holds. Death grants mortals a freedom that they do not know in life." His eyes shifted to hers, and they glowed in the darkness. "Imagine the control he could wield if he tampered with the threads of the living and the souls of the dead. Imagine the endless worship he could receive from immortal souls. This kingdom grows larger every day. Think of how he could manipulate the Olympians if he held the threads of a God in his grasp. He would not need the golden blade."

Persephone frowned at his words. "He would be invincible."

He stopped and gestured around him. "As above, so below," he whispered. "The Gods, mortals, we were all formed from the dust of stars, and infinity lies within each of us. But Zeus could change all of that. The dead are the last free people, and Zeus wants them; he will do anything to have them. In death, souls need not bow at the feet of a God but stand as equals, as bright as the stars in the Heavens." Hades took her hand. "For mortals, death is a metamorphosis. The Olympians are too foolish to realize that the shedding of a mortal's body is not the end. Because death is incomprehensible to them, they abhor it, seeing only the evil in it. But souls, like Gods, are immortal. In death, life begins anew. Persephone, *this* is the Land of the Immortals Prometheus spoke of. Not Olympus, but the Underworld, where the souls live free.

"You know of my great sin, the splitting of the souls. Zeus does whatever he can to keep them apart, believing death is the ultimate separation. But here he again shows his foolishness, for in death, they have something they did not have in life. Time." He closed his eyes. "If Zeus gains control of the Underworld, he will separate them again and never allow the soulmates to unite. He fears the power true love wields. He feared it in Demeter and Iasion; he feared it in Theo and Selene." He brought her hand to his mouth, kissing the tips of her fingers. "He fears it in us. It is a power that is incorruptible and eternal. A power he can never have."

Light glimmered at the end of the cavern, and when they stepped through, they stood in the sunlight of Elysium.

"Persephone, I must tell you. Minthe… I would never have broken my vow with you."

"I know that now." She brushed her lips against his. "Do not think of it. It was not you."

His hands tightened on her shoulders. "I detested her. Zeus had taken her as a lover and promised her riches and a title. She was an accomplice in his crime and knew that he and not I now sat on the throne of the Underworld. She would sneak into my room, and Zeus would allow her to use my body at her pleasure." His mouth twisted in disgust. "I wanted to tear her apart with my fingers, slowly, so she would suffer. She was a rapist and delighted in it. A perfect companion to my brother. The Cocytus will side with Zeus in the war when the king finds out what has become of his daughter. They hoped to eventually replace you with Minthe."

Persephone's eyes flared. "I do not regret what I did."

He grasped her hand and began to lead her through Elysium. "Nor do I. My heart was delighted to see her wither to ash. Destroy your enemies when they come at you. Show no mercy. Minthe was too foolish to realize she was merely a pawn for Zeus. We will deal with Cocytus." They reached a large blossoming tree, and he helped her sit beneath the shaded branches. "At least I can be glad that I can speak the truth to you now." He closed his eyes tightly. "It was like a dagger to my heart."

"Hush," she whispered.

She bent forward, brushing his lips with hers, and he leaned into her. He traced the seam of her mouth with his tongue, and she shuddered in longing. A groan rose deep in his throat, and he angled his face for easier access, his lips moving like magic over hers. He was with her finally, the other half of her soul. She rose over him, wrapping her legs around him and pressing as close to him as she could. His hips rose to meet hers, and the pulsing part of him met the aching part of her, and she let out a whimper of longing. His hand moved down, tracing the edge of her breast, and she felt her womb tighten, and her nipples harden, and she wanted to give him everything—every part of her. Suddenly, he pushed her away, and she fell back, staring up at him in stunned surprise. He was hunched over, breathing heavily, shivers wracking his body.

"Hades," she said urgently, "what is wrong?" She moved to touch his arm, but he jerked away from her, her fingers trailing the edge of his robes.

"I am sorry. Just let me get under control." His black hair covered his face, but she could see the beads of sweat dotting his skin. "When I feel intense emotions, it draws him back to me. Especially when I desire you, it calls to him. I cannot touch you in that way without him taking over." He looked at her, and a self-deprecating smile touched his lips. "And since I always want you, it is very difficult to suppress that impulse. It is difficult to touch you at all."

Persephone drew back, trying to mask the hurt in her eyes. "I am sorry. I did not know."

Hades' hand reached out for hers, pulling her back. "Difficult, but worth it."

"He has taken everything from us," she whispered.

"No," Hades answered, "not everything." She lay against him, but her body was stiff, afraid to move in some way that could cause Zeus to regain control.

"Has there been any moment since my return, when I... when I lay with you, that it was not him?"

For a moment, he did not answer. When he finally spoke, his voice was slow and careful. "The first night, Zeus had partaken of Hypnos' poppy. But after that, I was aware," he said softly, "but it was Zeus who was in control of me."

Bitter tears and shame clogged her throat. "I hate him."

"You could not have known, Persephone. He thinks he loves you. He feels our connection in my body, and he is obsessed with having you. I have seen the bleakness of my brother's soul. For eternities, he has been unable to feel true emotion, and suddenly, he holds the purest emotion of all in his grasp. He is addicted to the sensation."

"He will never have me," she vowed vehemently.

"He knows that our souls are connected. He will use that to manipulate you. The line between him and I is becoming blurred." He lifted her hand again, and this time, his finger traced a line that ran down the center of her palm. He held their hands side by side, comparing them; her line was so long it extended all the way to her wrist; Hades ended abruptly, the line severed. "The line of destiny," he murmured.

She closed his fingers over his palm, unable to bear the sight of it. "Can you feel it when I am with him?"

"Yes," he whispered.

Her lips trembled, but she bit them firmly. "Then, at least I have some part of you."

He grabbed her fiercely, turning her abruptly. "No! Do not think like that. It is precisely what he wants."

She traced the edge of his jaw. "The flower cannot help but reach for the rays of sunshine."

"No." His voice was harsh. "Persephone, listen to me. Zeus will use your love for me to bend and break your will. Do not let him. He will use us to find the child you bore in the forest. If he finds him, both of us are disposable. The child must be kept hidden."

"Hades," she said in a quiet voice, "my child died. You know that."

"But think where we are Persephone."

"But he is not here," she argued, becoming agitated. "You think I haven't tried to find him? I have searched for any inkling of a connection. There is nothing. It is like he never existed."

He took her hand, entwining his fingers with hers in a comforting gesture. "But all souls go somewhere, my love." She considered this enigmatic statement when he continued. "He will do whatever it takes to find him. He will never believe you do not know where he is. When I die, my heart can no longer shield you from his hatred. He thinks he loves you, but when our connection is broken, he will be severed from our bond. When he wakes up from this euphoria, he will see you only as an enemy, and Zeus does not allow his enemies to survive."

"He should know me as his enemy." Persephone's green gaze moved down the length of her husband's form. "Show me your wound."

"But you have seen it."

She shook her head. "No, you showed me what you thought I should see. Show me your true wound. I want no more secrets between us."

He regarded her for many moments before standing slowly. His hands moved over his robes, leisurely drawing them from his chest and abdomen. When he turned to face her fully, he lifted his hands, and she finally saw the true horror of his flesh.

The juxtaposition of his beautiful pale skin adjacent to his gaping, mutilated abdomen was horrific. Creamy flesh abruptly transitioned to a mound of bloodied, seeping tissue. Deep black veins ran from the wound towards his legs and up towards his heart, pulsating rapidly. The blood and flesh were infused with gold that ran down his legs, soaking the ground in glimmering crimson. Persephone made a noise of despair and rushed forward, laying her hands over his abdomen, trying desperately to stem the flow of his life and stop the golden threads that fell like glistening drops of snowflakes.

"How could you hide this from me!" she cried. "Why didn't you tell me!"

"I was unable to," he said softly, touching her hands. "I, like Ares, was bound by his magic. Even if you had known, there was nothing you could do. You cannot fix this." She pushed his hands aside and tried again to force healing magic into the wound. "Persephone," he said. "Persephone," he repeated more firmly, drawing her hands away. He waved his palm over the wound, and the façade was neatly back in place. Only the small white scar remained, hiding his dying body from her view. He took her hands and wiped them clean on his robes, and as she reached for him, his face suddenly contorted in pain.

"What is wrong?" she asked urgently.

"He wants– back in." His pupils were dilated, expanding so far that no hint of purple was visible in his gaze. "Ares' distraction must be waning. Quickly," he urged, grabbing her hand. "Come, Persephone, we must hurry away from here."

Hand in hand, they ran through Elysium, fear making her heart pound as they raced through the kingdom. When they finally stopped at the edge of Elysium, he spun her around and held her tightly against him.

"Know that I am not leaving you," he breathed against her. "Until my last breath, I am here; remember Persephone."

She pulled away, urgent questions dying on her lips as she looked up at him. Amber eyes stared down at her. She stumbled away from him, her eyes wary as a smile curled her husband's mouth. No, not her husband. She could sense the change in his posture and how he carried himself—how could she not have seen it before?

"Hello, little wife," Zeus taunted.

Without a word, she turned on her heel. A rough hand pulled her back, and she was facing those enraged, golden eyes.

"Did you think to fuck him, wife, when my back was turned? Another man will never touch you," he snarled at her.

"My *husband* does not fuck me; what is between us is only love. It is an emotion you will never understand. Your soul has no mate; it is lonely and barren, and when the end comes for you, you will die as you have lived—alone. I only hope I am there to see it."

She enunciated each word and smiled as she saw the rage grow in his eyes. He bent his head and ground his lips against hers, roughly forcing his tongue into her mouth. She endured it because she refused to retaliate, knowing it was her husband's lips that would bear the pain. When he finally pulled back, it was her blood that she tasted on her tongue.

Hades' chest rapidly rose and fell, his fingers pressing tightly into her arms. "I own you. I am your sun, moon, salvation, and torment. With a single word from me, I can destroy you. Soon, your soulmate will die, and I shall take his place."

She jerked from his grasp, and he let her pull away. "You think we could never be happy together, but you are wrong. I have been looking for you nearly as long as he has. You resist me needlessly, Persephone." His voice was beguiling, as lovely as the demons from Aidoneus' imprisonment within Cronus. "Don't you see that you can do nothing to stop me? The only one who could ever defy me is dying. I could grant you any wish you've ever had. I would destroy the world for you. I will adore you, give you children, and treat you like the queen you are. You don't need to be separated from your mother. All I ask is that you embrace me as your king and husband."

His luminous eyes gleamed with an eerie intensity, and the insidious inflection of his voice wove a sinister spell around her. She stood paralyzed, ensnared by the deceptive allure of his beautiful yet malevolent promises. Was this his nefarious tactic to entrap the unsuspecting victims who came before her? Suddenly, a flame of purple flared in his iris, and she fell back, stumbling away from him.

"Come here," he growled.

Terrified by his words and her own vulnerability, she grappled with the daunting challenge of confronting such an omnipotent deity. The relentless specter of Hades, wielded as a weapon against her, seemed inescapable. Even in death, her torment would persist. His body would be used to ensure her perpetual submission. Panic seized her, constricting her lungs. As he reached for her once more, instinct overcame reason, and she fled like a startled deer, racing toward the embrace of the forest's edge. His laughter echoed behind her like a malevolent specter, a chilling reminder of the inescapable darkness that pursued her.

"How the rabbit flees from the fox. See how I indulge you," he called to her. "Any other, I would smite for defying me. Shall you make me hunt for my prize?" Hard rain began to pour from the sky, the drops like knives against her flesh.

"Come back, Persephone. You cannot hide from me. You should know that by now."

She dashed behind a sizable tree and crouched against its imposing trunk as lightning illuminated Elysium. The ancient trees trembled around her in response to the violent wind. Another bolt of electricity sizzled through the air, splitting several enormous trees in half, and they tumbled to the Earth with a thunderous boom. She began to move stealthily from her hiding place but took a sharp intake of breath as she saw her husband's dark shape through the branches of a nearby oak.

"I do not want to hurt you," he called. "I have waited so long for you to know the truth. To finally be with me as I am. Not as Ares. Not as Hades. To feel your hand wrapped around *my* cock. I offer you the chance to be with a king. To love a king, the highest of the Gods."

Another tree crashed down beside her. This time, she was too slow, and she knew that Zeus had seen the movement of her skirts as she hurried through the forest. His eyes focused in her direction even as she crouched low behind a copse of trees.

"Persephone?" His voice was closer now, and she could hear his heavy footsteps in the rain and the hitch of excitement in his breath. "Think of how happy we will be when the boy is found. Athena is looking for him. I know you know of the prophecy that your child will dethrone me. So long as your child is with me, I will protect him. But I could never allow it to live if it was *his* son. It is good he was barren."

A faint glimmer caught her eye, and she turned her head sharply, fearful that Zeus had found her. She wiped the water from her face, not believing her eyes. There was a figure at the edge of the forest, illuminated in gold, and she stared in disbelief, recognizing him. It was her husband beckoning to her. She pushed from the ground, running as swiftly and noiselessly as her feet would allow.

She was ready to fall into his arms when she reached him, but she pulled back at the last moment, realizing something was terribly wrong. His form comprised thousands of dimly lit threads, the gold barely glistening in the darkness. His soul's light was like a moth's wings, fluttering against the dying candlelight. He had warned her that his thread of fate was unraveling, but until now, she had not believed it. Her hand reached for his, tentative, and she gasped as they connected. She was reminded of how they had clasped hands in Cronus's captivity when she had been within Janus.

"Hades," she whispered, "how are you here?"

He smiled at her. "I will explain to you later. But for now, run to Iasion's home," he urged softly. "I protected it with a cloaking spell many years ago. Run there, and I will find you in the morning."

She took his hand, bringing it to her face. "Come with me," she begged his aura. "Please."

"I cannot," he whispered. His fingers traced her face, and golden dust fell from his hands, dancing like fireflies on the wind. "Run, Persephone."

"Don't leave me!" she sobbed, but his form flickered, and their connection was severed.

A solitary footstep pierced the forest's silence, and she knew she had waited too long. Swiftly, she fled the woods, running until she reached open meadows. Her father's hut stood nearby. She ran to it, racing through the entryway, tumbling to the ground as she slammed the door behind her. A puddle pooled beneath her, but she lay still against the door, unaware of the cold or darkness.

The storm grew more violent, and she knew the instant Zeus realized he'd lost her, the wind howling viciously as rain and sleet ripped at the small hut that concealed her. As the wind roared, she lost track of time, sitting motionless in the shadows, a phantom in the night. Finally, as though in a dream, Persephone stood, rising from the floor. She pulled off the wet clothes absently, letting them fall to the ground until she stood naked. Shivers danced over her skin as she moved through the dark house, restless and dazed. Finding a shawl near the hearth, she wrapped it around herself. Persephone sat against the wall, with a clear view of the door and windows. Hours passed, and the storm began to ease, turning to a gentle rain until all became silent.

"Hades," she whispered into the darkness, "where are you?" The night remained still. "Please." Her voice wavered, and she lowered her face into her hands. "Just give me a sign that you are still with me."

The heartbeat was so faint that she barely noticed it at first, lost in her reverie, but as it grew in amplitude, she raised her head. A faint glow illuminated the room, and as the rhythm of the heartbeat grew, so did the golden light. It was as though individual threads were being spun faster and faster until a shape began to emerge, and she caught her breath. She recognized the heartbeat's cadence and felt her heart accelerating to meet its call. Finally, Hades stood before her, his aura pale as it had been in the forest, a ghostly apparition haunting her. She leaned against the window as he drew closer, afraid to move lest he vanish suddenly.

"Hades," she whispered. "Where is your body? What has happened?"

"My body is resting," he murmured, his voice as insubstantial as his form. "Zeus has exhausted my physical being." His gleaming fingers tightened around hers, pulling her from the floor and leading her to the darkened sleeping chambers. Gently, he pushed her back against the bed, sliding the shawl from her shoulders. "You need rest."

"Show me," she pleaded, "show me your threads."

She kept her voice soft, afraid that if she spoke too loudly, she would scare away this lonely spirit. He raised his hands, and the black toga that had covered him vanished, revealing his true form. Thousands of dark scars stood out against the pale gold of his soul, the largest pulsating, agonizing wound against his abdomen and a deep, furrowed gash on his chest, directly over his heart.

She traced the wound across his chest. "Is that from the arrow or..."

He pressed his hand against hers. "This is the burden I promised to carry."

Her head hung, ashamed. "Does it hurt?"

"Only a little."

She rubbed the scar as though trying to erase it. "You should never have had to carry that weight; it was never yours to bear."

His hand tilted her face up so their eyes collided. "I was born to carry this injury for you. This scar protects us both. Zeus cannot stand the trauma of it. He does not understand pain as we do—that it is a part of life and love."

"It weakens you, though, doesn't it?" Her eyes closed tightly, and a single tear fell to her cheek. "If I could take it back, I would."

"You want to know a secret?" he whispered, leaning over so his lips brushed her ear. She shivered at his touch. "Scars make us stronger. This scar shields both our hearts from him. Just as my brother craves to feel love, he cannot tolerate the other emotions that encompass it. Pain, loss, even death. Love is nothing without sacrifice. Life is nothing without death. I do not fear death, Persephone."

He moved over her, his lips capturing hers. She stayed still beneath him, frozen, afraid to move and breathe lest she break this spell. She took an unsteady breath when she felt his smile against her lips. "Kiss me back, Persephone."

"But I thought that this would hurt you."

"But I have shed my Earthly body. For now, my soul is still my own. Now, kiss me."

Tentatively, she moved her lips against his, and he groaned deep in his throat.

He brought her fully beneath him, the sensation so acutely pleasurable that she could feel an orgasm growing just at the touch of his lips against hers. Her body arched, and she relished the heavy weight of him over her. His length was hard and thick, and she rubbed the sensitive part of herself against him until she was throbbing, the wetness dampening her thighs. When his mouth lowered over her breast, tugging her nipple hard with his teeth, she cried out, her moan loud and urgent. She brought her hands to his face, pressing his mouth back to hers, and he smiled against her.

His lips were ferocious and urgent, but so were her own. She could feel the large head of his cock so close to the source of her wetness, teasing her and tormenting her, and she whimpered in need. Dark smoke billowed around them, the tendrils pulling and teasing her flesh as sensually as his fingers. She felt his spirit touching her everywhere, claiming every piece of her. He drew back from her suddenly, and his eyes were closed, his brow furrowed in pain.

"What is wrong?" she asked urgently, sitting up.

"I must go," he whispered. "Tomorrow, find me in the forest. Tonight, stay here and dream of me."

"I will come with you!"

But as his apparition faded from the room, his lips locked with hers again. The black smoke stroked Persephone over and over, reaching inside of her, filling her, until her back arched, her body clenched with intense pleasure, and as she shook with her release, darkness overcame her.

CHAPTER 23
THE PROTOGENOI

As the first pale ray of light shone over the horizon, Persephone's eyes flashed open. She flung herself from the bed, furious. He had said to seek him and then forced her into a dreamless slumber! She rushed from the small hut, her heart beating wildly. It was a beautiful morning in Elysium; the morning dew dampened her legs as she ran, the lush landscape shining in the morning's light, but Persephone noticed none of it. Where was he? She knew she had to calm her mind and take a moment to center herself, but the fear of what Zeus had done to him made it impossible. With every step she took, the sense of panic continued to escalate.

She wandered through the woodlands, tears of frustration and fear streaming down her face until she finally found him. He was almost stripped bare, his arms held above his head, and a sword speared through both palms, pinning him to a large tree. His eyes were closed, and she was overcome with fear. She leaped up with a muffled cry, yanking out the sword and awkwardly bringing him to the ground. Desperately, she placed her fingertips against his neck and found what she sought. A pulse. As she exhaled a ragged sigh of relief, her gaze shifted downward to his torso, and she gasped. A message had been cut into the skin across his belly.

Persephone,

Why must you be so difficult? If you continue to anger me, I will take my frustration out on his flesh, and I promise I will not be so kind next time. I will burn this world to the ground to find you. Have the decency to speak with me. After all, I am the father of your child.

Zeus

"Bastard," she whispered hoarsely, her fingers trembling as she traced his mutilated flesh.

She glanced at Hades' face, but he was still unconscious. That was perhaps for the best. Leaving Hades beneath the tree, she quickly ran to a nearby stream, searching the foliage. Her mind was too troubled to grow healing herbs, which disturbed her. She needed to be at her best if she would find a way to defeat Zeus. Instead, she was barely able to even summon her most basic magic. She found moss growing in the swirling water and quickly grabbed a handful, returning to clean off the clotted blood and attempting to heal the cuts in his flesh as she did so. His eyelids began to flutter as the last words faded from his skin.

"Persephone," he murmured.

Relief filled her as she looked into his eyes. It was still him.

"Can you sit up?" she asked, keeping a calm tone that she did not feel. She helped Hades lean against the tree, and she couldn't help but notice how weak he was and how much of her strength was required to lift him. "Why didn't you tell me last night? I could have stopped him! We cannot keep letting him do this to you."

He took her hand and brought it to his chest. "He is using me to lure you out. You cannot give in to his games. I would gladly hang from that tree a thousand years before I became bait for you. "He gave her a crooked grin. "This is nothing. I have been through much worse."

She did not smile back at him. "You still should have told me. I am tired of him controlling every move. "

"And if I had told you, then what? You would have sought me out, and he would have found you. And what do you think will happen, Persephone, after he discovers you? Do you think he just wants to talk? "

Her brow furrowed. "But I have already been with Zeus."

Hades' smile faded. "No, Persephone. You were with him when he was pretending to be me. He has been holding himself in check, but now that is all over. You have not yet begun to witness the depravity of the King of Olympus. And I will be unable to protect you."

She glared at him and reached out to grasp his hands in hers. She took a deep breath before sending healing heat towards their center, and the large, gaping wounds began to close. "Perhaps I do not worry about protecting myself; perhaps I worry about protecting you."

"There is nothing more important than your safety."

Her stare was vehement. "I disagree. Nothing is more important than *your* safety."

"An impasse," he murmured.

Gently, he extracted his hands from hers before staggering to his feet, his perfect backside on full display. He leaned heavily against the giant oak, breathing as rapidly as if he had climbed a mountain. As he stood, the small, intact remnant of his toga toppled to the ground. He looked down at himself and grimaced.

"While I have no objection to being nude, I do think it may shock my subjects." He lifted his hand, but it quickly fell, and he slumped against the tree. "Then again, perhaps I am too tired to care."

She rose abruptly, her tone matter-of-fact. "No magic is needed. My dress is far too long as it is." Hurriedly, she ripped the bottom off her dress and fashioned a short skirt around him. "There," she finished with a smile, "we are a match."

He smiled down at her and pulled her against him. They stayed like that for some time, simply enjoying the touch of their skin against one another. "Come," he said finally, leading her through the forest. "Let us return to the palace."

As they walked, he was silent, and she looked up at him. His face was pensive.

"What are you thinking?"

"I am thinking of Prometheus. I believe your son is alive."

His words triggered a dual reaction within her heart—it broke and simultaneously soared with fragile hope. "Why do you say that?" she asked breathlessly.

"For months, I combed the land in search of him, in search of his soul. I have scoured every nook and cranny of the Underworld. I went over each thread in the cave, and it was as if his thread had never existed. I spoke with the Fates, who confirmed that they had never seen his thread."

Her eyes welled with tears again. "But what does that mean? Did someone steal it?"

He shook his head. "No," he said emphatically. "What it means is that his thread is unique in some way. All threads leave a trace, some indefinable footprint, but the Underworld has no memory of him. It was never here. The Fates and I came to the same conclusion. Persephone," he whispered, "he is a God who is uncontrolled by Fate."

She gaped at him. "But that cannot be. And even if it were, he is dead; he died almost instantly in my arms."

"He is not dead. The Fates told me I must find his thread to save the kingdom. Your son is alive. Prometheus said that you would bear a son stronger than the sire. Stronger than Zeus!" He grasped her hands. "Your son is alive, Persephone."

"But then where is he? Why can no one find him? I have never sensed him again, never felt even a hint that he may be alive."

Hades paused, turning her to face him. "He is not in the Underworld. I searched deep within Chaos for answers, but my search was fruitless. My intuition tells me he is in the heavens or with the Protogenoi."

Persephone's brow furrowed at the unfamiliar word. "Who are the Protogenoi?"

"The Protogenoi are the very fabric of the Universe. They are ancient deities who hold the knowledge of creation within them. We younger Gods must look quite mortal in comparison, and compared to them, there is much we still do not understand. The cosmos are infinite. And the Protogenoi hold sacred wisdom."

"But *who* are they?"

"Nyx is Protogenoi."

"Nyx!" Persephone murmured, shocked.

"Yes," he smiled. "But Chaos is the original. The first being ever breathed into existence. He is the Master of Fate, from which all other creation sprang, and because of that, our lives can never be without Chaos. It is said that the true forms of Protogenoia can be quite terrifying." He outstretched his other hand, and a small, glistening galaxy appeared in his palm. She stared at the lovely, minuscule Universe rotating before them. "We are made from Chaos, and we cannot live without him in life."

"Have you asked, Nyx? Wouldn't she know if my son were with them?"

Hades shook his head. "She did not know. Some of the Protogenoi reside deep within the realm of Chaos. It is there that I believe your son may be hidden." He waved his hand through the tiny stars, and they glittered against his touch, reflected in the darkness of his eyes. "We all exist in the aether. Every soul is a minute light in the Universe, and we all have our part to play in it, big or small. Every soul has their reason for being here."

Gently, she lifted her fingertips to the cosmic dust, staring at the iridescent gold that coated her fingers.

"It is beautiful," she whispered in an awed voice.

"This is life, Persephone. And you hold the key to it. Only you have the power to find your son."

"Protogenoi," she murmured. "Why would they hide him there?"

"I believe to protect him." Hades clenched his fingers, and the lovely Universe vanished. He pulled her hand gently, and they began walking again.

"The figure from the forest," she murmured, "the one who took him from me. Do you believe that was a Protogenoi?"

"I do."

She was silent as she considered all that he had told her. "How have you been able to keep such a secret from Zeus?"

"I hold the information in my heart. These secrets he cannot access because of the scar that I took from you the night in Elysium. It fills him with unimaginable pain. That trauma you felt at his hand is the kind of suffering that terrifies him, for he only feels the shallowest emotions. You have protected my heart well." He grabbed her tightly, looking deep into her eyes, purple shining around his iris. "He might have control of my body, but my heart belongs only to you."

"As mine belongs to you."

She stood on her toes to kiss him. As her lips brushed his, the symbol of Pluto appeared on his forehead, and she traced it with her fingertips even as it vanished from his flesh. He took her hand and entwined his fingers with her own.

"Why do you dislike the name Pluto?" she asked.

His eyes darkened. "That name, since the first time I heard it, has filled me with an incomprehensible feeling. As though the moment it was uttered, it spoke my death into existence. Pluto is a promise of an ending I can never avoid."

"How long have you been called that?"

"Nyx has always called me by that name, even before my title changed." He paused, and she knew he was thinking of his mother's death. "There have been others as well."

For a moment, they walked in silence.

"Persephone?"

"Yes?"

"The time is coming when nothing will stand between Zeus and you. I have repeatedly seen how Zeus somehow forces his victims to believe they are in love with him. He will try to do this with you."

"Ares warned me as well, but that would never happen," she replied fiercely. "Never! You must believe that!"

"Do not think I question your loyalty. My brother has a power that is as irresistible as it is dangerous. He has an extraordinary ability to transform his victims from the unwillingly pursued to the devoted pursuers. I have witnessed both Gods and Goddesses scorn him only to prostrate themselves at his feet the next day. Intelligent, powerful deities who become little more than his playthings. It is despicable to watch."

"I could never, would never, love someone like him."

"But it would not be love, Persephone. What is between him and any other being is only ownership and addiction. Once he has what he wants from them, they are discarded in whatever way is easiest. For the time being, he sees you through my eyes. However, if he is not within my body if I am not his vessel, he will feel nothing but loathing for you, and he fears the power you wield over the people of this land—the power that lies within you. He wants to kill you, and without the love in my heart, he will. I am not his end goal. When you shot that arrow on the mountaintop, you slowed down Zeus' spell, but you also opened your soul to him to infest. There is a link between our souls, and through me, he will use that connection to invade you.

"While you sleep, your defenses are at their most vulnerable, and that is when he makes his most determined attempt to infect you, a never-ending barrage of darkness threatening to consume you. Every night, we battle over your immortal soul." He gave her a speaking look. "You, stubbornly, have refused to let me fight alone."

"My dreams," she whispered.

"No, not dreams, Persephone," he whispered." In our subconscious minds, a profound struggle unfolds—an ethereal battlefield where our souls engage in warfare for your soul."

She shivered. "I thought I was going mad," she whispered, her eyes lit with hope. "You must let me help you! If we can battle him together in that realm, we can defeat him."

"No," Hades said flatly. "You cannot touch him there; I have kept his magic from reaching you. The moment you let him in, it is over." His fingers tightened over her arms, turning her to face him. "Do you understand, Persephone? You cannot invite him in. Your soul is lost if you do. He will own you!"

Her enchanting mouth contorted into a defiant frown. "Then what are we to do?"

"Two tasks. First, I will continue to keep Zeus from your soul. You are safe as long as I can do so." He could practically taste the protests on her lips as her mouth opened.

"And *I* reserve the right to protest if I think your plan jeopardizes your safety in any way. You will not sacrifice yourself for me any more than you already have."

"A battle for another day, I think."

"And the second task?" she asked through gritted teeth.

"You must get ready."

Her brows drew down in confusion. "For what?"

"For the second task, of course. We have a party to host."

CHAPTER 24
THE QUEEN'S TRIAL

"Are you sure you want to have a party now?" she asked for the millionth time as they stood in her room.

"I can think of no better time," he replied, his voice muffled as he searched the wardrobe.

"But I thought we were to avoid Zeus?"

"We are," he agreed, poking his head out. "He is not here right now."

"But shouldn't we be planning war? Recruiting allies? A party seems entirely fruitless!"

"Oh no, not when I want to use it to formally bequeath you my authority and power."

"But Hades," Persephone protested. "We must think about this."

"But Persephone," Hades countered, mimicking her tone, that damnable dimple appearing by the corner of his mouth. "I have already thought about it."

Finally, he turned, drawing out a long gown made of such dark green velvet that it almost appeared black. Holding it up against Persephone, he studied it speculatively.

"I think this will do," he murmured. "But a little addition is in order." His palm slid across the gown's fabric, and hundreds of tiny emeralds materialized, nestled in the soft velvet. His gaze lifted to hers, and he grinned. "To match your eyes, though no stone can ever quite capture the uniqueness of that shade. I shall attend to you since you no longer have any servants within the castle."

Slowly, he turned her, unfastening her ruined gown. His fingertips were gentle on her back as he drew it down. The fabric fell to the floor, and she knew his gaze was on her naked flesh. She turned her head, seeing his dark eyes dilate as he stared at her intently. Knowing that he was stimulated by undressing caused her cheeks to flush. His fingers caressed her sensitive flesh as he brought the velvet gown over her head, the soft material brushing against her breasts.

The spell was broken as a loud rap sounded, and the door was abruptly opened as Ares sauntered into the room. He paused, observing the couple shrewdly, Persephone's flushed face telling him more than she wished.

"Ares," Hades greeted distractedly as he carefully adjusted the folds of the gown.

"I had a meeting with Nyx this morning," the War God said. "It has been arranged for her to guide us through Tartarus tomorrow." Hades gave a brief nod, carefully placing a laurel wreath atop Persephone's head. Ares' eyes narrowed as he watched the couple. "I never knew you to be so attentive to dressing before, Hades."

Hades' eyes flickered to Ares, but his attention quickly returned to his wife. "But this is no mere occasion. It is a party to celebrate the official transfer of my power. This is for her safety." He adjusted the crown slightly, then stepped back to survey his work. "There, I think you are ready."

Ares stepped closer, but Persephone noted that his eyes remained fixed on Hades. "If you had told me, I could have invited Nyx. You know my father fears her. She could ensure the safety of this evening."

"But the ball is at sunset. Nyx will be performing her nightly duties on Earth. It would have been pointless to ask her." Hades stroked his fingers over Persephone's long hair and smiled at her. "You look so beautiful. Are you ready, my Goddess?"

He extended his hand to her, and Persephone smiled back, lifting her hand to him. But suddenly, Persephone was staring at the massive, broad back of the War God, who had positioned himself firmly between Persephone and her husband.

"I do not think you should go with him."

Persephone gave Ares' back a slight push. "Move, Ares."

"I do not think this is your husband, Persephone. Let me see your eyes, *uncle*."

"This is unnecessary," Persephone said with a frown. "He has clearly proven to me that he is my husband."

"And now he needs to prove it to me," Ares replied stubbornly, crossing his arms. "Look at me," he demanded again.

Persephone leaned over Ares and saw the slight smile on her husband's lips. "So untrusting," Hades murmured. "But if you feel you must." The God of the Dead moved closer to Ares, and the War God grabbed Hades by the shoulder, turning him so that the light of the fire illuminated his pale face. Hades' eyes were fathomless, black pools with no hint of purple or amber reflecting in their ebony surface.

"Satisfied?" Hades softly inquired.

Ares grunted as he released him. "What did you tell me when you first asked me to guard Persephone?"

Hades paused for a moment, observing his nephew with a veiled expression. "I asked you to do whatever was necessary," he replied.

"And that is what I am doing," Ares said, stepping closer to Hades. "I do not trust you," he snarled.

"Ares," Persephone interjected, looking between the two Gods. "Perhaps you could tell us why you do not believe this is Hades?"

Ares' blue eyes moved over the God of the Dead. "I cannot say exactly; it is only a feeling. An instinct that is telling me not to trust him."

"Perhaps we need an unbiased party?" Hades murmured. "Cerberus." The pup leaped over to Hades, eagerly smelling his proffered hand, and after inspecting carefully, gave it a gentle lick.

"See Ares," Persephone said, "Cerberus does not appear to have any concerns."

"That mutt," Ares scoffed. "He also licks his own arse, so his viewpoint is dubious."

"Ares," Hades began in an exasperated voice, "I have few opportunities when Zeus is not using my body as a puppet, and I would like to proceed with my plan to ensure that Persephone is safe. Moreover, why would I have sent for you if Zeus had been planning this? Do not be foolish. This is to ensure the safety of our kingdom through Persephone." Music began to sound from the throne room. "May we leave now?" Hades asked in an ironic voice. "Or would you like to examine my brain to ensure it meets your standards? Come," he finished, extending his arm towards his wife.

Persephone took his arm without hesitation, but she felt Ares move close behind them, his doubt and suspicion casting a gloom over what had been jubilation at being with her husband. She turned back to Ares with a reassuring smile as they exited the room, but he only returned a ferocious look, shaking his blond head.

"Be careful," he mouthed.

She glanced at Hades but saw no trace of Zeus in her husband's face. Still, Ares was suspicious, and she should not discount that.

"Hades," Persephone began, "perhaps—"

Hades looked down at her with raised eyebrows, and a smile tugged at his full lips. "Oh, not you too, Persephone?" he asked in mock horror. "Please, just trust me a little more. What we are about to do is not just for you but for the kingdom. And it must be done while we still have time."

Persephone bit her lip but nodded her head in agreement.

They were now at the doors to the throne room, which were flung open at their approach. As the king and queen entered the room, uniformed guards stood alongside the door, garbed in formal black attire. Ares snarled as a guard suddenly obstructed his view of Persephone, and when the War God went to skirt around him, the King of the Dead turned just slightly, his black eyes flashing amber. Ares snarled, rushing forward just as the doors began to close. He shouted Persephone's name, but the guards concealed the War God from Persephone's view, and the throne room was loud with music. Hades flashed Ares a mischievous wink as a voice entered the War God's mind: *Farewell, son.* Ares surged forward with an unholy yell, but his last sight of the throne room was his father's eyes as the doors slammed shut in his face.

The throne room was filled with hundreds of souls and court members who eagerly awaited the arrival of the royal pair. As Hades and Persephone stepped into the room, a loud cheer swept through the hall, and Hades raised his hand, acknowledging the crowd. Persephone scanned the faces, but she found none that she recognized. A moment of trepidation filled her, and she turned, looking for Ares, but the throng was too large. A gentle pressure on her arm guided her forward.

The room had been completely rearranged so that a large marble staircase led to a massive hall. The large stone throne had been relocated to make space for dancing. The couple descended the magnificent staircase, and Persephone lifted her hand to trail down the balustrade, causing lush, red roses to spiral to the room below. The crowd gave a murmur of pleasure at the sight of the crimson bouquet. Unfamiliar music played as Hades guided her to the center of the room, and they paused before a large marble platform. Persephone wondered if there would be a performance.

Hades inclined his head in her direction. "Are you alright?" he inquired softly.

She nodded her head, maintaining a serene smile. "Where is Ares?"

Hades surveyed the room before shrugging. "I do not know. He must be lost in the crowd. But do not worry," he murmured to her. "I have no intention of allowing you to escape from me." His hand caressed her arm, causing Persephone to shiver as she searched his face. The words seemed ominous, but she still saw no trace of Zeus. Was this how their brief time together would be, constantly searching for any sign of Zeus' possession? "Ready?" he asked with a smile.

"As much as I will ever be," she whispered back.

Taking her hand in his, he led her to the platform. With only a slight hesitation, she followed him onto the dais.

"Welcome to you all." Instantaneously, the audience grew silent, and expectant faces turned toward the God of the Dead. "Gods of below, Judges, and spirits of the kingdom. We welcome and thank you all for coming to this special occasion. Tensions between the kingdoms are higher than ever. We have never been closer to war, and we have never been closer to losing all we have worked so hard for. Our kingdom is in jeopardy as individuals outside the realm attempt to undermine it. But it is not the outside forces that need to worry us.

"I have recently learned through trusted allies that there is a saboteur within our gates, one who is working to destroy the very fabric of our lives." The audience audibly gasped, and Persephone gave Hades a bewildered look. He took her hand, giving it a reassuring squeeze. "You wonder perhaps why I have gathered you here? I intend to expose the traitor and those who wish to harm the innocents who merely wish to live out their lives within our gates." Hades paused and surveyed the crowd. "Shall I denounce the traitor? Or should I show them compassion, grant them mercy?"

Outraged cries flooded the room.

"Show no leniency!"

"Consign them to Tartarus!"

The jeers grew louder and louder until they formed a nauseating vortex of noise in Persephone's mind. Hades raised his free hand, and the crowd grew silent once more. He turned toward Persephone.

"What say, my wife?" Hades asked. "What should I do with a traitor against the king?" She stared at him, and a dangerous hint of gold flickered in his eyes. She gasped and tried to pull her hand from his, but his fingers tightened painfully. "What do you think, Queen Persephone?"

She raised her chin. "All accused deserve a trial."

"A trial," Hades repeated for the crowd. "My wife demands a trial for a traitor, for a criminal who seeks to injure each one of you."

He quickly grasped her other hand, then raised them both high, turning her to face the crowd, his fingers a painful vise on her wrists.

"The queen has betrayed you. She refuses to bear an heir for our kingdom and has destroyed a most valuable alliance with the Underworld. She has worked with outside forces to attempt to bring down the kingdom."

When he abruptly released her, her hands fell to the ground, and she realized with a shock of horror that heavy, black chains were holding them down. The crowd advanced with angry faces.

"He is lying," she said in a low voice. The crowd stepped closer. "He is lying!" she called louder.

"Tensions are mounting between the upper and lower realms, and she is feeding strategies to Ares, Zeus' son and her lover."

"He is lying! He is not my husband! Listen to me; he is not who he appears to be!"

"She spews madness. She is unfit to rule as Queen of the Underworld."

Persephone shot him a look of hatred; he looked so strong and virile, every inch a king, and she knew the crowd would never believe her. The only individual who could corroborate her account was nowhere to be found, and she sincerely doubted anyone would listen to the surly, bloody God of War; he did not have his father's silver tongue.

"If my wife desires a trial," Zeus continued, "we shall have a trial. You, my people, will judge whether you find Queen Persephone innocent or guilty. I summon the King of Cocytus as the first witness to her heinous crimes!" An icy blast moved through the throne room, and the King of Cocytus drew near.

Hades' body bowed low. "King Cocytus, I implore you to discuss the sins Queen Persephone has committed against you and your people."

"Persephone murdered my daughter," King Cocytus called to the gathering. His statements drew gasps of shock from the crowd. "My beautiful, compassionate daughter, Princess of Cocytus, was murdered in a fit of jealousy by the Queen of the Underworld because she dared to be more beautiful than the queen.

"She was to learn under Queen Persephone's tutelage and return to her homeland prepared to reign and marry. Instead, I discovered my daughter was slain by a maniac." Cocytus raised a bony finger toward Persephone, his pale blue eyes brimming with emotion for the first time: loathing. "As long as *she* roams the Underworld at will, no one is secure. She is a serpent of deception."

Hades gripped Cocytus' hand and then turned towards Persephone. "Do you deny this crime?" With his face turned away from the crowd, a subtle smile graced his lips as he tilted his head. It was evident that he anticipated her reaction to his unexpected twist in the game, relishing in the unsettling drama.

"I do not deny it," she answered. The crowd emitted horrified cries. "But since you and your mistress were fornicating on the corpses of slain mortals, murdered at her hands, I think that more than justifies my actions."

A glint of almost admiration flickered in his eyes, only to be swiftly concealed as he turned back to the crowd. His countenance transformed into that of a grieving, betrayed king. "What lies will she not tell?" Hades addressed the crowd. "To accuse a virgin princess of such vile crimes is beyond comprehension." He looked towards Cocytus. "Speak now of the alliance between our kingdoms."

"Queen Persephone was invited as a guest to the palace in Cocytus. She challenged my daughter to a risky race there and threatened to sever the alliance between our kingdoms if Princess Minthe refused to participate. My daughter had no choice but to lose to the queen or risk severing a critical alliance.

"To further punish her, the queen took her beloved horse from her. Despite Queen Persephone's unstable behavior during her visit to Cocytus, I kept the alliance because of my faith in King Hades. She then butchered the horse in a fit of fury. I wish to the Gods I had never allowed Minthe back, but the queen demanded her return. I know why now. She lured her from the safety of my palace to be murdered."

Hades once more turned towards Persephone, who raised an eyebrow at him. "And what does the accused say to this?"

"I did win the race," Persephone agreed coolly, "but I am afraid the only crime committed that day was the riding skills his daughter exhibited. I assure you, I made no attempts to sever alliances between the two kingdoms."

Cocytus' eyes bulged, but Zeus quickly intervened. "She jests at the possible ruination of a critical alliance. I thank you, Cocytus, for your bravery and the truth you have spoken this day." Hades bowed to Cocytus, and the lesser king vanished into the crowd. "I call forward three souls: Leon Pappas, Sebastian Filo, and Chloe Gataki."

The room warmed slightly in the absence of the King of Cocytus, and three souls materialized before the stage: a younger man with dark hair, an older man with graying blond hair, and a young woman with curling black hair. They looked apprehensively towards Persephone, but Hades gestured them forward.

"Do not be afraid; I will ensure no harm comes to you. Have you seen the queen before?" Reluctantly, the souls moved forward. Persephone made eye contact with the young woman, who hastily averted her gaze.

"No harm will come to you; you need only answer my questions honestly," the king continued. "Have you seen Queen Persephone before?" he asked again. The two young souls looked towards the older man, who nodded slowly. "And can you recount your interaction with the queen?"

"It was the day we were being sorted, Your Majesty," the older soul began. "The souls had been made to wait many days, and it had been said..."

"It had been said?" Hades prompted.

"That it was the queen who had caused the delay, that she had no interest in allowing the court to be held." His blue eyes lowered. 'On the day we were finally allowed entry into the palace, we could see the king and queen arguing. A man had been brought back to the Underworld whom the queen had attempted to allow to return to Earth."

The crowd gasped at his declaration. The soul paused and looked at Hades, who nodded for him to continue.

"When the king attempted to explain that such an occurrence simply was not allowed, that it jeopardized all of our safety, and that Ares would use the man to infiltrate the kingdom, the queen seemed all at once to lose her temper, and she blasted a portion of the wall, which would have fallen on us had the king not ensured our safety by flinging the fragments away from the crowd."

"And is this how you all remember this account?"

The three souls nodded their heads.

"Thank you for your testimony." The king turned toward Persephone. "And have you anything to say to this accusation?"

Persephone looked towards the crowd and was reminded of Olympus when the Muses told the fabricated story of Hades and Persephone. There was no room for truth when the story being told was so enticing. A mad queen always made for exciting fodder, though the truth in this case was even more fantastical. A king possessed by his brother, the God of Olympus, who was determined to overturn the rule of the Underworld. But it was too late; an expert deceiver had already painted her character, and there was no way to remove the ink.

"I think it would be rather useless to protest at this point, don't you?"

"Oh, entirely useless, my sweet," he murmured softly. Facing the audience again, he called in a loud voice. "I now call the Judges, Minos, Rhadamanthus, and Aeacus."

As the three ancient entities advanced, they gave Persephone similar expressions of cold contempt. The three Judges would gladly send Persephone to Tartarus and discard the key. Zeus had selected his witnesses wisely.

"Minos, please describe the day the rivers froze over. The day the queen worked with her mother to destroy the Underworld."

Advancing eagerly, Minos moved with such haste that he momentarily stumbled. Persephone couldn't help but release a somewhat wild giggle, though she quickly stifled it. Laughing during her trial would undeniably contribute to her seemingly erratic behavior. And she wondered whether her ability to find amusement in such a somber occasion was a genuine reflection of insanity. She listened as Minos delivered a lengthy, laborious, but damning account of how Persephone had assisted in freezing the Underworld's rivers with Demeter and Ares, resulting in turmoil among the kingdoms.

The audience, which had before been so quietly attentive that Persephone nearly forgot they were present, now appeared to lean forward in unison, desperate not to miss a single syllable.

"I obtained further proof of the queen's treachery," Minos continued, "during a story of a prisoner's escape from the River of Fire. Ares and Persephone stormed the prison together and demanded the release of a prisoner. When the guard refused, she employed shadow magic against him, after which he awoke to find the prisoner gone. No one has ever escaped the River of Fire before. It means that our protection against the criminals of this realm is no longer safe. If the River of Fire can be breached, why not Tartarus?"

The king regarded Persephone, who was murmuring beneath her breath.

"What?" the king asked.

"I said that there was no magic involved," she added in a louder tone. "Ares merely struck him over the head." She held Minos' gaze. "And if the gates of Tartarus can be so easily breached, then you may as well surrender now."

She turned to Zeus. "You think implicating me will secure your victory. Yet, this kingdom will *never* bow to you," Persephone vowed. "Your ambition is to govern these entities as effortlessly as those above, but souls aren't possessions you can own."

Drawing nearer, his eyes transformed into a fiery amber. "In that, you are mistaken," he whispered softly, his words intended solely for her ears. "This kingdom and every soul within it will be mine." He turned to address the watching audience. "Including you.

"You are faced with these accounts," the king continued loudly. "I could continue to summon witnesses, but I have already presented a king, souls, and the Underworld Judges. All were impartial and without prejudice toward the queen. How am I to proceed? Do you, the citizens of this realm, consider Queen Persephone guilty or innocent of the alleged offenses? All those who believe the queen guilty of the crimes against her crown?"

Almost every hand in the ballroom was raised.

He softly said, "I think that's the majority, don't you? How disappointing that they were so readily convinced against you! I had hoped for a bit more fight, but this is often the way. It is why pawns are so discardable. They have no substance in their marrow." Suddenly, his voice was booming as he addressed the crowd. "Queen Persephone, you are found guilty of crimes against the Underworld. You have committed murder, sought to undermine a valued alliance, threatened the safety of the souls of this land, and attempted to topple the very foundation of this world. You sought to install the God of War as the ruler of this world after committing adultery with him.

"As a prisoner of the crown, you will not be permitted to leave the palace grounds. If it is discovered that you attempted to abscond from the palace, you will be captured and banished to Tartarus."

He lifted his hand amid repeated cries to throw her into that dark prison. Persephone could feel the eyes of all the subjects burning into her. He had certainly ensured it would be unsafe to show her face within the Underworld.

"And yet, if I further punish my mad wife, would that make me better than her? Before all of you, I will determine that I will show her leniency as long as my wife remains within the palace's borders. I will be a forgiving king so that her crimes end tonight."

The crowd looked mutinous but did not protest; they were too entranced by Zeus' silver tongue. His ability to manipulate people and command a crowd was legendary. She suddenly realized that, though Zeus could wield thunderbolts, that was not the source of his power. The true power that lay within him—the reason he was God of the Gods—was his ability to manipulate, and it was far more dangerous than Ares' sword, Aphrodite's arrow, or her mother's storms. With a single word from him, this throng would happily rip apart her body or declare her Queen of Olympus. They would do whatever he asked of them. Persephone felt a shiver run down her spine. What a dangerous, immoral power to possess, this ability to sway the minds of others.

"You may all rest certain," the king continued, "that I will have the queen in my sights at all times, ensuring that no further damage comes to the kingdom and that we can start to repair her damaged psyche. To demonstrate to the world above that we do not fear Ares' intervention, we will proceed with the ball and ask all of you to rejoice to the maximum extent of your abilities. Nothing is off limits when it comes to bringing pleasure tonight."

He raised his hands, and the music began again. Immediately, members of the crowd started to whirl across the ballroom. Zeus turned to face Persephone. He smiled as he drew near, and with a wave of his fingers, the shackles turned into light, almost translucent chains. He pulled her stiff body against him, looping her arms around his neck.

Nestling his face against her face, she felt his lips brush her ear, and he whispered, "Did you miss me?"

"No."

He laughed. "I missed you. You never cease to surprise me. I find I am anticipating your response, which is so different from the tedium of the mortals and the other Gods. You are unexpected in this predictable world."

She said nothing, allowing him to spin her around the floor like a helpless doll as she was filled with impotent wrath. She inhaled deeply, attempting to push the emotion back down.

"What did you think of my performance? I think it was one of my finer acts." His brow furrowed. "Not my best, perhaps; there are simply too many to choose from, but still very good." His eyes moved to her face again. "You left me no choice, you know. Now you can't run away again. You have a rather vile habit of running. It is quite annoying."

She regarded him with an unyielding stare, maintaining her composure even as a deliberate, hard elbow jabbed into her side from a passing dancer. She wasn't foolish enough to consider it accidental. She was now the most hated woman above and below.

"If you think for a moment that I will feel any other emotion towards you than contempt, then you are sadly mistaken, *Zeus*."

He gave a quiet chuckle. "Come now, that is not true. You and I both know how intimately you have enjoyed being with me. I have felt your sweet sheath quiver around my cock."

"Not your cock," she replied coolly, "my husband's. You may attempt to take his body and his emotions, but they will never be yours. You will never really feel anything; no matter how many lives you ruin or how much corruption you spread, you will only ever remain a bottomless pit that will never be able to be filled."

His hand tightened at her waist, and a flash of blue appeared in Hades' black eyes. Cruelly, he bent her backward, a sinister parody of an intimate movement of the dance, and she could feel the implied threat of his lips against her throat.

"Well, then I will just have to keep trying, won't I?" he murmured. "Let's see how I feel when the last of your husband's soul dies within this body." He brought her back up, pressing her breasts painfully against his chest. "I will enjoy fucking you tonight with no pretense between us."

His words terrified her. She could not endure the twisted farce of his arms wrapped around her, touching her, and forcing her to comply. But beneath the anger was panic, for some weak and horrible part of her still craved the touch of her husband's body against hers even though Zeus controlled him.

In a sudden surge of insight, she recognized the opportunity he unwittingly handed her. A mad queen—yes, she could play that role. She threw back her head with a roar of raucous laughter. Several nearby dancers halted their movements, eyeing the royal couple with curiosity and trepidation.

"What are you doing?" he murmured, his fingers tightening into the soft flesh of her arms.

Forgive me, Hades, she pleaded in her mind.

Suddenly, she reared forward, butting her head hard against the king's as she shrieked with laughter. He was so astonished that he released her, and she could slip the chain from around her neck. Once free, she began to twirl across the ballroom, the frightened guests falling back with a gasp of fear. She raised her arms, and a mighty wind ripped through the room, tearing down walls and decorations. All the while, she laughed until tears fell from her eyes as she ripped apart the room. Hard hands yanked her back, and she smiled up into her husband's face, hating the blood that dripped from his nose, but she knew Hades would understand. Looking up at him lovingly, she spit on his face with expert precision.

"Your Majesty," Rhadamanthus cried, stepping forward. "She must be put away until she calms down. For everyone's safety." Persephone was humming serenely, smiling at a nearby woman, who drew back with a gasp of terror as she let fire smolder in her eyes. "She is unsafe to be among the people."

"I can control my wife," the king growled.

Persephone performed a perfect twirl, using Hades' arm to guide her.

"Stop it," the king hissed.

"Stop it!" she echoed, shrieking the words. "Where is my husband?"

"I am here," he snapped.

"You aren't my husband! Where is Ares!"

Cocytus stepped forward, bringing an icy chill in his wake. "Your Majesty, she must be isolated. It would be putting yourself in danger to let her go free."

The crowd's cries began to murmur their assent, with all three Judges of the Underworld and Cocytus watching Zeus with expectant eyes.

"She will not harm anyone."

Very well, Persephone thought with a sigh. She charged forward and landed a decisive blow on Minos' jaw. Blood splattered over the floor as he slumped to the floor, and Persephone spun into the air, growling at the throng as she floated above the ballroom. She lifted her hand absently, and stinging hail began to fall. The crowd scrambled over one another, shrieking and wailing in terror. As the brothers hurried forward to assist Minos, guards gathered underneath Persephone.

She dropped her hand with a gleeful smile, enabling them to attach chains to her wrist as she floated about the room. She yanked her arms and sped rapidly around, causing the soldiers to trip over one another and battle to retain their hold. While the guards chased the queen, roughly shoving members of the crowd, the audience rushed out of the chamber, falling over one another in their hurry to escape. The palace was in complete and utter disarray. Persephone smiled serenely at the Chaos.

"Enough!" Zeus bellowed, his powerful chest heaving. Cocytus, the Judges, and a few brave crowd members surrounded Hades to protect him from the queen. The remaining guests paused, staring wild-eyed at the floating Persephone.

"Your Highness," Minos said quietly, "she cannot possibly be allowed free tonight. I fear there would be a riot if word were to get out that you had not contained her after such behavior. There are too many witnesses."

Persephone felt elation as she watched Zeus evaluate his options and knew when he came to the inevitable conclusion. She had outwitted the master, and though she would only receive a night's respite, she was ecstatic. Tomorrow, she would find a way to free herself, but tonight, he would not touch her.

"Lock her in the dungeons," he said in a low voice, "while I decide what is best to do with my *wife*."

Persephone allowed the guards to lower her to the ground. As they led her away in chains, Persephone glanced back, her hair partially shielding her face, and as she looked into Zeus' enraged eyes, she smiled.

CHAPTER 25
THE KING OF TARTARUS

An urgent hand shook Persephone awake. She had been led deep underground in the palace and chained in a dark, fetid prison. Persephone had tried to force herself to stay awake, afraid Zeus would change his mind, but eventually, she slept, unable to fight her exhaustion. She had been dreaming about a woman beckoning her deeper into the darkness, urging her into the darkest shadows. She shivered, her thoughts sluggish and disoriented.

"Get up," a harsh voice commanded. Persephone looked up to see the brilliant, blonde beauty of Ares. The picture was ruined by his furious glare.

She let out a shaky sigh of relief. "What happened to you last night?" she whispered as Ares bent to pick the locks of the enchanted chains.

"What do you mean what happened to me? The question is, what happened to you? You were stupid to trust him! You can never fully rely on Hades now. He is weakening, and at any time, Zeus might appear when you least expect it. You refused to listen to my warnings, and now you are a prisoner."

Persephone opened her lips to argue but bit back her acerbic response. He was correct. She had allowed her love for Hades to blind her to the danger of being with him.

"There are worse prisons," she finally answered, mostly to herself. "And where is Zeus now? "

"After you went like a lovesick lamb to the slaughter last night, I raced back to Olympus. I worked during the night to plant a seed of doubt in my mother's mind regarding a possible new conquest of Zeus'. Just as the dawn rose, she was in an absolute frenzy and delivered such a ferocious slap to Zeus' slumbering face that he was immediately transported back to his body." Ares gave a satisfied chuckle. "You should have seen how furious he was when he realized he was back on Olympus, facing his ferocious wife."

The chains clattered to the ground, and Persephone instantly rose to her feet, heading for the door. "Then Hades is back."

"Hold on, you little idiot!" He shoved a cloak over her head and pulled on a large hood to shield her face. She realized he was similarly attired as he quickly threw up his hood. "We are outcasts now in this world. You can no longer show your face."

She glared at him. "I was hoping that since we are friends, maybe you could temper your rudeness a little."

"I'm only rude if I like someone. Consider it a compliment."

Persephone's eyes narrowed. "And if you don't like someone?"

"I typically stab them. Now come on."

"What about the guards?"

"Don't insult me. They were child's play."

She rolled her eyes. "Where is Hades?"

"That's where I am trying to take you if you stop blabbering."

They began the ascent from the dungeons, bickering in whispers as they moved efficiently but cautiously over the unconscious guards that lined the corridors.

"It is taking Hades longer than before to come fully to himself," Ares said. "I have left him resting in his bed. By the time we reach him, he should be fully present."

Persephone hurried, Ares' words causing panic to constrict her throat. He is dying, her mind whispered to her. She sped up the stairs, Ares close on her heels. As they reached the main halls, they had to pause several times to avoid the guards stationed at various points throughout the palace, but finally, they reached Hades' chambers.

Persephone flung back her hood as they entered and rushed towards Hades, who was just partially beginning to sit up from the bed, clearly having sensed their presence. Her lip trembled as her eyes quickly moved over his face, his dark eyes standing out abruptly against his pale, almost translucent skin. She rushed forward, falling to her knees to lay her head on his lap.

"I am glad you are back," she whispered. Hades' hands stroked her hair, and then he stood up from the bed, lifting her with him.

"I should have been more cautious," he replied, settling his arms around her. "One moment, I was there, and the next, I was not. I could always feel a warning before he took control, but it is becoming more effortless for him. Are you all right?"

She nodded her head. "I am fine."

Hades cocked his head in the direction of Ares, who was seated on a chaise near the fire and devouring a brilliant red apple. "How much time do you think we have?"

"Enough," Ares replied. He picked up another piece of fruit and hurled it towards Persephone. Hades caught it in one hand before it collided with the back of her head. He shot Ares a menacing glance, at which Ares chuckled. "She should eat before we head into Tartarus."

"We?" Hades repeated with a raised brow. "I am not sure I trust you inside Tartarus."

Ares batted his eyelashes. "I promise to be a good little boy and not cause unnecessary trouble."

Hades rolled his eyes. "I think you and I differ as to what we consider unnecessary trouble."

He returned his attention to his wife, handing her the apple. She studied it for a moment, then took it reluctantly, biting into the fruit. When she offered it to Hades, he shook his head, and she sighed.

Hades bent to her. "Just because I cannot eat doesn't mean you should feel guilty. You must eat."

She furrowed her brow at his easy reading of her thoughts. "Why are we going into Tartarus?" she asked, changing the subject quickly.

"Isn't it about time you met your father-in-law?" Ares said before Hades could respond.

Persephone's eyes widened as she stared into Hades' face. "Cronus," she breathed. "We are seeking out Cronus?"

Hades shot Ares a furious look. "Perhaps you could leave while I speak to my wife so we can get dressed. You know where you may hide while we get ready." Ares laughed as he stood, tossing the remaining apple core into the fire. "And don't forget to cover your pretty face," Hades said. The War God lifted his hood, raising his hand in a rude gesture, before slipping from the room.

Hades led Persephone to the closet. "Dress in red. It is good camouflage down there. The heat is extreme." He withdrew a red silk toga with a matching cape and passed it to her. Bending low, he pulled out golden vambraces. "We are entering the most dangerous part of Tartarus, so we must be careful."

"Hades," she said, placing her arm on his hand. "Is it not dangerous to seek Cronus? How will he help us?"

"Nyx believes that he may carry knowledge regarding Zeus' curse."

She lifted her hand, brushing his dark hair from his forehead. "And what do you believe?"

His eyes closed briefly at her touch, and then he brought her hand down to his chest, pressing it against his heart. "I believe that he will not help. But I have exhausted my choices. Moreover, Ares may be correct in what he said, though his delivery leaves much to be desired. My father and I are long overdue for a confrontation."

She scrutinized his pale face carefully. "And are you ready to confront your father?"

He smiled ruefully. "I do not know if I will ever be ready for that, but sometimes life propels you forward, whether you are prepared or not."

As she dressed, he averted his gaze, and she recalled that it was more difficult for him to retain control while aroused. She swiftly slipped the dress over her head. When he turned back to face her, he held an archery strap.

"Your preferred weapon," he murmured with a grin.

She strapped it around herself. "Where is my bow?"

With a wave of his fingers, her ruby bow, a quiver of arrows, and the Acheron knife he had given her so long ago materialized. He hurriedly donned his armor while she prepped her weapons before attaching his whip. He raised his hand, and the silver bident appeared in his grasp. With another wave of his wrists, the golden and blue blades appeared in the scabbard on his back. She paused in her preparations, studying them carefully. These swords were as much her enemy as Zeus. How much suffering had occurred due to these beautiful weapons? She could almost imagine them as living, breathing things calling her closer. The trance was broken when he turned towards her, and she hastily averted her eyes, pretending to study her bow.

"Almost ready," he murmured, "but one more thing." With a final wave, he pulled his helmet from the shadows. He extended it toward her. "Under no circumstances, allow Cronus to see you."

She gave him a furious look. "I will not be a coward. I will stand with you in plain sight."

He shook his head. "You will wear the helmet, or you will not come."

They regarded each other stonily until Persephone saw that Hades' hand trembled as he clutched his bident. She could protect him more easily if she was invisible. She would not allow his father to harm him again.

"Very well," she relented with a frustrated sigh. "I will wear the helmet, but if Cronus even looks at you the wrong way, I retain the right to shoot him, helmet or no helmet."

The three Gods sped through the Underworld at breakneck speed. Hades and Persephone rode atop Cerberus, while Ares chose to run on foot. With Hades' knowledge of the Underworld, they met no resistance on their journey, and they reached the entrance of Hell relatively soon. Gyges greeted them at the gates, and Ares gaped up at the creature, Gyges' single stern face scowling angrily at the War God while the other faces focused on his nephew.

Hades urged Cerberus forward.

"Uncle, this is my wife, Persephone."

Gyges' faces broke into broad smiles, and he bent as low as his massive body would allow him, causing the ground to tremble beneath their feet.

"We have heard much of you, Queen Persephone." She placed her hand on one of Gyges' fingers. "Kind Goddess, you have my loyalty today and eternally."

"Gyges, from this moment forward, Persephone is to be given full access to Tartarus." Persephone glanced at him in surprise but said nothing. Gyges' heads nodded in agreement. Hades leaped down from Cerberus and caught Persephone as she dismounted as well.

"We go on foot." He gave Persephone a speaking glance as he took her hand. "Helmet on."

His final view of his wife was of her spitting out her tongue before she vanished. He chuckled, turning to Gyges. "Open the gates, uncle."

The quartet moved through the gate, and Persephone took a step back as Tartarus's oppressive, putrid smell drifted to her nostrils. Hades kept her hand securely in his, propelling her forward.

"Ah," Ares sighed, taking an eager sniff, "it smells just like I imagined." His alert blue eyes took a careful perusal as though searching for an enemy he could attack.

"Focus, Ares," Hades murmured. "Come, let us join together." Hades gathered the four of them into a circle. "Persephone, touch Cerberus, Ares," he continued, "grasp onto my forearm." He indicated the hand in which he held the bident. "With your other hand, grasp Cerberus. We must be linked." Cerberus' nearest head gave Ares a gleaming, golden stare, and Ares hesitated only briefly before laying his hand on the beast's wiry fur.

"Frightened of a little dog?" Persephone's disembodied voice asked sweetly.

"There's nothing little about him," Ares growled back at her.

"Be quiet, children," Hades admonished. "We are going deep into Tartarus, to the castle of the Titans, and we don't want to draw attention."

"She started it," Ares muttered rebelliously.

Finally, all was quiet, and Hades closed his eyes. A wind began to blow around the foursome, picking up speed as the land around them remained stagnant. The damp hair lifted from the back of Persephone's neck as her body seemed to sizzle with a current of electricity. She glanced at her husband. On Hades' forehead, the emblem of Pluto emerged, and the bident in his hand shimmered and vibrated as he whispered, "πορεία Cronus."

Persephone felt herself spinning into Tartarus's suffocating, sweltering heat as a stinging wind pulled them from the ground. The voyage lasted just seconds, but it was excruciating; the wind was so harsh against them that it sliced through their flesh like a diamond's sharp edge. They materialized near the castle, and their grasp on each other broke, causing Ares and Persephone to stagger forward. Ares tumbled to the ground, colliding into Cerberus, and the dog growled, snapping at the War God. Only Hades' strong grip on her wrist prevented her from falling.

Persephone surveyed the surrounding landscape. The sky was darkened, and lava spilled from the ground's fractured rock below, with treacherous gusts carrying the molten liquid in its wake. She gasped, as what she had mistaken for mountains were actually the huge, malformed legs of the Titans. Heavy shackles imprisoned them in this Hell. As Hades advanced, the ground trembled from the Titans' venomous roars.

"Blood Betrayer! False King! We curse you!"

"As you can see," a calm voice said, "you are not their favorite person, Pluto." Nyx stepped forward, her lovely, incandescent eyes lingering briefly on where Persephone stood beside Hades. "I am glad you came. And gladder still that you did not come alone."

Her magnificent eyes shifted to Ares and Cerberus, who stood a short distance away. Ares was wiping dirt from his robes while Cerberus shook his gigantic bulk, periodically sending gusts of dust to land on the War God.

"You did that on purpose, mutt," Persephone heard Ares mutter.

Nyx looked towards the palace. A black, jutting tower seemed to grow like an ominous malignancy from the large obsidian gates. "As you well know, Pluto, Cronus is the timekeeper. Nothing is as it seems inside his palace, and even those of sound mind may emerge irreparably transformed."

A slight grin pulled at Hades' lips. "Are you suggesting that I am not of sound mind, Nyx?"

"More than insinuating it, Pluto," Nyx replied with a sweet smile that swiftly vanished. "Be cautious. Are you sure you are ready to meet your father again after so much time has passed?"

Hades looked up at the enormous black gates. "But perhaps inside the palace, no time has passed at all. It often feels that way to me; even after all these eons, it feels as though it was just yesterday." He turned to look at Nyx. "I do this part alone. I have things to say to him, as I am sure he does to me."

Nyx's iridescent gaze moved over Hades' visage. "I'm confident that you both do. We will be waiting for your return. But remember," she added while she looked Persephone in the eyes, "two heads are superior to one. There is power in numbers and protection in those who seek answers with a pure heart."

"I will keep that in mind," Hades murmured, "but I am still going alone. Lower the gates!"

Two large, winged creatures flew high into the skies of Tartarus to reach the pulley that controlled the obsidian gates. Even Ares and Cerberus paused in their battle to watch, awestruck as the enormous gates lowered. Here was a forbidden palace, the stuff of legends, and inside was one of the most powerful beings that had ever roamed the Earth or Heavens. A heaviness seemed to pulse from the entryway, a warning that something deadly and ancient lay just beyond the threshold. Voices danced on the wind, murmurs in a forgotten language that Persephone did not understand but still sent a shudder of foreboding down her spine. Hades paused and then inclined his head toward Persephone.

Stay here, his voice demanded inside her head. He moved forward, letting go of her hand, and his dark form vanished within the shadows. Almost instantly, the gates began to rise.

"You had best hurry," Nyx stated calmly to no one in particular, "it would not do to get stuck in those gates."

Persephone sprang off the ground and slid through the little space that remained before the massive gate slammed shut behind her, trapping her in possibly the most perilous location in Tartarus.

The King of the Underworld walked the abandoned halls of his father's palace. After the war, a harsh punishment had been dealt to Cronus: he would be left alone with his thoughts for eternity. Death would have been more merciful; Cronus' power revealed images of lives that could never happen but might have been had fate been more benevolent. He was tortured by what-ifs at every turn, perpetually alone in his kingdom of one.

Through the obsidian pillars that lined the corridors, Hades saw shadows and glimpses of lives that, but for a small, seemingly inconsequential decision, had never come to be. The faces and images were unfamiliar until he moved further into that lonely hall, and his breath caught in his throat. It was Hades as a child, not as he had been imprisoned within his father's filthy, corrupted body, but smiling and happy, embraced by a loving and benevolent Cronus. Rhea was nearby; other ghostly children were sitting in her lap. The phantom Cronus suddenly bent down to her.

"I love you," the ghostly father whispered, echoing those powerful words into an eternity that was never to be.

As if a candle had been suddenly extinguished, the images abruptly transformed into shadow, and the hall was once more gloomy and sinister. Hades shook his head, wiping his face impatiently to find that there was moisture on his cheeks. He must not stay here too long.

"Cronus," he called. As he continued down the dim hallway, he received no response. "Cronus," he said again, this time louder. But instinct told him that the Titan would not answer to that name. He knew what he waited for—he would want to further defile his son. "Father." Hades almost spat the word; the taste was vile on his lips. It was a degradation of all that endearment meant.

"My boy," a voice echoed.

Ice ran up Hades' spine. It had been epochs since he had heard it, yet it still had the power to make his heart pound in fear. Every poisonous memory and excruciating torment flooded back as if he had never escaped his prison. How that voice had laughed as demons had torn apart his body, how it whispered to him that he was nothing as the flesh had been ripped from his bones, day after day.

Against every instinct in his body, Hades moved towards the sound. Fragments of the shadows began to coalesce, and a black throne rose from the darkness, and there sat the King of Titans, the once-powerful Cronus, a shriveled old man bound to the stone, his body so feeble that it appeared it would crumble to dust at the merest touch. Silver ribs glistened beneath his thin skin, and if not for his eyes, Hades would have believed he was dead. But his eyes—those horrible, watching silver eyes—were as piercing and filled with venom as they ever had been.

"Murderer."

The hissed word was hurled from the throne, and Hades felt the pain of it more than a physical strike. He forced himself to stare at the being who had so willingly assisted in his destruction and willed himself to feel nothing, to remember that this man no longer held any power over him. What lies he told himself, Hades thought with a bitter smile.

"Like father, like son," Hades replied coolly.

"My firstborn," snarled Cronus. "The traitor."

Cronus twisted his fingers, and sand particles materialized between his fingertips. The sand started to flow over Cronus' decrepit body, wiping away the evidence of time on his flesh until he sat, magnificent and silver-haired, with healthy, shining skin. He was stunning. The King of Titans slowly rose from the throne, enormous and formidable. Slowly, he approached his son, the huge golden chains that shackled his wrists and ankles dragging on the floor behind him. The restraints prevented him from reaching Hades, but they stood nearly nose to nose.

Hades could feel the strength that still flowed from this ancient entity—a barely controlled wrath that could only be restrained by his sons' combined, potent magic. Cronus pointed to the floor beneath them, and Hades glanced at their reflections on the mirrored surface. Next to his father's beautiful silver-haired splendor, Hades felt insignificant, a peasant next to a king.

The Titan's voice was soft as he spoke. "It was you who drove the sword into your mother's heart. You alone carry this sin." As he spoke the word' sin,' images flashed through the room, a young Hades, who was holding the blue-flamed sword aloft before viciously thrusting it into his mother's chest.

"No," Hades cried, closing his eyes tightly. When they opened, they blazed purple. "It was you I meant to slay that day."

Cronus laughed bitterly, the sound echoing across the hall. "Foolish boy," Cronus snarled. "Ineptitude does not provide you with absolution. You took the one thing I loved from me—the only other being who meant anything to me. I cursed the day you were born—the day my seed took root in your mother. Would that I could have stamped you out in her womb to prevent you from ever being brought into existence."

"Well, you certainly did your best to make up for that after the fact, didn't you?" Hades could not keep the bitter hatred from his voice.

"Why are you here, *son*?" Cronus snarled the last word. "Come to finish the botched patricide?" Cronus studied his son, and then a cruel smile lifted the corners of his lips. "Oh no, you need something from me." Cronus once more twisted his fingers, and Hades tensed as he felt time twisting itself across the room, shattering memories of the past, present, and future, wrapping itself like shackles around his body.

Cronus closed his eyes, and the symbol of Saturn flickered on his forehead. "You need my aid. You…are infected." The silver eyes flashed open, illuminated in the darkness. "You are dying."

Hades kept his face impassive. "Yes, I am dying; the people of the Underworld need your help."

Cronus gently laughed, interrupting his son. "Oh no, *King Hades*, I will not help you. You are as dead to me as Rhea is. *More* dead to me than she will ever be. I am a widow, and you are an orphan. And soon,

you will be nothing. It seems almost unfair that you should be allowed to enter the sweet bliss of oblivion when you have so much to answer for."

All around them, the moment that Hades' had struck Rhea down played again and again, their images dancing like ghostly figures around him. Hades fell to his knees, covering his ears as her endless screams echoed through the halls.

"Please!" Hades cried. "No more!"

Cronus bent to stroke his son's ebony hair. "You must remember as I remember. Her dying screams greet me in the morning and are the last sound I hear as I fall into sleep. In dreams, she finds me, and I watch you plunge your blade into her again and again and again." He touched his fingertips to his son's temples. "Ah," he murmured, "how fractured you are. It is your fate to die with the sword that you wielded so carelessly. You will die a thousand deaths before you breathe your last breath. Karma is at last coming for you, and the dark night of your soul is close at hand. You are death incarnate, and you will die by the blade you murdered my wife with."

Hades suddenly pushed away from Cronus, landing hard on the floor at his father's feet. "She was my mother!" he gasped in a low voice, his entire body trembling. "And she loved her children. All that happened and transpired was a result of your selfish cruelty and your own madness. You are right; she was good and pure, but you sowed twisted seeds, which have come to fruition. I am not the only abomination you created. I will die, but Zeus will not be stopped. He will destroy the humans."

Cronus nostrils flared at the sound of his other child's name. The emblem of Saturn reappeared on Cronus' brow, and when he raised his hand, Hades saw visions of his own destruction dancing about him. Cronus lifted his arm higher, and the sights flooded Hades' mind, permeating every cell within his body. His future. He experienced his death a hundred times, a thousand times, ten thousand times. The God-killing sword repeatedly severed his life in innumerable ways, his life essence ebbing away. Death was unavoidable; over and over, it came for him. It was his destiny—to die. There was no escape. Suddenly, Hades was back in the present, gasping for air as Cronus stood over him.

"These are your options; in every possibility, in all your lifetimes, you die by that sword," Cronus stated coldly. "It is too late for you. You, more than anyone, should know that you cannot cheat death. What you should be asking me is not how not to die but how you prefer to die. There is no future for Hades; his story is written."

Hades' body trembled, lost in the memories of the past and the future. Cronus leaned forward to hear the words tumbling from his lips: "Mother, I'm sorry."

Cronus drew back with a snarl of revulsion. "You dare to feign remorse! She was never yours to mourn. You never even knew her. She was mine, and you took her from me. Among all your siblings, you were the one I attempted to keep close, the one I vomited last, the one who should have remained in your prison. I witnessed you repeatedly murder her before you were conceived, and I knew my raven-haired son would kill her. I repressed the image for fear that the nightmare might come true if I spoke the words out loud." The sound of his laughter rang with insanity. "And look at us now. She is dead, and you are dying. What was the purpose of it all?"

Cronus leaned forward, pressing his hand against his son's face, and Hades' face contorted in anguish." Yes, how does it feel, my child? To see her die again and again, as I do? I may have imprisoned you within my body, but I never attempted to kill you." Cronus dug his fingers deeper into Hades' flesh. "Feel it! Feel the pain of your wretched life as I do!"

Hades' voice was a broken whisper. "I feel it every day. I watched her die in my arms. I see it every day. I close my eyes, and it is there. Please stop; I beg you."

Cronus pushed the vision deeper into his son's mind until Hades thought he would go mad. He felt his being begin to shatter, unable to withstand the weight of regret and sorrow, until Hades' eyes suddenly glowed purple, and Pluto's emblem emerged on his forehead. Rising fast from the ground, he raised his hand and blasted his father with such a massive wave of his own suffering that the castle trembled. Hades put all the agony he had experienced when he had pierced his mother's heart into the blow that threw Cronus off balance, and as he fell, Rhea's last words echoed in Cronus' palace: "I do not want you to be a murderer like your father."

Cronus crumbled, a glistening tear falling from his beautiful silver eyes.

"Leave me," Cronus whispered.

Hades' eyes moved over the broken form of Cronus. "Father," he began.

But when the silver eyes rose to meet Hades' black gaze, they were filled with dark hatred.

"I am happy to know death is coming for you. No matter how you try to change your fate, it only has one outcome: your destruction. When the time comes, I will be watching." Slowly, he stood and returned to his throne, his feet disturbing the sand at the base. "Say hello to your mother for me."

Hades paused, standing uncertainly in the long hall. As he moved to go, he turned, his dark hair obscuring his face. "You know," Hades said quietly, "all I ever wanted was for you to love me."

Cronus withered before his son's eyes, again an old man hunched on the throne. "I do not care."

Hades left the room, his feet silent on the floor, but Cronus had lost interest. A memory was playing of Rhea kissing her husband repeatedly on a loop, and Cronus watched it out of his silver gaze. His voice abruptly broke the silence. "Helmets of invisibility are only useful if you can manage to control your outraged huffs of breath. Are you planning to introduce yourself?"

Persephone yanked the helmet from her head and stared stonily at Cronus's withered form.

"Come closer, child." His eyes moved over her, studying the ring on her finger. "You are his wife."

She inclined her head coolly. "I am Queen of the Underworld."

"And do you make a habit of listening to private conversations? Not a very queenly attribute."

"I make it a habit of listening when I think my husband is needlessly confronting a madman." She gave him another polite nod. "Such as yourself."

Cronus gave a croaking laugh, bending to lift a portion of the sand from his feet. He let the granular material play between his palms, closing his eyes. "Queen Persephone," he murmured. "Ah, yes, there you are. He has done well for himself. A Goddess of the forest. A true descendant of Gaia."

As the sand shifted between his hands, the wrinkles again vanished from his face, the thinning white hair turning a dark silver that glistened like snowflakes around his masculine beauty. Persephone noticed that fragments of silver glistened beneath his flesh as though silver blood coursed through his veins. Cronus' eyes shot open, and he caught Persephone studying him.

"Do you find us alike, my son and I?" he asked. "Much as I despise it, there is a likeness between us, more than even the physical. Both are destined to be unhappy, both despising our fathers. Both of our mothers helped to shape our fate, but in my case, I was the only one with the courage to do what my mother wished— to slay my mad father. My mother even handed me the weapon so that I could accomplish my task. I did what my brothers could not, and this is my reward." He lifted his hands, the chains rattling in the quiet room. "Uranus cursed me as he fell. Nothing was ever the same again after that day. No good deed goes unpunished, after all." His eyes narrowed. "Maybe that is our destiny—sons killing fathers and fathers despising their sons. Though my son was not successful, as you can see."

"You are wrong, you know, to blame Hades for his mother's death. I think that Rhea did not want her child to suffer as you did. She sacrificed herself to break a cursed cycle." His eyes blazed at her, but she stared boldly back. "You may not like what I say, but in the end, it was Rhea who made her choice. She would die for him as many times as necessary to protect him and endure any pain for him. That is a mother's love; it is what any mother would do."

"Not any mother," Cronus replied coldly. "You speak freely to me for someone so young. Are you not afraid?"

"You, above all, know that there is little fear left when the only ones you love are taken from you."

An unpleasant smile tugged at Cronus' lip. "Oh, youngling, you still have much to lose. But perhaps it does not matter. You have entwined your fate with a cursed lineage. My father, the God of the Heavens, was a beast. He was as treacherous as a serpent; his words were poisonous. It seems logical that he would produce a cursed seed. But my eldest, after all, is impotent, so there is such a thing as small blessings. I wish I had seen fit to ensure the rest of my sons could not bear the tainted fruit of Uranus. Would that I had been unable to." The silver eyes of Cronus returned to her as she stiffened at his cruel words. "There is mortal blood within you," he stated abruptly.

"Yes."

"I loved mortals, you know," he whispered.

"I know."

"How are they now? My people?"

"They suffer."

Cronus gave a low laugh. "Of course they do." He gazed moodily into the shadows, silent for some moments. "What do you want from me?" he asked finally. "I will not save your husband."

"Will not or cannot?"

His eyes were cool. "Perhaps both."

"I heard what you told him," she replied. "I won't ask you for help when you are so obviously unwilling. I never thought you would support him. I will save Hades without you."

"And yet you want something."

"Yes, I want something," she admitted. She peered along the shadowy corridors where peaceful images of Cronus and his family played. "I feel that had you not been cursed, your fate would have been different. Just as with my husband." Persephone moved forward. "I had a son." Cronus regarded her with those strange silver eyes, saying nothing. "I thought he had died. But…" Her mouth quivered with emotion, but she firmed her lips and continued. "But it may be that I was wrong. I want you to help me find him."

"Your son?" Cronus inquired with a raised eyebrow. "But not my son's offspring?"

"He was not Hades' son," Persephone replied, her voice reluctant.

"Even so, why should I feel compelled to help you?" Cronus asked. "Have you not pledged your allegiance to the person I despise above all others?"

Persephone bit her lip. "For the mortals..."

"They are damned."

She exhaled a frustrated breath. "Don't you understand you have another son who is just as responsible, if not more, for what happened to Rhea?"

Cronus stood, and his face was terrifying. "Do not speak to me of her!" he bellowed. "I was there that day! I saw who slayed her!"

His hypnotic silver rage captivated Persephone, and she could not turn away from the agony in his eyes. Suddenly, a sense of pity consumed her. Pity for this mighty creature who had lost the only person who had ever meant anything to him; pity that he had suffered so horribly at the hands of a curse; the knowledge that he might have been good and whole had not fate intervened. Something sparked in Cronus' eyes as he looked at her, and the tension dissolved as he sat, his powerful chest heaving with emotion as he stared ahead at the ghostly image of Rhea. When he regarded Persephone again, his fury was once again under control.

"I will search for your son while you try to come up with something that would be of interest to me."

Persephone's mouth gaped, shocked by his sudden acquiescence. She stood as still as a statue, fearing that any movement would disturb Cronus's concentration. Cronus only continued to look forward without expression as time passed. She almost jumped when he suddenly let out a surprised laugh, his eyes narrowing as he watched the shadowed halls. She quickly scanned the darkened passage but saw nothing.

"Well then," he murmured, "well then." As he peered deeper into the darkness, a peculiar expression crossed his face, almost as if he were startled by what he saw in the shadows. His eyes gleamed with silver fire. "Mourn, torn, your son has yet to be born."

Persephone stepped back, shaking her head. "No, I gave birth to him in the forest. He was taken from me after he died. What do you see?" Persephone asked, stepping closer to the darkness. "Tell me what you see!"

"Your son has yet to be born," he repeated again. His pupils had dilated so that his gaze was almost black, so much like his son's, as he stared avidly ahead, enthralled by the vision only he could see.

"I told you," she said, frustration filling her voice, "that is impossible. I bore him in the forest, and he died there. His body was stolen from me."

Cronus laughed, reluctantly shifting his gaze to hers. "How young you are to the deep magic, Goddess." He regarded her thoughtfully. "Have you heard of the Islands of the Blessed?"

"No."

"It is located in Elysium. It is where the truly worthy go. Do you know how one gains access to this realm?"

"No. How?"

"First, you must enter Elysium after you die, then you must choose to be reborn, and if your soul lives another worthy life and you choose to die and be reborn a third time, your soul can finally rest in the most beautiful realm in the Universe."

"But what about it? There is still much of the Underworld I do not know. What has this to do with my son?" she asked impatiently.

"These brave souls choose to die and be reborn again and again. Imagine if an immortal was that brave. To die even once."

She stood very still. "Are you saying my son is on this island?"

A small smile lifted the edge of Cronus' mouth, and fury sparked in Persephone's heart. "Is this a game to you?" she cried. "My child died, my husband is dying, and I have nothing. I only wish to know where my son is so that at least I may find his body and bury him. I have no hope that he is still alive, but can you imagine what it does to a mother to not even know where his body is or why it was taken? Even now, Zeus searches for him. I cannot allow that monster to find him." She walked to his throne, lifting the heavy chains from the ground. "I am held in a prison, put there by the same man who now sits on your throne."

Compassion flared in Cronus' eyes. "You grieve as deeply as I do, though you hide it so much better," he murmured. "Give me your hand, child." She hesitated, then dropped the chains, stepping so close that she could see the flow of silver in his veins. She placed her much smaller hand into his larger, rougher one.

Cronus closed his eyes at the contact, letting out a slight noise of surprise. "Your future is much clearer than Hades." He started laughing, astonishment in his voice. "No wonder I could not see... But it is impossible. I must be wrong." His eyes flashed open, and his fingers tightened around her wrists. "Your husband, how bad do you want to save him?"

"More than anything. I would give anything—my life—for his."

Cronus looked at her with his silver eyes. "Such a sacrifice will not be necessary. I have found my price. The Islands of the Blessed, give me that realm, and when the time comes, I will assist Aidoneus."

"But Elysium is precious to Hades."

"Hades will be dust at your feet without my help." He leaned down low toward her, his stunning beauty overwhelming in such close proximity. "You need me. You know that. Why else would you be here?"

"How will you help him?" she asked warily.

"By aiding his wife." Cronus stood, releasing her hand. "How does Zeus succeed? What has Zeus built up? It was by freeing his family that he was able to fight me. And now his heirs fight at his side. Why did he tear your family apart? Why did he kill your father and separate him from your mother? Why did he try to alienate you from your husband?"

"He did it to isolate us," she murmured thoughtfully. "But–"

"Precisely," he beamed down at her as though she were a prized pupil. "There is strength in the family. It is why Uranus cursed me to destroy my own. It was the beginning of my end. This is how you will defeat him in battle. Without one, you will fail. Promise me this kingdom in Elysium, and I will aid you in your fight. You need my help. I will find your son. I might have been a bad father, but I will not be a bad grandfather."

"How do I know I can trust you? I do not understand your sudden change in heart; you have not explained."

"And I will not explain, not right now." He stared down at her, an enigmatic creature from another world. "You must have faith that I will keep my word. Do I strike you as a man who would betray a promise?"

She studied him carefully. "I do not know," she answered honestly. "I can only imagine you want very much to be free of this prison."

He laughed. "I do. *Very* much."

"*If* you save him, the isles are yours. If not, you will rot in here forever."

"And will you be telling my son about our bargain?"

"No," she admitted reluctantly. "He does not value his safety, and I do. He would not agree to this, so, no, I will not tell him I made a deal with you."

"Secrets have a way of revealing themselves," Cronus murmured, his eyes veiled. "Nevertheless, keeping our truce a secret for now would be best. I accept your terms. Now, we must get you back before Hades returns."

"But Hades already left some time ago."

Cronus smiled. "Did he? You will find that time is not always linear. Put on your helmet. If you need me, call me." She just had the helmet over her head when suddenly Cronus' voice echoed as the light flashed, and she was standing next to Nyx. *Remember your promise,* he had whispered into her mind.

Nyx gave no indication that she was aware that Persephone was next to her. The gate was lowering, and Hades was just exiting the palace.

"How did it go?" the elder Goddess asked Hades.

"He offered no solutions." Hades' voice was calm, giving no indication of what had transpired within the room. Persephone's heart ached for him at the cruel words that Cronus had leveled at him.

"Perhaps I can persuade him," Nyx said softly.

"No, it would be pointless. Come, let us leave this place. It was a waste of time to believe he would ever help anyone." His eyes were on

Persephone, and he motioned for her to follow him to Cerberus.

She moved, but not before Nyx leaned closer to her. "And did *you* find the answers that you sought?"

"I think so," Persephone murmured quickly. "I bargained with him." Nyx made a quiet noise, and uncertainty swept over Persephone. "Do you think I made a mistake by trusting him?"

Nyx raised her head, staring up at the high tower of the King of the Titans. "Oh, my dear," she said softly, "whatever bargain you made, you made in love, and already that is a good start. I do not know if we can trust Cronus, but we must try." Her eyes shot to Persephone's. "When you need me, you only need to call. Now, I think it best to return to your husband, lest he realize such antics as invisibility helmets are only effective on younglings and idiots."

CHAPTER 26
DINNER WITH THE KING

Persephone and Ares trained for the rest of the day. Blood adorned her arms and feet, and her hands, now raw, bore witness to the God of War's relentless tutoring. Ares delivered one hard blow after the next, and by the time they finished, Persephone's muscles were trembling with exhaustion as she limped back to her room. She wanted nothing more than to fall into bed, but she was too filthy. With a groan, she pulled off her ruined toga, tossing it into the fire, before dragging herself into the pool in the back of her room. A hiss of pleasure escaped her lips as the water alternatively burned and soothed the cuts across her flesh. With a wave of her hands, jasmine, and roses filled the bath, infusing the air with a sweet fragrance.

But even as she willed herself to relax, her mind still reeled with possibilities. Her promise to Cronus haunted her, and uncertainty gnawed at her resolve. Was the Titan a pawn in the Gods' cruel game, or just another master manipulator? Steeling herself, she dismissed the questions with fierce determination. Her commitment to saving Hades and finding her son must eclipse all doubts. She could not regret her promise to Cronus. She would do whatever it took.

Her eyes drifted shut, the water's soft swish a soothing lullaby. She shook off the drowsiness and pulled herself out of the pool. She had to sleep, whether she wanted to or not. Quickly donning a simple cotton toga, she suddenly paused, straining her ears. A whisper seemed to linger in the air, calling for her—*Persephone.*

Her hand hesitated on the door before she slid it open, and she caught the image of a fleeting, shadowy figure disappearing around a corner. The cape trailing behind them stirred a mix of familiarity and doubt. Hades. Was it indeed her husband or some deceptive manifestation? Uncertainty gripped her, and she bit her lower lip, torn between trust and suspicion. She was exhausted, but she needed to check on Hades.

Determined, she advanced cautiously down the hallway, each step echoing her internal conflict. A muffled thud guided her, and she followed the sound until she arrived at an open doorway. Peeking inside, she entered the room, her senses heightened.

The room was a rotunda shaped of pale marble, the walls lined with extravagant golden trimmings. An intimate feast had been set up; roasted peacock, parrot, oysters, salads, wild boar, and honied cakes glistened on the table. A sizable plush bed with furs and exotic silks had been immaculately arranged. The large marble fireplace flooded the room with a warm glow, and candles lined the table and floor, gently illuminating statues around the tower. As the door suddenly thudded shut behind her, Persephone jumped in surprise, turning to see her husband. He latched the entrance with a large golden key that hung around his neck, and her heart sank as she studied his face.

"My queen," he purred, a sly grin playing on his lips. He advanced, his predatory gaze never wavering from her. In the dimly lit chamber, his eyes glowed golden with a hunger that mirrored the flickering candlelight. Persephone's breath hitched. She turned away, but he closed the distance, encircling her shoulders with possessive fingers. "My *elusive* queen," he whispered. He yanked, spinning her in a circle, and she landed hard against him. His eyes were cruel as he looked down at her. "You think you were clever, outwitting me in our little battle. But your defiance only makes me hungrier for you. It is fortuitous that you came looking for me. We have much to discuss."

Her eyes met his, and the amber fire within them sent a shiver down her spine. She tried to push against him, but his fingers tightened around her back. "I was looking for my *husband*," she retorted, enunciating the word. "But I found a monster instead. Release me."

"But I *am* your husband," he replied. He abruptly let go of her, and she stumbled back. He gestured wide with his arms. "This is your prison." He smiled, and the malevolence in it made her shiver. "Remember your sentence? You are the most despised woman of the realm. You must be locked away for your own protection. But don't worry, little queen, I will find a way to pass your time." He raised his hand, and a translucent gown floated towards her. "For tonight," he said. "Put it on." She eyed the door, contemplating escape, and he laughed softly. "Oh, do try to run. Your resistance makes it so much more fun. It reminds me of our first time together. Remember? You fought like a wild cat."

Fury shimmered inside her, and she turned, striking him hard across the face before she could think better of it. His head whipped to the side, and when he looked back at her, he was licking a trail of blood from his lower lip. She stepped back, trembling in shame that he had goaded her into hurting Hades.

The King of Gods gripped her arm. "Force it shall be then," he hissed. His hands were painful on her as he ripped apart the back of her gown. As it dropped to the floor, his fingers explored her back, his lips grazing the soft skin of her neck. She struggled wildly against him, but he was too strong and subdued her easily. One hand held her still while the other explored her breasts, the vee between her legs, the flesh of her thighs. He was breathing heavily behind her, and she could feel his erection pushing into her. With a sudden snap of his fingers, the gown covered her body, and he released her.

She whipped around to face him, and his gaze was hungry. "Perfection," he declared. With a flourish, he sat at the table, pouring a glass of white wine. He took a deep drink, watching her over the rim. "I am famished after a day of plotting, and I don't want to rush this. I will satiate all of our appetites tonight." He raised his glass. "To you, my fugitive, my wife, my Queen of the Underworld." He laughed, the sound carrying a promise that lingered in the heated space between them.

With a fiery glare, she crossed her arms, putting distance between them. "I refuse to share a seat with you," she hissed. "You're delusional! Thinking that by masquerading as my husband, I'll suddenly buy into your twisted charade. Well, play make-believe all you want, but I won't entertain the notion that you're anything other than a monster."

His eyes were amused as he surveyed her over the table. "Oh, you will play the game with me, one way or another." He began to stand with a sigh. "But if you are so eager for bed, I will accommodate you." Her eyes widened, but she quickly stormed forward, a tempest of fury and resentment, her every step resonating with defiance. Reluctantly, she lowered herself into the seat. He, in turn, resumed his place with a smirk, a mock smile dancing on his lips. "How charming of you to join me. I shall prepare you a plate."

"I'm. Not. Hungry," she spat.

Ignoring her protests, he arranged a plate of succulent meat. Passing it to her, he leaned in, his breath tantalizingly close. "I spent such care arranging the dinner. See how I love you." She didn't move. "Eat, or I will take you to bed." She shot him a look of pure hatred as she plucked a piece of food from the plate. His gaze drifted down to her breasts. "After dinner, I will sup between your legs; you taste far better than wine, better than the ambrosia of Olympus."

With a forceful slam, her hand came down hard on the table, shattering her plate. "You're disgusting! You will not touch me!"

"You are in no position to make demands," he asserted, his laughter resonating with a dangerous edge. "I will touch you how I want when I want. Don't you know that by now?"

Her hands clenched into fists as she stared ahead, refusing to look at him. "I hate you."

His laugh was low." Oh no, Persephone. You love me, don't you? It's a love so consuming that it steals your very breath. Look at me and say the words – tell me you hàte me."

His words cast a shadow of fear over her. As her gaze met him, she found herself trapped between conflicting emotions. Before her was both the man she loved and the man she abhorred. Her husband and her attacker. It left her trembling, confused, and disturbed. The room seemed to close in, shadows dancing in unsettling patterns that mirrored the Chaos within her. She could feel the pull to him, an invisible force tugging at the frayed edges of her resolve. As his possessed eyes bore into hers, a flicker of recognition mingled with an unsettling malevolence, and her body trembled.

"I will never love you," she managed to whisper, but her voice betrayed the uncertainty that gripped her soul. The words hung in the air, anguish, and confusion swirling within her, leaving her torn between the love she once knew and the terror that now wore his face.

He smiled, cutting another piece of nearly raw meat, and the sight nauseated her. "My dearest, I was your first. The first inside you. The first to have a child with you."

"You are a rapist," she spat.

"Don't be foolish, that was Ares."

She stared at him, realizing he was utterly unhinged. "But *you* controlled his body."

He waved his hand. "A minor nuance. I will be your husband. And when Hades is gone, we can combine our kingdoms to be unstoppable. In the Underworld, the souls, without their mortal bodies, can be split as many times as I desire. We will have them erect statues, and the people can dance and sing our praises as they do on Earth. When our child is found, they will worship him as well. He will be a prince."

At the mention of her child, her cheeks flushed with fury. "Do not speak of my child. You had nothing to do with him!"

"I assure you I had *everything* to do with him. Tell me about him again, what happened that day."

"I told you," she spat. "He died."

"I refuse to believe that my child has met an untimely demise," he declared with repugnance. "My seed is too potent. I am not the father of lifeless offspring. Athena is diligently scouring the realms in search of him. Our suspicion is that a cunning and elusive Titan has clandestinely hidden him away." Casually, he popped a grape into his mouth from a platter of sparkling fruits piled high. "Now," he insisted, his tone demanding, "describe the boy's appearance."

She toyed with the peacock on her plate, its lifeless eyes seeming to observe her from across the table. As lifeless as her son's eyes that day. "He was beautiful—pale locks and dark, tiny lashes."

Zeus smiled. "*Our* son would be perfect." He grabbed her hand from across the table, squeezing her fingers tightly, and her hand convulsed beneath his grip. "I love you in a way I never thought I could love, in a way I have never loved before. Our child will unite the upper and lower world. He will sit on my throne."

She sat stiffly. "Hades is the father of any children I have."

He ignored her. "I can come down here in winter," he mused. "We will move the kingdom to Elysium. In the summer, you will stay with me on Olympus." He laughed with amusement. "My little scheme has worked out better than I planned. Your beloved's body will be reborn– a vessel for all my desires."

"The Underworld will never follow you! You have forgotten why the Underworld is so beautiful, why the souls are so happy. Hades. They love Hades for listening to their pain and allowing them to live a simple life. They will notice the difference. Souls are not as easily fooled as mortals."

He looked at her flippantly, lifting his arms wide. "But *darling*, I *am* Hades."

"You might wear his body, but you will *never* be him."

He seized her hair, tilting her head back, his finger tracing the contour of her jawline. "So much like your mother. So passionate and full of fury. I anticipate guiding you in the art of passion," he murmured. His intense gaze bore into hers. "I'm a masterful lover. You'll revel in the ecstasy I can offer."

"I will never want you," she promised, jerking her head from his grasp.

"You speak in such absolutes," he murmured. "Black or white; good or evil. Don't you know life and morals are best lived in the gray area? My sweet, naive Persephone," he chuckled, the sound grating on her nerves. "I am as much your husband as he is now. Do you not see the gift I offer? Your husband's strength, his allure, his very essence amplified by my powers. Embrace it, and you will bask in my glory."

"I will not!"

"You don't comprehend the game. Your mother raised you as delicate as the flowers you tend, incapable of grasping our ways." He carved another succulent slice of boar, the knife stained with blood, taking a bite and licking the crimson fluid from the blade. Her gaze lingered on the blood trickling down his chest, and he caught her watching. He laughed softly, toying with the knife, tilting it back and forth. "My brother is concerned you might just fuck me."

She gasped, her heart twisting painfully. "He's watching?"

He leaned forward, resting his chin against his hands. "Yes. Always. But not for much longer. You should be rejoicing. Your husband's body, with my power, will be ambrosia for you. I've set him free from the chains of his weakness, unshackled from the constraints of his foolish morality."

She stood abruptly from the table, turning her back to him, and she felt him move close behind her. Conflicted emotions tore at her, the love for her husband clashing violently with the horror of Zeus' possession. She longed to flee, to escape the wicked whispers that echoed in her mind, yet an inexplicable pull tethered her to this room. Hades. Her hands trembled, torn between wanting to strike down this monster and yearning to touch the man she loved.

She could feel the strength of his body pressing against her, and his hand trailed down her arm, entangling his fingers with hers. As Zeus spoke through him, his words were a poison dripping into her soul. "I can make him yours... for a time," he purred against her ear. "Imagine the ecstasy, his cock inside you, but it will be my power pulsing into your womb. But only if you surrender to me. Embrace the wickedness, and together, we shall revel in pleasures beyond mortal comprehension. It is still him touching you," he whispered, trailing his fingers down her breasts. "It is still his hands, his cock. It is not wrong to lay with your husband."

And God's help her, despite his wicked words, the touch of her husband's body against her comforted her, aroused her.

"I don't want you," she whispered.

Zeus' laughter reverberated, mocking her resolve. "Oh, dear Persephone, you want your husband very much. You think I don't know when a woman is aroused? You are dripping with need of him. I am him, and he is me. We are one. To reject me is to reject him. You cannot escape the inevitable." He spun her around to face him. "I know you ache for him," he said, taunting her with an intimate knowledge that sent a shiver down her spine. His hand reached between her legs. "Let me ease your pain," he whispered into her mouth.

A surge of anger overcame Persephone's fear. "No!" she exclaimed, her voice rising. "I won't let you destroy what we had. You're not him! You're just a parasite feeding off his soul."

Fury flashed in his eyes, but then a sinister smile replaced it. "Parasite? No, my wife. I am the catalyst, the key to unlocking the depths of his true potential. Just as I will unlock yours," he declared with an unsettling confidence. Studying her intently, Zeus continued, "I can feel his pain, his torment." She shut her eyes, shielding herself from his serpent-like words, tears tightly held against her eyelids. "Be with me. No more pain, no more heartache. Just an eternity of blissful darkness with the one you cherish beside you. Why make him suffer?"

The room seemed to shrink around her, a palpable weight on her shoulders. Zeus, cunningly aware of her vulnerability, preyed upon it. In that suffocating moment, she was forcefully reminded again of his true power—the uncanny ability to identify weaknesses and manipulate them to his advantage. Panic surged within her; she needed to escape from him immediately.

She looked around the room, and then her heart froze as she saw the large lemurian seed crystal filled with blood. "From my room on Olympus," Zeus explained with satisfaction. He smiled, tracing his fingers down her arm. "To think I kept that crystal for years thinking it was Demeter who witnessed the terror. Little did I realize it was her delicious daughter. How perfectly it planted the seed of distrust in your mind. The only soulmates in the Underworld will be you and I. When I take command, the Mourning Fields will be eradicated. We do not need to put the souls back together."

"You have meddled in my life before I was even born." Her voice trembled. "And it stops now! I won't let you stop me from uniting the souls!"

His facade of seduction gave way to fury. "Stubborn fool! You cannot save him. Your love blinds you to the ecstasy that awaits you. Reject me, and you reject him." He pushed her down on the bed. "Submit to me! Submit to your king!"

Her eyes locked onto her husband's face, his features contorted between the agony of possession and the familiarity of the man she loved.

He laughed harshly. "The longer you resist, the more he suffers, the more his soul unravels as he fights me."

She felt a pull, a magnetic force drawing her to him, compelling her to submit to the twisted promise. *I love you*, she whispered to his consciousness.

He fell back suddenly, grunting. Scratches appeared across his chest, and Hades' face twisted in a macabre grin. "Your husband–" He grimaced. "He is trying to claw his way to the surface."

She stared down in horror as she saw blood welling from the marks. "Hades?"

His grip tightened around her. "You will surrender every time, Persephone. I know it, and my brother knows it."

His dark eyes shimmered with tears as he looked down at her.

Persephone. I am dying.

"Do not leave me alone," she cried.

He grabbed around her wrist. "Don't fucking talk to him," he snarled. "You are mine!"

His golden eyes flickered with a glimmer of purple resistance, a desperate struggle against the wicked presence that ensnared him. Persephone's heart leaped at the flicker of recognition.

"No!" Hades growled, the words a guttural battle cry, as he clawed at his own chest. His body trembled. "Get out of me! Leave her alone!" Hades' fingers were vicious, with long claws tearing and ripping into his own flesh.

Zeus snarled in frustration as Hades' eyes flashed golden. "You weak fool! You are mine!" Zeus roared.

Golden dust flew across the room as her husband's eyes, now a battleground between darkness and fleeting clarity, locked onto Persephone's with a desperate plea. "Run," he rasped, a sliver of his true self surfacing.

Persephone leaped from the bed, torn as Hades and Zeus fought an internal struggle. As his eyes flashed gold and purple, she lifted her hands and summoned that darkness within her. With an unholy cry, she began to tear apart the room, screaming her rage, her sorrow, her love, until a chunk of the wall hit her head, and she fell into darkness.

CHAPTER 27
HIDING

Persephone was dreaming, falling in and out of consciousness. She was a child, and her mother was stroking her hair.

"I am scared, mother," the child Persephone whispered.

Demeter leaned forward, kissing her forehead. "Do not be afraid of the dark." But her voice was another's, and Persephone drew back in fear as she saw dark, gleaming eyes staring back at her. "Persephone," the stranger whispered, "do not be afraid. There is something I must tell you."

Suddenly, Persephone was in the forest giving birth, her baby cold and still. As her mind rejected the agonizing memory, the image split and shattered like glass, tearing at her heart as it crumbled from her dreams. She was married to Hades, hating him, loving him, and grieving him. Shivers wracked her body, and she watched him die, bleeding in her arms as a forest of pomegranate trees burst from the ground, all connected by a single root that grew from her own heart.

She saw it suddenly in the distance, in the void, a single dangling cord sparkling amid the darkness, and as she reached for it, she began to fall, descending into darkness, deep into oblivion, into death.

Rough hands were on her shoulders, shaking her urgently. "Persephone," his voice called. "Persephone, wake up!"

She gasped, air rushing into her lungs, her heart pounding wildly beneath her ribs. Strong arms encircled her, and she looked up to see Hades staring down at her. He gave a shaky exhale.

"Thank Gaia, you are awake," he murmured, bringing her tightly against his chest.

"What happened?" she asked in a trembling breath, reveling in the feel of his strong arms wrapped around her. Shamefully, she could not bring herself to question if it was Hades or Zeus. She needed it to be Hades, and for a moment, she would allow herself this weakness.

"You blasted an entire room of the castle into pieces. Zeus fled before he hit the ground. Thankfully, Ares was there to yank you from the room."

She glanced over to see the War God polishing his sword with an unhurried air. She nodded at him in thanks, and he returned a brief nod, a slight smile curving his lips.

Suddenly, a thought occurred to her, and she grasped at his clothes. "Are you hurt?" she asked urgently. "Did I hurt you?"

"Shh," he murmured, pulling her hands down his mouth to kiss the tips of her fingers. "Do not distress yourself so." She saw Hades cast Ares a glance, who stood slowly and casually strode away from the couple. He stared down at her and then closed his eyes tightly. "I've been so foolish to think I could conquer this. He holds custody of me now, and my free will is almost gone. I love you so much."

"And I love you." His words held regret, and they made her heart accelerate with dread. He seemed so far from her, so distant. Untouchable. Resigned. Her grip tightened as though she could force him to stay near her.

He looked down at her again, and his mouth was set in a tight line. "And in love, mortals and Gods are fools. I have been far too foolish, allowing my love for you to make me selfish, knowing what I needed to do but unwilling to do it. I can no longer let my love blind me to what is right. I am ready now."

Hades glanced behind his shoulder, and Persephone suddenly sat up.

They were lying in a field of poppies at the entrance of Hypnos' cave. She stood, pushing herself from the ground and locking her knees so that her shaking legs did not give way beneath her.

"What aren't you telling me? What are we doing here?"

Hades stood slowly, facing the entrance of the cave. Hypnos was gliding from the darkness toward them. Persephone started forward, but Hades placed his hand on her forearm, both a shackle and a comforting gesture.

"Take her somewhere safe," Hades addressed the God of Sleep. "A place where I cannot find her. Promise me."

"What!" Persephone cried.

"It shall be done." Hypnos' voice was quiet behind the veil. "Is there anywhere she should not venture?"

"You can take her above; you can keep her below. But keep her safe, for she is no longer with me. Make sure she is far beyond my reach."

"Has it progressed that far then?" Hypnos asked softly.

"Yes. Zeus will not stay away long. Hide her somewhere so she will not be harmed. We haven't much time."

Persephone's face was flushed crimson with anger and betrayal. "You have no right. I decide where I go, and I am not leaving you. I will not be forced to go. I will not be forced to go somewhere I do not wish to be. I have had enough people telling me what to do!"

"You will not die because of me."

"So I am to let you die instead?" she asked with an incredulous laugh. "I am your wife; I will not leave you!"

"He is right," Ares' voice said behind her. "Zeus is entirely in control of him. You cannot stay with Hades."

Persephone wheeled on her heel, giving the War God a furious look. "Stay out of this, Ares! This does not concern you." She whirled around to face Hades. "You think I will just go that easily, that I will just let you walk alone back to your death? You think so little of me?"

"Oh no, my sweet darling, "Hades said, his voice soft and sad. "I know you would not. I know you would follow me into the darkness until it swept both of us away. You are brave and loyal, and that is why I know I can take no chances." He kept one hand firmly on her arm and raised his other. A cup appeared in his palm, and dark mist flowed from the goblet. She recognized the water of the Lethe with shocked dread.

She became a wild animal. "No," she cried, fighting him wildly. "No! You will not take my memories!"

"If I do not, you will come back to me."

Ares' powerful arms abruptly seized her from behind, and she watched Hades move nearer, eerily similar to her wedding night but so different. Now, she would die for him, but instead, she would have to watch him die. No, he'd be far away from her when it happened, and she'd never get to see him, let alone embrace him as he breathed his final breaths. He would die alone, and she would be abandoned with not even the memory of love within her.

As she struggled violently against the enormous God restraining her, cold perspiration streamed down her brow, and suddenly, she felt the fire scorch down her flesh, and Ares drew back, gasping in pain. She let out a little cry of despair and fled across the field, dashing through the wild poppies like a wounded deer.

She saw the Lethe ahead, and a dark figure stood near the river's edge, watching her. Hades. He would never let her escape. She halted abruptly and stared at him, gasping for breath.

He extended his hands.

"Come, Persephone," he cajoled. "I will not force the Lethe water upon you. I only wish to speak with you. Trust me, just a little longer."

She did not move, eyeing him warily. "I will not agree to it. I will never agree to it. I will not drink from that cup."

"I know," he answered softly. "I should not have tried to force you. Just let me talk to you." She still didn't move. "Please."

She'd never know if she was compelled or if responding to his request was as natural as beating one's heart; it simply had to be. She placed her hand into his when she reached him, and he curled his fingers around her wrist. Together, they walked along the river's edge until they reached a large, jutting rock. They might have been a young couple simply enjoying a stroll, as she had so often seen mortal lovers do. But such uncomplicated pleasure was never to be their fate. Happiness had never been theirs to keep.

The water of the Lethe was calm and smooth, and the tranquility of it filled her with a terrible emptiness. A river should be bursting with life, flowing with the essence of it; instead, it was still, empty, and endless. As she would be. She pressed her body close to his, reassuring herself that he was still there. His body was still solid, but his flesh was cold against hers. Dying, her mind whispered, he was dying.

"I do not want to be as empty and still as these waters," she said quietly.

"You could never be empty. Life flows within you and always has. But your memories of me are no longer safe." His voice was a dark whisper in the stillness, and she shivered against him.

"I would rather live in Chaos with you than have no memory of our lives. I would rather suffer together than live a blissful existence alone."

"You would rather be together in Hell?"

"Yes! If you are in the light, that is where I will dwell. If you are in darkness, that is where I will live. I do not want to be without you!" She turned and lifted her hands, bringing his face against hers. She leaned her forehead against his, tears falling from her eyes. "And if you are nothing, I'll be nothing, too. Do not do this. Do not separate us. My soul is tied to yours; no matter what you do, you cannot alter that. My cord is interwoven with yours."

"Persephone," he whispered. He brushed his lips against her face, and she closed her eyes at the touch of his mouth on her flesh. "Persephone, I cannot let you be nothing. My very soul rejects such a thought. The knowledge that you may survive is the only thing..." His voice broke off abruptly, and she tried to lean back to look at him, but he held her tightly against him. "It is the only thing that brings me peace." He bent, kissing each eyelid, the tip of her nose, until he finally reached her lips.

When his lips touched hers, she gave a shuddering breath of pleasure. At first, it was just the barest touch of his mouth against hers, as though he feared the contact. But at the first touch of his tongue against the seam of her mouth, she gave a quiet whimper and opened her lips against his. And it was so very much like what she had dreamed and missed for so long that she was lost in it. Lost in the taste of him, the feel of his tongue against hers, the grip of his hands against her body.

She did not notice until it was too late that tendrils of mist were flowing from her mouth to his. He was taking her memories. All arousal fled her as she was suffused with panic. Tears streamed from her eyes as she strained against him, but he was unyielding, refusing to let her take her mouth from his, even when she bit hard, tasting their blood in her mouth. She tried to bring forth that blistering power again, but all she could feel was overwhelming panic as memories slipped from her mind.

The mist flowed endlessly from her till her heart violently clenched as the last memory of him was wrenched from her, and his lips finally released her. She could feel her chest constricting, a terrible, heavy weight pressing against her body for something she could not remember, but it was a terrible pain, this absence of memory. Her eyes dilated as she stared up at the beautiful, dark angel that held her in his arms. He was so sad, with tears in his eyes as he stared down at her.

"I am a casualty of war," he whispered. "Tomorrow, begin again. When the sun rises, know that, in the end, I finally found the courage to let you go. May you do the same when our paths cross. Sacrifice is the highest form of love."

His voice was the last sound she heard as she fell into a dreamless slumber.

He sat by the river, holding her in his arms, as he stared ahead at the endless flow of the Lethe—empty, infinite, and pointless, so much like his own existence. He had lived for so long and, for a brief moment, had held eternity in his palm. And how he had squandered that time. No, worse, he had committed atrocities, allowing himself to be manipulated by a master puppeteer. How many precious seconds had been wasted on what had never mattered? In his final moments, he held what truly gave his life its purpose, and she no longer remembered him. But he could remember her and fight to protect her from what was coming. It was enough, he told himself, cursed monster that he was; it had to be enough.

He traced the soft edge of her jaw before standing abruptly, carrying her in his arms as he made his way back to Hypnos' cave. Ares stood on the outskirts of the field but grew alert at the sight of Hades. The War God followed close on his heels as Hades laid Persephone gently onto the field of soft, rubied poppies. The King of Death lifted his hand, and a thin golden thread appeared, linked from her heart to his. Then he lifted his hand into the air, and the blue flame sword appeared in his grasp.

"What are you doing?" Ares asked in a harsh voice.

"I must cut our soul connection. Otherwise, I will find her again."

Ares moved around quickly, standing between Hades and Persephone, the shimmering golden thread between them. "You cannot do that! That is lunacy."

Hades' gaze narrowed. "You were agreeable enough about removing her memories."

"That was different. This is permanent. You and I both know she is not the first to have her memories taken, but to sever a cord connection, you know the danger of that. You've seen it firsthand with the mortals! It is irrevocable. It could shatter her mind and yours!"

"You think I do not know that?" Hades replied, his voice cold, the blue flame mirrored in his black eyes like a living entity. "But she will not be safe without removing all traces of me."

"Safe?" Ares laughed. "Gods, at least give her the choice! You would cut her soulmate tie? You would selfishly make the choice when, as you said, she wants to go through Hell and back with you? You have not changed from the God on the mountain all those years ago if you sever her from this connection, and you cannot mend it once it's broken."

"And what am I supposed to do!" Hades yelled, his voice rough, his chest heaving with the power of his emotion. "Look at what I have put her through. Look at what has happened all because of me. When I die, Zeus will never stop using me to find and destroy her. This bond between us is cursed and has only ever brought her pain. She will be better without it. I need her to survive."

"She may survive, but she will not be living! She will be dead inside, having no memories of your love. You are a fool if you think this will protect her from Zeus. He will kill her in front of you, and she will die without a trace of the happiness you both shared. You are so desperate to save her that you will destroy her." Ares turned to see Hypnos standing silently at the entrance of his cave, watching the discussion. "Don't just stand there, you fucking ghost! Tell him I am right!"

Hypnos glided forward with no trace of hurry in his movements. He stood beside Ares, staring down at Persephone. "Much as I hate to agree with the butcher, I believe you know what he says is true. The connection between you has brought much pain, but from suffering comes a powerful bond that not even death can destroy. Look at the cord, Your Highness; does it look tainted to you? It still glows as brightly and powerfully as the day it was constructed. Why do you believe that is? That link has never been broken or tarnished despite all that has happened. You must not cut your ties with her."

The blue fire grew in Hades' eyes until his pupils gleamed with sapphire power, his gaze filled by the strength of the sword. The dazzling cord shimmered between them, delicate, frail, and forever, and Hades approached it, gazing at its splendor. His eyes dropped down at the sleeping Persephone, and his face softened. Hades clenched his fist, and the sword vanished. He bent down, kneeling beside her in the fields of Hypnos' poppies. As he opened his palm, a thin golden ring appeared in the center, a more delicate counterpart of his own. The golden skull's rubied eyes glittered as he slid the ring onto her finger, over her wedding ring.

"This ring signifies that you are the legitimate heir to this world." He traced the contours of her hand, lifting it to his mouth. For a long moment, he merely sat beside her in the quiet night, holding her hand against his chest, letting his eyes take in the sight of her lying in the field of flowers, this Goddess of the Spring. "How many times can you say I love you?" He whispered the words softly so that only she could hear them. "A lifetime is not enough."

He thought of the Cyclops' words, and a grim smile curled his mouth. "The longer you live, the more you cling to life. Goodbye, my beautiful wife. Forgive me for all I have done and all that I still will do." He lifted her into his arms and bent once more, lightly touching her lips with his own. When he finally stood, his face was empty, a careful blank mask as he faced the Gods of Sleep and War.

"As long as our spirits are linked, I shall look for her—for the rest of my days, whatever remains of them. You both must make certain I do not find her. I must return now." His eyes moved again to Persephone, and the careful mask slipped, revealing a burning anguish that stole Ares' breath away. "If something happens to her, Hypnos, I won't be the only one with a death sentence hanging over my head."

With those words, the King of the Dead vanished. As the scent of poppies wafted gently in the night air, the God of Sleep and War stood over the slumbering Goddess of Spring, but Ares' gaze was fixed on Hypnos.

"Where are you going to take her?"

Hypnos raised his head as though contemplating the night sky. "To the Dark One."

Ares' scowl became even more fierce. "Who is he?"

"She," Hypnos corrected serenely.

"Who is *she*? And will Persephone be safe there?"

"Safe?" Hypnos repeated it as though tasting the word. "Oh no, she will not be safe. In fact, she will be decidedly unsafe. It will be precisely what she needs." Hypnos bent and lifted Persephone easily in his arms, already moving towards the cave. "Come, young butcher. Your adventure in the Underworld is about to begin."

CHAPTER 28
THE CAT & THE WITCH

S he was warm, cocooned in blankets, and a gentle, rhythmic noise lulled her deeper into sleep. The fragrant scent of herbs tickled her nostrils; the smell was soothing, adding to her sense of tranquility. She knew she should get up and help her mother with the chores, but a little longer in bed wouldn't hurt anything. Persephone snuggled deeper into the blankets, turning onto her side, when suddenly her eyes shot open as tiny talons dug ferociously into the flesh of her arm.

"Ow!" she cried, her eyes jolting open to stare into an amber-colored gaze.

The cat's coat was a beautiful, deep black, like that of a raven's wing, and it looked at her with haughty disdain, uncaring of the small, bleeding punctures it had left on her flesh. Persephone stroked the cat's face, and it closed its eyes, resuming its soothing purring once more. The claws were retracted as the feline presumably determined Persephone had been suitably punished for having disrupted its slumber.

"How did you get into the temple?" she asked softly.

Her mother did not care for cats, as they often dug and disrupted her plants, but Persephone had a fondness for felines. Perhaps it was their disdain for the rules that amused her so much. If she had her way, she would let them move into the temple. Her eyes widened in surprise as she glanced at the blankets covering her. She fingered the soft, ancient quilt that had been patched in many areas, giving it a haphazard appearance. The handiwork had been very poor indeed, and her mother would surely not have tolerated such shoddy work. Persephone surveyed the room in which she had been sleeping.

"What–?" Persephone murmured in confusion.

She was in a twin-size bed, the mattress made of hay. The room was small and cluttered; bookshelves were stuffed with strange containers of various shapes and sizes, and the books, which should have lined their shelves, lay open in haphazard piles on the floor as though the reader had simply been too busy searching through the pages to bother putting them back. Dried herbs hung from the ceiling, dangling to meet the enormous stacks of papers that littered the room.

It reminded Persephone of a cave, with the stalactites and stalagmites that grew from the ceiling and ground to meet in the middle. But when had she been in a cave before? She brought her hand to her head, an intense pain tearing through her mind at the memory, and she let out a murmur of distress, closing her eyes tightly. Breathing deeply, she took in the scent of incense and rosemary that seemed to fill the chamber.

"Is Calypso bothering you?"

Persephone's eyes shot open and took in the young woman who stood in the doorway. Long, ebony hair curled past her hips, and her skin was as pale as the moon. Persephone blushed as she realized the woman was entirely naked, her curvaceous body on full display. Lush breasts with dark nipples gave way to a narrow waist, culminating in the lovely curve of womanly hips and a patch of black hair covering her maidenly parts.

In one hand, she held aloft a large torch, with which she proceeded to light various candles around the room, which to Persephone seemed exceedingly dangerous considering the clutter that filled the tiny space. As the woman settled the torch into a sconce, she turned to survey the shelves with a slight frown, yanking a bottle from the shelf. Dust mites danced about the room like flowers on a fresh spring morning.

"I've been looking for this," she hissed in an ominous voice, shooting Persephone an accusatory glance. It took her a moment to realize the woman was looking at the cat. The ebony-haired stranger shook the jar emphatically, jangling the assortment of crows' feet within. "Move my things again, Calypso, and I will see about using cats' feet next time!"

But the cat merely yawned, unimpressed by the show of fury.

"That cat has become an absolute menace," she muttered darkly.

The woman's golden eyes flitted back to Persephone again, and Persephone had the startled thought that they were an identical shade and shape as Calypso's. Even the pupil was similar, almost vertical. She turned abruptly, giving Persephone a scandalous view of her posterior as she bent to retrieve a crumpled robe from the floor. After loosely securing it around herself, she unceremoniously plopped down on the end of Persephone's bed. The cat immediately moved to its mistress, curling contentedly in her lap. A pale hand stroked the edge of an ear distractedly.

"Sleep well?" Her voice was husky—a soothing, sensual sound. Persephone opened her mouth to answer, but she had the sneaking suspicion she was asking Calypso. She tucked a piece of hair behind her ear self-consciously as identical sets of golden eyes surveyed her with keen interest.

Persephone cleared her throat. "Where am I?"

"Where? You are with me."

"Um– but where are you? I mean, we?" Persephone blushed as she stumbled over her words. "I mean, where *are* we?"

The woman leaned forward suddenly, brushing her hand against Persephone's forehead. Persephone felt a strange tingling in her head like a buzzing bee, and the sensation was both unpleasant and obnoxious. The beautiful woman frowned at her.

"What is the last thing you remember?"

Persephone's forehead furrowed as she tried to sort through her throbbing head. "I remember... I remember it was raining. It was so hot, and I felt stifled. And there was something that was calling to me— something on the wind. It led me to a field. And there was a golden flower, and then..."

"And then?"

"And then, nothing." Persephone searched her mind, panicking at the emptiness that met her. The more she tried to recall, the tighter the pain wrapped around her until it was like a vise on her brain. Persephone lifted her hands to her head, closing her eyes tightly. "What is wrong with me? Did I hit my head?"

Cool hands wrapped around her own. "There is no need to strain yourself," the soothing voice said. "You had an injury, little bird, but we will soon get you as right as rain."

Persephone opened her eyes once more, searching the room before landing on the golden eyes that stared so intently into her own.

"Who did you say you were again?"

"I didn't."

"Oh," Persephone said, discomforted. "Well, will you? That is, will you say who you are?"

The cat and the woman merely continued to stare, and Persephone felt herself flushing at their strange, intent regard. She shifted uncomfortably on the bed, the pillow lumpy against her back. Distractedly, Persephone reached behind her, searching for the source of the lumpiness, to discover a large satchel of dried herbs.

The black-haired woman quickly snatched the herbs from her hands. "You found them! I wondered where I had placed them. What a clever girl you are." She grinned, securing the herbs into a pocket of her robe. "I am Hecate, and you are in my cave in the Underworld."

Persephone gaped at her, thinking she had misheard her. But Hecate merely smiled serenely back at her. "The Underworld! But that cannot be. Why would I be in the Underworld?"

"You have been placed under my guidance to polish up your magic and potion skills."

"My mother sent me to you?" she asked, disbelief edging her voice.

Hecate grunted. "I was to take you away from the watchful eyes of the malevolent Olympians. I was coming to collect you when you tripped and fell. Thankfully, not a scratch on your lovely face."

A sly smile curled Hecate's lips, and Persephone wasn't sure if she was making fun of her or not. Compared to this beautiful Goddess, Persephone felt plain and unworldly. And Persephone wasn't quite sure if she liked Hecate. There was something disconcerting in those golden eyes. Hecate gave a quiet laugh as though she could read Persephone's mind and was amused by it.

"Why would my mother ask a stranger to train me?"

"A stranger!" Hecate scoffed, standing up abruptly, much to the chagrin of Calypso, who jumped quickly to the ground with an indignant hiss. "I am no stranger. Your mother has grown and given me herbs for my potions for years. I am doing her a favor and will teach you great magic in return. You should be grateful. You *will* be grateful.

"Now, no more talks of aching heads." Hecate leaned forward, touching two fingers to Persephone's temple, and the pain instantly vanished. "We have more important things to do than discuss your throbbing mind. Throbbing minds, like any other throbbing organs, do us little good." Hecate was already moving to the door, and Persephone hurried to follow, stumbling slightly as she stood.

"But then, you are a Goddess, are you not?" Persephone called to her, still uncertain of whom she spoke to.

"My dear girl," Hecate said, turning in the doorway, her profile in shadow, those enigmatic golden eyes lowered. "I am made of bones and ghosts and the deepest shadow of the darkest night. Hecate, the Necromancer; Maiden; Mother; Crone; Guardian of Crossroads. I am the Witch of All the Night, the Wielder of the Shadowed, Forbidden Magic." The golden eyes lifted, and for a moment, Persephone was staring into the face of an ancient woman with drooping, wrinkled eyes. Persephone blinked, and Hecate was young and beautiful once more. The witch smiled. "You could not be in better hands."

Persephone followed behind Hecate through a narrow, cluttered hall. More books and trinkets lined the corridors, and Persephone felt claustrophobic, almost suffocating in the confined spaces. Finally, they stepped into a larger living area. Hecate had called it a cave, but it had been so completely transformed that it appeared more like a mortal's house. Well, perhaps not completely like a mortal's house. Traces of magic made it quite clear that this was not a human dwelling.

The hearth was filled with a roaring fire, with hues of purple and pink sometimes appearing in the crimson glow. A giant black pot simmered over the flames, and Persephone had a sinking feeling that whatever was bubbling inside was likely their breakfast. The outside of the pot appeared very stained indeed, and she could not imagine Hecate adhering to any rule of cleanliness. Persephone brushed up against the wall, and an outraged hoot caused her to fall back. A tiny, feathered owl glared at her indignantly, clearly having made a home within one of the cluttered shelves.

"I am so sorry," Persephone murmured anxiously, "but I did not know you were there!"

The owl ruffled his feathers and settled more securely on his perch. Persephone's eyes narrowed at the writing on the spine of the book: *Mastery of the corpse: re-amination of the unanimated.* And then scribbled in more frantic, sloppy writing: *Did not work, do not open.*

"Pay no attention to Agraulus," Hecate was saying. "At his age, you can hardly expect him to be polite. Now come, help me dry some herbs by the fire, and we can have a little chat."

Persephone stepped further into the room. Cats of all shapes and sizes sat on every surface of the space. The large wooden table in the center of the room was covered with stones and scrolls, and several of the felines were pawing at them with keen interest. Hecate shooed a few of the cats away before sitting on a tattered chaise, and two large black dogs hurried to lay at her feet. Persephone noticed that each of them had the gleaming, golden eyes of their mistress. In fact, she noticed with a shudder that every animal in the room had the same golden gaze.

"You may sit where you like," Hecate was saying. "Just mind who you sit on. Basil would not enjoy it, and I must admit, you would not enjoy sitting on Basil."

The sight of two cats scratching at a book that appeared to be fighting back by hissing green sparks diverted Persephone's attention from Hecate. "Basil?" Persephone repeated, feeling like a dimwit. "Which one is Basil?"

Hecate jerked her head towards the fire. "That is Basil."

An enormous black snake was coiled near the fireplace, clearly enjoying the warmth. At the sound of her name, a gleaming, golden eye opened lazily, followed by a slither of her tiny, pink-forked tongue.

"Oh," Persephone said a little breathlessly. "I haven't had many occasions to see such a large snake before."

Hecate was reading one of the scrolls from the table with a frown, scribbling notations. She looked up, and her reed continued writing independently as Hecate clasped both her hands under her chin thoughtfully.

"Of course, how rude of me not to introduce you. Basil, this is Persephone. You must be nice to her, as she hasn't had much occasion to meet one of your brethren." Once more, the golden eye opened and then closed. "Well, there you have it." Persephone glanced at Hecate, baffled. The witch grasped the reed, which attempted to pull free of her grip, clearly intent on resuming its writing without the help of its mistress. "Go on then; Basil won't mind if you pet her."

Persephone sat on the thick, woolen rug before the fireplace, gently stroking the smooth scales of the snake. "You are very beautiful, Basil," Persephone said softly. Basil once again admitted her small pink tongue, acknowledging the compliment.

"Here," Hecate said. She passed her a stout, spiced wine with a sprig of a leafy plant on the side of the goblet.

Persephone tasted the leaf, delighted by its cool, aromatic flavor. "What is this?"

Hecate smiled coyly, and she took a large sip of her own wine. "You do not recognize it?"

"No," Persephone replied, studying the small green leaf. "Should I?"

"That is a mint leaf. It's a new plant, I believe, and delicious in drinks. But one must be careful with mint; it has a tendency to outgrow its confines rather quickly, making it a bit of a pest. A rather unfortunate trait, do you not think?"

"A new plant," Persephone mused, lifting the leaf. "Did my mother make it?"

"Not exactly. You could say that it turned up somewhat unexpectedly."

Persephone's eyes moved to the large hearth of the fireplace. Candles, stones, and a small box with a goblet on top stood in the center.

"That is my altar," Hecate said, once more giving Persephone the impression that she was able to read her mind.

"Oh," Persephone said, understanding. "Where you can commune with the humans that pray to you in the shrines. The Olympians have that, too."

Hecate's eyes flashed with anger. "Do not compare me with that drivel. I have no shrines, little bird. Those who need me may seek me in their kitchen as they break their fast or in their bed, in the dark of night, when wicked thoughts fill their mind."

"And what do they pray to you for?" Persephone asked breathlessly, taken aback by her fierceness.

"It depends," Hecate murmured as she chewed the mint leaf rather viciously. "Some seek me so that I may help them attain that which should not and cannot belong to them. Those are the ones who regret calling on me, but once my name is uttered, the call cannot be revoked. Then, there are others—so many others—who seek me because they need guidance and have nowhere left to turn. When all the golden Goddesses have turned their backs on them, they come to me, the Witch of the Shadows. In the end, I assist them all, though not always in the way they imagined. Transformation is painful, even for those pure of heart, and it takes unintended turns. Sometimes, even I do not know how it will end."

Persephone watched her warily. "But why must it be painful?"

"Because it is a form of death, and death is always painful. You, too, may one day have such a shrine."

Persephone shook her head. "I cannot imagine that mortals will ever seek such guidance from me."

"Is there nothing transformative that has happened in your life? No darkness that lingers within you?"

"Nothing," Persephone answered immediately. "Nothing has ever happened to me."

"Ah, perhaps I am mistaken then. You are just a gentle Goddess of the

Spring; there is no darkness hovering at the edge of your soul."

They sat in silence for a little, Persephone letting the warmth of the drink fill her, warding off the chill that Hecate's words had instilled. Rain spattered somewhere near, and all the animals seemed to hunker down in the warm, protective enclave, settling in for a nap as the weather raged outside around them. Persephone glanced about the room at the cobwebs hanging from the ceiling. Little spiders were enjoying the quiet morning, spinning intricate webs in the corner of the cave. Persephone's eyes began to drift closed—the wine and warmth of the fire, the gentle scratch of the reed as it wrote, the beautiful angel with the sad, dark eyes. Her chest suddenly tightened painfully, and Persephone jerked, clutching her hand to her heart.

"Something wrong, dear?" Hecate asked without looking up.

"No, no, nothing is wrong." Persephone rubbed her chest. "It just aches a little."

"In your heart? Perhaps it is heartache."

"No," Persephone said with a laugh that was tinged with just a little bitterness. "There is no one in my life for my heart to ache for. Just my mother and myself." Persephone frowned as she thought of her mother. "Perhaps I should go home. Mother will be worried."

"Nonsense, duckling. Sit here and grow some sage; I am almost out. Your mother will be glad you are with me."

"I still find it hard to understand why she sent me here without saying anything." Persephone weaved her hands together, growing a lovely bouquet of green sage. Hecate snapped her fingers, and the sage floated towards her. She wrapped her fingers along the stem, examining the plant carefully. Apparently, it passed inspection, for she laid it on the cluttered table.

"Sage purifies the air when burned; did you know that?"

Persephone frowned. "Mother and I do not burn plants."

"Oh, don't you?" Hecate asked with a laugh. "Well, that will change. Grow me some lavender."

Persephone complied, studying the fragrant purple flowers that appeared in her hands. She touched the soft, purple petals thoughtfully.

Hecate snapped her fingers, and once more, the bouquet was wrenched from her hands, floating towards the witch as several cats attempted to swipe at the herbs as they whizzed past. As the flowers dropped to the table, a glistening rock tumbled from the bouquet.

Hecate held it up to the light. "Amethyst," she murmured. Her golden eyes flashed at Persephone. "Do you often grow crystals with your flowers?"

Persephone looked bewildered. "No, never. I have no idea how that got in there."

"How interesting," Hecate said lightly, setting the crystal amongst the herbs. "Now grow me some mugwort."

The time passed, with Hecate demanding certain herbs and Persephone growing them. Hecate would tell her the properties of each of the plants—secret uses that Persephone had never heard of. Herbs for casting spells, herbs for curses, and herbs and flowers for the lightest and darkest magic.

"When you mix the rosemary with thyme under the full moon, it creates a powerful aphrodisiac. However, you must cut the leaves with the edge of your blade, or your potion will make the drinker grow body hair in the most unsightly of places. You must learn precision if you wish to spellcast. The slightest alteration, the wrong turn, may have deadly consequences. Carelessness cannot be tolerated. Here." Hecate had bent and tossed a crumpled scroll to Persephone. "See if you can follow this. If you do it correctly, your potion should be a thin green liquid by the end."

Persephone opened the thin, ancient paper and read the title of the spell. Elixir to cause pain. Persephone looked up, giving Hecate a dubious look. "Why would I want to make this?"

"Why?" Hecate asked, her dark brows arching ominously. "Because sometimes you must cause pain because sometimes you need a diversion, because sometimes you need to feel pain yourself in order to grow, and a potion is the safest way. Now stop asking questions and start brewing!" Hecate clapped, and the ingredients flew towards Persephone, landing on the table.

The Goddess of Spring wrinkled her nose as she surveyed what was required. Scale of the Scylla, fermented liver of an enemy, hair of the

Hellhound, flower of the wolfsbane, two drops of the brewer's blood... Persephone stopped reading the list to glance at Hecate, who had already settled back onto her chaise, furiously writing again.

"Whose liver is this?" Persephone asked, holding up the tiny glass jar of watery brown tissue with disgust.

"As long as it's not yours, that's all you should worry about," Hecate responded without glancing up. "Brew! No more questions!"

Persephone sighed and then became engrossed in the spell. It was extraordinarily complex. The wolfsbane flower had to be drained precisely, its leaves cut with the edge of the knife and then added to a mixture of moon water and blood. Giving another sigh, Persephone held the knife to the skin of her forearm and, with a grimace, made a tiny cut, careful to let her blood first drain into a glass container before wrapping her arm. Time passed, and Persephone's stomach growled with hunger, but she dared not mention it before completing her potion. Finally, she reached the last stage, and she anxiously surveyed the tiny amount of green liquid at the bottom of the glass.

"Perfect," Hecate said behind her, snatching the vial from Persephone's fingers. "You are quite good at making potions. Have you ever done this before?"

"I have with poppies."

Persephone frowned, and it felt as though everything around her was moving slowly, like a dream slipping from her grasp. But she could never have made a spell with poppies. She had never even seen a poppy before; she must have read about them somewhere. This was reality, and the poppies were a dream. Hecate was watching her, those gleaming golden eyes seeing so much more than they should. Persephone brought a shaking hand to her forehead, wiping at the cool sweat on her brow before smiling at Hecate, who watched her with her unblinking cat-like stare.

"What I mean," Persephone continued, "is no; I have never done this before."

"How interesting," Hecate murmured. "There is a sister spell to this one." Hecate clapped her hands, and a scroll zoomed towards Persephone. She leaped up to grasp it from the air before it hurtled past her. Dust partially covered the title, and Persephone rubbed it away gently.

Elixir to Cause Pleasure. "I won't ask you to make this one today, but tell me, Persephone, which of these two spells do you think does more harm to the victim? Pain or pleasure?"

"Well," Persephone said slowly, "I would think the pain."

"Do you? What do you think causes soul growth? Enduring hardship or hiding behind enjoyment until one's soul is reduced to nothing more than a means of carnal pleasure? Adversity changes you and fortifies the very marrow of a person, changing their composition. It is like a tiny explosion of a star that comes back together to reform a new galaxy. There are those in this world whose greatest weakness is that they will refuse to allow pain to touch them, to allow themselves to suffer, to shatter. They have never given themselves permission to enter the shadowy area where we split apart before coming back together. It is a weakness to do that. A weakness that can be exploited if necessary."

"But wasn't that a potion for physical pain?"

Hecate shook her head. "I never said that. I said it was to *induce* pain." Hecate lifted her hand to Persephone's head. "The greatest pain lies here. It is where we keep our enduring sorrow, as well as a reminder of both the things we have lost and the things we do not want to lose. What would you be willing to die for? Life without pain is a selfish life. Pain comes with sacrifice, with putting the ones you love and the principles you stand for above yourself, above your very life."

"A creature that is fundamentally selfish will never comprehend it or be able to bear it. They will never be able to love, for in love, we make ourselves the most vulnerable. It is a strength that they could never recognize." She bottled Persephone's potion and quickly labeled it before tucking it into her robe. "Shall we break our fast?"

Persephone blinked at the abrupt change of topic but nodded eagerly, her stomach aching with hunger. Even the filthy pot could not dim her appetite. Hecate served them both from the cauldron that was still simmering over the flame. It held a thick, hearty stew, and Persephone was too hungry to care what it was made of. She took several quick gulps, burning her mouth, before turning to look at Hecate. The witch was watching Persephone speculatively, and Persephone blushed, wiping her mouth with her sleeve.

"Um," she began awkwardly, "do you like living down here?"

"The Underworld?"

"Yes! I mean, it seems like a rather dangerous place to live. You must have a lot of courage."

Hecate laughed. "It does not take courage to live here. There are many more dangerous things that lurk in the light; they have just learned to adopt a pretty face. I prefer the twisted beasts of the shadows. They do not pretend to be anything other than what they are."

"But King Hades, I have heard he is quite wicked. Does it not scare you to live in his realm?"

"Oh, he can be *quite* wicked, but I do not fear Pluto; after all, it was I who taught him his gift of shadow magic. In fact, he slept in the very bed you sleep in now when he was my pupil."

Persephone stared at her, overawed. "You taught him magic?"

"He became my lover, and in exchange, I gave him all my knowledge of the dark arts. He was a very adept pupil."

"Your lover!" Persephone's heart gave a rapid thump at the same time as her stomach, and she frowned at the unpleasant sensation. "And you were not frightened? I had heard that he was... dangerous."

"Oh, I was not frightened of him, but rather the other way around, I think a little. He was lost, almost shattered from what had transpired, and yet deep within him was a burning desire for revenge. He was filled with all manner of emotions." Hecate's eyes flamed. "It had been some time since I had met someone so broken and yet so filled with purpose. He needed someone to care for him, and I was more than happy to oblige."

"And so he convinced you to allow him to become your lover in exchange for your magic."

Hecate threw back her head, laughing loudly. "Again, you have it wrong. I convinced him. He was a virgin when I met him. I traded my secrets for his virginity. Yes," Hecate said, nodding her head at Persephone's wide eyes. "I mean exactly what I said. He was no longer a virgin, and I was once more milky-white and pure." Her smile was beautiful. "Now I am a virgin Goddess with children. Can you think how angry that makes Athena, she who preaches wisdom and yet places so much stock in an arbitrary piece of flesh between a woman's legs?"

"Erm," Persephone replied, as Hecate seemed to expect a response. "I suppose she considered it cheating?"

"Nonsense," Hecate replied with a wave of her hand. "I cast a spell, and now it is so. If my arm was severed and I grew myself another, is that cheating? Is it cheating when your flesh heals after an injury?" Hecate leaned forward, and there was fury in her golden gaze. "Why should any part of my value be determined by it? Why should it matter for any woman?"

"But Athena is a champion for women; she has often helped my mother and me."

"Athena, Artemis, and their ilk promote their anointed priggish club of chastity, falsely claiming to champion womenkind as innocent women like Medusa are punished for being raped. They will support a woman so long as she is virginal; meanwhile, they turn a blind eye to what occurs every day at the gates of Olympus—what their *king* does to innocents. The chaste Goddess who supports the tyranny of rapists. So, when I walk amongst them, and their eyes flood with anger, it is with great pleasure that they are aware of how easily that piece of precious flesh can be restored again and again and again."

"I have never heard someone speak of Athena with such dislike."

"I do not like hypocrites."

"You should be careful," Persephone said softly. "My mother told me that it is dangerous to speak ill of the Gods of Olympus."

"Why must I be careful? Will she put *my* head on a shield? I think not. Like all of them, they choose their victims carefully. They only fight those they know cannot fight back. I welcome them to try. I would crush their very hearts to dust."

Persephone considered her words. "You are right," Persephone said softly. "It is wrong to preach tolerance and then punish innocent women in the same breath. There is much I do not know of those who live on Olympus, and I was foolish not to consider that I do not fully understand their characters."

Hecate leaned back, her golden eyes gleaming in the shadows. "You admit when you are wrong. Rare for a Goddess from above."

"I hope I am not so ignorant as to not admit that there are many things I do not know."

Hecate made a hmphing noise, and it could have been agreement or indigestion. Persephone studied the flames in the hearth, their dancing hues mesmerizing. What a strange and unusual life the witch had lived. She had seen so much and knew so much more than Persephone. Hecate had been the lover of Hades. What must it have been like to have embraced such a powerful God in such a way—such a dark, enigmatic being? How did it feel to have a lover like him?

"Your face is flushed, sparrow. You shouldn't sit so near the fireplace."

"Oh, of course." Persephone leaned back, blushing more furiously at the strange turn of her thoughts. "What was he like?" she blurted out before she could think better of it.

"The King of the Dead, you mean, of course." The witch drank deeply from a silver goblet of wine that had appeared in her hand.

"Yes."

Hecate closed her eyes and smiled. "He was perfect. Pluto was a natural and so large. He was voracious. It is no wonder his brothers despise him."

"Why do you call him that?"

"That is his name; it is who he is. You have many questions about the God of the Dead; it is not good to remain ignorant." She outstretched her hand, and a thick book was pulled from the floor to land on Persephone's lap, dust flying like a tiny explosion. "I will leave you with an assignment. Read up on star divination. Astrologia." Hecate's eyes narrowed as she studied Persephone speculatively. "For instance, I can tell that you were born under the rule of Virgo."

"What does that mean?"

"Typical Virgo, "Hecate huffed. "Always demanding answers. Astrology extends far beyond the simple alignment of stars and planets; it is the very essence of the cosmos that shapes each of us." Hecate unrolled a circular chart adorned with celestial bodies. She carefully drew angles and lines to the various planets, her movements quick and sure. "This is your personal ephemeris, your birth chart," she explained, "a snapshot capturing your strengths, weaknesses, and the essence of your entire existence —a fixed moment in the grand continuum of time.

"Do not dare to dismiss astrology as nonsense; it's a profound discipline demanding years of dedicated study and mathematical understanding. Each astrological sign carries elemental and modal qualities, and within the cosmic ballet, major and minor aspects unfold—sextiles, trines, squares."

Intrigued, Persephone gently traced one of the lines. "What do these signify?" she asked. Hecate shooed away a cat who was attempting to nest on the chart.

"At the time of your birth, planetary alignments shape the narrative of our destinies," Hecate clarified, her gaze focused. "A planet's journey begins at zero degrees, marking the start of a new cycle, and concludes at twenty-nine degrees—the Anaretic degree, a fated realm signifying karmic endings. At this point, a soul has fulfilled its Earthly potential and is ready to transition to the next phase. To understand a person's birth chart is to comprehend the intricacies of their being—a key to their soul, revealing both their origin and inevitable conclusion." Hecate decisively rolled up the chart.

"Study this," she instructed, "for it holds a mirror to your inner self, providing profound insights." The witch had moved to one of the overflowing bookcases, shoving items aside until she made a noise of satisfaction as she pulled out several weathered scrolls. She shoved the large pile into Persephone's hands. "Here, take these too. These were some of Pluto's musings while he stayed here with me. Now, go and read while I finish wrapping the rest of the herbs. I have been in your company too long and require some solitude."

Persephone returned to her room. She surveyed the cluttered area with dismay and frowned before coming to a decision. Hecate would have to tolerate a little organization. She made the bed and then set about tidying the room as much as she could, organizing the stacks of books and scrolls, sneezing profusely as she dusted the bookcase. She was very careful with the contents of the shelves, making sure all the bottles were secure before touching them. Finally, when the room was a bit more tidy, she was able to settle onto the bed. Calypso joined her, his purring a soothing sound in the cozy space.

"You know, the persistent urge to organize is a Virgo compulsion," Hecate's voice called. "It would do you good to resist it now and then."

"I thought you wanted to be left alone," Persephone responded. A loud hmph was the only answer she received, and Persephone let out a quiet laugh, turning her attention back to the study material.

She spread open the books and scrolls, and after both she and Calypso finished sneezing from the dust, began reading. Pluto was the planet of change, secrets, death, and destruction. It also signifies rebirth and the soul's journey. A powerful connection to Pluto meant a journey of destruction and transformation. She shivered as she remembered Hecate's words. Along the pages of the book were occasional tiny handwritten notes, and Persephone turned the book so she could read more easily.

Am I worthy of redemption? Can an evil man be redeemed? The souls have run amok since their splitting. I will have twice the souls to sort now; on top of the horror, they die much faster than they did under the rule of Cronus. My punishment is certainly not undeserved. Twice the number of people and twice the work, all because of my weakness and hatred. I cannot grieve here much longer. If I am to be their king, then let me be a good king.

The scrolls revealed blueprints of how the souls would be organized and sorted. There was a list of who would be best suited for each task and a contract with three other individuals: Minos, Rhadamanthus, and Aeacus. She realized with shock that she was reading the history of how Hades had organized the Underworld, and the knowledge made her hands tremble. What a responsibility for a young God—or for any God, for that matter. Had he built the entire foundation of this world? What had he meant by the splitting of the souls? She read on, passage after passage, of Hades' plans for this kingdom. The palace of the Underworld would be built on neutral territory between two worlds, and the River Styx would be utilized for the safe passage of the souls from above.

Persephone traced the word **Charon**, which was written next to the river. There were passageways of laws that were written with heavy edits, clearly read again and again by the writer, and several of the scrolls contained final contracts. A contract between Hades and a king called Cocytus; a contract between Hades and the Goddesses of the Rivers. A tiny drawing of a three-headed dog lay in the corner of one page, and Persephone smiled at the depiction. The illustrator had clearly loved the tiny beast, and Persephone realized his name was depicted on the margins: **Cerberus**. There were drawings of the division of the kingdoms: Elysian Fields, Asphodel Meadows, and Tartarus. Persephone was captivated by his charming artwork of the first two, but she gasped as she turned to the rendition of Tartarus; it was horrible, and the images depicted bodies distorted in the throes of torture. Underneath was a passage:

The wicked need a place to live out their days after death—a place separated from the others. Tartarus. The souls must be protected at all costs.

Persephone leaned back, closing the book, overwhelmed. "How sad he was," she said to Calypso. She felt a strange kinship for this powerful king, who had once slept in this same humble bed. She stroked the blankets, which, knowing Hecate, had not been washed since Hades had slept there. "I hope you are happier now," she whispered, "wherever you are."

Time passed, and within weeks, Persephone was spellcasting. Hecate insisted she learn the ancient dialects and refused to translate the spells for her.

"If you cannot learn the language, you cannot perform the spell. Study or perish."

So, Persephone studied, learning the hard way what happened when one of Hecate's spells went wrong. Her hands were covered in burns, and her arms were scarred in some areas from magical cuts that did not heal as they normally should, but she was making fewer mistakes now; pain was the best teacher. Hecate also expected her to continue to study natal charts, and Persephone argued with her about this.

"Why must I study the stars?" Persephone complained. "I have not found them to be particularly useful."

"Foolish girl!" Hecate chided. "That is because you are horrible at it.

Everything that has happened and everything that will happen is written above. Only a fool discounts their knowledge. You will not only study the natal charts, but you will also learn to respect them."

And so she did. As the days went by, Persephone was content, if not happy. When she was alone, in her tiny room with Calypso, a strange melancholy would settle over her, and she would twist the ring on her finger, longing for something she herself did not understand.

One day, Persephone was introduced to Nyx, a beautiful, ancient Goddess whose gaze held the power of the Universe within them. At first, Persephone was shy around such a powerful being, but Nyx was like a calming balm, and her gentle nature coaxed Persephone from her natural reserve. Nyx began to visit the cave regularly and would help to teach Persephone as well. It astounded Persephone that such a powerful being would condescend to assist in the training of a trivial Goddess, but when she tried to question Hecate, the witch only laughed and said, "You're as suspicious as Hades! Why am I only gifted with suspicious pupils? Be grateful for the teachings."

They would sit just outside Hecate's cave as Nyx showed her how to weave shadows and how to call darkness from the void.

"It is all connected, Persephone. From light, there is shadow, and from shadow, there is light. They cannot exist without each other. All you must learn is how to manipulate the shades so that you can use them to your advantage. One day, it may be necessary for you to hide or even to hide others. You should be able to call the lightness or the shadows at your will. It begins as a tiny spark within yourself. Never let it control you; you control it; it is part of you, two sides of one coin. Call it to you; let it grow."

Nyx lifted her hand, and the dark Underworld exploded in a sudden flash of blinding light so powerful that Persephone feared she might lose consciousness. The moment passed quickly, and she stared in awe at the Goddess.

"I could never do that."

Nyx smiled. "You will do that... and more."

They would meditate for hours. "You must learn to be comfortable with the lightness and darkness within yourself. You do not trust yourself yet. Let go of the fear. Let yourself feel all the parts of your soul;

trust who you are."

And then, one day, it finally happened. While she was deep in meditation, Persephone could feel the perfect balance of her soul—all that was light in her, all that was dark—and she pulled upon both forces as she raised her hand, and the world exploded into a brief flash of blinding light before she pushed covering darkness over the land.

When the world righted again, Nyx was smiling at her. "How did that feel?"

Persephone was breathing rapidly as if she had just finished a race, but she returned the Goddess' grin. "That felt... good," she laughed, her voice incredulous.

Nyx taught her how to summon the power of sleep without using poppies. Persephone was reluctant to try, but Nyx assured her that she would be able to awaken any creature that Persephone had put to sleep. When they tried it on Hecate one afternoon, the witch awoke with a furious sputter, which quickly turned into laughter as she saw the terror on Persephone's face.

"Just don't do it again," Hecate muttered, but her eyes were sparkling with mischief as she and Nyx exchanged pleased grins. It both delighted and confused Persephone to see how invested they were in her education.

As time passed, Persephone began to notice a difference in the kingdom. While Hecate's cave remained cozy and protected, the Underworld outside was growing more chaotic. Lightning sparked and thundered in the greenish skies. A powerful, icy wind drifted through the land, and Persephone would sometimes see lines of guards on the rugged horizon. Hecate said they were looking for fugitives, but anytime Persephone left the cave, Hecate would wrap Persephone tightly in dark robes, casting a spell to make the Goddess' hair pale blonde and her face that of a human soul. "Just in case," she would reply vaguely when Persephone questioned her.

Hecate's own appearance was unpredictable; she would sometimes appear as a young child with mischievous eyes and at other times as an elderly, ancient lady with deep wrinkles obscuring her features.

"Do others not find it disconcerting when your appearance changes so rapidly?" Persephone asked when Hecate had walked into her bedroom one day, bowed over with age.

"Oh, yes," Hecate responded, a toothless grin on her face. "Imagine their displeasure when they go to bed with a nubile Goddess in her prime and wake up with *me*." The witch threw back her head, howling with laughter. "Oh, oh, oh," Hecate gasped out." You should have seen their faces; one of my lovers actually jumped from the window. He was fortunate that the tree was nearby, or he would have been smashed to bits. It's such a lovely way to get rid of a lover who overstays their welcome."

Persephone could well understand the shock, but she grew accustomed to Hecate's changeable appearance over time. In any case, the witch's gleaming, golden eyes and the danger hiding just beneath her surface would always be enough to identify her.

The witch began to lead her across the land, taking her a little further from her cave each time. Sometimes, she would merely take Persephone with her as she muttered ancient words or collected samples of the soil or horticulture. Other times, Hecate would simply stand, staring intently at visions Persephone could not see, and Persephone would practice meditation until the witch was finished.

On one trip, while Hecate was hobbling along as an elderly woman, the witch stopped suddenly and gestured wildly with her walking stick. At first, Persephone was concerned she was having some type of conniption but realized the witch was trying to draw Persephone's attention to the ground.

"This is where I want it."

"Oh." Persephone paused, glancing around. Hecate's train of thought moved quickly, and Persephone was frequently caught off guard by what she was saying. "Want what, exactly?"

"I have written a list for you." And she pulled out a lengthy, scribbled list from her robes. "We need crystals around this area to provide protection."

Persephone sighed, preparing for an argument. "But I cannot grow crystals."

Hecate simply frowned ferociously, pulling the sagging folds of her cheeks into a grimace, and continued on as if she had not spoken. "I want large Birch and Rowan trees made of obsidian, amethyst, and black tourmaline," the witch demanded. She toed the dirt beneath them, contemplating the soil. "Scatter them around the west to protect the cave. When you are finished, bring these herbs." She thrust the list into Persephone's hands.

"But what about the herbs I already grew?"

Hecate's sagging eyes bulged, and she waved her staff wildly. "They are putrid! They are measly! They would turn my spell sour!"

Persephone raised her hands in surrender. "All right, all right, I will grow you new ones!"

"I will also need some of the crystals as well for protection spells. Collect them and bring them back to me when you are finished." Though covered in folds of ancient flesh, the golden eyes flashed as dangerously as ever. "Do not return until my list is complete."

"But why does the cave need protection? I thought you said the Underworld was not dangerous," Persephone protested, perusing Hecate's extensive list with dismay.

"It is not dangerous for me," Hecate replied, "but for a little bird like you, it could be deadly. Remember the entire list. Consider the cave locked until you do so." And with a snap of her fingers, the witch was gone.

Persephone sat down on the rock with a groan. She could not grow crystals; she had told her that innumerable times. Persephone stared over the desolate horizon, a chill moving down her spine at the gathering greenish clouds that seemed ever-present against the darkened landscape now. Would Hecate really not let her in if she could not grow crystals? Persephone sighed again, closing her eyes, determined to at least try to comply with Hecate's unreasonable request. She followed Nyx's instructions, calling the light and darkness to herself and turning inside herself until all was still and quiet.

She was deep in her meditation when she felt something brush across her, something powerful and ancient. Her voyage into the meditative state had so far been filled with shadows and light, nothing concrete, but ahead in the darkness was a solitary, gleaming cord that hung from the nothingness. The cord swayed gently as Persephone approached. She could feel the gentle hum of it and the flow of energy passing through the light. Persephone hesitated, then lifted her hand to touch the pulsating light. The cord instantly lifted, connecting to her own heart, and Persephone heard a single voice whisper:

Aeternus

Power swelled in her, the cord filling her with its light and consuming her, and she could see it so clearly now: the connection between living things, that thread that ran between all beings, all creation, united, connected, and eternal.

As with the Universe, so with the soul, the voice whispered.

The connection was severed as Persephone's eyes opened and she gasped. A cove of crystalline trees encircled her. Was it possible that she had done this? The cord had generously shared its power with her; she trembled in the aftermath, almost bereft after the loss of their connection. She lifted her hand to one of the trees. The crystals felt alive, humming with vibrations. In a daze, she collected the crystals, mesmerized by the beautiful, glistening forest she had seemingly helped create.

When she returned to Hecate's cave, the witch was waiting at the entrance with her enigmatic smile and gleaming golden eyes. Hecate turned on her heel, and Persephone followed her inside with her bounty, her mind still fixed on the gleaming light that had felt so much a part of her.

Soon, the west side of the Underworld was covered in precious minerals and crystals. Waterfalls cascaded down into strawberry quartz, turning the water a beautiful, rich pink, and crystal trees glistened in the night sky. Persephone would collect baskets filled with rubies, emeralds, and sapphires the size of apples, bringing them to the witch for spell practice.

She walked further east one day, away from the safe forest she had created. Her feet led her to a calm river that ran quietly, and Persephone gazed into its soft, churning depths. It appeared to be an innocuous river, but it had to be the River of Forgetfulness that Hecate had warned her about. What pain could drive someone to drink from its depths?

Persephone followed the river until she came to a cave, where the ground was covered in brilliant, ruby-red flowers, and the air smelled nutty. Poppies. She recognized the bloom right away, and she rubbed her head at the buzzing, searing pain that suddenly pressed into her mind. Glancing over the horizon, Persephone could just make out the dark kingdom where the king presumably presided.

Pale lights danced in the castle's distant windows, reminding Persephone of the mourning candles that mortals would light when death had visited their homes. As lightning arced across the sky, it lit the greenish clouds, and Persephone gasped, stumbling slightly as she looked towards the skies. She had seen a face in the clouds, scanning the horizon, searching for her. Another clap of thunder clouded the sky, and Persephone shivered as a chilly rain began to fall, the apparition vanishing from her view. How fanciful she was becoming, she admonished herself.

"Persephoneeee," a voice hissed.

Terror and anticipation warred in her as she heard her name spoken like a low cry in the wind. She had been expecting this in some way, waiting for a call she would answer. The wind yanked her, drawing her attention to a rocky cliff in the distance. A man sat astride a raven-black horse, looking over the precipice. His hand was lifted, and electricity sizzled around his fingertips as he surveyed the land below, his long, black hair blowing in the ferocious wind. She watched as his back tensed, and her heart beat faster as he began to turn. She knew something monumental was about to happen; if only she could see his face, he was calling to her, and she was reaching for him.

A black mist whirled around her, tendrils of smoke pulling her back and obscuring her in darkness. She cried out in anguish, knowing she would not be able to find the man again.

"You should not have wandered this far," a tranquil voice interjected from the shadows.

Persephone waved her hand, clearing the mist, and she was facing a tall, hooded figure, once more standing in the endless field of poppies. She turned abruptly, scanning the horizon, but the figure near the cliff had vanished, and the sky was clear once more. Anger pulsed through her at the lost opportunity. He had been searching for her; she could feel the urgency in him—a driving need to find her. What had he want-

ed to tell her? How did he know her name? Frustrated, she turned back to the shrouded figure.

"Who are you?" Persephone demanded.

The figure bowed low. "I am Hypnos, the God of Sleep. You have wandered into my domain."

"Who was that man on the cliff? Where did he go?"

"What man on the cliff?" he inquired serenely.

Persephone's gaze narrowed suspiciously. "You pulled me back; you must have noticed him!"

"I feared that you would continue to wander near the edge of the precipice. You should return to Hecate's cave now."

"How do you know so much about me?"

"I am acquainted with the witch."

"That man seemed to be looking for someone or something." *For me,* her mind whispered. "I wish to help him."

"There is nothing you can do to help him."

"So you did see him! Who is he?"

"He is a ghost," Hypnos replied softly, "far beyond the reach of any of us. You would do well to stay within the confines of the safety you have built. There is nothing that can be done for him."

"Does this ghost have a name?" Persephone persisted stubbornly.

"He had many names once, though none that he would answer to now. He is neither alive nor dead but in between worlds. It would be unwise to attempt to join him there."

Persephone made a frustrated noise. "He needed help."

"He is beyond your help."

But the declaration from the God of Sleep only made Persephone more determined. The man on the cliff needed *her* help, and therefore, she could not just let him go. It had been a mistake to engage in conversation with this strange God. She would leave him and go in search of

that lonely figure.

"You are distressed," Hypnos said, gliding closer. "Let me help you."

"No!" Persephone cried, backing away, knowing that he intended to send her back to Hecate.

She must find the stranger on the cliff! It was more than a desire; it was a compulsion, and she could not allow anyone to stop her. Turning to run, she reached out a hand, her fingers brushing against the poppies, and a flame burst from her fingertips, lighting the field on fire. She let out a gasp of horrified shock as she surveyed the burning red field, the flame spreading rapidly across the once beautiful meadow. Unbidden, her conversation with Hecate danced in her mind as she stared at the destruction she had caused, paralyzed by the dancing flames: *We don't burn flowers.*

"You draw too much attention to yourself," Hypnos said, only the slightest edge in his voice as he surveyed his burning home. "That is never a wise thing." Lifting his hands, the field of poppies turned to ash, and the flame was suddenly extinguished. He turned to face Persephone. "You will go back to Hecate now."

"I will not!"

But his hands were on her, and then they were fighting, and the reasonable part of her mind was shocked, shouting at her to stop brawling with a strange God in the Underworld. But as they struggled, all reasonable thoughts fled. She would not go back! He was very strong, but clearly trying not to hurt her, so she had the upper hand. Between her well-placed jabs and kicks, one of her hands shot up, determined to reveal the face of her adversary. She paused in her fury as she pulled back his hood to stare up at the most beautiful face she had ever seen, transfixed by the absolute beauty. Small white wings obscured his eyes, and she wondered why before she collapsed into a deep, dreamless slumber.

CHAPTER 29
PREPARING FOR BATTLE

Persephone awoke on the straw bed in her room. She tried to sit up, then fell back, alarmed at the paralyzing weakness in her limbs. She frowned at her legs, willing them to move, but they remained stubbornly still. The last thing she remembered was fighting with Hypnos, and then… nothing.

"She is lucky that she was not put into a permanent sleep. Few are able to look upon Hypnos' face and live to tell the tale." Hecate's voice was matter-of-fact as it drifted through the open door.

"But she is not just anyone, is she?" Nyx said.

"And now *he* expects her to know how to handle a sword. It is not a weapon that will determine this fight."

"He never says anything without reason," Nyx warned. "He must foresee her in battle."

"The fate of this battle does not rest on a blade," Hecate insisted stubbornly.

"Nevertheless, we need to heed her husband's warning. She cannot be too prepared. It will do her no harm to practice the sword."

Persephone's brow furrowed. Husband? Who were they speaking of?

Hecate snorted. "I think her time could be better spent. Persephone," Hecate called suddenly, "do not strain yourself so hard trying to eavesdrop. Come out here, and we will tell you what we are discussing."

Persephone blushed. She tried again to stand from the bed, but her legs gave way beneath her, and she tumbled to the ground. It took every ounce of considerable resolve she had to pull herself up, and she was sweating by the time she was upright. She leaned against the wall, her languid body impeding her every move.

Suddenly, she was knocked down from behind, and Persephone gave a gasp of shock as she fell into an enchanted, tattered chair that was whisking her towards Hecate's sitting room, unceremoniously knocking down piles of parchments and books as it sped through the halls. Cats and dogs jumped from its path, and when she finally reached the doorway, both Goddesses turned to survey her, Hecate's eyes shining with golden fire and Nyx's luminous with concern.

"How are you, my dear?" Nyx asked in a soft voice.

"I am—well, I think I must congratulate Hypnos on the power of his gift. I feel I can barely walk."

"The effects will wear off in due time," Nyx said kindly.

"What did he look like?" Hecate asked. Her gaze gleamed with the curiosity of a cat's.

Nyx tsked. "I hardly think that matters, Hecate."

"Fine," the witch huffed. "She will tell me later, anyway."

"How much did you hear?" Nyx asked, redirecting the conversation.

"I wasn't trying to eavesdrop. I couldn't help but hear." Hecate merely regarded her stonily, and Persephone sighed. "Just you discussing me and another woman. Hypnos and me, and then a woman whose husband wanted her to train with swords—"

"Not two women," Hecate interrupted. "One."

Persephone's brow furrowed. "But–"

"*You* are married," Hecate replied bluntly.

Persephone laughed, but her laughter died away as she stared at the two Goddesses, neither of whom were smiling. She looked between them both incredulously. "But—but—I am not married. I think I would remember if I had a husband."

"Suffice it to say that you are, in fact, quite married," Hecate said.

"That is impossible! You are mistaken."

"The marriage is legal and consummated, to both of your satisfaction, I believe."

She may as well have been telling Persephone about the weather instead of revealing that she had some long-lost husband. As she realized they weren't joking, she felt a wave of fear wash over her. "All right," Persephone said. "Let's say I do have a husband. Why don't I remember him?"

"For your protection," Hecate continued, "it was decided that it would be best if you did not remember him."

"How?"

"Why does it matter?"

Persephone gave an incredulous laugh. "It matters to me! I would like to know how and why these supposed memories were removed."

"For both of your protection, they were removed. As to how all I can tell you is that it is not permanent and, at the right time, will be restored." Nyx interjected softly. "But he is sick."

Persephone froze. "Sick? I am married to a mortal."

Nyx lowered her eyes. "He hid you here to protect you. You are in danger, and so is he."

"Who is he to have such power? How is it possible for a mortal to have such intimate knowledge of the Gods?"

"For now, he must remain unknown to you. Persephone," Nyx leaned forward, her eyes imploring. "I can only imagine how hard this must be for you to understand. I know that you have questions, and I understand that you feel betrayed by him and by us, but I promise you, whatever my own soul is worth, that there is a reason for all of this subterfuge, and it was not decided lightly. In time, we will reveal all to you, but you must trust us. There is little time left. To help him, you must not seek him out. It is imperative that you do not try to find him."

Persephone pressed her hand against her heart. "I could feel it," she whispered. "All the time that I have been here, some piece of me has been missing. It is as if the very fabric of my soul was torn."

Nyx looked to Hecate. "Do you think her soul is in danger?" Nyx asked.

Hecate's eyes were speculative as she stared at Persephone. "I do not know," she answered. "Pluto's specialty is souls, not mine. It is possible she is just heartbroken. But she shouldn't have remembered enough to know that her heart should hurt."

Persephone's eyes shot open. "Does Pluto know about my husband?" The two women glanced at one another. "I am not a child! If you will not give me the answers I seek, perhaps he will."

The Goddess of the Spring stumbled from her chair, staggering towards the door, when rough hands pulled her back, and Persephone was staring into the wolfish gaze of the witch. "Foolish child," Hecate hissed, "you truly think the King of the Underworld would help you?"

Persephone's green eyes blazed back at her. The faces she once thought were those of trusted friends now seemed like co-conspirators in a clandestine plot to withhold a crucial part of her own existence, leaving her adrift in a sea of betrayal and confusion. "I think that I deserve to know what is going on! I refuse to be kept in the dark!"

Hecate's hair practically sizzled with outrage. "Sometimes the dark is the safest place to be! We have told you as much as we are able."

"You refuse to tell me?" Persephone asked, standing toe to toe with Hecate.

"Little brat, I told you, you know as much as I am able to say."

Persephone opened her mouth as Nyx stood from her seat, her hands raised. "Enough," she intervened, her firm voice cutting through Persephone's fury and Hecate's indignation. "Sit down, both of you." They sat like two furious children, reprimanded by their mother.

Nyx moved to stand before Persephone. "I understand your anger and your distrust. But war is coming, and we must do whatever it takes to prepare you. The stakes are greater than any of us. Greater than me, greater than Hecate, and greater than you. You want answers we cannot give."

Persephone was about to argue, and Nyx shook her head. "No, Persephone. We cannot tell you, though I wish we could. I know you may not believe it. I understand you do not like it, but we do not like it any more than you. I have no wish to bring you distress, nor does Hecate. We have done our best to guide you while ensuring you are kept hidden. A promise we made to someone who loves you and someone we both respect and care for. You may not like what we have to say, but right now, we are your only allies, and you have to trust us."

"My mother–"

"Your mother has no authority here. You are stuck in this world for now, and it is a world that Hecate and I understand."

"What do you mean the war is coming?" Persephone asked reluctantly. "Against who?"

"It will be the fight for all souls against a powerful evil. And you will play an integral role in it."

"I don't understand."

"I know, but before we go any further, I need to know if you are willing to continue to place your trust in us. There are things that may not make sense right away, but I promise that they are done for a reason. But you must continue to trust us; otherwise, none of this works."

"You are asking for blind trust."

"Yes."

"Why tell me this now? Why keep me in the dark for so long only to reveal this secret?"

"Because somehow parts of your memory are still present. Your run-in with Hypnos proved that. You are in greater danger by us not warning you. We are adjusting our plan a bit."

Persephone looked at Hecate, who watched her with furious golden eyes, and then at Nyx, who regarded Persephone with her luminous, incandescent gaze.

"Do we love each other?" Persephone asked in a quiet voice, looking at Nyx.

"Oh, yes," Nyx replied softly. "You love each other very much."

Persephone brushed her hand over her face, wiping away the moisture on her cheeks. "And if I seek him, would it harm him?"

"It would destroy him. And you."

"Do we have children?"

"No," Nyx answered. "Not yet."

Persephone did not understand why the answer hurt her so much. Slowly, she stood from the chair. "I would like some time alone. I will come back when I am ready to tell you my answer."

Hecate hissed, but Nyx raised her hand, inclining her head. "Very well, Persephone. We will wait here for you to tell us your decision."

As Persephone slipped from the room, Hecate turned to Nyx, her eyes narrowing. "We waste time!"

"We cannot proceed if she does not trust us. I believe her heart will tell her the right course."

"And if it doesn't?"

Nyx stared into the sparking flames of the hearth. "Then we are all lost."

Some time later, Persephone returned to the sitting room. Her face had shadows it had not held before, but her eyes were clear as she looked at the Goddesses of Night and Witchcraft.

"I do not like that you were dishonest with me and that you would hide something so essential from me. Despite your warnings, something in my heart is calling me to him—something that compels me towards him, that drew me to search for him even before I knew he existed."

Nyx watched Persephone steadily. "And yet?" she prompted.

"And yet," Persephone repeated softly. "I cannot deny that there is something within me that confirms the truth of your words because when I look for him, there is not only a blankness but a warning. A warning that if I pursue this, I will not only harm myself but my husband. I felt a shadow in my mind—an evil that searched for me as I sought him. I am willing to place my trust in you." Persephone glanced toward Hecate. "In both of you. But I ask for no more deception. If you can't tell me the whole truth, then I want to know, but I deserve to know at least that much."

"I can promise you that," Nyx replied.

Hecate was already standing, and she snapped her fingers. A tall, broad-shouldered figure materialized next to the hearth, a brown hood pulled low over his face. Persephone had the impression of a full mouth and strong jaw, but he quickly stepped deeper into the shadows.

"A little forewarning would have been nice, witch," the man greeted, his voice sardonic. "Did you even consider that I was, perhaps, in the middle of something?"

"Never mind that," Hecate replied with a dismissive wave of her hand. "There is no time to waste. Do you have the weapons?"

"Luckily, I came prepared." He lifted the cloak from his torso to reveal an array of swords, daggers, spears, and a bow strapped to him.

"Very good," Nyx said approvingly.

Hecate handed Persephone a dark cape. "Cover your face."

Persephone quickly donned the cape. "Where are we going? Why do we need so many weapons?"

"We are taking you to one who can teach you the way of the sword." Hecate laughed at the expression on Persephone's face. "Come, little Goddess, let us go into the Heart of Hell."

They moved through the dark like shadows until the heat became intolerable and the terrain grew desolate. As they reached the tall gates of Tartarus, the ground trembled beneath their feet, and Persephone gasped in awe as a massive, many-headed, many-limbed creature approached. But his smiles were warm when he saw her, and she nervously smiled back. The gates began to open, and Hecate shoved Persephone through, causing her to stagger. She gasped as the rotten air of the prison filled her lungs.

"Quickly, quickly," Hecate urged. "Before we are noticed."

The quartet moved as one. Persephone was flanked on either side by Nyx and Hecate, and the newcomer followed behind them. Every now and again, she saw the movement of something in the darkness, shadowy creatures that seemed to follow their every step, but Hecate would mumble under her breath, and the creatures vanished like ghosts.

Persephone gasped as a castle appeared in front of them. Nyx raised her hand, and an enormous black gate lowered. Gigantic creatures next to the palace came into view, but she was whisked inside before she could process what she was seeing. They moved until they stood in a gigantic greeting room, and Persephone's eyes widened as she saw the throne. A beautiful creature sat there, enormous, silver-haired, and silver-eyed. He seemed unsurprised by their sudden appearance.

"Well, well, so many visitors I am receiving lately," the stunning creature murmured. His gaze moved over Persephone speculatively. "You do not remember me, do you, child?"

Persephone's eyes moved down, and she realized in shock that he was chained to his chair. He was a prisoner.

Nyx stepped forward before Persephone could respond. "You know why we have come. Only you can give us the time we need. She needs to learn to be a warrior. Aid us in her training. I am sure she can arrange a shorter sentence if you do."

Persephone shot her an incredulous glance; she was sure of no such thing, but Nyx gave a subtle shake of her head, and Persephone bit her tongue. The magnificent creature leaned back, glancing between the motley group.

"I will aid her," he replied finally, his molten gaze fixed on the young Goddess, "but Persephone and I will discuss my terms of sentencing when her memories are returned. I do not believe in negotiating when a person is not in full possession of their wits."

Hecate snorted, but Nyx stepped back with a bow. "Very well. We are in agreement. Persephone," Nyx said gently, taking the young Goddess' hand. "You will be safe with him. He will help you so that you may learn to be a warrior."

"But I don't even know who he is," Persephone protested. Things were happening too fast, and she was afraid. She felt safe with Nyx and, strangely enough, with Hecate, but she feared this silvery being.

The beautiful creature laughed, and as his laughter echoed in the halls, he grew larger and larger until he filled the entire room. Persephone stared at him in awestruck fear.

"I am Cronus, child, the Keeper of Time. And we have met before, though you remember not." Persephone gasped as she realized she was standing before the King of Titans. He lifted his enormous hand toward her. "Come," he said. "The minutes tick by, and there is little time left to learn all that you must. Experience is the best teacher. Into the past, you shall go to fight on the side of the Titans. To fight against Aidoneus and Aene'ius."

Persephone's eyes widened at his words, her heart quickening with panic. This was madness! She looked back at Nyx. "But how am I supposed to fight in that war?" Persephone protested. "It happened centuries ago before I was even born. I do not know how to fight; I cannot!"

"My child," Cronus interrupted. "I am the Time God. I will return you there. And it is precisely because you cannot fight that you must go."

The Goddess of the Night stepped forward and wrapped a reassuring arm around the young Goddess.

"I know you are scared," Nyx whispered, "but he will protect you. I promise it. You must learn how to fight, Persephone; the fate of the world depends upon it. I am sorry that, yet again, we ask too much, but without you, we lose. Without you, the entire world loses."

Persephone cast a peek towards Hecate, who was not smiling and had a worried expression on her face.

"I am coming too," a deep voice interjected suddenly.

"Ah," the silver God said, looking past Persephone. "The brat grandson."

The hood was pushed aside, revealing a magnificent, golden-haired God. Persephone recognized him with a start: Ares, the God of War. She had seen him as a child in the mountains of Olympus. What in Gaia's name was he doing in the Underworld?

"And why do you wish to return to the Titan Wars, grandson?"

He came to stand beside Persephone. "I will help to watch over her."

"And you have done such a magnificent job of that so far."

Ares muttered something foul under his breath, and Persephone stared at him curiously.

"But very well. I accept." Cronus smiled, but the expression was far from reassuring. "When you reach Mount Othrys, you must keep your identities hidden, and you must leave before the Titanomachy is over; otherwise, you will be sent to Tartarus with the rest of us. You wouldn't want to be shackled here." He looked toward Persephone. "You will go by the name Kore. And you, Ares, shall be called Enyalius." Again, his gaze turned towards Persephone. "You should search out Aidoneus; he will instruct you in the sword's way. Do not reveal that you are assisting the Titans. He will not view any creature who aids me favorably."

Persephone blew out a breath. "I do not know if I can lie! I dislike being dishonest."

"You are indeed a child. In addition to the weapon, you will learn that, in order to protect others, it is sometimes necessary to conceal the truth. A word of warning, though, Goddess. Let Aidoneus train you, but do not fall in love with him. A lover cannot properly teach you.

"Furthermore, it is imperative that when you fight against the young Zeus, you cover your face." He waved his hands, and a helmet materialized in her grasp.

Nyx's lovely face was creased with concern, and Hecate looked mutinous. "Cronus," Nyx interjected quickly, preempting Hecate's less diplomatic remarks, "do you believe this is wise? Does it not affect the future?"

"Whether or not it is wise is irrelevant. It is required." Cronus continued with a knowing smile, "Moreover, the witch has taught her shadowed magic." Hecate regarded him with flashing, golden eyes but said nothing. "Persephone will erase Aidoneus' memory before she leaves. I will give her a warning before I retrieve them." The Titan bent lower.

"If she is going into battle," Hecate muttered, "then she should at least take this." The witch opened her hand, and a beautiful mahogany bow with rubied fruits dripping from it appeared in her grasp. "Take this with you, Persephone."

"Now, enough conversation," Cronus said as Persephone took the bow from Hecate. "Climb atop my palm."

Ares and Persephone exchanged looks. She was grateful that the God of War had agreed to accompany her, but she did not understand why; though his eyes blazed with the call of battle, she knew she hadn't imagined the trepidation in his gaze. Gods, how was she meant to accomplish this if even he was scared? Despite her misgivings, they moved forward onto the Titan's palm. His enormous fingers fisted loosely over them, obscuring the sliver of light that had been present in the dim hall. As a blue light swirled around them, the room began to spin, and when Cronus opened his palm, they were gone.

CHAPTER 30
THE KING & THE WARRIOR

"Where is she!" The king screamed at the bowed Judges, hurtling a precious vase in their direction. Aeacus narrowly avoided having it smash against his head, giving a cry of pain as it shattered against the wall, shards ricocheting against his face.

Minos nervously took a step forward, his eyes darting anxiously. "My Lord, the Underworld is vast, and she is a Goddess; she is difficult to track. We are doing everything we can to locate her. We have already burnt down Elysium searching for her."

Hades advanced menacingly. "Find her," he bit out. "Or I may find that you have outlived your usefulness." Minos paled and fell back to stand with his brothers.

A look of consternation passed over the Judges' faces, and they eyed each other until Aeacus finally spoke. "Your Majesty, you are... bleeding." The king wiped impatiently at his nose, carelessly smearing the crimson stain garishly across his mouth.

"Find her," he repeated. "Scour the Underworld, burn it all to the ground if you must. Someone is aiding her, shielding her from me. If you find them, you find her. If you do not succeed, I will throw you into Tartarus myself," he finished with a snarl. He stormed from the halls, his black robes billowing around him like deadly wings.

"Where have you hidden her, you royal fuck of nothing?" Zeus spat as he tore through the palace halls.

He could hear Hades' low laugh in his mind. "Such a temper tantrum, little brother. You will not find her."

Zeus turned, screaming in frustration as he blasted the wall with black electricity. A guard nearby started, and the king turned towards him. "You," he spat, pointing at the young man, "bring me a nymph!"

"Which nymph, Your Majesty?"

"Any nymph. A group of nymphs, preferably. Let us see how much you laugh as your fucking someone other than your wife."

"Your Majesty?" the guard stuttered in confused terror.

"I'm not talking to you, you idiot!" Zeus snapped. "Bring them to my room." When he reached the chamber doors, Zeus went to stand before the mirror.

Hades' reflection stared back at him, his eyes shadowed.

"Did I hit a nerve, *big* brother?" Zeus laughed. "Good. I will be hitting a very sensitive spot inside a few nymphs soon. Now, undress. We do not want to keep them waiting."

"No."

"Then bring me Persephone." Stony silence met his demand. "I see, then your infidelity will continue. You will enjoy it when a nymph's lips are firmly around you in worship tonight. I will be sure to regale your wife with tales of it when I locate her."

But Hades said nothing.

With a sinister smile, Zeus locked eyes with his despised brother in the mirror, his voice dripping with malice. "Dear sibling, your feeble attempts to resist me have been amusing, but I grow tired of this game. I shall find Persephone, with or without your help, strip away every ounce of happiness she brings you and revel as I watch your pathetic world crumble into despair. Prepare to witness the true extent of my power. But in the meantime, I will make you suffer in every way possible. Let's start with this."

Zeus' eyes gleamed amber, and he pulled the blade of Acheron, forged from the river of pain, and Hades prepared for a long night of torture. As the blade ripped through his chest, he let his thoughts drift, remembering Persephone's face, knowing she was far from his touch and that he was happy.

Nyx and Hecate stood in the hall of the King of the Titans. Hecate was eyeing the silver-eyed creature with palpable hostility. "Certainly, we do not have to wait ten years for her to finish her training," she snapped into the silence. "The war will have been fought and lost by the time we leave."

From his throne, Cronus observed the two Goddesses. "You must learn patience, witch. You know how readily time may be changed. She has, in fact, already spent over twenty years in the past." He let a sliver of sand pass through his fingers. "I have just sent them back for another battle."

"Twenty years!" Hecate shrieked.

Nyx placed a restraining hand on her shoulder as she stepped forward. "And is that safe? That they should experience so much in so little time?"

Cronus eyed them serenely, sprawled leisurely in his chair. "Little time for us, but not for them. And, no, it is not safe. But no matter where she travels, Persephone is never safe; despite her mother's and Hades' best efforts, despite yours, Persephone's life is constantly in danger. It is time to abandon this pretense of safety and embrace the fact that life when lived, is dangerous. Manipulating time is the only way she could learn to be the warrior she needed to be." He smiled down at the Goddesses. "Another five years, perhaps?" The sand moved again across his palm, and Hecate hissed.

Nyx stood silent while Hecate prowled across the throne room, her eyes moving over the shadows that danced like ghosts in the corridors.

"If Persephone has sex with Aidoneus, then she will be the one to take his virginity" the witch fumed.

Nyx looked at her blankly.

"It will unravel my chastity spell!"

"I hardly think that matters, Hecate, given all that has transpired," Nyx answered with a sigh.

"It matters when I think of Athena's smug face!" Hecate snarled.

Minutes ticked away, the silence deafening, until finally Cronus sat up and clapped his hands. Hecate jumped, surprise causing her to morph into an elderly woman, while Nyx merely tilted her head as though asking a question of the Titan.

"I think that is enough. Shall we see what our warriors have learned?"

He opened his hands, and Hecate and Nyx eagerly leaned forward. Two minuscule figures stood in the center, and as they stepped from his palm, they grew to their normal stature. Unsurprisingly, Ares was covered in blood stains, his swarthy face glowing with the joy of battle, but it was Persephone who drew both of their gazes.

She stood with a bloodied sword held high above her head, her bow and arrow slung across her back as though she had been in the middle of cutting down her enemy. Her skin was bronzed, her arms and legs lean and muscular, but the most changed were her eyes. They were the eyes of war, eyes that had decided who should live and who should die, eyes that had killed. She removed the helmet, letting it slip from her hand to drop onto the floor. Both of the warriors glanced about the room, and Persephone turned abruptly to look back at Cronus. The Titan stood, advancing towards the Goddess. He touched Persephone's chin, turning her face so that he could look into her eyes.

"She is ready." Cronus smiled, but there was a touch of something in his eyes that looked curiously like regret. "Have you learned what you needed?"

Persephone looked down at her sword, then back at Cronus, her fingers tightening over the hilt of the blade. She gave a brief nod as Nyx moved forward and placed a comforting arm around Persephone's shoulders.

"Welcome back, Persephone," Nyx greeted gently. She looked again toward the Titan. "Thank you for your assistance, Cronus. We shall take her back now."

Cronus said nothing, but as Hecate wrapped a dark cape around Persephone, the Goddess of Spring turned back to look at Cronus.

"I was not ready to leave. I didn't get to say goodbye."

The Titan shot her a stern look. "To whom?"

Persephone didn't answer, and Cronus sighed.

"I warned you, youngling," the Titan said, "not to become attached to Aidoneus." Persephone flushed. "He is in the past, and you have great difficulty ahead of you. You must forget him. As you confront the approaching darkness, you cannot afford to be distracted. Go now, for time is no longer on your side, Goddess."

Persephone's mouth firmed, but she allowed Hecate to begin to lead her from the palace halls. Persephone heard Cronus speaking in low tones to Ares behind them.

"Go back to the king," he was saying, "but remember, not a word of this. Her skills must be hidden from Zeus."

After securing Persephone in Hecate's cave, Nyx departed with a soft murmur to Persephone, telling her that she should rest. The Goddess of Spring sat before the fire pensively, staring silently into the colorful flames. When she turned to look at Hecate, she found the witch's eyes already fixed on her.

"Tell me what you learned," Hecate demanded.

Persephone turned her head. "Even all that time ago, when I fought against the Olympians, Zeus was already undefeatable. Though he was known as Aene'ius, I recognized him easily when I saw him for the first time, from the days I had spent as a child on Olympus. He already seemed to rule, though he was very young. My blade nearly shattered when it came into contact with him. He must have only gained power since then. I do not know how we will defeat him."

Hecate made a non-committal noise. "But you did not spend all your time fighting," she prompted.

"No," Persephone admitted softly. "At night, I would remove my armor and wander into the forest. In the woods, I met Aidoneus, and I let him train me as Cronus instructed. We spent many hours together. He taught me the best way to grow crystals. He never realized that I aided the Titans."

"That is good; that is what Cronus told you to do."

"I did not realize he would be so..."

"Charming? Handsome? Tantalizing?"

"Yes," Persephone acknowledged in a soft voice. "All those things."

Hecate eyed her shrewdly. "And how did you leave things with him?"

"As I felt Cronus calling to us, I erased his memories with magic."

"But you were tempted not to, weren't you?"

Persephone turned back, staring into the flames. "Yes, I was tempted." She lapsed into silence before finally asking, "What happened to him? Why have I not heard of him before?"

"Oh, he is still around...somewhere. Aidoneus was never one to seek fame."

"You knew him!"

"Yes, I knew him."

"Do I love my husband?" she asked abruptly.

Hecate's eyebrow arched. "From what I hear, you love him very much."

Persephone let her head drop into her hand. "I feel as though I have betrayed him in some way, and yet I cannot even remember him."

"Did you lay with Aidoneus?" Hecate asked bluntly.

"No!" Persephone answered quickly. "Tell me something; tell me something about my husband that is real."

Hecate moved abruptly to sit beside her. "Turn around. Your hair is a knotted mess." Gently, the witch began to untangle Persephone's blond, streaked hair. "Your husband fights for the Underworld. For Hades. It is his kingdom that is in danger." Hecate paused. "He would understand, you know, your feelings for Aidoneus."

"Would he?" Persephone asked miserably. "Then he is a very forgiving man, for I myself do not understand them." The crackling of the fire was the only sound for many moments. "How am I to defeat Zeus? Even after decades of battling him, all I learned was that he was not able to be defeated. I do not understand why it is that I play such a role in this fight."

"It is true," Hecate continued slowly, "that Zeus is formidable, though I do not enjoy saying it. Even the most powerful being, however, has a weakness. You must keep in mind that, despite his physical strength, he has significant limitations. You must discover a way to take advantage of them. You have a magic within you that Zeus could never comprehend."

"And what is that?" Persephone asked miserably.

"Deep within you, there persists a resilient flame of hope, glowing steadfastly amidst the storms of suffering you've endured. Even with the formidable power you possess, you choose not to wield it against others."

Persephone laughed bitterly. "That sounds more like weakness."

"No!" Hecate turned Persephone around to face her, and the witch's face was ferocious. "It is not a weakness to choose not to use your influence over others!"

Persephone took the witch's hand. "Thank you for having such faith in me." Hecate stared down at their hands as though shocked at the gesture of friendship. "I do not want to disappoint you all, but I don't even really know what you are asking me to do."

Hecate squeezed Persephone's hand before releasing her. "When the time comes, you will have to face Zeus. Not Nyx, not Hades, and not myself. You will be the one."

"But why must it be me?"

Hecate hesitated, something Persephone had never seen her do before. Finally, she nodded as though making a decision. "Zeus has harmed a significant number of people. It is one of his greatest skills—the knowledge of how to hurt the deepest. One of these people he hurt includes you." Persephone's eyes widened. "He attacked you in the forest, and you gave birth to a stillborn child. Zeus is still looking for you, and your husband has hidden you to keep you safe."

Persephone felt the blood drain from her face. "I bore a child?" she whispered.

"Yes."

Persephone stood abruptly, moving to stand to the hearth. When she turned back to look at Hecate, her eyes were blazing. "What happened to the baby? Why did it die?"

Hecate shook her head. "I do not know."

Persephone pressed her hands tightly against her stomach. "Why?" she said, her voice hoarse. "Why did he attack me?"

"Why has he committed any of the atrocities that he has? Because he can, Persephone, because there has never been anyone to stop him. My mother was a Titaness, you know. Ancient and powerful. Zeus pursued her relentlessly. He scorned her for turning down his advances, so he decided to take her by force. She dove into the sea to escape him, and all that remains of her are the islands my cave resides under. Her ancient magic was not enough to save her against the lightning wielder. And now all I have left of her is this cave; it is as close as I can ever get to her." Her golden eyes were filled with emotion. "My sweet mother, gone forever."

"I am so sorry," Persephone whispered.

"He has touched so many women, yet no one dares to question this rapist who has been proclaimed king. I spent my life learning magic in order to become so powerful and fearsome that Gods would never dare touch me. Do you know why Zeus regards me so highly?"

"Why?"

"Because he is afraid." Her eyes glowed yellow. "As he should be afraid, for I have welcomed destruction across my threshold, and I have taught her all I know. Potions for love, spells for defense, curses to destroy." She held out her hands, and the blood-red bow appeared in her grasp. "A weapon will not decide the fate of this battle. I have tried to tell them this."

Persephone moved closer, her fingers tracing the bow and a frown between her brows. "But a bow is a weapon."

"This bow was created with magic, with *your* magic."

"Mine!" Persephone gasped. "But how."

Hecate shook her head. "You made a powerful sacrifice that created it. This is no weapon; this is a key. This bow practically hums with life and with creation. He could never create life, but he always wanted to. It is you who holds the power of creation." Her golden gaze mirrored the red glow of the bow. "How will you wield such power?"

CHAPTER 31
KING IN THE CASTLE

In the midst of the heated debate between the Furies and the River Gods over war strategies, Hades remained seated, his gaze carefully navigating the room's animated occupants. While the Gods of the Underworld argued, Charon, standing just a step behind the others, maintained a stoic silence, absorbing the discourse with unwavering attention. Nyx hovered closely behind Hades, her presence acting as a formidable deterrent to Zeus—for the time being. Her strength functioned as a potent shield against Zeus' persistent attempts to wrest control of Hades.

A disquieting restlessness gripped Hades, an unusual itch coursing down his spine. His own flesh felt strangely foreign as if it no longer belonged wholly to him. Dark thoughts clouded his mind as he acknowledged the inevitable: very soon, Hades' body would not be his. Zeus was closer than ever to total dominion. A morose realization settled within him—he was on the precipice of losing everything. Soon, nothing would prevent Zeus from claiming complete control and, with it, Hades' very existence.

Hypnos moved forward, his voice serene as he interrupted the heated dispute between the Underworld Gods. The God of Sleep was assisting in the creation of a plan to wreak havoc on Olympus in order to give them the time they needed to prepare the Underworld for combat and temporarily release Hades from Zeus' captivity.

"It will take an enormous amount of power," Hypnos was saying.

"It is the only way," Hades finally answered softly, drawing himself from his reverie. "If we succeed, it will give us the time we need to strategize our next move and prepare the Underworld for Zeus' arrival. They need to know Persephone is not a fugitive but their leader."

"This might not work, Your Majesty," Hypnos cautioned.

"It has to. Ares has already begun to set plans in motion. I swear by the ancients that we will succeed. I will drain my life force if I have to."

"Very well. I will use the strongest poppies I have. He will be asleep before he detects the draught."

"Very good. We only have one chance at this; therefore, it must be done correctly." The king shifted in his seat, placing his palm on his brow. He shifted his gaze slightly to Nyx. "I am weary. Let us commune again tomorrow."

"Would you like me to accompany you?" she asked softly.

"No," Hades answered. "Your mind is best left to help strategize. Besides, if I go too long now, it is uncomfortable. Best to let him back in."

Only because he knew Nyx so well could he see the fleeting flash of sorrow in her eyes. But her expression cleared quickly, and she was bowing with the other Gods as they exited the chambers. He needed solitude to calm his aching mind.

"Persephone," he breathed out like a prayer. "Does any part of you remember me?"

The throne door flew wide suddenly, and Eurynomos entered, dragging his shattered wing behind him. A black hood shrouded his disfigured face, and shadows enveloped the monster. Hades felt an involuntary shudder as the memory of his time spent with this demon festered like an old wound. The devil had relished in Hades' ruin as a child and again after his mother's death. And all this time later, Eurynomos had discovered him once more, waiting in the shadows for Hades to become vulnerable so he could attack. This creature held no virtue or light within; he reveled in extinguishing the radiance of others until they mirrored his own darkness. His greatest joy thrived in the shadows of their darkest moments.

"I know where she is, the Goddess," the demon hissed.

Hades lifted a brow. In the creature's haste, Eurynomos had assumed he was Zeus. Hades quickly raised his hand, cutting off the demon's words.

"Is she well?"

"Yes," the creature answered.

The king's voice sounded like gravel and smoke combined as it echoed in the vacant throne room. "Good."

"Give me my blood price," Eurynomos breathed.

Hades lifted his arm casually and said, "Come, Eurynomos, claim your prize."

The demon stumbled closer to the throne for his reward, and the king stood, turning his back to him. A sword appeared in Hades' hand, and he ran his finger down the blade. The doors slammed shut with a resounding thud, and the demon raised his head as if he could smell danger.

"She told me to spare you, and so I did," Hades continued quietly. "I knew you would return from the shadows to haunt me." When the king turned around, the symbol of Pluto glowed on his forehead, and his eyes shone purple. The sword gripped tight within his grasp burned blue.

Eurynomos let out a howl of denial as he finally recognized his mistake. "To harm me is to betray her, just as you betrayed your mother." In his dread and desperation, his voice alternated from that of a beautiful angel to his true, hideous cadence.

The king smiled. "You truly believe your twisted words still hold power over me? Defiler. Consumer of flesh that was not freely given. Preying on those who are most defenseless. It is time for me to repay my debt to you."

Eurynomos was panting now. "Let me live, and I will assist you. I will provide you with information. I will give you information on Zeus. Whatever you want. Whatever you desire."

Hades drew nearer, dragging the blade across the floor behind him. In a desperate attempt to escape, Eurynomos climbed the wall; his deformed body dangled like a bat, his talons digging into the wall. His head leaned back, and the cloak fell, exposing his deformed, decaying visage. The demon's body was jerking swiftly, as if he were drunk, as he desperately attempted to evade his own mortality.

"You will not touch me," howled the demon. "I made you exactly as you are! I robbed you of everything until you became my own inner darkness. You are composed of my blood and my body! You and I are both the shadows!"

"But I made friends with the shadow, Eurynomos. It molded me until I discovered all of its secrets. Who, then, do you believe the darkness answers to?"

"You are nothing!" the demon wailed. "Nothing without me! Your soul belongs to me!"

"My body has been defiled, but not my essence. Know that regardless of your actions, I was able to love and was loved in return. I'd like you to also know," Hades continued almost amicably, "that this sword will not only kill you but shred your soul, leaving no trace of you. So you are aware that your darkness will perish with you and that you have no significance in this lifetime. You are worthless, and you will shortly be forgotten. Die quickly, Eurynomos. This is my contribution to humanity."

Hades lifted his hand and, with a fierce slash, cut Eurynomos down with the blade. Dark, viscous blood splattered across the king's face as the demon collapsed to the ground in a heap of garments and rotting flesh. Hades regarded the corpse of the creature that had tormented him for millennia. This was the first face he had seen within the belly of his father. The creature's venomous words had declared him unworthy and unlovable, attempting to obliterate even the faintest glimmer of hope within him. Hades felt the old rage simmer, a hatred that had coursed through him since the first day of his existence—familiar, searing, as intrinsic as his own skin. He allowed it to surge through him, to consume him entirely, feeling the fiery grip of bitterness that had been a relentless companion.

Then, with a deliberate exhale, he chose a different path. He allowed the flame of hatred to dwindle, releasing its scorching hold. In that moment of catharsis, he let out a shuddering breath, wiping away the final tears for the innocent, suffering child who had borne the weight of this creature's cruelty.

"Time to let it die," Hades said softly. He raised his hand, and the doors to the throne room opened. "Guards!" Hades shouted. The soldiers rushed in, staring in horror at the decaying, dead creature. "Throw this carcass in the fire to burn. Mind the blood. It will burn you."

"About time," a rusty voice noted with approval. "Glad you finally disposed of that vermin."

Hades did not turn, watching the soldiers gingerly drag the corpse to the large fire. "Ares," the king greeted. "The beast found her; Zeus is still looking for her."

Ares made a noise of disgust. "Of course he is." There was only a slight hesitation before he continued, "Did he tell you where she was?"

"I killed him before he could. But I am able to deduce that she is somewhere in the Underworld since Eurynomos was able to find her."

Ares grunted but said nothing.

"I should not think of it. I should not think of her; my resolve is growing weaker." Hades said, lifting his hand. The blade vanished into the shadows. "Tell me of your progress."

"The arrangement is proceeding as planned."

They watched the guards heave the corpse into the flames. "I have been thinking," Hades said finally. "I have a proposal I think you will not refuse."

"I am listening."

"The blood moon is approaching. If my life is eclipsed and my death does not destroy the weapons, you and I both know Persephone stands no chance in hand-to-hand combat against Zeus. A millennium would not be enough time to prepare her. Zeus is a ferocious fighter, and Persephone is still a young Goddess."

Ares merely nodded his head, uneasy that the king might discover that

Cronus had aided his wife in training.

Hades intertwined his fingers, wrestling his chin on top of his hands. "I am not blind to the fact that you want justice for your daughter."

"More than anything." Ares' voice trembled with emotion.

"My proposal is this. If you defend Persephone, you may pull my weapon, and if you succeed in protecting her, I will turn a blind eye to the justice you seek with it."

A slow smile spread across Ares' swarthy face. "Deal."

"Good. Go now, Ares. He will return soon."

The God of War departed with an ironic bow, and with one final glance at the fire charring the remains of the corpse, Hades swept from the throne room. He walked through the corridors until he reached the large, abandoned hematite hall. Large columns rose to the stone vaulted ceilings, and his footsteps echoed loudly throughout the vast room. Hades approached the reflective silver stones that adorned the walls. Shadowed eyes stared back at him. He raised his hands and wiped the demon's blood from his face. When he lifted his gaze again, he was staring into Zeus' eyes.

"Your informant is dead," Hades stated bluntly. "Persephone is still safely hidden."

"You lie!" Zeus hissed.

"You know that I do not."

Zeus' eyes were aflame with rage, but he forced a sly smile onto his lips. "How weary you look, brother. Why do you not eat something? Perhaps a glass of wine or a delicious boar? I will let you eat again when you bring her back."

Hades' hands trembled as he tried to avert his gaze from the reflection. "I won't let you control me!"

Zeus leaned close. "Control you? No, my dear brother, I aim to break you. To revel in the fragments of your shattered will. Though I must own, your futile resistance is rather amusing."

Hades gritted his teeth, grappling with the internal struggle to maintain the hold on his control.

"Feel that, oh brother? The tendrils of my influence weave through your every thought. Your resistance crumbles in the face of my dominion. Your pain is my pleasure, and I shall feast upon it until the end of time."

"I won't... I won't let you..."

"Let me?" Zeus laughed mockingly. "You have no say in the matter. I can sense how you long for my possession. You are so weak now you can barely stand without my influence." Zeus studied him. "And yet, you continue plotting. Why can I not see it? Are you hiding it in your heart, the heart she protects?"

"But I thought you were all-knowing," Hades answered softly.

"You have always been secretive, dear brother. Never telling the people that it was you who destroyed them. Never telling your wife it was I who fucked her. Never telling the other Gods that you killed your own mother."

"Be silent," Hades hissed.

"I will fuck her in my own skin soon enough when you are gone. She will beg for more once she feels the touch of my cock."

"I said enough," Hades snarled.

The room grew black, and Hades lifted his hand, balling his fingers into a tight fist. Zeus gasped, wrapping his hands around his throat as if trying to pry his hands away from his neck. His blue eyes bulged as tiny red arteries danced like serpents in the whites of his eyes. The dark king moved forward with a laugh.

"You have the regrettable tendency to speak excessively," Hades continued with a smile. "You are so eager to demonstrate your cleverness that you never consider how easily your little kingdom could collapse. You still insist on playing games with me, sharing far too much of your plan, but I no longer have anything to lose. You have so much that could be taken."

"There is plenty I can still take from you," Zeus gasped out.

"You are quite desperate in your search for my wife. I assume you have not found the child and that you have no heir to sit on my throne." Finally, Hades let his hand fall, and the reflection of Zeus fell to the ground, gasping for air.

"I will simply wear your body on the throne," he spat in between deep gulps of air.

"Ah, but thanks to you, my body can be destroyed." Hades drew a knife from his sleeve and drew a long gash down his arm. Fresh blood poured from the wound, and Hades' knew that he did not imagine the panic in Zeus' eyes. "A corpse cannot sit on the throne."

"You will not end it a moment before you have to," he spat. "You would never abandon your precious Persephone."

"You think you know me, but you do not. You are so afraid to die. I have made my peace with it. Your little scheme will never work without an heir to guard the throne while you dally in Olympus."

"You will have no choice," Zeus answered in a guttural voice.

"We will see."

Hades surged forward with both hands, smashing the hematite wall into innumerable tiny fragments that littered the floor, shattering the reflection of Zeus. The King of the Dead collapsed to the ground, gasping for air. His reflection flickered in the fractured glass, and he saw bruising across his own throat. He closed his eyes and leaned his head back, uncaring that the tiny shards dug against his flesh.

"Child," he called. "Where are you? Show yourself, for your mother's sake. Where is your thread?" There was no answer. "I am growing weaker," he announced to the emptiness. "I need to see her; I can feel her yearning." He lowered his head and spoke dark, ancient words. "Please allow me to see her. Allow me to go to her. *Morpheus viatorem.*"

Persephone lay in her room's little bed, watching the dust mites dance across the floor. She shifted on the hay mattress, unable to find a comfortable position. Even Calypso had abandoned her, growing tired of Persephone's restlessness. As she flopped on her stomach, she kicked at the blanket. How was she going to defeat Zeus? A million ideas flashed through her head, each one more implausible than the last.

According to Hecate, the King of Gods had molested Persephone, and she had eventually given birth to a child. Her child had died. The words caused physical pain, and her heart ached from the emptiness within her. Persephone closed her eyes tightly, hoping it would quiet her tumultuous thoughts. Aidoneus' black gaze flashed in her mind, and she hit her head against the pillow, wishing away the sight of his beautiful face. He'd been all she could have wanted in a husband, but it was not meant to be. He did not belong to her, and she did not belong to him. Besides, he no longer remembered her. She groaned in misery.

Hours later, she finally fell into a restless sleep. Strange dreams haunted her, shadows spinning in the dark, something just out of reach. Suddenly, she was moving through a large, shadowy palace, and instinct warned her to stay quiet. As she passed through a hallway, one of the doors creaked open slowly, almost like a subtle invitation. She hesitated, her heart beating like a wild tattoo before she slipped cautiously inside. The room was dimly lit by a roaring fire, and she could just make out an obsidian bed.

Her skin prickled with awareness as she sensed a presence behind her—someone as familiar as her own flesh—that she had known since before her soul was created. As she turned to face him, arms surrounded her from behind, and she sobbed a sigh of relief, tears flowing down her cheeks as the heat of his body warmed her.

"You found me!" she cried.

"I will always find you," he whispered.

She whirled in his arms, but he was only a shadow, his face cast in darkness. "Who are you? Please," she begged, "tell me who you are."

"I am the one who loves you, who has always loved you."

"Why can't I find you? Where are you?"

"I am in Hell," he answered, "and you suffered alongside me until I could bear the sight of it no more."

"I don't understand why I must be kept from you."

"It is dangerous to be by my side."

"They said that you are sick; is that true?"

"Yes, but I am better now that I am near you. Come," he murmured, taking her hand in his shadowed one. "Our time is short; let us be together."

She knew she should protest and demand explanations, but was it so wrong to want a little moment of happiness? And besides, this was only a dream. He led her to the bed, and they lay side by side until the shadow pulled her into his arms. He brushed kisses over her face, and she sucked in her breath, filled with longing.

He lowered his mouth to meet hers, wrapping his arms tighter around her. "There is something I must tell you. Tomorrow, there will be a coup on Olympus. Hypnos will put Zeus to sleep, and we will invade Olympus through him. If we succeed, I will find you."

"I want to help!"

"No. For now, you must stay hidden. For your safety."

"But I want to face Zeus."

"The time will come when nothing stands between you and Zeus. But, for now, you must remain hidden from him." Then he kissed her again, and her protests faded on her lips. He trailed his fingertips over her arm, and as he drew back, golden threads swirled between their flesh.

"Is this reality or a dream?" she whispered.

"Being with you has always been a dream." For some reason, the words made her inexplicably sad.

"Promise me you will find me again," she begged, drawing his shadowed figure closer to her.

Instead, he pressed his lips against hers, his tongue probing the seam of her mouth, before abruptly pulling back. "This is far too dangerous. I must go."

"No!" she cried. "Do not leave me!"

"But you must wake up, Persephone."

"No," she whispered. "Please, just a little bit longer. Stay with me."

"You must learn to let go," he answered gently.

"Promise you'll return to me."

"Let go, Persephone. Remember, you will never be alone."

And when her eyes opened, he was gone, and she was alone in the darkness once more.

CHAPTER 32
THE COUP

Persephone leaped out of bed, trembling from adrenaline. Abruptly, she came to a decision. She could not sit and wait while her husband risked his life for her. She moved stealthily through Hecate's cluttered cavern, and as soon as she disarmed the protection spells, she fled into the night. He said he was in Hell, and there was only one palace there: the King of Hell's castle. She raced through the night until suddenly, a rough hand yanked her back, and Persephone found herself staring into the witch's glaring eyes.

"Where do you think you are going?" Hecate snarled. The dogs of Hecate appeared as twin shadows, and they barked and howled in response to their mistress' rage. "You idiot! You'll destroy everything!"

Persephone returned the witch's gaze with a glare of her own. "I am not an idiot! I am weary of others risking their lives for me while I sit idly by. I know about the coup!"

Hecate's golden eyes narrowed. "And how did you learn that? Of course," she surmised, "he told you. Allow me to alleviate your concerns, then. None of us jeopardize our lives for you; we do this for ourselves and humanity as a whole. If you confront Zeus too soon, your efforts will be in vain. What was your husband's instruction?"

Persephone hesitated, annoyed, but she eventually responded, "He told me to wait."

The witch raised her hand and smacked Persephone on the head. As she did so, they both returned to the shelter of the cave.

"Why won't you let me help? This is my fight, too!" Persephone glared at the witch as she felt a rare fury growing inside her. "If I am not able to do something, I am going to go insane."

"Calm yourself! You are working yourself into a rage, and it is unnecessary. I said you were not going to the palace, but I did not say we would not assist your husband." Hecate shooed off the cats that had been reclining on the chaise before settling herself in the middle. Methodically, she began to roll up her sleeves. "This is a perfect moment to test your new skills."

Hecate waved her hands, and salt appeared in her palm. She drew the symbol of Jupiter on the ground and then scattered salt in the sign of Pluto over it. "There are those who fight with swords, those who fight with words, and those who fight with magic. We're going to use a little witchcraft to aid their plan. Lay on the symbols."

Persephone's heart felt considerably lighter, and she hurried over, eager to assist in any way she could. "On the floor?"

"Yes, that is exactly what I said; on the floor, go go." Persephone reclined on the emblems, and Hecate knelt beside her. "We will require some lavender. A beautiful, tranquil flower." Persephone waved her hand, and a bloom of the fragrant flower erupted from the Earth, filling the room with its sweet fragrance.

"Is that enough?"

"Perfect. Now lay down on your back and close your eyes." Hecate breathed in deeply. "I can see their plan clearly. They are going to invade Zeus while he is sleeping and use his body to wreak havoc on Olympus. For their plan to be successful, they need him to stay asleep. That, my dear, is where you come in. You need to lure Zeus far into dreamland. Let him chase you. Do whatever you can to keep him asleep. Remember, Zeus' weakness is women. Use that to your advantage."

Persephone's eyes shot open. "What if he catches me?"

"Do not let him."

"But what if he does?"

"Then stall him." Hecate reached her hand into her robe and drew out a tiny vial filled with green liquid. "This may come in handy." Persephone recognized the bottle; it was the Elixir of Pain she had brewed. Taking it carefully from the witch, she tucked it into her robes.

"Use your magic and keep him asleep in the dreamworld. Remember what we taught you." Hecate paused. "Are you sure you want to do this? You do not have to. We can simply let their plan proceed without our interference."

Resolve firmed Persephone's lips. "I want to do this. I am ready."

"Very well. Then take this too." Hecate extended her hand, and as her palm unfurled, a delicate necklace appeared in the center. A slender chain held six vacant gem settings, and a radiant golden locket dangled at the end.

With the utmost care, Hecate pressed the necklace into Persephone's palm, who touched it gently. It was warm against her flesh and seemed to hum with a subtle rhythm. "It is beautiful," Persephone murmured. "It is familiar to me somehow."

"Someone you loved gave that to you."

"But who—"

Hecate waved her hand. "There is no more time for questions if we wish to do this." Persephone bit her lips, knowing well that the mulish look on Hecate's face meant she would tell her nothing else. With a sigh, she secured the necklace before laying back.

"Be careful, Persephone. Do not get trapped within the dream."

Hecate moved across the room, and she suddenly split into her three forms: Past, Present, and Future; Child, Mother, and Crone. The child winked at Persephone. The three beings lifted their arms high into the air, chanting together: "Hypnos, Oneiroi, guide her to Zeus' slumber. Let her assist in his sleep and ensure the safety of the Underworld. Guide her safely from this dream when she is ready to return."

Persephone suddenly felt an overwhelming desire to sleep, and her eyelids began to droop. When she awoke, she was in Elysium; however, the surroundings were unnaturally vivid and brilliant. This was a dream. She looked down and noticed that she was no longer wearing her dark garments but rather a pale, flowing gown with her breasts visible through the fabric. Her long hair curled past her waist. A bolt of lightning streaked across the azure sky, and it dawned on her: This wasn't her dream. She was in Zeus' dream.

She glanced around, worry creasing her forehead. How was she supposed to find Zeus? She scowled; she should have asked Hecate more questions. Hesitating, Persephone began to walk through the fields and noted with chagrin that the skirt had slits that opened high to her waist, leaving little to the imagination. She clutched them tighter around her when a sound stopped her.

She turned to see Zeus staring at her in shock, and for a moment, she let herself feel the fear that terrorized her heart. He was as huge, intimidating, and powerful as he had been during the Titan Wars. This was the God she was supposed to defeat. This was the God that had tormented her, they said, that had made so many suffer. But then, she remembered Hecate's words. This wasn't about her. It wasn't for her. So, she forced a coy smile to curve her lips and let her skirts drop. She saw his eyes move hungrily over her thighs.

"You found me," she whispered breathlessly.

"I have searched the Underworld for you. Is this where you have been hiding?"

"Yes," she lied breathlessly. "They hid me in the skies of Elysium, but today I escaped. You were right. They have been keeping me from you, but it is you who I want. I can see that now." Zeus opened his arms, but she stepped back from him, shaking her head. "I waited and waited, but you never came. If you loved me as you say you do, you would have found me. Your love was all a lie."

"That is not true. I love you more than any woman I have ever been with. I want you so badly I feel drunk from it." He stepped towards her, and she pursed her lips in what she hoped was an adorable expression.

"If you love me, then catch me."

She began to run, and she heard him give chase behind her, his feet thundering on the ground.

"You cannot outrun the King of the Gods," he yelled.

Her heart was pounding in her chest. It was easier said than done to escape Zeus. He was incredibly fast. She could almost hear the voice of the witch saying, "Use your magic, you idiot!" Persephone interlaced her hands, and numerous copies of the Goddess separated from her own body and darted off in various directions. She abruptly veered left and heard Zeus let out a frustrated call from behind her. His yell of triumph as he caught one quickly turned to rage as the ghost Persephone vanished in his arms.

As Persephone ran, visions flashed in her mind, and she knew the witch was revealing to her what was happening on Olympus.

Zeus' body sat next to an empty chalice, the nutty scent of poppy heavy on his breath. Hypnos, with clever finesse, had slipped into the intoxicated God's realm through the intertwining dreams shared by the King of the Underworld and the King of Gods. Some time back, the Underworld's ruler strategically cultivated radioactive crystal minerals in Olympus—monazite, uraninite, carnotite—in hidden spots, casting a peculiar unease among the Gods. This subtle disturbance had slowly rippled through Olympus, creating an unprecedented tension. The higher Gods now found themselves susceptible to manipulation, a shift in dynamics that hadn't been present before.

Suddenly, Zeus stumbled from the throne room, his arms and legs moving strangely, his robes disheveled and stained. Incoherent laughter tumbled from his lips as he carelessly knocked over priceless vases and ornate decorations that adorned the royal corridors. The scent of wine clung to him like a heavy cloak, emanating from the goblet he clutched in a hand that trembled with intoxication.

As the Gods of Olympus approached, concern evident on their beautiful faces, Zeus became wild-eyed. He smacked Hera on the arse. He bellowed that Athena was a plain, small, tittied Goddess who was no child of his. He bent Apollo's lyre. He stomped Hermes' staff. The king's speech slurred as he drifted through the chambers, becoming a jumbled medley of half-formed sentences and inappropriate jests. His eyes bulged suddenly as he shouted that he would never allow his children to sit on his throne.

When the Gods attempted to restrain him, he summoned a wicked bolt of lightning and struck Athena viciously. As Artemis held her uncon-

scious form in her arms, the Gods viewed Zeus with fear.

And then Hypnos delivered the final blow, the flame to the kindling. "Anyone who isn't with me is against me!" Zeus bellowed. "I will send you to Tartarus to be chained with my father!" he snarled. He pointed to Athena. "Bastard daughter, born of foul seed, you will not take my throne!"

Pandemonium ensued as Olympus descended into Chaos, the once-glorious realm now the battleground for a bloody and tumultuous clash.

So entranced was Persephone with the visions that she forgot to be cautious, and she let out a gasp of surprise as Zeus' large body suddenly covered hers.

"Got you!" he shouted triumphantly. She lay beneath him, and she made her eyes slumberous with desire as she gazed up at him. He gasped with sudden pain. "My head," he moaned. "It aches!"

"Allow me to comfort you, my king," she whispered as she slid her hand from his temple to his neck, her lips nibbling his earlobe.

Intoxicated with lust, he bent to her, brushing his lips against hers, before flipping her on top of him. "What finally made you see reason?"

"My mind was clouded, but time alone helped me see more clearly. You are the one I desire, the one I've always desired."

She brushed her fingers against his cock, eliciting a moan of ecstasy from Zeus. He pulled back suddenly, his eyes wild. "Can you hear it? It sounds like a battle."

"I hear nothing. My poor king, you have worked so hard; you simply need to unwind. Let me look after you."

He scanned the area. "How is this possible? I destroyed Elysium searching for you, but there are no traces of the fire here."

"I am the Spring Goddess. I am capable of restoring even the most desolate regions." His pupils dilated as she lowered her gown, unveiling her creamy breasts and pale nipples. "Just as I am capable of bearing you the strongest of heirs. Let me show you how much I want you. Give me your seed, and I will harvest it deep within my womb."

Before he could object, she straddled him more tightly, her gown riding up to her hips. She rubbed herself against his jutting cock, and his eyes closed in ecstasy.

"I have wanted you so badly," he groaned. "Fuck me."

She lifted her hands and grew thick, green vines around his wrists as he reached for her. "I brewed us an aphrodisiac," she whispered. Pulling the elixir of pain from her robes, she poured it into her mouth, pretending to swallow. Leaning forward, she brushed her lips against Zeus', teasing him, biting him before she let the sweet, wicked potion trickle between his lips.

Persephone abruptly leaned back, pulled her dress back over her breasts, and swiftly stood over him. She regarded him coolly.

"What are you doing?" he demanded.

"Waiting."

His brow furrowed again in pain. "What is happening on Olympus?" He pulled at his wrists. "Release me!"

"No," she answered.

"You bitch, you tricked me!"

The witch spoke in Persephone's head. "Let me in, and I will aid you; I will help you remember what he fears the most." Persephone allowed her mind to expand, and she felt the instance that Hecate connected with her. Persephone smiled as the witch shared Zeus' private, shallow fears.

Zeus broke through the vines and endeavored to ascend into the sky while lightning arced around him. But his abilities were diminished and distorted in the dream. Persephone leaped after him and dragged him down by the leg. She knelt next to him, taking care not to touch him as he fell to the ground with a resounding thunderclap.

"This must be a dream," he sneered, breathing heavily. "You would never be so strong in real life."

"Not a dream, but a nightmare. *You* have given me nightmares," she whispered. Her eyes glowed crimson. "I would like to repay the gift."

Attempting to ascend into the heavens again, he was abruptly pulled back to the ground by Persephone while lightning sparked between them. Though they were briefly thrown apart, she quickly regained her hold on the king. In Elysium, the sacred trees started to melt like molten lava, their blossoms and bark shriveling in the intense heat.

"You have been my nightmare," she hissed again. "Now I will be yours."

Persephone snapped her fingers, and as a mirror materialized in front of Zeus, the light was sucked from the air. The Universe had gone completely dark when a single ray of light suddenly shone upon the King of Gods. He scanned the area desperately but saw no sign of the Goddess.

"What are you doing?" he spat, attempting bravado. "Show yourself, you little bitch."

Reluctantly, his eyes were drawn to the mirror. He was pale, sweat beading his forehead. He turned suddenly, straining his ears. Murmurs emanated from the shadows, and his complexion grew paler as he realized what it was saying.

"Father," the small voice called. "Father, you have forsaken me." He could hear the voice of the child he had consumed, the one that still lived inside him. Small, cold hands tugged at his legs, causing him to tremble.

"Do not touch me, you filthy spawn! You are gone; you cannot touch me!"

"You will join me," he whispered. Suddenly, the voice was not that of a child but of a horrifying, malicious demon. "You will join us in death." The word death echoed over and over, in a million cadences, for a million lifetimes.

Zeus was abruptly plunged deeper and deeper into darkness, passing through the lifetimes he had lived and the atrocities he had committed. Suddenly, he landed hard on the ground and was back in front of the mirror.

"Look," she whispered. "Look at what you have become."

Zeus stared at his reflection and screamed in horror as he observed the once beautiful planes of his face becoming sunken and sallow with age. His blue eyes were concealed by the sagging folds of his flesh; his stomach enlarged while his cock shrank. As his body was bent with age, his screams of denial merged with those of his child until his body became so frail that he collapsed to the ground.

Suddenly, Zeus was running, his old bones groaning in anguish, and something was gaining traction behind him: a shadowy figure. He knew he would die the instant those hands touched him, and he desperately tried to outrun it. However, he was old, and the figure behind him was swift and powerful. He knew in his heart that he could not escape it. Death had finally come for him. As he ran, he was surrounded by the voices of the women and children he had harmed, condemning and degrading him. Their fingers reached for him, and they were like knives on his flesh, cutting him, draining him of his life force.

"Let this end," he pleaded. "Let me wake up."

But he knew not to whom he prayed, for what deity lay above him? Who would hear his cries?

His knees ached as he ran, and he abruptly realized it was too late. *It had found him.* He turned to face it, dread filling his heart, when he felt the icy fingertips of death on his shoulder, and he gasped. It was *her*. The crimson eyes gleamed with rage as they bent towards him, and she held the golden blade high.

"All things die," Persephone promised.

And then he knew nothing.

Persephone awoke with a start, her eyes wide, confusion flooding her senses. The dimly lit corridor that surrounded her was foreign and disconcerting, and the absence of Hecate plunged her into a state of panic. A nagging thought insinuated itself into her mind—what if this was still a dream, and she was trapped in an endless labyrinth of her subconscious? She should have asked Hecate more questions!

Suddenly, a voice shattered the silence: "Follow his cord," it whispered.

Persephone strained her ears, yet the silence was undisturbed. Persephone sighed. Faced with no other option, she stood. Moving with care, she navigated through the halls, pausing after a while to listen intently. She could make out the sound of distant voices. Stealthily, she followed the voices until she reached the entrance of a dark room. Within, a tall, shadowed form stood over a bed.

"You must rest, my King. You are weak from the invasion."

Golden dust shimmered around the dark figure on the bed. "Bring her to me," he whispered, his voice resonating with a longing that drew her irresistibly closer.

"I will," the other promised, "but first you must sleep. Sleeeeep, my King."

The voice, lulling and slumberous, compelled Persephone's eyes to close against her will. When she reopened them, the figures had vanished, and she stood before a staircase, the surroundings cloaked in shadows.

Suddenly, the locket around her neck began to glow; a golden light seemed to pulse with unseen energy. She felt a subtle vibration, a gentle pull that tugged her in a specific direction as if it were a compass guiding her toward an answer. A small part of her wanted to turn around, her heart urging her to search for the source of that voice, to retrace her steps back to him, but she knew she had to continue forward. As she moved up the stairs, the locket levitated, and it seemed to guide the direction of her feet. A large, heavy door unlocked, and she gasped as her body lifted from the ground. She was flying over a river until she levitated before a doorway, facing a stone enclosure that hung over the swirling waters below. Was it a prison? She tried the handle, but it was locked.

Examining the doorway, she ran her fingers along the intricate carvings that adorned it—ancient engravings, constellations, and stars meticulously woven into the structure. A revelation dawned on her as she touched the locket, feeling the delicate cosmos embedded on its surface. With one hand connected to the locket, she placed the other on the door, and an ancient, profound power surged through her. The constellations came alive, swirling and dancing as if caught in the intricate choreography of a turning wheel. The Sun moved to Scorpio; the moon moved to Scorpio; Venus moved to Scorpio; Mercury moved to Scorpio; until, at last, all the planets converged on Scorpio.

"A Stellium," Persephone gasped, and with a click, the doorway opened.

Stepping into a vast, empty room, she saw doorways lining the walls, each marked by an ephemeris. The first door; Scorpio at zero degrees, the second; Scorpio at one degree, the third; Scorpio at two degrees and so on. Thirty doors stood before her, and a whispered intuition hinted at a single chance to choose the right doorway. But how was she supposed to know?

The locket glowed brighter. Closing her eyes, Persephone whispered, "Fate," recalling the witch's words about the Anaretic degree. Her gaze fixed on the last doorway—twenty-nine degrees, the degree of fate.

She walked to the last door, her feet echoing with a strange cadence in the cavernous room. Hand on the doorknob, she hesitated, then flung it open.

Millions upon millions of threads hung from the ceiling, and three ancient women were huddled together, their gnarled hands working frantically on ancient spinning wheels. Their eyes, wide with an almost manic intensity, darted between the threads, weaving an intricate tapestry that seemed to pulse with life. The creaking of the spinning wheels and the frenzied hum of cords merged into a dissonant symphony echoing through the chamber. Shadows danced on the walls, casting grotesque shapes that mirrored the chaotic urgency of the women's movements. It was a scene both mesmerizing and unsettling.

Persephone gasped as she took in the scene, realizing she stood in the presence of the Threads of Fate. Just as the thought appeared in her mind, the room was abruptly plunged into darkness, shrouding Persephone in shadow, even the locket silent and still.

Persephone.

Abruptly, a light pierced the surrounding darkness, beckoning her forward. Hastening toward it, she discovered the luminous light shining over a pomegranate tree bent low over a lake, its reflection dark in the unfathomable depths below. As she neared the tree, she noticed the fruit pulsing and contracting like hearts. The pomegranates oozed blood, creating scarlet ripples in the water below.

Persephone, the voice called again.

Suddenly, something fell from the branches and settled at her feet, and she knelt hurriedly to retrieve it before it sank. Her hands grasped the smooth wood of a bow engraved with pomegranates. A bow made of the pomegranate tree. The same bow Hecate had shown her. The same bow she had used and knew intimately from the Titan Wars. The witch's voice echoed in her mind, "This is no weapon; this is key." The engravings glittered on the surface as she brushed her fingertips over the bow, and she felt a pulse within the weapon as if it beat in the rhythm of the tree.

"It's a key," she whispered.

She stepped into the water, letting her hands trail over the bark of the tree as the bow pulsed. Persephone searched carefully until she found it: an engraving of a bow, an indentation etched deep within the tree's bark. Lifting the pomegranate bow reverently, she inserted it into the tree and heard a click. It was a perfect fit. The pomegranates beat wildly, and an opening appeared from the tree. She took a deep breath, her heart accelerating, and with barely a moment's hesitation, she pushed through the narrow entrance, entering the darkness within.

Persephone was in complete shadow. Her heart pounded faster; the darkness frightened her, yet something told her she had to continue farther into the shadows. As she ventured deeper inside, she noticed something in the distance: a dazzling light. She rushed towards it and saw the source of light. It was a translucent pitcher filled with a shining, golden fluid. The liquid rippled and seemed to come to life as she drew near. Tears welled up in her eyes as she stroked her fingertips reverently over the edge of the glass. This was somehow connected to her, something so precious that her heart filled with love beyond her comprehension.

"Persephone."

She whirled around to face a figure in a dark hood. The being was filled with a power so ancient and divine that it glowed in the dark, and Persephone fell back in awe.

"Who are you?" Persephone whispered.

"I am the Goddess of the Generations. I have traversed the corridors of time in search of you. I led you again and again to the pomegranate tree. I have a secret I have been waiting to share with you." Persephone gasped as the figure drew back her hood. Though she had the shape of a person, she was composed of spinning galaxies rather than bone and flesh.

"Why can I not see your face?"

"My body died long ago. To humans, I am nothing more than a belief in the ether. I reside with the Protogenoi now. I approached you in the shadows, but you were not yet ready to enter the darkness."

"But why?" Persephone asked. "Why do you seek me? I am only a minor Goddess."

"No, Persephone, you are *so* much more. Though you do not yet remember, you once made an incredible sacrifice. You bravely ate the pomegranate seed, giving up your freedom for love." Persephone gasped in astonishment. "You chose love over liberty. No other in this entire Universe has willingly eaten the seed of the Underworld. This act holds a unique power—a strength that comes from deep, selfless devotion. It's a sacrifice that goes beyond time, demonstrating the extraordinary strength found in the simple act of putting love first. It is everything, more powerful than any Godly might. And it is why one of profound importance has traversed the celestial realms, tirelessly searching for your essence."

She raised her hand, and Persephone noted that even her fingers were made of minuscule planets and stars. The figure pointed to the glistening container. When Persephone touched the glass again, the golden liquid inside shone.

"Why does it feel so familiar to me?" Persephone asked.

"You know *who* this is."

"My son," she sobbed in response, tears streaming down her cheeks.

"Zagreus. His spirit is not woven from thread. That is why those who searched for him could never find him. Even the Fates could not locate him. He is the very essence of existence."

Persephone ran her fingertips over the cup. "Zagreus." A soft heartbeat resonated against the glass, and though the memories had been taken from her, her heart was filled with love for this child, a bond that no magic could remove. "I loved you before you were born, and I've loved you every day since you died." She raised her eyes to the divine Goddess. "What happened to him?"

"He chose to have his body perish, and so it did. He was never supposed to be Zeus' son. You went down to the river that night in search

of another man, and he is Zagreus' true father. When Zeus intervened, Zagreus had no choice but to let his body die. And we arrived to take him away. We have kept him safe since then, shielding him from Zeus. He was destined to be the child of you and your husband."

She gestured to the cup. "This is Zagreus' soul, his divine essence. You must drink from the glass," the Goddess of Generations continued as she lifted the container, "to hold his soul within you so that Zagreus can be reborn and the weapons can be destroyed."

Persephone gently received the pitcher from the Goddess, her fingers tracing over the glass with reverence. As she closed her eyes and sipped from the vessel, tears welled up, moved by the profound warmth of the soul that moved within her. It was a sensation she intimately knew, reminiscent of when she cradled this very child within the sanctuary of her womb.

"There's an unparalleled love that only a mother knows, a love so deep that it transcends any boundary. We would do anything for our children, wouldn't we?" the infinite Goddess asked.

A quiet agreement escaped Persephone's lips, her response infused with emotion. "Anything. Everything."

"The next time you meet, you must lay with your husband, and he will give you a child. He'll send for you, and you must lie with him tomorrow if you want to conceive. But tell no one of Zagreus, especially your husband. Zeus must not learn of him. Protect the child at all costs."

Persephone held her hands over her womb. "I will protect him with my life," she swore, her voice trembling.

"Go now, Persephone. He is waiting for you."

Nyx flew through the door, ecstatic. "You saw!"

The witch sat by the fire with a glass of steaming wine in one hand, and a tray of crumbs beside her, and her eyes were luminous with excitement. "I watched in the flames! All that fighting made me rather peckish. Give me the gory details."

The Goddess of the Night smiled at her eagerness. "The poisonous crystals Hades planted on Olympus the night he took Persephone have worked their magic. As of late, a pervasive malaise has settled upon the upper echelons of the Gods. They have been wondering about the source of their illness and have been looking for someone to blame. Zeus, during the coup, provided them with the perfect villain."

"Go on," Hecate urged breathlessly, clutching Calypso to her chest. "It's too dreadful, I long to hear more."

Nyx laughed softly. "Ares persuaded his mother that his father has been acting strangely lately. Hera, at Hypnos' recommendation, was provided with a draft in order to put Zeus into a deep slumber and prevent him from leaving Olympus. Pluto was then able to use his connection to Zeus to allow Hypnos to enter Zeus' mind, producing turmoil, while Pluto infiltrated the Olympians' thoughts, implanting a plan of descent against Zeus." Nyx smiled. "I've never seen Hypnos so animated. He entered Zeus' body and caused quite a scene on Olympus, and there was a coup for power."

"The privileged are fighting amongst themselves," Hecate sneered. She took a deck of cards from her robes and spread them across the floor. Closing her eyes, she drew a card from her tarot deck. As Hecate flipped over the first card, she placed it on her left. "The emperor card in reverse. The corrupt king." The witch drew her second card. "The card of judgment. They've already started a trial against Zeus. It will last several weeks. This will allow us to work without interruption. Zeus cannot abandon his throne again, believing that the other Olympians are after it." She hissed as she flipped over the third card, placing it on her right. "A world in reverse. The end is near, but there will be much fighting. Not everyone will survive."

Nyx's smile faded. "But we always knew it would probably come to that."

Hecate picked another card while closing her eyes firmly and mumbling under her breath. She flipped it over, her gaze fixed on the card. Nyx drew nearer, but Hecate quickly cleared the deck away. "I suppose you are right. A battle is inevitable."

"Where is Persephone?"

Hecate pointed to the chaise, where Persephone was asleep beneath a pile of cats. "She had to confront him today. Whatever occurred, she was successful."

Nyx frowned, concerned. "Does Hades know?"

"He would never have permitted it, but she was prepared. She's still asleep, but I can feel her approaching the surface. She'll be awake soon."

"With the palace safe, I suppose he will want her back."

"I am sure he will." The Goddesses stood over her. "Let them enjoy the time they have left together. They have earned a little happiness."

"Why, Hecate, I do believe that is the most sentimental thing you have ever said."

The witch snarled. "If you tell anyone, I will turn you into a toad."

And Nyx smiled, but as Hecate returned her gaze to Persephone, the witch's eyes were filled with sorrow. Her last query to her tarot card was whether Hades would survive the battle. She took another look at the last card, which was still clenched tightly in her palm. The death card. In this fight, Hades would die.

CHAPTER 33

HOMECOMING WITH THE KING

A crow let out a startled cry as sudden shouting reverberated from the witch's cave. Inside, Hecate was fiercely arguing with a serene Nyx about Persephone's attire, but the Goddess of Spring was hardly paying attention. Persephone was overcome with apprehension after the King of the Underworld had summoned her. Hypnos entered the room and retreated into the shadows, but the Goddesses scarcely noticed, distracted as Hecate waved her hands emphatically. It felt like yet another hurdle before she was allowed to see her husband, and after confronting Zeus in the dream, she felt drained.

"She cannot wear yellow!" Hecate was shouting. "It will make her look like an old dishrag!"

That caught Persephone's attention, and she glanced up, meeting Nyx's twinkling eyes. "I don't understand why I must meet with Hades before I see my husband," Persephone said as Hecate pulled a lock of her hair and pointed vehemently to it.

Nyx smiled reassuringly and gently removed her hair from Hecate's grasp. "You and your husband will be reunited, but Hades must speak with you first. He will explain everything. Which color do *you* wish to wear, Persephone?"

"Oh," Persephone replied, gazing glumly at her reflection. "It doesn't matter. Though I suppose I don't want to look like a dishrag."

"See! She is indifferent. The gown must be black!"

"You know," said Nyx with a sudden grin, "I believe that will suit her perfectly."

Hecate made an oomph of satisfaction. "And her hair must be worn long with a slight wave." She lifted her hands, causing Persephone's long hair to curl. Nyx bent forward and applied rose blossoms to her lips. The witch smiled with satisfaction as she revealed a dark mesh toga adorned with precious gemstones. After placing it over her head, the witch fussed with the gown, ensuring every line was clean. Persephone reverently tucked the locket into the bodice, obscuring it from view, and Hecate eyed her with a smile as Nyx adorned Persephone with gilded jewelry. They applied gold glitter to her eyelids before stepping back and smiling.

Persephone scarcely recognized herself in the mirror. "I never imagined that such powerful Goddesses would dress me."

Nyx took her hand and squeezed it. "I am so proud of you. You have matured tremendously. Thank you for having faith in us. It is a gift that surpasses all others in value. Your mother would be very pleased with you."

"Thank you," Persephone answered tremulously, squeezing Nyx's hand back.

"Remember your training and your magic," Hecate said gruffly. "Do not let romance drive all your lessons from your head."

Persephone smiled and then wrapped her arms around the witch, giving her a brief but fierce hug.

Hecate's scowl turned deeper. "And remember, if you find your husband tiresome, you can always return here. Calypso will miss you."

Nyx smiled. "I think you will miss her a little too, Hecate?"

Hecate murmured, "Hmph," as she walked away to sit moodily before the fire.

"We must leave," Hypnos announced serenely.

Persephone wanted to say more to the two powerful Goddesses whom she had come to regard as dear friends, but Hypnos ushered her away; Hecate's gloomy visage was the last thing she saw as they began their journey through the Underworld. Hypnos appeared to be aware of her preoccupation, as he did not initiate conversation with her. They walked for some distance before reaching the Styx River. A boat rested in the water, and a hooded figure stood at the helm.

"Charon will lead you the rest of the way." To Persephone's surprise, Hypnos bowed low to her. "It has been my pleasure, Goddess."

"Thank you," replied Persephone. "And Hypnos?" He rose. "I am sorry– that I attacked you."

Hypnos laughed quietly. "No doubt I deserved it. Until next time, Goddess." He helped her step into the boat, and his dark figure stood on the shore until she lost sight of him.

As he paddled them through the river, Charon remained silent, and Persephone peered into the water. The River Bearer led her across the Styx, and she gasped in wonder as she saw shimmering spirits that followed the vessel. Soon, hundreds of souls trailed behind the boat, gleaming like starlight, as if escorting her into the palace of the dead.

The boat finally docked, and a guard hurried forward to assist Persephone in exiting the craft. She turned back to the River Bearer.

"Where am I to go?"

Charon indicated a large staircase, and Persephone, accompanied by the guard, began her ascent into the palace. Guards lined the corridors, and she did a double-take of astonishment when she realized that they were bowing to her as she swept through the long, dark passage. Blue-flamed torches illuminated the scenes on the walls with each stride she took until she reached massive obsidian doors. Two spectral soldiers, bowing, opened the door.

Persephone heard a deep, smoldering voice as the doors opened, and the sound caused her heart to race; it sounded like a voice from a dream, haunting and familiar.

"We will prepare the surrounding area for the forthcoming battles in the event that the conflict spreads beyond the palace. We will do everything possible to assure your safety."

At the opening of the doors, the entire room turned towards her. The audience suddenly knelt, their heads bowed low as they faced her. Her eyes widened in bewilderment. Was this portion of the Underworld simply overly courteous? She turned to observe the monarch seated on his throne. His dark, handsome face was illuminated with surprise and delight.

"Aidoneus," she whispered.

After the Titan Wars, Aidoneus had somehow ascended to the throne of the Underworld. He must be King Hades! She wanted to rush forward and embrace him, but a sudden spark of recollection prevented her from rushing to him. No, he would not recall her; she had ensured that. Self-conscious of the strange attention of the crowd, she clenched her fingers tightly and stepped back, attempting to blend into the throng.

"And so," King Hades continued, "all my powers, all my magic, and my throne pass to the queen."

The gathering bowed in unison, and Persephone involuntarily let out a gasp of astonishment. Was the king bequeathing his legacy to his wife? Confusion rippled through her. And where was the queen, Persephone wondered, eyeing the empty throne beside the king.

"Long live the queen," the crowd echoed.

Hades rose from his throne, and she realized he was coming towards her. Her heart raced like a wild tattoo. With a wave of his hand, the crowd between them vanished, and then he stood before her, and she lowered her eyes, unable to look at him. She thought she would never see him again after the Titan Wars. He had come to mean so much to her during that time, and now he stood before her, about to reveal who her husband was. She felt her cheeks flush at the absurd, painful irony of the situation. Hecate could have warned her!

"Persephone." His voice was a tantalizing whisper against her flesh.

"King– Hades," she choked out. "Thank you for letting me come to your palace. I am told that you know my husband." She finally lifted her face to his, and her blush grew deeper as her stomach did a curious flip. He was just as she remembered, and yet, somehow, so much more. Time had gifted his masculine beauty with wisdom and darkness that had not been there before. He was staring at her intently, and for a breathless moment, she wondered if he remembered her, but that was impossible.

"Yes, I know your husband," he answered.

"How is he?"

"Right now, he is better."

She had to escape him because he was too potent, too masculine, and too much of everything she still desired. It was a betrayal of her husband that she could not allow. She must get away from the king. "Will you take me to him?"

He took her hand, and she jumped. The irresistible attraction she felt since the first time she saw him persisted. Did he feel it too—this pull between them? He smiled down at her, his dark eyes enigmatic.

"There are things I would like to discuss with you first."

She once more gazed down at their intertwined fingers and noticed his wedding ring. Her heart wrenched in agony at the painful reminder he was already married, and she scolded herself severely. She ought to be happy that he found someone. On his other finger was a golden signet ring, and she frowned as she regarded her hand intently. It was the same ring that she wore herself!

He noticed her eyes on the rings. "Dance with me," he cajoled, his voice as dark as a raven's wing. "I will explain everything."

She swallowed and nodded, allowing him to lead her to the floor's center. He placed his hand around her waist and pressed her against his body. Oh Gods, help me, she pleaded silently. He began to spin her across the floor, their bodies pressed tightly against one another.

"I've missed you so much," he whispered, and as she jerked back in surprise, he brushed his lips against hers, and she gasped.

Memories all around them came to life, joining them like ethereal dancers. Persephone reading his letter, a joyful smile on her face; Hades defending her against Eurynomos; Hades confessing his love for her at his temple; the night in Elysium as they touched each other for the first time. Words echoed from the past: "I love you" and "Let this be my burden to bear." The words built to a crescendo into a million intimate moments with her husband and all the little ways she loved him. This was her love. Aidoneus. Hades. Something sinister emerged

from the shadows, filling her with dread. With a cry of denial, she remembered that he was not just sick; he was dying.

She wrenched herself away, tears streaming down her face, but he refused to let go, pulling her into an embrace.

"Welcome back," his voice was tender, a balm against her tumultuous emotions.

She struggled to create distance, needing to see the truth in his eyes. "You took away my memories!"

He nodded, unapologetic, yet his eyes revealed a depth of unspoken emotion. "I had to."

As he caressed her hair, she yielded, wrapping her arms around him and burying her face against his chest. "Never do it again!" she commanded sternly, but her voice trembled with the depth of feeling. Her hands moved over his face, tracing the lines of his lips, a silent plea for assurance. "Are you alright? Are you finally free of him?"

"For now, I no longer have to fear his possession. We have time to plan," he reassured her.

Suddenly, he was kissing her and tasting her, and she moaned in need, yearning for him.

"I want to take you somewhere I seldom go," he murmured against her lips. "The highest of the realms. Will you come with me?"

"Yes," she responded, bringing his mouth back to hers. "You know I will go anywhere with you."

The moment he waved his hands, they found themselves standing on a cliff overlooking the ocean. He gently drew her back and helped her sit on the ground, then raised his hands again and drew the outline of a door in golden threads until an enormous golden archway hung from the sky. He extended his hand, and as soon as the gates opened, they entered a world ablaze with golden light.

Persephone shielded her eyes as the landscape came into view, gasping. The entire horizon glowed with a brilliant light. The terrain was lined with luxuriant, leafy trees that bore enormous, golden fruit framed by purple mountains. Turquoise water glistened in the distance, painted golden by the reflection of the sun. She squealed in surprise as he abruptly lifted her into his arms.

Hades ran up a steep landscape until they reached a magnificent golden palace atop a cliff. As he slid her down his body, his lips toyed with hers. Together, they explored the palace until they reached an enormous, pale bedroom with a view of the sea. Red roses climbed the walls while pale chiffon curtains gently fluttered above the bed in the wind. Hades walked over to the bed and plucked a solitary rose from the covers.

"Where are we?"

"This is the Isles of the Blessed."

She regarded the land solemnly as she recalled her promise to Cronus. Her gaze lowered. "The Isles of the Blessed," she murmured. "It is beyond description. The most beautiful land I have ever seen."

He guided her to the balcony overlooking the sea. "Only the bravest and most pure of hearts are allowed here. Elysium souls have a chance to be reborn. If their next life is just as courageous and pure of heart, they will re-enter Elysium. If they reincarnate a third time and live that life with the same honor and valor, they can enter these lands."

"How many have achieved that feat?"

"Only a few. It is difficult to abandon the paradise of Elysium for fear of never returning. It requires tremendous bravery to enter the land of the living once more. Being human is one of the greatest gifts because mortals experience life so deeply. However, they also experience great loss and anguish. Such emotions can corrupt and cause such bitterness that good people do bad things." He grasped her hands and remarked, "And what suffering I have caused you. All of your suffering is my fault."

"No! You have never brought me anything but the greatest joy. Zeus is the one who has hurt me, who has hurt so many ."

Hades pulled her tight to him. "You have been through so much, but you did not wither away and die. Your soul is stronger than ever now. We do not grow from idle happiness. Pain, trauma, and death, as wretched as they might be, push our souls to grow in ways we never believed possible, and with that growth, people change the world. If Orpheus had never lost Eurydice, would he have ever written music

that inspired the world? Our suffering can make us better if we are brave enough to rise up and allow it."

She turned in his arms, resting her head against his chest, letting his heartbeat steady her. "You have such faith in me," she murmured. "More than I have in myself."

His lips caught hers. She felt a pulse deep in her womb, and she pressed her fingers against her abdomen. Had it just been a dream? No, it had been real. Even now, she felt a shimmer of that other soul within her—the tiny hum of his being. She longed to tell Hades that she had finally found the child and that their search was over, but Zeus would return, and it would endanger Zagreus. It was yet another secret she must keep from Hades. The promise to Cronus. The location of the threads. Her training with him in the Titan Wars. How much she had to conceal from him so that the King of Gods did not learn their secrets.

As Hades lowered her to the bed, she encircled his head with her hands and drew him tight against her, all thoughts of Zeus fleeing her mind. She closed her eyes in rapture when their love finally reached its climax, and she felt him arch inside of her. They fell asleep, and it was not until later in the night that she felt a change within her, a spark of life.

She sat up, taking care not to disturb her husband.

She whispered, "I have missed you, my sweet child," as tears of joy rolled down her face.

How she longed to wake up Hades to tell him! But she knew she mustn't. She could not endanger Zagreus. But, still, she would treasure this moment. She took Hades' hand in hers, placing her other hand over her womb, and at that moment, she felt genuine happiness, however fleeting, to be with her little family.

CHAPTER 34
WAR

As the days flowed by, Persephone found herself desperately trying to savor each moment with Hades, yearning to slow down the relentless march of time. But they had little time alone together as they prepared for war. Frequent gatherings with the other Gods of the Underworld had transformed the once-stately throne room into a bustling tactical war room. Tables were adorned with maps and intricate battle plans, setting the stage for the impending challenge against the Olympians.

Ares was more animated than she had ever seen him, and his eyes gleamed with anticipation as he instructed the Underworld Gods in various combat poses. Meanwhile, Hecate, Nyx, and Hypnos wove intricate magical strategies, while the River Gods and Charon delved into discussions about techniques to safeguard the ethereal waterways. Cerberus would periodically rise to sniff at the parchments, but he otherwise remained tethered to Persephone, one head always fixed on her. She knew he could smell the child that grew within her and that the Hellhound was determined to protect him.

During one of the meetings, Ares pulled out a map of the Underworld and spread it across the table. Hades moved away, taking special care not to view the map.

"Here are your battle positions," the War God announced.

Hypnos drew closer. "Where is my mother going to be?"

"This battle will take place during the Blood Moon," Hades announced from the corner of the room, and Hecate drew in a sharp breath. "Zeus will ensure Nyx will not be there."

"The Blood Moon is in Scorpious," Nyx said softly. "It falls on the day of your birth this year." She exchanged a meaningful glance with Hades, and Persephone's heart lurched at the look in the Goddess' eyes. They were full of sorrow.

"A birthday present from my brother," Hades said ironically. "We will have to make do without Nyx."

"But Zeus will find the pathway back to you more easily without her," Hypnos protested.

"He would always find the way back to me," Hades answered. "This was only ever temporary."

A tense silence followed his words. "Nonetheless," Nyx continued softly, "I have taught Persephone well. The Underworld will triumph with her leadership."

Persephone's heart raced in response to Nyx's words, tormented by the weight of their trust in her, an overwhelming fear gripping her that she would fail them.

"Queen Persephone will lead us to victory, I have no doubt," Hades said, moving to stand beside her as Ares rolled up the map. His fingers gripped hers, offering her comfort. "The Olympians are going to attempt to breach the gates," Hades continued. "They will likely position Poseidon near the Cocytus River. I suspect that they will melt the frozen waters so that the Underworld floods. Your mission is to prevent them from entering the palace. The threads must be safeguarded."

"Only Persephone knows their exact location," Hecate interjected.

"Yes," Hades agreed. "And all will safeguard the threads, except Ares, who will watch over the queen."

Persephone bit back her protest, knowing arguing would only waste time. He would never allow her to jeopardize her safety, but she would find a way to protect Hades as well as defeat Zeus.

Hades would often be absent during tactical discussions to ensure that whatever was discussed could not later be passed to his brother. He instead devoted most of his time to assisting Persephone in crafting speeches for the souls of Elysium and Asphodel Meadows. Overwhelmed by a fear of public speaking, Persephone's voice quivered as she rehearsed her words, but Hades remained a steady presence, his reassurance a comforting balm.

"I do not want to give speeches," Persephone protested glumly. "I am wretched at it."

"It's vital they trust you, see you as their queen and protector," he reminded her gently. "You can do this, Persephone. Just as you have conquered everything that life has thrown at you, this is simply one more obstacle you will defeat."

And so she practiced until her voice was strong and clear, until she placed the perfect enunciation on each word, and Hades deemed she was ready. As she faced the varied assemblies in Elysium and Asphodel Meadows—children, the elderly, tightly-knit families—she felt their eyes turn to her with trust as she pledged protection against Olympus. Yet, beneath the surface, a growing dread took hold. The weight of uncertainty pressed on her, knowing their lives rested in her hands, and she had no clear strategy to defeat the King of Gods.

Adding to her discomfort was the intensifying morning sickness, which was becoming harder to conceal from Hades. She attempted to attribute it to the anxiety of public speaking, but his perceptive dark eyes made her wonder how much he suspected. Her abdomen already had a subtle but definitive swell, and she dressed carefully to conceal the bump. His attentive care—washing her face, brushing back her hair—made her long to confide in him. But a lingering fear held her back; she couldn't risk endangering her precious baby.

Hades discussed the golden and blue blades with her. "Zeus will do everything he can to take the golden blade from me. I will hold him off as long as I can, but in the end, he will find a way to retrieve his sword." He grasped her arms, and his eyes were fierce as he stared down at her. "Persephone, you must do everything you can to avoid combat with him once he holds the golden blade. He will not hesitate to use it on you, and then he will own you, truly own you. Do not even let the smallest cut on your flesh."

But they both knew that the time was coming when she would have to battle Zeus alone. Would she have the strength to use the blue-flamed sword to destroy Zeus' soul? To smite him out of existence? It went against her deepest nature to take a life in such a way. And yet, in the face of such putrid evil, was there an alternative? She harbored an intense loathing for him, a visceral despisal for all he represented and the countless wrongs he had inflicted upon not only her but all of humanity. The idea that he deserved such a fate festered within her.

But a small voice whispered to her, reminding her of the tainted nature of the swords. If she were to employ them in such a way, would she be any better than Zeus? And what right did she have to consider her personal values when the entirety of humanity hung in the balance. The conflicting voices within her reverberated, creating a dissonance, a conflict as great as the impending battle that would reshape the fate of Gods and mortals alike. Why now, at this critical juncture, was she suffused with doubt about the inherent wrongness of the blades? The swords occupied more and more of her thoughts, and she found herself thinking of them as almost living and breathing entities, capable of tremendous evil. Even without her internal uncertainty about the blades, the truth was that despite all her training in the Titan Wars, she may be no match for Zeus, who was a master sword wielder. It was far more likely the battle could end with him ramming the golden blade through her heart.

At night, she and Hades would make passionate love until he collapsed into an exhausted slumber, but Persephone found no solace in rest; fear clung to her like a relentless shadow, and while her husband slept, she remained vigilant, eyes wide open, wrestling with uncertainty and dread. At all moments, Persephone kept the precious locket around her neck, and she would often touch it to reassure herself of its safekeeping. Desperation coursed through her veins, urging her to seize every moment with Hades. Her fingers brushed against his skin, seeking the reassurance of his pulse, a tangible proof that he was still with her. Yet, with each passing moment, her mind churned with the question of how to protect him. Strategies flitted through her thoughts, only to be discarded as quickly as they emerged, and as the sun rose each morning, she found herself no closer to any viable answers.

The Gods would gather in the throne room, utilizing their powers against one another for practice. One day, while Hypnos and Ares were battling, Hypnos sneezed, and Ares collapsed in a sudden swoon.

"How unfortunate," Hypnos mused, lightly tapping Ares with his foot while Nyx graciously handed him a handkerchief. "I have always been allergic to barbarians."

To everyone's surprise, Ares swiftly awakened with a resounding roar of approval. "By the Gods, I can't wait to see you use that on Athena! Fuck the powers of Olympus. Hypnos has more power in his sneeze than most do in their little finger!"

"Thank you, young butcher," Hypnos answered, and as he blew his nose, Ares collapsed again to the ground.

Styx, Lethe, the Furies, and Persephone, who had been training together, giggled, and Hecate was roaring in merriment, her boisterous laughter causing even Charon to smile grimly. As Persephone surveyed the room, she marveled at these once-enigmatic and powerful beings who had transformed from strangers into cherished friends. She could not fail them. While the other Gods trained, she would often vanish with Ares, resuming sword training and perfecting the techniques she had learned during the Titan Wars.

As time passed, Persephone grappled with a surge of restless energy, haunted by the absence of a plan to thwart Zeus and how to keep him from obtaining the golden blade. While the other Gods seemed to place implicit trust in her ability to navigate the impending battle, the daunting reality was that she had no idea how to overcome the King of Gods. Persephone bore the weight of her burdens in solitude, hesitant to disclose her lack of understanding to anyone. The unwavering support they provided only heightened her reticence, leaving her paralyzed by their reliance on her. She would spend as much time as possible by herself in solitary study, poring over ancient texts and scrolls for answers.

To compound her distress, as the days passed, Hades' complexion grew paler, his dark eyes ablaze with fever—a stark reminder of Zeus's encroaching return. A relentless mantra echoed in her mind every time she gazed at him: He is dying, he is dying. The mere thought of his death shattered her, and she found herself paralyzed by fear, unable to think.

But time pursued its relentless march, and on the eve of the impending war, Persephone lay in Hades' arms. With a tremor in her voice, she confessed, "I'm scared," the words barely audible against the gathering darkness.

He gently pressed her hand to his lips. "You're ready. You already possess everything necessary to beat him."

"I'm so afraid of losing you," she admitted in a small voice. "I can't bear the thought—"

He sat up abruptly, turning her to face him. "No, Persephone! Tomorrow, you must not think of me. Think only of the kingdom, of yourself. You cannot let anything interfere with that." His cheeks were flushed in his pale face, and Persephone's heart twisted in concern.

"Hush," she said, soothing him. She pushed him back to the bed, brushing his hair away from his flushed face. "Hush, I promise I will stay focused on Zeus," she lied.

"You must not—let him—distract you." His breath came in quick gasps. "He will try to – he will use me to bait you, or he could try to—"

"It's all right, Hades," Persephone murmured. "There are a million possibilities that he could do. We will be expecting him to attempt to separate us tomorrow."

"Remember, Persephone." His hand gripped hers tightly. "He will attempt to gain control of the golden blade. Do not let him use it on you; do whatever it takes to stop him. If he does, it is over. Once my – once he no longer is connected to me, he will hate you more than he has ever hated anyone. He will blame you when he loses the high from our connection. Promise me," he demanded, his dark, feverish eyes blazing at her. "Promise me when the time comes, you won't let anything stand in your way."

"I promise," she whispered.

Hades gently traced her face. "You have been everything to me. I could never imagine that someone like you could love me. Thank you," he whispered softly. "Thank you for the gift of your love, for never turning your back on me." For a brief moment, his hand tenderly lingered on her abdomen, and she tensed, wondering again if he knew about the child, but then he brought his fingers to her face again. "I love you."

Persephone's eyes blurred with tears. "Don't you dare say goodbye to me," she demanded fiercely, her lips trembling. "We are both walking off that battlefield tomorrow."

He placed his hand over her heart and moved her hand to his own chest. "We will always be together. We live inside one another, always, a light that no darkness can extinguish."

"I love you," she whispered. She hurriedly wiped at the tears on her cheeks. "Rest now," Persephone insisted practically, her voice a soothing balm. "No more talk of goodbyes. I simply won't allow it. We will need our strength tomorrow."

But sleep was again elusive for Persephone. She held onto her husband, watching him slip into an exhausted slumber, her heart quivering with a potent mixture of anticipation and dread. Occasionally, he would mutter in his sleep, fevered ramblings, and Persephone had the terrible feeling she was witnessing a man's last night on Earth as his disease reached a fever pitch. A sob broke from her lips, and she covered her mouth. Olive curled against her, and she buried her face against him, his soft fur absorbing her tears.

She clutched the chain against her neck, holding the locket tightly in her hand. "I will find a way to protect you," she vowed, closing her eyes. She placed a kiss on the necklace, her tears falling on the golden metal. "I won't lose you."

As the first faint light of dawn filtered through the window, she shivered, not only from the cold but also from the looming horrors that the day would bring—a day that threatened to take away everything she held dear.

Hades helped her to dress in armor, his fingers lingering over her skin. A gleaming golden breastplate, intricately engraved, encased her torso, and her arms were clad in polished gleaming bracers. She readied her weapons, and her fingers lovingly traced the pomegranate bow before she placed it into the sling on her back. A helmet embellished with symbols of the Underworld covered her face, so only the intensity of her green gaze was visible. Beneath the helmet, cascading curls of hair fell, trailing down her back.

He drew back, surveying her with a smile. Hades was similarly attired, and on his back, he wore the blue and golden blades. "You look like a true warrior. The Olympians should tremble to look upon such a fierce queen."

But Persephone was unable to return his smile. Instead, she lifted his hand and brought it to her face, closing her eyes tightly. "Happy birthday," she whispered. "I am so glad that you were born, that I found you. I love you so much."

"As I love you. Persephone," his deep voice rumbled. "Look at me."

She shook her head. A torrent of tears choked her voice as she grappled with the overwhelming weight of expressing what he truly meant to her, the paralyzing fear of losing him engulfing her. "I don't know what I'm doing!" she gasped suddenly. "I'm afraid! I– I cannot bear the thought of losing you. It would have been better if you had never known me," she whispered, a tear streaming down her cheek.

His fingers traced her jaw, gently tilting her head up. "Persephone." Finally, she raised her sorrowful green eyes to his. He leaned forward, brushing his lips against hers, and when he drew back, she saw all the love she felt within her own soul reflected in his eyes. "I cannot fathom altering a single chapter of our history. If reliving every ache and sorrow was the price of having you by my side, I would pay it willingly, over and over. I carry your love in my heart, and it is my shield; let mine be your armor." He brought her hand to his chest. "It lives on here, eternal, enduring." His lips brushed against hers. "Forever," he whispered.

Their embrace was furious; all the hurt, all the love, all the pain that had happened between them was expressed in the simple touch. But the moment was interrupted by an abrupt knock as Ares let himself into the room. He was clad in his habitual armor, and his handsome face was gleaming with excitement at the coming battle.

"I have gathered the Gods for a final discussion before tonight." He observed the pair, noting that they did not share his exuberance. "Or it can wait."

Hades brought Persephone's hand to his mouth and then firmly gripped her hand, slipping the Archeon blade into her palm. "Just in case," he whispered. "Are you ready, Queen Persephone?"

She nodded her head. Giving Olive one final kiss, they strode from the bedroom. Cerberus rose from the doorway where he had kept vigil each night, his paws a soft tread behind them. As they moved down the hall, a treacherous voice whispered that it would be for the last time. She bit her lip hard, refusing to listen to that wretched whisper inside her head. Her hand moved to the locket around her neck, and she clutched it like a talisman.

Hades waited outside, and as Persephone entered the throne room, the Gods of the Underworld were already gathered. All wore armor except for Hecate, who was dressed in long, black robes. They reviewed the plan for what felt like the millionth time, but this time, when Ares asked, "Are there any questions?" there was only silence.

"Very well," Ares said. He rapped on the door, and Hades walked in, moving to stand next to Persephone. He gave a brief nod of his head, and she stepped forward, preparing to give the speech that they had written together. As she moved to the center of the room, all eyes were fixed on her, these powerful, ancient Gods trusting her with their loyalty, with their lives.

"Today is the day that we fight against tyranny," she began, her voice unsteady. She closed her eyes, and she felt Hades' hand in hers. *Speak from your heart,* he whispered to her. *Fuck the rules.*

She tightened her fingers against him, the conflicting emotions within her threatening to spill over. Laughter and tears tugged at the corners of her consciousness, yet she held both back. When her eyes reopened, they blazed with a fierce crimson fire, and she stood resolute before her brothers and sisters in arms.

"Today, we stand united against the enduring oppressor of generations—Zeus. This is more than a mere struggle for our survival; it is a profound battle that will echo through the realms above and below, encompassing all creatures on this Earth. Tonight, our war is waged for every soul, a fight unlike any we have faced before. We acknowledge the power of the golden blade and the possibility that Zeus could erase our very existence. That we could die." She paused, closing her eyes briefly before they flashed open with determination.

"We understand the risks," she continued, "but still, we choose to fight. Each of us has felt his impact and suffered losses at his hand. We fight not only for those he has taken and harmed but also for the innocence yet to be born, ensuring that no others suffer as we have. As we enter the battlefield, let us reflect on the bonds of friendship we've forged, the honor we've experienced being part of this collective mission, and the profound privilege it is to stand beside you in this moment. Tonight, we shall emerge triumphant against the grip of tyranny!"

As the Gods cheered and readied themselves for the impending conflict, she felt the comforting presence of Hades' hand in hers, and she clung to it desperately, closing her eyes to savor the simple joy of him beside her.

While the other Gods took their positions, Persephone, Ares, and Hades waited in the throne room. Cerberus had stubbornly refused to leave Persephone until, finally, the witch threatened to turn him into a cat. Persephone had intervened, assuring him that no such thing would happen, when Hades suddenly knelt before the Hellhound, stroking his soft necks and whispering something in his ears. The Hellhound seemed to understand whatever he said, for he whined gently as he looked at his master, his dark eyes sad, but he abided, trailing behind the Underworld Gods until only the trio was left.

And that had been hours ago. The suspense weighed heavily on Persephone, threatening to drive her to the brink of sanity. It was necessary that Hades rested as much as possible before the battle, and while they knew it would happen tonight, they did not know exactly when. While Hades sat on the throne, Ares sat beside him on the floor, polishing his weapons, but Persephone couldn't sit still; she alternated between pacing, studying maps and scrolls, and every now and then, she would peek at the swords across Hades' back – shooting them a look of intense hatred.

Her ears strained for any sign of the impending battle. She both longed for and dreaded the war's heralding sound, her nerves wound so tightly that a scream threatened to escape her lips. Hades remained seated on his chair, seemingly serene, abiding by their agreement to await the battle in the throne room. Despite her overwhelming anxiety and the fear of the unknown, she adamantly refused to leave his side. But the uncertainty gnawed at her sanity.

Ares quipped suddenly, "If Zeus was the floor, then the battle would already be won with your stomping," as he absentmindedly cleaned his sword for what must have been the hundredth time.

"How is it that the God of War can sit so still?" she asked with a scowl.

"People think that war is constant fighting, but it's just as much sitting and waiting. I've had to learn patience over the years."

Just as she made a grunt of disbelief, a loud noise reverberated through the chamber, and the entire Underworld shook. Hades stood, his eyes blazing.

"The war has begun!"

The trio rushed from the palace, and they saw hands reaching through the gates, laden heavily with armor. Persephone kept pace with Hades, Ares right behind her.

"Will the gates hold them?"

"It is not the gates that concern me. Listen." She closed her eyes and heard it, too. Ice cracking and shattering.

"They're melting, Cocytus!" Persephone cried out. As a frigid wind blew through the Underworld, an enormous wave of icy water rushed towards them, and the noises of ice shattering grew louder.

"Styx!" Hades bellowed.

The River Goddess appeared as if she had leaped out of the air, her long gray hair billowing behind her. "The rivers are on the rise," she said quickly. "Lethe and Acheron are endeavoring to contain their waters so as not to inundate the souls with suffering and amnesia."

Styx closed her eyes and began weaving her hands, re-freezing the massive wall of the thawed river as Persephone grew enormous trees with large roots that consumed the remaining water. They were able to avoid being submerged by the icy wave, but the water level continued to rise.

"The threads!" Hades shouted. "If the threads are submerged, the mortals of Earth will drown."

Persephone knew what Zeus was doing. He was weakening his opponent before the battle. Hades' was already sweating and trembling; she panicked, sensing the unraveling of his thread.

"Hades, let us deal with this!"

"They cannot flood the Underworld if there is no water," he hissed.

"Hades, no! We can hold it!"

"You cannot hold the wall forever, Persephone."

Before she could object, he had already extended his arms and clapped his palms together; the Cocytus' water vanished. Hades' legs buckled beneath him, causing him to fall to his knees. He quickly placed both of his hands deep into the Earth, his eyes closing tightly as he muttered beneath his breath. Golden embers fell to the ground behind him, and the veins in his hands pulsed, black and gold dancing beneath his skin's surface. Persephone flew to his side as he collapsed.

She drew him into her arms, supporting his head on her lap.

"Hades," she said urgently. She placed her fingertips on his wrist and nearly wept with relief. There was a pulse there, though it was erratic and weak.

His eyes suddenly opened wide. "Ruined me," he murmured.

"What?"

"You have ruined me." The iris of his eyes glowed gold when he turned to gaze at her. He asked with a smile, "Did you miss me?"

"No!" she gasped. His hand shot towards her, and she quickly jumped away from him, landing on her feet in a crouch.

He faced her while still wearing that condescending smile. She looked behind her but saw no sign of Ares. "You have failed," the king said. "It is already too late for him. Come along, Persephone. Leave this mediocre existence behind and begin a new one with me. I love you more than I have ever loved anyone else."

"You do not understand the meaning of the word," she hissed. "I will watch you lose everything," she promised as she drew her sword.

"Very well then." The king reached his hand behind him and finally touched the golden blade on his back. "There you are." He raised his hand high, and she heard the Underworld's gates open. Just as she was about to attack, she heard the voice of Hades in her mind, saying, *Let them in.* She swiftly made the agreed-upon gesture, elevating her right hand to her temple so that the Underworld Gods would not yet reveal themselves.

The Earth rumbled as the Olympians entered, and an army of mortals marched behind them. Athena rode up to the palace with a smug smile on her face, guiding Zeus' horse with a golden rope while Zeus meditated atop the animal, a laurel wreath of gold glistening atop his head. The King of Gods' eyes suddenly flashed open, and her husband collapsed to the ground. She rushed quickly toward Hades, standing guard over him, as Zeus smugly gazed down at Persephone from his large steed.

"Surrender," he commanded.

As she looked up at him, her eyes were malevolent. "Never!"

"You are fighting a losing battle." Persephone heard Hades speak simultaneously with Zeus as he spoke from his steed, their mouths moving in unison. "I have already won." Zeus' covetous gaze shifted from her to the golden weapon that adorned Hades' back and then to Persephone. "I finally have everything I want."

Athena suddenly spoke, her cool voice echoing loudly. "King Hades, we have come to take you to Olympus to stand trial. Your co-conspirator, Hera, has already been hung high in the sky for her transgressions to stare at the abyss of Chaos. You are charged with conspiring against the King of Olympus, possessing him, the attempt to destabilize his kingdom, as well as the abduction and rape of Persephone. If you are proven guilty, you will be sentenced to Tartarus. Give Zeus the weapon and deliver his daughter to him."

"Never," Hades choked, his face creased in agony.

He struggled to rise, and Zeus laughed, his eyes dancing with pleasure. "By the Gods, there is nothing left of you. Your soul is nearly shattered."

"You will not touch him!" Persephone shouted. She lifted her blade high and yelled, "Now!"

Suddenly, Chaos ensued as the Gods of the Underworld emerged from the shadows. Hecate came first, appearing like a spectral phantom, accompanied by an army of golden-eyed shadow creatures. She approached Athena with fire in her eyes. "Impetus," she hissed. And the

Goddess of Wisdom gave a shriek as shadows enveloped her, pulling her from her steed and covering her from view.

Hypnos was battling the twins, Artemis and Apollo, countering whatever battle moves they made with a wave from his hands, making their movements sluggish. The God of Sleep eyed Dionysus as he suddenly stumbled near him, but he was drunk and appeared confused, clearly having wandered down with the other Gods by accident. Hypnos contemptuously threw a poppy at him, and with a single shriek of terror, the God of Wine collapsed to the ground.

Further from the palace, the River Gods united against Hephaestus and Hermes; they bent and manipulated the waters of their rivers, and the Gods of Olympus were on the offensive, terrified that those treacherous waters would touch their skin. Cerberus and the Furies teamed together against Pan, Halirrhothius, and the mortal army. Enyo suddenly raced through in her chariot, and an enormous Cerberus rushed towards her, howling with rage as he tipped her over, flinging her body in one of his mouth's like a rag doll.

But Zeus had eyes only for the Underworld's king and queen. Persephone looked again for Ares, but he was nowhere in sight. Hades stood unsteadily, and she gripped her sword more tightly as he raised his head. As though in a dream, Hades closed his eyes, muttering ancient words. Shadows moved from every direction, moving towards him and into him. The darkness of the world grew, and when Hades finally opened his eyes, they glowed purple.

Zeus snarled. He extended his hand and said, "Come to me!" The golden blade flew from the scabbard on Hades' back towards the God with the silver hair. Hades outstretched his hand, and the blade stopped between them, both Gods grasping with all their might for the weapon as it levitated in the air, spinning rapidly.

"You no longer have enough power to keep it from me!" Zeus shouted.

"I will hold onto it until my dying breath," Hades hissed.

"We shall see," Zeus answered slyly.

Persephone's body abruptly jerked, and she staggered towards Hades. He looked at her in concern but could not release his tenuous grip on the sword.

"Ha--Hades!" she stammered. "Move!" Suddenly, he felt a searing agony along his side. Persephone had slashed him with the Acheron blade. She gazed at him with horror, her green eyes rimmed with gold and tears, as she grasped the hand holding the blade with her other arm. Her body contorted like a doll recklessly bent by a child as she attempted to fight for control of her limbs. "What is happening to me?"

Hades' eyes narrowed on his brother, who was perspiring from concentration, but a wicked grin curved his lips. "Persephone," Hades said urgently, "Zeus is controlling you through our soul connection. Resist it!" He kept one arm extended toward the sword and wrapped the other securely around her. "You must break the connection now!"

Her face was creased with agony, and her entire body trembled. "I'm trying, but I cannot!"

"You must! Fight it, or you will end up like me. Fight it, or you're already dead!"

"Let me go! I am afraid I will hurt you again," she begged, but he did not loosen his hold on her. She cried out in desperation as she stabbed him again, and as he let out a scream of anguish, his hold on the golden blade weakened, and it finally flew to its master into the King of God's grasp.

Zeus roared in triumph, surrounded by arcs of lightning that crackled around him. Clasping the golden-flamed sword between his hands, the radiant gold hue illuminated his face and hair, casting an ethereal glow that made him gleam like the sun itself.

"No!" Persephone cried in anguish, burying her face in her hands as Hades held her tightly against him.

"It is all right, Persephone," Hades murmured. "Stay here," he instructed before lowering her to the ground and drawing the blue-flamed sword from the scabbard on his back. He flew in the direction of his sibling, and Zeus raised the golden blade with a growl of pleasure.

"Time to die, brother!" Zeus taunted.

When the swords collided, the air exploded with green, cataclysmic energy, propelling the brothers in opposite directions. Zeus' eyes glowed white with electricity as he extended his arm, sizzling Hades in the back with a gigantic burst of white lightning. Hades let his shoulder absorb the power, then drew his other arm back, propelling black energy towards Zeus.

"You have started a war for nothing," Hades growled. "You should have been happy with your life on Olympus! You had all a God could have wanted."

Electricity arced around Zeus' hands. "No," Zeus hissed. "I couldn't let you be happy. I told you. You will have nothing."

The brothers raced towards one another once more, blue colliding with gold, while thunder and lightning echoed throughout the Underworld. Massive boulders fell from the mountains and into the Styx, causing the river's waters to gush around them. Hades abruptly leaped into the air and, in a fit of fury, brought his weapon crashing down on Zeus, knocking him to the ground. As he stood over the King of Gods, his breath came in quick, short spurts, his silver blade hot with blue fire. But as Hades gazed down, his brother was smiling at him. A voice entered Hades' mind: "I will take everything from you, beginning with your love. Consider it a supreme blessing from the King of Gods. *Kill her!*" he commanded.

Hades raised his weapon high and abruptly turned around, unleashing a dark blast of pulsating energy at Persephone, who had been struggling to reach them, weakened after resisting Zeus' possession. She fell back with a shocked cry, and Hades flew towards her, lifting the blue-flamed blade high above his head. She scrambled, dodging to safety, her eyes wide with fear. She was on the offensive, defending herself but trying not to harm him. He, however, was aiming to kill, and that gave him the upper hand.

"Hades, please stop!" she cried. But there was no recognition in his dilated eyes as he advanced towards her.

Suddenly, he drove the blade into the ground, and the rock beneath her began to crack. She leaped to avoid plummeting into the fractured Earth below, and he unleashed a barrage of devastating blows against her. Persephone evaded blow after blow, narrowly escaping the blade's contact. Finally, she lifted her hand, twisting as she grew a covering forest. She scurried behind a rock, gasping for breath.

"I knew you were too weak to fight me." Zeus' voice echoed loudly. "Love has made you weak. It is the greatest weakness. Love has killed your husband, and unless I show you mercy, your husband will kill you."

Suddenly, a rough hand yanked her by the hair and pulled her from her hiding place. She gave a cry of pain, looking up at her captor. Hades. Tears streamed down her face as she stared into his vacant gaze.

"Please remember," she whispered. "Our love is more powerful than his, than any dark magic. Remember me, Hades," she pleaded desperately.

Hades raised his free hand, and lightning arced to the ground, burning her forest to ash. As he pulled her roughly back towards the palace, she reached up, her fingers frantic as she searched for his wrist. His skin felt cold against her hands, and his pulse was erratic. Suddenly, he threw her down and waved his hand over her. Thin chains made of diamonds held her down, immobilizing her. She sought desperately to find her power, but panic filled her, fear overcame her, and she stared up at the man she loved, the man who held the blue-flamed sword above her. The man who would kill her.

The Olympians and Underworld Gods paused in their battle, shock on their faces as they saw the King of the Dead attacking his wife. He suddenly lowered the sword to his wife's throat. She stared into his face, at his cruel smile, and then into his eyes as a tear fell down his pale cheek.

Fight me, his mind begged her. *Take the sword.*

No, I cannot, she cried back. *I cannot move; I cannot escape his hold either.*

Then I have failed us both.

"Kill her," Zeus whispered.

She watched him struggle against himself as he clutched the blue-flamed sword in his hand. His nose began to bleed, and blood dripped from his ears and his eyes. He lifted the sword high, and she wanted to close her eyes and prepare for the pain of death, but she would not leave him alone. She stared up at him with love shining in her eyes as the blue blade drew nearer, lighting her face with its radiance.

"I love you," she whispered.

And with a cry of pain, Hades re-directed the sword, forcing the blade through his own heart. Suddenly, she could move, and she leaped towards him with a cry of denial on her lips, catching him before he could fall on the hard, cold ground.

"No, no, no," she sobbed, wrapping her fingers around the cold steel of the blade. His precious blood was dripping from the mortal wound, pooling below him. She tried to press healing warmth into it, but it did nothing. "Hecate!" she cried. "Hecate, please, help him!"

The witch rushed to them, Hypnos covering her as she ran. Hecate knelt beside her, brushing her hands against Persephone's.

"I am sorry, little bird," she whispered, tears on her cheeks. "There is no magic that can aid him."

Hades' eyes suddenly flashed open, and his gaze was filled with an overwhelming love as he looked up at Persephone. The world outside seemed to fade into obscurity as she clung to his hand, their fingers entwined like the roots of a centuries-old tree.

With great effort, Hades offered her a bittersweet smile. "It's over," he whispered, his breath coming in ragged gasps. "His hold on me is gone. But now he will turn against you. Persephone, you must be ready. The greatest battle is yet to come."

Persephone's sobs came in ragged waves, but she forced herself to listen, her heart aching with the weight of his words. "No, please; I can't bear to lose you," she pleaded, her voice breaking. "Please don't leave me!"

"You have already given me everything, Persephone," he said, his voice filled with tenderness. "Your love, your devotion—those are the greatest gifts I've ever received." He lifted her hand from his chest. "I am free now. Let me die."

"No," she cried. "It cannot end like this; it cannot all have been for nothing! I will not let you leave me!"

"Nothing? No, it has been everything; you have been everything." His eyes widened suddenly, and he abruptly clenched her hand. "Persephone, lead me to the Styx. Only you. Do not let any others near us."

Persephone looked at the Olympian Gods. As the battle raged on, Zeus lay on the ground; he had been flung back as the sword pierced Hades' heart, and Athena helped him to stand. Persephone saw the horror and emptiness in his eyes as he rose. The malevolent gleam in his eyes flickered, replaced by a hollow gaze that betrayed the abrupt void left by the shattered enchantment. She knew that the "love" he had felt from his connection with Hades had vanished.

Persephone turned to Hecate. "Will you help me?" she asked in a trembling voice.

"Yes, we will ensure no one disturbs you. Take him," Hecate hissed. Her eyes began to be covered entirely by black. She lifted her staff high, and Persephone watched as her being was split into three forms, each surrounded by her own shadowy army of beasts. With an unholy cry, the trio joined the other Gods of the Underworld and launched Hell on the Gods of Olympus.

Persephone levitated Hades' body over the rocks to the river, clasping his hand and sobbing as she walked. Suddenly, she stumbled, and his body collapsed on the jagged rocks below.

"I am so--sorry," she stammered, her words broken, her teeth chattering. Desperation etched across her face as she tried to conjure her powers once more, but she was unable to summon them.

"It's all right, Persephone," he gasped through the pain. "Can you drag me?"

"No!" she cried out, a sob of despair escaping her lips. "The rocks will cut you."

"We have little time left; drag me. A few more cuts will not hurt me," he said in a strained voice, but a weak smile curled his lips.

With another sob, she pulled him over the rocks, being as gentle as she could, until finally, they reached the shore of the Styx. She lowered him into the water, sinking into it beside him, and the water around them turned crimson with his blood.

"This had to be a, life for a life. I was always destined to die," he whispered. "Gaia, please." He lifted his hands, attempting to pull the blade from his chest, slicing his fingers open on the wicked sword.

"Do not pull it out!" she cried.

"Persephone," he said softly, "I must. I must destroy the blades, or he will kill you." He held out his hand. His face creased in frustration. "I have severed the link between Zeus and I. Your soul is safe. But in doing so, I can no longer grasp his weapon. I will not be able to destroy it." His eyes closed for a moment, and his fingers brushed against the silver blade in his chest, smearing the blood. When they opened again, they were fathomless black pools. "But I will not leave you defenseless. This weapon is yours if you will claim it." His hand tightened over hers. "You must pull it from my chest, Persephone."

Zeus was watching the battle with a scowl on his face. Chaos had been unleashed on the battlefield, and the witch's infernal army of freaks was blocking the Styx from Zeus' view. He had no choice but to stand beside Athena as he gathered his strength, supported on either side by Apollo and Hermes.

"He is truly dying?" Athena asked her father coolly.

"Yes," Zeus spat, finally gaining enough power to push the Gods off him. Apollo bent to retrieve the golden blade. "Do not touch it, it's mine!" he bellowed. He bent, snatching the sword from the ground. The golden light reflected greedily in his eyes.

"Leave us," Athena said to Apollo and Hermes. "Take down the witch." Hermes gave her a mock salute as they rushed back into battle. "How did you do it? How did you kill a God?"

Zeus' face turned cunning as his grip on the sword tightened. "I will share with you after the battle, daughter." He looked towards the Styx. "Something is happening there."

She turned her cool gaze to the river, observing the couple. "Your war is all but won."

Zeus' eyes narrowed. "No, he is still plotting." He flexed his fingers, and electricity arced between the tips. He smiled with satisfaction. "Deal with the witch. Time for me to deal with the little bitch."

Persephone wrapped her fingers tightly around Hades', shaking her head, tears pouring down her cheeks. "But if I take the sword, you will bleed to death," she whispered.

"I am already bleeding to death, Persephone." He closed his eyes suddenly. "Before I go, there is something I must tell you." He raised his hand.

The water in the Styx bubbled around them, and she was reminded of the strange movements she had seen in the waters. Suddenly, it was splashing around them, growing higher and higher, until a soul clad in armor stepped from the dark, bubbling waters. Behind him, an army of other souls knelt, silent and waiting as though listening for a command.

"Who are they?" she whispered in amazement.

"They are the army of the dead, and at your command, they will attack," Hades answered. "Until then, only you and I are able to see them. I think you may know their leader."

The head soul suddenly rushed forward, bowing next to Persephone. He took off his helmet, and Persephone gasped. "Father!" she cried.

He reached for her, pulling her tightly into his arms. "My daughter," he said, his eyes filled with tears as he pulled back. "When Hades sent me away, he told me a battle was coming—a battle for all souls. He instructed me to train an army and that when the time came, he would call for us. He sent me into the Styx, and that is where I have been since." His sad eyes moved between Persephone and Hades. "I am so sorry that it has come to this."

"Are they ready?" Hades asked.

"Yes. They are awaiting her command."

"Good," he whispered. He turned his eyes back to his wife. "Persephone. I need you to pull the sword and claim what is yours."

She shook her head. "No! I cannot do it!" she cried. "I will not do it. I cannot be the one to do it!"

"You must. If you do not do it, you and our child will die!"

She gasped and began sobbing. "You–know– then?"

"Yes," Hades whispered. "I felt him in you that very night I laid with you. Our love is growing within you." His hand brushed her face. "I am–so lucky– to have had a family. It was all I ever wanted. A wife. A son. You will be such a beautiful mother. I only wish I could have been there."

She put her hand over his, closing her eyes. "It was all I ever wanted too. To be with you," she whispered.

"Pull the blade for him. Pull it now."

"I am not ready. Please, I am not ready to be the one to take your life!"

Footsteps splashed in the water, and she turned her head. Fear suffused her as she saw Zeus towering over them, the golden blade clutched tightly in his hand.

"Still alive, I see," he remarked with a sneer. "Why don't you just go ahead and die already?"

Persephone glanced anxiously at her father, who was staring at the King of Gods with intense hatred, but, as Hades said, Zeus was not able to see him.

"I think I will take the blue sword too," Zeus was saying. "It will complete my collection." He jumped, putting his foot on Hades' chest, and tried to yank the sword from him. Blood poured from Hades' lips as his upper body lifted off the ground.

"Get off of him!" Persephone shrieked, pushing the King of Gods back, but Zeus' face was fixed on Hades', who was smiling up at him with blood-stained teeth.

"You cannot pull it, brother," Hades explained softly. "Our connection is broken. The sword is no longer mine. Everything is hers." He tilted his head toward Persephone. "It is hers and hers alone. The entire Underworld belongs to her. Only she can pull this sword from me."

Zeus turned his head to Persephone and said, "She doesn't have the courage." His icy eyes gleamed. "She is no opponent. I told you the queen needed to protect her king. Without the king, she's just a weak little bitch. You do not know how to play the game. She is barely a player in this match. So weak. But very well. When I take her life, I will take the sword from her."

She looked up to Zeus with gleaming eyes. "Cronus," she whispered.

"What?" he snapped, barely paying her attention.

"Cronus shall be my successor."

She finally had the King of God's focus. His blue eyes narrowed. "She cannot be serious. Hades would not allow it."

"But I am already the ruler of this world. Perhaps you will find him a more suitable opponent." She closed her eyes, sensing that heavy, waiting presence in the depths of Tartarus, his seething rage. "He is quite angry and ready to be released from his prison."

"Foolish bitch!" he growled. "You jeopardize all worlds with your absurdity."

"Come now, Zeus; you have no need to worry about Cronus unless I die. If I survive, he will stay safely locked in Tartarus. However, if you kill me, the Gates of Tartarus will unlock, and he will come forth riding Typhon. Your happy little life depends on me, alive and drawing breath."

"I defeated him once, and I shall again," Zeus snarled. "Once this battle is finished, you will join Cronus." He kneeled beside his brother in the dark waters. "I told you your gates could not keep me out. The Underworld is mine."

Hades began to laugh, choking on the blood in his throat. "Brother. I did not build the gates to keep you out." He twisted his hand, and they heard the large doors seal shut with a thud that echoed across the land. "I built them to keep *you* in. Only Persephone can let you out. Her death will leave you a prisoner."

His eyes shimmered with rage, but then he smiled. "You think you are clever, don't you?" His eyes turned to Persephone, lingering over her and the hand that rested on the slight swell of her abdomen. "Everyone has a weak point. And that weakness can be exploited. I do not think I have taken *everything* from you yet."

Persephone, she heard Hades' desperate whisper in her mind, and she turned to him, kneeling down beside him. *He knows of our child. He will kill him. He will kill you to get to him. Take the weapon. Claim your kingdom. He knows.* Persephone looked into Hades' eyes. In their dark reflection, she could see Zeus lifting the golden blade behind her.

Persephone. His mind whispered, *Now!*

"I love you," she sobbed, and then she grabbed the heavy hilt of the weapon and when she pulled out the blade, she could feel the shattering of his soul, his death, and she screamed in anguish as she turned to face the King of Gods. A haunting howl merged with her own as Cerberus flung back his heads, howling in endless sorrow for the death of his companion. A giant blast of golden energy burst from Persephone, shattering rocks and mountains and flinging every God backward as she flew toward Zeus in a fury, striking blow after blow against him.

He looked at her in astonishment and then smiled. "You fight like a Titan."

"I fight like a mother, like a wife, like a queen," she shrieked. Golden tears flowed down her cheeks as she battled the pale-haired God. He blasted electricity towards her, and she formed a dark crystal to shield herself from the attack.

The battle raged behind them with a deafening clash of steel against steel, arrows cutting through the air like deadly whispers, and the ground trembled with the thunder of charging warhorses. But Zeus cared only for the Goddess of Spring, who held the blue-flamed sword.

Zeus' face was contorted with anger. "You finally got pregnant. I will not allow his child to live!" He lifted the sword, shattering the dark crystal.

She flew from her hiding spot high into the sky, and he lifted his hands up towards the heavens. Rain beat against her, and lightning sizzled through the air. With a wave of her hand, the raindrops transformed into a fury of dark crystals that rained down, stabbing the Gods of Olympus and their army below. The King of Gods bellowed as his body was impaled by the large crystals. Yanking them from his flesh, he pulled electricity from the sky and flung it towards her like a lasso, yanking her down. With a cry, she waved her hands, and Cerberus leaped, catching her. She twisted from his back, the wind carrying her high as she flew towards Zeus once more. As they met, their blades

crossed into an X, cataclysmic energy flashing around them.

She lifted one hand from the blade, twisting it to grow dark bloodstones. With a nod of her head, the crystals arced toward him, cruelly piercing his flesh. He gave a cry of anguish, falling back. As he pulled them from his skin, blood poured from the large wounds. Even as the injuries began to close, he pulled white-hot light from the sky, spinning it in his hands, creating a whirlwind of sizzling lightning, and pushed it towards her. She blasted it back with a wave after wave of black energy. With her other hand, she plunged the Underworld into darkness, aiding the Gods of the Underworld in their battle. They were used to seeing in the shadows, but the Gods of Olympus lived in the sunshine. Lightning arced across the sky, and the battle raged on.

Over and over, it repeated. His powerful lightning against her dark energy. Zeus was so powerful that she was unable to keep an eye on the other Gods of the Underworld; all her attention focused only on him, and she prayed to Gaia that they were all right. As he unleashed yet another series of devastating attacks against her, Persephone was too slow, and his blue eyes gleamed in triumph as he met his mark. The searing lightning surged through her, and with a gasp of agony, she summoned the last of her strength to erect a shield crafted from black tourmaline against his ferocious onslaught. Her hands trembled as she felt the deep burn on her legs. With gritted teeth, she attempted to infuse healing warmth into the injured, mangled flesh.

"Gaia," she whispered. "I am not strong enough. Help me." A tear fell from her cheek. "Help me," she begged again.

Persephone, release me.

She knew who that voice was that called to her, and she gave a sob of relief and despair. With the snap of her fingers, she could hear the shackles of Cronus fall to the ground; a great wind pushed through the world. He was free. Suddenly, a heaviness pulsed in her abdomen, and she grasped her stomach. A long, agonizing contraction forced her down to the ground. She gave a cry of despair: the baby was coming far too early. Had Cronus betrayed her? But thought fled her mind as she dropped the blue-flame sword and the crystal shield, screaming in agony as another contraction ripped through her.

Zeus laughed as he approached her. "Ah, the epitome of weakness and fragility: a mother. It's no wonder your kind is so easily broken. Now, die!"

He brought the golden blade high when a tanned hand caught his arm, halting the descent of the sword. Ares, his blue eyes hot with righteous anger, stood before the King of Gods. He shoved his father back, flinging him away from Persephone, then bent, lifting the silver blade from the ground. The blue of the sword glowed azure in his gaze, the blade nearly singing in his hand.

"You will not touch her," Ares spat as Zeus turned to face him, standing in front of the Goddess.

"Ah," Zeus hissed. "My snake of a son. How I am looking forward to this."

"My entire life," Ares said softly, "you have been the darkness that loomed over me, the storm that never passed. You made me the God of War, hoping that I would be shaped in your image, and I thank you for your lessons, for I've learned from you what I should never become. Your family should have been everything to you. Instead, you have used us as tools, discarding us when we are no longer useful."

"Traitor!" Enyo shrieked, her ragged voice carrying across the battlefield. "Blood traitor!"

"Silence!" Zeus snarled. He lowered his voice. "I plan to enjoy watching you die."

Ares turned and took one final look at Persephone. "Go," he whispered. "Hide. Protect the child." Then he was racing towards Zeus, the blue-flamed sword held high.

Persephone had crawled into a small cave next to the Styx, and she was bent over, gasping in pain. Frantically, she ripped the armor from her body until she lay clad only in a thin undercovering. She cried out in despair as she felt the warm liquid between her thighs. Blood. Her hand gripped the locket around her neck.

"Hades," she whispered. "Hades, please."

He cannot help you. Remember our promise. Cronus' voice echoed in her mind.

"The baby is too soon," she sobbed. "Please, save him."

Her contractions were closer and more severe, and blood began to pool beneath her as she screamed in agony. She searched for the tiny heartbeat within her.

"Please," she whispered, "do not leave me again. Not when you are all that is left of him. I give you his kingdom; I give you all my powers and everything I have for you to live. Take my life in your place; only live. Gaia, let him live!"

Remember our promise, the voice called again.

"I remember! Save my son! I beg you!"

Then push, Persephone. Push.

She gave a cry of shock as her abdomen began to rapidly swell, and she screamed in anguish, pushing with the contractions, pulling her legs back to ease the passage of her baby. As she bore down, she saw the hand of a small child emerge from her, grasping onto the hard stone of the cave. She gave a gasp of shock that turned into a scream as another powerful contraction coursed through her. A second hand emerged, the size of a man's. Persephone felt herself ripping and tearing, but she did not stop bearing down. She pushed, letting her tissues split, her womb shatter, until finally, she bore her child.

She sat up, her lips pale, her face drenched with sweat, to look at her babe, the young man lying on the cold stone, covered in blood and fluid. His hair glowed white in the darkness. Blood and sweat dripped off his skin, and when he lifted his head, she gasped. He was so like her husband—so beautiful and dear—and as she reached for him, she remembered the words from Janus: the white-haired God, the high God.

"Mother," he whispered.

He stood, using his muscular legs for the first time. His eyes glowed gold as he looked down at her. "Zagreus," she breathed.

He kneeled before her, wrapping his arms around her. One of his hands moved to her abdomen, pressing healing warmth into her.

"Mother, I have waited so long for you."

She held his face, studying it, memorizing the lines and planes as her eyes blurred with tears. "You found your way back to me," she sobbed.

"No matter the ebb and flow of time or the distance between us, I will always come back to you. I am born of your blood, of your love, and my very heart beats with the power of your creation." Their hands entwined fiercely. "Cronus sped up time so that I would be able to fulfill the promise that he made to you. You have been so brave, mother."

"No," she whispered, closing her eyes tightly, a tear trailing down her cheek. "I have failed your father, failed you." Another tear streamed down her face. "I failed the world. I was not strong enough to defeat him."

"No!" Zagreus said fiercely. "Strength lies not in the clash of swords or skill on the battlefield. You are stronger than any God. You have sacrificed so much for those you love. Your power lies far beyond your Godly abilities. There is no other God who would do what you have done. The love you carry in your heart," Zagreus pressed his hand against her chest. "This is where your true power resides. It makes you incorruptible. It makes you a queen the world needs." He brought her hand to his face. "It makes you a mother any child would love with all their heart."

"Zagreus," Persephone breathed, bringing him against her. "I love you so much."

"As I love you, mother," he said softly against her ear. "But I must go," he said reluctantly. "There is someone I must look for."

She grasped his arm, her face creased in concern. "Who? Where are you going? If Zeus finds you, he will use the golden blade on you!"

"I will be alright," he said gently. "You must stay here, mother. Do not leave the cave."

"Zagreus, no!" Her voice was a raw cry, but her precious son was already stepping from the entrance, a halo of light surrounding him. "Zagreus!" she called again. She tried to crawl after him, but she was too weak, and she gave a sob of despair as she watched him leave.

Outside the cave, Zagreus came to a halt, a fleeting pang of pain etching across his features as his mother's cry reached him. Despite the compelling urge to linger and offer solace to her, he had a promise to

fulfill. Wiping the tears from his face, he resumed his sprint toward the Styx, his eyes shifted to the battlefield. Amidst the Chaos, he spotted the unmistakable, powerful figure of the King of Gods. Zagreus paused, directing his intense gaze toward Zeus. The force of his scrutiny held as Zeus slowly turned his head, scanning the horizon, until he locked eyes with Zagreus. Zagreus watched as confusion turned to a potent mix of fear and fury in Zeus's piercing blue gaze.

"It is the boy, the child from the river," Zeus whispered, and his voice trembled. Zeus pointed the golden sword towards Zagreus and bellowed, "Bring him to me!"

As Zagreus dove into the waters of the Styx, the Olympians gave chase.

Hades' soul floated above the battle. He looked down at his hands, and they shimmered, golden and iridescent, weaved of infinite, miniscule threads. Around him was a kaleidoscope of stars, and he was suspended in them, floating in the ethereal ether of eternity. He was nothing and yet everything, free of the broken body that had bound him, relieved of the burdens that life had shackled upon him. As he gazed down at the battle, death gave him clarity on how senseless it all was. He searched desperately for Persephone, but he could not see her. Desperation filled him, a need to protect her still, but an insistent force seemed to tug at him, urging him to go. He struggled against the call until a delicate black moth fluttered towards him, drawing his attention.

"Come," it whispered. "I have been waiting for you."

Hades recognized the God of Death, Thanatos; he had come to greet him on this, his last journey. The moth's wings fluttered, leaving tendrils of smoky blackness in their wake.

"Persephone," Hades said.

"You cannot stay here, king. Your time in this world is over. Come," the voice cajoled. "Come."

Darkness enveloped him, and the tumultuous battle below disappeared as Hades trailed the moth through the expansive realms of the Underworld. They glided through the shadowy landscapes until they arrived at the statue of Janus. Drawing nearer, the moth's delicate flutter prompted the Two Faces to open, unveiling a concealed doorway. With a solemn gaze, Hades' soul traversed the threshold. As the doors began to seal behind him, Hades cast one last lingering look at the familiar world he was leaving behind.

"Persephone," Hades whispered.

The flutter of the black moth's wings was the last thing he saw.

"Farewell, king," it called softly. "Farewell."

Hades traversed the desolate expanse until the boundless blackness of Chaos loomed ahead, an insurmountable void that his physical form had been unable to breach. Now liberated from his corporeal constraints, his soul effortlessly navigated through the inky abyss. Moving towards the distant glistening white island that had once eluded his touch, it drew nearer until a small, pale temple materialized in the darkness.

Two hooded beings stood perfectly still, like pillars, and he somehow knew that they had been waiting for *him*. As he reached the shore, he waded from the ether and gasped at the world around him. Millions of stars illuminated the darkness; he was standing in the constellations within the very center of the galaxy. The taller figure moved forward and flung back her hood.

Hades trembled as he beheld her face. "It cannot be," he whispered.

"My son," Rhea whispered, her voice like a soothing lullaby. As he fell into her arms, she embraced him like a wee babe, drawing him close to her. "My darling boy," she said gently as she stroked his hair. "It's over now. Rest here for a while. Let me hold you."

"Mother," he whispered, and he could feel the hot tears on his face. "Forgive me, forgive me." He repeated those two words over and over, the phrase he had whispered in his dreams, in his nightmares for millennia.

"Aidoneus," Rhea said softly, lifting his head. "Look at me, my son. There is nothing to forgive. I made my choice. The burden of my death was never yours to bear." Her eyes filled with tears. "You have suffered so much. I am so sorry I was not there to protect you, that I failed you. But I would do it all again, you know; I could not let you take his life–sons killing fathers–I could not allow it. It would have shattered you."

He pulled back to look at her. "Mother," he whispered, touching her face. "Are you real?" She was more beautiful than he had remembered, the lines of her face somehow sharper, and the colors of her hair and eyes perfected in this other world.

"Yes, Aidoneus, I am real," she answered with a smile.

"How did you come to be here? How does my soul still exist after I – after the blade?"

"There was some truth to what the Cyclops said. While the swords they created may kill a God, they did not fully understand the weapons they had forged. Souls cannot die; they are the eternal threads of the Universe, intricately woven into the cosmos. They cannot be broken, for they are the timeless echoes of the divine. The sword returns us to our purest state." She spread her arms wide, indicating the cosmos around them. "We are made from the very stars themselves, and we return to where we were created, the realm of the primordials, the Protogenoi. Aidoneus," Rhea said, turning her head. "There is someone I would very much like for you to meet."

The diminutive figure hobbled forward, and a wrinkled hand lifted, drawing back her hood to reveal cascading, silken strands of long, soft white hair. Her hands bore the weight of millennia, veins heavy, fingers twisted and bowed like a gnarled tree. Her face, etched with deep creases and wrinkles, stood in stark contrast to a world filled with eternally young Gods. As her profound cerulean eyes met Hades', he gasped and fell to his knees.

Before him stood the embodiment of primordial power: Gaia, the Goddess of All Creation. The pure divinity in her countenance overwhelmed Hades, and a solitary tear traced down his cheek. Time had woven its intricate patterns on her face, sculpting it with the imprints of every loss and sorrow. It was, without a doubt, the most beautiful sight he had ever witnessed. Gaia gestured for him to rise, beckoning with a twisted finger.

"We've been anticipating your arrival, Hades. Observing and waiting," she spoke solemnly. Her hands gently traced the darker aspects of his golden form, the scars etched into his soul until she reached the deepest one over his heart. Bowing her head, she studied it intently.

"Chaos has engulfed the entire world. This was not how it was meant to be. Zeus intervened, altering your destiny. Zagreus was supposed to play a crucial role in setting things right; his conception was meant to occur the day you met Persephone. However, Zeus interfered. When Zeus attempted to thwart destiny, Zagreus, in his unique way, took action. To be reborn as your son and reshape his destiny, he embraced death. Yet, despite everything, he has always been your son, only *your* son."

Gaia shed a tear, and it fell into the galaxy, exploding and spawning a thousand stars. "The world has not been well since my husband unleashed evil upon it. Uranus: blood betrayer, murderer of innocents. Only one was brave enough to stand against him. He had the purest heart of all my children," she whispered sadly. "But as Cronus confronted Uranus, my husband cursed the Universe, and a million ills sprang forth. Now, the same darkness looms in his descendant—Zeus, who views his children as tools for manipulation, not as blessings."

Rhea approached, taking Hades' hand. "Hades, forgive your father and let go of this hatred. He was a good man, punished for his bravery—the sole child brave enough to stand against Uranus. His courage spared the world from tyranny, and though history paints him as evil, there are those who know the truth."

"Uranus and Zeus are two faces of the same coin," Gaia said. "They don't care who they damage in order to acquire what they desire. But they fail to see that, despite the power they hold and all the suffering they cause, life—" She raised her hands, and three beautiful women with long golden hair appeared beside her, each weaving strands and long spools of golden light. "Life is infinite; no matter how hard you try to control or take what belongs to others, Fate has already woven their promise into the stars, and she will demand payment for what was not freely given."

Astounded, Hades moved closer. As the lovely, golden-haired women toiled, the threads united to form a glittering golden tree, and the roots spread infinitely through the Earth below them.

"The Fates," Gaia said quietly. "In their true forms." She smiled. "The threads visible in the Underworld are merely the roots of the tree of life. Every thread and every being is interconnected. A singular heartbeat resonates within each of us, emanating from a solitary tree from which all life sprouts. While you've witnessed a thread being severed, have you ever observed one being woven? The Gods emerged from Chaos, the Master of all Fate. However, your son, Persephone's child by the river—the one I claimed on the day Persephone gave birth to him—he is the High God, unrestrained by Fate, his destiny inscribed only by his own hand."

"He should be here by now," Rhea murmured.

Hades drew his eyes from the women, looking at his mother. "Who?"

Suddenly, a light pierced the Universe, and Hades shielded his eyes against the blinding brilliance. As the brightness faded, Hades exclaimed in fury, for a young Zeus, white-haired and shining, stood before him.

"Why are you here?" Hades demanded, stepping forward to shield his mother and grandmother. "Leave this place!"

Rhea placed a restraining hand on Hades' shoulder. "Do you not recognize me, Father?" the young man answered.

Hades remained motionless, gazing at the face that so much resembled his own. "Son?" he whispered, his voice trembling.

"Yes."

In an instant, Hades surged forward, enfolding him in a tight embrace. "I could only dream you were real. Holding you—it's more than I could have ever asked for." He pulled back to look at him. "You are so beautiful."

"I didn't want to leave you, but I had no choice. I never gave up searching for a way back to you." Zagreus turned to his grandmother, smiling. "Rhea returned me to my mother so I could live again."

Hades tightened his grip on his son's forearm, but his words were halted by Rhea's gentle touch. "We must act quickly," Rhea urged. "Time is running out."

"Before what?" Hades inquired.

"Before Zeus locates Persephone. She has given Zagreus her powers and is defenseless."

"No," Hades exclaimed harshly. "Why would she do such a thing?"

Gaia interjected, "She did it willingly to ensure Zagreus' survival. Zeus seeks her for those very powers, and she makes the ultimate sacrifice for her child. Those who love give up their power freely. As you did for her."

Hades, still grappling with the revelation, clenched his jaw. "We cannot let Zeus harm her! What must we do?"

Gaia peered at him, her sparkling blue eyes shining beneath the folds. "The swords need to be eradicated—but not through destruction. It is life that will end this war. Not death."

"But how do we do this?" Hades cried in frustration. "I have wracked my mind and was not able to find an answer, and now I am unable to help her!" He turned to his mother. "How do I help her?" he begged.

"Through the love of your family—Zagreus, Persephone, and yourself," Rhea said softly.

"But I hold no power over creation," Hades stated.

"Your power lies in your family," Gaia interjected. "Persephone and Zagreus' powers will aid you. They will flow from Zagreus to you. You gave her your magic to protect her, and now she has given everything to bring you back. How many have died at the hands of this corrupt king? How many lives have been needlessly taken? Life is the answer. Creation is the answer. Through Zagreus, *you* will hold the power of creation in your grasp. The swords beat with life; I know you have felt it. Heroes do not burn the world; they build it back from the ashes of villains. From the blades, good can be made." Gaia's eyes twinkled. "Do not forget, Hades, souls are your specialty."

She nodded to Rhea. "We must act quickly." She motioned Zagreus forward. "Your body is still warm, Hades, but your threads have been severed. We shall weave you from Zagreus' lifeforce to stitch you back together and repair your threads, and you will live once again."

Hades stepped away from them, shaking his head, horror in his eyes. "I will not do that! I've lived a lifetime; I'm not going to take the life of my son."

"Hades," Rhea said softly, "through you, Zagreus will be reborn again."

Hades stood frozen, his heart torn between love and anguish. The air around them crackled with a mixture of divine energy and the weight of an impossible decision.

"I cannot watch you sacrifice yourself for me," Hades choked finally, his eyes pleading with Zagreus.

Zagreus met his father's gaze, a mixture of determination and sadness in his eyes. "You gave everything for Mother, and she, in turn, sacrificed for me. Now, it's my turn. This is the only way, Father. I know you feel pain, but it's the path we must tread, the only way forward."

Hades' grip tightened on Zagreus' arm, his voice breaking as he spoke. "I would give the Universe to keep you safe. I cannot bear to lose you again."

Rhea placed a gentle hand on his shoulder. "Hades, if you refuse, we will lose not only Zagreus but also Persephone and countless others. The very essence of humanity is at stake."

The weight of the world pressed down on Hades' shoulders, the responsibility of a decision that could shape the fate of all existence. But he knew he could never sacrifice his son, no matter what was at stake.

"Father, do not mourn for me," Zagreus whispered, his voice a soothing balm to the Chaos in Hades' mind. "This is my choice, just as it was yours and Mother's. Our family is bound by sacrifice but from sacrifice blooms renewal."

Abruptly, Zagreus reached into his chest, pulling a golden light from his heart.

"No!" Hades shouted, gripping the light tightly in his hands. "Stop this!"

Rhea stepped forward, her voice steady but filled with compassion. "Hades, this is the only way to end the cycle of destruction. Zagreus' sacrifice will not be in vain; it will forge a new beginning for all."

"No!" Hades shouted, trying to push the light back into Zagreus' body.

"Too late, Father," Zagreus replied softly, placing his hand over his father's. "I've already started to unravel myself. You have no choice now. What is done cannot be undone." He smiled sweetly. "I will find my way back to you," he whispered.

"Fix him!" Hades pleaded to Gaia.

"I cannot, my child. Zagreus is in charge of his own destiny. Don't let this sacrifice be for nothing."

Tears shimmered in Hades' black eyes. "I did not want this."

Gaia reached out her hand to Hades. "For the time being, saying goodbye is the most difficult thing to do. But trust in the Universe. It will bring you together. We must hurry. Zagreus has begun the process. Take hold of your son's hands."

Zagreus clasped Hades' hands.

Hades' entire body was trembling, powerless to halt the unfolding events. Anxiety for Persephone and the fear of losing his child overwhelmed him, leaving his head spinning.

"It's all right, Father," Zagreus reassured in a soft tone. "We'll face this together."

"You shouldn't have to make such sacrifices for us," Hades answered in a hoarse voice. "It's not the natural order, children sacrificing for their parents."

"I would do it again," Zagreus whispered. "For her. For you. For the world."

"It's time," Rhea said softly.

"A word of warning, king. Hades has died," Gaia uttered. "You will be permanently changed tonight. After we reweave your threads, you will no longer be Hades. It is the beginning of a new era, and you will never be the same again. Do you understand?"

A prickle of fear tingled Hades' spine. "But who will I be?"

"Only you can decide who you will be when you are reborn. You will be you, and yet not you. Hades has died. He can never return. Now, let us begin. Stand beside one another."

Rhea and Gaia started to sway side to side, weaving their hands; the movements were hypnotic.

"Watch us." They spoke in unison, their pitches harmonizing and mesmerizing. "Watch how we weave you."

Rhea touched Hades' heart, pulling a thread from his core. Gaia took hold of the light Zagreus had freed. Then the Goddess' hands intertwined, linking the threads and weaving Hades' threadbare cords with Zagreus' thick ones. They raised their hands, and the golden cords danced, millions, billions of threads intertwining under the light of the Universe, where the dawn of creation had begun. Hades raised his eyes to his son's. He could see Zagreus flinching in pain as his light spooled from him to his father's body.

"No!" Hades called abruptly. "It's hurting him; we must stop!"

"Hades, watch us. Look only at us," Rhea said calmly. Suddenly, both the Gods were lifted, and they levitated together high into the cosmos. Rhea and Gaia flew with them, but they never paused their frantic weaving.

"We need to move faster. Fates," Gaia called, "help us weave."

The golden-haired sisters took to the heavens, lifted the strands, and began to spin. The cords were moving so fast that they were nothing more than flashes of glinting light, and the women's hands blurred from the speed of their movement. Suddenly, the Fates' faces and bodies contorted, swelling and expanding as their primordial forms appeared.

They weren't women; they were the very foundation of the Universe, huge, ever-changing nebulas reforming Hades' entire being. The Fates were the pillars of creation and the pillars of destruction, healing every scar and wound in his spirit. Star clusters, light, and darkness encircled him. At the last moment, he covered his heart with his hand as they approached the scar on his heart, the one he had taken from Persephone. "No, leave this scar. I want to keep it." The nebulas paused and resumed their spinning, but they left the dark mark on his heart.

He turned his eyes back to his son, and he cried out in anguish. Zagreus had almost faded away; only his eyes remained in the dust of the nebulas. Soon, he would be nothing. It caused Hades' to gasp in pain, agonized that his child suffered for him.

Zagreus' voice suddenly entered Hades' mind: "Father, you were never alone. We will meet again. I love you." Hades closed his eyes, a tear trickling down his cheek, and when he looked again, Zagreus was gone, and then Hades fell into darkness.

He was in the Styx when he opened his eyes, Iasion kneeling beside him.

"Hades!" Iasion exclaimed, his eyes wide with astonishment. "You are alive!"

But the king felt different—he *was* different, and that was not his name anymore. Abruptly, he began swimming towards the shore. Iasion hurried after him, desperately crying out his name, but the king did not respond. He could feel her spirit calling to him. Persephone. It was time to end this.

CHAPTER 35
THE SCAR

"Persephone!" Zeus' voice bellowed. "Show yourself, or I will ram my sword through his heart!"

"Ares," she whispered.

Persephone tried to stand, but she slipped in the still-warm blood that lay beneath her, the afterbirth she had delivered smeared on her tunic and skin. Finally, she was able to stumble to the entrance. Her body trembled with the need to rest, but she would not run away like a coward. She forced herself to stand upright, breathless, as she surveyed the battleground in front of her.

The Gods of the Underworld were engaged in fierce combat, and she realized that they were losing. The forces of Olympus were too many, and while they fought, the palace was unguarded. And now she was unable to summon her father's army because her powers were gone. She searched for Hecate. Cerberus was fighting beside the witch, and suddenly, Hecate paused, her golden gaze scanning the distance until she found Persephone. Horrified disbelief reflected on her features, and she knew Hecate sensed that Persephone's powers had vanished.

Persephone gave her a trembling smile before issuing her last command as Queen of the Underworld. "Do not allow them to take the castle," Persephone mouthed to the witch. "Keep the threads safe."

She knew Hecate wanted to dispute the edict and rush to protect Persephone instead, but in the end, she obeyed, knowing there was no other choice. The humans must be protected, humanity must survive.

"Retreat!" Hecate bellowed, raising her staff high in the air. "Get to the palace!"

The Gods of the Underworld began to flee, battling as they went, but Cerberus did not move, his golden gazes fixed on Persephone.

"Go, Cebbie," she commanded quietly.

He whimpered before following the witch with a sorrowful howl, and Persephone heard the sounds of the battle become more distant. The breeze ruffled Persephone's hair as she remained still, only her bow remaining of her weapons.

When her eyes opened, Zeus stood in front of her, clutching the golden blade. The blue-flamed blade lay on the ground far in the distance, too far from her reach. Ares lay beside it, gagged and bound in shackles, and she feared the blade had been used on him, but then she saw his blue eyes flash. Another body lay behind the War God, and Persephone recognized the slain body of Poseidon's son, Halirrhothius. Ares had exacted his revenge on him. She was glad.

"Surrender the Underworld to me," Zeus hissed. "And the sword."

"No," she answered softly.

He leaped towards her, slapping her hard across the face. "This fight is over. Open the gates now, and I will be merciful with your friends. Or shall I start with my traitor son and run my blade through his heart?"

"I will not open the gates."

He reached for her, his fingers tightening around her neck. "Give me the sword and open these gates, you selfish bitch, or I will use my blade to kill Demeter," he snarled.

"But how will you reach her?" she choked out with a taunting smile. "I will not open these gates."

His grip around her neck tightened. "Then I shall use my blade on you and enter your body. You will be helpless against my possession."

"So–be–it," she gasped.

He threw her hard to the ground, his eyes moving over her in disgust. "Look at you, revolting, covered in the filth of childbirth. To think I ever thought to make you my queen."

He kicked her hard, and she fell into the mud, but she did not resist him. When his foot made contact with her a second time, she felt her ribs crack, and she drew a gasping breath, choking on blood. And then he unleashed the ferocity of his fists and legs on her. She curled into a ball, letting her thoughts wander as she had learned to do with Nyx. And so, despite his violence against her, her thoughts were far from his. Finally, she realized he had stopped.

"Let's begin your lesson," he said. "I think I am going to enjoy this."

He lifted his hand, summoning lightning, and it sizzled around her wrists and ankles, holding her down. She screamed in agony as it cruelly burnt her flesh.

The golden blade was lifted high over his head, the light dancing madly in his eyes. "First, I shall use the blade to possess you," he promised. "And then, after you open the gates, I will kill your mother in front of you. And then the fun shall begin. You will beg for death in the end, and merciful God that I am, I will grant it for you."

She pushed away the overwhelming fear, thinking only of Hades. Her eyes drifted shut, and she breathed in this moment. She would resist Zeus' possession as long as she could, which, realistically, would not be long. Persephone acknowledged to herself that she was afraid, so afraid that it took her breath away, and she let that fear consume her, fill her, and then– she let it go. Her mind flashed over her lifetime—all the blessings that had been bestowed upon her. A mother and father who had loved her. A husband that she had loved and who loved her in return. Her precious son. A smile curved her lips; how lucky she had been. A soft, golden glow illuminated her face, and she noticed her locket suspended in the air, radiating light; she brought her hand against it, caressing it. How was it possible?

The wind began to pick up, tossing her hair from her face, and she turned her swollen, bruised eyes towards the river. She imagined that voices resonated from those dark waters, that she could hear marching and shouting, but there was no one on the water. The waves beat rapidly against the shore, and a storm grew from them, bringing a torrent of rain from the waters. The sky grew blacker and blacker, the clouds swirling low until they turned to mist, until, at last, a dark figure emerged. His black hair was blowing in the wind that surrounded him, and she realized that the storm had come from him; he was the wind and the rain; he was the storm; he was life.

"Hades," she whispered, but the storm blew her voice away, carrying the sound far from her.

The edges around his eyes glowed, and behind him was an army of the ancient mortals who had existed before their souls had been split, four legs marching, four arms holding swords and shields, and right in front was Iasion. This couldn't be real, her mind rationalized even as her heart soared. He was dead. Perhaps she was dead, and this was some sort of afterlife. It didn't matter; she wanted to be with him. Zeus was still over her and had not noticed what was coming from the water. He kept talking to her, outlining the order in which he would murder her friends, but she was not paying attention.

"Hades," she called louder this time, her swollen throat croaking the word.

"He's dead, you idiot," Zeus snapped. But, finally, he followed her gaze and saw what was marching towards him. "No!" he gasped. "It cannot be!" Zeus let out a bellow and then shouted, "Fire on the insurgents! Protect your king!"

In the distance, the Olympians lifted their bows. Dozens of golden arrows were flung at the dead king. The arrows came to a halt in the skies as the King of the Dead lifted his hand. With another twist of his fingers, the arrows began to turn in the other direction, racing back toward the Olympian army. The blue flame sword materialized in the King of Death's grasp as he raised his hand.

As the army of the dead raced past Zeus, heading for their prey and guarding the castle, the King of Gods' eyes bulged as his brother drew nearer. "No!" Zeus exhaled. "It can't be. I killed you."

The blue-flamed sword in the King of the Dead's hand was raised high, and he twisted his other hand, releasing Persephone from Zeus' hold, gently levitating her away from them. "I was reshaped and woven from the Universe itself, from the darkest shadows of the brightest star." He raised the blue-flamed sword. "I was sent back to ensure that your reign of terror ends."

Zeus growled. "Hades, the hero who refused to die," he snarled. "I thought I'd cast you into the pit of nothingness. But here you are, like a persistent weed that will not be pulled. This time," he spat, "I'll thrust my sword so deep into your heart that you'll beg for the mercy of death!"

"I am not Hades," corrected the dark God. "I am Pluto, and I deal in souls and shadowed magic. I've come for vengeance."

"What nonsense you always spout; I grow tired of it! Hades, Pluto, it matters not; you all bleed red!" Thunder blasted through the Underworld as Zeus charged towards his brother, and a tremendous light burst as the swords clashed. As they ground their swords against each other, Zeus bared his teeth at him. "I will make sure the Muses write of your death and how you ran like a coward."

"But I do not care what is said about me," Pluto replied with a smile as they fell apart, circling one another. "I do not hunger for power." The blade's blue glow was mirrored on his face. "I don't need a multitude to bend down and adore me as their king."

"You are no king; you only have this realm from my benevolence. I am the High King, the God of Gods!"

"Your legacy is one of self-love. Worship and adoration, wielded through fear, built on the tears and sorrow of the ones you oppressed. A true king does not rule by fear but by caring for their people. Your wickedness was a seed that took root, but now it's time for it to wither and die." Pluto twisted his hand, and golden threads began to unweave from the swords.

Zeus gasped. "What are you doing? Stop!"

"You will not hurt my people," Pluto promised. "You will not touch the souls of the Underworld. You will not touch my son. You will not touch Persephone." Zeus raced towards him, hitting at the blue-flamed sword with his blade, but the golden threads continued to unravel from their blades. A green light flared as the swords collided again, and Zeus shrieked as the golden blade unraveled before his eyes.

Zeus fought more desperately, his movements growing clumsy and frantic. Pluto fought with one hand while controlling the threads of the swords with the other. He twisted and turned his palm, unwinding the blades as they clashed. The swords flashed blue. The swords flashed gold. The swords flashed green. As the threads danced about them like golden rays of light, both blades shrank and thinned.

Through these weapons, you have given life to death, Pluto whispered into Zeus' mind.

Zeus fell back, dropping the spindly remnant of the golden blade as it grew white-hot in his hand, and when Pluto raised his eyes, he saw stark fear in Zeus' pale gaze. The battle at the palace paused; the threads high in the sky, weaving around the kings, had attracted the attention of both Olympian and Underworld Gods. And Pluto knew that as they looked towards Zeus, they saw what he saw—cowardly fear in the King of God's face. Suddenly, Zeus tried to fly upwards back to Olympus, abandoning his own soldiers, but Pluto leaped up, dragging him back down. They landed hard on the ground with a thunderous clap.

"You came here without invitation, and now you cannot leave without my permission," Pluto hissed. He turned and bellowed loudly to the Olympian fighters. "Is this who you are willing to die for? A king who would leave you here to perish, to rot behind these gates!"

Behind him, Zeus grasped the tiny piece of the golden blade, aiming it at Pluto's back with an evil roar. Pluto heard Persephone call out, and he instantly turned, extending the thin remnant of the blue-flamed sword. As the blades collided for the final time, emerald light illuminated the Underworld, and then... nothing. The weapons were gone, and all that remained of them were the golden threads that floated high above.

Zeus stood still, staring down at his empty hands in disbelief. "No!" he shrieked.

Pluto looked towards Persephone, who lay on the ground against her father. He walked to her, lifting her hand in his, and her hand trembled in his grasp. And as it had so long ago, time slowed down, the background around them blurring until they stood as golden figures in the darkness.

"Who are you?" she whispered as he pulled her close against him. "I know you, and yet, you are a stranger to me."

"I am the one who loves you; can't you feel it?

Tears welled up in her eyes as he put her palm to his heart. Persephone saw everything that had transpired and grieved at its beauty. Rhea. Gaia. She sobbed as she witnessed Zagreus' sacrifice. When she gazed into Pluto's heart, she saw the scar he had kept—a dark, agonizing wound that pulsed with grief, loss, and suffering. And Persephone realized why he had not given it up. It was a pain that only those who had experienced love could comprehend, an agony that only love could make endurable.

"Do you understand?" he asked quietly. "True power lies not within the Gods, but in the power of sacrifice. This is the true gift granted by the Universe, the vast riches hidden within not just immortals' experience of life but all souls. It is in the love we bear that we discover a strength beyond our own, a power to endure the unendurable." He brushed her face. "The loss of a beloved child; the death of a parent; the grief of a widow. In love and sorrow, our souls grow and expand like the light of a star. You hold this strength inside of you."

"I understand," she said quietly.

And when she brushed her lips against his, their thoughts merged into one, forming an unbreakable force of purpose. Suddenly, Pluto soared through the air and summoned it, and time was restored as he placed it into her hand, the golden arrow. Persephone's fingers moved with reverence, delicately tracing the contours of her name emblazoned on its surface. This arrow had been the catalyst that drew Hades to her side; shot by Demeter and damned by Aphrodite, the curse of the golden arrow had irrecoverably altered their fate. Her eyes lifted to his. "It began with an arrow," she whispered.

"And ends with an arrow," Pluto finished.

Their eyes held, green to black, and then she turned to face Zeus, stripped of her immortal power, lacking the Earth's might and the Underworld's influence. But as she stood before this mighty God, possessed only with the love of a wife, the devotion of a daughter, the sacrifice of a mother, she had never felt stronger.

His eyes bulged as he looked at her. "You think to defeat me with that?" he laughed. "My Gods, you are dumb. Even with no sword, I can pulverize you. Before now, you were merely a womb for my seed, and now you're no longer suitable for that." Electricity crackled around him. "I plan to make you pay for that."

Other powers melded with hers—Rhea, Gaia, and Demeter. Yet, it wasn't just the Goddesses; it was also hundreds of souls, thousands of men, women, and children—everyone Zeus had harmed. Their voices united with hers, creating a harmonious resonance, and together, they formed an army that stood behind her. Zeus staggered backward, emitting a terrified cry.

"I bear the weight of countless generations." The voices poured from her lips in a million cadences. "Those who came before me and I carry the fruit of the generations who will come after; I am life; I am death; I am the reckoning itself."

"Zeus," she whispered softly, and the other voices hushed, leaving the King of Gods and the Queen of the Underworld in a solemn quiet. "With this arrow, I weave a spell." As she uttered the words, she sensed Pluto merging with her, and lightning echoed through the realms, the wind tearing through her long hair. "Mighty Zeus, you who know no fear, no pain, no feeling. You, who have inflicted suffering on others for your pleasure, yet remain untouched by pain."

Abruptly, Pluto materialized beside her, and she thrust her hand through his chest, extracting the scar from his heart and entwining it around the arrow. The golden shaft now glowed crimson, pulsating with intensity. "Now, you shall bear the weight of the pain we endured. When you contemplate this world, you will experience what you made us feel," she hissed. "Fear. Despair. Agony."

Zeus screamed, desperately trying to ascend from the Underworld, but she yanked him down, drawing upon the technique Hades had taught her when she had captured the soul of a deer. Pluto seized Zeus by the arms, intoning ancient and potent incantations. As she stepped forward, her face inches from Zeus', she could discern the gold outlining his azure eyes.

"For all those who have come before us, for those who will come after us. For my mother," she hissed. "For my father, for my husband, for my child." She let her fingers trail over the golden shaft. "And for myself." And she hoisted the golden arrow high before sinking it deep into the heart of the King of Gods. As thick, scarlet blood flowed from the wound, Zeus screamed in agony. "When you look at us," she hissed, "you will feel such pain, such excruciating fear, that the thought of this world will be unbearable. You will never return to this realm. Persephone," she whispered her name, smiling.

The word caused the King of Gods' knees to buckle, and his face creased in agony. "No," Zeus moaned, "no more; I cannot bear it. Make it stop."

"Look at me," she urged softly, gently raising his face, compelling him to meet her gaze. He screamed in anguish, tears cascading down his cheeks. "This is my gift to you. For the king without a heart, I bestow upon you the power of feeling." Her eyes glowed crimson, and her voice resonated with a growl, "Let my pain now become yours—for all eternity."

Pluto released Zeus, and as he extended his hands, a loud click echoed. The gates swung open, and the Gods of Olympus scattered, fleeing in terror towards the sky. Zeus stumbled towards the exit, babbling madly until he, too, vanished into the white light.

"It's over," she whispered in disbelief.

"Not quite yet," Pluto said with a smile, "but I must work quickly. Zagreus' powers are fading."

His back was turned, and he was entirely focused on the intricate weaving of the golden threads that were still cascading from the sky. His hands worked frantically, and as the final thread vanished, he gently lowered his hands, holding something tenderly in his arms. She approached, puzzled, then gasped as he turned around—a sleeping baby lay against his chest.

"Makaria," Pluto said softly. "My gift to the upper world: a merciful death, a peaceful death." Persephone moved forward in wonder, letting her fingertips trail gently over the dark-haired newborn. The infant opened her eyes—one golden, the other blue—and fixed a thoughtful gaze on Persephone.

"But how?" Persephone asked in amazement.

"The swords were living beings." He brushed his hand over the infant's dark hair. "She was re-woven from the threads of the blue and golden blades, life from death. The sacrifice you and Zagreus made allowed her creation. Our beautiful daughter."

"Oh!" Persephone exclaimed, tears welling up in her eyes. How could something so beautiful and pure emerge from such darkness? This tiny being was crafted from the profound evil that had plagued the world, yet she carried none of its burdens. The sins of the father seemed to have perished with her birth, leaving behind only goodness. Perhaps, in the end, the swords had never been inherently evil; they may have been tainted by those who had wielded them. "She is so, so beautiful. Can I hold her?"

Pluto tenderly placed the infant in his wife's arms.

"I have to work quickly. Zagreus' talents will not last long; come with me."

He gestured, and in an instant, they materialized before the pomegranate tree. Pluto closed his eyes, pressing his hand against the bark while the scarlet fruit swayed gently in the breeze. Stepping back, he raised his hands, drawing soil and boulders from the ground, causing the Earth to fracture until he came to a halt. With a graceful motion, he summoned Rhea's body from the ground, unchanged since the day of her passing—radiant and beautiful. Pluto closed his eyes once more, placing his hand on Rhea's chest, and her eyes flared open as she gasped for air.

Rhea released a joyful cry upon seeing their faces. As her gaze fell on Makaria, she burst into tears, leaping from her grave to embrace her son tightly. "Oh, my boy, you did it! You truly did it!"

"Yes, Mother," he replied, enveloping her in his arms. "*We* did it. Her name is Makaria."

Rhea drew back slightly, gazing at Persephone and the child, before extending a hand to her. Persephone took it, and Rhea's eyes welled with tears again. "I am so, so glad to see you again, Persephone," she said softly.

"And I am so very happy to see you, Rhea. Thank you for everything you did for Zagreus, for all of us."

Rhea wiped her eyes, gently brushing her hand over the baby's sleeping head, then began to weep once more. "She is perfect. Makaria suits her perfectly. And have *you* decided on a name?" she inquired, turning to face her son.

"Pluto."

"Pluto," Rhea whispered. "Yes, it suits you very well." Her brow furrowed as if a sudden realization struck her. "But you should not have wasted time on me! Zagreus's powers are already waning. This was not part of the plan."

"It was always part of my plan. Come, Mother," Pluto urged gently. "There is someone you must see."

Approaching the Gates of Tartarus, Gyges swung open the door, revealing Cronus, his eyes brimming with disbelief as he beheld them.

"It can't be," he gasped, the King of Titans crumbling to his knees in shock as he beheld Rhea. "I watched you die." Rhea hurried forward, enfolding him in her arms as he wept uncontrollably.

"Hush," she whispered. "Hush, I am here now. You are not alone anymore."

Persephone felt a lump forming in her throat, her eyes stinging with tears. The baby in her arms cooed gently, and Persephone bent, brushing her lips against her sweet face.

Pluto raised his hand, and they materialized in Elysium, standing before the resplendent golden gates suspended in the sky. With a soft smile, he said, "For you, Father. For you and Mother. The Isles of the Blessed." Persephone laughed in quiet amazement, fully aware that her husband could unravel even the secrets she had held with the King of Titans.

Cronus, still awestruck, stood slowly before his son. His gaze, once clouded by a curse born of anger and hatred, now seemed to clear. As he looked upon Pluto, it was as though he saw him for the first time—reborn and free from the shackles that had bound them. Deep shame etched his expression, his eyes filled with horror, and his silver eyes filled with tears.

"Pluto," he breathed, his voice breaking. "How I have wronged you. I cast you away. I failed you as a father."

"No, Father," Pluto replied gently. "It was the curse."

Cronus shook his head, his entire body trembling. "I let the curse fester in me, fueled by anger and hatred. I failed you." He sank to his knees, taking Pluto's hand in his. "I have no right to ask for your forgiveness, but I do just the same. Forgive me."

Pluto, feeling a mix of emotions, pulled his father to his feet with a trembling hand. "We've both suffered," he whispered. "But now, we can rebuild what was shattered. Father, it's not too late for us. We have the power to rewrite our story."

Cronus, gazing into the eyes of the son he had wronged for so long, managed a fragile smile. He embraced Pluto again, and for the first time, they held each other. The Isles of the Blessed bore witness to the mending of a fractured bond, the redemption of a love that had endured trials beyond mortal comprehension.

Cronus and Rhea had entered the golden door, but Pluto gently held Persephone back. "We will join them later," he said softly.

"Where are we going?" Persephone asked.

"To the palace. But first, there is something I must return to you."

Her gaze fell upon the sleeping baby. "You have given me the most precious gift. What else could I ask for?"

In response, he bent forward, pressing his lips against hers. As her eyes closed at his touch, she felt a rush of power and knew that her magic had returned. Pluto drew back, looking at her solemnly. "The sacrifice you and Zagreus made allowed me to create our daughter. I used the last of Zagreus' powers to bring back Rhea." He touched her face reverently. "When the time is right, Zagreus will return to us."

Persephone's eyes filled with tears. "I know he will," she whispered. "I feel his life within me, even now, waiting."

Pluto smiled, and her heart caught as she saw the dimple at the corner, the familiarity of it warming her very soul. "Come, wife," he said, "someone is waiting for us."

"And who might that be?"

"You will see soon."

They took their time returning to the palace, walking through Elysium. The shouts of joyful cheers echoed in the distance, and they smiled, knowing that the souls had learned of their victory against the Olympians.

"We all have cause to celebrate today," Pluto said, entwining his hand with hers.

In her other arm, she cradled the newborn, and her heart surged with joy. For so long, she had been afraid to embrace the notion of happiness, and now, it flowed effortlessly. Perhaps, she mused, that's how happiness should be— not a struggle, but a joy found in the simplicity of a moment, the feeling of his hand in hers. She would never take for granted these quiet moments. They meant everything to her.

As the palace came into view, Persephone gave a startled gasp. Demeter stood at the castle gates, locked in an embrace with Iasion, tears twinkling like stars in her eyes.

"Now that Zeus cannot enter the Underworld, Iasion no longer needs to hide," Pluto said softly. "He will live with us in the palace, and Demeter will be free to come and go as she pleases."

"Oh," Persephone gasped, clutching her hand to her chest. "I never imagined I could feel such joy."

She pulled Pluto against her, careful of the baby between them, her eyes tightly closed as tears seeped down her cheeks. "Thank you," she whispered.

His hand stroked her hair. "You better go say hello," he said softly.

Persephone gave a shuddering gasp and then ran towards her parents, embracing them and sobbing. Olive and Cerberus, who was now puppy-sized, delighted in the commotion, playfully biting at their robes. Her parents were overjoyed at the baby in her arms, showering her with kisses. Persephone saw Hecate emerge from the castle. The witch, bruised and battered from battle, smiled at Persephone, her lips trembling with emotion, and Persephone felt her own eyes fill with tears once more.

"Come join us," the witch called. "We are preparing a feast for our victory. Hypnos is attempting to make a cake depicting the battle, and Ares is roasting the meats. We may all succumb to food poisoning,"

she finished cheerfully.

As her parents moved to the entrance, Hecate bent her dark head to the baby. "Well, well, you are a little witch in the making. You can never start learning the ways too soon." And Makaria cooed as though expressing her agreement.

With a nod at Persephone, the witch led Demeter and Iasion into the palace. There was much to discuss, but for now, the joy of being together was enough.

Turning to face her husband, Persephone's breath caught, her heart so full it felt ready to burst. He was not the same man she had first met, he had been rewoven and respun into something different. He was still made of shadows, shaped from dark magic, a king of the darkness. No, he would never be a golden prince of Olympus, but that had never been what she wanted. He was the other half of her soul, the shadow and the light, and everything she needed. She ran to him, and he caught her, pressing his lips against hers.

"Well, my Queen, what do you think? Shall we live happily ever after?"

"Oh yes," she whispered.

And they did.

THE END

Made in United States
Troutdale, OR
03/09/2024

18337748R00401